"THIS WAS GILLIAM NESS'S FIRST STEP INTO THE LITERARY WORLD,
AND IT WAS A DOOZY."

"THE ACTION WAS NON-STOP, THE CHARACTERS WERE WELL DEVELOPED, AND THE
PLOT LINE WAS FASCINATING TO SAY THE LEAST. I WOULD CERTAINLY READ THE
AUTHOR'S NEXT WORK WITHOUT HESITATION."

"THIS TRILOGY KEEPS YOU ON THE EDGE OF YOUR SEAT RIGHT FROM THE START AND
WHEN YOU THINK IT CAN'T GET MORE EXCITING IT JUST KEEPS ON GIVING."

"MR. NESS TAKES US ON QUITE THE ADVENTURE, CREATING A PAGE TURNER THAT IS
DIFFICULT TO PUT DOWN!"

"THIS BOOK CAUGHT ME FROM THE 1ST PAGE AND DIDN'T LET GO!!"

GILLIAM NESS IS AWESOME! HIS WAY OF DESCRIBING WHAT HAPPENS, KEEPING THE
STORY MOVING, AND JUST PLAIN STORYTELLING IS AMAZING, ESPECIALLY FOR HIS
FIRST BOOK."

"DON'T MAKE PLANS FOR THE WEEKEND."

"A SPIRITUAL SCI-FI TECHNOTHRILLER THAT LEAVES YOU WHITE KNUCKLED AND
HOLDING YOUR BREATH!"

"DISTURBING, DARK AND GUT WRENCHING AT TIMES.
STRAP IN AND ENJOY THE RIDE!"

"I ENJOYED THIS BOOK FROM THE FIRST PAGE."

"THIS SERIES IS DEFINITELY ONE THAT I WILL BE READING MORE THAN ONCE."

"FAST PACED, LOTS OF ACTION, AND IDEAS THAT MAKE YOU KEEP THINKING ABOUT THE
BOOK EVEN AFTER YOU'VE PUT IT DOWN FOR THE NIGHT."

THE LAST ARTIFACT

A TRILOGY BY GILLIAM NESS

Published by POLYMATH PUBLISHING
Toronto, Canada.

POLYMATH PUBLISHING and the portrayal of the letter "P"
within the box are trademarks of Polymath Publishing.

ISBN 978-1-988145-08-2

August 2019

BOOK ONE
THE DARK RIFT

…And then the final days arrived,
When all the wild imaginings of men came to pass.
When the myths, theories, and legends were made manifest,
And the prophecies and suspicions were fulfilled.

In those final days they trembled and cried:
"How came we to conceive of such monstrous inventions?"
For the gods and demons they had imagined were all realized.
And a great shadow spread across the world.

-The Great Fall of the Angels
(From the Compostela Manuscripts, circa 865CE)

The Cantabrian Mountains – 2243 B.C.

A heavy mantle of fog clung to the surface of the small mountain lake, its dark waters emitting a profound stillness. Amid the gurgle of a slow-moving paddle a primitive dugout made its way out into the gloom, its two occupants dwarfed by the looming peaks that encased it on all sides. There was not a soul in sight.

The boy with the paddle completed another stroke, the boat sliding effortlessly forward. Their destination lay just ahead; a tiny island enshrouded in mist.

"It's certainly strange here," said the girl in the boat, chewing her lip, "but it doesn't seem as dangerous as they say."

There was something otherworldly about the place. It was sending waves of excitement through her. Like the boy, she too had turned twelve that day, and to celebrate their birthdays they had decided to investigate the mysterious island, knowing full well that they were forbidden to do so. She studied its dense tangle of trees.

"I want to go ashore."

The boy frowned.

"That wasn't the plan," he said. "We only came to look."

"We don't have to go into the shrine. We can just find it and see what it looks like."

The boy shot a suspicious glance at the island and then made up his mind.

"All right," he said, passing a hand through his shaggy hair. "Let's go."

They circled the island until they found a place to land. Above them a veiled sun was already beginning to dip behind the mountains and the girl felt a sudden twinge of fear. The shadowy trees were dense and ominous.

"It's getting dark too fast," she said. "Maybe we should go back."

"We're here already," said the boy. "Let's have a quick look."

He jumped from the dugout and dragged it up onto the rocks, holding out his hand for the girl to take.

"Very well," she said. "But only for a moment."

The island was unkempt, and the vegetation quite dense. Lush ferns covered most of the ground, and many of the rocks were rounded over with moss. From where they stood, a path could be seen climbing into the foliage. It picked its way through the rocky terrain in a series of natural steps and landings and the two were soon finding it quite easy to navigate their way up.

"This was a mistake," said the girl, following behind.

"Why?"

She peered into the woods. She thought she had seen a shadow moving through the trees.

"What if the Druid Fathers are right?"

"The Druid Fathers are old fools," said the boy. "Nobody believes their stories anymore."

It was not long before they arrived at a small, circular clearing, not twenty feet in diameter. There was a large, flattened boulder directly at its centre, and as they made their way forward, they could see the ancient image of a maze carved into its surface. There was a crude figure of a man standing at its entrance. It was unsettling, but more disturbing still was what lay at the outer extremities of the clearing: A grouping of fourteen standing stones, each as tall as a man, and forming a perfect circle around them.

"What is this place?" asked the girl.

The boy shook his head and frowned.

"I don't know…"

The sound of a large bird taking flight startled them, and as the girl's eyes followed it up through the tangled boughs, she saw how dim the sky had become. There was a darkness growing in the woods.

"I'm scared," she said, clutching the boy. "Let's go. I don't like the way this island makes me feel."

"Just a little while longer," he said, taking her hand. "Come on. We've got to be close to the shrine by now."

She followed him reluctantly, deeper and deeper into the thick. It seemed to her that the island was swallowing them alive. After a five-minute hike the boy stopped suddenly, his heart pounding with excitement as he pulled her into another clearing.

"This must be the place," he said, refusing to acknowledge the fear he felt.

"Wait," he muttered, his eyes straining. "What is this?"

He could see the standing stones looming in a circle around them again. They had somehow returned to the same place, and something felt terribly wrong. It was too dark. At some point the overcast sky had transformed into a starless void, and only the muted light of a crescent moon leaked through the twisted branches above.

"We've been walking in circles..." he stammered.

A shrill pitch of the purest fear was ringing through his body now. He could not understand. The air had become frigidly cold.

"The Druid Fathers were right..." he whispered, shaking his head in horror. "By the gods, what have we done?"

A deep and inky void had appeared where the central monolith had been, and just then, something even more unsettling came into view.

Shadowy figures were materializing behind the standing stones. They were stumbling forward, their arms hanging limply at their sides, and their gazes vacant and cold. The boy's eyes opened wide. These people were dead. Their flesh was crawling with worms, yet somehow, they still lived.

"No!" he grunted, unable to move. "This is impossible..."

It was only then that it came. An invisible force of unimaginable potency. It moved over them with the momentum of an ocean tide, forcing them to the ground and driving the sight from their eyes.

CHAPTER 1

Istanbul, Turkey.

Professor Agardi Metrovich staggered out of the examination room and into the hall of the private Istanbul hospital. He was a large, bearded man in his late seventies, dressed in an old tweed sports jacket with frayed cuffs. The door closed behind him as he exited, shutting out the chanting priests as they continued with their archaic ritual.

Through the walls, the weary professor could still hear the spitting curses coming from his patient, a sensation of pure evil crawling over his skin. As he had expected, he was instantly approached by his patient's father. Isaac Rodchenko was an inpatient at the institution as well, and stricken with paranoid schizophrenia. Over the course of the evening, the unearthly cries of his son had driven the poor man into a state of despair.

"Professor Metrovich!" he whispered, his eyes straining with worry. "You must tell me what is happening to my son!"

Metrovich could only stare back at him, his own face pale and drawn with fear. After decades of medically overseeing exorcisms, the seasoned professor had yet to overcome the horror the rituals consistently provoked in him. He struggled with his emotions, finding comfort in the words of an ancient text he had long ago unearthed in his research.

Fear is an illusion, a ghost without substance. It is easily dispelled.

In many cases, suspected victims were merely suffering from severe psychotic dementia, but on rare occasions such as this, events could not be explained so readily. Demonic possession was an anomaly that defied all rational thought. It was something not of this earth.

"Please, sit down, Mr. Rodchenko," the professor managed to say, and following his own advice, he collapsed heavily into one of the waiting armchairs. "You must give me a moment to regain my strength."

Isaac Rodchenko sat down at once. He had a healthy complexion for his sixty odd years, along with thick salt and pepper hair and black eyebrows. He wore an elegant charcoal grey suit and had an air of humble confidence about him, despite his distress. For a long moment Isaac waited obediently but could contain himself no longer.

"My son has spent thirty-three years in a vegetative state," he said, rubbing his hands together nervously. "How is it possible that he should have awakened from it now, and in this condition? I know you are keeping something from me, Professor. Have pity on a suffering father. Tell me, please!"

Metrovich held Isaac's gaze for a moment, but then let his eyes fall.

How could I possibly tell this man what I suspect to be true?

"Sir!" insisted Isaac. "You must tell me at once!"

The old professor looked up, his tired eyes scanning the distressed face before him. He opened his mouth to speak but an unearthly scream split the silence. It was followed immediately by a call from one of the priests inside.

"Professor! Come quickly!"

In one clumsy motion Metrovich rose from his chair and passed into the examination room, a stench of rot and suffering engulfing him as he entered. There in the half light, he could see two priests hunched over the possessed patient, his obese body contorting in a series of slow and twisting seizures.

Having already been severely deformed since birth, the effects of the possession had transformed the victim into something utterly horrific. Metrovich looked to the priests. They stood there in quiet resignation, praying silently over the poor beast.

"We are losing him, Professor," whispered the ancient Father Franco.

The professor's eyes found the electrocardiogram and saw that the old priest was not mistaken. The patient had entered into cardiac arrest. In his weakened state, there would be no way of saving him.

His joints creaked woodenly as he lurched and twisted, his enormous body becoming still before moving into a violent death rattle. When it was over, the heart monitor gave off a flat, uninterrupted tone, and crossing himself, Father Franco muted the alarm.

With the death of the patient, a deep silence had fallen over the room, a residual feeling of the supernatural hanging in the air like a pall. In all his years of overseeing exorcisms, Metrovich had never witnessed a ghastlier case than this, and judging by the expressions on the two priests, he could see that they had not done so either.

Metrovich moved towards the corpse. He had been plagued with a gut feeling since early that evening. It warned of something so unlikely that it seemed ludicrous that he should even be considering it, but it could no longer be ignored.

He reached down to take hold of the urine-soaked gown that covered the patient's lower torso but froze instantly in the act. He thought he had felt a slight tremor running through the corpse, and in that instant a fresh wave of fear rippled through him again. He looked more closely. The cadaver was visibly trembling. His eyes darted to the ECG. It was still showing a flatline.

This is impossible. The body is dead...

Metrovich looked back in time to see the ghastly corpse jerk to life.

"Ahreimanius!" it hissed menacingly, its upper body lurching violently towards him.

All watched in horror as the restraining straps gave way, the thrashing corpse coming dangerously close to the professor before collapsing back onto the bed. A final quake ran through the body.

Struggling to keep himself composed, Metrovich reached forward to resume his task, drawing slowly aside the gown that covered the lower half of its torso. What he saw filled him with horror and disgust. Father Franco gagged and coughed.

Plainly visible before them, grotesque and utterly malformed, were a pair of lacerated genitals, disproportionately large and belonging to both the male and female sexes. It was at that moment that a shaft of light split the darkness and Isaac's swaying form appeared in the doorway. He stared blankly at the scene before him. The professor's eyes remained glued to the patient.

"You did not tell us that your son was a hermaphrodite, Mr. Rodchenko…"

Isaac seemed to wince at the statement.

"Is he dead?"

Professor Metrovich turned to face the grieving father but said nothing, his expression containing a mixture of compassion and confusion. With this latest development, twenty years of skepticism had been suddenly stripped from his mind. The evidence was now irrefutable, the coincidences far too numerous to discount.

Through the death of this unfortunate victim, an ancient and obscure prophecy had somehow been made manifest. The impossible had somehow transpired.

"I know this is difficult for you, Mr. Rodchenko," said Metrovich slowly. "Can you remember where your son was conceived?"

The professor's words struck Isaac like a dull blow. He was too drugged to sense any pain, but the question probed one of the primary causes of his mental illness. The mother of his child had died giving birth to their misshapen son, and he had never recovered from the loss of her. Over the years he had progressively lost his mind. He slumped to his knees, rocking himself to and fro.

"My wife and I were on a religious pilgrimage in the mountains of Northern Spain," he muttered, his eyes squinting ever so slightly as he remembered. "We were on a small lake. We had found a little island…"

Metrovich tore his gaze from Isaac and turned to face Father Franco. The old priest looked back at him, his eyes alight with foreboding.

"God help us all," he said solemnly.

Outside a rumbling chorus of thunder sounded. The storm that had long been approaching had finally arrived.

CHAPTER 2

Florence, Italy.

The thirty-two-year-old **Dr.** Natasha Rossi sat amid the clutter of her small restoration shop. Before her on a battered workbench lay the ninth century tabernacle she was working on. It was almost finished, and behind it a large monitor displayed a three-dimensional infrared scan of the piece. She was using it to spot tiny deposits that had been missed during the restoration process.

Playing in the background was one of her many self-help audiobooks.

...for this reason, traumas in our past relationships can be part of the reason why we keep attracting selfish men into our lives. We feel compelled to fix what went wrong the last time, and this can happen over and over again until we finally become aware of the cycle...

Natasha applied solvent to a tiny deposit of paraffin lodged in the tabernacle's base, nodding in agreement the whole while. She pondered the seven months she had just wasted on her ex-boyfriend, amazed by her ability to find the tiniest flaws in artifacts, yet be utterly blind to the most blatant flaws in men. Or maybe she was aware of their flaws, and simply thought their imperfections were something that could be removed if she was meticulous enough, like stripping dirt from an old artifact.

"He really was a jerk..." she whispered, blowing a lock of hair out of her eyes.

It was a dark chestnut colour and it fell thick and curly around her shoulders. Natasha's accent was Italian, but three years at

Harvard had tempered it nicely. She ran through her positive affirmations, feeling another wave of depression coming on.

I'm strong and powerful. My thoughts and actions create my destiny.

Christmas was approaching and Natasha was dreading it. There would parties and church functions to attend, and she would be alone the entire time. It seemed to her that she was always alone, even if she happened to be dating someone.

She only ever felt happy when she was dancing, but even her love of the ballet had brought her disappointment of late. Her role in this years' production of *The Nutcracker Suite* had disappeared when poor ticket sales had forced the show's cancellation. Months of grueling practice had been lost in the blink of an eye.

Natasha gazed out her shopfront windows to see the little piazza outside. Its stalls were uncharacteristically quiet for a December's night, and she found herself thinking how magical Christmas in Florence normally was. The reason for the sad state of things was quite understandable.

Following a horrendous terrorist attack in Los Angeles, the United States economy had collapsed like a house of cards, leading the rest of the planet into a severe economic depression. In addition to the sweeping devastation it caused, the heinous attack had left the streets of Florence bereft of tourists and holiday shoppers alike.

Natasha chewed her lip as she returned her attention to the artifact, reminding herself how fortunate she was. Despite the global crisis, the Vatican had continued with its museum renovations, providing her little restoration shop with dozens of artifacts needing to be cataloged and cleaned. It was a tedious job, but one that was constantly reenergized by the small chance that something new might be revealed as the layers of dirt were stripped away.

It was this act of revealing, and her strong passion for it, that had inspired Natasha to work in artifact restoration to begin with. Having grown up surrounded by religious relics, it seemed a natural extension to the doctorate she held in theology.

Natasha laid down her tools and rose wearily from her chair, stretching as she did so. Across from her a sixteenth century mirror reminded her of how many hours she had been working.

"I look horrible," she whispered.

As always, she absently arranged her hair to cover a pale, dime-sized scar at the centre of her forehead. It had been there for as long as she could remember; the remnant of abuses she had suffered in an orphanage as an infant.

There were other burn marks on her body as well. Plastic surgery had made them almost imperceptible, but they still haunted her. They were ghosts of an evil that had touched her before her earliest memories. They made her feel malformed and inadequate, even though they were practically invisible.

Continuing with her stretching, Natasha approached the windows in time to see a mass of heavy clouds rolling in. They blanketed the starry sky within moments, and heavy drops of rain began to spatter the cobblestones outside. After a barrage of thunder and lightning, Natasha turned to find that her computer had shut down, along with all the lights in the room. Outside, the storm exploded into a deluge.

"I forgot to save that scan…" she said gloomily, and her eyes darted to the front door.

A gust of wind had just blown it open, letting in the torrential rain. Natasha wasted no time. Priceless artifacts were getting wet. She arrived at the breach in seconds, reaching up to take hold of the outer door and slamming it down with a crash. The workshop plunged into darkness, and it was only then that an irregular banging could be heard coming from the back room.

"What is that?" she whispered, and a wave of fear ran through her.

Natasha was not one to be easily frightened but she could not deny the eerie feeling that accompanied the banging sound. With a decisive effort she dispelled her fears and made her way into the darkness to find its source.

For almost a hundred years, the back area of the workshop had been used as a storeroom; a place that she rarely ventured into. It was cluttered with thousands of religious artifacts, and bric-a-brac of every kind, its few naked bulbs never providing enough light to dispel the fears she had always held for the place. Nevertheless, she found herself venturing into its depths, groping forward with nothing but a flashlight to illuminate her way.

"Is someone there?"

A crack of thunder sounded in response. She could feel the little hairs on her neck standing on end as she navigated the maze of cluttered shelves. It was as if something had invaded her workshop; something paranormal; something demonic. She knew this was a ludicrous thought, but she frowned in confusion nonetheless. Her instincts were telling her to flee, yet there was something drawing her forward as well.

It was not long before she found the source of the banging, and she breathed a sigh of relief. The same gust of wind that had blown open the front door had opened the back door as well. She could see it swinging in the dim light of a gas lamp outside, banging the old frame at irregular intervals. Its rusted latch had obviously given way under the jolt of wind.

Natasha looked down suddenly and swallowed hard. There was a street dog crouching in the shadows by the threshold, its eyes glowing cold in the reflected light. It stood as if ready to pounce and Natasha felt her body go limp with fear. It was only then that she realized it was not growling at her, but rather at something else; something *behind* her.

She jerked around, the dog lunging as she did so, but there was nothing there. Turning again, Natasha saw the animal pacing nervously, the hair on its back still on end. She knew that animals could see things humans could not, but what had it seen?

Her mobile phone rang suddenly just then, and the shrill tone of it startled the dog. With a loud bark it bolted off, rushing through the door and vanishing into the storm.

"Pronto?" she said, bringing the phone to her ear.

She was hurrying to the door now, wanting nothing but to close it. Outside a sheet of lightning lit up the sky.

"Is this Natasha Rossi?" said a crackling voice.

It spoke in English but bore a heavy Spanish accent.

"Yes..."

"Miss Rossi, this is Sergeant Alberto Martinez of the Spanish Civil Guard. I am afraid I have some very distressing news, señorita."

"Yes, I'm listening," said Natasha, a sick feeling growing in her stomach.

She closed the door and locked it shut. Darkness engulfed her.

"I am so sorry, señorita. A private plane chartered yesterday by Professor Agardi Metrovich and Father Franco Rossi has crashed in the mountains southwest of Santander. All including the pilot have been killed. Father Franco was your legal guardian, no?"

"What have you done with him?"

"We managed to land a paramedic to see if there were any survivors, señorita, but there were none. Their plane is very high in the mountains, and it is in a very dangerous position to access due to the high winds. We have been unable to retrieve their bodies. This might not be possible for some months, señorita."

"I see," said Natasha, lost in a daze. "Thank you, Sergeant."

Natasha sank to the floor, the musty storeroom plunging into blackness as the light from her phone went out. Father Franco had cared for her since she was a little girl, and if those at the church orphanage had been her family, Father Franco had been her father. Now he was gone, and her heart burst with grief.

Natasha's thoughts went also to Father Franco's lifelong friend, Bishop Marcus Di Lauro. He lived close to the orphanage and had been like an uncle to her all her life. He and Father Franco had been inseparable since they were boys.

How can I tell him what's happened? He's too old. The shock will kill him...

Suddenly, from within the inky hollows that surrounded Natasha, the sinister presence she had felt only moments before returned. It flooded over her like fetid water.

"Please, God," she prayed. "Make it go away."

But the evil remained. In her sorrow, she almost welcomed it.

CHAPTER 3

Boston, Massachusetts.

Dr. Gabriel Parker tilted the bottle and watched as the golden liquid tumbled over the ice in his glass. It was shimmering in the halogen light of his bedside lamp, and he threw himself back onto the oversized pillows, bringing the glass to his lips and inhaling deeply before downing its contents.

He gazed up to see a beautiful young blonde working her way into a pair of tight jeans at the foot of his bed, and then watched expressionlessly as she slipped on a lacy bra. A second later she was back on the bed, straddling him and delivering a deep and sensual kiss.

"Yum," she said, savouring the whiskey on her lips. "You taste like a man."

Gabriel's hands explored her curves.

"I taste like whiskey," he said, giving her bottom a gentle slap.

The girl kissed him again and when she pulled away Gabriel noticed she was pouting.

"What's wrong now?" he asked, stretching over to refill his glass.

"What's wrong with *you*, Gabriel?" she said, her eyes downcast and sultry.

Her fingers were tracing over a dime-sized scar at the centre of his chest. It had always intrigued her. Gabriel took another gulp of scotch and then lifted her chin to have a look at her.

"Nothing's wrong," he said. "I'm just tired."

She raised an eyebrow.

"You've never been tired before…"

The girl ran her fingers through his shaggy hair and passed them over the stubble on his chin. He had a strong jaw, perfectly at home with his rugged features. On his throat she found another familiar scar, and pushing aside a lock of hair, she traced her thumb over yet another on his forehead.

"Are you getting tired of me?" she asked, concentrating on the mark.

Gabriel put down his glass and sat up.

"Listen, Mica—"

"Mica's my working name," said the girl with a frown. "You know that. I'm Mary."

"Mary—" began Gabriel, but she cut him off.

"You still haven't told me about these scars," she said, kissing the one on his forehead.

Gabriel felt the usual pang of discomfort at the mention of the blemishes, and it annoyed him as always. He was thirty-two years old. Should he not have got over this nonsense by now? A recurring scene played itself out in his mind.

"Hey, Ashtray!" cried one of the bullies who surrounded him. *"Has daddy been using you to butt out his smokes?"*

"Ashtray did it to himself!" said another. *"Faggets love pain!"*

The group of boys exploded into laughter.

"Ashtray's gay! Ashtray's gay!"

"Earth calling Gabriel..." said Mary, looking down at him intently. "The scars...?"

Gabriel drained his glass and pretended to be serious.

"Electrode torture marks from an Iraqi prison."

She slapped him playfully.

"You're never going to tell me, are you."

Gabriel reached over and poured out some more scotch. Time, and his general hairiness, had made the scars almost imperceptible, but it had not been like that when he was a boy. Back then they had stood out starkly, like bumpy red cigar burns.

Gabriel told himself the mysterious marks had made him strong, but the truth was they had only made him proud. As a boy, the constant taunting had turned his feigned apathy into arrogance, a defensive trait that still plagued him to this day.

"Tell me..." whispered the girl, nibbling at his ear. "You know how much I care about you."

Gabriel forced himself to be patient. He hated hearing this kind of thing. It was not necessary.

"You don't care about me, Mary," he said. "I'm just a regular customer who treats you well."

Mary smiled naughtily, her pretty hands finding his crotch.

"You treat me *very* well."

Gabriel gave her a playful shove that sent her tumbling to the other side of the bed with a squeal. He got up and pulled on a pair of baggy brown trousers and a sleeveless undershirt, securing his belt as he made his way to a nearby table. He had a flat stomach and a strong chest, his body shaped by a lifetime of deep-sea diving. He took hold of a battered leather duffel bag and opened it slowly, double checking what he had packed inside.

He was not having a great day, or a great month for that matter. Something in Gabriel ached with emptiness, and it was not just the recent death of his father that was responsible. He was feeling a general weariness with the world, as though everything were losing its meaning. He could not understand what was causing it because nothing had changed.

He had been happily living a full life for a decade now; lecturing at the university, researching and locating sunken ships, entertaining beautiful women, and getting together with friends and colleagues on a regular basis. Life was exciting, but even still, something was not right. He would be turning thirty-three soon and something was lacking, even if he could not say what it was.

"Where are you going this time, Gabriel Parker?" asked Mary, her voice sounding timid as she came up behind him. "Take me with you. I hate Boston."

Gabriel turned around and looked at her, forcing himself to smile. It was not difficult. The girl was riveting. He took her by a belt loop and pulled her close, giving her an assertive kiss. When he was done, he opened her hand and gave her a roll of banknotes, carefully closing her fingers around it.

"You don't have to pay me this time," she said quietly. "We haven't done anything."

He walked her to the front door, producing a buzzing phone as he did so. His electronic boarding pass had just arrived.

"I'm sorry to kick you out, Mary," he said, opening the door for her. "I've got a plane to catch."

CHAPTER 4

Rome, Italy.

To anyone else, the distant knocking would have been impossible to hear, but even in his eighty-third year of life, Fra Bartolomeo's hearing had remained as acute as it had been when he was a boy.

"A blessing and curse you have given to me, Father," he prayed aloud.

His accent was thickly Italian, but years spent in the service of a British-born bishop had made English his habitual tongue.

"Where is Suora when one needs her?"

The old Christian brother gave a sigh of resignation. He was in the kitchen's pantry, attempting to extricate a box of tea biscuits from the back of a cluttered shelf. The distant knocking was persistent, and he knew that it was coming from a rarely used service door located at the back of the rectory.

"Nobody ever knows which door to use..."

He made his way along ancient hallways belonging to what had once been a small monastery, centuries before. Located in the centre of Rome, it was now the private residence of the retired Bishop Marcus Di Lauro, a man who, despite his advanced age, was still very active in church matters, especially those pertaining to the paranormal.

Fra Bartolomeo accelerated his pace, arriving at the door as the knocking stopped. Opening it, he saw a delivery man walking away.

"*Pronto!*" he exclaimed, scratching the back of his head where a little bit of silver hair still grew. "Can I be of assistance?"

"I have a delivery for the bishop," said the courier, turning around.

Fra Bartolomeo gave a patient nod.

"I will take it to him, my son."

The old, white-bearded Bishop Marcus was at his desk when he heard the quiet knock on his door. He took one last look at the framed photograph he had been studying and then turned to place it back on the credenza behind him.

It was an image of himself standing before Mont St. Michel in the company of his two dearest friends: Father Franco Rossi, and Professor Agardi Metrovich; both recently deceased.

"I am an old man now," he whispered, producing a well-used handkerchief from his pocket. "I will see you both very soon, my friends."

He evacuated his nose in a series of short, staccato salvos and then cleared his throat.

"Come in," he said in a perfect British tenor.

Fra Bartolomeo appeared at the door. As always, he wore threadbare corduroy pants, a flannel shirt, and a tattered woolen cardigan, each article a different shade of the same muted grey. He held out a small parcel in both hands.

"A package has arrived for you, your Excellency."

"Thank you, Fra," said the bishop, smiling kindly. "Come in, come in. What say you to having our cognac a little early today?"

When their drinks were done, and the old brother was off on his business again, Bishop Marcus leaned forward and picked up the package.

"Father Franco," he said quietly. "What could you possibly have sent me?"

In the package the old bishop found the battered leather-bound journal he had so often seen the professor with. He picked up the accompanying letter and scrutinized it through a brass rimmed magnifying glass. It was from Father Franco, and written on the day of his death. He held it under his desk lamp and proceeded to read.

Istanbul, November 29.

My dear friend,

The exorcism was a failure, with our patient passing away several hours into the ritual. We were however, shocked to discover that he was intersexed; a hermaphrodite. Impossible as it seems, last night's possession reflects the professor's myth perfectly. He is now certain that the Cube of Compostela exists, and has deduced that it is residing in the archives of the Museum of Antiquities in Tangiers.

As I write, we are awaiting a chartered plane that will be taking us to the place of the hermaphrodite's conception, an island on a small lake in the mountains south of Santander. We fear that this is the same island mentioned in the prophecy. There is a deep dread in me.

The professor believes that the time has come to unite Gabriel and Natasha. He does insist, however, that the two of them be united before the Cube is recovered. He has asked that I send you his Cube diary so that you might study it with them. As you know, everything he has learned concerning the artifact is contained within it.

Enclosed you will find the name of the professor's contact at the Vatican Museum. He will assist you in obtaining the Cube from the Moroccan authorities.

Your faithful friend, F.R.

The old bishop laid the letter out on his desk and fell back into his chair, releasing a long, drawn-out sigh.

"I feel you are here with me, old friend."

He reached forward and took hold of the journal. On its tattered cover were the remains of what had once been a gold embossed stamp.

The Cube of Compostela
Reality or Myth?

Bishop Marcus hesitated a moment, and then taking a deep breath, proceeded to immerse himself in the mysterious lifetime obsession of his dear friend and colleague, the late Professor Agardi Metrovich.

CHAPTER 5

The Atlas Mountains, Morocco.

Gabriel grumbled under his breath. He was dragging himself through a copse of dry bushes that served as his only means of cover. He knew that the lack of a moon, coupled with the dark fatigues he was wearing, would make him invisible to the armed guards, and he was glad of the fact. They would, at that very moment, be scanning the castle's perimeter, including the place where he presently found himself.

Gabriel pulled down his cap. Invisibility was a good thing, and he thanked the dark night. If he were spotted, here in the shrubs, casing out the villa of one of the most powerful drug lords in North Africa, he would most certainly be skinned alive.

Completing the last leg of his approach, Gabriel arrived at his final position. He was high on a rocky perch now, hiding safely behind the cover of a dense grouping of shrubs. Below him, a panoramic vista of the Atlas Mountains spread out in all directions, lit from above by a star-studded sky that seemed to hover only inches above him.

Sandwiched as he was between that infinite glowing cosmos, and an earth that seemed to almost embrace him as he lay upon it, Gabriel felt a sense of safety that he had never before experienced. It seemed ludicrous. This was by far the most dangerous expedition of his career, yet instead of feeling anxious or worried, he was perfectly at peace. He whispered into his radio.

"I've reached the entry point."

"Well done, boss," came the muted reply.

It was his trusted assistant Amir who spoke, his Moroccan accent giving life to a peculiar fusion of British and American English. Amir was high in a tree, gazing at the castle through a pair of binoculars and chewing, as always, on a hot cinnamon toothpick. His build was agile and muscular, his groomed dreadlocks shoulder length and adorned with a few dark beads. He brought the radio to his mouth and whispered.

"They still haven't left the conference room."

"What's been going on in there?" asked Gabriel. "I thought I heard a gunshot."

"You did. Nasrallah shot one his guys in the stomach. The poor bloke's still there. They sat him right next to Nasrallah."

Gabriel shook his head in amazement.

"Let me know when they leave. As soon as that room's empty, I'm going in as planned. Over and out."

Gabriel settled in for what he knew could be a very long wait. Apart from illustrating Najiallah Nasrallah's cruelty, the shooting was an indisputable sign that trouble was afoot in the castle, and where there was trouble, routines would almost certainly be upset.

It could be hours before the smugglers vacated the conference room and settled into their nightly pastime. It was a ritual that would take place in what Gabriel had dubbed *The Opium Den;* a room filled with rugs and cushions where the men would lie nightly in drug-induced stupors. Across the gorge he could see the room's uninhabited window, a tiny black dot in a massive stone wall.

Almost two weeks had passed since Gabriel had left his home in Boston, and if anything, his feeling of world weariness was only getting worse. Adhering to his new habit, he locked away the painful emotions and focused on the many tasks at hand.

Over the past nine days he and Amir had photographed, filmed and recorded every event that took place in the castle, going to great lengths to gain every scrap of intel possible. At one point they had even entered onto the grounds in the guise of electrical repairmen, using the opportunity to map the areas of the castle pertinent to their mission.

Gabriel considered how the unexpected crisis in the castle might affect their plans, but he knew that ultimately it did not matter. It was too late to abandon the mission. Amir had laid explosive charges all over the castle grounds. Removing them would be impossible to do without being detected, and leaving them behind to be discovered at daybreak would make returning impossible. There was no turning back. All Gabriel could do was wait and hope for the best.

For more than ten years, Amir had been a close and trusted friend of Gabriel's. They had originally met in the port of Tangiers when Amir, then just a boy of fourteen, had approached Gabriel as his ferry had landed. Amir had been wearing a tie-dyed Bob Marley shirt, his messy head resembling a tangled brown mop. He had offered to be Gabriel's guide, and even though Gabriel had told him to go away over a dozen times, he had followed him all the way to the marketplace, singing *Everything's Gonna Be All right.*

"I will show to you the medina!" he had said as he jogged happily at his side. "I know best places to shop!"

To this day, Gabriel could not be sure if it was the long climb to the old Arab quarter that had finally broken his will, or if he had indeed taken a liking to the boy. In the end he had given in. It was the best thing he could have ever done.

"Very well," Gabriel had said, "but you won't get a dime out of me. You'll have plenty with all the kickbacks from everything I buy. Now where can I get a decent drink around here?"

"Kickbacks? No kickbacks!" the young Amir had said, a twinkle in his eye. "I work for free! I take you for drink! Very illegal. Best place!"

The medina's narrow streets had bustled around Gabriel in a dizzy tangle of crowded shops and bellowing merchants, and before long, Amir had led him into a secluded courtyard café. No sooner had Gabriel sat down than he was brought a forbidden bottle of Johnny Walker Black, coincidentally his favourite scotch. It had been the start of a great friendship.

Gabriel studied the castle through a pair of infrared binoculars, all the while thinking back on their long alliance. How many artifacts had they retrieved together? How many times had they narrowly escaped with their lives?

The reggae-loving Arab was truly fearless and had saved his life on more than one occasion, despite all the hashish he smoked.

What was more, Amir had been a favourite of Gabriel's adoptive father, Professor Metrovich, and that was a very difficult standing for anyone to have achieved. The professor had been very selective with those he consorted with.

Gabriel put away the binoculars and reached sadly into his pack, unfolding a loose sheet of paper covered in his father's scribbled handwriting. He had found it stuffed into a notebook in the old man's desk; a letter to his colleague Father Franco that he had forgotten to mail.

Gabriel's mind went over the mysterious events for the hundredth time. The professor had been on an assignment in Turkey with the old priest. For some unknown reason they had chartered a plane to Santander. Two days later Gabriel had received a phone call from the Spanish Civil Guard informing him of their deaths. That was all there was. He was still reeling from the news.

It was thanks to his father that Gabriel had the unique career he had. Just as Professor Metrovich had been in his younger years, Gabriel too, was a treasure hunter, and a very good one at that. His father had taught him everything there was to know about locating and retrieving lost artifacts, especially those found in sunken ships.

Being on the board of directors for the Vatican Museum, the professor had also ensured that Gabriel's pieces would be purchased with no questions asked. In this way, Gabriel had become a very wealthy man. Even still, he would have given it all up if it had meant getting his father back again.

The professor had been everything to Gabriel. He had rescued him from an orphanage when he was an infant and had over the years taught him what it meant to be a man. Under his constant support and tutelage, Gabriel had grown up to become a noted archaeologist. As a child, he had practically lived on the Harvard campus where his father worked, spending his nights on the restored, turn-of-the-century schooner that was their home.

Since boyhood, Gabriel's life had revolved around sailing, diving, travelling, and above all else, studying. He had read more books than the most diligent of scholars, and had visited more countries than he could keep track of. To Gabriel, acquiring knowledge was an effortless pastime, like eating or drinking. Travelling, treasure hunting, diving, and sailing, were just the things he did in the time that was left over. It had always been that way.

Under the stealthy red light of a military flashlight, Gabriel scanned his father's letter until he found the part he was looking for. He had examined it countless times, but seeing it here, on the top of that ridge, high in the Atlas Mountains, renewed his sense of purpose, and gave him the stamina he needed to go through with the task at hand.

On the paper before him, scribbled in the professor's barely legible hand, was a short paragraph concerning something that he was totally unfamiliar with. It spoke of a legendary artifact that Gabriel had never heard of before.

I've been turning over some rocks in Istanbul and have made an important discovery. The long-lost Compostela Cube might still exist. I have narrowed its location to one of three places. If it is found, the legend will be validated, and there will no longer remain any doubts concerning the mystery surrounding the births of Gabriel and Natasha, and their birthright to the inheritance of the Cube.

Below these notes, was a crude drawing of the cube that had been referred to. It appeared to be a medieval quadriform, measuring fifteen centimeters on each of its sides. In essence, it was a simple box. Jotted down next to it was a name.

Gutierrez de la Cruz
Priest / Cartographer
835 - 901 CE"

Below it three more lines had been written. Two had been scribbled over and were illegible but the last line was easily read.

The Museum of Antiquities, Tangiers, Morocco.

Gabriel folded the letter carefully and put it away. That was all there had been to go on, but given his passion for relics, and the knowledge that his father was not one to speculate on anything other than facts, it was enough to start him on a quest to find the Compostela Cube. Even still, there were so many questions left unanswered.

What was this cube? It appeared to be an important artifact, but if this were the case, in all his years of study, would he not have heard mention of it? And who was Natasha, and why was this artifact *their* birthright? Was it possible that he might have a sister? If only the professor were still alive.

All his life Gabriel had seen his father working in a battered old diary, but he had never been permitted to even look at it. His gut told him that the answers to any question he might have concerning the artifact would be found in that book, but where was it? Gabriel had turned the boat upside-down but had found nothing. He was perplexed, and his desire to learn more about the Cube had taken on an almost obsessive quality.

Within a few days of finding the scribbled letter in his father's desk, Gabriel had boarded a plane to Tangiers. At the Museum of Antiquities, he had learned that the Cube had been stored in the archives for as long as the museum had existed, but it had never been displayed to the public.

"It was a beautifully illuminated quadriform," the curator had told him, "but not particularly impressive when compared to other illuminated artifacts from the same period. For that reason, I was very surprised when the museum was broken into last year, and only that piece was stolen."

Not knowing where to begin his search, Gabriel's thoughts had naturally gone to his assistant. Amir had grown up in the streets of Tangiers. If anyone could find out who had stolen the artifact, it would be him.

It was not long before Amir and Gabriel were sitting in a busy café, sipping mint tea and talking to an informant that Amir had arranged to meet. He was a giant of a man, with a fleshy scar that bisected the entire left side of his face. His massive brown head was shaven clean, and a patchwork of scars and bumps covered it as though it were a piece of battered luggage. On his neck was the symbol of a moth; an artless image brought into relief by the crude branding of a primitive hand.

Gabriel had been impressed. Despite his rough appearance, there seemed to be a profound dignity to the ugly giant. There was a quiet wisdom in his eyes.

"Najiallah Nasrallah," he had said, his voice as deep as a diamond mine.

He spat in disgust.

"He is a dog, living in the palace of a king."

Gabriel could still remember the informant's face in every detail, and the way he had scowled when he had spoken that name. Amir had put a roll of banknotes into the enormous hand and exchanged a knowing look with the man. Moments later the dark giant had vanished into the milling crowds.

"Nasrallah's a powerful drug lord, boss," Amir had said, squinting up through his dreadlocks. "He's said to have a taste for archaeology. I should've known it was him. He employs a lot of people in this town, but everyone hates him."

"Where can we find him?"

Amir had slugged back the last of his tea and was holding out the glass, admiring the bright green leaves that filled it.

"He lives in a Moorish castle," he had said, sitting back in his chair. "It's high in the mountains, north of Tetouan. It's impenetrable, boss."

"Impenetrable," muttered Gabriel under his breath.

He was looking through his binoculars and had just seen the lights go on in the opium den.

"Impenetrable until the Moors decided to hook-up to the electrical grid..."

His radio vibrated.

"You're clear to go, boss. They all left the conference room. Be careful."

"All right, Amir," he said. "Here goes nothing."

Gabriel shifted into a low crouch and took a deep breath.

Everybody else gets lawyers to arrange their inheritance. Why does it always have to be so difficult for me?

Reaching up, he hooked an insulated zip-line trolley to the power line that hung above him. He could see it disappearing into the darkness, stretching across the gorge that separated him from the castle. Somewhere in the distance, the cable would end at a narrow sill where it connected to the castle's main power supply. He would have to drop ten feet to a rooftop below or be electrocuted instantly.

A flash of bright light spread out behind the castle just then, followed immediately by the buffeting sound of an explosion. Amir's distractions had been detonated, and for an instant the castle looked like it belonged in Disney Land. A huge starburst spread out behind one of the turrets, followed by another and yet another. The wheels were in motion. There was no going back now.

"I sure hope the brakes work on this thing," he said, leaping from the cliff face and sliding out into the starry night.

CHAPTER 6

Soho, New York City.

Christian Antov lay on the floor, curled into a semi-fetal ball at the foot of an enormous abstract painting. He was a middle-aged man, thin and pale, and as always, he wore a tailored grey suit with a white shirt and neutral coloured tie. Around him his art studio stretched out like a war zone, the lofty ceilings and exposed brick walls doing nothing to mask the sordidness of the scene.

It had been another night of debauchery, and the scattered debris of empty bottles and cigarette butts left no doubt that there had been a large gathering here the night before. Christian opened an eye to see the handful of guests who had spent the night. They littered the floor like scattered bodies after a lost battle, framed by a backdrop of the dark expressionist paintings that comprised the bulk of his work.

"Get the hell out," he said weakly. "Get the hell out of my house..."

He sat up with a groan and leaned back onto a fifteen-foot canvas.

"Get out you ungrateful pieces of shit!"

Christian's face contorted in pain from the effort of his cry, but he could soon hear groans and muttering, followed by shuffling sounds and the patter of footsteps. His guests were familiar with his unpredictable temper, and they made no delay in their exodus.

Seconds later, he heard the door slam shut and he cursed aloud, letting his head fall into his hands. His brain was still reeling from the drink, and his body trembled from the excessive cocaine. He swallowed hard, trying to control his loose bowels. At least he was alone now. All he needed was a cigarette and a drink.

He was bending to reach for an abandoned butt on the floor when he spotted two men at the door. They were wearing black suits.

"I told you to leave!" he screamed. "GET OUT!"

There was a long pause.

"That is no way to treat your guests," said one of them. "And it is certainly not the way you were raised to behave."

They were too far away for Christian to discern their faces, but he immediately recognized their Dutch accents. A feeling of hatred filled him as the last of his strength ebbed away.

"What do you want?" he said listlessly, falling back onto the canvas again.

He plucked the trampled cigarette and lit it, inhaling deeply.

"What the fuck do you want from me?"

He could see the men approaching. They were immaculately dressed, and they picked their way through the carnage of the party as though it were human waste.

"You will be grieved to know that your father is near death, Christian," said one of the men. "He has sent us to collect you."

Christian laughed coldly.

"He can die and rot for all I care."

"Get up, Christian," said the other man firmly. "The jet is waiting."

CHAPTER 7

The Atlas Mountains, Morocco.

"Amir!"

Gabriel's whisper sounded more like a scream. He was speaking into his radio, the sound of the fireworks outside still echoing through the castle.

"Can you hear me?"

"Where are you?"

"I'm still in the conference room. The Cube's not in the safe."

Amir threw down his toothpick.

"You gotta get out of there, boss. They're already starting to comb the place. You don't have much time."

"I'm not leaving without the Cube," said Gabriel, still searching through the safe. "Where are they concentrating their search?"

"Perimeters for now," said Amir, his normally smooth tenor beginning to roughen a little at the edges. "Guards are all over the grounds. They've even got dogs. It won't be long before they start searching the castle!"

"Where's Nasrallah?"

"I don't know!" he said, frustrated. "Inside somewhere. Boss. Truly. You gotta get out now. You're in a lot of danger. Your escape route could be cut off at any moment."

"I'm not leaving without the Cube."

Gabriel pocketed his radio and scanned the room. It was without a doubt the castle's most important chamber, its twenty-foot ceilings held aloft by four massive columns. On the room's northern wall ran a long arcade of elegant sandstone arches. They opened onto an expansive terrace. At some point the arcade had been glassed in, and it was through these windows that Amir had been spying on the meeting only moments before. In the centre of the room sat the large conference table where the criminals had gathered.

There was a pool of blood coagulating under one of the chairs there. It contents had been tracked all over the room, painting the stone floor as though it were an abstract canvas.

Gabriel stood before the empty safe he had only just blasted open. Its twisted door was laying on the floor at his feet. Next to it, he could see a set of footprints that stood apart from the other boot prints in the room. They were made by Nasrallah's dress shoes, and Gabriel followed them out of the room.

Whereas all the other traffic had gone in the direction of the opium den, Nasrallah had taken a different path. Gabriel could see traces of his prints leading down a long stone corridor and he followed them to a spiraling flight of descending steps.

Moving as silently as possible, he made his way down, arriving at a small antechamber containing a heavy wooden door. He could hear two guards calling out in Arabic somewhere above. He pressed himself against the wall and remained there motionless. Behind the door there was only silence. When the guards had passed, he tried the handle and found it was unlocked.

"Here goes nothing," he muttered, and then he slowly opened the door.

With nothing but the dim light from the stairwell to illuminate the room, it was difficult to see what lay within. Gabriel entered regardless, closing the door quietly behind him and making use of a large deadbolt to lock it shut. If the guards decided to come that way, they would have one more obstacle to get through before finding him.

With the door closed, the room plunged into darkness, but Gabriel had come prepared. In the green hue of his infrared goggles, he saw that he was in a storeroom of sorts. It was a narrow chamber, littered with cluttered tables and shelves, all laden with scales, cardboard boxes, and plastic bags.

"The packaging department," he muttered. "But no drugs anywhere. Weird."

There were three doors here. Two were shut and one was slightly ajar. From the open door came a cooler reading than the others, leading Gabriel to consider that the room might be a connecting chamber, and the one Nasrallah had taken. He approached it with stealth. In a chamber such as this, even the slightest shuffle would be amplified twenty times over. Gabriel eyed the door, listening intently for any sounds behind it.

"Let's see if you took door number three…"

He pushed the door open and switched off his night vision, turning on a black light scanner. Immediately he was able to see the glowing residue of blood from Nasrallah's shoes. It shone brightly back at him, leaving a track of irregular marks heading off into the chamber.

Gabriel entered silently and reactivated his night vision. He was in what looked to be the castle's original kitchen, the giant hearth before him still blackened by the soot of ancient fires. To his left, beneath a row of crudely hewn sinks, he noticed a drainage trough emptying into a narrow pit.

Gabriel cocked an eyebrow and pushed back his messy hair. A faint glow was radiating from an open doorway just ahead of him. He removed his goggles and approached it cautiously, pressing himself against the wall and peeking in.

Within was a medium-sized room, its worktables cluttered with computers and an assortment of scientific apparatus. What had once been a pantry had been converted into a laboratory of sorts, its tiled floors and walls providing the perfect hermetic environment.

He stepped forward silently. A particular table had caught his attention. It sat apart from the others and was the only one not covered in clutter. Above it hung a single halogen fixture, its dimmed light illuminating a very out of context piece of equipment.

What would a drug lord be wanting with a portable X-ray machine?

Gabriel made his way to the table and was almost disappointed by what he found. There, resting on a tray of lead, was the treasure he had been seeking, but it was by no means what he had been expecting. Under the halogen light he saw it for what it was: A typical quadriform cube, measuring some fifteen centimeters in width, and constructed from what appeared to be vellum or wood.

My God, is this what all the fuss is about?

Gabriel had seen countless treasures in his career; priceless works of art boasting outstanding materials and craftsmanship. Disappointingly, the piece before him seemed unremarkable, a mediocre artifact at best.

Typical of such quadriforms, each of its six sides were decorated with illuminations, but in this case, the illustrations consisted of six crudely rendered apples, their peels removed, but curiously left coiled around them. Gabriel was perplexed.

What kind of medieval subject matter is a peeled apple?

He bent closer to the relic, noticing only then the elegance of the framework that encased it. Constructed in time-blackened silver, it comprised an exoskeleton of intertwining branches, each section encrusted with what appeared to be heavily soiled rubies and emeralds.

It was not until Gabriel had carefully picked up the artifact that he was at last made aware of its uniqueness. Whereas most of the quadriforms he had encountered had been hollow and used for decorative purposes, this artifact was surprisingly heavy for its size.

Now I can see why he was trying to x-ray it. There's got to be something inside.

The artifact was not what Gabriel had been expecting to take hold of. In it he felt an inexplicable quality, something that defied any kind of rational description. As he turned it over in his hands, he would have easily lost track of time were it not for the vibration of his radio calling him back to reality.

"I found it," whispered Gabriel, snapping out of his trance. "Amir. I've got the Cube."

"Boss. You gotta listen very carefully."

It was the first time Gabriel had ever sensed fear in Amir's voice. By its varying volume, he guessed that Amir was running as he spoke.

"I had to give up my lookout point. There are guards everywhere. I just saw Nasrallah. He came out screaming. They know you're inside!"

Gabriel heard a violent pounding. The guards had arrived at the door he had bolted shut. He looked up, startled.

"Shit."

He could hear Amir's urgent whisper through the radio.

"Get to the escape route right away! You might still be able to make it there in time. Call me the minute you get through and I'll set off the charges. I'll meet you at the river rendezvous point."

"Amir," said Gabriel, his voice calm and steady. "I'll never make it out that way now. I'm deep in the castle. I want you to blow the escape route right away. With any luck it'll confuse them and give me time to get out of here."

"What? Are you crazy? That's the only way out. You know that! You gotta run!"

"Amir!" said Gabriel, a little too loudly. "There's no time to argue. Blow it NOW! That's an order. I'll meet you at the river. Just look out for me. I don't know where I'll be. Now do it!"

Gabriel turned off his radio. He could have no more distractions. He produced a plastic food container from his pack and put the Cube in it, sealing it tightly. He had got this far. He had retrieved the Cube; *his* Cube. He would get out of this place. He knew he could do it.

The pounding was getting louder. More guards had arrived at the door and Gabriel knew he had a minute at most. He sprinted back to the room he had just been in and approached the dark pit that the wash basins emptied into, producing a flashlight from his belt. The channel angled its way downward and looked to be unobstructed.

"The Moors were geniuses," he said to himself, trying to think straight. "Geniuses are practical people. Practical people always dump their shit into the closest body of water they can find."

He peered into the drain.

"If this goes anywhere, it goes to the river. It just has to."

Behind him, the banging had turned into a violent pounding. The soldiers had found something to ram the door with. They would be upon him in seconds. Gabriel tightened the straps of his pack. In the beam of his flashlight, he watched a six-inch millipede scurry into the pit. He passed a hand over his two-day beard and battled with his revulsion of the crawling insects.

Suddenly, the castle shook underfoot, jarring him to attention. Amir had just blown up his former escape route. Any other option he might have had for escape was gone now. Cursing under his breath, he lowered himself into the tight passage headfirst. At six-foot-two Gabriel was not a small man, but the channel was just big enough to wiggle through.

"Good thing I'm not claustrophobic," he muttered, lying.

CHAPTER 8

Los Picos De Europa, Northern Spain.

Only when the last throbbing beats of the rescue helicopter had faded away did Isaac Rodchenko regain consciousness. Before him, precariously perched on a cliff's edge, and set high amid a sweeping mountainscape, lay the wreckage of the chartered floatplane. Trapped in it were the bodies of Father Franco Rossi and Professor Agardi Metrovich (as well as the plane's pilot) all inaccessible to the Spanish Civil Guard's retrieval team due to the buffeting winds.

Only a single paramedic had been lowered on a cable to confirm there were no survivors. He had found the bodies of the dead but failed to locate Isaac Rodchenko. Having secretly stowed himself away on the plane, Isaac had not appeared on the manifest, and as he had been thrown clear of the impact zone, he had gone completely unnoticed. As it was, he lay pinned beneath a section of fuselage, with the corpse of his son emerging from a broken coffin at his feet.

Earlier that day, and much to the surprise of the professor and Father Franco, Isaac had listened attentively to their strange request and granted them permission to conduct a special burial ceremony for his son on the island where he had been conceived. Given his faltering mental health, it had been agreed that Isaac would not attend the ceremony, but unbeknownst to the professor and the priest, Isaac had secretly boarded the floatplane and hidden himself in the cargo area next to the casket.

The sun was low in the sky when Isaac began to slip once again into unconsciousness. His face was badly bruised, his dark grey suit torn in places but amazingly free of blood. Overhead a rushing mass of cloud sped past like a giant landmass, lulling him into a delirious half sleep.

Below the crash site, the jagged mountains of *Los Picos de Europa* stretched out like a mouthful of teeth, each peak a mountain unto itself. It was here in this wild place, far from the world of men, and surrounded by death on all sides, that Isaac witnessed something that defied all the laws of physical nature. To his utter horror, he could feel the corpse of his son jerking and twitching at his feet.

"Dear Father in heaven," he prayed, his eyes wide with fear. "Deliver me from this evil. Bring peace to the body of my child."

Isaac tried in vain to move his foot away from what he knew to be an abomination, all the while battling with his guilt for wanting to do so. This was his beloved son, his flesh and blood. But like a frozen stone, the malformed cadaver seemed to be drawing the life from him. Through the sole of his shoe, he could feel its malignance. This was no longer his poor and helpless son. It had transformed into something utterly evil.

Isaac looked down to see the body heaving and lashing about with great force. His son was dead. He had watched him die. What lay at his feet was no longer his progeny. It was a beast. A cold corpse that somehow still lived.

CHAPTER 9

Rome, Italy.

The rain was falling in torrents when Gabriel's cab pulled up to the old stone church. It was 6:30 a.m. and Rome was just waking up. In the distance he could hear the siren of an ambulance cutting through the humid air, the wet cobblestones at his feet reflecting the erratic flashes of headlights as a growing number of cars rumbled past.

"*Grazie,*" Gabriel said, handing the driver a fifty euro note.

With a nod of thanks, the cabbie passed him his luggage. A single leather pack, travel worn and battered.

Navigating his way through an obstacle course of puddles, Gabriel made his way into the shelter of the monastery's arcade like a child playing hopscotch. Before him a towering wooden door barred his way. He shook the rain from his jacket and sounded a great iron knocker that hung at the centre of the portico.

Within moments a little door opened within the larger door and Gabriel had to duck low to get through. An old Christian brother was waiting on the other side, and he shut the postern behind him as he entered, the clank of its deadbolt echoing through the empty chapel.

"Good morning, my son," said Fra Bartolomeo, embracing him heartily. "The bishop is presently at his toilet. He will be meeting you for breakfast very soon."

Gabriel released him but kept hold of his shoulders.

"Thanks, Fra," he said warmly.

He was always amazed by the strength in the old man's body.

"It's good to see you."

"And it is always good to see you, my dear boy. I see you have not yet discarded that decaying pack of yours."

Gabriel held up the leather duffel bag. The old brother was right. If it were not for the meticulous repairs he had made to it, the thing would have fallen apart then and there. As it was, it was fully serviceable.

"It's hard to part with an old friend," said Gabriel, and he thought it funny that within such an old and battle-scarred pack could be one of the most important artifacts he had ever come across.

They made their way along the aisle of a dark chapel, passing a large bank of candles flickering in little red cups. Their wicks sent up plumes of vapor that mingled with the incense, and Gabriel breathed deeply. He loved the smell of the old church, and although an unbeliever himself, he had always basked in the profound sense of peace that radiated from the place.

Up in the rafters, the sound of the pounding rain could be heard on the chapel's roof. It echoed through the space, giving life to the marble statues that looked down at them from their niches above. It was a familiar feeling to Gabriel, being under their gaze; something that had always comforted him as a boy. His eyes scanned their stoic faces.

A manmade fantasy to explain the inexplicable.

He had never been able to understand how anyone could dedicate their entire life to a myth, but at the same time, he respected their faith. It was a testament to the power of the human mind, be it sane or delusional.

Fra Bartolomeo made a quick turn into a small alcove, and within moments they had passed through a concealed door that led into a narrow passageway. With the arched ceiling only inches above his head, Gabriel found himself having to duck at regular intervals to avoid the naked light bulbs that stretched out before him. He could see a long line of them ahead, emerging from a conduit that ran the entire length of the tunnel.

Where did this route come from? I thought I knew every inch of this monastery...

"Please pardon my detour," said the brother over his shoulder. "This way we can avoid getting wet from the rain in the cloisters. His Excellency's chambers are just up ahead."

Gabriel had to rush to keep up with the old man's pace.

"That's quite all right, Fra," he replied cheerfully. "I've only just been in much tighter quarters."

Gabriel shuddered at the memory of his harrowing escape. Not twenty-four hours had passed since he had made his way through the Moorish sewer. It had been a hell he would soon make every effort to forget. For over an hour he had squeezed his way through the entrails of the castle, caked in sewage, starved of oxygen, and beleaguered by rats and insects of every kind.

On two separate occasions he had been forced to cut through iron bars using the mini acetylene torch he had thankfully packed among his equipment. The choking fumes had nearly made him lose consciousness. With the stench of waste still trapped in his olfactory, Gabriel followed the old brother, reliving the final moments of his trying ordeal.

Deep under the Moorish castle, when he had at long last reached the end of the tunnel, he found that the passage plunged into a reservoir of sewage water. In his pack was a breathing apparatus containing just ten minutes of oxygen. It was meant to have been used to cover the short distance underwater that had been part of his original escape route. On this occasion, he had no idea how long he would be required to stay submerged. With no other options available, Gabriel had donned the mask and proceeded.

"It won't be long now," said the brother, but Gabriel was too lost in thought to reply.

Nine minutes had already passed when he came upon a second set of iron bars. He knew he had less than a minute of air left and was unsure as to how much gas remained in the torch. He did not waste time finding out.

In the murky light of his flashlight, he could see that two of the three bars had already rotted in their mounts. He shook them and they fell away easily. The middle bar, however, was anchored quite firmly. In a moment his torch was blazing, cutting through the old iron. Even still, Gabriel wondered how much tunnel remained on the other side. His air had run out sometime ago now, and he had only been able to half fill his lungs. Suddenly the bar broke loose and he was through, feeling the surrounding water drop in temperature almost immediately.

With burning lungs Gabriel pushed his way upward, moving freely for the first time in over an hour. After what seemed an eternity he reached the surface, sucking in the night air hungrily. Somehow he had done it. He was out, and he was still alive.

"Boss. Is that you?" came the whispered call.

A large inflatable river raft appeared suddenly, and a strong hand grasped Gabriel's shoulder strap and hauled him aboard.

"Amir," said Gabriel, when they had landed on the river's edge at last. "If you'd shaved this morning, I'd probably be kissing you right now."

"Not smelling like that you wouldn't," said his faithful assistant, pushing aside his dreadlocks to get a better look at him.

He stuffed the raft under some bushes and covered it with twigs and dried leaves.

"Where the hell have you been anyway?"

Gabriel smiled and shook his head in disbelief.

"That was far too close…" he muttered under his breath.

"I actually thought it was quite out of the way," replied the brother, and Gabriel remembered how sharp the old man's hearing had always been.

Arriving at the end of the secret tunnel they approached a small wooden door that swung out effortlessly. Ducking low, Gabriel emerged into a large stone room. It was warm, and the furniture was plush and velvety.

"Wait here, Gabriel," said Fra. "The bishop will come down soon."

Gabriel made his way into the waiting room as Fra disappeared back into the tunnel. He had always loved this room, but he had never entered it as he had just now.

"Who would have thought," he muttered, looking back at the section of bookshelf as it swung closed. "A secret passage I didn't know about."

Gabriel walked into the carpeted room. Above him the vaulted ceiling rose solidly, with four gothic arches curving up to meet at a circular stone bearing the cross of St. George. Around him hung an assortment of detailed tapestries depicting great historical scenes. He approached his favourite one. It was a large work depicting the famous *Burning of Savonarola* in the Piazza della Signoria of Florence.

In the centre of the composition the puritanical priest could be seen chained to a great iron cross, with two of his supporters crucified to his left and right. At their feet, great flames licked upward. Savonarola had been a priest vehemently opposed to the Renaissance movement, and was infamous for his rampant destruction of what he considered to be immoral works of art. Below the scene, on the tapestry's ornate border, was an inscription quoting the executioner who had supposedly lit the pyre.

The one who wanted to burn me is now himself put to the flames.

"I see you are reliving one of the greatest victories of the Florentine artist," came a familiar voice from behind.

"Marcus!" said Gabriel turning. "Have I got something to show you!"

"Well," said the old man smiling. "I certainly hope it can wait until after breakfast."

The two embraced as they always did. A great love existed between them, and although the retired bishop had no blood relation to Gabriel, he had been a lifelong friend of his father, and as a result, had always been like an uncle to him.

Throughout his life, Gabriel had spent so much time in the old monastery that it was like a second home to him. He was familiar with the entire grounds. The bedroom he had always stayed in as a boy opened directly onto the main cloisters, and many a night he had sneaked out to explore the countless mysteries the old building had to offer.

Walking side by side, the two slowly made their way to the *breakfast room*, as the old bishop liked to call it. In truth it was a small overgrown greenhouse that opened into the monastery's private gardens. They arrived to find a little table set for two, complete with a linen tablecloth and full silverware. It sat amongst copious plants, and beside it a mossy fountain gurgled, silenced by the rain that pounded the panes of glass above. All around them finches chirped and fluttered.

"Your father and I breakfasted here quite often, as did you, my son," said the old bishop, sitting down slowly. "I can remember you as a boy, taking your sausages into the ferns, and feeding your crumpets to the birds on the sly."

Gabriel remembered too, and for a moment, a deep sadness took him. He missed his father dearly.

"Marcus, I've got something I want to show you."

"Tut-tut!" interrupted the bishop. "I know, my son. We have much to speak of, but first, we old men must have our nourishment. You forget the hour at which you come. I would normally still be sleeping."

"I'm sorry. I came here straight from the airport. I didn't think."

"Not to worry," said the old bishop with a reassuring smile, and just then, Fra Bartolomeo arrived carrying a large tray of food.

"Ah yes!" said the bishop, rubbing his old hands together. "God bless you, my friend, and thanks be to God. We have been graced with one more meal. Let us enjoy it. It could very well be my last!"

"If you continue to say such things, I will take this away and bring you lent rations," scolded the brother lovingly.

"God forbid such cruelty!" came the immediate reply.

Even perfect strangers felt a warm affection for the venerable bishop. It would have been impossible not to, and Gabriel smiled, knowing the old man's encompassing love for the gastronomical delights.

Looking down at his plate, Gabriel welcomed the hot food. As always, it had been lovingly prepared by Suora Angelica, a very competent Italian nun whom Gabriel had also known since childhood. It was the regular breakfast fare. Poached eggs, bacon, sausages, potatoes, fried fish, baked beans, fresh croissants, and coffee in a French bodum. The perfect continental breakfast, and the eighty-five-year-old bishop showed that he still had quite an appetite.

Gabriel was dizzy with sleepiness by the time he had finished the meal.

"Let us now retire to the library," said Bishop Marcus, noting Gabriel's fatigue. "There we can discuss your Compostela Cube."

"But how did you know?" said Gabriel, rubbing his eyes sleepily.

"I'm not as dumb as I look!" said the old bishop with a wink.

He scrubbed at his beard with a napkin, loosing a fragment of egg that had clung there the whole while.

"That is to say, I am much smarter than I appear!"

When they arrived at the library, Gabriel could barely keep his eyes open. The food was settling into his stomach, and his body was beginning to respond.

"Take off your shoes and lie yourself down on that sofa, my boy," said the bishop from the threshold. "I'll be right back. We've got a lot to talk about, you and I."

Finding himself alone in the room, Gabriel decided to take the bishop up on his suggestion. Wearily he kicked off his shoes and stretched himself out on the soft leather sofa. Beside him, thin orange flames flickered lazily behind the glass doors of a cast iron stove, and the familiarity of the room instilled a feeling of peace and security in him. As his eyes wandered around the paneled library, roaming dizzily from bookshelf to bookshelf, Gabriel began to feel a deep slumber take him.

"I'll just close my eyes for a second until he gets back..."

CHAPTER 10

Amsterdam, The Netherlands.

It was night when the private jet landed in Amsterdam. Christian had slept the entire way. He emerged from the executive cabin to find his two escorts standing on either side of the door, their arms crossed over their chests officially.

"I trust you had a good flight, Christian?" asked one of the men.

Christian walked past them as if they did not exist. He was a prisoner, and he always had been. Bending to look out the window he felt a distinct pang of hatred surface as he gazed downward. This was his hometown, and he did not know what he hated more, the city or his father. The mere thought of the man filled Christian with bitterness and scorn.

When the plane came to a stop beside a waiting limousine, Christian, familiar with the mechanism, opened the hatch in time to see a motorized staircase pull into place. He stepped onto it before it had come to a stop and made his way off the plane and into the car before his two escorts had time to follow.

"Take me to my family residence," he ordered, closing the door as the two guards approached.

"Now!" he barked.

The car sped off instantly, leaving the two men on the tarmac. Christian lowered his window, feeling a flow of cool, Dutch air wash over him. It was a familiar smell that he deeply despised. It was too fresh, too clean, and it smacked of the forward-moving mentality characteristic of the Netherlands. He lit a cigarette and passed a hand through his dishevelled hair.

The Antov family estate was located in the outskirts of Amsterdam, its manicured grounds, majestic stone walls and shining copper rooftops sending an instant message of power and affluence. How long these buildings had housed his ancestors Christian did not know, but if he was sure of one thing, it was that his family was much older than the stately Napoleonic residence: much older indeed.

"Take me to the west entrance," he ordered, "and call ahead to have a bath prepared for me. I want a bottle of red wine and Eggs Florentine waiting for me when I'm done."

"Very good, sir."

The car rolled down the long drive that led into the grounds, its wheels rumbling over the cobblestones. Christian lit another cigarette.

Maybe I'll get lucky, and he'll be dead already.

* * * * * *

"Your father has only just awoken," said the desiccated old butler. "Your timing could not be better, Master Christian. Please follow me."

Christian passed through the large oak doors to find his father lying on a great bed in his darkened chambers, a pair of nurses flanking him. A bearded doctor was there too, his patient's limp wrist in his hands. He looked up to see Christian enter the room and shook his head gravely. A feeling of relief sparked in Christian's heart.

Is he dead?

His hopes were soon dashed when he saw a brittle arm dart upward, its bony hand clenching the doctor's shirt and pulling him in with uncanny strength. Christian watched the doctor's face as his ear drew close to the patient's mouth, noting the change in his demeanor as the inaudible words were uttered.

"Everyone out," he whispered, coming to his feet. "The Baron wants a word with his son."

Christian remained motionless at the threshold, a knot tightening in the centre of his chest. In a matter of seconds, the medical entourage had flowed past, closing the doors behind them and leaving him alone with the man he most hated in the entire world. An instant later a deep fear was welling up in

Christian, conjuring up specters of childhood abuse, and reminding him of his despicable and worthless status.

The room was dimly lit now, most of the light having vanished when the doors had closed. It was a massive chamber, with the distant walls and towering ceilings dissolving into the gloom. Only the oversized four-post bed was fully visible. It was a dais-like structure encased in hanging textiles and ornate cushions the colour of dried blood.

Christian stood there silently, frozen with a fear that had been nurtured in him since he was a boy. He could hear the scratching hiss of his father's breath and his knees felt on the verge of giving out.

It was all Christian could do to remain on his feet. Real or imagined, his father's customary psychic assault was working its way into his brain, and it was doing so with unprecedented intensity.

All power is based in fear. Fear must be maintained at all costs.

These were his father's words; words that had been drilled into Christian for as long as he could remember. They filled his head with the power of a swelling ocean. He had always felt his father's repugnant presence within him, but never with such clarity. What had always been vague and hidden was suddenly plain to see. It caught him off balance.

"Come," came the hiss, and like a lamb being led to slaughter Christian obeyed, his hatred giving way to a silent plea for mercy.

"Father," he whispered, arriving at the bedside.

The sight he witnessed was ghastly, and he fought back an urge to flee. It had been more than three years since he had last seen the man, and the transformation that had taken place in that time was nothing short of demonic.

There before him, lying amidst the finest silks in the world, was the grey and wasted form of what could only be described as a dying lizard.

"You need not fear me any longer, son," hissed the beast, craning his corpselike head closer. "Now that you have learned fear, it is *you* who shall be feared. You will know power the likes of which no other man has ever known."

The implications of such a promise made Christian's head spin, and it was only after a few seconds that a full comprehension of his new situation struck him. He was the sole heir. His father's entire empire would be passed onto him alone.

Christian swayed on his feet. Along with the intoxicating realization of his approaching inheritance had come the unobstructed awareness of his father's presence within him. It was a feeling similar to that of being violated, and the clarity of it made him seethe with repulsion.

Since early childhood, his father had infested him body and mind. The problem had been that he had never known any other way of being, and as such, the defilement had always gone undetected.

A tsunami of rage suddenly flooded into Christian, erupting with murderous intent. He heard the words leave his mouth like a curse. It was as if someone else was speaking them.

"Get out of me *you piece of shit…* "

Never before would Christian have dared to utter such a thing to his father, but his words flowed freely. With unrestrained contempt he spat on the old man, and to his utter surprise he watched as the reptilian face broke into a dry smile.

"Nautonnier!" cried his father suddenly, and then his head fell back onto his pillows, only to continue speaking in a whisper.

Christian bent closer despite himself, a look of disgust contorting his features as he strained to listen.

"It is done, Nautonnier," whispered his father weakly. "The boy is ready…"

With these last words he released a long, rattling breath, and just then Christian spotted the brittle figure of a man emerging from the shadows. His head was hooded, but hints of an ancient face could be seen in the lamplight. He approached the bedside and removed a serpentine ring from his father's finger.

"Behold," he hissed, proffering Christian the band. "Your father is dead. You are master now. Use your power wisely."

CHAPTER 11

Rome, Italy.

Gabriel awoke suddenly. The only light in the room was coming from a wood-burning stove that glowed warmly in the corner. The same person who had covered him in a blanket had also turned out the lights.

"What time is it?" he groaned, looking down at his watch.

The dial glowed blue in the darkness. 11:23pm. He sat up stiffly and made the calculations in his head. It took him a while. He was still half asleep.

"Let's see. I got here at around six-thirty... Finished breakfast by eight..."

He stopped short.

"Crap. I've been asleep for fifteen hours..."

Gabriel found his way to the end table and switched on a lamp. There was a note there. It was written in the calligraphic script of the bishop, a little shaky but still assertive.

I hope this note finds you well rested, my son. You have been through quite an ordeal. Please feel free to make yourself comfortable in the visitor's room. I will see you for breakfast at eight-thirty sharp.
M.D.L.

Gabriel put the note down sleepily. Had he read it more carefully, he would have understood that it was not his habitual room that he was being told to use, but rather a guest room next to the chapel.

He had no sooner started off than he was taken by a strong urge to urinate. With a bursting bladder he rushed along the dimly lit corridor until he arrived at the door of his usual room. There he would find a toilet, and with no time to spare.

Not wanting to wake the sharp-eared Fra Bartolomeo in his chambers next door, he moved the latch slowly. After that there was no time to even reach for the light switch. He knew that just to the right, past the armoire, was the door to the bathroom. He entered without hesitation and the relief that fell over him was encompassing. He sighed deeply, reveling with satisfaction at the deep rumbling sound of his stream.

"Seventeen hours without a leak…" he muttered, shaking his head in disbelief.

Feeling invigorated, Gabriel moved to the sink and rinsed his hands. It was there he noticed something was not quite right. Reflected on the tiles he could see light where there should have been no light at all. It was coming from the bedroom outside, a fact that puzzled him greatly considering there had been no lights on when he had entered. A feeling of dread washed over him.

"Shit," he muttered, the last of his grogginess vanishing.

He recalled the bishop's note.

The Visitor's Room. Shit!

Turning slowly, Gabriel made his way to the bathroom door. It was still ajar. Through it he saw that a lamp in the room had indeed been lit. Whoever was outside was clearly awake. He stood there without moving. Listening.

"Hello?" he said at last. "I think I might have just used your restroom."

A young woman's voice replied.

"Yes, I believe you did."

Her voice was timid, her accent Italian but schooled in American English.

Gabriel was at a loss.

This is not good. There's a girl out there and I just barged into her room and pissed in her toilet. Marcus is going to kill me.

He tried to think of what to do next, but no solution came. She was clearly in her bed, so he could not just walk out, but he could not remain where he was either. His mind seemed to stall. There was an awkward silence.

"Will you be staying long?" she asked.

It took a moment for Gabriel to respond.

"No. I'm quite done."

There was another pause.

"You can come through," she said. "It's all right."

Gabriel stepped into the bedroom and froze. Wrapped in the blankets of the bed he had always slept in was the most stunning woman he had ever laid eyes on. The soft light of the bedside lamp made her look almost angelic, and her startled eyes were large and childlike. Thick chestnut hair fell over her slender shoulders in heavy ringlets. Gabriel swallowed hard.

"I'm Natasha," she said carefully.

Gabriel was silent for a moment.

"I'm Gabriel."

Her stern expression made him want to smile, but something told him to be careful. His eyes twinkled despite his best efforts.

"My apologies," he said as sincerely as he could. "It's just that I normally stay in this room. Bishop Marcus is like an uncle to me. I was half asleep."

"I didn't know that Uncle Marcus had a nephew," she said, sitting up and eyeing him distrustfully. "And you would think I would know, considering that he is like an uncle to *me*."

Gabriel was too unpolished for Natasha's tastes. He had a messy, travelworn look about him that made her want to throw him in a bath. She sat up a little more.

"And for your information," she added, "this is the room where *I* normally stay."

Gabriel's mouth hung open. He was about to speak when a soft knock sounded at the door. A second later Fra Bartolomeo poked his head into the room.

"Natasha," he whispered. "What is going on here? I thought I heard the voice of a man."

He looked around.

"Gabriel!" he cried. "What are you doing in this young lady's room? Have you lost your senses? This is completely unacceptable!"

"No, Fra. It was a mis—"

Gabriel's words were cut short as the old brother burst into the room and took hold of his collar, escorting him out with practiced agility. Fra Bartolomeo had long been a schoolmaster before his retirement.

"Fra!" pleaded Gabriel as he was removed. "I thought this was *my* room…"

CHAPTER 12

The Atlas Mountains, Morocco.

"You have betrayed me, and now you are lying to me. Tell me who stole the relic!"

It was Najiallah Nasrallah who spoke, his voice as greasy as his shoulder length hair. His accent was impossible to trace, and he wore a silky black suit under a blood-spattered apron. A shirtless, muscle-bound hulk was strapped to a barber's chair before him, slumped under a flickering fluorescent bulb in a windowless chamber.

"No, Master," muttered the giant of a man. "I would never betray you..."

His voice was deep and broken, but still dignified. He eyed the cattle prod in his captor's hand.

"There was talk in the streets," he continued, swallowing the blood that welled in his mouth. "An American was asking about your relic. His name was Gabriel Parker. There were leaks after the robbery. The informer could have been anyone."

"Do not lie to me!" snapped Nasrallah, pressing the instrument into the man's ribs.

The ensuing scream was deep and resounding, and much to Nasrallah's annoyance, the prisoner slipped into unconsciousness. Nasrallah jerked around to face a middle-aged doctor standing nearby. His lab coat was bloodstained too, his face pale from exhaustion.

"Why didn't the drugs keep him awake?" hissed Nasrallah.

The doctor pressed a finger to the prisoner's neck to check his pulse.

"I gave him a massive dose, sir, but he is still only a man. If you continue like this he will die."

With the prisoner's head tilting to the side, it was easy to see the large scar that bisected his face. In charge of two hashish production operations in Tangiers, and a smuggling ring in Algeria, he was Nasrallah's top captain; the only man left alive who had been involved in the Cube's robbery from the Museum of Antiquities.

Nasrallah scowled down at the unconscious brute, his upper lip tightening into a snarl.

"You're a slithering worm, Bahadur. You will pay dearly for your betrayal."

Within hours of Gabriel's escape, Nasrallah had ordered his helicopter to collect the giant and bring him to the castle. His family had also been taken, and they were currently locked in a cell within earshot of his screams.

Nasrallah stripped off his apron and turned to leave.

"He had a hand in this," he muttered under his breath. "I should have killed him along with the others."

Nasrallah's phone vibrated just then, and he stopped at the door to look down at it. His expression changed when he identified the caller.

"Father Vanderwerken," he said amiably. "How can I help you?"

His expression turned to shock and disbelief.

"But how can this be?"

He listened again.

"No sir, I do not doubt you. If you say the Cube is in Rome, then it must be. Yes, sir. Kindly relay your data and I will send a team out immediately. Yes, sir. At your service."

Nasrallah pocketed the phone and turned to face the doctor, his jaw tightening.

"Clean up Bahadur and make him well enough to work again!"

CHAPTER 13

Rome, Italy.

Gabriel sat in a plush leather armchair, scanning the guestroom he had just been escorted to. He was completely awake now, and he looked around with a refreshed alertness that was more in keeping with early morning than the time on his watch. His eyes fell on his leather duffel bag. He could see it resting on a rosewood table at the foot of his bed.

"Couldn't hurt to have a look," he muttered, rising from his seat. "Anything to take my mind off that girl..."

Even before Natasha had introduced herself, Gabriel had suspected that she was the woman named in his father's notes. According to the professor, the Cube was as much hers as it was his.

She said Marcus was like an uncle to her...

He rubbed the stubble on his face. It made no sense. Surely somebody would have mentioned her. What bothered him most was the way she had made him stop in his tracks. He shook his head and opened his duffel bag.

"She's got high maintenance written all over her. Another prissy little princess."

Gabriel shook off his misgivings and produced the container that housed the mysterious Cube. As he had noted before, it was surprisingly heavy, having a density that reminded him of an uncooked roast. A noise outside caught his attention just then and he turned to face the window. It had sounded like a dull thud. He remained motionless for a while, listening.

Most likely a tree bough downed by the storm.

The rain had yet to let up. Roman winters tended to be rainy, but this season had been particularly cold and wet. Outside, the downpour was pummelling the wooden shutters, and Gabriel was glad of the fire that burned low in the hearth. It was a foul night, and the room was quite comfortable. He moved to the desk and placed the artifact down carefully.

It was such an odd thing, this Cube, quite unlike anything he had ever seen before. When closely scrutinized it was easy to see that it was more than it appeared to be. Its density was of course the first give away, but surpassing this was the lack of attention that had been given to the illuminations that adorned it.

Compared to the detailed work that had gone into the carving of its external framework, the illustrations seemed overly crude. Each side contained the same image of an apple with its peel removed and arranged around it in a coil.

It was only then that Gabriel noticed something peculiar. Having studied similar quadriforms of the same epoch, he knew that their frameworks were always attached last, thus preventing any of the vellum from peeling off the artifact's surface over time. In this case, that precaution had not been observed. The edges of the vellum were peeling up, even if ever so slightly.

"Wait a minute..." he muttered, passing his finger over an upturned edge. "Is it possible there could be something behind these illustrations?"

Gabriel groaned as it dawned on him. These were not just pictures of peeled apples. They were instructions. He tested a loose edge with his pocketknife to find that the old vellum offered little resistance to being peeled back. He stopped himself immediately.

What the hell am I doing? I'm about to mutilate a twelve-hundred-year-old artifact...

Nevertheless, something drove Gabriel onward, and he was soon uncovering a golden sub-layer, one that was so well-preserved that in his excitement he forgot to breathe. He carefully pulled away the outer layers one side at a time, revealing a shining artifact beneath.

Adorned in intricately worked parchments of deep ruby reds and glowing emerald greens, it was a gold encrusted work of medieval art the likes of which he had never seen. Reminiscent not only of the Islamic and Christian works found in the cathedral of St. Sophia Hagia, the piece also reflected an uncanny similarity to the mystical arts of India, as well as the sublime elegance of those masterful works originating from the Far East.

"This is unbelievable..." he whispered, turning it slowly under the light.

The truth of the matter was that he had never laid eyes on such a masterpiece. It was beyond a doubt the finest example of medieval craftsmanship in existence, its authenticity unquestionable. It was only upon arriving at this conclusion that Gabriel noticed something that dumbfounded him.

"Wait a minute," he said aloud. "This can't be right..."

Reaching for his pack, he retrieved an examination kit and produced a large magnifying glass. After a moment's inspection there could be no mistake. On each of the six sides were miniature texts belonging to six distinct world religions.

"Buddhism," whispered Gabriel, turning the Cube under the magnifying glass, "Judaism, Islamism, Taoism," his eyes were wide with amazement, "Hinduism, Christianity. This is impossible..."

The likelihood of there existing a ninth century artifact that housed texts belonging to the six major world religions was unheard of. In this artifact was evidence of a cultural contact that, according to the history books, would not occur for another four hundred years.

Gabriel placed the Cube back on the desk and reclined in his chair, trying to digest what the existence of such a piece could signify. Who had made it? Why had they made it? Who in the ninth century would have had knowledge of the six major belief systems, not to mention knowledge of their languages? And what would have inspired them to want to unify them in such a manner?

"What the hell's going on here?" he muttered, taking his eyes from the Cube to look around the room. "Why is all this happening? Why did my father say the Cube was my birthright?"

All the while that Gabriel studied the Cube, and hours passed without him knowing, there resided in his heart a strange and disturbing familiarity for the object, one that he could not begin to explain. It was as though he had dreamed of the Cube, or perhaps seen it as a child. An elusive recollection of the artifact seemed to be hovering just out of reach, like a word on the tip of his tongue. Perhaps he had simply slept too much.

Sensing that he had had enough, Gabriel packed away the relic and headed for the bathroom.

It's almost two-thirty in the morning. I could use a shower and a shave.

Natasha jerked herself into a seated position. A scuffling sound had just awoken her. It was coming from outside.

What is that? Is it the rain?

The noise sounded again. Natasha frowned and left her bed silently, approaching the louvered set of doors that led to the cloisters outside. What she saw there made her rub her eyes in disbelief. Through the downpour she could see a dog sitting patiently in the shadows, its wet fur glimmering in the lamplight. He pawed at the door again and Natasha gasped aloud, her intuition peaking.

"You again? But how's that even possible?"

Natasha's rational mind was sounding its objections. Florence was almost three hundred kilometres away from Rome. There was no way the dog could have found her here. Nevertheless, she was certain of it. The animal outside was the same one she had seen in her storeroom. She took a deep breath and opened the door.

"Gabriel!" came the distressed call. "Get out of there and get dressed immediately. There is no time to waste!"

Gabriel shut off the water and poked his head out of the shower. Through the steam he could see Fra Bartolomeo standing at the door of the bathroom. In one hand he held a two-way radio, in the other, the battered old duffel bag that he had left lying on the bed.

"What's going on?"

The old brother held out a hand to silence him, bringing the radio to his mouth.

"It is true, your Excellency. There are men outside."

The bishop's voice sounded on the other end.

"Are the telephones still down?"

"Yes, and there is no mobile coverage either."

"Collect Gabriel, Natasha, and Suora Angelica. Meet me in my quarters immediately. I want all of you prepared to move. Bring warm clothes and any food supplies you can muster. Make haste!"

"What's going on?" asked Gabriel, donning a bathrobe.

"There is no time to explain," said the old brother, turning to leave. "I will wake Suora and get some supplies. Meet us at the bishop's study!"

The old brother handed Gabriel his pack.

"*E per tutti i santi*, Gabriel," he said. "Do not take your eyes off this. It is the Cube they have come for!"

Gabriel stayed looking at the door after Fra had gone.

What the hell's going on?

It did not take him long to get dressed. Begrudgingly he packed away his razor, rubbing at the three-day growth on his face.

"I'll get that shave if it kills me."

Making his way through the old familiar corridors, Gabriel found it difficult to believe there was an enemy outside. It was just the storm. It had to be. Even still, he was glad that Fra had left all the lights off. If there truly were men waiting for the right time to invade the monastery, it would be best to keep them thinking that everyone was asleep.

"Nasrallah could never have got on to me so fast," he muttered to himself. "It's impossible."

He made his way briskly towards the bishop's apartments, a thought occurring to him.

"Amir," he gasped aloud, his brow furrowing.

Had they captured him? Was that how they were able to locate him here in Rome? Could they at this very moment be torturing his friend? Gabriel stopped abruptly despite his urgency, an anger alighting in him.

If they've got him...

He shook it off and started walking again. He was just being paranoid. He had seen Amir installed in his Gibraltar flat not thirty-six hours before, safely out of Morocco and in one of the securest ports in the Mediterranean.

He brought his thoughts back to the matter at hand and just then arrived at the bishop's quarters. He burst into the room, forgetting to knock.

Gabriel found Natasha sitting on the corner of the bishop's desk, and he felt his heart skip a beat despite himself. She was dressed in blue jeans and a cream-coloured blouse, with a dark jacket that had an eclectic, military edge to it. Her black boots were soft-soled and low-healed, matching her little backpack perfectly. It sat next to her on the desk with a lit-up iPad sitting atop it. Oddly enough, there was a chocolate-brown hunting dog at Natasha's feet. Behind the desk sat the bishop, smiling as though there were no danger at hand.

"Well, well," he said in his British tenor. "It would appear that the long-awaited reunion has at last come to pass. I would introduce you if I had not already been informed of your accidental meeting earlier this evening."

The bishop shot Gabriel a stern look.

"You could have read the note a little more carefully, my son."

Gabriel gave a guilty shrug and then glanced over at Natasha apologetically. The bishop stood up and walked around the desk towards him.

"Do you have the Cube?" he asked in earnest, his untrimmed eyebrows gathering into a silvery mass.

Gabriel nodded.

"Would you like to see it?"

"No, no. Now is not the time. I must pack a few things."

With that the old bishop turned, instantly shaking off his seriousness. His eyes were alight with an almost youthful glow. In all the excitement, his eighty-five years of life seemed to have dissolved away. Even the old man's posture had changed, and as he walked across the room his gait seemed like that of a man twenty years younger.

He arrived at an antique armoire and removed a small pack from one of its shelves, whistling quietly as he filled it with some things. Gabriel glanced over at Natasha only to find that she was already looking at him, her eyes suspicious.

"I didn't see him in your room," he said, motioning to the dog.

"That's because he wasn't there."

She slid off the desk gracefully and kneeled beside the animal, scratching its proud neck affectionately.

"It's a very strange story," she said to the dog. "We met in my workshop in Florence about two weeks ago. I was sure he was going to attack me. Instead, he ran away, and I thought I'd never see him again. A few hours ago, he came to my door. I still can't believe it."

Gabriel frowned and then moved around the desk to sit in the bishop's chair. His body still ached from his ordeal in the sewage tunnel.

Why does her accent have to be so damn sexy?

He closed his eyes, opening them a minute later to find that she had taken up her place on the bishop's desk again. Gabriel frowned. She was looking directly at him; scrutinizing him again. He tilted the chair onto its back legs and closed his eyes.

"Shackleton's the reason why we're all up in the middle of the night," he heard her say.

Gabriel kept his eyes shut.

"Shackleton?"

"That's what I've named him," said Natasha. "He's quite the traveller."

"So it would seem."

Natasha examined Gabriel from head to toe.

"He led me to a little window in the bathroom."

She nudged his balanced chair with her foot.

"Maybe you know the one I'm talking about?"

Gabriel opened an eye and then closed it again. He had apologised enough times already.

"He got up on his hind legs and looked through the panes," she continued, chewing on her lip as she remembered. "He was grumbling. When I went to see what he was looking at, I saw two dark figures squatting by the fountain. Some of them were armed with rifles, so I woke up Fra. He says they're surrounding the monastery."

Gabriel opened his eyes and leaned forward.

"You're joking right?"

Natasha shook her head and Gabriel could finally see fear in her eyes. He rose to his feet, and just then Fra Bartolomeo entered the room. He was accompanied by a tiny old nun dressed in a pale blue skirt with a matching blouse and cardigan. She appeared to be laughing and crying simultaneously.

"Suora!" exclaimed Natasha, rushing to her and falling into her arms. "Don't be frightened. Bishop Marcus knows what to do."

Gabriel smiled despite his confusion. It felt odd that Natasha should be so familiar with Suora, and he felt a kind of childish jealousy seeing the two embrace.

"*Ciao, Bellissima,*" he said, giving the little nun a hug. "Don't cry. Everything's going to be fine."

"Ah, my child," she said quietly, her Italian accent as thick as Fra's. "I am an old woman awaiting death. What could I be frightened of? I am not crying for fear. I am crying because I am happier now than I have ever been. I never thought I would live to see the two of you united. It seemed to me it would never happen. Thanks be to our blessed Virgin Mary!"

Gabriel and Natasha looked at each other suspiciously. They were standing on either side of the nun, each of them holding on to one of her hands. Suora Angelica had been like a mother to them both; the only mother they had ever known. Crying with delight, the old nun brought Gabriel and Natasha's hands together, intertwining their fingers as she spoke.

"The bond between you will see no bounds," she said.

Natasha exchanged an uncomfortable glance with Gabriel before pulling her hand away. In the meantime, the bishop had finished packing, and was in the process of throwing a dark cloak over his vestments.

"The time has come, my dear family," he said, slinging a pack over his bony shoulder. "We must flee this place at once. Follow me!"

By the time the bishop had led them to the church's sacristy, Nasrallah's men were already making their move. With great stealth they entered the monastery and fanned out in every direction, their dark forms moving without a sound. Their orders were simple. Retrieve the Cube and kill everyone in the building. There could be no survivors; no one to relate what they had seen. For this reason, every square inch of the building would have to be searched.

* * * * * *

In the shadows of the sacristy the bishop used an old iron key to open a gate that stood before them, revealing a narrow flight of steps leading down into the darkness.

"We will be taking a secret underground passage that leads to what was once a convent, a very long time ago," he said in a barely audible whisper. "The tunnel travels for approximately one kilometre but I do not know if it is still passable. It is our only chance of escaping this place undetected. If nothing else, it will offer us a place to hide."

Natasha looked perplexed. A tunnel connecting a monastery to a nunnery defeated the purpose of each institution entirely. She looked over at Gabriel to find him digging through his duffel bag.

"We'll be needing these," he whispered, handing both her and the bishop a flashlight.

He produced a compass and yet another flashlight which he kept for himself. Fra approached suddenly, gathering the group together with his arms. His whisper was urgent.

"They are inside the building!"

All heads scanned the surrounding shadows. Even Shackleton was looking.

"Follow me," mouthed the old bishop, leading them into a chamber beneath the sacristy.

Gabriel locked the gate behind him, working the key as silently as possible. He was the last to arrive below and saw them standing in a small circular room. Its shallow domed ceiling was so low that he was forced to bend over as he descended into it. Gabriel knew that this was a burial place; a grotto containing the tombs of Christian martyrs from the second century.

The old bishop approached a round marble altar in the middle of the chamber. Around them, within evenly spaced niches, lay seven sarcophagi. The bishop embraced the dais and strained against it.

"We must slide this aside," he whispered. "The entrance to the tunnel lies beneath it."

Gabriel and Natasha jumped to his aid, and within moments the stone altar began to move. Fra Bartolomeo crossed himself, thanking God that the ancient hinges had somehow remained silent. Only a damp gust of wind escaped from the tunnel mouth, the thick air smelling of musty earth. It seemed terribly cold.

Suddenly from above, filtering down the marble steps, came the muffled padding of dozens of feet. All looked up. Nasrallah's men were just outside.

"We have no time to lose," mouthed the bishop. "I will go first."

One by one they climbed down a short ladder into the tunnel, including Shackleton, who surprised everyone by descending as adeptly as a circus animal.

The tunnel's walls were of raw earth, with the only support coming from crude timbers erected at odd intervals. Gabriel worked the altar's mechanism, delighted to find it swing closed with a quiet thump. Its mechanism had clearly been built for stealth.

* * * * * *

Bahadur stood dizzily beside the marble sacristy, his battered face pale and bloodstained. His scar looked gruesome in the sharp light of his flashlight, and the tattooed moth on his throat seemed almost alive, changing in shape every time he swallowed the blood that oozed from his broken sinuses.

The battered giant had been given no rest before being dispatched on his assignment, and his hulking body still trembled from its wounds. He watched silently as his men searched the small church. They had spread out into four lines and were combing the space, methodically checking every pew, every niche.

"My family will soon be safe," he muttered deeply, his elocution at odds with his brutish appearance. "We shall do this quickly. There is no other way."

Bahadur jerked his massive head around. He thought he had heard, or perhaps felt, something below, but he could not be sure. Moving with all the stealth he could muster, he made his way around the sacristy, his pistol at the ready. It was not long before he found the gate and saw a narrow passage leading down into the darkness. Finding it to be locked, he hissed at one of his men, motioning him to come.

"Open this," he mouthed, and within moments the soldier had picked the lock with an expert hand.

The circular chamber was empty, and Bahadur, weary with fatigue, approached the central dais and leaned on it heavily. He thought he had heard something, but he was no longer certain. Taking a final look around he pushed himself off the altar.

"There is nothing here," he said to his men. "Help the others. Search the rectory."

* * * * * *

Gabriel stood frozen atop the ladder; his left hand outstretched to the others in a plea for absolute silence. Above him he could hear the guards speaking amongst themselves. They seemed to be moving off.

"They've gone," he whispered back, wedging a spare battery into the hinge mechanism to prevent it from being opened from above. "We're safe for now. Let's get moving."

They proceeded into the tunnel, walking silently for some time. It was Natasha who broke the silence.

"Why was this tunnel made, Uncle Marcus?" she asked. "I thought that monasteries and nunneries were built to *separate* men from women."

"Right you are, my child," said the bishop, smiling. "But even under the most severe barriers, Mother Nature has a way of bringing together what was meant to be together."

"A tunnel of love," said Gabriel from behind.

The bishop's smile vanished when he shone his flashlight on the earthen walls.

"Yes, a tunnel of love," he said, "but also one of tragedy."

Under the roaming beam of light, all were able to see that the tunnel walls were lined with burial niches, or *loculi*, filled with the skeletal remains of infants.

"Behold the products of their love," said the bishop sadly. "The pregnancy of a nun could well be hidden under her habit, but once born, the child would be brought here and left to die."

Natasha cringed in horror. In the distance she could see the tunnel looming in the darkness, with row upon row of open graves in full view.

"But why didn't they cover them?" she asked.

"Penitence loves guilt," said Gabriel. "The corpses must have been a great way to remind them of their sins."

"Come," said the bishop. "Let us not linger here."

The group moved forward into the gloom, with Shackleton leading the way. Apart from the burial niches and wooden support structures, the tunnel offered very little to see. It worked its way forward, crudely veering around or beneath boulders, but always keeping to its general heading.

Gabriel followed with his compass, imagining what it must have been like for those who had dug the passage, and the decades of repressed sexual urges that had driven them to do it.

Ten minutes into their journey they approached their first major obstacle and both the bishop and Suora took the opportunity to rest. They sat down on some large rocks that had caved in from above. Fra was soon to follow. Their flight had been exhausting, and in the limited light offered by their flashlights, the obstacle looked impassable.

Gabriel lit a flare and the tunnel burst to life. Within their shadowy loculi, the sepia coloured remains of the infants glowed ominously, the flickering shadows bringing the skeletons to life. Whereas the addition of light would have normally made any place seem less oppressive, it was having the opposite effect here.

Behind them, at the fringe of the flare's reach, a curtain of impenetrable blackness loomed. Natasha concentrated on the obstacle before her, trying to forget the fact that they were in an expansive tomb filled with dead babies.

"We might be able to dig a way through up there," she said, pointing to an area below a collapsed support.

Gabriel shook his head.

"The dirt's too loose. It'll cave in on us."

"So what do we do?"

Gabriel looked into Natasha's eyes, lost in thought. She held his gaze for a moment and then looked away, recalling what Suora had said about the bond between them. She struggled to understand but drew a blank.

It was only then that she saw motion at the bottom of the caved-in section. In all the time that they had been looking for a way over the obstacle, Shackleton had found a way under it. Natasha's face lit up with delight.

"You're really pulling your weight this morning, Shackleton…"

The dog came out of the shadows and nudged her leg, spinning with wagging tail only to disappear back where he had come from. Natasha followed, shining her flashlight into the gap.

"It seems to go right through," she said, looking back at the others.

"Now who would have thought that I would be having such an adventure at my age!" said Suora, shaking her head in disbelief.

The old nun was on her hands and knees, halfway through the passage and laughing merrily. Gabriel watched Natasha as she helped Suora along with lighthearted words of encouragement. There was a sweetness about her that seemed sincere, and she was a lot like Suora too, able to laugh when anyone else would be scowling.

Gabriel felt a twinge of loneliness run through him, but he pushed it away swiftly. Deep down, he believed that women like Natasha were unattainable, at least to him. In so many ways Gabriel was self-assured and confident, but when it came to women, he was inherently crippled. There was something in him that prohibited any kind of fulfillment in a relationship, and as he was not one for *soppy introspection*, as he liked to call it, he clung instead to the same rationalization as always.

Wonderful girls only ever want assholes.

Of course, Gabriel had fallen for women like Natasha before, and every time he had been let down. He had long ago taken a more pragmatic road to companionship, and he believed that it was too late to go back now. All this being said, he felt emptier than ever.

It took the better part of twenty minutes for the party to traverse the obstacle, more than enough time for Gabriel to forget about his ruminations and get back to the task at hand. Being the last one through, he decided they should take a short rest, reasoning that they had all made quite an effort that morning, and that a break was well deserved.

"Fra Bartolomeo," said Bishop Marcus with a twinkle in his eye. "Might you have had a chance to bring along a few things to snack upon? Even your Lent rations would seem a feast in this place."

The brother's old face lit up at the suggestion.

"I did manage to put together a few items in our haste…"

He dug into his pack and arranged the contents on a nearby boulder. Around it a few large rocks had fallen, giving the elders a place to sit. Gabriel and Natasha found perches close by and soon all were resting.

"I see you found my pork roast," said Suora, shaking a finger at Fra.

The monk was carefully unwrapping the hunk of meat. He laid it down next to a crusty loaf of bread and then rubbed his hands together briskly, studying the thing as though it were a piece of sculpture.

"I know every one of your hiding spots, dear girl," he said, craning his neck to examine the thing. "And you'll not hide the crackling from me either!"

And then pulling out another wrapped parcel, he added, "Nor the gravy!"

Natasha clapped her hands in delight, her mouth watering.

"The pantry," proclaimed the brother proudly, "is the domain of the clergy!"

And with a magician's bow he produced a bowl of roasted potatoes.

"Dinner for breakfast!" he exclaimed, and all gave a cheer except Gabriel, who only rolled his eyes.

The old bishop pulled two bottles from his pack.

"And what is dinner, without water and wine?"

After a short prayer of thanks, the five of them dined happily under the light of a second flare. Shackleton laid himself down between Gabriel and Natasha and began working on the pork rind Fra had given him. Gabriel bent to speak into his ear, and oddly enough, the dog stopped chewing to listen.

"If faith is good for one thing, my canine friend," whispered Gabriel, "it's for the delusional sense of safety it offers. Anyone else would be trembling with fear, but these guys think they're on some kind of a holiday picnic."

Shackleton seemed to consider Gabriel's words before returning to his rind.

Their meal ended when the flare began to burn itself out. Fra and Suora busied themselves packing away the remaining food.

"That was exquisite!" said Marcus, rising to his feet and adjusting his vestments. "Excellent foresight, dear brother."

Fra bowed to the bishop and then passed Shackleton another chunk of roast before packing it away. The dog took it gently, looking up at him in thanks.

"You are certainly the most charming animal I have ever met," he said, patting Shackleton's back awkwardly.

Natasha gave the dog a potato and then bent down to kiss his head.

"Shackleton's saved us twice today," she said, ruffling his ears. "He's the best dog in town!"

The brown dog buried his muzzle in her lap and grumbled contentedly.

"All right guys," said Gabriel. "I hate to break it up but we really should get moving."

The tunnel continued on unchanged, and once the distressed areas had been left behind, it seemed no different to what they had already passed through. Inky blackness, eerie graves, and the unsettling skeletal remains of infants.

Gabriel calculated that they had already travelled more than a kilometre, and consulting his compass, saw that they were still headed in the same direction. Their pace was slow, but they were making headway. If they did not encounter any more obstacles, the chances were good that they would soon be arriving at the convent.

This being said, all hopes were soon dashed by yet another cave-in, only unlike the previous collapse, this one was most definitely impassable. Whereas the other had been comprised of boulders and loose rubble, the cave-in before them was formed entirely from earth and sand. There was simply no way through.

"It would appear that we have arrived at an impasse," said the bishop. "We will hide in the tunnel for as long as our food lasts, and then return to the rectory. Let us pray that the soldiers will have gone away by then."

"There's another option," said Gabriel, aiming his flashlight in the direction they had come.

Everyone turned to look.

"Not a hundred meters back I saw what looked like a tunnel leading off in another direction."

"Why didn't you tell us?" asked Natasha curtly.

Gabriel took note of her tone.

"Because I didn't think there was a need, Sergeant."

He looked over at the bishop.

"I thought we'd be arriving at the convent any moment."

"Well, my son," said the bishop, "it would seem there is a need now."

Gabriel gave a nod.

"Let's go back and take a look."

The opening was small, low, and crudely cut into the tunnel wall, almost as though the excavators had encountered it by accident. From within came a draft of slightly warmer air. Gabriel crouched and entered.

"I'll just take a quick look," he said over his shoulder. "Be right back."

The others stood by while Natasha squatted before the opening, gazing in. She watched as Gabriel disappeared past a curve in the passage, the light of his flashlight fading away soon after. All waited expectantly, but Natasha was the most impatient of all. As the minutes passed, she seemed to grow more and more anxious.

"What if he gets lost, Uncle?" she said, chewing her lip. "It's already been ten minutes and there's no sign of him."

"Have faith, Natasha," he said reassuringly. "Gabriel will be fine."

"Why do you say that?" she asked sharply. "I don't care what happens him. I'm only thinking of the three of you."

She rose to her feet and stepped away from the opening. Something was drawing her to Gabriel despite her distrust of him. In the end her concern proved impossible to resist and she made her way back to the opening.

"I'm going to take a quick look," she said, entering. "I'll be back in a moment."

No sooner had she gone in however than Gabriel appeared. There was not much room in the tight passage and his face was only inches from hers.

"Miss me?" he said with a smile.

Natasha looked daggers at him.

"What took you so long?"

"I wanted to make sure it was what I thought it was."

"Well? Was it?"

"I think it is."

The seniors watched them emerge from the passage.

"All right," said Gabriel. "There's a good chance we can get out this way, but it might take a while."

"Where does it lead?" asked Fra.

"To the catacombs," said Gabriel, glancing over at Natasha. "While those monks were digging their tunnel of love, they bumped into one of the largest necropolises in Europe."

"Good heavens!" exclaimed the old bishop, his eyes alight with excitement. *"The Catacombs of San Callisto!"*

CHAPTER 17

Amsterdam, The Netherlands.

Christian Antov walked briskly through the lobby of an opulent, five-star hotel. Around him were some of the most powerful people in the world, each of them members of a private organization that would soon be holding its yearly weekend conference.

He stopped at the reception desk, only to be immediately greeted by his new personal assistant. She was the youngest daughter of one of his father's associates, and she made no attempt to mask her innocent worship of him.

"Hello, Mr. Antov," she said flirtatiously. "Can I help you with anything?"

Christian did not return her smile, but instead looked down at the generous cleavage she seemed to be proffering. Cynthia had been a little girl when he had last seen her three years before, but she had since blossomed into a beautiful young woman.

"How old are you, Cynthia?"

"Seventeen and a half."

Christian paused, looking straight into her eyes.

"Email me a list of the guests who will be arriving today."

Christian moved off before the girl could respond, the hint of a cold smile on his lips. He would revisit her invitation in six months. For now, he would use her for other purposes.

All things considered; Christian was quite proud of how rapidly he was adapting to his new environment. It was a drastic departure from his decadent life as a New York City artist, but he was enjoying the power tremendously. It had only been two days since he had taken over his father's position as Chief Head of the Vanderhoff Group Steering Committee, but oddly enough, he felt completely at home with his new responsibilities, as though he had been born for the position.

Making his way through the lobby, he thought back on the previous day, still trying to digest all that he had learned from his uncle, Prince Vladimir Rodchenko. They had met outside the Vanderhoff Group Headquarters earlier that afternoon. It was a palatial residence in the centre of Amsterdam. The old prince had escorted Christian into the building, leading him through an opulent hall and up a sweeping staircase to his new offices. On the way Christian had been greeted by many staff members, each one offering their respectful condolences with regards to his father.

"Today I will be telling you many things you do not know, Christian," his uncle had said. "Things that will help you understand who you are, and why you were raised as you were."

Vladimir Rodchenko was the brother of Christian's late mother; a woman whom Christian could only vaguely remember. He was a brittle and impervious man, with a temper that could suddenly lash out like a whip, and then vanish just as quickly. Being the only relative that he had ever been permitted to meet, Christian was not sure who he hated more, the prince, or his father.

"This is your new office," the prince had said flatly, leading Christian into a luxurious apartment. "Everything here was your father's. It now belongs to you. All of its contents, along with the position your father held, are a part of your inheritance. It might seem strange to you, Christian, but you have been training for this job all your life."

When the prince had gone, Christian had settled into the leather armchair behind his father's desk. In the simple act of leafing through an appointment book, he had learned more about the man than he had done in the entirety of his life. Until that day, Christian would have been at a loss to explain exactly what it was that his father did for a living. His father had never told him. Nobody had.

Christian made his way into the hotel lounge and sat down at his private table, lighting another cigarette.

"Orange juice and champagne," he said as a waiter approached.

He checked his phone and saw that the guest list had arrived.

"Very prompt, Cynthia," he muttered, scanning the email.

He was soon lost in thought, smiling bitterly at what had always been kept from him. A scene played out from his childhood. He was in his bedroom, its minimal furnishings cold and sterile. With all forms of amusement strictly forbidden to him, not a single toy was in sight.

"Your father is a businessman."

It was his nanny speaking. She was laying out his clothing.

"That is all you need to know," she said dryly. "The rest is none of your business. You will not be disrespectful."

Having lost his mother as a child, the Austrian nanny had become Christian's only means of connection to his mysterious father, and indeed to the entirety of his family. She had been a cold and militant woman, following explicit orders to under no circumstances reveal anything to the boy concerning his relatives.

On one occasion, Christian had been told that his father worked with his uncles, but he had never been permitted to meet any of them. Prince Vladimir had been the only one; no grandparents, no aunts, no cousins. As a child, Christian had always been kept apart.

A barely audible alarm sounded from Christian's phone, bringing him back into the present and reminding him of the Steering Committee meeting he had to attend. He cleared his mind and made ready to be the new chairman. How they expected him to do this he did not know, but he would play along. As the prince had told him earlier that day, the machine was built and functioning. All that was needed was a steady hand at the wheel.

"All power is based in fear," muttered Christian, rising from the table. "Fear must be maintained at all costs."

The words were of course his father's, but Christian had long ago adopted them as his own, absently hearing them echo in his head more often than not.

Christian found himself thinking of his new position as he traversed the hotel's atrium, and all the responsibilities it would entail. There would be no person above him, and it seemed natural that it should be so. His father, it turned out, had been a leader of leaders, and all his life, Christian had been groomed to be the same. In his possession were the controlling shares of the Vanderhoff Group, arguably the most powerful organization in the world.

Smiling with self-satisfaction, Christian strode arrogantly to his first official meeting as the Chief Head of the Steering Committee. The Vanderhoff Group, he had learned, was named after the hotel where its first meetings had originally been held. What had initially started out as a handful of American, British and German businessmen working to smooth trade relations, had since grown into a collective of more than one hundred members, each of which dominated arenas in global business, media, and politics.

The group itself was an unofficial organization, regularly hosting annual conferences in five-star resorts in Europe and North America. This year, the conference would be held here, in the same hotel where it had all begun; a hotel that had long ago been purchased by the founding member of the Vanderhoff Group, Christian's very own grandfather.

Officially speaking, Christian's new responsibilities did not extend beyond the role of host and organizer. Unofficially, however, he was the chief administrator of a deeply enmeshed geopolitical agenda, one whose nefarious roots dated back centuries.

Plainly put, his father's Vanderhoff Group was a secret society, one whose primary objective was to centralize economic and political power with the sole aim of forming a single world government, corporately run by their own offices under a false mask of democracy.

Leaving the lobby, Christian made his way along carpeted hallways until he had arrived at his private boardroom. He entered to find it populated by men, who in their own individual positions of power and social standing, comprised the steering committee. There were twelve of them in total, each one a blood relation, and they sat around a large wooden table engaged in a variety of isolated conversations.

Noticing that he had not yet been seen, Christian took the opportunity to scan the faces of the twelve old men who filled the room, amazed at how each bore the same bitter and hardened expression. He entered and walked to his place at the head of the table.

"Good morning, gentleman," he announced confidently. "I believe we will be discussing items relevant to a new North American currency in this meeting."

CHAPTER 18

Los Picos de Europa, Northern Spain.

The section of wing that trapped Isaac Rodchenko was merciful. By collecting the splashing droplets of a nearby spring, it was channeling a meager stream of water close enough to his face to hold death at bay. For many days now Isaac lay trapped in the airplane wreckage. He was high atop a frigid mountain in the wildest regions of Spain, battling a new and invisible enemy.

From the corpse of his son had come an unspeakable blight. The same demons that had possessed his child, were now accosting him. Wave upon wave their relentless attacks came, and in his weakened state he feared that it was only a matter of time before they entered into him.

Even in his struggle with mental illness, Isaac Rodchenko had remained a staunch Roman Catholic, and he now clung to its doctrine like a drowning man to a piece of flotsam.

"Dear Father in heaven," he prayed fervently, "I accept this punishment. I know it is my past sins that have caused you to unleash these demons upon me. Had I not abandoned Christian and Alina, none of this would have happened. What I did was unforgivable."

Isaac went over the events of his life. At the age of twelve, his father had sent him to live at Vatican City for a year. Following the council of a venerable priest there, Isaac had chosen to remain in the city-state, taking his mother's surname and disinheriting himself entirely from his wicked father. The priest's name was Father Adrianus Vanderwerken, and he had consistently encouraged Isaac to forget his past and start anew.

"God has wonderful plans for you, my son," he had often said when sadness haunted young Isaac. "Have faith in His merciful will."

In not returning home, Isaac knew that he had abandoned his little brother Christian and his baby sister Alina to a hell at the hands of their abusive father. It was the guilt and regret stemming from this decision that had over the years become the root of Isaac's mental illness.

Despite Father Adrianus' smooth-tongued assurances that he had done nothing wrong, a dark specter of remorse had remained buried in Isaac's heart; one that would soon be growing in intensity as the numbing effects of his medications began to wear off.

Exposed to the elements and slowly dying, Isaac Rodchenko continued his hopeless battle against the demonic forces that accosted him. Unspeakable things had been happening of late. The corpse of his son was somehow reviving, its occasional twitches escalating into prolonged seizures that filled Isaac with horror.

Even now as it lay there motionless, Isaac could hear its icy whispers. The corpse was urging him to surrender; to let the demons take control.

CHAPTER 19

Rome, Italy.

"The most venerable and most renowned of all Rome!" exclaimed Bishop Marcus as he led the way through the dark tunnels.

He was quoting what Pope John XXIII had said of the catacombs of San Callisto in the early nineteen-sixties.

"When we were boys, Father Franco and I would sneak into the restricted areas of these catacombs!" he said brightly. "They might very well have been what inspired me to become a priest."

Natasha was amazed. That dark and tangled passages could be a source of religious inspiration dumfounded her. Even still, she had never seen her uncle so enthusiastic about anything before. It was as if the spark that had been rekindled in the old man earlier that morning had now blossomed into a beautiful flame.

"These Catacombs are a resting place for almost half a million Christians," he added. "As well as sixteen popes and many, many martyrs. The necropolis covers almost ninety acres!"

"That's quite daunting, Uncle," said Natasha. "Will we be able to find a way out?"

She was walking beside him now, trying her best to see the beauty he saw in the arched and crumbling passages.

"A way out? Oh, most definitely, my child!" he chimed. "We are presently on the lowest of five levels; an area off limits to the general public, but one that I explored at great length with my schoolmates."

Gabriel fell to the back of the group. Entertaining as the bishop's discourse was, he had become concerned about Suora. She was walking in front of him now, slightly behind Fra, and she seemed to be hunched over more than usual.

Her breathing had become laboured since they had entered the catacombs, and Gabriel could see she was having trouble keeping up with the group's already slow pace. Even Shackleton seemed to sense something. Instead of his normal place at the head of the group, he was lingering at the back, keeping near to the old nun and looking up at her every now and again with his gentle amber eyes.

"How's about a break, Suora?" asked Gabriel, trying to make it sound offhand.

"I am fine, my son," she said, giving her short little nods. "I was just listening to his Excellency. How incredible."

"There's no reason why we can't all have a rest."

"If I am not mistaken," said the old bishop, having overheard Gabriel, "we should soon be arriving at a wonderful little chapel. It would be a perfect place to take some refreshment."

Gabriel frowned. It seemed to him that his comment had made things worse for the old nun, reminding her of her fatigue. What was more, Fra had now brought his attention to her as well, and in the half light, Gabriel could see the concern on the old man's face. There was a great love between two.

As if in answer to the brother's prayers, the chamber the bishop had spoken of appeared suddenly to the right. Two heavy columns rose up on either side of the dark opening, with a crooked lintel holding them fast. The crumbling portal looked impressive. It was carved with what appeared to be Egyptian hieroglyphs, their strange shapes shifting under the roaming beams of their flashlights. A dark chamber lurked behind the pillars, radiating the scent of pungent mildew.

"How many flares do you have left, Gabriel?" asked Bishop Marcus over his shoulder.

"Just one."

"We had better save it then," he said, rubbing his chin. "If memory serves me correctly, this chapel has a hearth in it."

The crooked portico gave way to an open space that appeared palatial in contrast to the tunnels. Under a shallow domed ceiling they could see an altar adorned with peeling frescos. It sat between another two columns, with a life-sized wooden carving of a crucified Christ hanging at its centre. To the right and left of the altar, intricate freezes were carved into the stone walls. Natasha ran the beam of her flashlight over them, her background in historical artifacts piquing her interest.

"These carvings are obviously Christian," she said, "but they're Egyptian in style..."

Gabriel came up beside her as she passed a hand over one of the freezes. He could see she was not mistaken, and he was surprised by her knowledge.

Who is this girl?

"Christ is being portrayed as the Egyptian god Horus," she continued. "See the giant sun behind him? This is the traditional setting for a sun god."

Gabriel looked around, the beam of his flashlight finding a fresco depicting a scene of the Egyptian god being crucified.

"This chamber would have to have been built in the early fourth century," he said. "Most of these frescos would have been considered heretical any time after that."

Now it was Natasha's turn to be surprised, and she fought back an urge to look over at Gabriel. She had not imagined he could be interested in the early church.

"I can't believe I've never heard about this place," he continued, and Natasha noted the sense of awe in his voice. "It depicts clear parallels between Christianity and Egyptian mythology."

He looked over at the bishop.

"That's got to be why this level of the catacombs is off limits to the public," he continued. "The church has never been able to explain how the same stories in the bible were told in Egypt, thousands of years before they ever supposedly happened."

"That is a highly contested subject, my son," said the old bishop, his eyes wandering over the ancient paintings. "The fact of the matter remains that the early Egyptian Christians were of the most severely persecuted by the Romans. In all probability, this chapel was built as a shrine to them. If you look next to the altar, you will find a small doorway leading to a room that is filled with their bones."

It was not the first time that the old bishop had heard mention of the disputed pagan sources of Christianity, yet even though there existed a large body of archaeological evidence in support of this claim, he did not suspect it was a matter of simple plagiarism. He felt that there was a missing piece to the puzzle; a truth that would reconcile the chronological discrepancies, without destroying the essence of what Christianity stood for.

"Truly, though," he said, thinking of Suora. "All this is of no practical concern to us at the moment."

He turned away from the frescos and looked to the back of the chapel, shining his flashlight on something there.

"What *is* of practical concern," he continued, "is that the inspired gentleman who ordered this chapel built saw it fitting to equip it with a hearth. And as you can see, a long departed archaeological team has left us with plenty of material to burn in it!"

Gabriel and Natasha turned and focused their beams on the chapel's back wall. There, between two wooden scaffolds, was an enormous hearth under a full-sized statue of the god Horus. Its falcon's head was looking straight across the chamber to the crucified Christ that hung directly opposite. Scattered around the hearth were wooden chairs and a table. To the right of the scaffold was an old trunk filled with dust covered torches.

"Now there's a beautiful sight," said Gabriel, his beam focusing on the crate.

In no time the small party was huddling around a crackling fire, enjoying the first warmth they had felt in hours. Gabriel lit some torches and set them around the room. In the flickering light the chapel was brought to life, its mysterious purpose being revealed to them with utter clarity.

The chamber was clearly a sanctuary, but it also held a great secret, subtly revealing clues to a mystery that Natasha had always been fascinated by. The Egyptian roots of Christianity.

While Gabriel had been busy with the torches, Natasha had prepared a chair for Suora and placed it directly before the hearth, lovingly covering the old nun in a blanket the moment she sat down. Fra Bartolomeo, in all his foresight, had brought a small pot in which to heat the soup he had also stuffed into his pack. Only one portion could be prepared at a time, and against Suora's emphatic insistence to be left until last, the first bowl was given to her. The effects were nothing short of miraculous.

"Thank you, my dear ones," she said from beneath her blanket. "You are too kind to me. It was only these old bones and the dampness."

"Rest well, dear girl," said the old bishop gently.

He was lowering himself into a creaking chair before a worktable, an old leather-bound book in his hands.

"We will stay here for an hour or so," he said. "After that we will have a bit of walking to do. We are very deep, but I know my way. God willing, we'll be out of this place in time for supper."

Natasha was next to get her soup. She thanked Fra, and drew a chair up to the old worktable, sitting down close beside the bishop.

"What book is that, Uncle?" she asked, sipping her soup. It was warm and wholesome, and it drove away the last of her shivers.

"This is a book that belonged to Gabriel's father," he said, studying its worn cover. "I received it in the mail shortly after his death."

Gabriel was sharing some of the roast pork with Shackleton when he overheard the bishop's words.

"My father?" he repeated, his mouth full. "What book's that?"

"It is a book containing all of his findings concerning the Compostela Cube, my son. It is time that you both knew the knowledge it contains."

"The diary," said Gabriel. "I went crazy looking for that thing…"

"His life's work," nodded the bishop, pausing for a moment and then continuing slowly.

"Out of love, and an earnest desire to give you both an unburdened childhood and adolescence, much has been kept from you, but all will now be revealed. The time has come for you both to learn the truth about who you really are; a truth that we have long suspected, but one that has only recently been confirmed."

CHAPTER 20

Amsterdam, The Netherlands.

"Shall we get started, young man?" asked Prince Vladimir condescendingly.

He was seated directly to the left of where Christian stood, a sharp, hooked nose distinguishing him from the other old men in the room. He leaned over and stretched out a crooked finger, tapping a stack of papers on the table before Christian.

"It is all right there in front of you, boy," he said. "Right in the agenda."

Christian looked through the room's large windows and out onto the manicured gardens.

Boy? Go to hell you son of a bitch.

A group of men caught Christian's eye. At first, he thought they were gardeners, but as he looked more closely, he could see this was not the case. The figures were robed and hooded, and they appeared to be enveloped in a strange darkness, utterly out of context with the bright sunny day.

Christian frowned. Although they seemed to be standing still, the figures also appeared to be shifting from side to side. Their appearance was scratchy and difficult to discern, as though they were not entirely there.

A creeping fear was making its way up Christian's spine now, spreading through his body and making his eyes water. He tried desperately to control himself against the irrational emotion, but he found he was powerless against it, able only to maintain the outward appearance of calm.

"Well, Christian," said his uncle, humorlessly. "Shall we begin by discussing the first item on the agenda?"

Christian turned to face him. The prince's words had somehow broken the spell.

"Yes," he said. "Yes, of course."

Christian glanced back into the garden. The hooded figures had vanished, only to be replaced by a decrepit old man standing in the place where they had just been. He squinted at the figure, recognizing him immediately as the man who had been present at his father's deathbed; the same man who had given him his father's ring.

With unmistakable purpose the old man turned suddenly towards Christian, his cold reptilian eyes locking with his. A current of intense fear shot through Christian's body like high-voltage electricity. It nearly knocked him over.

"Pay no heed to the Nautonnier, boy," said the prince, his voice thick with disdain for the old man. "Father Adrianus Vanderwerken is a relic from the past. Look how his nurses come to change his diapers."

Christian watched as the old man was escorted from the lawns. His scalp was still itching from the cold sweat that had come over him when they had locked eyes. Why had he seen four figures where the Nautonnier had been?

He turned to face those in the room and gathered himself immediately. His mind was obviously playing tricks on him. He would give it no further thought. He had a meeting to direct. He would consult with his psychiatrist later. The dosages of his medications would have to be adjusted.

"Gentlemen," he said calmly. "I have been informed by the prince that the Federal Reserve will soon be replacing physical currencies around the world with a new digital currency. He also told me that the current economic collapse of the United States was engineered by the Vanderhoff Group as a means of ushering in this transition."

Christian moved closer to his chair.

"If I am to lead this committee, I need to know its motives, and its objectives. What kind of deal have we struck with the Fed to make us want to bring down the entire world economy?"

Christian sat down, glad of the opportunity to shake off the remnants of his disturbing hallucination. He heard an old man at the opposite end of the table clear his throat and make ready to speak.

"We have made no deals, Christian," he said condescendingly. "The Federal Reserve is not federal, but rather privately owned by us."

"What's that supposed to mean?"

"It means that every regional reserve bank is ours. They always have been."

Christian frowned.

"That means nothing. Those banks are all controlled by the Board of Governors, a *federal* agency."

The old man nodded patiently.

"Whose members are appointed by the President and confirmed by the Senate. In other words, by *us*."

Christian looked back at the man, remembering what the prince had told him about the multifaceted illusion that was called representational democracy. Centuries of finance, lobbying, and propaganda had given the Vanderhoff Group complete governmental control behind a façade of democracy, not just in the United States, but in every country that claimed to be egalitarian.

"It was the Vanderhoff Group that instituted the Federal Reserve system in 1913, Christian," added the old man. "Right after we engineered the banking crisis of 1907."

Christian was beginning to understand.

"So last month's terrorist attack in Los Angeles was our latest strategic crisis."

The old man clasped his hands over the table.

"A terrorist strike was needed to take down the U.S. economy and the greenback along with it," he said. "A standardized CBDC is the only global solution to the crisis now."

Christian smiled coldly. Fear and doubt had always been the two main weapons in the Vanderhoff arsenal. With them they had routinely manufactured crisis after crisis in order to implement their policies.

"And why a central bank digital currency?" asked Christian. "Are we not already in control of the existing currencies?"

"Our goal is to centralize power, Christian," said another man, his accent Texan. "A standardized CBDC will help us do that. The more we control monetary policy, the more we can shape other existing systems to suit our needs."

"This is what the United Nations is for, Christian," added another. "It provides us with a means to implement new infrastructures planetwide."

Christian could hardly believe what he was hearing.

"Are you saying the Vanderhoff Group created the UN?"

The Texan leaned forward in his chair.

"Our objective is a single world currency and a central world government, son. It'll be split up into four unions. The American Union, the Asian Union, the African Union, and the European Union,"

Christian shook his head in amazement.

"And we'll be the ones who appoint their *democratic* leaders."

A rumble of pompous laughter made its way around the table.

"Just like we've always done, Christian," said the Texan. "Just like we've always done."

CHAPTER 21

Gibraltar, Europe.

Amir stood on his balcony, looking out over the sunny rooftops of Gibraltar. He tilted his head to move aside his dreadlocks and then took a deep haul from his pipe. It was a ninth century chillum, the size and shape of a large carrot, and covered in ancient Vedic carvings. He had obtained the relic years ago while on an expedition in Thanjavur with Gabriel. It went everywhere with him.

Just as the wandering Hindu monks had done a thousand years prior, Amir had packed the pipe with a specially prepared mixture of hashish and kief. It was not for the novice smoker.

Amir glanced over his shoulder into the spacious flat behind him. His computer had just chimed an alert.

"Who could that be?"

Smoke lingered around his handsome features as he considered. Amir's skin was the colour of dark honey, and he had intelligent eyes that were bright and alert, despite his constant smoking.

He held in the vapours a little while longer and then released a billowing cloud of smoke, lazily watching it float out into the open air. When his computer chimed again, he groaned and turned to go inside. Someone was messaging him. He bent over the screen.

—*Amir. Something terrible has happened.*

It was Amir's cousin Abida who wrote. He sat down and began to type.

—*Abida, you shouldn't be contacting me like this. It leaves traces. What happened?*

Abida was the sister of Bahadur. She lived in Tangiers, and was constantly under the surveillance of Moroccan authorities, her family being directly connected to the smuggling cartel.

—*Men came late last night and took Bahadur. They took the whole family along with him.*

—*Are you absolutely sure?*

—*I speak with them every day, you know that. When I didn't hear from them, I went to their house, but it was empty. The neighbour told me what had happened. She said that Nasrallah's men had taken them all away.*

—*Was anyone hurt?*

—*I don't think so. She said she saw them get loaded into a van. Even Jadda.*

—*Even Grandmother? Did she have her heart medicine?*

—*I don't know. If it was the government, we could ask about them, but it was Nasrallah. The neighbour's sure of it. What should we do?*

—*Abida, listen carefully. I'll take care of this. Don't speak of it to anyone. You'll do nothing. Do you understand?*

—*Yes, Amir. Thank you. I know you'll fix this.*

—*OK. Get some rest. Everything will be fine.*

Amir rose from his chair and produced his phone. He paused a moment to think and then called Gabriel. It went directly to his voice mail.

"Boss," he said, stepping out onto the balcony. "There's trouble. Give me a call when you get this."

CHAPTER 22

Rome, Italy.

The firelight played on the old bishop as he sat before Gabriel and Natasha. Their eyes were glued to him as he spoke, his silvery beard and mustache picking up the hues of the fire that crackled behind them. Before him on the archaeologist's worktable lay the professor's tattered journal. On its leathery cover could still be seen the remains of a tattered, gold embossed stamp.

The Compostela Cube
Reality or Myth?

Fra and Suora had both fallen asleep by the hearth. They had brought their chairs together so they could share the same blanket, and now sat cuddled, the nun's head resting on the brother's shoulder. Bathed in the warmth of the firelight, the two old figures seemed to embody the objective of what the nunnery tunnel had attempted to accomplish so long ago: to unite what had always been meant to be together.

Shackleton was laying in front of them, his proud head held high as he gazed almost pensively into the flames. There was a consciousness in his eyes that seemed at odds with his species; a quiet wisdom that appeared almost divine. Within Shackleton's soul there was none of the conflict so common to the human condition, only a pristine desire to serve humbly and to protect.

He turned his noble head and looked at the three who sat there at the table, focusing his amber eyes on the speaking bishop. Entirely unconcerned with what was being said, Shackleton's satisfaction lay in seeing that everyone was safe, and getting the rest they so much needed.

"You see," said the old bishop, "if it were not for a legend, it is very unlikely that we would ever have found you."

"I don't understand, Uncle," said Natasha, snuggling into the dark wool of her jacket. "What does a legend have to do with it? I was very sick when I was a baby. Father Franco told me that he had arranged for the church to adopt me when they couldn't care for me at the orphanage anymore."

"That's more or less what the professor told me," said Gabriel, looking at Natasha and then back to the bishop. "After that he ended up taking a liking to me and decided to keep me."

"These stories are not lies, my children," said the old bishop, "but they also leave out much truth. Before I proceed, I must repeat that it was our intention to keep all the details surrounding your early months from you until we were certain of the facts.

"You must try to understand things from our perspective. We had recently taken on the responsibility of raising two beautiful children, and we wanted to ensure that the life we gave them was as rich and nurturing as possible. Of what good could it be to fill your heads with uncertain stories?"

"What stories?" asked Natasha.

Her face was earnest in the firelight, her eyes almost childlike.

"You mentioned a legend. Uncle Marcus, please."

The bishop smiled.

"I apologize," he said. "Be patient with me. There is much to convey, and I will start at the beginning. All I ask is that both of you never lose sight of who you are now, at this very moment. The things that happened in your past do not define you. They only explain how you came to be."

The bishop looked at each of them in turn and proceeded only after he was convinced they were ready.

"As you both know," he began, "I have, for many years now, held an office pertaining to church investigations of events that are often labeled paranormal. For me this term seems a contradiction to the truth, because things such as apparitions, demonic possessions, and other spiritual manifestations are indeed very normal, in that they have always existed, as opposed to the above-and-beyond meaning that the prefix *para* implies."

"Uncle Marcus!" cried Natasha, stamping her feet.

Gabriel was temporarily fixated despite himself. Natasha's display of impatience had displaced a lock of her hair. He watched it play around her lips for a moment before she tucked it away behind an ear.

"Yes, very well, my child," continued the old bishop. "I will get to the point. Thirty-three years ago, I received a phone call. I was at my desk, and as it so happened, Gabriel, your father was there with me. The call came from a deacon who was assisting me at the time.

'I have received two separate calls relating to suspected cases of demonic possession,' he had said. *'A girl in Argentina, and a boy in Taiwan.'*

"Now while it was not uncommon to receive calls such as this from time to time, the remarkable thing was that in both cases, the children were newly born; something that I had never heard tell of before."

"Possessed babies?" coughed Gabriel.

A twisted scene of a demon-infested infant was playing out in his mind.

"That's pretty damn creepy, Marcus."

Natasha's eyes were wide with a mixture of fear and concern.

"It was the first case I had ever encountered," continued the bishop, clearing his throat with a barely detectable wince. "An abomination of Satan. The two children had spent their first month in a coma, only to regain consciousness in severely agitated states."

The bishop paused, taking hold of the professor's journal as if to open it, but refraining from doing so.

"Now if this were not already strange enough," he said, folding his hands over the weathered cover, "I would soon learn from the deacon that the babies had not only been born on the same day, but also at precisely the same hour."

The bishop sat back in his chair.

"Now although I thought it a great coincidence, I would most likely have left it at that, were it not for the fact that Professor Metrovich had overheard our conversation.

"*'Where exactly were they born?'* he asked, and I saw him take up a globe that was sitting on my desk.

"*The boy, on an American military base in Taiwan,*' I repeated aloud, as I was given the information. *The girl, in the village of La Quiaca, in Northern Argentina.*'

"The professor had then juggled the globe around until he had found Taiwan, and then proceeded to locate the village on the very opposite side of the globe.

"*There could be more to this than mere coincidence,*' he said, and I will never forget the expression of concern that suddenly came upon him. I told the deacon I would speak with him shortly and hung up the phone.

"*The military base is directly on the Tropic of Cancer. Up here,*' the professor said, pointing to the place on the globe. *La Quiaca, is directly on the Tropic of Capricorn. Down here. And what is more, if you can see, they are exactly on opposite sides of the planet.*'

"I took the globe and looked for myself. I was amazed, for it was just as he said. The professor clearly knew something that I did not."

"And I was the little girl in Argentina," said Natasha timidly.

"Yes, my child, that was you," said the old bishop, smiling. "And the boy on the military base was you, Gabriel."

"I pretty much figured," said Gabriel, looking at Natasha and then back to the bishop. "So, what became of us?"

"Why we went out to get you!" said the bishop, smiling. "We brought both of you back to Rome, and Father Franco and I laboured for fourteen months exorcizing the demons that infested you."

"Demons?" asked Natasha, aghast. "There were more than one?"

"There were fourteen in total, my child," said the bishop rather plainly. "Seven in you, and seven in Gabriel. And as that particular ritual could only be conducted on the night of a full moon, it took us fourteen months to liberate the two of you. In the end we were successful, and miraculously, you only suffered minimal injuries."

"Injuries?" asked Natasha, leaning forward.

The old bishop nodded.

"Burn marks at the energy centres of your body," he explained. "These were the places where the demons were extracted."

Gabriel and Natasha turned to face each other in shock.

"Burn marks?" they exclaimed in unison.

Gabriel addressed the bishop with a frown.

"My father told me my scars came from someone who had abused me in the orphanage..."

Natasha was still looking at Gabriel.

"That's what they told me too…"

She reached over and pushed aside his hair. The scar on his forehead was in the exact same place as hers. Gabriel was confused until she moved aside her own bangs to show him. He had to bend close to see it in the firelight. The scar was barely recognizable, but it was nevertheless there.

"I've got them all over my body," he said, and then he turned back to the bishop, his frown deepening. "Why were we lied to?"

The bishop looked down at the table.

"I know that lying to you both was a sin but telling you the true story would have been extremely destructive. Knowing that you were mutilated as infants has been a cross you have both had to bear all your lives, my dear, dear children, but the truth…"

The old bishop's eyes became glassy with tears.

"We could not possibly have told you the truth."

Natasha fought back her tears as well.

"It's all right, Uncle," she said quietly. "You were right not to tell us. I always suspected that there was something more to the scars than I was told. When I was twelve, I learned about the seven Hindu chakra points, and I saw that all my scars aligned perfectly with them. It was not long after, that I found the one on the crown of my head."

"There's another one on our head?" asked Gabriel, searching through his messy hair with the tips of his fingers.

The bishop gave a single nod.

"That was from the last demon to be extracted," he said matter-of-factly. "He was by far the most tenacious."

"Lovely," said Gabriel. "Thanks so much for letting us know all these little details about our early childhood. Very nice."

The bishop only shrugged.

"Do not let it trouble you, my son," he said. "Let us continue with the tale."

Gabriel settled back into his chair, looking over at Natasha to find that she was already looking at him. She smiled and then turned to the bishop as he began to speak again.

"'*Is there something more that I should know about this coincidence?*' I asked the professor. He had become very quiet since he had last spoken, as though he were lost in thought. He continued to hold the globe between his two fingers, one upon each of the locations. At length he began to speak, and I was truly amazed by what he said.

"The professor told me of an obscure medieval artifact called the *Compostela Cube*. Unknown to but a handful of scholars, its story had grown to become a legend among certain monasteries in Northern Spain. The Cube was believed to be the true Holy Grail; a receptacle carrying the living blood of the Christ, which to the ancients was a metaphor for knowledge, or more specifically, *gnosis*."

"Gnosis?" asked Gabriel.

The bishop nodded.

"The secret alchemical knowledge of liberation and transmutation," he said. "A mystical, intuitive knowledge that can only be known when it is directly experienced, as opposed to the kind of knowledge that is gained through rational thought, or theoretical conjecture. It was said that within the Cube were stored the keys to the cosmos. There was also a prophecy, one that the professor found to be based on an ancient Egyptian creation myth."

"What myth is that?" asked Natasha.

"A rather obscure one, my child," replied the old bishop. "Originating from a pre-dynastic period. The myth tells the story of how the god Atum willingly sacrificed himself and let himself fall into the underworld so as to plant the *Seed Of Truth* for all mankind."

"Atum was the Egyptian god of completeness," said Natasha. "He was the embodiment of the Divine Androgyne, or the Alchemical Marriage; the merging of male and female forces. He was a hermaphrodite."

The bishop nodded.

"The myth goes on to say that from the seed that Atum planted sprung the Tree of Life. There are many such trees to be found in cultures around the world, but in our myth, the gods Osiris and Isis were said to have emerged from the tree in a state of earthly mortality."

"*Tep Zepi*," said Gabriel, remembering his Egyptology. "Also called *First Time*. The age of Osiris, when Egypt was believed to be ruled by gods in human form."

"Exactly," said the old bishop, gazing into the flames of the fire. "According to the myth, Osiris and Isis each represented one half of what had formerly been the god, Atum. In other words, his male and female aspects.

"They resided now in a dualistic world, where unity had been fractured into opposing states: Birth and death, high and low, light and darkness, good and evil, and so on."

"But what does the creation myth have to do with the Compostela Cube?" asked Gabriel. "And more importantly, with us?"

"Patience, my son," said the old bishop with a smile. "I will soon get to that. According to the myth, the Tree of Life also yielded a single piece of fruit, and this was symbolic of all the gnosis that had been lost after the fall of Atum; gnosis that Osiris and Isis would need to re-assimilate, if ever they were to resume their former state as the god Atum.

"Only then would the divided become whole again, and duality be transcended. After this, the underworld would slowly begin to be transformed into a heavenly place."

"Was the fruit an apple by any chance?" asked Gabriel, thinking of the images he had removed from the Cube.

"Indeed, it was," said the bishop. "The apple is present in many mythologies and cultures, and in almost every case, it symbolizes immortality, just as it does in this myth."

Natasha nodded and turned to Gabriel.

"Hercules travelled to the edge of the world to steal the apple of immortality," she said. "He took if from Hera, the Queen of Olympus. The apple's also identified with the Celtic god, Afallach, and his underworld home of Avalon. In folk tales and legends, the hero usually has to retrieve an apple to win the king's daughter and fulfill his destiny to be the one to save the world from evil. The apple's everywhere in mythology."

Gabriel feigned distrust.

"And how is it you know so much, anyway?"

Natasha was taken aback until she realized he was teasing her. She narrowed her eyes at him.

"Natasha is an accomplished theologian, my son," said the old bishop.

Gabriel was clearly impressed, but he continued with his playful scrutiny regardless.

"And from what Suora tells me, she's a professional ballerina as well. She's just full of surprises, isn't she."

Natasha rolled her eyes and looked away in a huff. Marcus sent Gabriel a playful wink.

"She could also inform you that in almost every story, discord soon arises with the appearance of the apple. Just like in the story of Adam and Eve."

Natasha smiled with satisfaction.

"Thank you, Uncle. Please go on."

The bishop looked at them for a moment before continuing.

"Similar to the Book of Genesis," he said, "our Egyptian myth sees the appearance of the devil. This is the god *Sutekh*, or *Set*, and in our myth, he comes in the form of a grotesque hermaphrodite beast; a desecration of Atum's divine androgynous state.

"Set was the embodiment of doubt and fear. He was both the creator and ruler of the underworld. He worked against Atum, filling Osiris and Isis with a fear of the knowledge that was housed in the apple. In short, Set drove the two further and further apart from each other, until they stood alone on opposite ends of the earth, lost in ignorance and misery."

The bishop paused for a moment to clear his throat.

"With each passing age, and to symbolize the cycle of birth and death, Osiris and Isis would emerge on precisely the same day, on opposite sides of the earth. Due to their longing for each other, they would be reunited, and made to traverse a great labyrinth. Within they would search for a stairway to the paradise they once knew, their only possession being a single apple to give them nourishment on their journey."

Natasha leaned forward, placing her hands on the table.

"And the professor believed that Gabriel and I are reincarnations of Osiris and Isis, and that the Compostela Cube is the equivalent of the apple spoken of in the myth."

The bishop looked over at her.

"To be incarnations of Isis and Osiris would be impossible, for they never existed. They are fictitious characters in a myth. The professor only saw an incredible similarity between your births, and the story told in the myth. The existence of a medieval prophecy surrounding the Compostela Cube only served to further his suspicions."

"Come on, Marcus. It's just a coincidence," said Gabriel, shaking his head. "How can we be expected to believe any of this nonsense? It's just a myth. It has no relevance to reality."

"A myth, Gabriel, is no small thing," said the bishop. "Housed within every myth is a wisdom incommunicable by any other means. Modern society has made the mistake of equating a myth with a lie, but nothing could be further from the truth. History, be it however well documented, will always be inaccurate, but the wisdom housed within myth will forever retain its meaning and purity."

The old bishop produced a crumpled handkerchief and proceeded to evacuate his nose in a series of brief, staccato rounds. He looked at Gabriel, considering his next words.

"Myths are not to be taken literally, my son," he said. "They are to be interpreted, so that the truth held within them can be understood and assimilated on a level much deeper than rational thought."

"Like the truth that's in the story of Narcissus," said Natasha, "and how he fell in love with his own reflection. Or of Icarus, flying too close to the sun because of his own hubris and pride. The fact that these events never actually happened doesn't change the fact that these traits can be found in every one of us."

"I suppose you've got a point," said Gabriel. "You could also go as far as to say that embodied in every mythical god, is a quality that can be found in the human psyche."

"Yes!" exclaimed the bishop. "And in its purest essence. Learn about any god, and you will only be learning about yourself, for the god is you. This was the great appeal of praying to a god whose qualities you desired. The patron saints of Christianity are no different."

"But what about the medieval prophecy you mentioned?" asked Natasha. "You've told us about the myth, but you haven't explained the prophecy."

"Right you are, my child," said the bishop with a wink. "The monks referred to it as *The Ascender's Prophecy*, and it stated that during the darkest hour, the Two would come again to release the gnosis that is locked in the Cube. In so doing, they would open a way for mankind to be awakened from its slumber of ignorance, and be initiated into the Cube's secrets."

Gabriel rolled his eyes and released a sigh of strained patience. The old bishop continued unfazed.

"Like Osiris and Isis, these two saviours would be born on the same day, on opposite sides of the world, and under the dominion of Lucifer. In other words, they would be demonically possessed when they were born."

"But that's an impossible coincidence," protested Gabriel.

"Yet an undeniable one!" replied the bishop firmly. "Even still, your father was not wholly convinced. It was not until he had witnessed the second half of the prophecy mirrored in reality that he finally accepted what he had always tried to explain as a freak concurrence of legend."

Natasha chewed her lip pensively.

"The hermaphrodite…"

The bishop nodded.

"The Ascender's Prophecy spoke of its coming too. It would be born on precisely the same day, and at the same hour of the coming of the Two. It would be a mockery of Atum and the sexual unity embodied in the divine androgyne. Unlike the Two, however, the beast would pass its entire life in a coma vigil, only to awaken and die on the first full moon before its thirty-third birthday. During this time, he would be possessed by the devil himself.

"The prophecy stated that once the body of the hermaphrodite had died, the Fourteen Emissaries of Lucifer would be released upon the world. They would come to command a mighty army and do everything in their power to prevent the Two from awakening humanity and unlocking the mysteries of the Cube."

Natasha leaned closer.

"These emissaries, Uncle. Are they the same fourteen demons that were removed from us when we were babies?"

"They were," said the bishop, shuddering at the memory of them.

"Fourteen," said Natasha, thinking. "There's something about that number. In another Egyptian myth, Set kills Osiris and divides his body into fourteen parts, spreading them throughout the lands."

Gabriel turned to the bishop.

"Who was it that made the Cube?"

"I can remember asking the very same question," replied the bishop. "*What is this Compostela Cube?*' I asked, *Why have I never heard mention of it before?*'

"'*Few have,*' the professor told me in response. *It is believed to be a Christian relic, but I suspect that it is much older.*'

"He went on to tell me how he had first come to learn of the Cube, deep in the archives of a monastery in Toledo. Curiously enough, it was an Islamic text that he had found, a single Arabic manuscript dating back to the time of the Moorish occupation of Spain.

"The Cube of Knowledge, it explained, was the central subject of a treasure known to the Moors as *The Book of Khalifah,* a secret codex that had been passed from caliph to caliph over the centuries. Finding this book became an obsession for the professor, but in all his years of research, he was only able to gather a few scraps of information concerning it.

"From the manuscript he had found in Toledo, the professor learned that the Compostela Cube held mysterious runes, and that the Book of Khalifah contained the only record in existence of their translations. It was said that without these translations, the Cube's mysteries could never be unlocked. The manuscript stated that the Book and the Cube were linked, and that whoever possessed one, would be led to find the other."

"Who authored this book?" asked Natasha, fascinated.

The old bishop shook his head in bewilderment.

"It is in part an Arabic translation of an ancient Greek text that was long ago destroyed," he whispered. "One that related to an ancient Mesopotamian tablet. This tablet spoke of a *lost Cube*, said to contain a wisdom capable of emancipating man from the confines of mortality and matter."

The bishop looked at both of them in earnest.

"As well as giving detailed descriptions of the artifact," he continued, "the tablet also spoke of the Cube's possible location in the mountains of Northern Spain, and of its original resting place at the entrance of a mysterious labyrinth; a place where it would one day need to be returned in order that humanity might be made ready to receive its secret knowledge."

Gabriel was perplexed.

"Exactly how old is the Cube supposed to be?"

"The professor could not say with any certainty," said the bishop. "He suspected it to be pre-Egyptian, and perhaps even pre-Mesopotamian. The Book of Khalifah describes the Cube as the most prized of all treasures and refers to it as the most ancient of artifacts.

"It was to the Moors, what the Holy Grail was to the Knights Templar, and the professor believed that the two were in fact one and the same thing. According to him, the Cube was the reason why the Moors invaded the Iberian Peninsula to begin with."

Gabriel pondered what the old bishop was telling him, nodding his head as he began to understand.

"Once the Moors had crossed over the Strait of Gibraltar, they made a beeline directly for the north coast of Spain. Historians have never been able to understand the need for their urgency. They cut their way through the Visigoths in less than a year."

"Theirs was a holy quest for knowledge," said the bishop, nodding. "Although it was not they, who in the end would recover the Cube."

"So who was it that found it?" asked Natasha.

"The manuscript states that a Catholic priest found it," said the bishop with a smile. "And that he found it while on the *Camino de Santiago de Compostela*."

"And that's where the Cube gets its name," said Natasha. "I thought it might be named after the city."

"Can somebody please fill me in?" asked Gabriel. "What Camino?"

"The *Camino's* a Christian pilgrimage," explained Natasha. "It follows an ancient Celtic footpath that makes its way through the mountains of Northern Spain. It ends at a big cathedral in the city of Santiago de Compostela, the place where the remains of St. James are said to be kept."

"It begins in France," said Gabriel, nodding. "I've always heard it referred to as the *Chemin de St. Jacques.*"

Natasha nodded as well.

"There's an old legend that tells the story of how St. James' long-lost crypt was found on that trail. It says that a goat herder named Pelaio stumbled on it in the ninth century; that he heard angels singing while out in the mountains at night. He walked towards the music and saw thousands of stars raining down on the tomb. That's why they call it Compostela. It comes from the Latin *Campus Stellae,* or *Field of Stars.*"

"Exactly," said the old bishop. "But the Arabic manuscript told a tale far more intriguing than the popular legend."

The fire crackled in the hearth as the three of them huddled closer together at their table. Encased as they were, deep within that sprawling tomb, it seemed to them that the very walls were comprised of the dead. Even still, the wooden planks from the old scaffolds were thick and dry, and they burned well, shedding a much-welcomed heat, and reassuring them that they were very much alive and well.

Taking a sip from the cup before him, the old bishop straightened his black cassock and continued.

"In the year of our lord, eight hundred and sixty-five, almost fifty years after the tomb of St. James was claimed to have been discovered, the Arabic manuscript tells of a church expedition that went missing in the north of Spain.

"Its objective was to survey an ancient Celtic route that ran the entire length of the mountains, and to map any potential sites where strongholds might be built against the ever-advancing Moors. The leader of the expedition was an Asturian priest and cartographer by the name of Gutierrez de la Cruz.

"Hours before dawn, while deep in the mountain wilds, Gutierrez and his expedition were said to have been overtaken by a potent demonic force; one that came upon them at the bottom of a dark valley, on the shore of a fog enshrouded lake. The party, it is said, heard the tortured cries of two children coming from out on the lake, but the evil that accompanied these cries was such that all but Gutierrez fled into the night, never to be seen again.

"Gutierrez then mounted a raft and followed the cries until he had landed on a small island. There he was overcome by a deep slumber and witnessed the apparition of two angels in a dream. They had taken the form of a boy and a girl, and they appeared hovering over a gaping fissure at the centre of the island. From within this fissure there was said to have come great flames, and a chorus of wailing."

"A gateway to hell," said Gabriel, swallowing despite himself. "Nice dream."

The bishop looked down at the journal, passing his hands over its worn cover and remembering what he had read therein.

"The legend goes on to say that the angels then spoke to Gutierrez about the fissure, referring to it as *The Portal of Ahreimanius*."

"Ahreimanius was a Zurvanite god," said Natasha, frowning. "A very evil one. He originated in the Sassanid Empire of Persia, around 400 BCE."

Gabriel locked eyes with Natasha and then turned to the bishop.

"But what about Gutierrez?" he asked. "How did he find the Cube?"

"The angels told him where it was," replied the old bishop with a shrug. "When Gutierrez awoke, he followed their directions, and arrived at a tomb. It was in this tomb that he found the legendary Cube, and it is here where the manuscript begins to take some unexpected turns. The tomb that Gutierrez supposedly found was said to have belonged to St. James the Just."

"The brother of Jesus Christ," said Natasha. "I can see the connection now. There were two St. James' in the bible. One was Jesus' famous apostle, but the other was James the Just. He was the biological brother of Jesus. The church has always tried to leave him in the shadows.

"Some historians believe that James the Just was the person Jesus chose to lead the church after his death. They claim that the Jewish high priests murdered him before he could take control."

"All right," said Gabriel. "I get how there were two St James', but so what? What does any of that have to do with the Cube? And why would the church make up a story that would put a lost tomb of St. James in the north of Spain to begin with? It's not like it was just around the corner from Jerusalem. It doesn't make sense."

"The church legend is a fabrication," said Natasha. "It states that after Herod beheaded St. James –the apostle, not the brother of Jesus– his body was put into an unmanned boat that made its way to the north of Spain under the guidance of angels. They say that a fisherman found the body at sea, and buried it in the mountains, where it stayed lost until Pelaio found it eight centuries later."

"It definitely sounds like they made it up," said Gabriel. "But what was the church's motive behind the fiction, and what's more, how could the Cube have been found with the body of James the Just? The Cube's medieval. I've got it right here in my pack. It's plain to see. A relic from the time of Christ could never have looked like that."

"Nevertheless," said the bishop, "the Cube is what Gutierrez is said to have found in the tomb of James the Just. The true motives behind the church's legend of St. James, and indeed the truth behind all of this, has yet to be revealed."

For a while, the three remained silent, with Gabriel and Natasha trying to digest everything they had learned thus far. There were so many questions, so many loose ends.

"Uncle Marcus," said Natasha at length. "You said the professor had been very concerned with the similarities between the Egyptian myth and the births of Gabriel and I. Even if all this is true, and we're somehow connected to the artifact, why would the professor need to be so concerned?"

The bishop looked up at Natasha, his silvery brow furrowed.

"Because of what the Ascender's Prophecy relates, my child," he said slowly.

"What do you mean?" asked Gabriel, bending closer.

"It states that the coming of the Two will be marked by a great, world-altering cataclysm. One that will mark the end of an aeon and the beginning of a new epoch."

"A metaphorical cataclysm is what you mean to say, right?" said Gabriel. "A symbolic destruction of the earth."

"The professor believed that it would be very real, my son," said the bishop, "and that it would take place on the winter solstice of the very year that we now find ourselves in."

"But that whole doomsday thing belonged to the Mayan calendar," said Gabriel. "That winter solstice came and went, remember? Nothing happened."

The old bishop only shrugged.

"The myth tells of how Osiris and Isis attempted to escape from the Great Labyrinth during this cataclysm and save the world from destruction."

"But the winter solstice is less than two weeks away," said Natasha. "It's on the twenty-first of December."

"The day we both turn thirty-three," said Gabriel. "What exactly is going on here?"

"I have no idea," said Natasha, a fear coming over her, "but thirty-three seems to be an important age in this prophecy."

She turned to the bishop.

"The hermaphrodite was one full moon away from being thirty-three when he died."

"Indeed, he was," said the bishop slowly. "Jesus was also thirty-three when he was crucified."

Gabriel shook his head and frowned.

"Genetically speaking, thirty-three is also the age when the human body reaches its full development. After that, our DNA begins to develop errors during mitosis."

The old bishop looked down at the tattered journal, his face growing dark.

"The Ascender's Prophecy admonished that if the corpse of the hermaphrodite were taken to the portal before the day of its thirty-third birthday, and buried there in a special ceremony, the Fourteen Emissaries would not be able to enter onto the earth-sphere, and humanity's transition out of the fifth age would be made less catastrophic. This was what both of your fathers died trying to do. They failed."

Gabriel pushed back his messy hair and gazed into the flames of the hearth.

"So, what you're saying is their deaths were no accident."

"It would appear not," said the bishop. "Something caused their plane to crash, and I believe that it was a supernatural force that did it; a demonic force to be precise."

Natasha looked at Marcus, her big eyes filled with fear. She had felt that same demonic force in her workshop just the other day.

"What did the myth say would happen if Osiris and Isis failed to find their way out of the labyrinth?"

The old bishop cringed at her question, and just then the catacombs seemed to close in around them. A frigid draft had suddenly entered into the chamber. It sent chills through them.

"The myth spoke of perpetual night," he said solemnly. "It spoke of a *Great Dying*, and the loss of all hope."

It was at that moment that Shackleton rose from his place before the fire. He approached the door with stealth, his nose raised and sniffing, and the hair on his back on end. He turned and focused an intense look upon Natasha, just as Fra was opening an eye and cocking his head to listen.

"Someone is coming," he whispered. "I think they have found us."

CHAPTER 23

Amsterdam, The Netherlands.

Christian awoke with a start, his heart racing from the remnants of a nightmare. Following the steering committee meeting, he had retired to his room to drink a bottle of wine. He had fallen asleep soon after and dreamed of the four hooded figures. He could still hear his father's voice echoing in his mind.

"Heed the Zurvanites! Heed them! Heed them well!"

Christian ran his hands over his face. He was drenched in sweat. The telephone rang.

"Christian," came the prince's dry voice. "Proceed to the Vanderhoff suite immediately."

"Bloody Christ," groaned Christian. "I'm taking a nap."

Prince Vladimir coughed angrily.

"Go there at once!" he hissed. "The Nautonnier has summoned you!"

Christian heard the line go dead.

The Vanderhoff suite was located in the same wing as Christian's penthouse, and it was not long before he found himself stumbling there, a tumbler of wine in one hand, and a lit cigarette in the other. He recalled what his uncle had told him of the Nautonnier earlier that day.

"He is a figurehead," the prince had said, his voice tinged with hatred for the old man. "He is a remnant of old traditions and outdated superstitions. In all my life I have never seen him do anything of any importance. Your father feared him. Why, I do not know."

Christian thought back to the first time he had seen the Nautonnier. It had been at his father's deathbed, and a sinister power had radiated from the man, one that he could still feel. The

Nautonnier's sudden appearance on the lawn earlier that day had only increased Christian's trepidation. The old man had been standing directly where the hooded figures had appeared, as though he and they were somehow connected.

Christian drained his glass and tossed it away. If his father had feared the Nautonnier, it must have been for a good reason. He made his way along the plush corridor, feeling the tyrannical presence of his father more poignantly than ever now. It settled around him like a cold fog, pressing down on him, suffocating him.

All power is based in fear. Fear must be maintained at all costs.

Christian arrived at a pair of towering doors, only to see them open of their own accord. He squinted into the darkness. The light from the hallway was doing nothing to illuminate the room within.

"Come in, Christian," said a brittle voice, and in that moment, Christian was filled with a deep and inexplicable dread.

Every instinct was telling him to flee but something held him fast.

"Fear me not, boy," came the voice again. "I am no stranger. Please be so kind as to close the door behind you. Your eyes will soon grow accustomed to the darkness."

Christian stepped forward and did as he was told, shutting the door and waiting for his eyes to adjust. It was not long before an ancient man materialized before him. He was seated at a small table, the light of a dim candle illuminating his strange and unsettling features. He sat regally, his brittle white hair as thin as cobwebs, and growing from a pasty grey head that appeared to be moulting.

With the exception of his long, hooked nose, the Nautonnier's bone structure was almost reptilian. He had no eyebrows or facial hair of any kind, and his tripe-coloured skin was like scar tissue, thin, and brittle as old parchment. He reminded Christian of a pagan oracle; powerful and merciless, and almost skeletal. The hard line that was the Nautonnier's mouth transformed into a slit when he opened it to speak.

"I have summoned you here so that you might fulfill the final part of your inheritance," said the Nautonnier. "In order to do this, you must be made aware of certain facts that have been kept from you. After this, you must make a special pledge."

"A pledge?" asked Christian, arriving at the table. "What are you talking about?"

"Sit down, boy."

Christian obeyed, lowering himself slowly into a chair.

"You are of an ancient linage, Christian," said the Nautonnier, his voice like dry leaves. "Your family has always held power over others. It is no coincidence that things have been this way. Many attempts have been made to usurp your family's control, but there has always been a force that has kept it intact."

"Yes," said Christian. "It's called ruthlessness."

The old man smiled slowly, and it seemed to Christian that his skin could be heard cracking as he did so.

"Yes," he replied. "And the driving impetus behind this ruthlessness has always been granted from below."

Christian cocked an eyebrow.

"What are you talking about?"

"I am speaking of Ahreimanius," said the Nautonnier. "The Dark Lord of Matter. The highest servant of Lucifer."

Christian stared into the Nautonnier's reptilian eyes and then began to rise from his chair.

"I'm leaving."

"*Sit down!*" came a sudden hiss, but it had not been the Nautonnier who had uttered it.

Christian felt something invisible push him back into his chair. His head swelled dizzily. His father was present. He denied it.

"You need not be fettered as you are, boy," continued the Nautonnier, more urgently now. "Forfeit your will to that of the master's and you will be more powerful than any man alive."

"*You will assume your responsibilities!*" hissed the voice.

Christian scanned the shadows. There was no denying it. The voice was clearly that of his father's. His mind reeled. His father was dead. They had buried him.

"What the hell's going on?"

The Nautonnier smiled dryly, holding up a wrinkled hand in a gesture of peace.

"I am a fair man, Christian," he said. "I will answer any questions you might have. When you are satisfied, you may proceed with the pledge, or you may choose to abstain from making it. Is this acceptable?"

Christian could feel the hold on him lessen in intensity and he took the opportunity to reposition himself in his chair. Whatever it was that was happening, he would have to play along. The man before him was obviously his superior. His father had feared him. He was beginning to understand why.

"What kind of a title is Nautonnier?" he asked. "What makes you so important?"

The old man nodded.

"Nautonnier is the title given to the leader of our ancient society. It means *The Great Navigator*. It is a lifetime position, and one that has been held by very important personages throughout the ages. It is a position that is held until it is taken away, for there can only be one Nautonnier."

"And who is Ahreimanius?"

The old man gazed into the flickering candle, his eyes betraying a deep fear.

"He is the greatest demon of the Luciferic Order. He is a son of Lucifer and was first called Ahreimanius by the followers of the ancient prophet Zoroaster. He is his father's arm and fist on the earth-sphere. Ahreimanius is merciless and terrible."

"And why can't Lucifer be terrible himself? Why does he need Ahreimanius?"

"Lucifer cannot access the earth-sphere in his bodily form. He can exist here only in spirit. For this reason, Lucifer bestows great power onto Ahreimanius, along with all the souls who are loyal to him. We are such souls, you and I."

Christian scanned the shadowy room. All the shutters and drapes had been drawn tight. Not a sliver of light could be seen anywhere.

"And what is there to gain by serving Ahreimanius?"

"By serving Ahreimanius, we serve ourselves," said the old man. "In exchange for our loyal acts we receive power over others, and great dominion over the matter that he is the master of. Everything that you have in this life, Christian, you owe to Ahreimanius."

Christian was not a spiritual person, yet he could distinctly feel a dark and sinister presence around him. He was certain he must be imagining things. The doses of his medications required altering. He would call his psychiatrist when he was done.

"Your soul is much older than you realize, Christian," continued the Nautonnier.

"What do you mean?" he asked, his fear and confusion mounting. "What are you talking about?"

"The soul of every being that inhabits this planet is ancient, to be sure, but whereas most of these souls are lowly, and of no importance, your soul has been in league with Lucifer since the time of the Great Fall. You are a prince among the fallen angels, Christian. It has always been so, and just as in each of your many previous life incarnations, the time has come when you must renew your pledge to the master once again."

Christian locked eyes with the Nautonnier. As irrational and superstitious as it seemed, he sensed that this was no trivial request.

"Have you any more questions?"

Christian remained silent in his confusion.

"Very well," said the Nautonnier slowly. "There will be other opportunities for you to learn more. As I promised, I shall now permit you to decide how you wish to proceed."

"I choose to sleep on it," muttered Christian, rising slowly from his chair. "I'll get back to you after the conference."

The Nautonnier gave a dry chuckle.

"Oh no, Christian," he said. "I made no mention of giving you time to deliberate. That is not an option. You will decide now. You are free to take any decision you choose but know this: Should you decide to abandon Ahreimanius, your special place at his table will naturally be taken from you. You are free to decide, but you must decide now and forever. Be sure not to err. Ahreimanius knows not the meaning of forgiveness."

Christian could feel the psychic tentacles of his father worming into him again.

All power is based in fear. Fear must be maintained at all costs.

"Follow your heart, Christian," whispered the Nautonnier. "What is it telling you to do? You are free to decide."

Hearing the old man speak had a great effect on Christian. He suddenly felt as though it were still not too late. A sense of urgency filled him. Around him the room had begun to warp and twist.

"What do you want me to do?" he whispered; his eyes wide.

"Merely to sign a contract," said the old man. "It is but a symbol of allegiance to Ahreimanius. A formality. It states that you align yourself with him and offer up to him all that you possess."

The Nautonnier placed a large book on the table and opened it. It was ancient and brittle, and Christian could see that it was a ledger of sorts; a record of all who had signed their souls into the service of Ahreimanius and Lucifer.

The Nautonnier took Christian's hand and pricked his thumb, filling the quill of a pen with the blood that emerged. He laid the pen next to the open book.

"You may sign it here," he said, his crooked finger pointing to a spot at the bottom of the page.

Christian took up the pen and watched his hand move the quill to the age-old parchment. A mark was made, and knowing that it was done, he quickly finished the stroke.

Christian felt a dizzying surge of dark power flood into him just then, and he shuddered unexpectedly. Something was awakening in him; something that should never have been disturbed. He looked up to see that the Nautonnier was watching him intently now, an expression of cold malice spreading across his repugnant features.

"It is done," he hissed, blowing out the candle.

"Wait a minute," said Christian, but the room plunged into darkness.

A sudden realization flooded into him.

"What have I done? What have you made me do?"

"The way to Ahreimanius has been opened," came his father's hiss. *"Behold the newborn son of Lucifer!"*

Christian staggered through the darkness, finding the door to the suite and jerking it open. The light from the hall filled the room, but the Nautonnier was nowhere to be seen.

"What's happening to me?" he gasped, squinting into the shadows, his eyes wide with panic.

In the corner of the room, he could see the shapes of four hooded figures, their bodies jerking violently from side to side, and coming in and out of existence.

"The Cube!" they hissed in unison. *"The Cube!"*

"No!" gasped Christian.

His fists were clenched, and his heart was racing.

"This is impossible!"

CHAPTER 24

Rome, Italy.

"We must move quickly!" whispered the bishop.

Gabriel tiptoed to the entrance and poked his head out into the cold, dark passage. He heard footsteps and then saw a light flash suddenly in the gloom. Within seconds, two figures had become visible. One of them was holding a lantern, but both were holding guns. They were clearly Nasrallah's men.

Gabriel darted back into the chapel. His intention was to wake up Fra and Suora, but he found them both on their feet. He motioned Natasha and the bishop to draw near.

"Nasrallah's men are just up the tunnel," he whispered. "I don't know how they got here. We should have seen them pass."

"They have come from above," said the bishop.

"But that's impossible. The only way they could have found us would be through the nunnery tunnel."

The bishop took hold of Gabriel's shoulder and passed him his father's journal. He had sealed it in an envelope. He drew Natasha nearer as well and spoke to them both.

"There are dark forces at work here," he whispered urgently. "Their knowledge of where the Cube is at any given moment is directly related to the amount of spiritual separation that exists between the two of you."

"What's that supposed to mean?" asked Gabriel, frowning.

"Listen carefully, my son," said the bishop. "When you retrieved the Cube without Natasha being present, it would appear that you inadvertently directed certain dark forces to her. These forces have been with her ever since, and according to the professor, they will continue to follow Natasha until you and she are able to fully merge."

"Merge?" whispered Gabriel urgently. "This is no time for superstitious nonsense, Marcus! The bad guys are just down the hall. What are you talking about?"

"The answers are in the book, my son. Until you resolve these problems, you will find that the enemy will always have a general idea of where you are."

Gabriel and Natasha looked at each other and then back to the bishop. He was gazing up at the scaffolding now. In the light of the fire it could be seen rising up the frescoed wall and ending at the ceiling. There was an old ladder strapped to its side.

"If memory serves me correctly, there is a trap door up there," he said, pointing. "I believe the scaffold is hiding it. It will lead to the next upper level. Go now. You must still find your way out of the catacombs. That will be no easy task."

"But, Uncle," said Natasha, her eyes welling. "The three of you could never make it up that scaffold..."

The old bishop noted her tears and reached into his vestments for his handkerchief.

"We will not be going with you, sweet girl," he said gently.

Familiar with the bishop's grubby napkins, Gabriel stuffed a clean tissue into Natasha's hand before the bishop could offer up his own. Being no stranger to her uncle's hankies, she shot Gabriel a teary-eyed look of thanks.

"What do you mean?" she sobbed.

The bishop pocketed his crumpled rag absently.

"The three of us will stay here and hide, my child."

Gabriel's frown deepened.

"They'll find you and kill you all."

"That is not certain, my son," smiled the bishop. "There are spirits of God here who are helping us. Have faith, and fear not for us."

"But Uncle—" pleaded Natasha.

"Go!" said Marcus, a rarely seen anger flaring up in his eyes. "There is more at stake here than you can possibly imagine, and there is no time!"

To everyone's surprise, Shackleton took to the ladder in a single leap, making his way to the top swiftly and without pause. From below the others watched him disappear onto the top platform, only to see him poke his head out and look down at them.

"Who would believe a dog could do that..." whispered Gabriel, shaking his head in amazement.

In a moment he had taken up both of their packs and was guiding Natasha to the scaffolding. She resisted at first, but Gabriel's touch seemed to reassure her.

The timbers were old but strong, and at the top they found the trapdoor the bishop had spoken of. It was barely big enough to squeeze through, but as Gabriel shined his light into it, he could see that it opened into a tunnel above. Shackleton had already passed into it. Gabriel could see him in the shadows, sniffing the air and looking around.

"I'll go first," he said, stuffing the packs up and hoisting himself through.

He held a hand down for Natasha to take.

"Come on," he whispered. "There's no time."

Natasha was looking over the edge of the scaffolding. She could see the bishop helping Suora into the tiny opening at the base of the altar. They would be hiding in the room that was filled with bones. Natasha saw him look up at her.

"Go!" he mouthed, motioning at her with his hands.

Natasha saw him smile reassuringly, and then disappear into the opening.

"I'll see you soon, Uncle," she whispered, and just then, Nasrallah's men burst into the chapel.

Natasha saw them make for the hearth. These were not the uniformed figures she had seen earlier in the courtyard. They were plainly dressed men and would have appeared to be tourists were it not for the guns in their hands.

Gabriel poked his head down and was going to say something, but Natasha silenced him. She gave him her hands and let him pull her up.

* * * * * *

"Radio Bahadur," said one of the mercenaries in Arabic. "Search every corner of this place. They were just here. They could not have gone far."

Bahadur arrived moments later to find most of his men in the chapel. They were all in plain clothes now, two of them emerging from behind the altar. They had found a backpack. They approached him with scowling faces.

"They were sleeping in that chamber, sir," said one of them, handing him the pack. "The room is full of bones, but there is a blanket spread out on the floor."

Bahadur took the pack from the mercenary and reached inside. He brought out a package, unwrapping it to find a large piece of cake dripping with honey. He smelled it and took a huge bite.

"Has this space been fully searched?" he said, chewing.

"Yes, sir," replied the soldier. "We have found nothing here but the traces they left behind. They must have been eating when they became alerted to our presence. There is still soup in the pot."

"Soup?" repeated Bahadur, raising an eyebrow in the direction of the hearth.

He had not received a morsel of food in more than twenty-four hours and his tortured body was in desperate need of nourishment.

"Continue with the search as planned," he said. "They are obviously not here. Go! The sooner this is over the better."

Within moments his men had vanished, leaving Bahadur alone before the crackling hearth. He sat himself down in one of the chairs, wincing in pain as he reached for the pot. It rested on an iron grating with hot embers still burning beneath it.

Beside the pot he found a slice of bread laden with what appeared to be slices of roasted pork. It had been Gabriel's, and only a single bite had been taken from it.

"Lentils," he said, blowing on a spoonful of soup. "And roasted swine…"

He paused for a moment, thinking.

"A sin to eat, but Allah will understand."

CHAPTER 25

By the time Gabriel had lifted Natasha through the trapdoor, Shackleton was nowhere to be seen. Gabriel shone his light down the passage in one direction and Natasha in the other. There was no sign of the dog anywhere.

"Shackleton!" whispered Natasha. "Shackleton!"

Gabriel turned to face her.

"He knows what he's doing," he said quietly. "We've got to keep moving. This place is crawling with Nasrallah's men."

"But which way do we go?"

Gabriel pulled out his compass.

"The main entrance is at the southern end of the necropolis."

"But we're still three levels beneath it," said Natasha.

"Good point. Let's just look for a way up then. Any preference in direction?"

Natasha pointed into the shadows.

"That way."

"West. OK. I'll always trust a woman's intuition. Let's go."

"I hope that Shackleton has the same intuition as me," said Natasha, but Gabriel had already moved off.

The tunnel they found themselves in was identical to the others. To their right and left were the countless loculi with their sepia-coloured bones. Unlike the tunnels of the lower level however, these wound and split, bringing them to many forks and junctures along the way. They stopped at every one, each time Gabriel asking Natasha for her first intuitive direction.

"Left," she would say after a moment's pause, or "Straight through," or "Left," "Right,".

They walked like this for what seemed hours, feeling themselves more and more entangled in the knotted passageways.

With each step, Natasha felt her hopes fading. She no longer felt the pressing danger of those who pursued them. Everything had been overshadowed by a desperate need to escape this place; to simply get out.

Natasha felt as if the dead were calling to her, and with every step she feared more and more that they would never leave this place alive.

"Is it true that some people have entered these catacombs and never found their way out again?"

She could see Gabriel up ahead, his dark form silhouetted by his roaming flashlight. He stopped and turned to face her, suddenly aware of how frightened she was. He pushed a hand through his hair.

"Come on," he said gently. "You're lagging."

Natasha came closer and Gabriel took her hands into his. In the darkness he could feel them cold and trembling.

"Everything's going to be fine," he said.

Natasha forgot her misgivings and fell into his arms.

"I'm scared, Gabriel," she said amid shivers.

"Now listen to me," he replied softly. "I've been in much worse places than this. Really, I have. I'm not worried. Believe me. We're going to get out of here."

Natasha chewed her lip.

"But what about Uncle Marcus, and Suora and Fra?"

Her eyes were wide now, staring out into the darkness that loomed around them.

"And where's Shackleton?"

Gabriel said nothing. He could already feel her calming down as the warmth spread between them. He was feeling something he had never experienced before. With their bodies pressed together, the inner void that had plagued him felt suddenly full.

Gabriel pushed her gently away but kept hold of her arms. Women like her were incapable of accepting the kind of love he had to give. It was a lesson he had learned the hard way many times. The objective here was simply to cheer her up a little. That was all.

"Never lose sight of the facts," he said.

Her scent was intoxicating.

"Marcus knows these catacombs well, and he's been full of surprises up to now."

He moved a lock of hair out of her eyes.

"You might have all your woman's intuition," he added, frowning at an unexpected surge of affection in him, "but I've got my gut, and it's telling me we'll be seeing them again really soon."

Gabriel was having a considerable effect on Natasha. In the few minutes they had been together, almost all her fear and coldness had vanished. As surprising as it was, she could not recall having ever felt safer than she did right now, lost as they were in that dark and dreadful place. She swallowed slowly and collected herself, stepping back and wiping away her tears.

"You have a way with ladies, Gabriel Parker," she said, giving him a smile that was suspicious and timid all at the same time.

Gabriel was going to say something, but she reached up and put a hand over his mouth. She could see a flickering light in the darkness behind him, not fifty paces away.

"Somebody's coming," she whispered.

Gabriel took hold of her hand and pulled her back into the shadows.

"Don't even breathe," he whispered severely, poking his head out into the tunnel.

He could see the light clearly now but was surprised to learn that it did not come from a flashlight. It appeared to be the light of a lantern, or several lanterns. It was illuminating a large area of the tunnel. Within moments the patter of many feet was echoing around them. A voice spoke out in an Italian accent.

"Now, please, ladies and gentlemen. We will continue to follow him, but keep together. We do not want anyone else getting lost."

Gabriel turned to Natasha.

"Did you just hear that?"

Natasha had a smile from ear to ear.

"Let's stay here," said Gabriel. "We've got to be absolutely sure."

Gabriel poked his head out again to see a group of a few dozen tourists behind their guide. Directly before the man was a handsome brown hunting dog, urging them all to follow him.

"Shackleton!" shouted Gabriel, jumping into the passage. "Come here, boy!"

Natasha burst from her hiding place just in time to receive the dog into her arms. He had come bounding down the passage like a horse at play, slowing only just before arriving, and gently finding his way into Natasha's embrace.

"Oh, Shackleton!" she said. "What would we do without you?"

* * * * * *

The setting sun was blinding as they emerged from the necropolis, and a relief flooded into them that could only be described as euphoric.

"What a beautiful evening," said Natasha, taking in a deep breath of the fragrant air.

Around them Rome bustled in its familiar way, oblivious to the damp graves and catacombs that lay underfoot. Shackleton let sound a deep bark.

"What is it, Shackleton?" asked Natasha, bending down.

"He's trying to tell us something," said Gabriel, squatting next to Natasha. "What is it, boy?"

As if in response to Gabriel's question, Shackleton raised a paw and laid it on Natasha's bent knee, nuzzling his head into her lap.

"Shackleton!" she said laughing. "What are you trying to tell us?"

The dog answered her question with a happy bark and then bounded off suddenly.

"Shackleton!" cried Natasha. "Come back!"

They stood up to see him trot past a group of tourists and disappear into the crowds. Natasha looked at Gabriel in distress.

"Now don't start worrying about him again," he said, holding out his hands. "I've got a hunch that dog knows more about what's going on than we do."

"But where's he going?" she asked, pouting.

"I haven't a clue," said Gabriel. "But if I'm sure of one thing, it's that we'll be seeing him again, and probably when we need him the most."

CHAPTER 26

Amsterdam, The Netherlands.

"Ladies and Gentlemen, I would like to introduce the president and owner of AuraChip Industries, esteemed member of the Vanderhoff group since nineteen eighty-four, Dr. John B. Middleton."

It was early evening, and the conference was concluding its second day. The keynote speaker stepped onto a podium in the hotel's main banquet hall amid a full round of applause. Before him were the world's elite, more than a hundred and twenty strong. They sat at large round tables, arrayed with the finest china, and lit by the warm light of massive chandeliers.

"Thank you," he said, waiting for the applause to subside. "It seems like only yesterday I was up here boring you all with the tiring details about radio frequency identification microchips, and their many biometric potentials. I can recall we were just about to have dinner, and that's probably why none of you left the room."

Laughter spread through the hall.

"You'll be happy to know I'm going to skip past all the technical stuff this time and go straight into what we at AuraChip have accomplished over this last year. Although our outlook is quite extensive, it can all be summed up in two words: Human Implantation."

He was forced to pause until the applause died down.

"Out of the veritable cornucopia of cutting-edge biometric technology, human R.F.I.D. implantation promises to be the ultimate game changer. Over and above the many ways it will improve health, lifestyle, and security, perhaps the most powerful will be in social guidance, and its ability to rein in outlaws, terrorists, and anyone who refuses to adhere to societal norms."

Another round of applause sounded. Population control was one of the Vanderhoff Group's primary objectives, and the group was delighted with what they were hearing.

"The moment laws are not followed, AuraChips will simply be deactivated, leaving deviants trackable, and without resources. In a world where all your money is on your AuraChip, and cash does not exist, what will a deviant do if he's offline?"

"He'll clean up his act and get *in*line, God damn it!" exclaimed an old American man at a nearby table.

His comment was met with a healthy round of applause.

"Yes, I'm afraid he'll have no choice but to shape up and become the kind of good citizen he was always capable of being," said the speaker. "Unless of course he wants to live like a caveman."

The laughter continued.

Christian took the opportunity to rise from his table and leave the hall. Over his shoulder he could still hear the speaker.

"Now the world at large is still unaware of our plans for the AuraChip, and this leaves us with a tremendously exciting, and extremely lucrative opportunity to be the ones to implement this new technology across a full spectrum of applications. What I'd like to go over now is a detailed plan of action that—"

Christian closed the door behind him. Any interest he might have had in the conference had by now been replaced by a cold contempt for all those attending.

"Maggots and parasites," he muttered bitterly. "Putting on airs of helping humanity when all they want to do is subjugate it. If they openly admitted to what they were doing, I could respect them…"

Ever since the proceedings with the Nautonnier that afternoon, Christian had been consumed with anger and hatred. Although intoxicating, these nefarious emotions also frightened him. They seemed to come from a dark personality within him, a previously dormant shadow-self that had been awakened when he had signed the ledger.

Christian began to tremble with rage the more he thought of it. The Nautonnier had tricked him into taking that pledge. He would make the old man pay dearly for what he had done.

I'll murder that son of a whore with my own hands...

As he marched towards the main lobby, Christian could not help but flinch when he saw his reflection in a passing mirror. It jerked him back into reality, checking his wrath almost immediately. He had never been a saint, this was true, but in his eyes he had just seen a cold-blooded killer.

He stopped in his tracks and walked back to the mirror, looking at his reflection with deep concern. For a fraction of a second, he could have sworn that his eyes were not his own, but rather those of a reptile. He produced his phone on an impulse.

"This is Christian Antov," he said. "I need to speak with Doctor Bennington immediately."

There was a pause as he listened.

"It does not concern me that he's on holiday in Paris. He will drop whatever he is doing and call me at once!"

CHAPTER 27

Rome, Italy.

Gabriel could not help thinking he was in a photo shoot for Architectural Digest. The minimalist pomp of the five-star suite was completely at odds with his tastes. Despite having managed to amass a considerable fortune retrieving lost treasures over the years, Gabriel had never been taken by the luxuries such wealth offered. With the exception of his love for Italian motorcycles, German cars, and American gadgets, his tastes had remained simple and down to earth.

In almost every case, Gabriel preferred the clay goblet to the golden chalice, and if he had brought Natasha to this hotel, it was only because he wanted to be sure that she would be as comfortable as possible. She was currently showering in the adjoining suite, the door that linked their rooms kept open on her insistence.

"I hope you don't mind," she had said timidly, "but Uncle Marcus said that those men will always have a general idea of where we are. And then there are those dark forces that he said were following me... I'd feel safer knowing you're close by."

Gabriel peered into her room uncomfortably. Over the sound of the shower, he could hear her singing an Italian pop song. He shook his head incredulously.

How can a nation that spawned the likes of Puccini possibly produce a song that bad?

He called the bishop's phone again. When the voicemail sounded, he decided to leave a message.

"Marcus," he said. "I hope you get this. Natasha and I are out of the catacombs and checked into a hotel here in Rome."

He paced around the room as he spoke, not knowing what to do with himself.

"Something's come up. It turns out the informant who gave us the location of the Cube was Amir's first cousin, a guy named Bahadur. Nasrallah suspects he had something to do with the robbery and he's holding their family hostage."

Gabriel moved to the enormous bed, looking down at its oversized pillows and sterile coverings.

How's anyone supposed to get comfortable in a place like this?

He reached down and pulled away the silken cover.

"Before we do anything about the Cube, I've got to get Amir's family out of there. I'm responsible for all this. Natasha's insisted on coming with me. We'll be flying to Gibraltar tomorrow, and then heading to Morocco from there. Call me the minute you get this. We need to know you guys are safe."

Gabriel pocketed the phone and laid back onto the bed's many cushions, his arms behind his head. He could still feel the grit from the catacombs in his hair and felt far too dirty to be lying where he was. He got up almost immediately, looking around the suite and feeling a growing anxiety for the three dear seniors. The fact that he had intentionally left them behind was proving difficult to bear, especially given the luxurious surroundings.

"We had no choice," he muttered to himself. "They'll be fine. Everything will be fine."

Gabriel paced aimlessly. He had promised Natasha that he would wait until she finished showering before doing so himself. He moved to a little glass table by the window and pulled up a chair. His battered old duffel bag was on the settee beside him, and as he took hold of it he noticed that it had already soiled the cream coloured upholstery with rusty catacomb dirt.

"Oh, man," he sighed, moving it onto his lap. "So much for the damage deposit."

He reached into it, carefully removing the Cube. There was something about the artifact that drove him to hold it, something that made him feel as though it needed his attention. It was as though it were somehow alive.

Removing it from its container, Gabriel was instantly made aware of its strange characteristics, and once again found himself unable to pinpoint exactly what it was. He had seen countless artifacts over his career, but there was something different about this one. Gabriel looked up suddenly. The shower had stopped.

"I'm almost finished," chimed Natasha, and another surge of affection filled Gabriel's heart.

Don't go there, buddy. She's not for you.

It was at that moment that he noticed something very peculiar. A glimmer of light had caught his eye, one that appeared to have originated from the Cube. He glanced up to the ceiling, expecting to find a recessed light that might have reflected in its gold leaf, but there was nothing there. He looked around the room and found no lamp that could have produced such a reflection.

"Do you see how quickly I shower?" came Natasha's voice, pulling him from his thoughts as she appeared at the threshold. "I'm just like a man that way."

She was wrapped in a thick white towel and in the act of brushing her liquescent hair. Gabriel was captivated once again. It took him a few seconds to register that her happy expression had changed into one of wonder.

"So that's the artifact then..." she whispered, stepping into the room and pointing to the Cube in his hands. "What makes it glow like that?"

Gabriel looked down and was unable to believe his eyes. There was a shimmering blue light emerging from the relic's surface. He jumped to his feet, dropping the Cube onto a chair and instinctively moving away.

"What the hell is that?" he said, shielding Natasha as though it might explode. "Medieval artifacts aren't supposed to glow..."

As one, they inched closer to the relic, intrigued by the magical quality of its light. Gabriel was perplexed. He had examined the piece on several occasions and had been certain of its authenticity. In a split second all that had changed.

"This is clearly some kind of hoax..." he said, moving to squat before it.

Natasha kneeled next to him.

"The light seems to be leaking through cracks at the edges of the parchment," she said, picking up the artifact and coming up close to Gabriel so that he might study it too. "Do you see what I mean? Right here, where the vellum meets the framework."

"It looks like there's another layer…" he said, intoxicated by the smell of soap on her skin.

"Another layer?" she asked, turning to look at him. "What do you mean?"

Gabriel felt himself falling into the depths of her big brown eyes. He was suddenly oblivious of the artifact. It was taking all his will to stop himself from kissing her.

"It used to have a crudely painted outer shell…" he muttered dizzily. "I removed it back at the monastery. I kept the pieces if you'd like to see them…"

Natasha was as transfixed as he was. Her vision seemed veiled in mist as she gazed back at him. Her reply came in a soft whisper.

"Are you saying this artifact had an outer layer?"

Gabriel nodded slowly in response.

"Why didn't you tell me…?"

"I was going to…"

"You were…?"

Gabriel nodded again, his eyes drinking in her features.

"I must have forgotten…"

Natasha glanced down at his lips.

"Well, don't let it happen again."

Gabriel's gaze deepened still, and Natasha felt herself being drawn into a vortex of sorts.

"Because if the Cube had one layer…" she managed to say, "It could easily have another…"

"I think it does…"

"I think it does too…"

It was only then that Natasha began to break from the spell. She had dedicated her life to artifact restoration, and here was the most mysterious artifact she had ever encountered, potentially ready to reveal another layer of itself. The realization filled her with a flood of urgency, and in a split second her eyes were alight with excitement.

She sprang to her feet with the Cube in hand.

"This is incredible!" she cried. "Where are the pieces you removed?"

Gabriel blinked up at her and rose with a groan. He pointed a thumb at his tattered pack.

"Go crazy," he said, a little annoyed for having let himself get caught up in her like that. "But don't be too excited. My guess is you're going to find a couple of nine-volt batteries in that thing."

"We can't be certain until we've studied it," she said, rummaging through his bag.

She produced the parchments and glanced up in time to see him walking away.

"Where are you going?"

"To take a shower," said Gabriel, feeling almost relieved that the Cube had turned out to be a hoax. "You know that drug lord really had me going. Apart from the silly light trick, that artifact's a brilliant forgery."

Bahadur mopped up the remaining soup with a crust of bread held between a massive thumb and forefinger. It had been the first thing he had eaten since Nasrallah had interrogated him, and although it had done him tremendous good, he was still not satisfied.

He hunched over and picked through Fra Bartolomeo's pack, wondering if he might have missed something. He found a bottle of water and a flashlight.

"This is very strange," he said to himself. "Perhaps they left their food and water behind in their haste... But how far could anyone go in this darkness without light?"

Bahadur tested the switch and saw that the batteries were still good.

"Something is not right," he muttered, and his voice seemed as deep as the catacombs.

Groaning in pain, he rose from his chair and made his way to the room where the guards had found the pack. In the roaming beam of his flashlight, he could make out the somber mounds of bones, finding at last the small blanket that lay spread out on the floor.

"Why sleep here when you could sleep by the fire?" he said slowly.

Grunting with effort, he bent low and squeezed himself through the tiny opening, unholstering his handgun as he went. He made his way to the blanket and pulled up the edge.

"Allah be praised..." he said in his deep basso.

There in the floor, directly beneath where the blanket had been, was a trap door made of old wooden planks. Holding his gun in one hand, he took hold of the door with the other and swung it open, his eyes opening wide at the sight before him.

There, lying trembling in the cold ground, he could see three figures looking up at him, their eyes wide with fright.

"What have we here?" he said, holstering his gun. "You all look quite old, but hardly ready for the grave."

Bending down, Bahadur took hold of Suora's arm, and, gentler than might have been expected, helped her out of the shallow pit.

"Sister," he said respectfully, his voice like a bass drum. "Please. Allow me."

He shook the blanket that had been lying on the floor and wrapped her shivering body in it.

"Why, thank you, my son," said Suora, more than a little surprised.

The enormous baldheaded man appeared to her to be a kind of monster. His scarred face was badly cut and bruised, and there was a gruesome image of a moth tattooed to his throat. He wore a black sweater and military trousers, his massive, horse-like muscles stretching the material taught. Strapped to his waist, on the opposite side of his handgun's holster, was a combat knife large enough to gut an elephant.

Even still, there was a keen intelligence and deep wisdom in his eyes, and the three seniors could see that this was no monster at all, but rather a tame and noble giant.

"Please," he said to the bishop and brother, reaching down to help them.

They each took hold of a massive hand and rose slowly to their feet. They had only lain there for ten minutes at most, but the ground was cold and damp, and their old bodies had not taken kindly to the accommodations.

Bahadur helped them out of the pit, looking back over his shoulder as he did so.

"You need not fear me," he said, his battered face at odds with his words. "I am not a murderer, and especially not of those in the holy service. I only ask that you assist me in my endeavor. Where is the Compostela Cube?"

"I am Bishop Marcus Di Lauro," said the old bishop, "and I thank you for your kindness and civility. I must say it is greatly appreciated. The Cube is not in our possession, although we were close to its keeper not so long ago."

"Gabriel Parker," said Bahadur, frowning. "Where is he?"

"That I do not know," said the bishop, "but I must confess that even if I did know, I would not tell you under any circumstances. You see, the Cube belongs to Gabriel by birth. It is his for the keeping and I will not betray him."

"Yes, of course, your Eminence," said Bahadur, nodding solemnly. "This I can understand, but you must also understand that if you will not cooperate with me, I will be forced to take you as my prisoners until the Cube is recovered. It is not I who decide it, but those to whom I am bound."

"You are a good man," said Suora suddenly. "In your heart you are true, my son. It is the wickedness of others that has led you astray."

Bahadur turned to face the little nun, his expression gentle.

"Thank you, Sister," he said deeply. "You are very kind and very observant, for ugly as I am, I try to be my best under the eyes of Allah. I have taken many lives, but never those of the innocent. You are safe while under my charge, but I cannot guarantee that my master will be so kind. Please now, you must come with me."

He led them out into the tunnel.

"I will give you a choice," he said, stopping and looking very serious. "I will be taking you to our headquarters. To do this we must first leave the catacombs. We can do this by going back to the monastery the way you have come, or we can take the much easier route up through the catacombs, and out the public entrance."

The bishop moved to say something, but Bahadur silenced him with a gesture.

"Were we to take the way through the catacombs, and enter into the general public, any one of you could easily scream out and draw attention to us. What kind of promise can you give me that you will not do this?"

"You have shown us mercy, my son," said the old bishop in earnest. "In exchange for your kindness, I give you my word that we will not cry out. We will go with you peaceably to your headquarters, or anywhere else you wish, and we shall trust in God, or Allah if you prefer, for He is the father of us all."

"And I will honour your promise, your Excellency," said Bahadur. "Please, come this way."

The sun had already set when they approached a black van parked on the roadside, meters from the catacomb entrance. Bahadur slid open the side door, much like a chauffeur might do, inviting the three to enter with a polite bow.

"Please," he said. "You will find the seats comfortable after your long flight."

"Thank you, my son," said Fra Bartolomeo, being the last to enter. "God bless you."

Bahadur closed the door and Fra watched him through the windows as he made his way around the van. He stopped just outside the driver's door and made a phone call. Fra listened in with his sharp ears.

"He must be talking to Nasrallah," he whispered to the bishop and nun. "Judging by his tone."

He listened intently.

"He is telling him that he has found us, and that his men are still searching for Gabriel and Natasha."

Fra looked at the bishop in surprise.

"He has been told that they are no longer in the Catacombs."

The bishop took hold of the brother's arm, a combination of joy and worry engulfing his features. The old brother held up a hand in a plea for silence.

"They do not know exactly where they are. Somewhere in the city centre. Bahadur is agreeing to regroup at headquarters."

Just then the driver's door opened, and Bahadur entered the van.

"Do you require food or drink?" he asked over his shoulder. "I am afraid I have eaten all of your provisions."

"A cup of tea would be very nice," said Suora. "If you might be so kind."

"It will be my pleasure, Sister," said Bahadur, "and a fair price for such fine lentil stew. The honey cake was also very good."

"Oh, I am so glad that you enjoyed it, my son!" said the old sister. "It is my specialty. The lentils, however, were Fra's humble invention."

She timidly pointed her thumb at the old brother and smiled ear to ear.

"I thank you," said Bahadur. "My employer had given me a sound thrashing and nothing to eat for more than a day."

"Oh, my goodness," said Suora, and just then the bishop's phone beeped.

"Excuse me, your Excellency," said Bahadur. "It would appear you have a message waiting. Perhaps you might put the phone onto its speaker mode, so that we all might hear it."

"Of course, Bahadur," said the bishop, fumbling with the phone. "I understand."

Gabriel's message played out and Bahadur turned in his seat to better hear it.

"-before we do anything about the Cube, I've got to get Amir's family out of there. I'm responsible for all this. Natasha's insisted on coming with me. We'll be flying to Gibraltar tomorrow, and then heading to Morocco from there. Call me the minute you get this. We need to know you guys are safe."

Bahadur nodded slowly when the recording had ended.

"If you will please excuse me for a moment."

With that he left the van and began pacing outside, bent in thought. He returned a few minutes later, speaking only after he had closed the door behind him.

"Amir is my cousin," he said deeply. "His family is my family, and it would appear that Nasrallah is an enemy to us all."

He rubbed the back of his thick neck and frowned as he thought.

"I can help Gabriel Parker," he continued. "But he will have to promise to help me in return. Nasrallah is a very dangerous man. If he learns of my betrayal, his vengeance on my family will be swift. He would have to be brought down quickly and decisively. Would Dr. Parker be willing to help me do this?"

Bishop Marcus, Fra, and Suora all nodded emphatically.

"I have known Gabriel all his life," said the old bishop in earnest. "He will most definitely help you, my son. Of this I am certain."

Bahadur gave a single nod. Amir had always spoken well of Gabriel Parker and had related more than a few tales of his bravery and loyalty.

"Then I will arrange a private flight to Gibraltar for us later tonight," said the giant. "While I do this, if your Excellency will please contact Dr. Parker and inform him that you are here with me, and that you are safe. Allah willing, we shall free my family, even if we must raise a small army to do so."

Suora squeezed her companion's hands excitedly, delighted with the new plan. Bahadur produced his phone and put it on speaker mode so that they all might hear. The connection went straight to Nasrallah's voicemail.

"Master," he said. "There has been a change in plans. I have extracted information from the hostages and killed them. A trap has been laid for Gabriel Parker at the Trevi Fountain tomorrow at twenty-three hundred hours. I have learned that he has hidden the Cube. For this reason, he must be taken alive and made to talk. I promise to have the artifact for you in thirty-six hours. Please call me if you have any questions. I am your humble servant."

Bahadur sent a text message and then made another call.

"Stop your search," he said sharply. "Regroup all the men. We will be laying a trap at the Trevi Fountain. I have sent you the details."

He was silent while the mercenary spoke.

"No!" barked Bahadur in his deep basso. "I have other business I must attend to. You are in command now."

Bahadur put away his phone.

"The game is afoot," he said, starting the van's engine and pulling out into traffic. "May Allah help us."

He accelerated up to speed.

"Now for more important matters," he added, tapping the navigation system. "British tea!"

CHAPTER 29

Los Picos De Europa, Northern Spain.

"To the Black Lake!" hissed a demonic voice.

The sun had already disappeared behind the mountainous peaks as Isaac battled his way down the rugged terrain. Around him the tangled branches of countless black trees encased him like threads in a spider's web. At his feet, a tarp covered sled fashioned from plane wreckage carried what was left of the rotting corpse of his son. The stench of it made him nauseous.

Dear Father, give me strength to endure this trial.

Isaac could do nothing to escape his fear. In the end the demons had won. They had taken possession of his faculties and left him with barely enough consciousness to know what it was they were making him do. He was in a waking nightmare, and while he had no control of his actions, he struggled desperately to keep control of his thoughts.

His memory told him that he had managed to free himself from the wreckage of the plane, and that he had been dragging the corpse for days now, crossing treacherous barriers, descending perilous rifts, and all the time being made victim to an icy voice that filled his mind like a swelling ocean.

"To the Black Lake!" it hissed over and over again. *"To the Portal of Ahreimanius!"*

It was his son who spoke, and if he knew this, it was only because he was of his own flesh and blood. Isaac had spent a lifetime at his side. Singing to him, caring for him, loving, as best he could, a child who had never once uttered a single word to him; a child who had caused the death of his beloved wife.

It had been a thirty-three-year-long vigil of parental duty, and even now in death, the child would still give him no peace. Isaac felt a deep hatred for his son rise up within him, and with it came an encompassing sense of guilt for feeling this way.

"To the Black Lake! To the Portal!"

It was a cyclical litany, minute after minute, day and night. It came as from a hungry infant; pleading, insistent, selfish, parasitic. On occasion the corpse would throw itself into violent tantrums, its stiffened bulk twisting and jerking beneath the battered tarpaulin like a great dying fish.

Isaac made his way downward into the woods. Below him he could see a tiny island, the place of his son's conception. He began to feel a great weight pressing down on him just then, and it drove the air from his lungs, and the sight from his eyes. He brought his hands to his face as a vivid memory flooded into him.

He could see his late wife Alina materializing out of the blackness. She was on the edge of a circle of standing stones, the tangled trunks of the little island's interior surrounding her. They had only just docked their boat. Alina had playfully run into the woods with a picnic basket and Isaac relived the intensity of his love for her. It ached in his heart and made any other pain he was experiencing seem insignificant by comparison.

Almost thirty-four years earlier, Alina had been introduced to him by Father Adrianus. She had been a beautiful girl, over a decade younger than himself, and deeply in need of love and support.

"It is time you took a wife, my son," the priest had told him one day. "You will take this young woman as your bride, and together you will raise a family."

As always Isaac had done as he was told. It was not long before he had found himself on his honeymoon, walking the pilgrimage of the *Camino de Santiago* with a young wife at his side.

Now, in his delirium, he was revisiting that time and place, and he saw that he and Alina were once again making love atop the great monolithic stone. A chilling fog had settled in and something seemed terribly wrong. He glanced down at Alina and found to his horror that the corpse of his son had taken her place.

Isaac broke from his twisted reverie, his eyes finding the cadaver at his feet. Through the tarpaulin he could make out its macabre form and a sudden desire to destroy the thing filled him to the quick.

CHAPTER 30

Rome, Italy.

Gabriel emerged from the bathroom, cleanshaven and wrapped in a plush white bathrobe. He found Natasha sitting cross-legged on his bed. She was wearing a pair of hotel pajamas two sizes too big, and her chestnut hair was piled loosely on her head, accentuating her graceful, ballerina's neck. A tray laden with food sat at the foot of the oversized mattress, its contents covered with silver lids.

"I asked room service to put it here," she said casually, reading his thoughts. "I hope that's all right. I thought it would be more fun this way. Like a picnic."

She smiled shyly.

"It looks like you ordered every item on the menu," said Gabriel with a wink.

Natasha beamed and then moved away a pillow that had been in front of her. Gabriel gasped in surprise. His new friend had been busy. The Cube had undergone a complete transformation.

The artifact lay there amid six, cross-shaped sheets of parchment, and a completely dismantled jewel-encrusted framework. All that remained was a perfectly formed cube that looked to be made of semi-translucent stone. As before it was glowing, and the colour it took on was an incredibly beautiful iridescent blue.

"Happy to see me?" flirted Natasha.

"I am…" Gabriel said, coming closer.

His eyes were glued to the artifact.

"How did you know?"

"Because it got brighter when you saw me."

Gabriel sat on the bed; his attention fixed on the strange relic.

"What the hell is this thing? Is this some kind of a joke?"

Natasha crawled to the foot of the bed and began to pour out some coffee. Gabriel glanced up for a moment, his stomach rumbling, but his eyes returned to the artifact like iron to a magnet.

"It's no hoax, Gabriel," she said plainly. "I'm certain of it. Whatever this is, it's authentic. Look at those parchments and you'll see why."

Gabriel examined them each in turn. They were cross-shaped, comprised of six, equally sized, square-shaped sections. Their creases revealed how they had previously been wrapped around the Cube. The parchments were beautifully worked, each one written in tongues belonging to the six great faiths: Islamism, Hinduism, Buddhism, Judaism, Taoism, and Christianity.

Gabriel could not understand. Their level of detail was tremendous. It would have taken a forger years to complete a work of this magnitude. The parchments simply had to be authentic.

"Look on the back of the one that's written in Latin," said Natasha, pouring out the coffee. "It's signed by Gutierrez de la Cruz. Do you remember him?"

"He was the priest in Marcus' story," muttered Gabriel, picking up the parchment with great care. "The guy who found the Cube. He appears to be representing the Christian faith in these documents."

Gabriel turned his attention back to the Cube itself, laying down the parchment and picking up the strange, semi-translucent stone. He was amazed by what he saw. Covering its glowing surface were strange and ancient symbols.

"These must be the runes that Marcus was telling us about," he said, looking up at Natasha. "The ones that were deciphered in the Book of Khalifah."

He returned his attention to the artifact again.

"This Cube isn't Sumerian, Natasha. It's Neolithic. By the structure of these runes, I'd say it was proto-Basque."

"How old do you think it is?"

"It's difficult to say," he said. "The origins of the Basques have always been shrouded in mystery. Many theories point to them being the first Cro-Magnon people to populate Europe, some forty thousand years ago. By the looks of these proto writings, they might be right. If it's genuine, this Cube could easily be that old."

"Can you read the runes?"

He shook his head as he studied them.

"They're abstract symbols," he said. "Proto writings. The Sumerians were the first to come up with an actual alphabet. Before that, people just drew pictures to tell stories. Whoever deciphered them must have been privy to some very specific knowledge. These symbols could mean absolutely anything."

Gabriel looked up at her before returning his attention to the artifact.

"At least this explains how Gutierrez could have found this in the tomb with James the Just," he continued. "This artifact would have been ancient even by their standards. It must have been Gutierrez and his contemporaries who built the framework and covered it in the illuminations. There's only one problem. How the hell can a forty-thousand-year-old artifact be glowing?"

Gabriel shot a baffled glance at Natasha and then returned his attention to the Cube.

"To produce this kind of light, a power source of some kind would be required. It's too bright to simply be phosphorescent."

The more Gabriel turned it in his hands, the more confused he became. The material it was comprised of had a strange, organic quality to it. What was more, there was still the matter of its bizarre density. More than ever, it reminded him of firm flesh, similar in density to the flank of a strong horse but looking very much like translucent stone.

"I've never seen anything like it…"

Natasha handed him a steaming cup of coffee.

"Would you like to see something really amazing?"

"Sure," said Gabriel, taking a sip from his cup.

"Empty your mind of any thoughts," said Natasha. "Just think of your coffee."

"All right…"

No sooner had Gabriel done so than the Cube ceased to glow.

"What?" he said, looking up at Natasha, only to see it come to life again.

She clapped her hands in delight.

"It's magical, Gabriel!" she chimed. "It only glows when we're thinking of each other."

"How on earth did you figure that out?"

"Because you stopped thinking about me when you went into the bathroom."

Gabriel paused before answering.

"As a matter of fact, I did," he admitted. "I was feeling a little overwhelmed about everything. I decided to have a timeout."

"Interesting," said Natasha, rubbing her chin. "And how do you feel now?"

Gabriel returned his attention to the artifact, his brow furrowed.

"Overwhelmed."

Natasha leaned forward and kissed Gabriel's cheek.

"I like you very much, Gabriel Parker," she said, rolling off the bed before he could react. "And just for your information, I'll be returning to my room as soon as we've eaten. So don't get any ideas."

Gabriel gave her a curious glance, his eyes following her as she made her way to the suite's balcony. Her words had sounded more like an invitation to him than anything else.

Don't even go there, buddy...

"You seem so familiar to me, Gabriel," she continued, gazing out over the glittering lights of Rome.

Gabriel tore his eyes from her and brought his attention back to the Cube. She seemed incredibly familiar to him too, but he would not allow himself to be drawn into this conversation. There were more important issues at hand. Namely, a forty-thousand-year-old artifact that somehow glowed.

Gabriel emptied his mind of Natasha and watched the Cube grow dim as a result. After a few minutes Natasha returned to the bedside to see that Gabriel had completely put her out of his mind. The Cube was like a lifeless stone.

"Earth to Gabriel," she said with hands on hips.

When he looked up at her the Cube burst to life again.

"This thing really can read our thoughts..." he said, returning his attention to the artifact yet again.

Natasha watched it grow dim.

"That's what I said..." she muttered dejectedly.

She climbed onto the bed and busied herself with the food, glancing over at Gabriel as she prepared the plates. She was unsure when the change had taken place in her, but at some point her suspiciousness of Gabriel had turned into a kind of fascination.

She caught herself feeling oddly jealous of the artifact for holding his attention, and she tried to understand what it was that drew her to him. Gabriel seemed to reside in his own universe, and did not seem to need anything from anyone, least of all her. He was like a planet, and she like a reluctant moon caught in his gravitational field.

I should never have let him hold me in the catacombs...

Gabriel continued to study the glowing Cube, oblivious of Natasha's thoughts. He was not one to believe in magical trinkets. There was a scientific explanation for its light, and another to explain its obvious thought reading, neurofeedback capabilities. The Cube somehow knew when they were thinking of each other, but that hardly meant it was magical.

He passed a hand over his jaw, absently looking for any stubble he might have missed. He could remember reading about brain-computer-interfaces, but he had never heard of wireless versions before. He could devise no hypothesis that might explain why an object of such seemingly advanced technology would be inscribed with Neolithic proto-writings and wrapped in thousand-year-old manuscripts. It simply did not make sense.

Gabriel noticed the lights in the room dim just then and looked up to see Natasha standing by the light switch. The sight of her sent the enigmatic Cube into a brilliant blue glow again, and he felt as though he had been freed from one trance only to be trapped by another.

He watched her climb gracefully onto the bed, taking up the two plates she had prepared. The delicious aroma reminded him of how hungry he was.

They ate mostly in silence, each of them lost in thought. Gabriel was trying hard not to think about Natasha, but he was failing entirely now, and the glowing Cube betrayed his attempts at indifference. It amazed him that they could be so comfortable together, sitting alone in a hotel room without having to say a word. Despite his dislike of the minimalist suite, he could not recall having ever felt more at home than he did right now.

When they had finished eating, Natasha piled the dishes onto a tray and carried them back to the serving cart. When she returned Gabriel had leaned back against the headboard and closed his eyes. She stood there silently for a moment and then gave a forced yawn.

"Well, I guess it's bedtime, then…" she said.

He responded with a drowsy grunt and pushed himself back into his pillows. Natasha watched him drift off to sleep, her eyes scanning his features. Every man she had ever loved had broken her heart, and she wondered if Gabriel would do the same.

Go to bed, Natasha. You're thinking too much.

She moved to the bedside to turn off the lamp and reached down on an impulse to touch his face. At the last minute she desisted and smiled softly at her silliness. Seconds later she was back in her adjoining suite, leaving the door slightly ajar behind her.

CHAPTER 31

Amsterdam, The Netherlands.

Christian stood on the terrace of his penthouse suite, a lit cigarette in one hand and a brimming glass of red wine in the other. A full moon was beginning to rise over Amsterdam, and far below he could see the last of the conference attendees boarding their limousines at the hotel's front entrance. He drained his glass as if to toast their departure and ended the farewell with a grimace of disdain.

Turning back inside, Christian took up the wine bottle and drew heavily from his cigarette as he poured out the Bordeaux. He could still hear the insistent voice of his father in his mind. It echoed only two words, over and over again.

"The Cube!" it whispered urgently. *"The Cube!"*

Having no idea what this could mean, Christian was content to suppress the message, using the familiar tools of denial and alcohol to get the job done. There was no need to worry. His doctor would soon be providing him with medications that would silence the voices completely.

He fell onto the sofa and clicked on the television. It was eleven o'clock and one of the many Vanderhoff-owned news channels was filling the screen, its famous slogan being proclaimed against a background of flashing imagery and hypnotizing graphics.

"GNN. The planet's most trusted news network."

Christian smiled wryly.

"What a joke," he said bitterly. "The only reason they're the most trusted is because they don't stop saying it."

He watched the introduction finish with a flourish, and soon the anchorman was announcing the top story.

"Today, leaders from around the world sign the final legislative documents ushering in a new age for global economics. On the first of January, the World Bank's "CREDIT" will become the new currency of the global marketplace, completely phasing out all forms of cash across the majority of the planet by the end of the year. Coming up, a rebroadcast of this evening's Presidential address from the White House."

Christian turned off the television. It disgusted him. He had only wanted to see that all had gone as planned, and it had. The machine he had so recently been given control of was working perfectly.

He threw the remote onto the coffee table, and just then heard a knock at his door. Rising slowly, he made his way to answer it.

"Hello, Mr. Antov," said the beautiful young woman.

She had an innocent, seductive smile, her hair red and curly.

"Good evening, whore," he said quietly, not even attempting to mask his disdain. "I want you naked on the bed, and I don't want to hear another word coming out of that painted mouth of yours for the rest of the night. Is that clear?"

The smile vanished from the girl's face. She nodded in affirmation and entered silently.

Christian watched her undress and climb onto the oversized mattress. She was perfect in every way, but he saw no beauty in her. He was drowning in hatred and violence. He could feel it churning within him like an alien entity. An unexpected knock sounded just then and Christian shot a glance over his shoulder, his hatred transforming into fury. He reached the suite's door in a series of aggressive paces and jerked it open.

"What part of *Do Not Disturb* do you not understand?" he said, but instantly he fell silent.

Standing on the threshold was none other than the Nautonnier himself. Christian felt the room suddenly reeling around him. He hated this man more than he had ever hated anyone before, and an urgent desire to snuff out his repugnant life flooded into him again.

"Perhaps it is not what I understand that is important," said the Nautonnier in answer to his question, "but rather what your master *requires* of you."

With a dismissive shove, the old man used his bony forearm to push Christian aside and enter the suite. No sooner had he passed inside however, than he raised his long nose into the air, taking two quick sniffs.

"You have a lovely scent, sweet girl," he announced. "Now put on your things and leave us. We have important business that need not trouble your pretty little ears."

Christian was puzzled by the Nautonnier's remark. It had been his specific request that the girl wear no perfume. Within moments she emerged from the bedroom, her clothes donned haphazardly.

Her head was lowered in humility and fear as she made for the door, but the Nautonnier's ancient hand shot out as she passed, clamping onto her arm with uncanny strength. He pulled her close, running his grey lips over her delicate neck and inhaling her scent deeply.

"Ah," he said, sniffing her as a dog might do. "I can see he has not got to you yet..."

And then shooting a glance at Christian he added:

"See the pretty redhead saved from a ravishing! You might thank me, little one."

The girl twisted under his grip, smiling politely while trying to free herself from the stench of his breath.

"Thank you," she said meekly.

"You do not know the thrashing I have saved you from, my sweet," breathed the Nautonnier.

He glanced over at Christian.

"Neither does our esteemed Mr. Antov. Now go! And never whore yourself again! Go to church, girl! Ask Jesus for forgiveness!"

He released her and she hurried to the door, fumbling nervously with the latch before finally escaping. The Nautonnier made for the door as well.

"Get your things together, Christian," he said over his shoulder. "You will meet me in the Vanderhoff suite in fifteen minutes. Is that clear?"

"Get out of my room," came Christian's reply.

His hatred and fury were merging into a barely containable wrath.

"You can expect me within the hour. If you don't like it, you can go to hell."

The Nautonnier turned slowly to look at him, smiling darkly the whole while.

"I see you are feeling the power of the dark lord Ahreimanius," he said knowingly. "We will be waiting for you."

Christian followed him to the door only to witness something deeply disturbing. As the Nautonnier had made his exit, Christian had caught sight of four quivering shadows being cast onto the carpeted floor of the hallway outside. He could not bring himself to look for their source. A feeling of deep foreboding was churning in his stomach.

What is this? What the hell's going on?

He closed the door quickly, but the low chime of an arriving elevator came to his ears just as it shut. The sound seemed a kind of death knell to Christian, summoning that dark self within him, and sending a jolt of hair-raising fear through his entire body.

Christian retreated into his suite on faltering legs, a snakelike voice whispering its unending message into every corner of his psyche.

"The Cube," it hissed. *"The Cube!"*

CHAPTER 32

More than an hour had passed, by the time Christian arrived at the Vanderhoff suite. He had purposely lingered at the hotel bar, wanting to make it clear that he was not one to be ordered about. He prepared to knock, but just as they had done on his first visit, the doors opened before he could do so. The dark and somber room came into view.

"You may come in, Christian," said the brittle voice of the Nautonnier from the shadows.

The doors closed silently behind Christian as he entered, plunging the room into inky blackness. He could feel a strange presence very close to him now, almost brushing his face and body. A subtle yet unmistakable stench filled the room. It smelled of death and rot.

A terror began to take hold of Christian, and it was only a sudden rush of anger, brought on by that dark self within him, that prevented him from collapsing to the floor.

"This is bullshit!" he barked, his fear transforming. "I didn't come here for a spook show. Turn on a bloody light or I'm leaving, and you can go to hell!"

He heard a match being struck, and saw a candle come slowly to life. It sat in the corner of the suite, illuminating a round table, along with its five shadowy occupants. They wore dark, hooded robes.

"I didn't know this was a Halloween party," said Christian dryly.

He saw the Nautonnier rise to his feet and throw back his hood.

"You will have respect!" he hissed.

"Fuck you."

The Nautonnier sat down as Christian approached, and the others remained motionless in their seats. The air seemed to crackle with energy.

There was an empty chair at the table, and as Christian arrived, he stood by it, looking down at the robed figures. It was the first time he had seen them up close, and their rate of oscillation seemed to have slowed, so that they almost appeared to be solid. Christian fought back an urge to vomit. They were repulsive to him.

"Sit down!" came his father's icy hiss.

Christian did his best to ignore it.

"Show me your faces!" he demanded.

As one, the four reached up and pushed back their hoods. Christian stepped away in shock.

What is this? How can this be?

Fluctuating between grainy ghostliness and solidity, he could see four visages before him, so ancient that their appearance seemed to defy the laws of nature. They stank of rot and decay. That something could be so old seemed to Christian utterly impossible. He bent forward despite his disgust. Their features were clearly reptilian.

"What the hell is going on here?" he asked, looking over at the Nautonnier.

"Our brothers are ancient by all standards," he said. "They belong to a race of beings that dwelt on the earth long ago. We are of their bloodline, Christian. Please, sit down. I beg you."

Seeing that the Nautonnier was finally assuming a respectful disposition had a calming effect on Christian. He had had enough of the old man's impertinence. He sat down and lit a cigarette, blowing smoke into the Nautonnier's face.

"Start talking," he said, feeling his self-confidence fading. "I'm a busy man."

"You are nothing without the master!" hissed the four in unison, each of them rising to their feet.

In that instant, it seemed to Christian like a great weight were suddenly pressing down on him, as though he had been submerged in very deep water. The pressure made his head reel in pain, but he could not cry out. He watched the Nautonnier rise to his feet and disappear behind him. The pain was intensifying. He could do nothing but grasp the arms of his chair and writhe in agony.

"Can you now feel what you are up against, boy?" came the icy whisper.

Christian heard the voice as though it were filtering up from the floor. The stench of the Nautonnier's breath curled over his neck and into his nostrils.

"Fuck you," he managed to utter.

"You will learn respect!" cried the brittle voice, and suddenly Christian felt a piercing pain burning into his lower spine.

It shot up into his ears, silencing his scream and sending all the muscles in his body into spasm. The room went black.

When Christian regained consciousness he found that he was still seated in the same chair. He looked up to see that the table before him was ablaze with candles, each one placed at the outer points of a pentagram that had been drawn crudely on its surface. At its centre lay a dagger with a serpentine blade. Surrounding the table were the four ancient figures, and the Nautonnier. He could feel their wicked eyes on him.

"Who are you?" muttered Christian at last, looking to the four.

"We are the Zurvanites of Ahreimanius," came the frigid whisper. *"We are the keepers of the Eternal Temple of Set."*

Christian passed his hands over his face. His head was spinning.

"They are *The Four,*" said the old sage, nodding. "Since ancient times they have served the Nautonnier and given him knowledge and power. They represent the four great forces of destruction and are the keepers of the four dimensions. They answer only to Lucifer."

"How can you expect me to believe any of this nonsense?" asked Christian weakly.

"You will believe when you witness the destruction they shall reap through you," said the Nautonnier. "You were always a disbelieving boy. It is time you opened yourself to the truth."

"How would you know what kind of boy I was?"

"Ah, but you forget, my child," whispered the Nautonnier. "We were great schoolmates."

In the depths of his heart, Christian felt a sudden pang of intense emotional pain. It seemed to come from a long way off; from another life, or from a nightmare. He squelched it immediately, denying it utterly.

"I see you choose to forget our special friendship," hinted the Nautonnier, a sly smile spreading over his face. "And after all the fun we had together..."

Christian battled with himself. Memories he had long ago buried were coming up from his dark childhood. His loveless father, his cruel nanny, the loneliness and isolation. They had sent him far away, to a horrible place. It was an institution. There had been teachers. *Brothers* they had been called. Catholic priests. Christian squirmed in his seat, feeling the cruel eyes of The Four on him.

"Oh," said the Nautonnier in a playful tone, "I think he is starting to remember those things we did together."

Christian squirmed. The Nautonnier's voice was like a scalpel.

"How could you have forgotten? You are breaking my heart!"

Christian looked directly at the wispy haired Nautonnier. The latter was staring back at him now, an exaggerated pout distorting his repugnant features. In his cold, cruel eyes Christian could see something vaguely familiar, and in an instant, long drowned memories came flooding back to him, as though a dark gate had been lifted, or a tired dike thrown down.

"Father Adrianus..." breathed Christian in horror, moving his head from side to side. "No... It can't be you..."

A darkness was enveloping Christian now. It came in from his periphery, engulfing everything in an inky blackness. Out of the shadows a scene materialized. He was remembering. He was a child. He was in a study room in the school's library.

"You've been a very dirty little boy, Christian," whispered a voice, and Christian knew at once that it belonged to the Nautonnier.

"What you have done to me is very wrong, and very dirty."

"No!" cried Christian in tears. "You made me do it! You made me!"

"Dirty boy!" scolded the voice. "Now you will do it to me again, or I will tell everyone what you have done!"

Christian jerked into the present. He focused his eyes on the Nautonnier, remembering fully what he had been made to do.

"You!" he said, trembling with fury.

A deep shame was making its way through Christian now, as though he were drowning in it. The seething hatred and anger that came in its wake threatened to consume him.

"I will kill you for what you did to me!"

"He remembers!" exclaimed the Nautonnier, clapping his hands in feigned delight.

Christian attempted to rise from his chair, realizing only then that he was completely paralyzed. He could move nothing but his head.

"And, yes, Christian," said the Nautonnier wickedly. "Your father knew very well of our little games, as did you your uncle Vladimir."

Christian was in tears of frustration. Through the Nautonnier's promptings he had now regained all the memories he had so thoroughly repressed. He could recall each and every cruelty perpetrated by those who were supposed to have loved him. The walls had broken, and all the subterfuges that Christian had created to hold onto himself were gone. There was nothing but the truth, and he refused to believe it. He refused it with all his will. He would never allow himself to accept this. Never.

As the Nautonnier came closer, something in Christian transformed. It arose from the depths of his soul, riding on a swelling wave of hatred and violence. It took form as a sudden surge of strength, and its power was intoxicating. Christian did nothing to repress it, choosing instead to observe the beast within him as a spectator might do. It felt primal and ancient, like something he had long ago once been, and since forgotten. In a fraction of a second Christian's dark inner self had taken full control.

Directly before him, Christian could see the Nautonnier's creased and wrinkled face. It was contorting with mock pity. He could smell the putrid breath, and the stench of it brought a pang of lucidity to his memories. Christian's childhood traumas were playing out before him. He was reliving every feeling, every sordid experience at the hands of this malevolent priest.

"You'll pay for what you did to me," he said in a low and trembling voice.

His rage was on the verge of explosion.

"Oh, he is upset with me," mocked the Nautonnier. "Is this a lover's spat?"

With one concerted effort, Christian broke from the spell that had held him paralyzed. He shot out a hand and took hold of the Nautonnier's wrinkled brittle throat. His strength seemed unreal.

I'm going to kill you, you son of a bitch.

To his surprise, Christian felt his fingernails perforating the cartilage of the trachea with a sickening crunch. Hot blood coursed from the Nautonnier's mouth in bubbling gouts, running down Christian's arm, and spattering his face and body.

Christian rose from his chair like an angry god, lifting the dying Nautonnier into the air as though he were a limp rag doll. He could see the old man's eyes bulging from the pressure, but there was still an icy smile on his bloodied lips, as though he were somehow encouraging his pupil to continue.

Christian was beside himself now. Running in his mind was a movie of all the torments he had suffered at the hands of this man. The humiliation. The sheer humiliation.

Christian reached down with his free hand and took hold of the serpentine dagger that lay on the table. Ever so slowly he sunk its blade into the Nautonnier's neck, sawing ineptly until he had at last severed the head. He dropped it onto the table along with the knife, and then watched the lifeless body crumple to the floor.

The Nautonnier's head had landed in the centre of the pentagram of burning candles. Its eyes were still blinking, and the stench of burning hair filled the room. Around the table the Zurvanites stood unmoving, flickering and shuddering in and out of existence.

Christian was in a kind of ecstasy. He felt sated and free, like one who had finally rid himself of a postulant wound, or pulled an infected thorn from his flesh. His hatred rang like a bell's note. He took a long, deep breath and looked up at the Zurvanites as they stood there before him, his eyes dark and reptilian.

"It is done," they said to him, bowing in reverence. *"The prophecy is fulfilled."*

Their voice was no longer a physical one. It came like a thought from somewhere deep in Christian's mind. A wave of fear and repulsion passed through him, for he knew in his heart that the Zurvanites were now inside him. He and they had somehow fused. He gagged and bent to vomit.

"Hail the new Nautonnier!" they hissed as he sank to the floor. *"All power to Ahreimanius, Lord of Darkness and Matter!"*

CHAPTER 33

Rome, Italy.

Natasha stood before the balcony in Gabriel's suite. The shutters were drawn aside, and eruptions of lightning could be seen painting the horizon, spreading sheets of light over the distant clouds. Framed as they were by the starry sky, they resembled mountains, dark and threatening. From them came an ominous rumbling that seemed to grow louder with every passing minute. An immense stormfront was drawing closer, and the busy streets of Rome seemed oblivious to its impending wrath.

Gabriel slept soundly in his bed behind Natasha. She knew that there was no reason to be frightened. She had only had a nightmare, but something in her seemed persistent in its warnings nevertheless. She passed her fingers through her hair.

"You're up," came Gabriel's groggy voice.

Natasha turned to find him propped on an elbow, his brow furrowing the moment he saw the expression on her face.

"What's wrong?"

She stood there without moving, looking helplessly back at him. Her eyes welled with tears.

"I'm so sorry for coming into your room like this, Gabriel."

He got up and went to her. He put a hand on her shoulder, not knowing what else to do.

"You're trembling."

"I had a dream," she said. "We were together in a horrible place. Then we became separated. Oh, Gabriel, I felt so lost…"

Natasha threw her arms around him and began to cry. Rolling thunder boomed outside.

"I can't understand," she sobbed. "Why is all this happening?"

"It was just a dream," Gabriel heard himself say. "Just a nightmare, that's all."

Natasha pulled her head back and looked into his eyes.

"Something unspeakable happened to us when we were babies…" she whispered, pushing aside his hair and tracing the tips of her fingers over the scar on his forehead.

An instinctive urge to deny what she was saying took hold of Gabriel, but he dismissed it. The idea that they could have spent the first fourteen months of their lives possessed by demons was extremely disturbing, but it had to be accepted. He reminded himself that it was only through this paranormal event that the bishop had found them. They were who they were today because of it.

Something unspeakable happened to us when we were babies…

He moved away from Natasha and stepped out onto the balcony. It was past midnight, but the streets of Rome were still bustling.

"I've had dreams too," he said slowly, facing out into the night. "All my life. I've always pretended that I didn't have them, but when they came, I always knew something was wrong."

"Then we're not alone in this anymore, Gabriel," came Natasha's voice, but this time there was a renewed strength in it. "That changes everything."

Gabriel turned to find that she had gone over to his bed. She was lying on her stomach, propped on her elbows and gazing into the glowing Cube.

Once again Gabriel was captivated. The Cube's blue light was washing over her face as though it were moonlight. He could see that she was no longer frightened, and her resilience surprised him, helping him to douse his own fears.

Gabriel shook his head in wonder. Just like the Cube, it seemed to him that deeper levels of Natasha were being revealed to him with every passing hour. This being said, it was getting easier for him to keep his distance from her. The more virtues he saw in her, the more unworthy he felt. She was intelligent, genuine, and compassionate, without ever coming off as prudish or self-satisfied, and he was, after all, a whore monger. He felt emptier than ever.

"Do you remember what Uncle Marcus said about the spiritual separation between us?" asked Natasha, her attention still fixed on the Cube.

Gabriel gathered himself before answering.

"He said there'd be dark forces attracted to you as long as we were not spiritually merged. Whatever that was supposed to mean."

Natasha looked over at him through dark, curling locks.

"Two days ago, I felt a supernatural presence in my workshop," she said, tucking her hair away behind an ear. "It was evil, Gabriel. That's why I went to stay with Uncle Marcus. It really frightened me. I thought I was going crazy."

"Two days ago," said Gabriel, letting himself fall into a chair next to the bed. "The same day I recovered the Cube."

"That would make sense," she said, sitting up and facing him. "Uncle Marcus said that dark forces were alerted to my presence when you retrieved the Cube without me being there."

Gabriel thought for a moment.

"Do you think the dark forces could be in tune with our separation, in the same way that the Cube is in tune with our togetherness?"

Natasha shrugged.

"Considering that all positive spirituality is based on unity, and that all negative spirituality is based on separation, it could be so."

"By negative spirituality, do you mean Satanism?"

"Among other things," she said. "There are two opposing belief systems. The right-hand path, and the left-hand path. Followers of the right look for integration with the godhead. They want to achieve divine creative power by achieving union with all. That's what *'All Is One'* means."

Gabriel nodded.

"And followers of the left?"

"They seek the glorification of the individual self, or the ego," said Natasha. "They want power over others, and fragmentation. That's what *'divide and conquer'* means. Throughout history the left hand has always been synonymous with evil because of these two different paths. As a matter of fact, in Latin, the word left means sinister."

"Dextra et sinistra," said Gabriel in Latin. "Right and left."

They both fell silent, caught up in their own thoughts. Natasha continued to examine the Cube.

"You know," she said at length, "I'm thinking we might find something if we could scan this with a BIRIS."

"What's a BIRIS?"

"It's a portable imagining scanner. I have one in my shop. It's on loan from the National Research Council of Canada. I'm using it to capture all the Vatican pieces I've been restoring."

"How does it work?"

"It uses three twin-aperture lasers to scan an object," she said. "Then it triangulates the data to generate a three-dimensional image. With translucent objects like this one, you can scan them inside too. A BIRIS is like an x-ray machine and an MRI, all in one."

Gabriel's face lit up.

"We've got to get that gizmo, Natasha," he said, a roll of thunder filling the room as he spoke. "It might give us a clue as to what makes this thing tick."

Gabriel's phone sounded just then, the name on the display filling their hearts with hope. Gabriel hit the speaker setting.

"Marcus?" they said in unison. "Is that you?"

"It certainly is!" came the familiar voice. "And I must say that I am delighted to be speaking with you both!"

"And Suora and Fra?" asked Natasha. "Are you all safe?"

"We are fine," came the humble voice of the old nun. "Our Father in heaven sent a noble giant to save us."

Gabriel and Natasha looked at each other.

"Bahadur?" asked Gabriel, following a hunch.

"That is correct!" said the old bishop. "He will be coming to Gibraltar to help us organize his family's rescue."

"I don't understand," said Gabriel. "I thought he was being held prisoner by Nasrallah."

"Bahadur was the leader of the men who invaded the rectory, my son. Nasrallah forced him to do his dirty work by threatening to kill his family. Bahadur has happily decided to join our side instead."

"You've got to tell him how sorry I am, Marcus," said Gabriel, frowning. "This is all my fault. I put his entire family in danger when I stole the Cube. I had no idea that would happen."

"It was not entirely your fault, Dr. Parker," came the deep voice of Bahadur. "Had I thought twice before giving you and

Amir the information, all this might have been avoided. Nonetheless we will free them all. Everything will be fine. Of this I am certain."

"So what happens now?" asked Natasha.

"I have chartered a private plane to Gibraltar," continued the giant. "We will leave Rome immediately. There is a storm approaching. You must come quickly."

"Is there any way we can meet you in Gib?" asked Gabriel. "We need to pick up some equipment from Natasha's workshop in Florence first."

"That should not be a problem," said Bahadur. "I can arrange to have a plane waiting for you in Florence. How much time will you require?"

Gabriel looked at Natasha.

"Feel up to it?" he whispered, covering the microphone.

Natasha smiled and nodded eagerly.

"Let's see," said Gabriel into the phone. "It's about a three-hour drive from here to Florence, but in a fast car I could do it in less than two. We'll need an hour to gather the equipment. How about three hours from now? That would put us there at around three-thirty in the morning."

"Consider it done, my friend," said Bahadur. "I will text you the particulars."

"If you don't mind me asking," said Gabriel. "How can you be so sure you'll find a plane on such short notice?"

"My position has its advantages, Dr. Parker."

"Very well then," chimed in the old bishop. "Off you go! At the *Pillars of Hercules* shall we meet!"

The elevator doors opened, revealing the hotel's pompous lobby. They had not taken two steps forward before they were approached by the concierge.

"Dr. Parker," he said formally. "The car you have requested is waiting in the courtyard."

"Thanks," said Gabriel, stuffing a hundred Euro note into the man's chest pocket. "It mustn't have been easy to arrange at this hour."

"It was my pleasure, Doctor," he said cordially.

A peal of thunder shook the air as Natasha led the way outside. There was a black sportscar in the courtyard, its sleek curves reflecting the silent flashes of lightning that lit up the night sky.

"Wow," she said to Gabriel. "I'm impressed."

"We needed something fast," he said with a shrug.

Gabriel led Natasha to the passenger door and held it open long enough for her to fall in. A moment later she felt a dense thud as the door sealed itself shut, the vehicle's interior reminding her more of a fighter-jet cockpit than a car. In a moment Gabriel had entered as well, quickly firing the engine to life.

He slipped the car into gear and Natasha felt herself being pushed back into her seat as they sped out of the hotel and into traffic. Following Gabriel's example, she clicked her seatbelt home, delighting in the car's sexy interior.

"Here's where she really sings," said Gabriel, entering the autostrada's onramp and gunning it.

The car lurched instantly into dizzying acceleration, but just then heavy drops of rain began to strike the windshield, smacking into it with the force of small stones. They were headed directly into the storm.

Gabriel gripped the hand-stitched leather wheel and settled back into his seat.

"Good thing we've got all-wheel drive."

CHAPTER 34

Rome, Italy.

The rain was pummeling the tarmac, sending water shooting upwards in a myriad of splashing torrents. In all his years in Rome, the bishop had never seen a time when it had rained with such profuse density. It seemed an almost tropical storm; an anomaly in keeping with the strange and catastrophic weather conditions that had been battering the planet of late. On this night there was not a breath of wind to be had, only a slight breeze being stirred up by the rain itself.

"How can we possibly fly in this?" muttered the old bishop to no one in particular.

They were making their way out onto a runway that looked more like a fast-moving river. Up ahead, the bishop could vaguely discern the shape of a plane materializing through the downpour. It looked to be an old twin prop, its engines running.

"Please, come along!"

It was the deep boom of Bahadur that called to them. He was guiding them forward through the downpour, their umbrellas heavy under the falling water.

"We are almost there!"

Through a wall of rain, the bishop saw a staircase appear. He moved aside to allow Suora to pass first. Bahadur stepped up to help her, taking her umbrella and making sure she did not slip on the wet steel.

"Thank you, my son," she said as they made their way up. "God bless you."

Fra Bartolomeo followed, with the old bishop slogging his way up last.

The aircraft looked to be a relic of the early seventies; a silver cargo plane built like a tank. The interior was no different. Single rows of seats lined a wide cabin, leaving a broad cargo area running down the centre of the fuselage. It was hardly luxurious, but it offered a welcome shelter from the rain. The bishop took a seat behind Fra, strapping on his seatbelt and settling back into his chair.

Bahadur had just finished assisting Suora on the other side of the fuselage when the plane began to move. The bishop watched him swing his massive body into the seat behind her, strapping on his belt and turning to look out the window with bruised eyes.

The pounding rain, combined with the roaring engines, made for a very noisy takeoff, but in the space of a minute they were airborne. The plane rose sharply and banked to the right.

Outside the night was black under the dense rain, only to ignite into a flashing landscape of cloud when the lightning struck. The frequent claps of thunder were sending shuddering quakes through the fuselage, and crossing himself, the old bishop joined his friends in their well-earned slumber.

He had long ago given his life to God, and he feared death no more than one might fear a future dentist's appointment. That is to say, without looking forward to it, but accepting that the time would come when he would find himself sitting in that chair with a bib tied around his neck.

* * * * * *

Gibraltar

Amir hung up the phone and then picked it up again, dialing a new number. He had just arranged hotel accommodations for the bishop and brother, and had also, at the nun's request, called ahead to the convent to let them know to expect her. He was now in the process of phoning an old friend, one of Gibraltar's most infamous smugglers. He could hear ringing but there appeared to be no one home. He was about to hang up when someone answered.

"Yeah, yeah! All right for Christ's sake!"

The voice was gruff from too much smoking, and aggressive, its British accent rounded by its marriage with the Andalusian dialect.

"I'll get the bloody phone, darling. Don't you move a leg! Hello!"

"Scotty," said Amir in his steady tenor. "Sorry to be calling so late."

"Is that you, Amir?" came the reply. "Late? The night's just beginning, mate! Bloody hell! This witch of mine has had me locked up in here with her all day and it's bloody tiring! I'm bloody-well knackered from it!"

Amir smiled.

"Women tend to keep you out of trouble, old friend."

Robert's reply was being directed at someone other than Amir.

"Well, if she don't shut up, I'm gonna lock her fat ass in the closet again!"

And then in a friendly tone it added:

"What can I do for you, mate?"

Amir's dreadlocks shifted as he shook his head, smiling despite himself.

"I'm in a bit of a bind, Scotty. Could you help me out?"

"Of course, mate. What's the problem?"

"Nasrallah's putting the screws to Bahadur. He's taken our family hostage. He's even got granny."

"That bloody bastard…" said Roberts, genuinely shocked. "That's heavy shit, man. How can I help?"

"Bahadur's flying in from Rome tonight. He's thinking about taking Nasrallah down and busting our family out. They're being held in Nasrallah's digs."

"Bloody hell, mate," said Roberts, a little shaky. "That's a bloody fortress. I'd love to see it happen, but that's a bleeding war you're talking about."

"Listen, Scotty," said Amir, frowning with concern. "A few of us are getting together at Dickey's shop down in the docks, sometime around sunrise. I know it's early, but do you think you could make it?"

Amir could hear the smuggler screaming at his woman in the background, the rubbing sound of his hand on the phone's mouthpiece doing little to mute the dialogue.

"Shut up, you bloody whore!" he bellowed. "Can't you see I'm on the bleeding phone! …What's that? Well I don't give a bloody shit what you think, so you can shut your bloody mouth is what you can do!"

"Amir, my mate," said Roberts, returning to his good-natured self again. "For you, anything. I'll be there. And don't you worry. We'll find a way to get them out."

Amir nodded.

"Thanks, Scotty."

He heard the screaming continue for a few seconds before the line went dead, and then shook his head and smiled. Some people never changed.

CHAPTER 35

Los Picos de Europa, Northern Spain.

Isaac dragged the bloated corpse of his son onto the island's shore, the air entering and leaving his lungs in great gasps. His feet slipped in the soft clay, his bleeding toes curling into the earth to find traction. Over the course of the crossing, the cadaver had almost doubled in weight, the water having found its way in through the decomposing rib cage, leaving it waterlogged and wretched beyond belief.

Isaac strained to heave it up onto the rocks. Above him a thick tangle of trunks and boughs dissolved into the grainy depths of the island. Somewhere outside of that cursed mountain range the sun would be rising, but it was invisible to him. He was in a low valley, the sky above dimmed by a somber mass of cloud that churned and boiled forebodingly.

"To the Portal of Ahreimanius!" came the icy hiss yet again, but this time with an insistence that was almost crippling.

A muffled cry escaped Isaac's tightened lips. The demons within him were frenzied, and the corpse of his son had begun to lurch and contort again, its limbs thrashing violently in great spasms. The stench of it was outlandish. Clotted masses of maggots, excrement, and vitriol were being pumped from the broken carcass with every freakish contortion.

"To the Portal!" commanded the voice, and the fiendish words stabbed like needles into his brain.

With a desperate and frantic tug, Isaac dislodged the cadaver from the rocky depression where it lay and proceeded in haste to drag it to the place of its incestuous conception. The rocks were slippery with the blood that left his feet, the incline steep and treacherous. Nevertheless, Isaac did as he was compelled to do, so that after an agonizing ordeal, he arrived at last at the clearing.

The circle of standing stones was better lit than the tangled path he had followed. Whereas the dense trunks had blotted out almost all the predawn light, the clearing itself offered a dead glow of filtered illumination. It fell over the place like a pall, and the central monolith seemed to call out to him from it. It lay there heavy and massive, its weathered top flat, and ready to accept what had burdened him for so long.

With his last ounce of strength, Isaac heaved the corpse onto its surface, a chorus of icy whispers driving away the last remnants of sanity from his mind. Around him, spread out in a perfect circle, were the fourteen standing stones, as tall as men and disfigured as though they had been subjected to tremendous heat.

Isaac produced a shard of metal and proceeded to disrobe the jerking body. Black shadows had appeared on its skin, showing him where to cut. Without a word he began to butcher the undead flesh, all the while gagging and vomiting from the stench of it.

No sooner had the cadaver made contact with the central stone than it had begun to tremble. It was as if each piece of the grisly carnage were somehow alive; quivering and contracting as the crude blade divided it up, the fingers gripping, the toes curling and uncurling. The tortured voice of Isaac's soul cried out helplessly.

Dear Father in heaven! Deliver me from this evil!

With the corpse now divided, Isaac proceeded to take up the fourteen butchered sections, placing each one at the base of a different standing stone. Overhead, a mass of heavy black cloud rolled in under the boiling sky, and a great clap of thunder shook the island to its roots.

With the grisly sections at last distributed, Isaac stood motionlessly at the centre of the ring, looking down at the top of the stone where he had done his butchering. It was crawling with the maggots that had been left behind, and beneath them he could see the image of a labyrinth carved into its surface, with the crude figure of a man standing at its entrance.

"What horrors have you been forced to commit, Isaac," came a voice of such cunningness that he was instantly lured into its spell. *"Where is your loving god now? How could he have allowed this to befall you?"*

Isaac teetered as though on the edge of an abyss. He was suddenly back in the hospital room with the demonically possessed body of his son in the bed before him. To his right and left he could see the stiffened corpses of two priests hanging by their necks in the cold blue light.

"I am Ahreimanius," hissed his son from the bed suddenly, and Isaac looked down to find a pair of wicked eyes gazing up at him. *"Your blessed Father has deserted you, Isaac, but I can give you powers beyond your comprehension. Come with me, and I will make you more powerful than God."*

Isaac's soul groaned in agony. Ahreimanius was right. Throughout all his tribulations, he had never once felt the presence of God. On the contrary, he had felt as though God had abandoned him when he needed him the most.

A great temptation to accept the offer arose in Isaac, and as he considered it, a vision of himself on high appeared before him. No sooner had he contemplated these things, however, than a voice within him cried out against the insidious offer.

"Never!" he exclaimed with all his will, and just then he was back on the island, released from the demons who had forced him to butcher the body of his son.

"You and your stupid Cube!" hissed the voice of Ahreimanius in fury. *"Did you really think I would ever allow you to do anything but serve my purposes? You will never assist the Two in their endeavors! You will die here tonight, and your pathetic life will have served no purpose but mine!"*

Isaac staggered backwards, looking around in shock. He could suddenly think clearly again. He struggled to understand.

"What have I done?" he gasped, bringing his bleeding hands to his face. "Lord Jesus Christ, what treacherous sin have I committed?"

Like the world returning to one who has awoken from a long slumber, so was the unholy scene revealed to Isaac. Forgotten now by the demons that had possessed him, he found himself stumbling to the edge of the circle, cowering in the dense undergrowth but unable to look away from the centre of the clearing.

Whereas each of the standing stones had begun to sink into the ground, the central monolith appeared to be rising ever so slightly into the air, its bulking mass levitating until it hung there weightlessly. Countless worms and other lightless insects were scurrying around beneath it.

Quite suddenly, in the depression where the monolith had rested, there appeared a rapidly growing pit of fire and ice. The surrounding circle of stones were being sucked into it, along with their grisly charges. A great chorus of wicked cries was issuing forth now, and from the black pit there arose fourteen demons, like dense clouds of earth and dust. These were the Fourteen Emissaries of Ahreimanius, and their forms were horrendous.

One by one they rose, churning in the air like blackened masses of cinder smoke; one by one screaming in hatred before shooting upwards into the boiling sky.

Only then did the floating stone fall, its ancient bulk fracturing suddenly into countless shards before being swallowed by the gaping portal as well. Isaac was trembling with fear. Deafening claps of thunder were assaulting him from above now, and just then a violent barrage of lightning crackled down around him, setting the island alight. The demonic chorus was growing louder and louder as well, until it seemed to Isaac that the entire world would be consumed by it.

"What have I done?" he moaned, his hands covering his ears.

Before him he could see that a conflagration had begun, and that the twisted trunks around the clearing were fully ablaze. Stunned and exhausted, Isaac stumbled wearily through the thickets to the water's edge, throwing himself into the black lake so that his death might come by drowning, rather than by fire.

"Forgive me for what I have done, Father," he said, his somber face lit by the flames. "Save my soul."

CHAPTER 36

Florence, Italy.

The black sports car rolled slowly over the cobblestones, its headlights cutting through the downpour. Natasha was looking intently through her window, scanning the shadows as they proceeded. They were driving along a narrow alleyway in the city centre, and the heavy rain was falling like a curtain around them.

Given the weather, the drive from Rome to Florence had taken more than twice what it should have. It was almost sunrise now, and they were only just approaching Natasha's workshop. They had decided to take the back entrance in the off chance that Nasrallah had eyes on the place.

"So far so good," said Gabriel, easing the car forward along the constricting laneway.

He pushed a button and Natasha watched as the side view mirrors collapsed inwardly.

"It looks like there's an opening in the wall up ahead," said Gabriel.

Natasha peered into the curtain of rain.

"This is it," she said. "We're here."

Gabriel pulled the car up next to the opening so that Natasha could open her door into it, then he climbed over to her side and followed her out. They were soon making their way along a narrow passageway. It led to a gate that opened into an inner courtyard, partially sheltered from the rain. Natasha produced an old iron key as they approached a timeworn set of doors.

"I hate this storeroom," she said, inserting it into the lock.

In a moment the smell of raw earth and ancient mildew was wafting out of the darkness to greet them. With the increased humidity, the musty air could almost be tasted on the tongue, and

Gabriel breathed it in deeply, savouring the antiquity like a connoisseur.

"We left the torchlights back in the car," he said, squinting into the darkness.

Natasha produced her phone and used its flashlight app instead. The last time she had been in this storeroom a sinister presence had accosted her, and she could still feel its residue lurking in the many shadows and crevices the jumbled space had to offer. Even still, with Gabriel so near, and knowing what she now knew, its effect on her was nothing compared to what it had been that day.

Gabriel followed close behind, producing his phone to help light the way. They made their way through a maze of laden shelves and cluttered cabinets until they reached the front room at last. It was not as dark here, and the bluish light from the streetlamps outside filtered in through the watery panes, casting shifting patterns on the wooden floor.

"Make yourself at home," said Natasha, beginning to fill a field case with equipment.

Gabriel's phone rang just then, and he remained on it the entire time that Natasha packed the supplies. She could see that he was doing more listening than talking, but it was not until she had finished that it looked as though his conversation might end.

"All right then, Amir," he said. "If all goes well, we'll be seeing you this afternoon. Stay in touch."

He pocketed the phone, turning to Natasha.

"What is it?" she asked.

Gabriel's mouth formed a straight line.

"Our flight to Gib's been cancelled," he said, "We've got some driving to do."

* * * * * *

Gibraltar

The old bishop awoke to find the plane in a sharp bank. It was no longer raining, and looking out his window he could see the Rock of Gibraltar turning slowly below him, its city centre twinkling with a thousand lights. Stretching out into the distance, the shimmering waters of its bay and strait could also be seen, dotted with freighters and ships of all kinds.

To the starboard side towered Gibraltar's majestic peak, silhouetted against a predawn sky. It was a time-sculpted rock formation, topped with the famous single white cloud that had come to be known as *El Levante*, named after the easterly wind that was responsible for its formation.

In minutes they had circled the small peninsula, levelling off to make their landing approach on the short strip of runway that separated the British colony from the Spanish mainland. The bishop smiled in delight.

"Gibraltar!" he exclaimed. "One of the two great pillars of Hercules! The fortified bastion of the British Royal Navy, and home to the largest per capita density of pubs in all of Christendom! Aye, but a pint of stout would be nice. That and a breakfast of steak and kidney pie!"

CHAPTER 37

Amsterdam, The Netherlands.

It was just past six in the morning when prince Vladimir Rodchenko arrived at the Vanderhoff suite. The front desk had awoken him with orders from the Nautonnier to go there at once. Christian met him at the door and led him into the room, locking the door behind them.

The old prince gasped in horror. On a table at the back of the suite could be seen the severed head of the Nautonnier, propped in a pool of clotted blood. Christian had lifted the headless corpse into a facing chair, and it sat there stiff and macabre, like a gruesome figure in a wax museum.

"As you can see," said Christian, positioning himself behind his mortified uncle, "there has been a change in command. The Nautonnier has ceded his position to me."

The prince seemed only then to come out of his shock. He would have fled the room had Christian not placed a heavy hand on his shoulder.

"Do you remember when you used to drop me off and pick me up from school, Uncle?"

"Before and after every holiday," stammered the prince.

"Was it ever difficult for you?" asked Christian. "Knowing that you were taking an innocent boy to be buggered by the man who is now dead before you?"

The prince froze, unable to respond. The psychologists had assured them that Christian's memories would remain suppressed for the entirety of his life.

"I had nothing to do with it!" he stammered. "It was something between your father and the Nautonnier."

"You had everything to do with it! You knowingly allowed it to happen!"

"I will not be held accountable for your father's actions!" said the prince with rekindling authority. "I am leaving!"

He attempted to move but found that an invisible force was holding him fast. He struggled to free himself from it, his eyes bulging from the effort. Christian looked on. In the space of a few seconds, the prince's face had gone from a pasty, ashen white to a vivid purple.

"Sit down," snapped Christian with icy hatred. "I'm the Nautonnier now. You will leave when I am finished with you."

"Please, Christian," he said, giving up his struggle and sinking into a chair. "I am your family."

It was on hearing this reference to his family that yet another deep, childhood wound surfaced in Christian. Impossible as it might seem, it had been the cause of more pain than all the abuses suffered at the hands of Father Adrianus.

Christian had once had an older brother named Isaac. He had been the only source of love and support in his deprived life. It was not long after the birth of their sister, Alina, and the subsequent death of their mother, that Isaac had been sent off to study at Vatican City. From that point onward, everything in Christian's life had changed for the worse.

He had lost all contact with Isaac, and two years later had been shipped off to boarding school himself, returning home on his first holiday to find that his baby sister had also been displaced.

"What happened to my brother and sister?" said Christian, trembling with a strange combination of fear and rage. "Tell me about my brother and sister!"

The prince remained silent until he felt the force of a vicious slap to the back of his head.

"Your father sent Isaac to be manipulated by Father Adrianus," he stammered. "He was persuaded to disown himself from the Antov family. Your sister Alina was sent to be raised in another household."

The prince held up a hand to ward off another blow. Christian obviously wanted the full story. He proceeded with trepidation. He could well imagine the effect that the truth would have on Christian, and he feared for his life.

"Your father repeatedly raped your sister in Satanic rituals, Christian," he began. "He drove her to madness, and then disowned her at sixteen. She became a prostitute.

"Years later, in accordance with their plan, she was recovered and brought to Father Adrianus at the Vatican. She and Isaac were made to marry. Of course, they did not know that they were brother and sister, but through their union a hermaphrodite child was conceived. Alina died giving birth to it."

Christian looked down in silence, unable to comprehend what he was being told. It made no sense.

"The child was created to fulfill a Satanic prophecy," said the prince slowly. "Your father and the Nautonnier were obsessed with the occult. They used our science facility in Jerusalem to genetically mutate the child while it was still in Alina's womb. They used the genes in our bloodline to create a monster."

Christian broke from his stupor and turned to face the prince, his eyes smoldering with deadly intent.

"And you knew all this?" he said, coming slowly out of shock.

The prince shook his head from side to side as Christian bent down over him.

"No," he gasped, his eyes wide with fear. "You do not understand..."

Christian's face was contorting with the pain of betrayal now. This was his uncle. His family. How could he have allowed this to happen to innocent children? He reached out a hand, as if to caress the prince's face, but instead took him by the throat and began to shake him violently.

"You did nothing to stop it," he snarled. "You didn't give a shit!"

Christian was beside himself with fury now. How could such a thing be possible? It was too repugnant to even imagine. He released the prince in disgust and spat in his face.

In that moment, the same dark self that had possessed Christian when he had beheaded the Nautonnier, paid him another visit. All he could do was watch as it took control. In the blink of an eye the intensity of its presence had grown into such a murderous rage that it was impossible to contain.

"YOU'RE RESPONSIBLE!" exploded Christian in a thunderous roar.

His verbal assault was directed solely at the prince's face. It sent him recoiling into his chair, his head jerking backwards in terror. A second later the old man was clutching his chest, his other hand thrust outward, beseeching his nephew to desist.

Christian was suddenly calm and sated. He positioned himself directly over his uncle and smiled cruelly.

The prince's unfocused eyes were blinking erratically in the candlelight now, his facial features contracting with pain. Christian knew he was having a heart attack, and he cocked his head in curiosity. In the prince's cold eyes there could almost be seen a cry for mercy, but it seemed wooden and insincere.

Christian drew closer until his lips were brushing the old man's ear. He smiled coldly again, and his wickedness rang like an icy bell.

"Dear, Uncle Vladimir," he said with mock innocence, his words twisting into the prince's head. "Now you will... DIE!"

The volume and intensity of that final word caused the prince's pupils to contract in fear. A look of surprised desperation was contorting his features as he tried frantically to ward off the icy hand of death.

Christian moved away from him in disgust. He could see the life force slowly leaving the body and watched with great satisfaction as his uncle fell into a long, drawn-out death rattle.

When all was over, Christian spat on the corpse, and then bent immediately afterwards to tenderly kiss the forehead, a tendril of saliva stretching and breaking as his lips pulled away.

* * * * * *

The morning was still young when the chief inspector left the Vanderhoff suite with Christian at his side. Behind them, in a shaft of sunlight, the dead prince could be seen sitting opposite the decapitated corpse, the Nautonnier's waxy head still on the table.

"A tragic incident, Mr. Antov," said the inspector solemnly, closing his notebook. "It is clear that your uncle died of a heart attack after murdering Father Adrianus. No investigation will be needed."

"Very good, Inspector," said Christian darkly. "Thank you for your diligence, and please have this mess cleaned up. I will have my assistant make the funeral arrangements."

"Very good, Mr. Antov," he said. "And a peaceful day to you, sir. You have my most sincere condolences."

Christian watched the inspector leave.

The matters of the Permanent Secretary are above the law.

No sooner had Christian had this thought than he felt himself being pulled back into the room, as though by an invisible hand. He made his way to the Nautonnier's body, and acting on an impulse, removed a bejeweled ring from the corpse. He placed it on his finger, directly next to his father's ring, and moved to look at himself in the mirror. A chorus of whispers were sounding in his mind again, but his time with unprecedented intensity.

"Hail the new Nautonnier! All power to Ahreimanius, the Lord of Darkness and Matter!"

Christian shuddered as an icy chill rushed up his spine. In the mirror's reflection he could see the repugnant Zurvanites standing behind him now. They were positioned around the Nautonnier's severed head, their grainy forms jerking violently from side to side, untouched by the sunlight that streamed into the room. Christian spun around suddenly with boiling wrath.

"Get away from me!" he bellowed, but they had already vanished.

It was only then that Christian fully grasped the dark truth. He had indeed become the new Nautonnier, and he recalled what his wicked predecessor had told him of the Zurvanites only days before.

"They are the Four. Since ancient times they have served the Nautonnier and given him knowledge and power."

Like a floodgate opening, Christian was at that moment made privy to many strange and mysterious things, and he was certain that the Zurvanites had been the ones to impart this knowledge onto him.

As though through churning mists, there came to him strange and formless recollections, and in the blink of an eye he had been taken back through time; past the days of Herod, past the rule of the Zoroastrians, and further back still to when the world was watery, and men were like reptiles; murderous and cruel.

This was his ancestry, the lineage of all the Nautonniers who had gone before him. With it came a knowledge of the things that needed to be done at present, so that the dark plans of Lucifer might come to pass.

He picked up a handset from its place on a table below the mirror.

"This is Christian Antov," he said. "Get me Cynthia."

"Hello, Mr. Antov," came her silky voice. "How can I help you?"

"We will be checking out tonight."

"Of course, Mr. Antov," she said. "I'll arrange to have your things packed immediately. Will you be needing anything else?"

"Dr. Bennington will be getting here shortly. Call me the moment he arrives."

"Yes, sir," she said seductively. "Anything else?"

Christian turned to study his reflection in the mirror again and for a split second saw himself shift and transform as the Zurvanites had done. He bent closer to the glass. For that fraction of a moment, he could have sworn that his features had become reptilian.

Christian ran his hands over his face. He was beginning to understand.

"Connect me with the head secretary of our Jerusalem office."

Cynthia was silent for a moment, surprised by the odd request.

"Right away, Mr. Antov."

Christian waited impatiently.

"Yes, Mr. Antov," came the voice of a man, his accent Israeli. "How can I help you?"

"We will be moving all operations to the Jerusalem complex this afternoon. Coordinate with Cynthia. I want our pilots ready for takeoff at thirteen hundred hours, and I want everyone in the Steering Committee on that plane.

"I will accept no excuses. Set up a group meeting for tomorrow morning. Have my private jet fueled and ready for immediate takeoff. Is that clear?"

"Yes, sir, Mr. Antov. Immediately, sir."

CHAPTER 38

Gibraltar.

The old bishop watched the barriers on either side of the runway rise into the morning air. They had been lowered to stop the flow of pedestrians across the tarmac while their plane had made its landing. Now, as they taxied towards the small terminal, the traffic had begun to flow again, a milling crowd headed by a cavalry of electric scooters.

"Your Excellency will be glad to know that Amir has arranged accommodations for you and your friends."

It was the deep voice of Bahadur that spoke. He was out of his seat now, and on his way to open the hatch.

"Excellent!" exclaimed the old bishop happily. "You must thank him for us."

"You may do so yourself, your Excellency," said Bahadur, pulling open the hatch.

In an instant Amir was inside, embracing Bahadur heartily.

"Good cousin!" said Bahadur, rubbing Amir's back with his massive paws. "Have faith in Allah. We will get them out safely."

"I'm not worried," said Amir, his dreadlocks swaying. "We've got a small army to help us do it."

Amir shot a welcoming smile at the three seniors.

"You were lucky to make it to Gibraltar," he said. "They've shut down air traffic across Europe."

Bahadur's brow knotted into a frown.

"Why have they done this?"

"Terrorist attacks," said Amir, addressing each of them in turn. "All in the last hour. Bombings. One in Madrid, two in London, two in New York City, one in Atlanta, and only ten minutes ago a massive explosion in Rome. Thousands are dead. They've declared martial law in the U.S."

The bishop stood up in alarm, as did Suora and Fra.

"We must contact Gabriel and Natasha!"

"I only just got off the phone with them," he said respectfully. "They're fine. They're on their way here."

CHAPTER 39

The French Riviera.

The black sports car screamed through a curving tunnel west of Monaco, its tuned exhaust reverberating off the chiseled walls of the mountain pass. To the left, flickering through a series of gallery openings, the Mediterranean was shimmering under a rising sun.

At long last the rain had stopped, and they were finally getting a chance to make up for lost time. Gabriel looked down at the speedometer and shook his head in amazement.

Two hundred and forty kilometres an hour, and I'm barely pressing the accelerator.

With all air traffic having been suspended after the terrorist strikes, they had been forced to drive to Gibraltar. It was now seven in the morning, with very little traffic on the autoroute. If they could maintain an average speed of two hundred, they would be crossing into Gibraltar seven hours from now.

"Maybe we can look at this now," said Natasha, producing the envelope containing Professor Metrovich's journal.

"Do the honours," said Gabriel.

Natasha opened the envelope and removed the tattered book. It was thick and worn, and it smelled of old leather.

"Wow," she whispered, opening it carefully. "It's filled with illuminations..."

She held it up and Gabriel shot over a quick glance. In the second he had looked, he had seen intricate medieval illustrations, glowing gold leaf, and precise calligraphy.

"I had no idea," he said, shaking his head.

Many times, Gabriel had seen his father working in the journal, but he had never been permitted to know what was within. When he had asked, his father had always given the same response.

"When it is time, Gabriel, and only then."

The journal had always disappeared somehow, and as a boy, no matter how thoroughly he had searched for it, Gabriel had never once found it.

"So what's in it besides pretty pictures?"

Natasha was studying the book as she spoke.

"Eighth and ninth century texts," she said. "Perfect copies, Gabriel. Letters, scrolls, papyri, ancient maps. Some are in Greek, others in Coptic, Aramaic, Arabic… Here's a Latin manuscript. Guess who it's by."

Gabriel shrugged.

"Gutierrez de la Cruz," she said.

"That guy's everywhere."

Natasha turned another page. It was covered in gold leaf.

"This book's a masterpiece," she whispered. "I can't believe your father created this. It's even hand bound."

Gabriel only nodded. He missed the old man terribly.

"Listen to what he writes on the very first page," she said. "It's an excerpt from the Pistis Sophia.

"And the spirit of the Saviour was moved in him, and he cried, 'How long shall I suffer you? Do ye still not know? Do ye still not understand that ye are all Angels, and Archangels; all Lords, and Rulers? That ye are from all; of yourselves and in yourselves in turn; from one mass, and one matter, and one essence?

"It refers to humanity's divine nature," said Natasha, "and the high places we held before the Fall. The page next to it only contains a single line of text, but it looks really important by the way it's been illuminated."

Gabriel looked over at her.

"What does it say?"

Natasha read it aloud.

"To transcend the Cube is to see it in all things."

Gabriel raised an eyebrow but was soon lost in his thoughts. He was thinking of his father. Natasha continued to study the book.

"This journal's divided into sections," she said at length. "The first treats with a medieval author named Chrétien de Troyes, and his book *The Quest For The Holy Grail*."

Gabriel paused to think.

"That was a fusion of Celtic folklore and Orthodox Christianity, wasn't it?"

Natasha nodded.

"Yes, and Jewish mystical symbolism too. It can be interpreted on many different levels. Some say it's an allegory of the secret teachings of the Alchemists."

"The ones who could turn lead into gold," said Gabriel.

Natasha nodded again.

"The Alchemists were Gnostic priests," she said. "The Church burned them all and destroyed their knowledge. It was called *gnosis*, and your father was obsessed with finding out what it was."

Gabriel smiled and shook his head.

"That sounds like Dad."

Natasha pulled an iPad from her backpack, her eyes wide with excitement.

"What are you doing now?" asked Gabriel.

"Researching," she said, tapping at the screen.

Gabriel gave a nod and let her surf the internet in silence. Several minutes later she had found what she was looking for.

"According to this," she said, glancing over at Gabriel, "the person who possesses gnosis becomes an immortal creator of heavenly worlds. His every desire is fulfilled, and life takes on a perpetual state of excitement and bliss."

Gabriel raised his eyebrows.

"Sounds like Las Vegas."

Natasha shot him a sidelong glance.

"The only problem is that there are practically no traces of gnosis left. The little that remains is veiled in legend and myth."

"So basically, it's a lost knowledge."

Natasha continued scanning the document she had found.

"Acquiring gnosis was an initiatory path," she said. "Pieces of the knowledge were given to the student as he or she advanced. The alchemists believed that gaining gnosis was the meaning of life. It was about remembering to be something that we once were, and still are, instead of trying to become something we're not."

"So what are we?" asked Gabriel.

Natasha looked over at him as he drove.

"It says we're all God."

"Gnosticism," said Gabriel, thinking. "The ultimate heresy. Christianity as myth."

Natasha nodded.

"The alchemists combined Judeo-Christian mythology with other ancient mythologies. To them, the story of the Garden of Eden wasn't so much the cause of the Fall, but rather the result of it. In their version, the serpent isn't even the devil. She's the benevolent Mother, and the knowledge contained in the apple is the gnosis that reminds Adam and Eve of the Virtue they lost as a result of the Fall."

Gabriel scanned the road ahead.

"Like in the myth that Marcus told us about."

Natasha put away the tablet and returned her attention to the journal, reading silently for a while longer before looking up at Gabriel. Her eyes were wide with the wonder that only a theologian can feel about such things.

"The next section's about Gutierrez de la Cruz," she said. "According to this, he wasn't just the one who found the lost Cube. He was also a member of an organization called the *Council of Six*."

"What's that?"

Natasha scanned the page.

"It was comprised of representatives from each of the six world religions. All summoned by the Moorish Caliph of Toledo in 866 to translate the proto writings inscribed on the Cube."

Gabriel recalled the parchments that had previously covered the artifact. They had been written in six different languages. He had only skimmed over them at the time, but it now occurred to him what they must have spoken of.

"Of course," he said. "That's what's written on each of the six parchments: Discourses on the translations they made. But why? Why gather scribes from the four corners of the earth to translate crude symbols that could have meant absolutely anything? Could there really be some kind of secret knowledge locked up in the Cube?"

Natasha shrugged.

"Your father suspected that everything would be explained in The Book of Khalifah."

"That's why he was so obsessed with finding it," said Gabriel. "That book must be pretty damn special."

Natasha looked over at him.

"We need to find it, Gabriel."

"I agree," he said, his eyes glued to the road. "Keep reading. I want to know everything my old man knew."

CHAPTER 40

Los Picos de Europa, Northern Spain.

Isaac woke to find a brown hunting dog licking his face. The sun was up now, and the terrible storm had passed. His mind worked to remember where he was, and how he had arrived there.

Where did this dog come from? What is happening?

He saw that he was on the shore of a small mountain lake. At its centre he could see a little island burning steadily. His memory returned a moment later. He reached up and patted the dog's head.

"It is thanks to you that I am alive."

Isaac shuddered as he recalled the horrific events that had transpired, and how he had waded out into the waters to escape the hellfire. He had been certain he would drown, and was on the verge of letting the lake take him, when a dog had swum up to him unexpectedly. He had lost consciousness shortly after.

As Isaac lay there, his mind went over all that had happened since the plane had gone down, and he was perplexed by his clarity of mind. It was as though he had regained his judgment, something his doctor had told him would never happen. He looked at the dog, puzzled by the deep intelligence in its amber eyes.

"Where did you come from, my friend?" he asked. "There can be no explanation for your appearance other than divine intervention."

The dog gave a round nod and barked. He put a paw on Isaac's chest as he lay there, and it seemed to Isaac that the animal was trying to communicate something to him. He examined the dog's collar. It was made of rough twine and passed through a crude hole in what looked to be the lid of an olive jar. Isaac saw that there was a name written on its underside.

"Sir Shackleton," he read, smiling. "A fitting title."

Groaning with pain, he sat up and took a deep breath of the fresh mountain air.

"I cannot recall when my head was ever this clear," he said to Shackleton. "Perhaps it was when I was a boy. Everything's so vibrant... So beautiful..."

Isaac looked around in wonderment, only then remembering his medication. He had not taken it for many days now. He searched his pockets, a panic beginning to take him. In over forty years he had never once missed a dose.

"I must find my pills..."

Just then he felt Shackleton's muzzle poke him in the side, and he turned to see that the dog's eyes were focused intently on him. There could be no mistake as to what the dog was trying to tell him. His failure to take his medication was the reason for his recovery. He looked at the dog, his brow furrowed with confusion.

"But Father Adrianus always insisted that I never miss a dose," he muttered. "He said that my sanity depended on it."

Shackleton gave him another poke.

"Very well," he said, frowning. "I will get up."

Isaac rose unsteadily to his feet, noticing only then that Shackleton had returned him to the very place where he had first embarked onto the lake. Not a few paces away was the makeshift sled he had used to drag the corpse from the crash site, as well as his shoes, and the pack of supplies he had taken from the dead Father Franco. Isaac looked down at the dog.

"Who are you, my friend?"

Shackleton let out a resounding bark in response. He trotted over to Father Franco's pack, picking it up in his maw and dragging it to Isaac's feet. Within, Isaac found cured sausages and biscuits. It was not long before he had sat himself down and was sharing a meal with his new friend.

"Something of great importance has happened, Shackleton," he said, looking out over the water. "I must try to understand."

The flames on the island were beginning to subside now, replaced by a thick plume of rising smoke. Even though the sight of it served to affirm the reality of the demonic horrors he had experienced, the smoke was also strengthening his faith in God.

That such a powerful evil could exist only confirmed the existence of an even greater force of good.

As he looked out over the lake, it seemed to Isaac that all the events of his life had led him to the place he now found himself. He took a deep breath and rose to his feet, scanning the mountainous peaks that encased them.

"I do not understand, Father," he prayed quietly. "Lucifer used me and discarded me. He left me for dead. I am an abomination. I dismembered the corpse of my own son. I released an unspeakable evil onto the world. Why do you spare my life? Why do you send this noble animal to help me? Should I not be despised and cursed by you?"

Isaac returned his gaze to the island, his eyes filling with tears.

"My life is yours, Father," he whispered. "Help me and guide me so that I might put right the terrible wrongs I have done."

CHAPTER 41

Gibraltar.

Bahadur was standing on the edge of a rusty dock in the shadows of the lower port. Around him loomed the clutter of Gibraltar's industrial marina, the smell of stale diesel fuel and brine filling the air. A dusty sun had just risen behind the rocky peak, but the sky in the west was still holding on to a few scattered stars. The dawn had come up blood red, and there would be hard weather today.

"A good day to storm a castle," said Amir, emerging from a dilapidated workshop.

He struck a match and stoked his chillum until they were engulfed in its fragrant smoke. He took a deep haul and offered the pipe to Bahadur, but the giant shook his head absently and turned to look out to sea. His broad face was a mask of consternation.

"They'll be fine, cousin," said Amir, noting his dread. "Nasrallah knows you. He'd never hurt them. He's a coward."

Bahadur glanced over at Amir.

"Where is Gabriel?"

"He's on his way. He says to expect him at around two or three."

"Your friend knows how to drive."

Amir released a billowing cloud of smoke.

"He's been averaging two-twenty all the way from Florence."

Bahadur nodded and then looked off to sea again, frowning.

"I am concerned about the men," he said in his deep basso.

"They'll all be here soon."

The brown giant shook his head darkly.

"It is not our men I am concerned for, cousin. It is Nasrallah's men I am thinking of. They are good men. They have wives and children. They work hard. They do not deserve to die."

"They know Nasrallah," said Amir, poking aside a wayward dreadlock. "If they choose to work for a murderer, they—"

"They do not choose!" said Bahadur, turning to grasp Amir's shoulder before proceeding more gently. "They have families to feed. It is that simple."

"Cousin," said Amir in earnest. "Maybe there's another way. Once Nasrallah's been taken out, our new coalition will be in control. There will be work for everyone. If we could somehow let Nasrallah's men know about our plan. They'd rather work for you."

"We cannot take that risk," said Bahadur gloomily. "It could easily go the other way. Men take what is real. They do not risk their lives on promises. Nasrallah pays them at the end of every month. That is all they are concerned with, and I cannot blame them for it."

"Then men will die," said Amir, spitting into the oily water. "Men will die."

CHAPTER 42

Costa Brava, Spain.

The rocky cliffs were racing past in a blur, and Gabriel was enjoying the drive tremendously. The purring sports car was finding no difficulty in maintaining a cruising speed of two hundred and forty kilometres an hour. It felt like the car was on rails. Natasha looked up from the journal.

"There's an Arabic document here your father transcribed," she said, bending closer to the book. "It's dated 661 CE and addressed to the Umayyad Caliph of Cordoba. It's from one of his clerics."

"What does it say?"

Natasha scanned it for a moment before answering. She wanted to make sure she was translating it correctly.

"It says that Arab forces found the Urn of Theophilus after taking Alexandria."

"I've heard of that artifact before," said Gabriel, scratching his head, "Theophilus found the Urn in the Great Library of Alexandria, just before he ordered it burnt to the ground."

"Theophilus the bishop of Alexandria."

Gabriel nodded.

"He led a Catholic movement at the end of the fourth century. Their orders were to destroy anything that was heretical. Sacred temples, priceless art, ancient writings."

He paused to remember.

"Legend has it there were some pretty old tablets in that urn. They were supposedly written by the first Mesopotamian kings."

Natasha was shaking her head in amazement.

"According to this letter, those tablets spoke of a Cube of Knowledge, Gabriel. It's there where the Arabs first learned of the artifact. Listen to this. I'll do my best to translate it.

Know, oh Prince of the Faithful, that at the time of the emperor Theodosius, the bishop Theophilus issued forth an order for the demolition of the great heathen library of Alexandria. From therein he was brought a golden urn of such beauty and richness that he could not bring himself to destroy it, but instead took it secretly as his own.

Within this urn were ancient tablets belonging to Alulim, who was the First King of Sumer, and who reigned for 28,800 years in the kingdom of Eridu, in Mesopotamia. The tablets spoke of a Cube of Knowledge, and of the Nephilim, who took the Cube from its resting place at the entrance of a great labyrinth and gave it to Alulim, to whom they taught many wondrous things.

At the End of The World this Cube is said to reside, oh prince, in the land of the warrior-priests. It was recovered by the Kristos of Judea and laid within the tomb of his brother who guards it until the day of reckoning.

"Kristos is Greek for Christ, right?" said Gabriel.

Natasha was still studying the text.

"It comes from the word *Krishna* in Sanskrit."

Gabriel thought for a moment.

"If the tomb belongs to the brother of Jesus, it means that this document is referring to the same tomb that Gutierrez found. Do you think there's a connection between the labyrinth it mentions and the one in the Egyptian myth that Marcus told us about?"

"I do," said Natasha, tucking her hair behind an ear.

"That would mean that the entrance to this labyrinth is on the same island where Gutierrez found the tomb..." said Gabriel, turning to look at her.

Natasha looked back at him and nodded excitedly.

"You said the markings on the Cube were Basque, right?"

"Proto-Basque," said Gabriel, squinting into the distance as he drove.

"Aren't the Basques and the Celts of Ireland related?"

Gabriel shrugged.

"That's what the DNA suggests..."

"Gabriel," said Natasha. "There's hard evidence that Christian evangelists landed in Ireland just four years after Jesus was crucified. They were led there by James the Just, and they succeeded in converting the Druids to Christianity."

Gabriel frowned.

"The Vatican deemed the Celtic Church heretical," he said. "They called it Insular Christianity. How could it be heretical if it was created by Jesus' own brother?"

He scratched the back of his head, his frown deepening.

"I see what you're getting at though," he continued. "The Druids must have known about the labyrinth. That's why the runes on the Cube are Proto-Basque, and that's why Jesus delivered the Cube back to them. The Druids must have been its original keepers."

"Of course it's just speculation," said Natasha, looking down at the journal, "but your father seemed to think the same. He was convinced that the end of the world was not so much a time, but a place; a Celtic place…"

"Finisterre, right?" asked Gabriel.

"Yes," said Natasha, looking up from the book in surprise. "How did you know?"

"Because it's not far from Santiago de Compostela. It's a small village on the west coast of Galicia, but it's also been called *The End of The World* since the time of the Druids."

Gabriel sped past a grouping of trucks.

"So, the labyrinth is in Finisterre…"

"Not exactly," said Natasha, "but your father believed that it was somewhere close. According to him, that whole area was considered to be the end of the world."

Natasha turned to a different part of the journal.

"This section's dedicated to the labyrinth. Your father refers to it as *The Great Labyrinth of Sarras*."

Gabriel raised his eyebrows.

"Sarras was the heavenly city in *The Quest for The Holy Grail.*"

Natasha looked up from the book and nodded.

"The place where Galahad saw the Grail and healed the Fisher King."

"Thus, satisfying the legend, and restoring life to the kingdom…"

Natasha nodded again.

"Some historians believe that the original Grail romances were written by members of *Rex Angelus*, and that they carried secret messages that contradicted the Church's doctrine."

"Rex Angelus?"

Natasha chewed her lip.

"A society that claimed to be the direct descendants of Jesus Christ, and the keepers of his original teachings."

"A bloodline of Christ…" repeated Gabriel, rolling his eyes.

"It's a well-known hypothesis," said Natasha with a shrug. "Gutierrez de la Cruz claimed to be Rex Angelus himself. Your father believed that he only became a priest to infiltrate the Church."

Gabriel had to break hard and wait for a car to get out of the passing lane.

Natasha read one of the professor's annotations aloud.

"To all Rex Angelus, the Holy Grail is a symbol of the original gnosis. It is the receptacle of the wisdom that Jesus himself taught, before it was distorted by the Vatican in order to control the masses.

In the story, when the Christ-like Galahad is pure enough to behold the Grail, he restores the Fisher King to full health, and in this way the wasted kingdom is restored.

If we follow the allegory, this is another way of saying that when humanity is ready, the true teachings of Jesus Christ will triumph over the greed and hypocrisy of the Vatican and result in a kind of heaven on earth."

Gabriel shook his head in astonishment.

"So, it's exactly as Marcus was saying back in the catacombs. The Cube and the Holy Grail are the same thing."

"It seems so, Gabriel," said Natasha, her eyes alight with excitement. "Your father makes the point that throughout history, the Grail has not only been described as a cup, or a chalice, but also as *A Stone Within A Cup.*"

She read from the journal again.

"A stone which fell from heaven and symbolizes the wisdom that is imbibed when one drinks from the metaphorical cup of the Kristos."

Natasha looked up from the book.

"According to Rex Angelus, there's only one primordial source of wisdom. It's a doctrine that became fragmented over the ages, with different parts being adopted by each of the six world religions.

"It would appear that the ancient Druids were the guardians of that original knowledge. They were the warrior-priests that the letter spoke of. The Keepers of the Cube.

"Your father believed that if the fragmented parts could be unified again, then there would be harmony between all the religions, and humanity would at last have access to the entire truth, instead of just small fragments of it."

"What exactly have we stumbled onto here?"

"Your father's life work," said Natasha in awe.

Gabriel rubbed his eyes to stave off the sleepiness. There was so much to consider, but his faculties were losing their edge. He needed to shut his eyes for a while. Natasha continued to carefully turn the pages.

"What are you reading now?" he asked at length.

"You're not going to believe me."

Gabriel looked over to see her flipping back to earlier sections of the journal, her head shaking from side to side.

"This is impossible," she muttered, "but you can see it everywhere in the diary."

"Try me."

She glanced over at Gabriel through a lock of chestnut hair.

"Your father claims that Gutierrez speaks of you and I in his writings. He refers to us as *The Two,* but that there's an ambiguity in the translation."

"What kind of ambiguity?"

"In certain Coptic dialects, The Two, also means *The Primal King and Queen.* Your father wasn't sure why this particular word would have been used, when a more specific numerical terminology existed."

"But how could Gutierrez know of us?"

"Uncle Marcus said we were a part of all this, Gabriel. Remember?"

"It's just a product of my father's overactive imagination. He was making assumptions, Natasha. Nothing more."

"Gutierrez refers to you as *Gabriel, Hero of God,* and to me as *Natalia, The day of the Saviour's Birth.* Your father writes that you and I are spoken of in the ancient prophecies as well. The same ones that speak of our heroic mission."

"Our mission?" asked Gabriel, turning to face her. "What mission?"

Natasha held up the journal to show Gabriel an illumination when a loose page fell into her lap.

"What's that?" asked Gabriel.

She fell silent as she read it.

"Well?" asked Gabriel again. "What is it?"

Natasha was shaking her head in disbelief.

"It's a reminder that your father wrote to himself, Gabriel. It's about us. It's so strange that it should have fallen out of the journal at this particular moment…"

"What does it say?"

Natasha read it aloud.

A Matter of Grave Importance

When the Cube is retrieved, Gabriel and Natasha must go immediately to the Bodega del Pi in Toledo to see Yuri. Any delay could have serious repercussions on their mission. I must inform Father Franco of this development.

Natasha lurched forward against her seatbelt, surprised by the sudden deceleration. Gabriel was braking hard.

"What are you doing?"

"We're taking this exit to Toledo," he said. "If we cut through the middle of Spain this *Bodega del Pi* won't even be out of our way. Besides, it's your turn to drive. I can hardly keep my eyes open anymore."

CHAPTER 43

Somewhere over the Mediterranean Sea.

"This is Galaxy Network News, the most trusted news network in the world. Spain is reeling this morning after a string of seventeen car bombs ravage Bilbao, Barcelona, Madrid, and Zaragoza. Hundreds are dead, and many more injured. As well, violent riots spreading throughout the Muslim communities of the United States and Europe. Is the war spreading into our homes? Stay tuned for a special GNN report: *The Fist of Islam. Christendom is Burning.*"

Dr. Bennington's attention was fixed on the monitor mounted to the cabin wall. He was in a private jet enroute to Israel, being taken there against his will.

He was an older man; lean, clean-shaven, and almost entirely bald. He wore rimless spectacles and a light beige suit with a golden cravat. His demeanor was exceedingly gentle and consistently calm, even in his current situation.

Three hours earlier he had arrived at Christian's hotel only to be stuffed into a limousine and driven to a private airfield. Under the care of three armed security guards, Bennington had then been escorted onto Christian's jet and made to wait there for over an hour. After arriving, Christian had disappeared into the cockpit, leaving Bennington alone in the luxurious cabin as the plane took off. The gentle doctor could not believe what he was seeing on television.

"Well, Steve," said the expert being interviewed, "this kind of fighting is nothing new. Taking shelter in populated urban sectors allows the terrorists to use civilians as shields. For the most part, these Muslim communities are made up of great people, but they've got some bad apples in the bunch, and it's these guys who have banded together to fight this war."

"This war you are referring to, Mr. Peterson. Who exactly are the fundamentalists waging it against?"

"Against whoever opposes them, Steve."

"Now isn't that the loveliest circus you've ever seen, Doctor?" said Christian, returning from the cockpit.

He muted the monitor and threw himself onto a leather sofa across from where Bennington sat. Much to Christian's relief, his father's whispers had subsided after the last appearance of the Zurvanites, and he was enjoying the reprieve tremendously. He reached lazily for his glass of wine.

"There's nothing lovely about war and chaos, Christian," said Dr. Bennington.

"They are a means to an end," said Christian offhand. "The lovely thing I was referring to is the instability."

"I don't understand."

"Can't you see that we're all in great danger?" asked Christian sarcastically. "The terrorists are very terrifying, and the population needs the government to protect them. *The Enforcer of Laws* has become our new hero. He will protect us, but we must do exactly what he tells us to do. This is war after all."

"And what will we be told to do, Christian?"

"We'll be told to comply, Doctor. The masses will soon surrender the majority of their civil rights."

Christian lit a cigarette and returned his attention to the television. They were showing footage of a Muslim uprising taking place in Washington D.C.

"It's all just propaganda of course," said Christian, yawning. "It's nowhere near as big as it looks. The Muslims are as docile as lambs."

"And how can you be so sure this is just propaganda?"

Christian gave a dry chuckle.

"Because my organization is producing these stories. We own the mainstream media, Doctor. We decide how people perceive things."

"How can you possibly expect me to believe that?"

Christian rolled his eyes.

"I hope you're not one of those people who refuses to believe in conspiracy theories."

Bennington held his gaze but remained silent.

"Well, it's time you revisited your opinions and considered the validity of at least one of them."

"And which one might that be?" asked the doctor.

"Do you know the one about the group of cigar smoking men in the dark boardroom who are secretly running the world?"

"Yes," said Bennington. "That theory is familiar to me."

"Well, it's true, Doctor, with the exception that all those men answer to only one man, and I don't smoke cigars, I smoke cigarettes."

Christian took a long draw from his cigarette and smiled with self-satisfaction. Bennington shifted in his leather seat, crossing his legs. He had garnered very little from Christian up to this point, and he wanted nothing more than to keep his patient talking.

Christian was showing every sign of megalomania, and Bennington's professional instincts could sense tremendous turmoil behind the confident facade.

"Christian, you must forgive me if I find it difficult to believe that you're the leader of a shadow government directing every nation in the world."

"I direct most of them, Doctor, but not all of them. Not yet. With regards to your doubt, consider that we're the only civilians flying over European airspace right now."

"I'm aware that there have been restrictions made on flights," said the doctor. "But I'm also aware that given your new position, you must have certain privileges."

"Yes, Doctor, I do," said Christian, gesturing towards the window. "Perhaps these privileges would explain our military escort."

Bennington rose from his seat, sliding the blind up as he bent forward. There, not fifty feet from their plane and staggered in perfect formation were three RAF fighter jets.

"Are you beginning to understand, Doctor?" said Christian, enjoying his new companion tremendously. "There are another three on our starboard side as well."

"Understanding would imply knowing, Christian," said Bennington, returning to his seat, "and I'm sure I know very little."

"Not to worry, Doctor, because I'm going to tell you everything. I feel like I have found a very good friend in you."

"Friends don't force their friends to accompany them to Israel by taking their wife hostage."

Christian sat up suddenly, an anger alighting in him.

"Your wife is staying in a three thousand-euro-a-night suite in the Paris Ritz. You would think that would be good enough for anyone. Perhaps you might show some gratitude, Doctor. I am your patient. I am in need of your help."

"You threatened to kill her, Christian."

"No one's going to kill anyone if you do your job."

"And what might that be?" asked Bennington. "Altering your doses to prevent hallucinations? That will not be sufficient to treat what ails you, Christian. You must talk to me. You must tell me what is wrong."

Christian rose from the sofa and walked to the bar to refill his glass. He lit a cigarette and focused his eyes on the doctor.

"Strange things have been happening... Unnatural things."

"Perhaps you could be more specific?"

Christian continued to stare intently at Bennington.

"I was tricked into making a pact with the devil," he said. "I savagely murdered the man responsible. I also murdered my uncle. After I did all this, four demons appeared to me and told me that I was the son of Lucifer, destined to rule the world, but that's not the worst of it."

Bennington nodded slowly. It was important that Christian did not feel judged.

"What is the worst of it, then?"

Christian took a heavy draw from his cigarette and then placed it carefully in the ashtray. He took a sip of wine.

"The worst of it, Doctor, is that I believe them."

CHAPTER 44

Toledo, Spain.

An ancient hand emerged from the shadows, unlatching the heavy gate and pushing it outwards towards them.

"This is the place," whispered Natasha into Gabriel's ear.

She pointed to the battered sign that hung above them.

La Bodega Del Pi

Gabriel studied the pale hand and saw that it belonged to an old woman.

"Buenos dias, Señora," he said. "I'm Gabriel, Agardi Metrovich's son."

"Indeed, you are," came the old woman's voice. "And an angel of hope you are too. Enter, my child. I have been expecting you."

Gabriel shot a puzzled glance at Natasha and went in first. Everything was draped in shadow, but the darkness was soon vanquished when a shutter squeaked open. In the dusty light of the window, he could see an ancient woman dressed as a gypsy. Her silver hair was covered in a crimson shawl, and her eyes were big and green, shimmering with mystical power.

"Come in, come in," she said in her thick accent. "You too, Natasha. Come in. You are even more beautiful than I imagined."

Natasha smiled politely and entered timidly, looking around her as she did so. They were in a small tavern, its walls and ceiling comprised of ancient stone masonry.

Centred under a massive arch was a dark wooden bar, behind which sat dozens of open wine bottles, lined up on oaken shelves with their corks stopped into their necks. There was a large roast on the bar, covered in a glass dome. The old woman took up a knife that was lying next to it and used it to point out two stools. Gabriel and Natasha obeyed her silent order and sat down.

"You have driven a great distance," divined the old gypsy woman, turning to face an antique espresso machine, "and at great speeds, I might add."

She worked the machine, the smell of coffee filling the room.

"There is confusion in your minds, and your bellies are empty. This combination is not conducive to learning. I will make you breakfast."

The old woman sliced some of the peppery pork roast and stuffed the meat into crusty rolls, pressing them in what looked to be a fifty-year-old panini grill. She watched in silence as Gabriel and Natasha ate, speaking only when Gabriel had finished the last dram of his caffè latte.

He nodded to her in thanks as he put down the glass.

"I sense that your father has crossed over," said the gypsy woman soberly.

"Yes, he has," said Gabriel, looking down into his empty glass and turning it pensively. "He died earlier this month in a plane crash."

"Only his body is dead, my child," said the woman tenderly. "Now if you please. Come with me."

They followed her to a wrought iron staircase in the corner. It spiraled up into the stone ceiling and down into the wooden floor. As the old woman approached it, she came to a stop, her ancient hand clasping and unclasping the handrail as she thought.

"My husband's body is also dead," she said, studying the stone wall before her. "His name was Yuri Blavatsky. He was a procurer of ancient texts and writings. For fifty-nine years he assisted your father in his research, Gabriel. Many were the secrets they unearthed together; secrets of wisdom and power."

Gabriel looked over at Natasha, feeling the same curiosity he saw in her eyes. What secrets was the old gypsy referring to? Why had the professor seemed so urgent in his note? Why had he never told Gabriel about Yuri Blavatsky?

The air became cold and damp as they descended, and they soon arrived at an old wine cellar. Rack upon rack of vintage bottles surrounded them, and each was blanketed in thick cobwebs and caked in dust.

"Toledo is an old woman," said their guide over her shoulder, lighting a battered lantern as she spoke. "But as you will soon see, her womb still bears fruit."

They had descended well into the depths of the cellar when they came upon a heavy, time-blackened rack, laden with bottles. It was built against a wall of living stone.

The old woman hung her lantern on a nearby hook and reached slowly into one of the racks, pulling on a lever hidden within. In an instant the sound of scrapping stone gave way to a mechanical rumble of gears and counterweights. The massive rack slid aside.

"For reasons of secrecy," she said, retrieving the lantern from where she had hung it, "no electricity has ever been installed in this room. Follow me."

She led them through a low tunnel that opened into a circular chamber, about thirty feet in diameter. In the darkness they could make out a few cluttered shapes, but it was not until the old woman had lit a large candelabra that they could truly see the wonders the space had to offer.

Circling the entire chamber was an unbroken line of shoulder-high shelves; oaken, and crammed with ancient books, codices, scrolls of papyrus, vellum, and treasures of every kind. Covering its stone floor were luxurious Persian rugs on which could be seen several leather wingchairs, and sturdy desks laden with still more books and scrolls.

The room looked to be a library of sorts, but it was the stone ceiling that gave the chamber its unique character. Masterfully built, it formed a perfect semi-spherical dome above them.

"This is *The Chamber of the Sphere*," said the old gypsy. "It was built by Toledo's first Caliph. Here we have stored our greatest treasures."

Natasha swallowed slowly and followed Gabriel into the space, her eyes wide.

"What's that?" she whispered, pointing to a strange spherical apparatus that lay glimmering at the centre of the room.

black holes spin at unbelievably high rates. Because of this, their projected gravitational field isn't spherical anymore. Instead, it gets flattened out and forms a massive spinning disc; kind of like a pancake. Ours is a hundred thousand light years in diameter, but only a few centimeters thick."

Gabriel bent his knees until his line of vision had aligned with the galaxy's equator. Natasha followed his example. To their utter surprise, the hologram's light vanished completely as their eyes passed through the thin disc of the galactic plane, only to return to its original splendor as their line of vision emerged from its underside.

"Why's this happening?" asked Natasha, lowering and raising her line of vision above and below the galactic plane.

"The gravitational field is just like the black hole," said Gabriel, doing the same. "It sucks up all the light that comes into contact with it."

"To the ancients it was known as the *Dark Rift*," said the old gypsy. "Our solar system will soon pass into it."

Gabriel and Natasha could see that the old woman was not mistaken. In the holographic projection, the magnified section that contained the earth's solar system was clearly moving closer and closer to the galactic plane.

"But what does this mean?" asked Natasha, looking at the old woman.

"It means the end of an age, my child," she said, walking towards them.

"You said that the ancients feared this," asked Natasha, "Why?"

Gabriel was the first to answer.

"Because every time our solar system passes through the galactic plane, the sun and the planets are exposed to massive magnetic and gravitational fields. Getting close to it would be devastating. Crossing it would be catastrophic."

Natasha considered the implications.

"So, all the strange weather we've been experiencing for the last decade, all the earthquakes and tsunamis and tornados and hurricanes, they're all being caused by our proximity to this gravitational field?"

"That's what it looks like," said Gabriel with a shrug. "Provided this hologram is accurate... According to astronomers, our solar system travels in a kind of wave pattern as it moves along its orbit. It dips up and down through the galactic plane every fifty million years or so. Every time this happens, our north and south poles shift in position."

"And how do they know this?"

"Core samples, mostly," said Gabriel. "They take them in Antarctica and use them to study the magnetic alignment of the molecules frozen into the ice. Every fifty million years they see massive and sudden changes recorded there. But that's not the only evidence. They also know that many of the places that are now arctic were once tropical, and vice versa. The earth hasn't always spun on the poles it spins on now."

"The end of each age is marked by a great cataclysm," said the old woman, nodding in acceptance.

"But why all the destruction?" asked Natasha in horror. "What causes it?"

Gabriel stroked his chin pensively.

"The earth isn't a hard ball of rock like everyone thinks," he said. "It's a ball of liquefied magma covered in a thin crust of stone. It's so malleable that when it spins, it actually bulges at the equator. Shift the locations of the poles and it'll bulge in different places."

"And the oceans and tectonic plates will shift to fill in the gaps," whispered Natasha.

"A natural occurrence for the planet," said Gabriel, "but one that's pretty devastating for all us insects living on its surface."

Gabriel and Natasha watched as the old gypsy removed the Cube from the astrolabe. The hologram vanished as suddenly as it had appeared.

"We pass through the Dark Rift on the twenty-first day of this month," she said, relighting the candelabra with a flaring match. "The cataclysm is unavoidable, but its catastrophic effects on both the earth and humanity can be mitigated, if you fulfill your purpose."

"What purpose do we have to fulfill?" asked Gabriel, drawing closer to the old woman.

"You must awaken humanity to a true knowledge of itself."

"And how exactly are we supposed to do that?" snapped Gabriel, frustrated.

The gypsy woman scowled back at him.

"You must return the Cube to the *Great Labyrinth of Sarras.*"

Gabriel moved to say something, but the old gypsy silenced him with an upraised hand.

"You must pass through the *Seven Portals* and open the *Seven Seals of Gnosis* to the world. In doing these things, you will save us from perpetual darkness."

Gabriel exchanged a look with Natasha. If it were not for what they had just seen, they would have thought this old woman a lunatic, but given the oddity of everything that was coming to pass around them, her words seemed impossibly valid.

"But how can you expect us to accomplish any of this?" asked Gabriel. "The labyrinth could be anywhere in those mountains, and besides, what possible difference could our efforts make? This is a geological phenomenon. It's unstoppable."

"The passing of our planet through the Dark Rift will affect changes on both physical and metaphysical levels. It will affect matter, but it will also affect consciousness."

"How so?" asked Gabriel.

"Every mind will be cast into darkness and confusion," said the gypsy with a frown. "Humanity's collective consciousness will come under great duress. We are in dire circumstances, my children. Over countless millennia we have unwittingly allowed the forces of darkness to penetrate our souls. These forces have twisted and distorted the truth about life and death. They have isolated us from one another, and more importantly, from our true selves."

The old gypsy woman looked into the flames of the candelabra.

"This coming age will mark the passing of yet another galactic year. It will be the first anniversary of the complete annihilation of our distant ancestors. If you fail in your mission, humanity will follow in their footsteps. Our souls will be drawn into the lower spheres of Hades and reside there for aeons to come."

"Wait a minute," said Gabriel, turning to face the old woman. "It takes two hundred and fifty million years to complete a galactic year. Are you suggesting that there were people on the earth back then?"

"The beings that existed then were not like us," she said, "but their society was as fully developed as our own."

"And what happened to them?" asked Natasha.

"They passed through the rift in a state of spiritual darkness, and the Great Cataclysm ensued."

Natasha looked at Gabriel to find that he was shaking his head incredulously.

"What's wrong?" she asked. "What are you thinking?"

"Only that two hundred and fifty million years ago was when the Permian–Triassic extinction event occurred. It's also referred to by geologists as P-Tr, or *The Great Dying*."

Gabriel began to pace back and forth.

"P-Tr was the mother of all extinction events," he continued. "It makes the one that wiped out the dinosaurs sixty-five million years ago look like a terrestrial hiccup. When P-Tr occurred, ninety-six percent of all marine life was completely decimated, along with eighty percent of all the terrestrial vertebrate species. Even most of the insects were wiped out, and that never happens..."

Gabriel scratched his head.

"It never occurred to me before, but P-Tr happened around the time of our galaxy's nineteenth birthday."

Natasha frowned and bit her lip.

"And this galactic year we turn twenty?"

Gabriel was still coming to grips with the realization.

"Astrophysicists would say, yes," he said. "Give or take a few thousand years... But if what Señora Blavatsky is saying is true, we'll be turning twenty when we pass through the galactic plane five days from now."

"This is our last chance to turn the direction of the spiritual spheres," said the old gypsy. "The Great Cataclysm is once again upon us. Succeed in returning the Cube to its original resting place before the crossing is made, and humanity will be preserved.

"Pass through the *Seals of Gnosis* and the knowledge held within them will be released unto mankind. Only then will the balance of our universe be tipped in favour of the Light. Our collective mind will then manifest itself in a new world of peace and societal evolution. If you fail, all will be lost."

"Release the gnosis from the seals?" asked Gabriel, perplexed. "How are we supposed to do that? You must forgive us, Señora, but we don't know anything about this artifact."

"And even if we did know," said Natasha, "how could it be done? The world can't change in less than a week."

The gypsy sat down in one of the leather wingchairs.

"To transcend the Cube is to see it in all things..."

Gabriel and Natasha looked down at her, their eyes filled with confusion.

"You must be in truth," she continued, nodding slowly, "but you must also be in love. Once you have fully merged, the exact location of the lost Book of Khalifah will be revealed to you. It is imperative that you find this codex. Within it are the six translations needed to unlock the Cube's mysteries."

"You said *fully merged*, Señora," said Gabriel, looking over at Natasha. "What does that mean?"

"You were both demonically possessed when you were infants. Did you know this?"

Gabriel and Natasha nodded slowly.

"And do you know the origin of your scars?"

"We do," said Gabriel uncomfortably.

The gypsy woman smiled darkly and continued.

"Before they were exorcised, the fourteen emissaries infected both of you with demonic parasites," she said. "These entities infect you still. They work to keep you apart. Find them! Bring them into the light of awareness! They will dissolve like smoke in the wind. Only then will you merge."

"How do we find them?" asked Natasha, her eyes glassy with concern.

"You must look within, my child," she said with a smile. "They will be hiding where you least want to look. They will be shrouded in your fear."

The gypsy rose to her feet.

"You must begin your search for the Book of Khalifah at once. You must find the Labyrinth and complete your mission."

Natasha sat down in a chair next to where the old woman had been sitting. Gabriel remained standing. He had packed away the Cube and was examining the astrolabe again.

"We will do this," he said solemnly. "But not before I fix the damage I've done."

"What are you saying, child?" said the old woman, turning to face him. "Of what damage do you speak?"

"Because of my efforts to retrieve the Cube, innocent people are being held prisoner by a very bad man. Their lives are in danger. I'm not doing anything until they're safe."

The old gypsy came up to him, a sense of urgency filling her.

"Gabriel Parker," she said firmly. "You will leave all else aside and fulfill your destiny! You know very well there is not enough time!"

Gabriel turned to look at the old woman only to feel her grasp his wrist. Her green eyes seemed to him just then like churning waters, and he was instantly drawn into their emerald depths. The room around him was suddenly transforming, a cataclysmic wasteland of oblivion and destruction materializing before his eyes.

Stumbling amongst the devastation could be seen throngs of twisted corpse-like figures. Their eyes were lifeless, their mutilated bodies riddled with festering wounds. By some unknown power the gypsy woman had filled Gabriel's mind with a vision of the despair that would befall humanity, should he and Natasha fail. He tried desperately to break from the enchantment. He had somehow been carried into the depths of hell.

"There will be time for everything, Señora," came Natasha's voice, and Gabriel was immediately released from the vision, opening his eyes to see Natasha smiling at him.

She had gently taken hold of the old woman's hands.

"But the Dark Rift approaches…" pleaded the gypsy, only to grow suddenly calm.

She took a deep breath and smiled, seating herself next to Natasha.

"Of course, my child," she said, patting her hand. "Your wisdom is true."

Gabriel looked gratefully at Natasha. She had pulled him from a horrible place, but it had nonetheless left its mark on him. The gypsy's dark future would need to be avoided at all costs, and an almost desperate sense of urgency filled him now.

Perhaps there would be time for everything, but they certainly had no time to waste. Gibraltar was still hours away, and they had yet to make their way to Nasrallah's castle and free the prisoners.

"Come on," he said to Natasha, shouldering his pack. "We're leaving right now."

CHAPTER 45

Somewhere over the Mediterranean Sea.

Christian opened his eyes to find the doctor looking down at him. He was lying on the sofa, the luxurious interior of the jet's passenger compartment reminding him of where he was.

"What happened?" he asked.

"I had you in a hypnotic trance, Christian," said Dr. Bennington, his gentle smile doing nothing to mask the concern in his eyes.

Christian's memory came flooding back to him. He rubbed his face and sat up.

"What did you learn about the Cube?"

Bennington sat down opposite Christian and scribbled some notes onto a pad of paper. Before the induction, Christian had told him everything that had transpired up to that point, beginning with the death of his father and culminating with the murder of the Nautonnier and his uncle.

Bennington had asked many questions, and Christian had answered them all, insisting finally that he be put under a hypnotic trance. He had wanted to uncover the meaning behind his father's incessant whispers, and to clarify his own role in the events that were transpiring. He had warned Bennington to conceal nothing, reminding him that the entire induction would be recorded on the jet's security system.

"Well?" asked Christian.

Bennington looked up from his notepad.

"It's important that we deal with this calmly and methodically," he said. "You're a very troubled individual."

Christian rose to his feet, snatching the notebook from the doctor's hands.

"I'd say that's pretty obvious, Doctor. Why don't you tell me something I don't know?"

Christian flipped through the pages, trying to decipher Bennington's illegible script.

"What did you learn about the Cube?" he demanded, flinging the book back at him.

"You told me many things, Christian, but we must be careful. You're not ready to know everything."

Christian's face grew dark and menacing.

"What did you learn?"

Bennington sat back in his chair, thinking of his wife. There was nothing he could do but comply. He would have to tell Christian all he had learned. He could not afford to take any chances.

"You repeatedly referred to an ongoing battle between good and evil, Christian. You spoke of Jesus Christ and Lucifer as being the personifications of the two opposing sides."

"And I'm on Lucifer's side."

"Yes," said Bennington. "Your task, as you described it to me, is to lay waste to the world. When this is done, you are to rebuild it in a way that removes all civil liberties and spiritual pursuits. In essence, you believe that your purpose here is to make the earth as much like hell as possible."

"And why am I supposed to do this?"

Bennington paused before answering.

"You believe that Lucifer demands it of you, Christian; that you are to do whatever is needed to prevent humanity from rising to its next level of societal evolution."

"Why?"

"You claim that it is the only way that our souls can be stopped from escaping into the higher realms."

Christian frowned in confusion.

"And why doesn't Lucifer just let the souls go? What does he care?"

"If he lets them go, he loses power," said Bennington. "An overlord is only as powerful as those he holds beneath him. Take away his subjects, and a tyrant becomes nothing. This, you said, is why kings and emperors live in constant fear. Lucifer is no exception."

Christian's eyes seemed to light up with understanding.

"I see," he said, crossing his arms. "Please, continue."

Bennington swallowed hard. He knew that what he would say next would give Christian a direction of intent that would be detrimental to his sanity. All his instincts told him to keep this information from his patient, but he knew it was futile. Christian's words would have been recorded by the plane's microphones regardless, and he had the safety of his wife to consider.

"You told me that many souls had already ascended since Jesus Christ opened the way two thousand years ago," he began. "Despite Lucifer's continuous attempts to stop them from doing so. You said these ascended souls no longer require to be incarnated again and again; that they have used Earth for the purpose it was created and have purified themselves enough that they can now live in the higher spheres. From there, you said they will assist other souls incarnating on earth and help them to ascend as well."

"Is that so?" said Christian quietly.

A deep understanding was penetrating him now, and it seemed to him that it came from those same churning mists that the Zurvanites had shown to him the previous day.

Bennington studied his patient's face with concern. It was as though a hollow darkness had come over it. Something in Christian was transforming before his eyes.

"You claimed that humanity is still very much bound to Lucifer," he continued reluctantly, "but that there is something that threatens to change this relationship."

Christian looked intently at the doctor.

"Yes," he said. "What is it?"

"A mysterious, cube-shaped artifact," said Bennington, holding Christian's gaze.

"Finally!" he exclaimed, beginning to pace excitedly. "The Cube! What is it? Who made it?"

"By some it is called the *Cube of Knowledge*," said the doctor. "By others, the *Compostela Cube*. You said it's an artifact that is ancient beyond reckoning. You asserted that humanity only requires a consolidated push in order to move up to the next level of societal evolution, and that this Cube is capable of giving us this push."

"I don't understand," said Christian, looking intently at the doctor. "How can an artifact do that?"

Bennington held his gaze.

"You were not sure, Christian," he said. "You claimed that it is not so much a question of what the Cube does, but what humanity does with it. You explained that the Cube is a tool of sorts; a key, or a map, if you will. You admitted that you know very little about this artifact."

Bennington stood up and put a hand on Christian's shoulder.

"Do not lose sight of the metaphorical meanings behind your delusions, Christian. The Cube would appear to be a container of knowledge, and knowledge is always symbolic of freedom."

"I see," said Christian, nodding. "And this is why the Cube must be destroyed."

"The Cube does not exist, Christian," said Bennington. "It is a creation of your unconscious mind. What is important to note is that you have endowed your creation with the capacity to dissolve all fear, and to liberate humanity. This is a very positive construct."

"First of all, Doctor," said Christian, turning away, "the Cube *does* exist. It's very real, and so are the stories I've told you. Secondly, I have no interest in dissolving fear. Fear is what we use to control people; to make them do what we want them to do. I have no interest in liberating the masses. That would be pointless and stupid. How could any wealth be generated without the masses to do the work?"

A blank expression filled Christian's face.

"All power is based in fear," he uttered by rote. "If fear in the masses were ever lost, everything we have worked so hard to build would be destroyed. Fear must be maintained at all costs."

"But can you not see that those are not your own words, Christian?" pleaded the doctor. "Can you not see that you were programmed to say them? I know that this all seems very real to you, but you must believe me when I tell you that it is all in your mind. It is myth. If you make the effort to understand the stories, you will be able to make sense of them, and find peace."

"What else did you learn, Doctor," said Christian, turning to face Bennington. "You will tell me everything."

Bennington let himself fall into his armchair, defeated.

"You told me that your brother and sister conceived a hermaphrodite child so that an ancient prophecy might be fulfilled. You said that this child was born so that a portal to hell might be opened, and a great host of demons be unleashed onto the world.

"You told me that your brother would accomplish this by returning the corpse of his son to the place of its conception, where he would divide it into fourteen pieces, just as the Egyptian god Set had done to his brother Horus."

"I see," said Christian, squinting ever so slightly. "I remember now. There's a tremendous symbolic meaning behind this division, Doctor."

He looked down at Bennington, his arms hanging limply at his sides.

"Fragmentation is Lucifer's way…"

As Christian spoke these words, a dark roll of thunder sounded ominously outside the plane. With this last piece of information, it was as if a curtain had been drawn aside for Christian, and all the knowledge of which he had only previously glimpsed, was at last made fully available to him.

The jet banked and began its descent into Jerusalem.

"What are you going to do, Christian?" asked Bennington, his voice fearful and unsteady. "Surely you will not act on these mythical constructs."

"I will do what I was born to do, Doctor," said Christian, already becoming lost in his thoughts. "I feel I am finally ready to begin."

BOOK TWO
THE LOST LABYRINTH

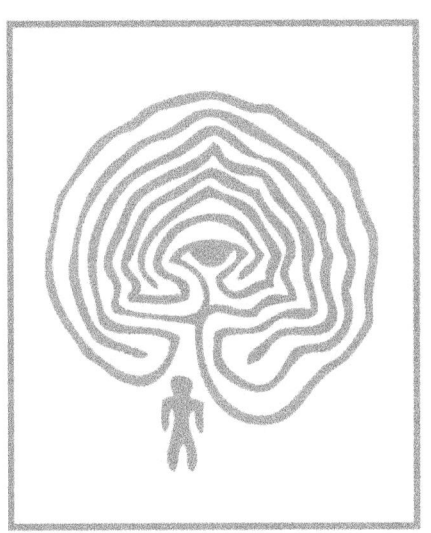

CHAPTER 1

Gibraltar.

Major Richard Roberts, aide-de-camp to the Governor of Gibraltar, sat at his desk, his task book open before him. He was a ruddy faced man, a little on the plump side but powerful and tall, with a stamina on the field that could put soldiers half his age to shame. He wore simple khaki barracks fatigues, had never once lost his temper, and possessed the kind of relaxed, confident demeanor that put people at ease.

He reached over and took hold of his mug without taking his eyes off his work, sipping the milky tea and wincing.

"Bloody hell," he muttered. "It's gone cold..."

It was only six hundred hours, but Roberts already knew what kind of day it was going to be. Along with the latest terrorist strikes in Spain had come an endless list of security tasks that needed to be accomplished, and the governor himself was of absolutely no use.

The old man had been bedridden for three days now and was showing no signs of improvement. His doctor had been the first person to call that morning, insisting the old man be taken to the naval hospital at once.

"You will please understand that I have insisted, Doctor," Roberts had said, his right eye winking nervously. "Sir William will have nothing of it. He seems quite content to die in his bed rather than be transferred to any hospital."

The military doctor had not offered much resistance. He knew the governor's stubborn streak. He had instead scheduled another visit for later that day, hoping to at least be able to collect some urine samples. The prognosis did not look good.

Major Roberts shook his head in exasperation as he looked over his agenda. What had been described to him as a ceremonial role was turning out to be the most challenging position of his career.

Since 1704, a governor had always been appointed to Gibraltar as a representative of the British monarch. He was the de facto head of state, responsible for the swearing in of the chief minister, who was officially the man in charge.

The trouble was that of the few duties still assigned to the governor, Gibraltar's defence was one of them, and during times of terrorist threats such as the ones of late, the governor's administration had been a very busy one to say the least.

The governor's residence, or the *Convent,* as it was also known, was located at the southern end of Gibraltar's busy main street. It was a majestic stone and brick building that had originally been built by Franciscan friars in 1531. Since 1728 it had been the command centre of the Royal Gibraltar Regiment and had not seen any military action since the Second World War. It was more of a ceremonial place than anything else, its dining room renowned for the most extensive display of heraldry in the entire British commonwealth.

"I understand, sir," said Roberts into the phone, "but you must understand that this change in policy will have far reaching implications for Gibraltar. To be told with no warning whatsoever—"

He paused to listen.

"Yes, sir, I understand, but you must see that it comes as quite a shock."

Another pause.

"No sir, I'm afraid the governor's truly quite sick, sir. No, the doctor is not sure what it is. Very well sir, I'll let him know."

Roberts hung up the phone, a look of disbelief blanketing his ruddy features. He could feel his right eye blinking as it always did when he was nervous, but he knew that this time it had good reason.

In the span of just two minutes, Gibraltar had been pushed from her imperial nest, and it had happened on his watch. Roberts made his way down the long corridor to the governor's suite, knocking softly on the heavy wooden door when he arrived.

"Come in," said a voice from within.

Roberts entered quietly. A clean-shaven old man lay in a large bed before him, a stack of snow-white pillows propping him into a semi-seated position. Behind him was a prominent, oaken headboard. It was carved with the crest of the Gibraltar Regiment, a castle and key under a crown. It gave him an air of regal importance.

The room itself was spacious and brightly lit, the curtains drawn aside to reveal a view of the lush gardens outside. The chirping of birds made its way in through the open window.

"Good morning, Major," said the old commander in chief from beneath his blankets.

He had a Roman nose, dark hair, and deep-set blue eyes that still twinkled despite his poor health. He had always held a deep fondness for Roberts, and never seemed to tire of his company.

"Good morning, sir. How are you feeling? Do you sense any improvement?"

"Perhaps a little," smiled the old man, lying. "The new nurse only just left. She was quite pretty, really. Quite nice. And speaking of pretty women, how is that little wife of yours, Major? Is she managing the renovation well? You must remind her to be very careful. A woman in her condition should not tax herself."

"I tell her that every day, sir," said Roberts. "Anita decided that she wanted to renovate the oldest house in Andalucía and have a baby all at the same time. Even still, I think she's managing remarkably well, sir. Thank you."

"It will be a seaside retreat to be reckoned with," smiled the governor. "Only yesterday she was telling me all about her new kitchen."

"The one she had to have custom made in England," said the major, exasperated. "It cost a fortune, but if it makes her happy it's well worth it, I suppose."

"Indeed, it is, Major. Indeed, it is."

The governor's voice trailed off. His tone was more serious when he spoke again.

"What news have you for me, Major?"

Roberts looked down for a moment to choose his words.

"I only just got off the telephone with Lieutenant Williams in London, sir. The news is not good. I'm afraid they've cut our military support. We'll not be seeing any British security forces here any time soon, sir."

"No, of course not," said the governor nodding. "Well, I do say this does not come as much of a surprise, now does it?"

"No, sir," said the major. "We both feared it would happen someday. Given the state they're in after the strikes, we've been told to do our best with what we've got. The lieutenant hinted that there would soon be a need for all His Majesty's forces in a retaliatory strike. Against whom or what, I'm not quite sure, sir.

"The truly shocking news is that Britain's completely given up its directorate. Gib's become her own republic, sir, at least for the time being. I was told to inform you that the Gibraltar Regiment is now under your exclusive command."

"Oh, my," said the governor, groaning in pain.

He had attempted to change his position on the bed but failed. He motioned the major to come closer.

"Richard," he said softly, patting the major's hand. "My faithful aide-de-camp. It has begun. For the time being, you must take command of this ship. I know you've got it in you. You were born and bred on the Rock, and you're my best officer. If anyone can protect Gib, it's you."

"Surely you'll be fine in a few days, sir."

"We will see, Major," said the old man weakly. "Now off you go and get to work. Remember everything I taught you."

The governor closed his eyes and immediately fell asleep, leaving Roberts sitting quietly in his chair. The major hoped against hope that the old man would recover soon. He was a true gentleman, the last of a dying breed.

Roberts walked through the Convent in a state of disbelief. The many events that had transpired that morning were still turning over in his mind. Not only was Gibraltar on its own, but in a matter of minutes, the governor had completely handed over the responsibility of its defence to him. This was no small thing, yet oddly enough, he felt up to the task. For the past three years the governor had been more a teacher and mentor to Roberts than anything else.

"Richard, I will tell you a secret," he often said. "There are powers behind the throne that seek to dominate the world by destroying it first. When they rebuild it, things will not be the same as they were before. Dark times will come, and Gibraltar will be left to defend herself. She must be prepared for the worst."

Roberts had always taken the old governor's warnings with mixed feelings. On the one hand he knew of the governor's vast political experience and his high connections. He was, after all, a Duke, and an influential one at that. But on the other hand, he was also an old man who, like many old men, thought the world was going to its destruction.

One thing was certain, however. The governor had always been in love with Gibraltar; her people, her history, and her culture. The Rock's best interests were always at the forefront of his mind. He would often refer to Gibraltar as a big magnet.

"No matter where you go," he would say with a fond wink, "she's always pulling you back to her."

Today it would appear that the governor's gloomy projections had been proven correct to a certain degree at least. Only yesterday they had received orders from England to be on high alert, a terrorist strike imminent.

The major shook his head. They were truly on their own now, and as if to punctuate his thoughts, he heard the pounding thunder of jet engines overhead. The RAF was wasting no time in bringing its fighters home.

Roberts felt a vibration in his pocket and pulled out his phone. It was his young wife calling.

"Hello, cookie," he said.

"Oh, darling," said Anita caringly. "I just got your message. What's wrong?"

"The UK's left us high and dry," he said. "Just like that. No more military support. No more governmental support. Listen, cookie, it looks like it's going to be a long day, I don't think I'll be able to make it over tonight. Why don't you come down and we'll have a nice dinner here?"

"All right," she said. "Oh, no, I can't Richard. The plumber's coming to connect the appliances. You know how long it took to get him to come. I simply can't cancel now."

"Don't even think of it," he said. "You're better off in Spain anyway. The *Levante* is terrible today."

"The bane of Gibraltar," said Anita, referring to the easterly wind that often formed a somber cloud over the Rock. "Are you sure?"

"I wouldn't have been much company tonight anyway. I'm bogged down with work. How's our little soldier?"

"He just gave me a kick," she said. "I think he knows I'm talking to you."

"Well, tell him to take it easy, and you do the same. He could come any day now."

"He's still three weeks away, you worry wart."

Roberts reached down into his pocket and produced a beeping two-way radio.

"I've got to go, darling. I've got a call coming in. We'll have a nice lunch tomorrow."

"I'll miss you."

"I'll miss you more. Now run along, I've got a million things to do."

Back at his desk, Roberts ran a hand through his short-cropped hair. He picked up the receiver of an old military telephone and used the back of his pen to punch in some numbers, giving a sigh of resignation.

One step at a time, Richard. One step at a time.

Renewed strength was pouring into the major as the shock of the news wore off. Things were not that bad. He had a full battalion of superbly trained men and plenty of ammunition and supplies, much more than would ever be needed to stave off a few random terrorist strikes. He heard the phone line engage.

"Captain Brown," he said in a commanding voice, his right eye giving a quick twitch. "I want all the officers assembled in the mess for lunch today."

There was a short pause before he continued.

"Stop asking questions. Make the necessary preparations. As of now we're on high alert. Don't screw it up."

CHAPTER 2

Sierra Nevada Mountains, Spain.

"We're on our way to visit some friends in Marbella," said Gabriel to the Spanish Guardia Civil agent.

The latter was poking his head into the car, eying Natasha as she slept. It was the third time Gabriel had been asked where they were going, and he was not about to tell them the truth.

Three hundred years after Gibraltar had officially become a British colony, the Spanish were still silently disputing its ownership. Gibraltar was not a good word to be saying to paranoid soldiers. Gabriel watched the ensign walk away and then looked over at Natasha, glad she was getting some sleep.

Having left Toledo far behind, they had been driving through a mountain pass north of Granada when they encountered the checkpoint. It had been set up at a toll station, something that did not normally occur.

The lieutenant had returned Gabriel's documentation, but for some reason they were not allowing them to depart. Having been stopped for over half an hour now, Gabriel was beginning to grow impatient.

"What a load of crap," he muttered quietly, pushing back his shaggy hair.

His eyes followed the ensign who had just been questioning them. He was walking over to speak with one of his commanding officers. Gabriel heard Natasha stir.

"What's going on?" she asked sleepily.

"They've declared martial law in Spain, and most of Europe by the looks of it."

He pointed out the commanding officer.

"That guy over there says that all foreign plated cars need special permits to circulate. Our plates are Italian. He also says that we need to produce papers that confirm our reservations in a hotel tonight. There's a curfew in effect. Nobody's allowed to be on the streets past ten."

"Gabriel," said Natasha, looking out her window. "I'm scared. This has never happened before."

"Sure, it has," said Gabriel. "Curfews were in effect during the entire second world war."

Natasha chewed her lip.

"Is that what this is? Another world war?"

"I don't know if it is technically, but if it isn't yet, I'd wager it's going to be soon. There appears to be a global crisis developing. The agent was just saying that Islamic militias have surfaced all over Europe. He says they're armed and aggressive. The newspapers published those cartoons again, and this time all hell broke loose."

"So, what'll happen now?"

"We'll wait and hope the lieutenant gives us a break," said Gabriel, turning on the radio and searching through the stations.

"You're listening to the Galaxy Network News International Radio Broadcast."

He turned up the volume. They were giving a report on the latest developments. Another nuclear suitcase bomb had detonated, this time in a Boston university. It had incinerated more than a thousand people. China had invaded Taiwan, simultaneously declaring war against the United States coalition, and condemning their attacks on Iran. Already there were scattered skirmishes happening between Chinese and American troops all over the Middle East. Many had been killed on both sides, and Russia had officially sided with China.

"This is so strange," said Natasha, still trying to come to grips with the dread she was feeling. "All our lives we've feared this would happen, and now it's happening. It's World War Three."

"It sure seems that way," said Gabriel, looking over at the ensign who had just been questioning them.

He was a few stalls over in the next toll booth and Gabriel could see him talking with his commanding officer. There was a white van parked beside them, and it had just become surrounded by half a dozen agents, their assault rifles poised and ready. By the large tarpaulin-covered load it was carrying, Gabriel guessed that it was Moroccan.

"What's that strapped to its roof?" asked Natasha.

Gabriel kept his eyes on the scene as it developed.

"Moroccan men will often head up to France and work there for several years," he said. "They save up their money to buy a van and a bunch of stuff to sell back in Morocco. With the money they make they can usually buy a small piece of land and move up in the world. It looks like they're being given a hard time."

Gabriel caught a glimpse of the driver's hardened face and in an instant knew that something was terribly wrong. He had friends who were Moroccan merchants. They were good, family-oriented people. They did not look like that.

The momentary appearance of a weathered, bearded face in the passenger seat only served to confirm his suspicions. These men were militants. He was sure of it. What they were doing here in Southern Spain he could not even begin to guess, but he did not like it in the least.

"Look," said Natasha. "Someone's getting out."

A man emerged from the back of the van just then. There was a large pack strapped to his back, and heeding his intuition, Gabriel slipped the car into reverse, glancing into the mirror to see if the way behind them was clear.

Who wears a backpack while they're on a road trip?

Gabriel pushed the accelerator to the floor and popped the clutch, keeping his eyes glued to the van as the sportscar lunged backwards. The man with the pack had just closed his eyes. He reached over and pushed Natasha below the safety of the dashboard.

"Get down!"

The rest unfolded rapidly. Seeing the terrorist's intentions, the civil agents had opened fire immediately, but the bomb detonated nonetheless, sending broken bodies and shards of metal in all directions. A second later the van itself exploded, its hidden store of ammunition igniting to produce a massive, mushroom cloud of fire and smoke.

The sportscar continued to speed backwards, shaking under the force of the blast. To the right of the van that had exploded, a delivery truck came about with squealing tires, its doors opening as several masked men spilled out. They too were armed, and they immediately opened fire on the remaining Guardia Civil troops. In a matter of seconds, a small war had erupted; a war that Gabriel wanted no part of.

"Hold on!" he said, slamming on the brakes and throwing the car into first gear.

Natasha peered up cautiously. Instead of driving away from the melee, Gabriel was heading right into it. He was accelerating directly for the tollbooth.

"Are you crazy?!" she screamed. "You're going to get us killed!"

"Not if I can help it!" barked Gabriel, flying through the narrow gate at full throttle.

The engine roared and dozens of bullets zipped past them on all sides as they flew from the toll booth, not one finding its target. In an instant the rattling machine guns had been left behind, and before them, stretching out like a promised land, lay a sunny, traffic-free autoroute. Gabriel released a long breath of relief and set the cruise control.

"Are you all right?" he asked, looking over to Natasha.

"I think so," she said, sitting up in her seat.

Gabriel shook his head.

"That was close. Sorry for screaming at you like that. I guess I got a bit spooked."

"Well, that makes two of us," she said, fixing her disheveled hair. "That was fast thinking, Gabriel."

"I just wanted to get out of there as quickly as possible. Besides, we've got to make it to Gib. Hopefully we can still get across the border."

Gabriel turned up the radio. The journalist speaking sounded more like a sports commentator than a correspondent. He shook his head again, but this time in disbelief. There were crises unfolding across the entire planet.

"This just in from the Middle East: U.S. and Pakistani forces have been overwhelmed by rogue militants in Islamabad. There are no confirmed reports, but it is feared that the entire Pakistani nuclear arsenal has fallen into terrorist hands. London Heathrow Airport has been destroyed by a series of missile attacks launched from somewhere in the United Kingdom."

Gabriel lowered the volume and used the car's voice control to dial a number.

"Boss," said Amir. "Where are you guys?"

"We'll be in Malaga soon," said Gabriel looking at the GPS.

He tapped the screen.

"If we can keep up this pace, we should be in Gib within two hours."

"Head to Estepona," said Amir. "We'll send a launch to pick you up. The Gib border's a mess. I doubt you'd get through."

"Where in Estepona do you want to meet?"

"Bar Jimmy."

"Done," said Gabriel.

"Boss," said Amir. "Are you guys all right? There are skirmishes happening everywhere in Spain. It's one of the most unstable regions in Europe right now."

"Tell me about it," said Gabriel. "We only just managed to slip out of a gun fight about fifty clicks back."

"Just take it easy. You're doing great for time. Everything's ready on this end. I'll send out a boat right now. It should be there waiting for you when you arrive."

"Amir."

"Yes, boss."

"Put a bottle of Johnny Black in the launch, would you? I'm dying for a drink."

"No worries, boss."

Gabriel terminated the call and let out a sigh. The day was turning out to be beautiful. They were heading due south now, descending out of the mountains. Straight ahead and far below the Mediterranean shimmered like a gemstone. Above them a wide-open sky cradled a warm, yellow sun.

"Look at it out there," said Gabriel. "I'd roll down the windows but at this speed we'd probably get sucked out."

They drove along the rocky coast for about an hour, the autoroute eventually winding around the city of Malaga and heading south-west along the arid Costa del Sol. The day was well under way now, and the growing traffic prevented them from achieving the speeds they had reached up to that point.

At long last they exited the autoroute and made their way into the *Puerto Deportivo* of Estepona. It was a nicely constructed marina complex, filled with bars and restaurants, and nestled amongst groupings of shady palm trees and spurting fountains.

Gabriel steered off the main path, navigating the car through some low buildings and into a hidden area where fishing boats were docked. He parked in front of a crowded little bar, filled with darkly tanned fishermen and their families. The lively sounds of *Sevillana* music filled the air.

"*Bar Jimmy,*" said Natasha, reading the sign.

Gabriel shut off the engine and unhooked his seatbelt.

"If we didn't have to storm a castle, I'd treat you to some *Chanquetes.*"

"What are *Chanquetes?*" asked Natasha, climbing out of the car with bright eyes.

"They're tiny little fish, no bigger than minnows," said Gabriel, exiting the car as well.

He opened the front hood to take out their equipment.

"They pass them through flour and deep fry them. It's all very illegal," he added with feigned severity.

"Why?" asked Natasha, stretching her body after the long drive.

Gabriel was taking up the bags, but he could not help watching her out of the corner of his eye. He loved the ballet and could recognize a schooled dancer when he saw one. Even in the simple act of stretching, Natasha's movements were elegant.

"Because the fish are just babies," he said, turning his attention back to the luggage, "and babies should be allowed to grow into fish before you eat them, I suppose. But if you know the owner of the bar, you can usually get them. It's always been like that, and they've never run out of fish."

Natasha reached for her backpack, but Gabriel shouldered it first.

"We'll have some next time," he said, leading her forward. "That and some *tinto con gaseosa.*"

"That I've had before," said Natasha, walking close by his side. "Red table wine with carbonated sugar water. It is a Spanish staple!"

They squeezed their way through a crowded dining room and around an equally busy bar. It was clad in the ornate blue and white tiles typical of Andalucía. The countertop was stainless steel and cluttered with countless varieties of tapas, its perimeters delineated by hanging legs of ham and other cured meats.

At the rear of the establishment, they passed through a door that opened onto a beachfront patio. Gabriel scanned the shore. There was no launch in sight. He looked at his watch.

"I think we might have made it here faster than Amir thought," he said. "Come on. We can grab a table and keep an eye out for them. Looks like we might have time for a little bite after all."

Gabriel pulled out one of the aluminum patio chairs and invited Natasha to sit down.

"It's so beautiful here, Gabriel," she said, scanning the shady terrace and breathing in the fresh sea air. "It seems you know this place well."

Gabriel waved at a waiter and then sat down.

"I used to live close by," he said. "I came here almost every day."

When the waiter arrived Natasha could see he was not lying. The two embraced like old friends, dealing heavy blows to each other's backs.

Gabriel spoke to him in fluent Spanish, introducing Natasha and ordering their food. In no time they were dining on the tiny fried fish he had promised. They came piled on a large plate and looked more like thinly shaved potato frites than fish. Gabriel took a big lemon wedge and squeezed it over top of the dish.

"Give them a try," he said, skewering half a dozen of the *chanquetes* with his fork.

He popped them into his mouth along with a chunk of crusty bread, leaning back in his chair as he chewed with delight.

"You eat the heads and tails too?" whispered Natasha in surprise.

Gabriel gave her a wink and took a gulp of his *tinto con gaseosa*.

"Trust me on this one," he said.

Natasha took a tiny fish on her fork, looking down at its two little eyes. They were not even the size of poppy seeds, and all was covered in light, golden batter. Her eyes lit up the moment she had placed it in her mouth. It was light and crispy and the most delicious seafood dish she had ever tasted.

"Wow," she said, tearing off a piece of bread. "I see what you mean. It's so simple, and yet so good!"

They ate contentedly, with Gabriel telling Natasha all about the time he had spent in Estepona. He had found the town while looking for a base to head up a treasure hunt. The objective had been to locate a sunken ship just off the coast. The story was fascinating.

"It was a tenth century Moorish patrol boat, about a kilometre out and thirty meters down," he said, pointing to sea. "The research we did said it was carrying twenty kilos of plundered Visigoth gold. It took us the better part of a year, but we found it."

Natasha was captivated the entire time that Gabriel told the story. She had never met anyone even remotely similar to him. His tale was engaging, his voice almost musical, and with no trace of pretension. He gave most of the credit to Amir, or to the local fishermen they had contracted to help them. In this way he related their fantastic accomplishments without seeming even remotely boastful.

Natasha laughed at the predicaments he described, and listened intently, making the occasional comment when she felt she had something to add. In the end their lunch together proved one thing to Natasha: Gabriel was a true gentleman, in every way. When her glass was empty, he filled it. Once, when her napkin had blown from her lap, he had retrieved it for her. He had even stood up when she left the table to use the restroom, and done it again when she had returned. This was unheard of.

There was only one problem with Gabriel, and it plagued Natasha the entire while. He showed no signs that he was sexually interested in her. Gabriel's indifference took her off guard and she began to feel self-conscious.

"Do you have a girlfriend, Gabriel?" she asked when a gap appeared in the conversation.

Gabriel shifted slightly in his seat.

"I have friends," he said carefully, "but nothing serious."

Natasha smiled.

"What about you?" he asked. "Have you got a *ragazzo* waiting for you in Florence?"

Natasha looked down.

"I did, but we split up a few months ago."

Gabriel nodded.

"You left him."

"I did," said Natasha. "How did you know?"

Gabriel looked out to sea.

"Only a dummy would give a girl like you the boot, and you're way too smart to date a dummy..."

Natasha arched an eyebrow.

"Was that a compliment?"

Gabriel shot her a wink.

"Simply an observation."

Natasha smiled and rubbed her chin pensively. Gabriel seemed pensive as well.

"He was a jerk, right?"

Now it was Natasha's turn to look out to sea.

"And a liar, and a cheat."

Gabriel was scanning the horizon to the southwest.

"Even though you tried to fix him."

Natasha looked over at him in surprise.

"It seems you know me well."

Gabriel shrugged.

"I've known one or two pretty women before."

"So, you're saying we're all the same," said Natasha, a little perturbed by his remark.

Gabriel remained silent.

"In what ways do you think we *pretty women* are all alike, Gabriel?"

He turned to face her, his expression serious.

"Do you really want to know what I think?"

"Yes, I do."

He poured himself some more *tinto con gaseosa* and drained the glass before speaking.

"Pretty girls always move from one boyfriend to the next," he said. "If they've been more than a month without one, they start coming apart at the seams. But that never really happens because there's always a long line of guys waiting for their turn."

Gabriel sat back and put his feet up on a neighbouring chair. Despite his best attempts to remain indifferent he could already feel old resentments coming on. He grimaced slightly.

"The only time a pretty woman ever feels good about herself is when she's got a fancy man at her side to make her feel that way."

Natasha was shocked by Gabriel's words. He was making sweeping generalizations, but despite her reluctance to admit it, they were bitingly true, at least in her case.

"Is that so," she said peevishly.

"I'm pretty sure it is," continued Gabriel, masking his bitterness with a yawn. "But instead of giving the asshole the boot, pretty girls always try to fix him. Turn him into a real man. You see it makes a girl feel noble to be so selfless. Really all she's doing is trying to compensate for the guilt she feels for having betrayed herself in the first place."

"Betrayed herself?"

Natasha could not believe Gabriel was saying these things, but she wanted to hear him out regardless.

"Sure," he said. "She betrays herself by needing to be dependent on a jerk to make her feel good about herself. She acts confident and self-assured, but she's not, and she knows it. That's why she punishes herself."

"Punishes herself?" blurted Natasha.

Gabriel was blind to her exasperation. He just nodded and looked out to sea.

"By rejecting the real guy when he comes along."

The pain in Gabriel's voice was unmistakable, and Natasha felt her anger slipping away, despite her indignation. Gabriel obviously had issues with past relationships, but this still did not give him the right to say what he had just said, as though it were true of all attractive women.

"It seems to me a pretty girl once broke your heart."

Gabriel ignored her remark and continued to look out to sea. At length he spoke, voicing a thought that had only just occurred to him.

"Maybe deep down inside pretty women don't think they're worthy of real love. So they reject the real guys, and keep trying to change frogs into princes…"

He glanced over at Natasha and then back out to sea. There was no cynicism in his words anymore, just a desire to understand. Natasha knew she had been right about his broken heart.

"So naturally, you'd never get involved with a pretty girl then."

Gabriel sat up in his chair. He had just spotted a boat coming towards them.

"I don't get involved with *any* girls," he said over his shoulder. "Period. Life's simpler that way."

Natasha cocked a suspicious eyebrow.

"You don't seem like the celibate type to me."

"That's because I'm not."

Natasha frowned. His words had opened a painful wound.

"So, you're *that* type of man, then."

"What type of man?"

"The kind who uses women for sex. The kind who are liars and cheats."

Gabriel turned and looked directly at Natasha, mirroring her frown.

"Now wait a minute," he said, leaning forward in his chair. "If I offended you, it certainly wasn't my intention. You asked for my opinion, and I gave it to you. There's no reason to be insulting."

Natasha clasped her hands over the table.

"Generally speaking," she said in earnest, "if a man wants to sleep with a woman, he has to make her believe it might go somewhere. In your case, that would be a deception, and that would make you a liar. You'd become a cheat the moment you seduced more than one woman in this way."

Gabriel held her gaze. He could see he had offended her, and it only confirmed what he already knew. Wonderful women like Natasha were off limits. Something in him prohibited them, though he could not say what it was.

"Listen, Natasha," he said. "I'm not going to tell you I haven't done what you're saying. I have, but I stopped it a long time ago.

There was always someone getting hurt or feeling used, no matter how well they hid it. It got ugly."

He could hear a boat approaching behind him. By the sound of its engine, and the hull slapping against the waves, he knew it was a fast launch. The smugglers had finally arrived, but he did not want to turn away from Natasha until he had explained himself.

"So you stopped seeing women then," she said, smiling curtly. "Somehow I doubt that."

"No," said Gabriel bluntly. "I started paying women to have sex with me instead. Things have been working great ever since."

Natasha had to consciously stop her jaw from dropping. She was speechless. She would never have guessed that this would have been his response. She could only stare at Gabriel as though he were a stranger.

"I'm a whoremonger, Natasha," he said. "I know that must disgust you, and I don't blame you. It's just what I am."

He rose to his feet and Natasha followed him up, her eyes wide the entire time. She was surprised by her reaction.

Since when did I become so innocent?

"What kind of prostitutes?" she heard herself ask.

Gabriel looked at her with strained patience.

"The expensive kind, Natasha. Does it make a difference?"

They heard Amir cry out and turned to see the launch coming up on the beach. Its engine roared louder for a moment as the prop was pulled from the water.

"If it makes you feel any better," said Gabriel, looking at the boat, "you're not the typical pretty girl anyway."

"I'm not?" asked Natasha.

Gabriel shook his head.

"You're more like a plain girl who happens to be pretty."

Natasha frowned in confusion and came up speechless. Gabriel pointed to the fast launch to change the subject. It was coated in matt black anti-radar paint, and it had a stealthy, military look to it.

Together they watched Amir hop onto the sand and jog towards them, his dreadlocks contained by an Indian print bandana. He was wearing khaki cargo pants and a dark, loose-fitting sweater. A pair of military goggles hung from a strap around his neck and there was a combat knife strapped to his belt.

A serious, black-dressed pilot remained in the launch behind him, scanning the coast through a pair of binoculars.

"I can see you made good use of the downtime," said Amir, scanning the empty plates on the table as he arrived.

He and Gabriel clasped hands and embraced heartily.

"You're late, my friend," said Gabriel.

Amir shrugged and gave Natasha a courteous nod.

"A pleasure to make your acquaintance, Dr. Rossi," he said, taking her hand regally. "Gabriel failed to mention your beauty..."

Natasha smiled, still coming out of her earlier shock.

"He also failed to mention your charm, Amir."

"Jealousy and envy," he said with a charismatic wink. "He's always had a burning desire to be just like me."

Gabriel tossed a lemon wedge at him.

"What the hell took you guys so long?"

Amir shook his head in trepidation.

"It was a close call, boss. We ran into some trouble with customs boats. Two of them chased us for over an hour. The entire coast is crawling with Guardia Civil. Something's up."

Gabriel was reaching for his wallet when the owner of the establishment appeared. He was a large Andalusian man, with a generous belly and a jolly countenance.

"Dr. Parker!" he said in a thick Spanish accent, smoothing down his apron as he approached.

He propped his big hands on his hips.

"Thinking of taking off without paying again, are you? I'll have to keep that fancy car of yours!"

Gabriel laughed and gave the fat man a wholehearted embrace.

"Could you do me a favour, Jimmy?" he asked quietly.

He passed him the car keys and some folded bank notes.

"Could you put her somewhere safe for me until I get back?"

Jimmy took the keys but refused the money.

"She will be safe in the boat shed," he said. "Would you mind if I take her for a spin?"

"Go crazy," said Gabriel. "Just stay around the port. We ran through a check point back near Malaga. They might still be looking for the car."

"Some things never change with you, Dr. Parker," he said, rubbing his chin and frowning. "Always with somebody at your heels. I think I will pass on the ride, old friend, but thank you just the same. The Guardia Civil are back in their fascist element again. I want no trouble."

CHAPTER 3

Los Picos de Europa, Northern Spain.

The sun was setting rapidly as Isaac hurried to finish setting up the tent. He could see Shackleton lying next to the fire and he marvelled at the dog's ingenuity. Earlier that evening he had disappeared for twenty minutes only to come back with a plump goose in his maw, the same goose that Isaac was roasting over the fire.

It had been a full day of hiking and they had covered much ground. That morning, having eaten a good breakfast, Isaac had found himself feeling much better and strong enough to follow Shackleton's lead. Putting his trust in the dog, he had followed him faithfully, never once doubting that he would lead him to safety.

"That should do it," he said, securing the final stay and moving to the fire.

He rolled down his sleeves and put his suit jacket back on. Shackleton opened an eye as he approached.

"Shall we eat, old boy?"

Shackleton sat up immediately, licking his chops as Isaac pulled the piping hot goose from the skewer. He divided it and placed half of the steaming carcass before the dog.

"There is nothing like a barbeque to lift the spirits."

Shackleton responded with a round nod, and a lick of his chops. It was clear that he preferred his food cooked, but as the bird was still too hot for him, he laid his head down before it, his snout resting on his two paws while he waited for it to cool.

The sun dipped down and out of sight as the two of them ate, until at last they found themselves engulfed by night. Above them the Milky Way hung like a snug blanket, growing brighter with each passing minute. They had made camp in a sheltered pocket on the side of a crag, and the fire crackled merrily.

After dinner, Isaac fought back his sleepiness and took out the notebook that he had found in Father Franco's pack along with the tent. He hoped he might find some explanations in it. He desperately wanted to know why all this was happening. He produced a flashlight and shone it down on the book, opening it to its final entry.

Wednesday, December 5. – Santander – Waiting to board the floatplane.

I feel somehow comforted to know that regardless of what shall happen to us, the professor's Cube journal is safely in the post and on its way to Bishop Marcus. There have been many unexpected turns of late, and I cannot guess what awaits us at the island. The professor seems optimistic, but I fear the worst. Dark and powerful forces are at work here, and I doubt very much that they will allow us to bring an end to their sinister plan without considerable resistance.

The body of the hermaphrodite has already been loaded onto the plane, along with all the equipment we will need for both the burial, and our hike to the monastery. Mr. Rodchenko was nowhere to be found when we departed. I am convinced that his mental illness is a blessing in disguise. How could any man live with the knowledge of having conceived a child through such abominable means?

Isaac looked up from the book, a sickening dread welling in the pit of his stomach.

What does he mean?

He shrugged off his drowsiness and flipped through the book, finding many entries pertaining to something referred to as the Compostela Cube. It was not long before he came upon a loose sheet of paper. It was a photocopy of a child adoption form. Isaac had worked extensively with church orphanages before his illness. He was no stranger to their paperwork.

"This comes from the Istanbul orphanage…" he muttered, his brow furrowing.

He scanned the document. He could see that it was dated the same year that his own son had been born. He would have been in Istanbul at that time, working at the very orphanage from which the document had originated.

What are the chances of this happening? And why are two names on this paper circled?

"Gabriel Parker and Natasha Rossi..."

He had only just seen these names in one of Father Franco's previous entries, and even then, they had sounded familiar to him. He flipped back through the book until he had relocated the entry.

With these latest developments, any remaining reservations we have held concerning the connection of Gabriel and Natasha to the Compostela Cube have now been put to rest. Every element of the Ascender's Prophecy has been fulfilled.

Isaac pocketed the book and crawled into the tent. As strong as his desire to know more was, his exhaustion from the day's travels won out in the end. He could no longer keep his eyes open.

"We'll have another look tomorrow," he said, giving a gaping yawn.

Seeing that Isaac had retired, Shackleton moved to the threshold of the shelter and laid himself down. He gave the night one final sniff and then lowered his head onto his paws, loosing a long sigh before abandoning himself to sleep.

CHAPTER 4

The Atlas Mountains, Morocco.

Najiallah Nasrallah sat at his desk, his unwashed hair pulled back into a tight ponytail. He was wearing a designer suit, its shiny black material expensive, but as gaudy as his mustard-coloured shirt. He was in the act of examining an ancient map that was spread out before him.

"Where are you hiding?" he muttered.

The richness of the chart's Islamic illuminations sent thrills of excitement through him, but they also filled him with pangs of frustration. It had been this very scroll that had led him to the Compostela Cube, but despite all his efforts, he had been unable to locate the second treasure marked on its surface: A fabled Islamic codex known as the *Book of Khalifah*; an artifact he knew was inextricably bound to the Cube.

Nasrallah ran his fingers over the ancient parchment. At its centre, surrounded by Islamic texts, was an ornate diagram of the Strait of Gibraltar, showing the location of a secret cave hidden somewhere beneath the Mediterranean Sea. In that chamber resided the Book of Khalifah, hidden for centuries and impossible to locate.

He picked up the jewel-encrusted cylinder that housed the scroll and marveled at its workmanship. Even if he could never use the map to locate the Book, the scroll itself would fetch him a fortune when a buyer for it had been found. His mobile phone rang and he answered it with a curse.

"Everything is ready, Master," said a man's voice.

"Where is Bahadur?" he hissed, remembering his anger.

"He is somewhere in the plaza, sir. I do not know his exact location. We determined where we should position the snipers over the phone should Parker decide to flee."

"He is to call me immediately. He is consistently out of coverage!"

Nasrallah terminated the call.

My captain is keeping something from me...

He got up from his desk and crossed the room. These were troubled times. Each of his last hashish shipments had been intercepted by the police, and he had lost hundreds of thousands of Euros as a result. His mind raced. Who had tipped them off? There was a rat in his organization. Nasrallah rolled up the scroll and carefully inserted it into its bejeweled cylinder.

I will try to sell this to Antov along with the Cube...

Not ten days had passed since he had been approached by three Dutchmen while dining in a Tangiers hotel. They had somehow learned of his acquisition from the museum of antiquities the year before and were curious if it might still be for sale.

"Our employer has a mild curiosity for artifacts belonging to that period and would find it entertaining to purchase it from you."

Nasrallah had gone into dealings with them immediately, and by the end of the evening had settled on the cool price of one million Euros. They had arranged to make the exchange the following week, but Gabriel Parker had robbed him of the Cube before this could happen. Nasrallah ground his teeth.

He came into my home and stole from me. He will pay dearly.

Nasrallah passed a light hand over his slick head. He would not mention the scroll until the deal with the Cube had been finalized. He could not help feeling ill at ease about the transaction. His original contact, a Catholic priest named Adrianus, had been replaced by a cold and unpredictable man named Christian Antov.

Nasrallah could not afford to make any mistakes. Already his men were complaining. They had not been paid in months, and the treasury was empty, the last of his money being diverted to settle an overdue account with furious Afghani suppliers.

Nasrallah paced around his office, unable to concentrate. There were too many things going wrong. He left the room and marched along a corridor until he arrived at a small balcony. Below him lay the boundless majesty of the Atlas Mountains. For anyone else it would have been a breathtaking view, but for Nasrallah it meant nothing. He grasped the iron railing as one of his mobile phones rang again.

"What is it?" he barked.

"Word just in from Tripoli, Master."

The man's voice was trembling nervously.

"Speak up, imbecile!"

"Our operation there has been raided," he said. "Interpol has seized everything."

A rage consumed Nasrallah. He had already arranged to sell that operation. Everything was now resting on the sale of the artifact; an artifact that he still did not possess. Unable to control his anger, he hurled the phone over the railing and into the sweeping gorge.

CHAPTER 5

Central Jerusalem, Israel.

"The Compostela Cube is not in Rome, Mr. Nasrallah," said Christian into his phone. "My predecessor might have trusted in your abilities to find it, but I do not. I'll be using my own men from now on."

Christian made his way along a sunny atrium in the Vanderhoff Group's bustling Jerusalem complex. A tired Dr. Bennington followed two paces behind, struggling to keep up.

"But there is no need, sir," implored Nasrallah, knowing that he would receive no payment if Christian's men were to find the relic first. "I have confirmation that the Cube is in Rome. My men will intercept it at any moment."

"The Cube is in the south of Spain, you imbecile!" snapped Christian, his voice tight with impatience.

"But that's impossible…," said Nasrallah. "I can assure you it is in Rome."

"You can assure me of nothing!" hissed Christian angrily. "I, however, can assure you of one thing. If you don't produce the Cube in twenty-four hours, you'll be taken prisoner and tortured."

Christian pocketed his phone. After Bennington's hypnotic trance, he had not only become fully aware of the Cube, but also of the previous Nautonnier's dealings with Nasrallah to obtain it. No sooner had their plane landed than he had called the drug lord and demanded its delivery. His father's urgent whispers were commencing in him again, fueling a frantic desire to complete the transaction.

Christian and the doctor were now descending a broad, spiraling corridor, its paneled walls lined with beautiful works of art. Below them lay a massive underground complex, housing hundreds of employees, each working in departments ranging from finance to advanced biochemical research.

This was the Vanderhoff Group's central hub of operations, a maximum-security control centre buried deep beneath the city of Jerusalem. What had emerged in the late nineteen-fifties as a crude operations fallout shelter, had grown into a state of the art, and exceptionally elegant, corporate fortress.

Christian led the doctor to the door of an elevator, oblivious of the respectful nods he received along the way. He blinked into a retinal scanner and stood aside as the doors slid open.

"After you, Doctor," he said, ushering him in.

Minutes later the elevator doors slid open again, this time revealing a luxurious lobby, flanked by two walls of heavy glass shimmering under a rippling film of water. Directly before them was the beautiful young Cynthia. She stood behind a reception desk of polished granite.

"Good morning, Mr. Antov," she chimed as he approached. "All are present and waiting for you in the main boardroom, sir."

The thirteenth level was also the deepest level and reserved exclusively for the members of the Vanderhoff Steering Committee. Here could be found not only their offices, but their living quarters as well, along with all the amenities of a five-star hotel.

Christian proceeded at a relaxed pace. He felt truly in command of himself now and was possessed of a confidence that he had never known before. As he had expected, they arrived at the boardroom to find its occupants in an outrage.

Being ordered to the Jerusalem complex on such short notice was utterly unacceptable for the venerable committee members. They had barely had time to pack. In addition to this, the current state of the geopolitical arena was spinning out of control. Global chaos was bad for business, and this fact, coupled with Christian's irrational orders, made for a very hostile environment.

All rose in anger as Christian appeared, each one reprimanding him with heated words. They were the ones who gave the orders here, not some inexperienced boy with an ego the size of Manhattan.

Christian moved to the head of the sprawling table with Bennington a pace behind, a tranquil smile on his face. All could immediately sense that their angry words were having no effect on him. This was not the same novice they had met in Amsterdam. He exuded a confidence and strength that was illusive, yet undeniable, and there seemed to be a latent power in him that struck fear into their hearts, no matter how vehemently they denied it. Within a few moments their strong words had trailed off into a murmur of muttered curses.

"I thank you all for arriving on such short notice," said Christian, inviting Bennington to sit next to him as he spoke. "I can understand that it must have been difficult for you and your families."

He gestured towards Bennington.

"This is my personal advisor, Dr. Bennington."

"Just what are you getting at, Antov?" barked an old Texan on the opposite side of the table. "Where do you get off ordering this relocation without our approval? We're on the verge of a bloody world war, boy; one that's five years ahead of schedule!"

"I have arranged both this war and this relocation with perfect timing," said Christian dryly, "and if you give me an opportunity, I will explain."

The room burst into surprised dialogue. Who did this man think he was? It had not been two weeks since he had taken his new position. What did he know that they did not? Christian waited patiently for everyone to become silent and then continued.

"As you all know, our organization dates back far beyond the fifty years that the Vanderhoff Group has been in existence," he said. "It was founded by a society that is traceable to the time of Herod, with roots that go as far back as Ancient Egypt and Mesopotamia."

All were silent. Christian knew this would not be easy, but an explanation would have to be given in order to facilitate the next stages of his agenda.

"Throughout history many have tried to wrestle our power from us, but we have never given it up, and we never shall.

"There was, however, one man who succeeded in threatening our retention of power in a way that no other has been capable of doing. Despite our greatest efforts to undermine him, he continues to be a thorn in our side. He is a threat to our ultimate plan of world domination; a plan that we have been working to fulfill for more than two thousand years."

The group of octogenarians listened intently.

"His name, my colleagues, is Jesus Christ."

At the mention of the name the room burst into a series of guffaws and outright laughter. Had this debutant lost his mind? Next, he was going to force them all to attend Sunday school. This was preposterous. Several men stood up with the intention of leaving.

"You will sit down," said Christian with icy severity, "or everything you hold dear shall be stripped from you."

So poignantly malicious were Christian's words, that the old men fell immediately back into their seats.

"It matters not whether you wish to believe in Jesus Christ or not. This is of absolutely no relevance. What is of relevance, are the original teachings that this historical figure spread; teachings that our society has been very successful in repressing and distorting over the centuries.

"As you all know, if we are to remain in power, fear must be maintained in the masses. Unfortunately, a dangerous political and spiritual movement is about to be born, and it will undermine this fear if it is not stopped."

"Christian," said an octogenarian seated close by. "Please be more specific. What movement do you speak of? Surely, you're not referring to the Christian faith?"

"The Christian faith offers no threat to us," continued Christian. "On the contrary, our alterations have made it an invaluable vehicle through which to spread the fear and guilt needed to secure subservience.

"No, gentlemen. I am not referring to Christianity, but rather to the pre-Egyptian body of knowledge that was promulgated by the upstart Jesus Christ more than two thousand years ago. A body of knowledge that will be delivered to the entire world if the Compostela Cube is not recovered and destroyed at once!"

Again, the room burst into a frenzy, but this time one of utter disbelief. The lost Compostela Cube was a name familiar to them all. It belonged to a legend that was as old as their society. It was the harbinger of their doom. It was their nemesis. But this was only a legend, nothing more.

"With all due respect, Christian," said an old man, attempting to be reasonable. "You are now going too far. How can you expect us to take you seriously? The Cube is a myth."

The man looked around at his counterparts.

"Next you'll be telling us that the extra-terrestrials are coming."

They all laughed.

"The Cube of Compostela has been found," announced Christian amid their jeers, and in a split second every mouth had become silent, their faces aghast with disbelief.

Like any secret society, theirs too had its traditions and ceremonies, but they had lost their original meanings long ago. For generations the same words had been uttered: Ahreimanius, the Zurvanites, the Compostela Cube; but only as one might utter the name of an obsolete god. They were not real. They were stories. Fictions.

Nevertheless, many eyes fell on the coat of arms inlayed in the centre of the sprawling conference table. It bore an image of Set, the Egyptian god of chaos, surrounded by fourteen red eyes. Under Set's foot was the Cube of Compostela, and in the demon-god's upraised hands a spherical cage could be seen, with the fettered earth within it. It was from this image that the symbol for the United Nations had originated.

To all but very few, the secret society of Set had long ago become a society of business and politics, the Vanderhoff Group becoming its new face. Even still, in their vows of initiation, each member was made to swear a pledge of allegiance to their lord and master, Ahreimanius.

In this pledge, a promise was duly made to recover the Cube and destroy it. This was the first mission of every priest upon inception, a ceremonial rite that appeared, only now, to be revealing its true purpose.

"The Compostela Cube is a legend!" asserted a baldheaded man, breaking the silence. "It does not exist!"

"It is as real as this table!" affirmed Christian, bringing his fist down on the dark wood. "Our deceased Nautonnier, the late Father Adrianus Vanderwerken, was on the verge of acquiring it when it was stolen from under his very nose! It currently resides in the south of Spain and is in the possession of *The Two*!"

"Impossible!" exclaimed another man.

The Two had been mentioned in the legends as well. They were the sworn enemies of their society.

"Oh, come now!" exclaimed yet another. "Enough of this nonsense!"

"What proof have you got?" demanded the old Texan.

"The appearance of the Zurvanites is proof enough," replied Christian more quietly now.

"The Zurvanites?" balked the old man. "Are you mad?"

Christian watched as the men at the table began to whisper and chuckle quietly amongst themselves. He could sense the fear that lurked beneath their laughter, and as the merriment increased, it became clear to Christian that they were all in denial.

"Why, we're the Zurvanites!" cried one of them in jest.

"Be silent!" bellowed Christian, and his fury silenced them all. "I am the new Nautonnier!" And just as the prophecy foretells, I come to lay waste!"

With Christian's final words, there came an end to the merriment. Any remaining smiles had now vanished from the faces of the committee, replaced by their usual dry expressions. Time was money, and the destruction of the earth was bad for business. Their new director had obviously lost his mind.

In unison, every member of the group rose to his feet and proceeded to make ready to leave, shaking their heads in disbelief.

"If you're the Nautonnier, then I'm Peter Pan," said the old Texan.

"We'll be contacting the extended Vanderhoff group and informing them of your resignation, Christian," said another. "You've been reading too many of the initiation books, son."

"They're just stories, boy!" said a member who must have been in his nineties. "What you need is a nice long vacation."

Christian had anticipated such a response and had made the necessary preparations. He produced his mobile phone and sent a text message. Within seconds, armed security guards appeared at the door, sending a wave of surprise through the group of old men.

"Have you lost your mind?" exclaimed one of them. "Have you forgotten who we are?"

"You are nothing!" snapped Christian.

"This is madness!" cried another, holding the side of his head.

He had attempted to make his way past the guards and been delivered a backhanded blow.

"You will receive no assistance from us!" said another of the group, outraged.

"Oh, but I will," said Christian, growing calm again. "Of this you may be certain. You see gentlemen, you all possess something that I do not: Loved ones. Every one of you has family members who happen to be my guests in this facility, is that not correct?"

"What are you getting at, Antov?" said the old Texan. "By God, if you do anything to them—"

"I will rape your little virgin granddaughter before your very eyes, you arrogant fuck!" said Christian viciously. "You will all comply! The Zurvanites have come, and together we will destroy the earth! And when it lay in waste, we will build it up again as the Great Prison Planet of Ahreimanius!"

"You're mad!" cried out several of them in unison.

All eyes found Dr. Bennington.

"What have you done to him?" they demanded. "You're responsible for this!"

Dr. Bennington looked back at them pleadingly. It was true. He was responsible. Had he not hypnotised Christian, none of this would have transpired. He had awakened a slumbering fiend.

Bennington's eyes scanned the group of octogenarians. They were surrounded by security personnel, and he could not help but feel a certain compassion for them. As unscrupulous as they might be, they did not deserve to be used as pawns in the destruction of human civilization. The doctor hung his head in defeat.

"The Vanderhoff Group will lead the world into oblivion," said a fully composed Christian. "And just as the masses are molded by our media, so will the extended Vanderhoff Group be molded by those in this room. Like the rest of humanity, they too will serve our needs, ushering in a New World Order that will secure our dominion forever."

Christian moved to the centre of the table and planted both hands down on it in a dictatorial pose.

"I am the new Nautonnier," he said through steely eyes, "and from the ancient chamber of the *Kadosh Hakodashim* I shall rule the world. You will all bow to me."

And looking past their pale faces, Christian directed his attention to the head guard.

"Take them away," he said, yawning. "And bring me wine."

CHAPTER 6

Gibraltar.

Major Richard Roberts opened the throttle of his motorcycle and accelerated past the traffic that clogged Winston Churchill Avenue. It was always a busy route to the Spanish frontier, but today it was at a standstill. A foreboding dread had engulfed the Rock that morning, and it was not just the growing storm clouds that were responsible for it.

Roberts squinted into the gloom. Gibraltar, it would appear, was on the verge of being invaded.

"Major," came the crackling voice over his radio. "More Guardia Civil forces are arriving."

"Keep them on their side," he said into the receiver, his right eye twitching. "Form a line if necessary. Under no circumstances are they to cross the frontier. Is that clear?"

"Yes, sir," said the officer. "We will hold them back."

The major traversed the long stretch of tarmac that comprised the airport runway and blasted through the gates, racing alongside a queue of pedestrians. Thunder assaulted him as he arrived at the frontier, and even though he had known what to expect, seeing so many Spanish agents so close to the Gibraltar side of the border sent a wave of surprise and anger through him.

They've gone too far this time.

He navigated his motorcycle through the crowds until he arrived at the main border crossing. It was there where he found Captain Brown. Just like Roberts, he was clothed in dessert combat dress and body armour.

"Where's their commanding officer?" asked Roberts, dismounting.

"He's standing beside the customs entrance, sir," said Brown, pointing to the place.

Roberts nodded and turned to see several Gibraltar Regiment troop transports approaching fast. They were on the runway, their engines roaring as they raced towards them. Roberts put his hand on Brown's shoulder.

"Follow me, Captain."

"You will remove these men and let us pass at once!" ordered the Spanish officer, gesturing to the two dozen Gibraltar regiment troops that blocked the way.

"We'll do nothing of the sort," replied Roberts. "You've no authority to occupy positions on Gibraltar soil."

"We have been authorized by the European Union to deploy anti-terrorism forces throughout the entire Spanish Peninsula!"

The officer handed Roberts an official looking document stamped with the seal of the Spanish Civil Guard. Among many things, it stated that being a geographical part of the peninsula, Gibraltar fell under Spain's anti-terrorism jurisdiction.

"This does not originate from the government of Spain," said Roberts, returning the paper. "It comes from the Spanish Civil Guard. You have no authority to be conducting this operation."

"Yes, we do!"

Roberts shook his head in disbelief.

"I will consult with the E.U. concerning this issue. Until then, stand down. This is an official border crossing, and it must remain open."

"Spain's border is closed! It will only be reopened when we have occupied our positions!"

A violent clap of thunder shook the air.

"This is British soil," said Roberts, turning to leave. "I won't have it occupied by fascist paramilitary forces."

He had no sooner said this than things changed very quickly. A man emerged suddenly from the crowds on the Spanish side, not ten meters away. He wore a backpack and was crying out in Arabic. Before anyone could react, he had crossed the border and moved into the crowds on the Gibraltar side.

"Get down!" bellowed Roberts.

A deafening explosion shook the earth, and the crowds dispersed in both directions, leaving a mass of mutilated bodies littering the tarmac. Seconds later, a deluge of rain exploded from above, the coursing water mixing with the blood of the victims.

A handful of Guardia Civil agents took advantage of the resulting mayhem to cross into Gibraltar, taking up positions in one of the customs buildings along the frontier. Shots were exchanged, and within seconds a small war had erupted.

With the arrival of the Gibraltar Regiment troop transports, defensive positions were immediately established. All knew exactly what to do. The defence against a possible Spanish invasion at the frontier was one of the first scenarios to be learned by any new soldier in the regiment.

In a matter of seconds, the major and captain had retreated to a defence post that they knew would be there when they arrived.

"Captain!" bellowed Roberts over the rattling gunfire and thunder. "Relay these orders! Full deployment of *Siege Defence 1704*, effective immediately across the entire Rock perimeter!"

"Yes, sir!" bellowed Brown through the downpour.

Roberts watched the captain disappear into the tumult and made his way to where the temporary command post would soon be set up. He arrived to find it almost entirely assembled.

In the ten minutes that had passed since the skirmish had begun, tents had already been set up with important equipment rolling out of trucks, and a flurry of military technicians buzzing about.

The countless drills had proven effective, and in another five minutes the command post would be fully operational. As it was, they had already set up Roberts' field desk.

"Good work, boys," he said, watching as a battery of monitors lit up before him.

They contained feeds from cameras along the entire frontier, as well as from up the rock. Roberts studied the images more closely, not liking what he saw.

A dozen Guardia Civil agents were installed in the Gibraltar customs building. By taking this position, they had flanked the first defence post, and were currently exchanging fire with them. Roberts knew that it would not be difficult to flush them out. The tricky part would be doing it with as few casualties as possible.

They had been fired upon, and one of their men was down. He had the legal right to retaliate. The surveillance cameras would prove it. But this was not about killing. He wanted no more blood spilled. At that moment Captain Brown entered the tent, breathing rapidly and drenched from head to foot.

"Major Roberts, sir," he said. "The perimeter is now secured. We have isolated the forces in the customs building. What are your orders?"

Roberts pointed to one of the monitors.

"It looks like they could be planning a frontal attack to the west of the frontier," he said, and just then a violent thunderclap shook them. "I want that customs building hit and hit hard. Flush those bastards out of there immediately. Use delta tactics. I want them taken prisoner before the Guardia Civil gets any ideas of what to do with them."

"Yes, sir!" said Brown, turning to leave.

"And Captain," said Roberts, his right eye giving a quick wink. "Get me a casualty report."

"Yes, sir."

Roberts sat back in his chair and took a deep breath. It was imperative that he think clearly. As additional monitors were set up, he could see more and more of what was happening around the entire Rock. Gib was no stranger to attacks, and it was now fully mobilized.

Historically, Gibraltar had always been a bastion of British sea power, controlling virtually all naval traffic into and out of the Mediterranean Sea. The six square kilometre rock had been designed to withstand attacks from land, sea, and air, and housed a labyrinth of more than eighty kilometres of internal tunnels.

There were also massive caverns blasted out of the limestone. They comprised what was, in essence, a small underground city; barracks, mess halls, theatres, offices, a fully equipped hospital, and room for all of Gibraltar's thirty-three thousand residents. Roberts released a long breath.

Calm, cool, and collected, Major.

On the array of monitors before him, Roberts could see as much activity happening within the rock as without. Scattered over much of Gibraltar were gun installations. The Rock was literally bristling with them. Dozens were housed within heavy fortifications, many others cut into the sheer cliffs themselves, and all were fed by an extensive network of supply tunnels that were coming to life as he watched. Roberts could not help but smile.

The complex was extensive, boasting heavy ordinance, anti-aircraft guns, and state of the art surveillance systems, not to mention huge caches of ammunition, food, fuel, and medical supplies. Over the past three years the governor had worked diligently to revitalize the tunnels and bring the underground city back into a fully functioning military complex, something it had not been since the end of the Second World War.

"There are hard times coming," the governor had always said when asked about his tunnel restoration project. "When the crisis arrives, we must be ready to meet it."

It had been the governor's personal assets that had funded most of the renovations, including the excavation of residential galleries in the new lower level. Having never had a family of his own, the governor had adopted Gibraltar as his heir, and could see no better way to use up his enormous fortune than to prepare her for a storm that he was convinced would come.

"Casualty report, Major," came a voice from behind Roberts. "One KIA. Three more WIA."

"Who did we lose, Private?" asked Roberts, turning to face the soldier.

A series of lightning blasts lit up the tent, followed by an earth-shaking clap of thunder. Roberts saw the man's lips move but heard nothing.

"Who?"

"Private Morrison, sir!" he repeated.

Roberts slumped back in his chair, running his hands over his face. Morrison had only been twenty-one years old. He looked up at the monitor in time to see the customs building falling under attack. Tear gas was being used to flush the enemy out.

So far so good.

Roberts looked down at his pocket. His mobile phone was ringing.

"Is everything all right?"

It was Anita who spoke.

"Where are you?" asked Roberts, sitting up with concern.

"I'm still here," she said. "Gibraltar was just on the news. Everyone in town is talking about it. They're saying there's been a terrorist attack at the frontier. What happened?"

"Just that, cookie," he said, rubbing his eyes. "A suicide bomber. The problem is that the Guardia Civil are using the attack as an excuse to try and put anti-terrorism troops on our soil."

"Are things very bad?"

"Not really," lied Roberts. "They could be a lot worse. We'll have things set straight soon enough."

"Oh, darling," said Anita. "I'm scared."

"Don't be, cookie," said Roberts. "Everything will be fine. I'll call you later today and let you know how things are going."

"Be careful."

"I will."

CHAPTER 7

In the Strait of Gibraltar.

"Something's up," said Gabriel to Natasha.

They were sitting at the back of the fast launch. He had to speak into her ear to be heard over the roaring engines.

"I'll be right back."

Although unsure of the cause of the disturbance, Natasha was certain that something was not right. They were in open seas now, and the distant coastline was barely visible under a mass of angry black clouds. Amir was with the pilot at the front of the launch. He was talking on the radio.

Natasha watched Gabriel make his way to the bow of the lurching boat, his shaggy hair flying in the wind. Amir had just put down the radio. She could see them talking and could feel Gabriel's sudden concern.

Far to the right she could make out Gibraltar, rising from the sea like a faint triangular mountain. Above it, black clouds rippled with lightning. The Rock was under a massive stormfront. Perhaps this was why they were so far from the coast.

"There's been a change in plans," said Gabriel when he returned.

"What's happened?"

"A renegade branch of the Guardia Civil has used a terrorist strike as an excuse to occupy Gibraltar. The government of Spain's denouncing them, but they can't do anything about it. They can't spare the troops."

"That's insane. Did they get in?"

Gabriel sat down next to her.

"A dozen or so are holed up in a customs building. The border's closed and a Gibraltarian soldier's dead."

Natasha looked out at Gibraltar's grey-blue form. It seemed more like a ship of war than a land mass.

"So what happens now?" she asked. "That looks like a dangerous storm."

"It's coming from the south and moving northwest," said Gabriel, squinting into the wind. "We should be all right if we stick to our heading. Bahadur and his men left the Rock as soon as the trouble started. The sea around Gib is crawling with patrol boats now. It's a full-blown siege."

"Where's Uncle Marcus?" asked Natasha with concern. "And Suora and Fra?"

"They're in Gib but I wouldn't worry. That rock is the ultimate fortress. It's never been taken."

"And Bahadur and his men?"

"Moving towards the Moroccan coast as we speak. Our paths should intersect in about forty minutes. There's good news though, a chance we might be able to get the hostages out without doing any fighting."

"Really?" asked Natasha. "How can that be?"

"It would appear Nasrallah's belly up," said Gabriel. "He's broke. Hasn't been able to pay his men in months. Bahadur's already started secret negotiations to hire them all."

"Bahadur must be rich."

"He hasn't got a cent."

"Where will he get the money?"

"It looks like my father gave Marcus a stash of unstamped gold coins to keep for him," said Gabriel, shaking his head in amazement. "He'd found them in a sunken Roman merchant ship back in the day, and as they had no historical value, he decided to hold onto them. They were going to use them to buy the Cube, but since we've already got it—"

"We can use it to hire Nasrallah's men out from under him," interjected Natasha.

Gabriel shrugged.

"The gold should get Amir's family out safely," he said. "And some of those new recruits could help us get up to that labyrinth."

Natasha nodded in understanding.

"Spain's become a very dangerous place these days. An escort would be good."

Gabriel frowned.

"Marcus also hinted that some powerful people want us dead."

Natasha's expression mirrored his.

"They want the Cube…" she said, looking out to sea.

She recalled an entry she had skimmed over in the professor's journal. It had spoken of the existence of a dark organization, sworn to destroy the Cube. When she turned back to face Gabriel, he was holding two glasses and a small bottle of whiskey.

"Would you like a cocktail?"

Natasha remembered how he had asked Amir to bring it along and smiled at his foresight. She hated whiskey but a drink would probably do her good.

CHAPTER 8

The Mediterranean Sea, North-African Coast

It was only when they were right upon them that Natasha could make out the dozens of launches speeding over the sea to the south. She saw Amir point to them just as the pilot aimed the boat in their direction, its hull responding with an explosion of foaming seawater.

Unbeknownst to her, they had converged precisely as planned, not two kilometres from the city of Tetouan, their designated landing point.

Covered in their light absorbing anti-radar paint, the smuggling launches were difficult to see at first, even in the broad daylight. As they drew closer, Natasha was at last able to study them in more detail, observing the many occupants that filled them.

"Look, Gabriel!" she cried out, pointing to the launch at the head of the pack.

Sitting at its stern were three tiny figures, oddly out of place among the pirate-like men surrounding them.

"What the hell are they doing here?" exclaimed Gabriel, laughing with surprise.

It was as if the unexpected occupants had heard him speak. No sooner had Gabriel cried out than he could see them waving happily. Bishop Marcus, Fra Bartolomeo, and Suora Angelica, all smiling excitedly.

In fast launches, and on open seas at that their age? Have they gone insane?

Despite their concern, Gabriel and Natasha's hearts were filled with joy at the sight of them. In a matter of seconds, the boats had drawn together, their hulls bobbing up and down in the mid-sea swells.

"Ahoy!" cried the old bishop. "Well met, my dear ones!"

"Uncle Marcus!" cried Natasha in delight. "You're crazy!"

The bishop feigned consternation.

"Do you think I was going to let this man run away with all of our gold?" he exclaimed, resting a hand on Bahadur's massive back.

His response was deep and booming.

"Never have I met three more delightful bankers! Now follow our boat! The sooner we land, the better!"

They were soon speeding their way into Tetouan, its shining white beaches drawing nearer with every passing second. It was a small city, ancient by all standards, and built at the feet of the Atlas Mountains. Its clutter of whitewashed walls and green tiled roofs could be seen perfectly from their vantage point, a tangle of tight little streets and ornate balconies covering the hilly terrain like a textured quilt. The sky was clear and blue.

"What happens now?" asked Natasha over the roaring wind.

Gabriel shrugged and looked her way just as an explosion of seawater came up to douse them both. Natasha was having to hold on tightly now. The waves were getting choppier as they approached the coast, and it seemed like the speeding launch was spending about half its time in the air. Gabriel moved a little closer.

"We'll land in some dodgy place, no doubt," he cried, studying the lie of the approaching land. "Then we'll be shuttled off to Nasrallah's digs by a pack of cutthroats and pirates!"

Natasha beamed.

"How wonderful!" she cried. "And where exactly might these *digs* be located?"

"Up there!" cried Gabriel, pointing to the towering peaks, "About a three hour drive in from the coast!"

Gabriel's prediction proved to be more accurate than he had expected. After entering a sheltered fishing port, the procession of launches was soon taxiing into a grouping of dilapidated boat houses that stank of fish.

They were greeted by a motley group of rogues, the leader of which spoke only to Bahadur. Ten minutes later the same men were leading the way into a neighbouring garage where several Land Rovers were parked. Gabriel, Natasha, and the three elders entered one of the trucks, with Amir taking the driver's seat.

"Together again!" exclaimed the old bishop from the back seat, adjusting his vestments.

He reached forward, excitedly rubbing Gabriel and Natasha's shoulders.

"It would appear the adventure continues!"

"I'd say," said Gabriel, turning in his seat to face the three of them. "And what made all of you decide to come along?"

"I'm afraid it was my idea," said Suora timidly. "I felt that Mother Mary wanted us to come along. Why, I cannot say..."

"I only hope that we will not be a burden to you," said Fra, squeezing the old nun's knee. "When this woman gets set on something, there is no changing her mind."

"You could never be a burden, Fra," said Natasha. "And I'm glad that you acted on your intuition, Suora. An inspiration from the Blessed Virgin should never be ignored."

Compared to the strife that plagued the rest of the world, Morocco was a bastion of peace and tranquility. As they made their way up into the fertile mountains, one would never have suspected that the world was at war.

They were entering into Berber country now, home to an ancient people who lived in ways little changed from their original culture. The keepers of these lands spoke the same language and farmed using the same methods they had used since the times of ancient Egypt.

"The home of *Taric el Tuerto*," said Gabriel, rolling down his window to let in the mountain air.

"Taric the who?" asked Natasha.

"Taric the one-eyed," he said. "At least, that's what the Spanish called him. He was the Berber general who led the conquest of Visigothic Spain in 711, one of the greatest generals in history. His invasion was the best thing that could have ever happened to Spain, and to the rest of Europe for that matter."

"Why's that?" asked Natasha.

Gabriel surveyed the passing countryside, his shaggy hair blowing in the wind.

"The Moors brought everything that was needed to pull Europe out of the dark ages," he said. "No small feat considering the stranglehold the Vatican had on everybody at the time. It's thanks to the Arabs that European culture is what it is today."

As they bounded and bumped up the twisting mountain road, Gabriel talked about the Golden Age of Islam, an age of freedom and enlightenment, and he outlined some of the numerous influences that would eventually find their way into every culture on the planet.

For seven hundred years, he explained, Islam would cultivate art, science, philosophy and literature in Spain, making monumental advances in agriculture, law, medicine, technology, astronomy, and economics.

"It's no small coincidence that the Renaissance coincided perfectly with the re-conquering of Spain," he added. "As each of the Moorish cities fell into Christian hands, so did their vast libraries. Think about it. The world would never have known about Plato, and all the ancient Greeks for that matter, if it wasn't for the Arabic translations the Christians had captured. The Church had destroyed everything heretical centuries before."

Their convoy plodded its way higher and higher into the mountains. Behind them, and across a shimmering sea, lay a spectacular view of the Spanish mainland, with a storm enshrouded Gibraltar standing majestically at its prow. It would not be long now before they arrived at Nasrallah's castle. Its structure could be seen directly above them, a small square of timeworn stone atop a ragged peak.

"I sure hope Bahadur fixed things right," said Amir, a cinnamon toothpick clenched in his teeth. "I'd hate to have to get into a gunfight now. It would ruin our little trip."

Gabriel looked skeptical.

"I saw them loading an arsenal of weapons into the Land Rovers back at the boat house."

"Bahadur doesn't like taking chances, boss," said Amir. "But things'll go smooth. Gold makes people pretty friendly when they're passing it around."

Amir pulled up behind Bahadur's truck. The convoy had come to a stop and a pack of thirty or so armed ruffians had already assembled on the road, kicking up dust and checking their weapons. Bahadur approached Amir's side of the Rover, motioning for them to remain inside. Moments later his big head was poking in through Amir's open window.

"I trust that everyone has had an agreeable ride and that my cousin's driving was not too unpleasant?"

"He has done an excellent job," said Suora, her face lighting up at the sight of the giant.

Bahadur smiled tenderly at the old nun.

"It pleases my heart to hear that, Sister."

He turned his attention to Gabriel and Amir in the front seat.

"I will be continuing on foot with my men," he said, his voice taking on a deep and serious tone. "Amir, you will come with us. The rest of you will remain here until we send word. Please do not leave this truck."

"What are you talking about?" asked Gabriel. "I'm the one who caused this whole mess. You can't expect me to just sit here and do nothing."

"Dr. Parker," said Bahadur in earnest. "I can understand your wanting to help but your presence would only confuse the men. This is not about the Cube or my family for them. It is about changing their loyalty. You have done enough by financing this endeavor. Stay here and leave the rest to me. This is more a political exercise than anything else."

"Listen to him, boss," said Amir, clasping Gabriel's forearm. "He knows what he's doing."

"If all goes as it should," said Bahadur, "we will meet with our contacts outside the castle and show them the gold. After that, the only remaining objective will be to capture Nasrallah. For that we have more than enough men."

With that Bahadur reached in with a massive hand and gave Gabriel a heavy pat on the shoulder. He bounded off before Gabriel could respond.

"Stay put," said Amir, tying back his dreadlocks and leaving the truck. "Everything will be fine."

From their vantage point in the Land Rover, they could see Bahadur strapping guns and ammunition to his bulking body. Though he was by far the most powerful man in the group, his authority was founded more in respect than in his physical size. Bahadur was not like the other smugglers. He was intelligent and well-spoken, and would have led the life of an academic if the fates had been more kind. As a boy, he had dreamed of becoming a university professor, but being the son of a smuggler captain had made that impossible.

Having watched the armed party disappear into the rugged terrain, Natasha turned in her seat to face the old bishop.

"Gabriel and I only had a chance to skim through the professor's journal on the way down. Did you read it all, Uncle Marcus?"

"I did, my child," said the old bishop. "I spent all of last week studying it but I could hardly say I know it well."

Gabriel turned in his seat and told them everything he and Natasha had learned from the old gypsy woman. He explained the extinction level event that would soon take place, and told them of their impossible mission to find the Labyrinth of Sarras before the crossing of the Dark Rift occurred.

Suora immediately began to pray silently, but Bishop Marcus seemed more concerned with the note that had led them to the *Bodega Del Pi.*

"I must have missed it entirely," he said, baffled. "And I was of the belief that I had visited every page in the journal. It is a good thing that it found you."

Natasha could not bear the suspense any longer.

"Where is the Labyrinth of Sarras, Uncle Marcus?" she asked. "Did the professor know?"

The old bishop frowned.

"Yes," he said, "but that information died with him and Father Franco I'm afraid. All that we know is that the entrance to the Labyrinth is located on the same island where the tomb of St. James the Just was found."

"Yeah," said Gabriel. "We already figured that part out."

"So how do we find the island?" asked Natasha. "And even if we do find it, and we somehow manage to return the Cube to its original resting place, how are we supposed to pass through the labyrinth and open all the seals?"

With the day moving on, the sun fell heavily on the truck. The bishop looked over and spied a shady patch of grass beneath the cover of some trees. It was not far from where they were parked.

"What say you all to a picnic?"

"But your Excellency," said Fra, his Italian accent particularly thick in his distress. "Bahadur has told us not to leave this vehicle."

"Oh, come now!" said the old bishop, nudging the brother with his shoulder. "Don't be a stick in the mud! Since when were you one to follow orders from anyone but our divine Father in heaven?"

"Fra," said Suora, delivering a weak blow to his other shoulder. "A picnic would be lovely."

"Well," said the old brother reluctantly, thinking of the cooler in the back of the truck. "I did pack a bit of lunch before we left Gibraltar. Now would be a good time to eat it I suppose..."

"Done!" exclaimed the bishop. "Bring out that journal, child! We shall study it over a nice bottle of wine and some food. I am certain that it will yield all the answers we require!"

CHAPTER 9

Central Jerusalem, Israel.

Dr. Bennington followed Christian through the complex, but he was hard pressed to keep up with his pace. In the fifteen minutes since the boardroom meeting had ended, they had done nothing but walk. During that short span of time the doctor had witnessed a drastic change come over Christian.

It was as if a metamorphosis were taking place before his eyes. Gone were the subtle traces of Christian's self-doubt and fear. They had been replaced by a cold wickedness that seemed to radiate from every pore in Christian's body. Even his facial features had altered to suit, his paleness intensifying, and his eyes becoming hard and cruel.

Bennington battled his fear with professionalism. The dark self that Christian had spoken of had clearly taken over. It was difficult to pinpoint, but there was something about Christian that reminded him of a reptile, a cold-blooded predator. It was as if Christian's inner-demons were altering his physical appearance. Bennington had seen similar transformations in patients before, but never to this extent.

"Please, Christian," he said, breathing rapidly. "I cannot keep up this pace."

Christian made no reply but in that instant the doctor felt as though something were suddenly pushing him along, as though a strong wind were now at his back.

This is uncanny. Is it possible that he has developed telekinetic abilities? What other powers has he been given? Where is he taking me?

"I have been given nothing that was not mine to begin with," said Christian. "And in answer to your second query, I am taking you to a laboratory. Our scientists have been working on a virus for more than fifteen years now, and it has come to my attention that they have at last been successful with it."

They arrived shortly at an elevator and used it to ascend several levels, moving past a crowded reception desk and into a broad and sterile looking hall. To their left were the entrances to the employee decontamination rooms. Christian did not pass into these chambers, but instead approached a door situated directly next to them.

On the wall was a glowing hologram, a semi-spherical dome about the size and colour of an orange, positioned at head level. Christian stopped before it, a series of pulsating lasers scanning his face to confirm his identity. Seconds later he was leading the way through a thick metal door. It opened into a long glass tunnel, and Dr. Bennington was amazed by what he saw.

A dozen meters below them was an enormous underground cave, teaming with bustling scientists amid batteries of equipment.

"This is where some of the world's most advanced scientific research is conducted," said Christian, resuming his brisk pace as they made their way along the tunnel. "As you just saw with the facial scanner, we have already perfected the holographic interface, but there is much, much more."

"Why have you brought me here?" asked Bennington, struggling once again to keep up.

"Because I enjoy your company, Doctor," said Christian dryly. "I need to be here, and I thought you might come along."

They walked until they came to a second door of thick steel.

"This is the executive decontamination room," said Christian, blinking into another holographic scanner. "Here we will not have to remove any of our clothing. Instead, we will be exposed to a mild radiation. I assure you it is completely safe."

They entered what looked like a perfectly normal waiting room, containing several armchairs and a sofa. Christian invited the doctor to be seated, and then sat himself down as well. The only thing that seemed out of the ordinary in the room was a monitor over the door. On it were digits counting down from ten minutes. Bennington made himself comfortable in his chair. He was thankful for an opportunity to rest.

"Tell me, Christian," he asked. "How is it that you can know my thoughts?"

Christian raised an eyebrow. The answer to Bennington's question had only just occurred to him.

"Thoughts inhabit a field that exists outside of physical parameters," he said. "You might compare this field to magnetism. Both are invisible yet detectable by other means. If the mind is free of its own thoughts, it can sense the thoughts of others.

"Your thoughts appear to me as if they were my own, but as I know that I am not generating thoughts in my mind, it becomes clear to me that these thoughts belong to you.

"Like your thoughts, I can also feel your emotions. You are becoming more interested in me, Doctor. You are puzzled at how I can be so congenial, and yet so wicked at the same time."

"Yes, Christian, I am," said Bennington. "You've changed, and I'm hopeful that you'll now choose to use this newfound power to aid humanity instead of destroying it."

Christian smiled coldly.

"Humanity will be aided through its domination. This is what humanity wants and needs."

"How can that be, Christian?" asked the doctor. "The wish for freedom resides in the heart of every man, woman, and child."

"Yes," said Christian, "this is true. But the wish to obtain this freedom without paying the price for it also exists in every man, woman, and child."

"What do you mean? What price?"

"The price for freedom is responsibility, Doctor. I would think you would have discovered that by now. Humanity does not wish to be responsible for itself. It wants to do as it pleases, much like a child, and suffer no consequences for its actions. At best, people want an efficient government to carry the burden of their lives, at worst, they yearn for some god that will serve them like a magic genie. What rubbish."

Bennington was amazed. In all the years he had treated Christian, he had never heard him speak like this.

"The irony is that every living person could have all the freedom they desired, if they only took their lives into their own hands, but they are too lazy and frightened to do so. Because of this humanity requires a master, and a master it shall have in its new government."

"But your new government is built on lies and deception, Christian. How could that be good?"

Christian laughed coldly.

"In this world there is only one thing that is good," he said. "The good that comes from holding power over others. This is Earth, Doctor, not some fairy-tale land. Wake up. Your god is dead, and even if he does live, he doesn't care about us. The state of the earth, with all its poverty and injustice, offers clear enough proof of that."

Bennington considered his words before replying.

"Faith, hope, and perseverance empower us to evolve out of these conditions."

"There is no hope!" asserted Christian. "There is no faith! There is only survival. You and me and every other pathetic creature on this planet belong to only one master. We vowed allegiance to him aeons ago. His name is Lucifer, and he is our jailor."

Christian produced a cigarette and lit it, inhaling deeply.

"This is our lot, Doctor," he concluded, releasing a cloud of smoke. "Domination is our only saviour, not some weak little man hanging from a cross. Not some Indian telling us to weave our own clothing. What nonsense!"

Just then a chime sounded, and Dr. Bennington looked up to see that the time on the clock had elapsed.

"Come with me," said Christian rising. "I will show you the future."

CHAPTER 10

Los Picos de Europa, Northern Spain.

"How I would love to know where you are taking me, my friend," said Isaac, looking above him to see Shackleton standing at attention.

The dog was perched atop a large boulder not ten meters away, and at first glance it seemed to Isaac that there was an aura of light surrounding the animal, one that disappeared the moment he attempted to verify its existence.

"Just give me a chance to catch up," he complained, resuming the climb. "A slave driver is what you are..."

Considering Isaac's weakened state, they had made very good progress. Two days had passed since they had left the island behind, but instead of making their way down to the coast, Shackleton had been leading them higher into the mountains. Isaac followed faithfully. It was clear the dog had a plan, and that he would soon be finding out what it was.

In the meantime, Isaac was simply content to be alive. He could not help but marvel at how quickly his mental health had returned since he had stopped taking the medication. Everything sparkled with clarity, and it seemed to him that both he and the world had been reborn. He found himself perplexed as to why Father Adrianus had been so insistent that he never miss a dose. The old priest had been adamant about it, and for the first time in his life, Isaac felt an unmistakable distrust for the man.

He had spent the better part of the day going over all the events that had transpired since the plane had crashed, giving particular attention to the tribulations he had suffered at the hands of the demons. He recalled how Ahreimanius had mentioned a Cube, and how he had told him that he would never allow him to assist the Two in their endeavors. Ahreimanius had clearly been referring to the same Cube that Father Franco had written of, but who were the Two? Isaac looked searchingly at Shackleton as he arrived at his side.

"Who are you, my friend?" he asked. "And why did you come to save me?"

Shackleton looked back at him playfully, as if telling him to stop thinking and enjoy the scenery. They had been following a narrow goat herder's path for most of that day, and it was clear that the dog was enjoying the trek tremendously.

Isaac looked out from their perch. Around them the land had taken on a barren and rocky character, foreign to the lush green that had been their surroundings up until now. Here the earth was dry and of a russet colour, with only tangled and brittle shrubs dotting the otherwise barren sections of rock. Isaac used a hand to shield his eyes from the sun and gazed far into the south and west. There was not a village in sight.

Abandoning his search, he saw that Shackleton had decided to lie down and take a break. He joined him happily, and after sharing some water with the dog he pulled out Father Franco's diary, deciding to have another look at a map he had found there the night before. He used the sleeve of his tattered suit jacket to wipe the sweat from his brow.

There simply must be a way of locating our position in these mountains...

Over the past two days Isaac had found many puzzling things in the notebook, but none more so than the existence of the two orphans named Gabriel and Natasha. After much struggling, he had remembered why their names seemed so familiar. It had been his secretary who had first called his attention to them, more than thirty years before, when he was still in the employment of the church.

"This is very peculiar," she had said, holding up a document. "Have you seen this week's adoption summary?"

Isaac had been gazing out the window of his office at the time, lost in grief. It had not been a month since his young wife had died and he was still reeling from the loss.

"It says that two newborns were admitted into our agency this morning," she told him. "A boy named Gabriel, in our Taiwan orphanage, and a girl named Natasha, in the Argentine shelter. The bizarre thing is that both of them were born in comas, just like your child, Mr. Rodchenko. What a strange coincidence, wouldn't you agree?"

"Yes, indeed," he had said. "And the circumstances?"

"Unwed teenage mothers. Both gave birth to their babies on the same day that your child was born."

Isaac looked out over the mountainscape, turning the event over in his mind. Gabriel, Natasha, and his own son had all been born at precisely the same hour. The church document confirmed it beyond a doubt. What was more, all three children had been in rare coma vigils at the time of their births. The chances of this happening were incalculable, and that they should all be connected directly to him made the coincidence impossible to ignore. Isaac frowned. What did it all mean?

Flipping back to the map, Isaac could see that it covered a section of the north coast of Spain. At its centre was a circle marking the general vicinity of the island where they had just been, as well as another mark a good distance from it that was labeled *Monastery*. Isaac squinted at the page. Scribbled beside the map was an itinerary.

Day 1: Final rites and burial at the island.
Day 2: Make camp and rest.
Days 3-5: Expedition to the Rex Angelus Monastery.

Isaac was baffled.

What monastery?

He looked up from the book to see that Shackleton had risen again. He was sniffing at the air, scanning the horizon and growling at what he saw. A wall of heavy cloud had amassed in the east. It was advancing like a great curtain, its darkness accentuated by the white gulls that flew up against it. Isaac rose with a groan. What approached them was nothing short of a tempest. They would need to find shelter at once.

CHAPTER 11

The Atlas Mountains, Morocco.

Bishop Marcus insisted on not uttering a single word about the mission until they had each had at least one glass of wine and some of the crustless cucumber sandwiches that Fra had brought along. The day was turning out to be magnificent, and from their shady picnic blanket beneath the olive trees they could easily reach the nearby Land Rover should a speedy retreat be required. Bahadur would not be too upset with them.

"I must apologize for my initial reluctance," said the old brother as he proceeded to slice a leg of lamb. "Your Excellency has once again made a wonderful suggestion. This is beyond a doubt the most glorious spot in all of Morocco. Thanks be to God."

Everyone watched as the old brother worked on the lamb.

"After all," he added, "it could be hours before Bahadur returns, and why not have a nice lunch in the meantime?"

"We will be sure to save him a portion!" chimed the bishop, popping the cork from a second bottle of wine.

The birds sang happily in the trees above, and the lazy afternoon soothed their bodies like the best of tonics. Gabriel breathed in the fragrant air. He was sitting with his back to an olive tree, in one hand a glass of wine and in the other a savory hunk of brie folded into a piece of crusty bread.

"How about it, Marcus?" he asked, languidly looking over at the old bishop. "You've got the Cube and the journal sitting right there, and you've already had two glasses of wine. No more excuses. Tell us about our mission."

"Most certainly," said the bishop, draining his glass. "Now is the time."

Hearing the bishop say this, Natasha came over and sat down beside Gabriel. Suora began to cry with happiness.

"For more than thirty years I have prayed to the Blessed Virgin to see them together," she said, and immediately Fra rose from his place and came to comfort her.

"Their love is true," he said, caressing her back. "Blessed be their union."

Natasha turned to look at Gabriel only to find him frowning into his glass of wine. The bishop noticed too but said nothing. Suora was meanwhile letting Fra guide her to their place on the blanket. They sat down side by side and continued with the preparation of the food.

"Well," said the bishop. "Let us speak of your mission, no?"

"Sounds good to me," Gabriel said petulantly, snapping out of his reverie. "How do we find the Book of Khalifah? How do we open the seals?"

The bishop held out his hands in a gesture of patience.

"Before I can attempt to answer those questions," he said, "you must first understand what your overall objective is. You said that you have gone over the journal's contents?"

Natasha shook off her funk and sat up a little.

"We've only skimmed through it, Uncle."

"Very well," said the bishop, nodding. "We shall begin at the beginning. Are either of you aware of the philosophical concept of the Divine Spark?"

"Of course," said Natasha. "It's our higher-self. The Cosmic Consciousness. Our God-self. It resides in all of us."

Gabriel rolled his eyes.

"Indeed," said the bishop, noting Gabriel's reaction. "And all these names refer to our true, albeit forgotten identity; the very essence of ourselves. Put simply, your primary objective is to re-establish contact with this inner-being."

"And how are we supposed to do that?" asked Gabriel. "That sounds a bit abstract, don't you think?"

"That is where your mission comes in," said the old bishop. "As you move to the centre of the Great Labyrinth, so too will you move to the centre of your own being. With every passing stage, communication with this perfect inner-being will become less and less obstructed, until your higher-self will finally and completely express itself through you."

"And then we'll know all the answers and we'll be able to pass them on to everyone else," said Gabriel in a disbelieving tone.

"Yes," said the bishop. "That is more or less the idea."

"Well, excuse me for being so blunt, Marcus, but what's the point? Why do we need to establish contact with this inner-being in the first place? Everybody seems to be getting along quite fine without it. What's the big deal?"

The bishop paused to consider, sipping at his wine and looking up into the trees. A nice breeze was rustling through the leaves now. It sent fragments of golden sunlight over their picnic blanket.

"Connecting with the higher-self is the most empowering thing that anyone could ever possibly do, my son," he said, bending towards Gabriel and lowering his voice. "It is the true meaning and purpose of life. Anything that we have ever accomplished that has had any value has always come from our higher-self."

He leaned back and studied Gabriel's face.

"The trouble is that most of us are only connected to a fragment of our higher-self at best. Making a full and unobstructed connection to it is the reclaiming of a long-lost, god-like power."

Gabriel moved his glass into a shaft of sunlight, watching the little pool of wine shimmer and glow.

"That sounds really great," he said. "Too bad it's all nonsense."

The old bishop smiled patiently and turned to Natasha.

"Did you have a chance to study Gutierrez de la Cruz's version of *The Great Fall of the Angels*?"

Natasha shook her head.

"Very well," said the old bishop. "I will quickly go over it then. There are many variations of this story in cultures around the world, but Gutierrez's version explains our human condition quite well."

The bishop reached for the bottle of wine and filled Gabriel's glass, topping up his own as well.

"According to the story," he began, "the souls that constitute humanity originally abided in the higher spheres, or in heaven, if you will. Countless worlds existed there, with an endless variety of experiences to be had.

"You see, God had given to each of his created beings tremendous power, and the free will to use this power as they saw fit. He had also, however, warned them against using certain aspects of this power, stating that they ran contrary to his universal laws, and that they could ultimately be destructive."

"And this is a myth, right?" said Gabriel. "We're not supposed to take this literally."

The old bishop nodded patiently.

"These things can only be related through myth, my son. What actually happened would be impossible for us to understand. The spirit world is quite simply inconceivable to us. The function of this myth is to embody the essence of the event of the Great Fall so that it might be understood. In this respect it is very truthful."

Gabriel nodded and motioned him to go on.

"According to the story," continued the bishop, "the first to test out the forbidden powers that God had warned us about was one of God's highest angels. His name was Lucifer, and he was the *Archangel of Illumination*, also called *The Morning Star.*

"Lucifer had shown great promise and was destined to be one of the greatest beings ever created. The trouble was that he had long been questioning Christ's supreme position and wondered why he should have to occupy a place inferior to that of the Christ.

"None of the other angels thought there was much danger in Lucifer's observations, but over time, like a bad seed, Lucifer's contentions grew into pride and envy, and were the eventual cause of the fall."

"And exactly what was this fall?" asked Gabriel. "Mythically speaking, of course."

"It was a mass exodus of spirit entities from paradise, my son. Spirit entities that would later incarnate on earth as human beings. To put it simply, Gabriel, we are all the once fallen angels. Every human being ever to have lived was an angel in heaven before he or she was lured away by Lucifer's lies and promises.

"You see, by tapping into the power that God had warned him not to use, Lucifer generated a force that ran in an opposite direction to divine law. He used this dark power to tempt us into following him, and of our own free will we did just that.

"The tragic consequence of this power was that every divine aspect of God was turned automatically into its opposite when it was used. New *dualistic* universes were created as a result.

"In these spheres, harmony gave birth to disharmony, light created darkness, love spawned hatred, and so on. After that, wholeness split further still, and the more the pull of temptation proceeded, the worse the fractured state became. Eventually, the spheres of Hades came into existence."

"I remember reading an entry in the professor's journal that mentioned this," said Natasha. "It said that the fallen angels made hell for themselves."

"How does that work?" asked Gabriel.

"A universal metaphysical construct," said the old bishop. "According to Gutierrez, every spiritual entity creates his or her own physical world, and that world expresses the state of mind they happen to be in.

"When like-minded entities gather together, their collective states of mind construct the worlds in which they collectively live. One world may be heavenly, while another may be hellish; it all depends on how spiritually evolved the entities abiding there are."

The bishop took another sip from his glass.

"In the case of hell," he said, "the spirits abiding there had fallen to such a degree that the world they created was utterly opposite to that which could be found in heaven. It was a reptilian sphere, and utterly evil. The darkness there was so complete that they could not even conceive of having once been creatures of the light."

Natasha looked over at Gabriel.

"In the journal, your father said that countless spheres exist between the extremes of heaven and hell. He said that the earth sphere is one of them, but that what makes it unique is that it's perfectly in the middle. Humans are equally exposed to good and evil forces here. That's why our world is the way it is."

"It is precariously balanced, my child," said the bishop. "One push will send it spiralling either upwards or downwards, and that push will come at the time of the crossing of the Dark Rift. The outcome will depend on the mindset of humanity as a whole."

"That's a crazy concept..." said Gabriel, thinking. "It basically states that the physical exists as a result of the spiritual.

He looked over at the bishop.

"It's the opposite of what everyone thinks."

The old man smiled.

"The spiritual is nothing other than a state of mind," he said. "It is the state of mind that creates the state of body, and all things material."

Gabriel paused to consider the implications.

"Consciousness creating the physical world," he pondered. "It reminds me of the double-slit experiment."

The bishop and Natasha both gave Gabriel a puzzled look.

"It's a quantum mechanical experiment," he said with a shrug. "It's boggled the minds of scientists since the beginning of the twentieth century. It uses an electron gun and two slits in a metal barrier to isolate the basic principles of what you're talking about.

"In a nutshell, the experiment points to a conclusion that states that it must be our minds that create the physical universe, and that we do this simply by *observing* things; by being conscious..."

The bishop nodded.

"Can you both now see the connection that Gutierrez is making?" he asked. "If our state of mind creates the world in which we live, then it would be necessary to possess a more evolved state of mind in order to create a better world for ourselves to live in."

Gabriel rubbed the stubble on his face. As mind boggling as it was, the concept seemed logical enough, even on a personal level.

"Like good days and bad days..." he said, thinking. "The world seems to literally transform around you when you're in a good or bad mood. The natural tendency is to blame the day's events for the mood you're in, but what if it was the other way around?"

"Moods are born from mindsets, my children," continued the bishop. "And mindsets are what heaven and hell are made of, along with all the worlds that lie between them. The higher spheres are simply societies of purified entities living together in heightened states of mind.

"Whether we are aware of it or not, it is the goal of everyone on this planet to restore these forgotten states of mind and return to the paradise we left long ago. It is your mission to unlock the knowledge that will help everyone to achieve this goal. That knowledge resides in the Cube."

"And we release it by re-establishing contact with our inner core being?" asked Natasha. "With our Divine Spark?"

"Precisely!" exclaimed the old bishop. "This will happen as you make your way through the seals and into the centre of the labyrinth."

"Opening up a stairway to heaven..." said Gabriel, shaking his head. "Pardon me for saying this Marcus but that sounds absolutely ludicrous."

"If you say so," said the bishop, smiling. "But keep in mind that the heaven we search for does not lie outside in the clouds, as Michelangelo would have us believe. The true heaven lies within and is a very long journey away for most.

"Heaven is arrived at one step at a time, and according to Gutierrez, humanity is now ready to take its next step towards it. Let us concentrate on moving humanity to the next higher sphere, shall we? No need to go barging straight into heaven. There will be time enough for that."

"And what will this next sphere be like?" asked Natasha. "Does the journal say anything about it?"

Fra and Suora had by now finished preparing the lamb sandwiches. They placed a tray of them on the blanket and the old bishop's eyes lit up.

"It says that the next higher sphere, or the next *inner* sphere, depending on how you decide to look at it, will be much like it is here, only better," he said, picking up a sandwich and biting into it. "There will be no more war. Neither will there be greed or envy. There will be abundance for all."

He took a sip of wine.

"People will live in peace and prosperity," he said, "and the situation will be such that greater, and more purified states of mind will be achievable. More and more people will understand the universal laws and live by them. Our upward cycle of evolution will continue."

"And what about death?" asked Natasha, taking a sandwich. "In the higher spheres do people still die?"

"Nobody ever dies, child," said the old bishop with a gentle smile. "Death is truly an illusion. Gutierrez does, however, state that reincarnation will still be necessary in the next sphere, as will the death of the physical body, but aging will occur at a much slower rate. People will stay younger longer."

"And what about sickness?" asked Natasha.

"Sickness will take on different forms, but it will not entirely disappear either. Gutierrez states that physical sickness is a direct result of spiritual sickness, and while we are evolving, it is sure to exist, even in higher spheres.

"Pain and suffering will also continue to exist in the next higher sphere, for they are a necessary means of spiritual purification. Even still, our tribulations will be looked at very differently once we have made the transition. They will be accepted and embraced with maturity, because the truth behind them will be fully understood by all. Humanity will see things differently by and large. We will be more evolved."

"Gotta like that," said Gabriel, rising to his feet with a pessimistic smile. "I think I could really get into accomplishing this mission.

"Become my inner god-self and then move up to a higher sphere where everybody's chilled out and enjoying life to the max. Sounds like a blast."

Natasha glanced up at Gabriel only to see the smile vanish from his face. Coming from very close by could be heard the roar of engines, and the rattle of automatic weaponry.

Gabriel frowned when he saw two Land Rovers speeding past on the road below them, one in the lead and another giving chase under heavy fire. As they passed, he saw a hand emerge from the leading truck and lob something into the window of their parked Rover.

"Incoming!" he cried, pushing Natasha and Suora to the ground and covering them with his body.

The ensuing explosion shook the earth. Luckily, the hillock on which they had laid out their picnic gave more than adequate protection from the blast. Even still, their ears rang painfully.

Gabriel jumped up and ran to the roadside in time to see the Rover that was giving chase lose control and swerve off the mountain road, its wheels destroyed by the blast. The sick crunching of steel was soon followed by a massive explosion, the flames of which engulfed the entire switchback below.

It was from out of these flames that Gabriel saw the leading Rover emerge unscathed. It roared past the wreckage and sped off and out of sight.

Returning to the picnic spot, Gabriel saw that although everyone was considerably shaken, no one had been injured. Natasha ran to him.

"What happened?"

Gabriel was trying to collect his thoughts, his head still reeling from the explosion.

"I don't know for sure," he said. "My guess would be that Nasrallah was driving the truck that got away. The guy at the wheel was too well-dressed to be a guard."

"And who was in the other Rover?" asked Natasha.

"I don't know..." said Gabriel, a shadow of worry engulfing his features. "I couldn't see them clearly, but one thing's for sure. They were our guys."

"Bahadur..." said Suora, bringing her hands to her face.

"I don't think so," said Gabriel. "I would have recognized him by his size."

"What about Amir?" asked Natasha with concern.

Gabriel did not reply. He squeezed Natasha's arm and ran off in the direction of the flames.

CHAPTER 12

Bahadur made his way into the safety of the castle amid the incessant clatter of gunfire. He moved briskly but silently, scowling with worry.

Nasrallah knew we were coming. There must have been an informer.

He played the events out in his mind as he hurried forward, thinking back to when he and his men had first arrived at the rendezvous point.

As arranged, they had been met by a small group of smugglers who had taken a handful of gold coins to show the others. Not twenty minutes had passed before they had returned, stating that all had gone well, and that the men were now officially under his charge.

Bahadur had been delighted. To make such a change in command with absolutely no bloodshed was unheard of. He had followed his men to the castle's entrance where they were happily greeted by all.

"We have locked Nasrallah in his quarters, Captain!" said one of the smugglers, slapping him on the back. "There he will remain until you decide what to do with him!"

What happened next had shocked everyone. They had no sooner entered the courtyard than three guards began to open fire on them from the watchtower above. Most of the men had scattered into the shelter of the surrounding arcades, but two had been killed instantly.

Bahadur had managed to find cover behind a column, while Amir, along with three other men, had taken shelter beneath a large bronze basin, located in the centre of the courtyard. There they had remained, trapped beneath the gurgling fountain amid a rain of bullets.

Perched as the snipers were, it had been impossible for the men below to strike back at them, and all were forced to remain under cover, unable to retaliate.

With his enemies trapped in the courtyard, Nasrallah had appeared outside the castle gates. Accompanying him were three men, but the hostages were nowhere to be seen.

From their respective vantage points, both Amir and Bahadur could see that Nasrallah was on the verge of getting away, but to pursue him would be suicide. The snipers in the tower would cut them down before they were halfway out.

Bahadur saw Amir talking to his men. They appeared to be studying the round basin under which they were hiding. Something was afoot.

"Free our family!" bellowed Amir to Bahadur.

Seconds later, he and his men had given the basin a consolidated shove, succeeding in separating it from its stone base. In moments they had perched it on its side, effectively creating a moveable shield. Bullets bounced off the heavy bronze as they rolled it out of the courtyard, making their way to the front gate where they exchanged fire with Nasrallah and his men. The villain had only just boarded one of the many Land Rovers parked there, and in seconds he and his men were off, with Amir and his team in pursuit.

After seeing this, Bahadur wasted no time. With Nasrallah gone there was only one thing left to do: Find his family. Screaming orders to his men, he disappeared into the castle, an intense feeling of dread filling him to the quick. Nothing was going as planned. Why would Nasrallah not have taken the hostages with him? Was his family already dead?

Bahadur arrived at the entrance to the lower levels and descended into the dungeons at full speed. The surroundings were familiar here, and he thought back on his life as a smuggler. Everything seemed so different now.

The fact that his dealings had reached a point that the lives of his very own family had become endangered had changed everything. What had he been thinking? Stealing, lying, killing, cheating. How could his actions not have come back to him? As it was, the people he most dearly loved were in tremendous danger, if not already murdered, and it was entirely his fault.

Bahadur rounded a corner and knew instantly that he was in the right place. It was not the dark stone arches and crudely hewn ceilings that gave him this certainty, but rather the damp stench in the air. It was an odour that only years of incarcerated humans could create. There was a pungent density about it, one that could be sensed on the tongue.

Making his way slowly forward in the dim light, Bahadur tripped over something lying on the ground. It was a smuggler, the body still warm. He squatted down, checking for a pulse. There was none. In the shadows by the door he spotted yet another body, a pool of dark and glossy blood spreading out around its head.

Bahadur readied his gun. To his left he could see a looming passage and he suddenly realized how Nasrallah had appeared outside. The passage led to a secret exit, one that opened onto the castle grounds not a stone's throw from the main gates. It had been built by the Moors centuries before as a means to flank enemy forces attacking the castle. Today, Nasrallah had used it for his own purposes.

Bahadur inched his way forward, pressing his massive body up against the damp stone. Caution would be necessary. If Nasrallah had been able to secure the loyalty of the men in the watch tower, he could easily have left a guard or two behind.

Bahadur was in the process of berating himself for not having brought a few men along when he heard a faint moaning coming from just ahead. He rounded the corner, inching his big head out to see a man sitting on the floor, his back against the wall. He was holding his stomach, and his shirt was soaked in blood.

"Elakhdar…" whispered Bahadur, frowning.

He was Nasrallah's second in command. He was a good man, and Bahadur had known him since childhood.

"My dear friend," he said quietly, kneeling at his side. "You have been hurt."

Elakhdar winced in pain.

"He asked me to betray you but do you know what I said?"

"What did you say, my friend?" asked Bahadur, smiling tenderly.

"I said that you were too big and too ugly to betray."

Bahadur frowned at the joke. There was too much blood.

"Where are you hurt?" he asked, looking for the wound.

"Nasrallah's a dirty swine," said Elakhdar. "He wanted to kill your family one by one until you gave him the Cube and the gold. He sent three of his men down the tunnel to prepare the escape and ordered me to kill your Jadda and leave her body hanging for you to find. When I refused, he ordered his men to shoot me, but I shot them first."

"It would appear they shot you also," said Bahadur, finding the wound and attempting to staunch the flow of blood.

"When I looked up to kill that pigdog, I saw him running away into the tunnel like a coward. I shot but I did not strike him."

Elakhdar swallowed hard. He was fighting to stay conscious.

"Bahadur," he said quietly. "We are not murderers. Perhaps we are criminals, and mercenaries too, but we are also fathers and sons and husbands. We are just men. We do the best with what we have been given."

At this point the captain began to tremble uncontrollably, the blood welling up into his mouth. Bahadur knew there was no hope for him. He held his shoulder, his other hand pressing down on the gushing wound.

"My dear friend…" he coughed.

"Quiet now," said Bahadur in a voice as soothing as he could muster. "Do not speak."

"Go to your family, Bahadur," he said. "They are well. They will be happy to see you."

Bahadur looked up hopefully, peering into the dimly lit tunnel where he knew their cell would be. When he returned his gaze to his friend he saw that he was dead.

Passing a hand over his open eyes, Bahadur bowed his head and thanked him silently. If his family was alive, it was because of Elakhdar's great sacrifice. It would never be forgotten.

CHAPTER 13

Central Jerusalem, Israel.

Dr. Bennington peered out into the adjoining space. A second door in the decontamination room had just slid open, revealing an expansive laboratory beyond. He followed Christian out into it, and immediately noticed the quality of the air. It was utterly clean, bereft of even the slightest odor.

Around them milled dozens of scientists dressed in white overcoats and wearing face masks and head coverings. They nodded respectfully to Christian as they passed, some even bowing.

"It is just up ahead, Doctor," said Christian, leading the way into a high security area labeled *Biological Defence.*

Christian approached a heavy glass door secured by a holographic scanner. Its pulsating lasers mapped his face and then sounded a soft chime, opening the way before them. Within they passed through a maze of blinking machines and apparatuses, arriving at last at what looked to be a large holding tank situated in a corner of the space.

Although it was covered by a thin curtain, Bennington could still see motion within, and he immediately sensed that something dark and sinister was at play. When they were approached by a white-robed scientist he knew his fears were about to be confirmed.

"Mr. Antov, sir," said the scientist, excitedly pulling aside the sheet. "Your timing is perfect."

Having caught a glimpse of what lay within, Bennington instinctively turned and walked away.

"We were only just going to call you, sir. I can now state quite confidently that we have at last perfected the virus."

Christian raised an eyebrow.

"Its genetic propagation has been stabilized?" he asked, moving towards the glass container.

"Why, yes sir, it has," said the scientist, surprised by Christian's knowledge of the project. "The dead tissue has been fully reanimated. By modifying the double-stranded RNA to suit this specific species, we have completely eradicated any traces of DNA polymerases, thereby increasing the mutation rate. The virus is in a constant state of healthy propagation, sir. This is quite unique, given the highly irregular host environment."

Bennington moved towards the tank reluctantly, knowing that a ghastly sight awaited him, but unable to curb his curiosity.

Dead tissue reanimated? What on earth are they talking about?

He arrived at Christian's side in time to see a savage attack occurring. Within the glass tank could be seen a line of seven monkeys, each one chained securely to its base, yet free enough so as to be able to make contact with its immediate neighbours.

Whereas the monkeys to the right of the tank seemed healthy, those to the left appeared to be wounded and rabid. They jerked and strained against their bonds in savage bursts of energy.

What in God's name are they doing to these poor animals?

There was something very unsettling about the enraged monkeys. Their eyes were bereft of life, and the many wounds they had were grey and bloodless. Their emaciated lips were drawn back like those of a corpse, and there was something utterly unnatural about the way that they jerked and twitched, something that seemed completely alien to the natural fluidity of motion characteristic to their species.

"You will be amazed to know, Doctor," said Christian dryly, "that the monkeys to the left of the tank are all clinically dead."

Dr. Bennington was speechless. The evil he was witnessing had left him trembling, yet he could not avert his eyes. The three animals to the right of the tank were clearly still alive, their eyes wide with panic. Directly to their left however, one monkey lay dying, its face utterly destroyed. The grey-faced beast responsible for its wounds was straining against its bonds, licking frantically at a pool of blood that was emerging from the dying monkey's head.

"Watch," said Christian. "The virus will propagate the moment the monkey's brain dies."

To Dr. Bennington's horror, no sooner had the wounded monkey ceased its death rattle than its eyes opened once again, a new savage energy beginning to imbue its body. In a matter of seconds it had leapt to its feet, savagely attacking its healthy neighbour until it too lay dying at the base of the tank.

"What have you done?" gasped the doctor, looking to Christian pleadingly. "What madness is this?"

"We have raised the dead," said Christian, smiling coldly. "Just like Jesus did. It is a miracle. By introducing a specially engineered virus into the dying tissues, we have in essence genetically reprogrammed every cell in the body to conduct itself according to very specific criteria.

"By extracting energy from the host's very own cells, the virus propagates itself into all tissues, mutating them in a way that they begin to function once again, only this time without the need of blood flow or a brain to command them."

"But how is this possible?" asked the doctor. "What is giving them the innumerable orders needed to maintain life?"

"There is only one order to obey, Doctor," said Christian casually. "That is the order to feed. As long as the monkey can introduce more cellular fuel into itself, it will not need to consume its own cells. As far as the intelligence needed to govern cellular activity is concerned, this has been programmed into the virus itself. Virally secreted neurotransmitters mimic the brain's natural messages throughout the organism."

"But how can this be?" asked the doctor, aghast.

"Technology," said Christian dryly. "Technology and dogged perseverance."

He turned to face the scientist.

"Show me the humans."

"Yes, sir," stammered the researcher, surprised by Christian's demand. "We have set up the experiment, but we were waiting to conduct further tests on the monkeys before proceeding."

"There is no need," said Christian. "We will conduct the experiment at once."

* * * * * *

Dr. Bennington sat in his armchair. Above the door he could see the clock counting down from forty minutes.

"I apologize for the length of this decontamination," said Christian, "but leaving the facility is considerably more dangerous than entering into it. I am sure you can understand why."

The doctor looked at Christian but did not reply. He was still in a state of shock. What he had witnessed was more than any man could possibly be expected to endure.

Those poor people. What had they done to deserve that?

He sat shaking in his armchair, unable to remove the grisly images from his mind.

"Why, Christian?" he heard himself asking. "Why are you doing this?"

Christian yawned.

"The earth's population must be culled to a more manageable size," he said plainly. "The virus will help to kill off two-thirds."

Bennington could not muster the will to respond. Christian continued.

"The spirit of the world must be broken as well, Doctor. All hope must be annihilated. Seeing the dead walking and consuming the living will aid in this endeavor. A new age is dawning, one that has been meticulously planned since the creation of this pathetic planet. When all hope has been destroyed, the world will bow to its true master."

"You won't succeed," said Bennington at last. "God won't allow it."

"God has no choice in the matter," said Christian gravely. "His laws require that we use our own free will to liberate ourselves. This will not be possible when all hope is lost."

Christian crossed his legs casually.

"You see, one cannot ask for liberation if one does not know what liberation is. And if one does not ask, one cannot receive. Total darkness will once again return. God's foolish plan of salvation will have failed, and what was once Lucifer's, will return to Lucifer, only this time he won't make the mistake he made before. His new prison will be made inescapable."

"You will never succeed in destroying all the love and hope in this world, Christian."

"Even love and hope will eventually die in the absence of light."

"There will always be light!"

"Maybe so, my good doctor," said Christian, "but not for those on Earth. My society is making very sure of that."

"What do you mean?" asked the doctor. "What are you saying?"

"I'm saying that dark days are coming. They are already upon us. As the decades pass, more and more people will forget what it was like to be free."

"Nevertheless, there will always be scores who will oppose you," said Bennington. "How will you do away with all of them?"

"The only way to truly destroy your enemy is to make him use his own power against himself. In this way you guarantee his complete demise."

"And how do you propose to do that?"

"Propose?" smiled Christian. "Yes, perhaps at one point we did propose, but now things are much further evolved than that. Where should I begin? Perhaps in the protocols that our founders laid down. Each of them revolves around the same basic principle: *Take the best in man and distort it so that it becomes the worst in man.* The desire for freedom, for example, is the strongest desire, but it is prone to corruption by its very nature."

"Is that so?"

"Yes," said Christian. "Because along with the desire for freedom, comes the dread of slavery, and when threatened by this fear, a man can be made to destroy the very freedom he longs to preserve."

"And how would you make everyone on the planet feel so threatened?"

Christian smiled.

"With the mainstream media," he said. "We have already done it as a matter of fact. We have changed the content of traditional entertainment and shifted the trends in pop culture so that they reflect the decline of society. We have given the masses antiheroes instead of heroes; vampires instead of angels. We have made innocence and purity look sickly, and wickedness look strong and sexy.

"We have flooded them with a regular stream of scandal in the government, pointed out every lie, every deception, every lowly act by our leaders, and turned it all into cynical humor on night-time talk shows. We have shown them the hypocrisy that resides within the very political institutions that were once deemed the envy of the free world.

"We have begun to destroy the dream, Doctor, and replace it with the image of a fallen nation; a fallen world. People will soon long for a return to the Golden Age. They will hunger for it."

"And that's why you've given us President John F. Abbot," said Bennington. "You even used JFK's first two initials. Our President is a false King Arthur..."

"You are beginning to understand, Doctor," said Christian, smiling coldly. "In his false attempts to restore freedom, the President will dissolve the constitution and extinguish the last of what used to be the United States of America. He will officially usher in the North American Union, and this union will be a police state.

"There will be no elections of any consequence, and he will remain in office as a dictator. Biometric technology will monitor everyone. There will be no more freedom. This is the birth of the Fourth Reich, Doctor, just as it was planned to be. It will be a New World Order."

"But how can this be true?" asked Bennington. "You are telling me that our demise has been planned since the beginning of the world itself. That there is no hope..."

"Hope for power over others, Doctor," said Christian, "and learn to hate me, for you will soon have great cause to do so."

With these last words the chime announced the end of the decontamination period. Dr. Bennington watched Christian rise to his feet and leave the chamber. Very slowly the old doctor forced himself to stand. He would follow his captor. He had nowhere else to go.

As he made his way down the long glass corridor, he could see the scientists milling about below him, and the memory of the horrific human experiment came flooding back into his mind.

"They have no idea what they are a part off... God forgive them."

CHAPTER 14

The Atlas Mountains, Morocco.

Natasha pushed open the door to see Gabriel sitting next to the bed, his eyes glued to Amir. The latter lay there unconscious, his head wrapped in blood-soaked bandages. His face was severely lesioned, and his naked upper body was covered in burns and lacerations.

Gabriel's dear friend was dying and there was nothing anyone could do about it. The nearest hospital was in Tetouan, over three hours away, and the signs of internal bleeding were everywhere. He would never survive the bumpy ride. He had but hours to live.

Gabriel looked up at Natasha and the events played out in his mind again. He had sprinted down the perilous incline, taking a direct route to the burning truck. Before reaching it, he had found Amir on the ground, his head dashed against a stone. There had been no breath in his lungs, and only the faintest trace of a heartbeat. In a matter of minutes another Land Rover had arrived, and working together, they had loaded Amir into it and sped him back to the castle.

Natasha laid a gentle hand on Gabriel's shoulder, looking down at Amir's battered face. There was a regular flow of clear liquid coming from his ears and nose, and his pupils were dilated to different sizes. These, among other things, were indisputable signs of a brain hemorrhage.

"We're losing him," said Gabriel, his voice choked with grief.

Natasha sat down next to him. She could see he was battling with anger and frustration. In the little time she had known Gabriel, she knew he was not one to sit around idly, but this time there was absolutely nothing he could do.

Natasha remained silent. She was holding the professor's journal in her lap, trying to find the right way to tell Gabriel what she had just learned.

He'll never accept what I must tell him. He'll say it's nonsense...

Even still, she knew it was Amir's only chance.

"Gabriel," she said slowly. "Would you try anything to save him?"

Gabriel nodded silently, reaching over to wipe some of the fluid that oozed from his ear.

"There's nothing we can do, Natasha," he said, smiling sadly. "He's a goner."

Natasha opened the book.

"I was just talking to Uncle Marcus," she said gently. "He believes that there's a way to save him."

Gabriel looked over at Natasha, his haunted eyes penetrating hers.

"Praying isn't going to do it this time."

"Uncle Marcus was saying we could use the Cube to make Amir well."

Gabriel's expression changed. He frowned in confusion but there was a trace of hope in his eyes.

"What are you saying?"

Natasha opened the book to the page she had marked.

"He showed me an entry your father made several years ago. It speaks of the Cube's power to heal."

Gabriel glanced down at the book but remained silent.

"It says all we have to do is intend to heal him and the Cube will make it happen."

Gabriel sat up in his chair and then rose to his feet, his mind beginning to awaken. The Cube harboured a strange technology, this was indisputable. It could respond to their thoughts, but was that enough to perform miracles?

He recalled how it had exploded with energy when Natasha had kissed him in the Chamber of the Sphere, and it dawned on him that he could not begin to explain how any of that had happened. The hologram the Cube had generated was beyond any present-day technology as well. He stopped pacing and looked hard at Natasha.

"Tell me what I have to do."

Natasha smiled gently. Gabriel truly was a fighter. She proceeded with caution, knowing he would not like what she was going to say.

"We'll have to spiritually merge."

Gabriel fell back into his chair, his frustration returning with increased intensity.

"I can't make myself believe in unicorns and fairies, Natasha," he said through clenched teeth. "Just forget it."

He turned his back on Natasha and bent over Amir, his eyes filling with tears.

"Maybe it's not like that, Gabriel," he heard her say. "Maybe it has something to do with the neuro-feedback technology you were talking about."

Gabriel jerked his head around to face her.

"What are you saying?"

Natasha swallowed. Gabriel had frightened her.

"I'm sorry," he said quickly, seeing the effect his words had had on her. "Tell me what you're thinking."

Natasha looked down at the journal.

"When we were having our picnic, Marcus said there was no difference between what's called *spiritual* and what's called *state of mind*. They're both the same thing. The Cube seems to be able to sense our state of mind, so maybe if we both shared the same state of mind, that might be like spiritually merging…"

"And what state of mind would that be?" he said, his pessimism returning.

Natasha remained patient.

"Perhaps one where we are open to each other and not guarding ourselves so much?"

Gabriel frowned angrily.

"I'm not guarding myself against anyone!" he snapped.

Natasha sighed in resignation and stood up wearily. It seemed to her that she had been in this kind of conversation a hundred times before, and it had always gone nowhere. This time she had finally learned her lesson. She would never try to change a man's mind again. It was pointless, even if someone's life hung in the balance. She walked towards the door.

"I'm so sorry, Gabriel," she said gently. "Really I am."

Gabriel looked up.

"Wait. What did that gypsy woman mean when she said that we had been infected with demon parasites?"

Natasha turned around to face him. The room was dimly lit but she could see his eyes in the light of the bedside lamp. There was a tragic desperation in them, and Natasha had to fight back her tears. Gabriel seemed to her like a proud lion who had just been fatally shot. He was giving up, but there was something so dignified about his surrender. So noble…

She looked at Amir and wondered if he was not already dead. He seemed to have stopped breathing. She moved to Gabriel's side and knelt beside him, placing his father's journal on the bed.

"I think the gypsy woman was using a metaphor when she referred to the parasites," she said, opening the book again. "She was probably referring to a psychological malady that effects everyone to a greater or lesser degree."

Gabriel glanced down at the book and saw an illumination of a serpent above ornate Latin script.

"*Vermis Eorum Patebit Indignitas,*" he read aloud. "The Worm of Unworthiness."

Natasha looked up at him.

"That's what your father called the demon parasite. I've got it pretty bad, Gabriel. I never realized it until recently, but I've never felt I deserved to share a true connection with a man. I always felt myself unworthy of that kind of love."

Gabriel looked over at Amir, torn between his concern for his friend and for what Natasha was saying about herself.

"You're wrong, Natasha. You're more worthy of that kind of love than anyone I've ever met."

Gabriel was silent for a while, thinking.

"To be honest," he said at length, "I've always felt that way too, although I don't think I ever realized it until just now. It's so strange…"

Natasha was still kneeling beside Gabriel. She put a hand on his leg and looked up at him.

"What is it, Gabriel? Tell me."

Gabriel looked deeply into her eyes.

"I've lied to myself this whole time. You were right when you said that a pretty woman broke my heart. I always blamed her, but the problem was me. I sabotaged it all. I didn't feel I could actually have that kind of love."

Gabriel got up and began to pace. He needed time to digest all this, but he did not have that luxury. Amir was dying. If the Cube was truly their only chance at saving him, he had to get to the bottom of his neurotic behaviour quickly.

"For some reason I always felt I was prohibited to have the things I longed for," he said. "Love, riches, fulfillment... The way I dealt with it was to rebel. If I wasn't allowed to have riches, then I'd just steal them and the world could go to hell. That's why I do what I do, Natasha. I'm a grave robber. I do the same with love. Sure, I tried to make real love happen, but when I couldn't do it I decided to steal love as well, this time by paying women to love me."

Gabriel continued pacing.

"But lately it's all been falling apart," he said after a moment. "There's been this nagging emptiness in me, and my way of dealing with things hasn't been working anymore. All those girls, all that treasure... They couldn't help me..."

Natasha rose to her feet and peered into his eyes. She had never seen him looking so vulnerable.

"How do you feel right now, Gabriel?"

He shrugged and looked away.

"You make the emptiness in me go away somehow," he said, shaking his head in confusion. "I know I'm not worthy of you. I can't even consider... You're good and true and I'm... I'm a creep..."

Natasha smiled gently and took hold of his hands.

"You are many things, Gabriel Parker, but a creep isn't one of them. I think you're wonderful. And you're not a grave robber. You find things that were lost and you put them in museums where everyone can see them. You're the most amazing man I know. Can't you see? It's just this thing that we've been infected with; this *worm*. It explains everything."

Gabriel looked back at her in mild astonishment. He could sense the truth in her words but something in him still refused to accept them. Natasha continued before he could reply.

"And you were right when you said I wanted to punish myself for betraying myself. I always rejected every good man that came along. Can't you see, Gabriel? This is the parasite. There's no reason why either one of us doesn't deserve to love and be loved. We're both more than worthy of it."

Gabriel looked over at Amir, his brow furrowing.

"I can't let him die, Natasha. Not like this."

"Then we must make him well again. I know the Cube can do it."

Natasha walked over to her pack and brought out the artifact.

"Let's at least try, Gabriel."

Gabriel nodded and moved to stand facing her. Together they held the Cube and looked into each other's eyes.

"What do we do now?" he asked.

Natasha glanced over at Amir and then brought her attention back to Gabriel.

"Maybe we let ourselves love each other?" she asked timidly.

Gabriel could not stop himself from smiling with affection, despite his grief and concern.

How could I not love you?

"I suppose I could give that a try…" he said instead.

Natasha smiled back and in that moment it became irrefutably clear that something extraordinary existed between them. Neither could say exactly when the love had surfaced, or where it had come from, but it was here now and there was no denying it.

"Let's do this," said Gabriel in earnest. "Let's light up this Cube and fix Amir once and for all."

Natasha nodded slowly; her eyes misty as Gabriel's lips met hers.

In that moment the Cube exploded with energy. They could both see its light through their closed eyelids, but they paid it little heed. There was something far more magnificent igniting within and between them. It was an indescribably potent force of the purest and most passionate love imaginable; an erotic, pulsating, elevated vibration, exploding with the vigour of life itself. It seemed to them older than the universe, yet fresh and blooming, and it coursed through them with the strength of a thousand quasars.

* * * * * *

In the very same room that Amir had witnessed a man getting shot by Nasrallah, a meeting was taking place between Bahadur and the smuggler captains. On one side of the table sat the Moroccan contingent, on the other, the Gibraltarian.

Among them were Bishop Marcus, Suora Angelica, and Fra Bartolomeo at the insistence of Bahadur. It was they, after all, who had made the rescue of his family possible by providing the gold needed to contract Nasrallah's small army. Bahadur had not forgotten the agreement he had made with the old bishop before they had set out from Gibraltar.

"Gentleman," he said in his deep basso.

He was standing like a battered stone buttress at the end of the long table, his dark military fatigues stretched over his bulging muscles.

"Our mission is accomplished. The hostages have been liberated and Nasrallah has fled in defeat. We shall soon be back in business!"

In an instant the smugglers were on their feet, raising their glasses and sounding a cheer. When all were done drinking Bahadur motioned them to sit down.

"We will now have to restructure our new organization," he said, remaining on his feet. "This will prove to be no small task."

"That's why we brought you along, mate!" said Scotty Roberts.

He was reclining in his chair, his feet propped on the table as he casually lit one of his cigarillos.

"Just don't screw it up!"

Bahadur looked over at the unruly smuggler. He sat next to the old bishop, an infamous Gibraltarian, hated and adored but known to all. His ash-coloured hair was shoulder length, and a solid gold bust of Jesus Christ hung from his neck amidst a tangle of thick gold chains.

He drained his wine theatrically, breaking into a grin that would have made his worst enemies smile. Like the best of criminals, Scotty Roberts was extremely charismatic, and even the old bishop could not help but like him.

"I will try to not disappoint you, old friend," said Bahadur, crossing his arms and looking at the colourful smuggler with a twinkle in his eye.

"You'd better not," said Scotty, a deadpan expression on his face. "Or I'll have to take you outside and give you a sound thrashing."

The idea that Roberts could have given the giant a thrashing was ludicrous, and all burst into laughter. Bahadur feigned a worried frown and chuckled merrily.

It was amidst the laughter that Gabriel and Natasha made their entrance, and their effect on the gathering was considerable to say the least. No sooner had their faces been seen than the gaiety in the room ended. The old bishop rose to his feet.

"How fares that good-hearted soul?" he asked, his voice strong, but bereft of hope.

Gabriel and Natasha looked at each other and smiled.

"I think he's going to be all right," said Gabriel slowly.

Immediately the group burst into yet another cheer, rising to their feet and laughing aloud.

"It's a miracle!" cried someone.

"It'll take more than a bashed skull to stop Amir!" cried another.

When the cheers had died down, Bahadur addressed Gabriel and Natasha.

"Sit down, dear friends," he said, pointing out two empty chairs at the table's end. "You have brought news that I would never have dared hope for."

Gabriel shrugged and pulled out a chair for Natasha.

"He's completely healed," he said, sitting down and glancing over at the bishop. "There aren't even any scars."

No sooner had he said this than everyone became silent. These were tough men. Their lives were hard won, and if one belief tied them all together, it was that nothing in life was easy. Good things came at a price, and miracles belonged in fairy tales. Gabriel's words had filled them with disbelief. Scotty Roberts seemed to be having the most difficulty with the news.

"Now just hold on a bloody second, mate," he said to Gabriel, swinging his feet off the table and leaning forward in his chair. "Just what are you saying? I was there, comrade. I held his bloody crushed head in the Land Rover and he was as good as dead. What do you mean he's got no scars? That's bloody bullshit!"

Natasha could feel Scotty's fear and doubt. Before Gabriel could respond she stood up and spoke.

"Scotty Roberts and one of the Moroccan captains will come with me to inspect Amir's wounds. I would invite all of you, but I think it would be best to leave Amir as undisturbed as possible."

Scotty remained seated. He seemed to be struggling with himself.

"Come along, Mr. Roberts," said Natasha, crossing her arms. "I'll take you to him and then you can tell everyone what you've seen."

"Don't be frightened, my boy," whispered the old bishop with a wink. "This is just the beginning."

Roberts glanced over at the old bishop and stood up, his brow furrowed.

"Very well, Princess," he said, regaining his composure. "Let's go take a look at the Lord's handiwork."

"I will accompany them," said the Moroccan captain named Bahaddine. "I will bring word of the gifts of Allah."

The group remained silent until the three returned. Bahaddine appeared calm and collected, while Roberts' face was white, and clearly distressed.

Noting the silence that had befallen Gibraltar's most boisterous smuggler, all knew that something very important had transpired. Gabriel's earlier words seemed to take on a much more mysterious quality now.

"Well?" asked a Moroccan captain seated next to Bahadur. "What have you to tell us, Mr. Roberts?"

All watched intently as Scotty looked back at his questioner. He produced a cigarillo and lit it under the flash of a wooden match, his eyes still locked with the man.

"Bloody Christ in heaven," he said quietly, breaking at last from his silence. "If I hadn't seen it with my own eyes, I'd have never believed it was possible."

"Believed what?" asked another from the Gibraltar side.

He stood up and leaned over the table.

"Speak up, man! What did you see?"

"He should be dead," said Roberts, turning to look at his countryman. "I saw his head pissing blood all over the bleeding truck. His skull was crushed, man. I loved him like a brother but there's no way he could have survived that injury."

"What did you see?" demanded another.

An impish smile appeared at the corners of Scotty's mouth; his cigarillo still clenched in his teeth.

"By my word, mates," he said aloud. "I just saw that son of a bitch looking better than he has in years! When he gets home, he'll have a good shag waiting for him to be sure! Bloody hell, he looks so good I'd shag him myself if I'd had enough to drink!"

All remained silent, puzzled by his odd humour.

"I'm telling you, you thick headed rogues! It's just as our good archangel Gabriel here says, goddamn it! Amir's as right as rain! Sleeping like a bloody baby he is!"

In an instant the table exploded into excited amazement, each and every captain bursting into dialogue with his neighbour. Scotty's repeated affirmations rode over top of the din like a broken record.

"I'm not taking the piss, man! He's just like new! The son of a whore! He's as right as rain!"

Bahadur was the first to call for silence, and slowly the ruckus came to an end. Everyone gave him their undivided attention.

"My dear friends," he said, a great smile spreading over his broad face. "I can think of no better gift than having Amir back with us. I will not say I understand, but I am sure there is an explanation for what has happened, as sure as there is a sun in the sky.

"We will listen to what Gabriel and Natasha have to say, and we will begin to understand. Of this I am sure."

All looked to the couple, but Bahadur had not finished.

"Before I let them speak," he added, holding up a bearlike hand, "I will remind them that we are all in their debt, and that we will help them in any way we possibly can. Are we all in agreement?"

"Aye!" cried Scotty, bringing his fist down on the table.

And then looking to the bishop, and then to Gabriel and Natasha he said:

"Whatever you need, I'm at your service!"

"As am I," said Bahaddine, coming to his feet.

"And I!" said yet another, rising. "Long live our new captain!"

One by one, as was the way of their band, they rose and swore their loyalty to Bahadur, offering their help to Gabriel and Natasha as well. An unprecedented feeling of union and trust was being shared among the normally bickering smugglers. Something magical was in the air.

"So how about some explanations, mate?" asked Scotty, exhaling a billowing cloud of smoke. "And best try to keep the wording simple on account of all the numbskulls present, myself included," he added with a wink.

Gabriel and Natasha then told them all about the Cube, and how they had used it to heal Amir. They gave a detailed account of its history, and all the things that had happened up to then. They told the smugglers of the ancient myth that surrounded the artifact, of the Cube's mysterious powers, and its ability to unite the world in a new modality of peace and prosperity.

They also told the men of Nasrallah's dealings with a secret society who for more than two thousand years had sworn to see the Cube destroyed, and of their uncanny ability to know where the artifact resided at all times.

Gabriel and Natasha also warned them of the dark forces that this society was in league with, of the cosmic clock that was ticking as the earth made its way closer and closer to the galactic plane, and of the dark world that would ensue, should they not succeed in fulfilling their mission.

This was to return the Cube to its original resting place at the entrance of the Great Labyrinth of Sarras, and to open the seven seals of gnosis that resided therein.

In short, Gabriel and Natasha told the company of captains everything they knew, along with all the questions that still remained unanswered, leaving out no details so that everything might be open and transparent.

Not one of them doubted what they were being told. The artifact had brought Amir back from the brink of death and left him perfectly healed. This was proof enough.

When they finished speaking Natasha passed the Cube around the table for each man to examine.

"Wherever this labyrinth lies," said Bahaddine, turning the artifact in his hands, "my men and I will see that you arrive there safely."

"As will mine," said another captain solemnly.

"And mine!" said yet another.

From his new place to the right of Gabriel, Scotty was the last to examine the glowing Cube. He held it up before him while the others spoke excitedly, testing its strange density and studying the runes inscribed on its glowing surface.

On the smuggler's face was an expression foreign to all those who knew him. It bore a mixture of purpose and determination, oddly out of character with his normally carefree spirit.

While many discussed how Gabriel and Natasha might be brought safely through the war zone of central Spain and up to the northern coast, Scotty sat silently, weighing the severity of the situation at hand.

"You haven't said anything about the exact location of this labyrinth, mate," he said quietly to Gabriel, giving him back the Cube. "Only that it's on a small lake somewhere in the mountains. I've flown dozens of shipments to Santander. Lots of lakes up in those parts, comrade. Too many to survey in just four days."

Gabriel took the artifact from the smuggler and frowned.

"I know," he said, placing it gently on the table before him. "That's what worries me."

CHAPTER 15

Gibraltar.

Major Richard Roberts stood perched along the battlements at the highest point of the Rock, the earth curving along its horizon in a panoramic, nocturnal view. It was from this point where the extent of the siege was most visible, and a glance through his night vision binoculars confirmed the dozens of Guardia Civil vessels anchored around them on all sides. At the frontier he could see the Spanish troops amassed, a formidable force to be sure, but nothing they could not handle.

"Captain Brown," he said into his radio. "What's the status of the northern fortification?"

"Eighty-five percent complete, sir," came the crackling reply. "It's been fully armed and operational for twenty minutes now, sir."

"Very well," said Roberts, his right eye blinking. "Let me know when it's complete. I'd like to inspect it personally."

"Yes, sir," said Brown. "Anything else, sir?"

"That's all, Captain. Over and out."

Roberts resumed his surveillance of the Bay of Gibraltar below.

What the hell are they doing this for? What could they possibly have to gain?

Roberts' phone rang. It was Anita.

"Richard I'm scared," she said. "I wish I was there with you. The Guardia Civil are everywhere. They call themselves anti-terrorists now, but all they do is terrorize. They take away anyone who talks back to them, accusing them of being terrorist sympathizers. The old villagers are saying that it's even worse than during the times of Franco. I'm scared to get in the car. They've put check points up everywhere."

"Everything will be fine," said Roberts. "Just don't go out unless you absolutely have to, and don't draw any attention to yourself. The last thing we want is for them to find out you're married to a Gibraltarian officer."

"But I am Spanish!" she said. "I have my rights!"

"Listen, cookie," he said in earnest. "Just lay low. Please. Soon this will blow over and they'll open the border again. When that happens I'll come and get you, but until then be invisible."

Roberts knew that Anita was crying on the other end of the line. He waited patiently.

"On the news they're saying that the Muslims are rioting all across Spain," she said at length, "but it's a lie. I was just talking to Blanca in Madrid. She said there have only been a few demonstrations there, and that they've all been peaceful. She says the Muslims are all terrified. The news is making it look like a war's being waged between them and the Christians. Why are they doing this?"

"They want to scare everyone so they can put the army on the streets," said Roberts. "I'm not sure what's going on, but this is bigger than just Spain. The same things are happening all across Europe. Orders are coming from the highest levels of the EU. Something's up, and it doesn't look good. Until I can get you out of there I want you to lay low."

"Is that an order, Major?" asked Anita with a sniffle.

"Yes, it is," said Roberts, smiling tenderly.

"Well then I'll just have to obey my commanding officer," she said quietly. "I miss you."

"I miss you more."

CHAPTER 16

Los Picos de Europa, Northern Spain.

The storm had only just blown past when Isaac and Shackleton made their way into the tiny hamlet. The village sat on the peak of a mountain, and above it the fleeting clouds were already dispersing, leaving behind a clear and star-studded sky.

Isaac had spotted the village through the downpour before sunset, and he had resolved not to stop until they arrived. He approached a stone building that looked to be the village inn, his legs shaking from exhaustion. Its painted sign was well lit.

Pension Santiago. Comidas y Camas.

The door opened before he could reach for the bell, and an ugly, scowling woman appeared on the threshold.

"This village is not on the pilgrimage route!" she snapped.

She was eyeing Isaac suspiciously, taking note of his tattered suit and frayed white collar. They were stained with days of hard travel.

"We are not used to foreigners here!"

"Buenas tardes, señora," said Isaac, dizzily. "Do you have any rooms available for the night?"

The woman continued her surveillance. He and the dog were sopping wet, and she glanced past them in the direction they had come.

"Where are you coming from?" she demanded. "Who else is with you?"

"No one else, madam," said Isaac, a little confused. "It is just myself and my good dog."

Isaac gazed past her into the common room. Through the open door he could see several tables, all empty save one where a group of people sat eating, their dogs lying at their feet gnawing on bones. Behind them a crackling fire burned in a broad hearth. His stomach rumbled audibly.

"We have no rooms available!" barked the woman suddenly. "And there is no food here!"

She slammed the door and Isaac heard the clank of a deadbolt finding home.

"I suppose we'd best keep looking," he said to Shackleton.

The latter was sniffing at the door, as if unable to comprehend the woman's rudeness.

"Aren't you a noble one!" came a friendly voice from behind.

Isaac turned to see a young woman approaching. She bent and ruffled the fur behind Shackleton's ears, smitten by the enraptured expression on his face. She was fashionably dressed, her messy hair dyed blue, and her lips and nose pierced.

"*Buenas tardes*, young lady," said Isaac, with a weary smile.

In the background he could discern the tinny sounds that escaped her headphones, and he realized he had not been heard. Isaac waited patiently until the girl looked up at him and then pointed to his ear.

"My apologies," said the girl, removing her headset.

She stood up, continuing her play with Shackleton. He had clamped his teeth onto the end of her scarf and was engaged in a gentle game of tug of war.

"Do not pay any attention to our innkeeper," she said, squeezing his nose in an effort to get him to loosen his grip. "She is a horrible woman."

Isaac shot a glance at the closed door.

"Yes," he said. "I can see that."

"Are you looking for a place to stay?"

Isaac nodded.

"Then come with me," said the girl happily. "Your dog has won my heart."

They set off at once with Isaac having to make an effort to keep up with the girl's skipping pace.

"There are not many young people left in our village," she said, her Spanish accent becoming more noticeable now. "They have all moved to the cities."

Isaac peered around at the dark and lonely streets as they hiked along. The somber village seemed as old as the mountains, its squat stone buildings ancient among the hollow sounds of their footsteps. There was an indescribably morose atmosphere to the place; as if ghosts of the bygone Spanish Inquisition still haunted the damp gothic arches, and the wrought iron balconies.

They had not been walking long before a pounding rhythm could be heard rising from the ground, and soon the girl led them through an old wooden door and along a gloomy stone corridor. It ended at a spiraling flight of steps that took them into a dungeon of sorts. Isaac was very surprised by what he saw.

Deep in a cellar, the village youth had made a clubhouse, one that seemed more like a Barcelona booze can than anything else. In the blacklight he could see dozens of people huddled together in groups, the smell of hashish and tobacco filling the air. A large screen had been erected amid the dark arches, and a projector was illuminating it with strange images and video clips that mirrored the throbbing electronic music.

The girl entered ahead of them, moving into the space to talk with one of the two young men who appeared to be the creators of the show. While one was mixing the music, the other was using a laptop computer to compile the video sequences that were being projected.

It was with this boy that the girl spoke. Isaac saw him turn his head and look at them, a friendly smile on his face. He motioned Isaac to come closer.

"Welcome to our social club!" he said.

He was bobbing up and down to the music, but still managed to lay a friendly hand on Isaac's shoulder.

"I hear that you met *la bruja*."

He bent for a moment to ruffle Shackleton's ears. Isaac smiled and nodded.

"She should have been burned at the stake with all the other witches!" said the boy over the music.

And then looking to the girl he added:

"*Nena!* Take our guests to the Chamber of Honour and feed them!"

The girl clapped her hands in delight and wrapped her arms around the boy's neck, giving him a long and passionate kiss.

When she had finished, she tousled her blue hair and turned to face Isaac and Shackleton with a bright smile.

"Come along!" she hollered over the electronic throb. "I will show you your room!"

CHAPTER 17

Central Jerusalem, Israel.

Dr. Bennington glanced over at Christian and then down at his watch. They had been driving for almost fifteen minutes now and he had no idea where they were going. Christian was behind the wheel, steering the electric car along a tubular concrete tunnel that stretched off into the distance. Overhead, a steady stream of passing of lights marked their progress.

Bennington swivelled around to check on the young girl sitting in the back seat. She had been introduced to him as Cynthia, Christian's personal assistant, and the seventeen-year-old granddaughter of one of the Vanderhoff Group's oldest directors.

It was clear to Bennington that she had been sedated. He shot Christian a suspicious glance, wondering why he would have brought the girl along in the first place. Something did not feel right.

Where in God's name is he taking us?

Christian responded to his silent question.

"You shall soon see, Doctor."

They drove on in silence until the end of the tunnel came into view. There was a large cargo door there, with a smaller door beside it. Christian pulled the car up, the screech of its tires echoing around them. Leaving the car, he proffered his face to another of the ubiquitous holographic scanners. Bennington watched as the smaller of the two doors slid open.

"Please be so kind as to escort my assistant, Doctor," said Christian over his shoulder.

Bennington obeyed, exiting the vehicle and opening the girl's door.

"Thank you so much," she said through heavy-lidded eyes.

Her words were slurred and drawn out.

Bennington passed through the door ahead of Christian with Cynthia at his side. He was surprised by the masonry within. It lay in stark contrast to the poured concrete that had lined the tunnel, and was comprised of a light brown stone, crudely hewn but incredibly well preserved. He touched its surface.

"Babylonian sandstone," said Christian. "It dates back over two and a half thousand years."

"Where are we?" asked the doctor, studying the heavy arches that supported the ceiling.

"We are precisely ninety-three meters below the Temple Mount, in the centre of old Jerusalem," said Christian, moving off.

They followed a few paces behind.

"And what is this place?" asked Bennington, looking around in amazement.

"This is an exterior hall leading to an interior chamber," said Christian, arriving at a newly constructed concrete wall.

It was equipped with another cargo door, and no sooner had he placed his hand over a scanner than it slid upward to reveal a remarkable chamber within. With a high voltage boom a battery of lights switched on, flooding the space with a warm halogen glow. Bennington's jaw fell open at the sight.

"This is a Babylonian *Apsu*," said Christian, yawning. "It's nothing compared to what's coming."

Bennington stumbled forward in astonishment. The chamber was unlike anything he had ever seen. It formed a large open basin of sorts, as wide as two tennis courts, its domed canopy held aloft without a single supporting column.

Although crude and cave like, it was the room's colour and contents that filled the doctor with awe. Its floor was of the richest crimson imaginable, shining and liquescent, as though it were coated in a glossy film of ruby red blood.

The chamber's walls were made up of a series of arched colonnades and adorned in crystal mosaics of the richest blues, all deep and sensuous. Piled at its centre, as high as two men, were golden treasures of unimaginable worth.

"What place is this?" whispered Bennington, his face lit by the golden glow. "Where have you brought us?"

"This is an ancient storehouse of sacred treasure," said Christian dryly. "One of seven chambers that surround the Inner House."

"The Inner House..." repeated Bennington, glancing over at Christian intently. "Surely you're not referring to the *Holy of Holies?*"

"I am," smiled Christian. "*The Kadosh Hakodashim.* The dwelling place of God."

"The Most Holy Place..." whispered the doctor reverently. "But this is impossible. The site was destroyed centuries ago..."

"It was not, Doctor."

"And the Ark of the Covenant?"

"It's there too," said Christian blandly. "Quite tacky, really. Overly ornate."

"But how can this be?" stammered Bennington, taking another step into the space. "The Temple of Solomon was destroyed by the Babylonian's in five hundred BC."

"It was," said Christian. "And a second temple was built on the same site fifty years later. Contrary to popular belief however, the Babylonians did not destroy the Inner House. They built these chambers around it to hold their treasure and then held a public destruction of the outer temple to insure the chamber's secrecy. The secret died with their civilization."

"So how is it that we're here now?"

"Herod the Great discovered the Holy of Holies while renovating the second temple. You can only imagine his delight. He had all his worker's tongues cut out, and when the renovations were complete, he put them to death along with their families. The secret has been passed along by my ancestors ever since."

"But why keep it secret?"

Christian glanced over at Cynthia. Her sleepy eyes were focused on him in silent worship.

"You will soon see, Doctor," he said, looking down at his watch. "Come along."

Christian led them around the perimeter of the chamber to an archway that opened into a wide corridor. Opposite them was another archway revealing a perfect replica of the apsu where they had just been.

A short while later they arrived at a truly enormous hall, circular in shape with a towering ceiling. At its centre was a massive, crudely hewn block of dark stone. It was a perfectly proportioned cube, almost thirty feet in height and bombarded with spotlights. The sight of it reminded Bennington of a museum exhibit.

"The Kadosh Hakodashim," said Christian, pausing for a moment. "A cube not unlike our artifact, but one that is already in my possession."

"My God…" whispered the doctor. "This is unbelievable…"

Bennington followed Christian towards the massive cube with the girl at his side. High above them an expansive domed ceiling spanned the chamber. It was clad in blue mosaic tiles and dotted with countless golden stars, inlaid with astrological precision. Below their feet the ruby red floor gave the illusion of being wet with blood.

Christian motioned to a narrow descending stairwell at the base of the great cube.

"After you, Doctor."

Giving Christian one last look, Bennington proceeded slowly down the passage with Cynthia clinging to his jacket. At the end of a short tunnel a flight of steps appeared. They were bathed in golden light and led up into the interior of the cube.

A practicing Jew himself, Bennington paused for a moment, considering the importance of the place he was about to enter. The smell of ancient antiquity was in the air now, and an indescribable radiance of holiness filled every fiber of his being.

"Dear God," he whispered reverently as he climbed the last steps into the sanctuary.

What he saw within filled him with unbounded awe. The holy space was floored and wainscoted in what he knew from his studies of the Tanakh to be *Cedar of Lebanon*. Its walls and floor were guilt in pure gold, and directly before him stood two massive cherubim, guardians of the highest order. They were beautifully crafted out of what looked to be olivewood, and each stood almost fifteen feet high, their mighty wings spanning the chamber to meet at its centre.

Bennington stopped in his tracks and forced himself to breathe. His eyes had just found that which only legends spoke of.

This cannot be...

At the feet of the towering cherubs lay a gold and jewel encrusted table, upon which sat the Ark of the Covenant in all its glory. At its base was a small platform, not two feet high, and it was covered in purple and crimson linen. This was the chamber considered by the Jews to be the dwelling place of God, and both he and Cynthia fell to their knees instinctively, succumbing to a benign presence that filled their hearts to overflowing.

"Get up, you idiots," said Christian, spitting on the golden floor.

He approached the doctor and the girl and instantly they were brought to their feet by an invisible hand. Christian's eyes were black and reptilian now. A dark power was coursing through him.

"Cynthia," he said dryly. "Go to the platform and do what I told you to do."

She obeyed instantly, walking slowly to the place below the massive, winged angels and turning to take her seat.

Bolted to the dais was a chain, and Bennington watched as she picked it up. There was a sturdy dog collar attached to its end, and Cynthia proceeded to strap it tightly around her neck. Bennington shot a glance over at Christian and saw that he was looking at his watch.

"Why did Cynthia just put on that collar, Christian?" asked Bennington, frowning with confusion. "Why did you bring us here?"

"I wanted you to see what happens at three a.m.," he said, still looking at his watch. "Apparently there's going to be an alignment of planets."

"What are you talking about, Christian?" asked Bennington, only just then noticing Christian's strange, black eyes.

"Satanic superstition, Doctor," he muttered. "We're about to see if there's any truth to it. Here we are. Five, four, three, two, one."

In a clear and emotionless voice Christian called out.

"Cynthia. Use the knife I gave you to pierce your heart."

To the doctor's horror, she did exactly as she was told. Without hesitation she produced a ceremonial dagger from her purse and thrust it forcefully into her chest.

"No!" cried Bennington, trying to rush forward but finding himself held fast by some invisible hand.

He struggled against it, but every attempt sent a surge of excruciating pain through his body. Frozen with terror, he could only watch as Cynthia's lifeless body slumped to the dais. After that, everything began to lose its reality. Bennington felt himself teetering on the edge of madness.

"Don't be so melodramatic, Doctor," said Christian in a bored tone. "You didn't even know her. Don't pretend to be so attached."

Bennington focused his eyes on the dead girl. To his dismay, a transformation was taking place in her body. Similar to the human experiment he had been forced to witness in the secret laboratory, Cynthia's fingers were beginning to twitch. Moments later her cadaver was being gripped by a series of violent seizures. Her hands began to tear at her own flesh and her body twisted and contorted at impossible angles, amid sounds of cracking bone and shattering teeth.

Bennington looked on aghast, his face a mask of revulsion and grief.

"You infected the knife with the virus…" he stammered.

Christian gave a slow nod. He was still looking at his watch. Bennington's eyes darted back to Cynthia. Her body had almost fully reanimated now. Her dead eyes were moving around like a rabid animal's, her freshly lacerated skin hanging in shards the colour of wet ash.

The violent seizures had not only caused her to mutilate herself, they had also dislocated her jaw. It was straining open now, distending from her face on corded sinews and snapping hungrily at the air.

Bennington gagged and coughed. A stench of rotting flesh had suddenly filled the chamber, and over the dais an oily black vitriol was spreading like a black tide. In the blink of an eye it had engulfed the Ark of the Covenant and was already swallowing the two Cherubim that stood behind it. Cynthia's corpse jerked to its feet, straining dumbly against the collar and chain that bound it.

"Quite amazing," said Christian, smiling coldly as he glanced down at his watch yet again. "Kill a virgin on a full moon with the planets aligned and look what happens."

Bennington moved to speak but he was silenced by a hellish sound.

This is a dream… This is not happening…

What began as a single screech was soon joined by other voices, quickly producing a sound more abrasive and dissonant than anything he had ever encountered. Cynthia's corpse was jerking frantically against its bonds now, its gaping jaw snapping viciously with shattered, bloodied teeth.

The sacred chamber had transformed into a living hell, and out of every corner a chorus of demons was shrieking in rage and hatred. Their cries vanquished any hope of survival for Bennington and sent waves of terror through every fiber of his body.

"Dear God," he prayed, gagging from the stench in the air. "Protect me."

"There will be no protection from your Yahweh here!" cried Christian over the rising clamour. "His earthly abode has been desecrated! The virgin has been slain and resurrected! Just look at your god's pathetic Inner Chamber, his *Holy of Holies!*"

Black demonic shapes were whipping through the air all around them now, sending their clothes aflutter. The din was growing louder with every passing second, and Bennington knew that something unspeakable was about to occur. He braced himself instinctively.

"What have you done, Christian?"

Fourteen horrendously disfigured demons were materializing around them now, each as tall as two men, and as dense as iridium. They were in constant motion, their own substance belching out of them like black molten lead, only to be swallowed up as it was replaced by yet more. They were oscillating at an impossible rate as well, and the evil that radiated from them ripped through Bennington like toxic radiation. It was sending every fiber of his being into paralysis.

This is a nightmare! This isn't happening!

Bennington looked over to see Christian standing regally beside him now, his head held high like some dark emperor. It seemed to him that each of the fourteen demons was trying desperately to escape, and that it was only Christian's will that held them fast.

The fetid black shapes were flying faster and faster around them now, circling the chamber at dizzying speeds, and stirring up a scorching wind. At any second everything would explode in annihilation. Bennington was certain of it.

"Hail the Fourteen Emissaries of Lucifer!" sounded Christian's call over the mounting tumult. "They are my captains, and with them I shall command an Army of Darkness!"

The pulsing energy was reaching impossible levels now, yet still it was gaining in intensity. And just then, emerging from a bubbling pool of black vitriol at the centre of the dais, there appeared a lowly demon, twisting and grovelling. Like the fourteen emissaries, it too was comprised of dense matter, and it shot towards Cynthia's corpse, flowing into it like a colony of black maggots.

The change that took place in the cadaver was sudden and horrific, its movements becoming so savage and frantic that Bennington was sure it would break from its bonds.

"I am the Beast upon the Throne of Solomon!" cried Christian, his reptilian eyes fixed on the frenetic corpse. "The prophecy has been fulfilled! From this chamber I shall rule all nations! I will claim what belongs to Lucifer and take back for him what God stole!"

The rising clamour exploded in climax just then, and the Fourteen Emissaries sounded an earthshattering shriek, ripping through the ceiling of the chamber like a swarm of cindery locusts. The flying black shapes followed them, their sickening cries sending Bennington into a violent bout of vomiting.

The stench of death and rot had by now reached outlandish proportions, and what little breath the doctor had was taken by the buffeting gusts. A void had swallowed him, and bowing his head in defeat, Bennington gave up his soul to God. If this were indeed a nightmare, as he suspected it was, there would be no waking from it. Of this he was certain.

CHAPTER 18

The Atlas Mountains, Morocco.

Gabriel entered Natasha's chamber to find her standing on its little stone balcony. She was dressed in a silk nightdress and bathed in moonlight, looking out over a sweeping mountainscape under a star-studded sky. Her room was located above the opium den and sounds of men laughing and singing could be heard filtering up from below. A full moon had just emerged from behind the jagged peaks, and the night air was sharp and chill.

Gabriel approached wordlessly, leaning up against the stone railing behind Natasha and taking her into his arms. She slipped into his embrace with effortless ease, and he was amazed at how perfectly their bodies fit together. It was as if she had always belonged where she was now, and he kissed her neck, taking time to breath in her intoxicating scent.

In a similar way, Natasha could not recall having ever felt so complete. Using the Cube to heal Amir had not only altered her understanding of the artifact, it had altered her understanding of Gabriel, and of herself as well. The event had stripped away the last obstacles that had kept the two of them apart, and shown them, with perfect clarity, that they truly did belong together.

Natasha spun around to face Gabriel, and they fell into a deep kiss. It was like nothing either of them had ever experienced before, and its intensity took them both by surprise. It was as if they were melting into each other, their souls merging into a vibrating field of energy that seemed boundless and intimate at the same time. A desire to fuse further still, filled them both to the quick. It was impossible to resist.

Natasha took Gabriel's hand and pulled him onto the bed. What transpired next would be impossible to describe. The merger that took place between them transcended the parameters of body and mind, opening a way into a mystical reality beyond human comprehension.

* * * * * *

Gabriel awoke to find Natasha sitting up in bed and reading his father's journal.

"Anything interesting?" he asked groggily.

She smiled gently and reached over to run her fingers through his hair.

"You were sleeping so soundly, Gabriel. I didn't want to wake you. I've been studying Gutierrez's third manuscript."

Gabriel sat up beside her and rubbed his face awake.

"What's it say?"

"It talks about *Mithuna*."

He glanced down at the book.

"What's that?"

Natasha scanned his features.

"It's a way of making love, Gabriel. Have you ever heard of Tantric sex?"

Gabriel raised a curious eyebrow.

"I've heard of it," he said slowly, "but I've got to confess, I don't know much about it. Is that what Mithuna is? Tantric sex?"

Natasha nodded and brought her attention back to the journal.

"Mithuna means *Sexual Union* in Sanskrit. It creates a dreamlike trance when practiced. It looks like we'll have to use it to locate the Book of Khalifah and complete our mission."

Natasha pointed to the page. On it were drawings of figures surrounded by complex structures that depicted energy fields.

"That looks complicated..."

"It's really quite simple," she said, glad that he seemed open to the concept. "Tantra's based on polarity. Men and women are like electrical conduits that join together to make circuits. A bio-energy field runs through us."

Gabriel furrowed his brow and nodded.

"The Chinese call it *Chi*," he said, examining the drawing.

The image was of a sexless figure with lines of energy radiating out from the crown of its head. The fields arched downward, outside the body, only to curve up into the genitals again. From there a twisting concentration of energy spiraled up through the energy centres in the core of the torso and made its way back to the head to begin the cycle again.

"These are the two energy phases," explained Natasha. "Descending and ascending. When Chi gets down to the genitals it usually builds up as tension, until it's finally released through orgasm or ejaculation. The secret to Tantra is that sexual energy is encouraged to be retained in the body, so that it can ascend back to its source in the brain."

"The man doesn't ejaculate?" asked Gabriel.

"It's discouraged," said Natasha apologetically.

Gabriel gave a pained expression and feigned confusion.

"I could see a gasket blowing out down there…"

Natasha laughed and poked an elbow into his side. It was then that Gabriel noticed a smaller drawing that she had not referred to yet. He brought the journal closer to get a better look at it.

"What's this?" he said, pointing.

It was a drawing of a man and a woman standing face to face, encapsulated in energy fields.

"Those are the energy poles," she said. "If you look closely, you'll see that men and women both have positive and negative poles on their bodies, but they're inverted. The woman carries her positive pole at her heart, while her negative pole is at her vagina. The man has the opposite configuration. His positive pole is at his penis, while his negative pole is at his heart."

"And that's what makes the whole thing work," said Gabriel, understanding at last.

Natasha nodded and traced her fingertips over the illustration.

"The *Chi* energy circulates between the poles, creating what Gutierrez calls a *Circle of Light*. Mithuna's based on this. The woman's sexual energy flows out of the positive pole in her breast, and into the negative pole of the man's heart. From there it travels downwards through the man, until it emerges from his penis and enters the woman's vagina. From her vagina it travels upwards through her body and then leaves her breast again to start another cycle."

"I thought we were supposed to be circulating the energy within our own bodies, and not letting it go outside of ourselves."

"We don't want to release the energy," said Natasha, "but we do want to share it. Think of there being two energy circuits happening at the same time. In the end they combine to make a unified flow."

Natasha prepared to turn the page but paused to look over at Gabriel with a sly smile.

"I think you might be interested in this next part."

Rendered on the following leaf, in an ancient Hindu style, were illustrations of the progressive sexual positions they would need to assume in order to achieve Mithuna. Gabriel looked up from the book and gazed deeply into Natasha's eyes.

"You know... I think I'm really beginning to like this mission of ours..."

CHAPTER 19

Tangiers, Morocco.

Nasrallah scanned the luxurious hotel suite. Two blonde-haired Vanderhoff agents were sharing a table with him, and two more stood at the room's only exit. Each was wearing a dark blue suit, their muscles bulging through the cloth.

Having made his escape, Nasrallah had found himself in desperate need of money. It had not been difficult to entice Christian Antov with the promise of a map that pointed to the location of the Book of the Khalifah, but the resulting meeting had not gone as he would have liked. Rather than being given the security deposit he had requested, he had instead been taken prisoner.

"Where is the map?" asked one of the seated agents, his face heavy with malice. "You will surrender it to us at once."

"The scroll is safe," replied Nasrallah, "but its price is one million Euros and as I said, I will need a retainer."

He shot a glance at the other agent at the table. The man had a phone to his ear and Nasrallah knew that he was speaking with Christian Antov.

"No, sir," said the agent. "He does not have it with him but he claims that it is in his possession."

Nasrallah was forced to wait while the agent listened. After a few agonizingly long moments the man placed the phone on the table and activated its speaker setting.

"What lies are you spinning now?" came the voice of Christian.

"No lies, Mr. Antov," said Nasrallah. "I assure you. The scroll is securely hidden in my castle."

"Your castle is currently occupied by your enemies."

"Yes, sir," said Nasrallah, "this is true, but it would be impossible for them to find it. With your retainer I will be able to retrieve it."

There was a pause before Christian spoke.

"Because there is a remote possibility that you might be telling the truth, I am willing to be patient with you. I will most likely kill you, but there is a small chance that I will spare your life if you have pleased me."

"Oh, yes, Mr. Antov," said Nasrallah emphatically. "I wish nothing more than to please you."

"Then tell me where the scroll is hidden," said Christian dryly.

"You must understand, sir," he said, rubbing his hands nervously together. "If I reveal its exact location to you, I will lose my only bargaining chip."

"Would you prefer to be tortured?"

"No, please, I will tell you. It is in a safe, hidden deep in the castle's dungeons. It was my plan to retrieve it as I escaped, but one of my men betrayed me at the last moment."

"We will be executing a missile strike on your castle within the hour," said Christian. "Will this safe withstand a direct strike?"

"Target my castle?" exclaimed Nasrallah. "But why?"

"Will the safe withstand the strike?" repeated Christian menacingly. "I would advise you to be truthful."

"It is deep in the bowels of the castle," said Nasrallah, wiping the sweat from his brow. "It would not be damaged."

"Very well," said Christian. "The strike will be arranged. You will accompany my task force to your castle. When you arrive, you will retrieve the scroll and then I will decide whether or not to kill you."

"You are very generous, Mr. Antov. Thank you."

Nasrallah let out a muted sigh of relief when the agent pocketed his phone. Things had not gone as he had planned, but they could have also gone much worse. His enemies would be eliminated in the missile strike, and he would soon provide Antov with the scroll. For now, that was all that mattered.

CHAPTER 20

The Atlas Mountains, Morocco.

Gabriel awoke from a deep slumber to find Natasha asleep in his arms. Judging by the light entering through the chamber's window, the morning was well advanced.

His gaze passed lazily over the ornately paneled ceiling. A particular pattern had caught his attention and was serving to remind him of one of the night's mysterious revelations. It sent a vivid image of the Book of Khalifah into his mind's eye.

"The Book..." he whispered. "Of course..."

He raised himself on an elbow and passed a hand through his hair.

"Natasha," he said softly, kissing the top of her head. "Natasha. Wake up."

"Gabriel," she said dreamily.

A sweet smile enveloped her face.

"What did you do to me last night?"

Gabriel smiled roguishly and kissed her lips. She was still half asleep.

"We've got to go and get the book, baby," he said softly.

"Yes," she mumbled. "Yes, we do... We must go and find the book..."

"That's why you've got to wake up."

"That's why I've got to wake up..."

Gabriel could feel her tightening her embrace, only to let go suddenly and roll over top of him. In a second she was on her knees and straddling him, her eyes bright with excitement.

"Gabriel!" she exclaimed happily. "Let's go get it!"

She kissed him and jumped out of bed. Gabriel could not help but love her. He watched her patter naked over the cold stone to the safety of a Persian rug. Her skin was glowing in the late morning light, and her tousled chestnut hair was falling over her shoulders and down her back. He remained there unmoving, drunk with love.

"Come on!" she exclaimed, surprised that he was still in bed.

She was giving little jumps as she pulled on her jeans. Gabriel groaned as he sat up a little more.

"I feel like it's Christmas morning."

He threw himself back onto the pillows.

"I think I could use a little more sleep…"

"Shut up!" laughed Natasha, leaping onto the bed and falling into his arms.

"Oh, Gabriel," she said, hugging him tightly. "It was so beautiful last night."

"It really was," he agreed, kissing her neck and taking in a deep breath of her.

It had been something he could never have imagined before experiencing it firsthand. Together with Natasha, Gabriel had entered into a trance that transcended reality as he knew it. He would never be the same man again.

"Come on!" she said, taking his hand and pulling him from the bed. "Get dressed!"

* * * * * *

The bridge of the USS Stalwart looked like the helm of a starship. Like every Arleigh Burke-Class destroyer, it was among the largest and most powerful ever built, more heavily armed than any of its predecessors. Even still, its captain seemed unimpressed.

After decades of service, and countless seminars, the old admiral sitting in its command chair could still not get used to all of its new technology. It was as if the gadgets had suddenly appeared out of nowhere; as though he had woken up one day to find himself in the land of Buck Rogers. He seemed to constantly be studying manuals to keep abreast of the ever-changing technology. It was a task he abhorred.

"Goddamn bloody hell!" he cursed.

It had been a long night for Admiral Chester B. Sterling, and the morning was not proving to be any easier. As of late he had been having problems with his stomach, and he emptied another handful of Tums into his mouth in an attempt to curb the incessant burning.

"I picked a fine time to develop an ulcer," he complained in his southern drawl. "Smack dab in the middle of World War Three."

"Admiral Sterling, sir," said a communications officer seated before a battery of monitors. "We're being ordered to strike a target east of Tangiers."

"What's the target?" asked the admiral routinely.

"A terrorist cell, sir. They appear to be holed up in a castle."

"A castle...?" he asked, minutely interested. "Pull it up for me. Let's have a look."

The sergeant tapped away at his keyboard, instantly producing high-resolution satellite images of the target. The admiral looked at the various monitors spread out before him.

"Well, well, well," he said pensively. "That ain't gonna be an easy one to take out."

"Sir, they're calling for the use of fifteen Tomahawk missiles, sir."

"What?" he said, rising to his feet. "Have they gone mad? Who are those orders coming from, Sergeant?"

"The Commander in Chief, sir," said the sergeant, looking up at the admiral. "They're coming directly from POTUS."

"Well I'll be damned!" said the admiral, returning to his chair. "Wouldn't want to let him down, now would we? Soldiers, let's do a little castle demolition!"

Sterling worked the controls on the arm of his chair, magnifying the image so as to better determine the castle's structure.

"After five missiles, that place is gonna look like a pile of gravel in a Wisconsin prison quarry. After fifteen missiles, the President better get himself a beach towel, cause there ain't gonna be nothing there but silky-smooth sand!"

The communications officer shook his head in disbelief. Whoever it was they were hitting, they would not be leaving things half done, and at a cool five hundred thousand dollars per missile, it was clear the U.S. government was not scared of spending a little money to do the job right.

"Begin the preparation sequences, Sergeant," said the admiral, adjusting his cap. "And make sure you've got a live satellite feed open by detonation time. We've got cameras on every missile, and three up in space. I want to see 'em all. This is gonna to be quite a show!"

* * * * * *

"OK," said Gabriel, shouldering his duffel bag. "I'm ready."

"You're taking your pack?" asked Natasha.

"The Cube goes where we go," he said. "And so does my stuff."

"Do you have my toothbrush in there too?"

"As a matter of fact, I have your entire toiletry kit," he said with a wink.

Natasha moved to the door, shaking her head at Gabriel's over cautiousness. Opening it, she found Suora Angelica standing in the hall, a laden breakfast cart at her side.

"Suora!" exclaimed Natasha, delighted. "Oh, thank you, come in! It smells so good!"

"No, no, dear child," said the old nun, proffering the cart to Natasha. "I do not want to disturb you. I only came to give you this. Young lovers need their sleep, but they also need their breakfast."

Gabriel eyed the cart and was suddenly famished. The smell of coffee and bacon was already filling the room.

"There's no time to eat," he said, scooping some scrambled eggs onto a piece of toast and devouring it as he stood.

"Heavens me," said Suora, noticing that Gabriel had shouldered his pack. "Wherever are you going? And what could possibly be so important that you cannot even sit down to breakfast first?"

"Suora," said Natasha, looking intently at the old nun. "We think we know where the Book of Khalifah is."

"My child!" she gasped. "This is wonderful! Thanks be to the Blessed Virgin!"

"It's as if everything's led us directly to it," said Gabriel, shaking his head in disbelief. "That old gypsy woman didn't want us wasting our time coming here. It turns out it's the best thing we could have done."

"We think it might be hidden in the dungeons," said Natasha excitedly. "Why don't you come along?"

Suora stopped and turned.

"Did you say the dungeons?"

"Yes, Suora," said Gabriel. "Come on, let's go."

"Wait!" she said suddenly. "We must bring all of our things, as though we were going on a long journey."

"Why?" asked Gabriel. "We're just going down to the basement."

"No, my child," she said, her eyes glassy. "Mother Mary came to me in a dream last night, as she has often been doing of late. She said: *When you go to the dungeons, make ready for a long journey.* I did not know what she meant until just now."

"Well in that case, I'll take my backpack too," said Natasha, going to where her things were. "And the BIRIS as well."

"That's really weird, Suora," said Gabriel. "For some reason I felt like I had to take my things along too."

"We must heed our intuitions well in these times," said the old nun. "There are angels at our every side."

They entered into the corridor fully equipped and ready, and as chance would have it, Father Marcus and Fra Bartolomeo arrived there as well, having just finished their daily game of chess.

"Good morning, you two love birds," said the old bishop to Gabriel and Natasha. "I see that Suora is feeding you well."

"Gabriel's eating for both of us," said Natasha, motioning to him as he stuffed a bacon laden mini croissant into his mouth.

The bishop shook his head disapprovingly, as did Fra.

"And where might the three of you be going off to?" asked the old brother, looking curiously at Suora. "I see a pretty nun with a sparkle of excitement in her eyes, and the two of you with your packs on."

They drew closely together at Suora's insistence.

"We are going to look for the Book of Khalifah in the dungeons," she whispered excitedly. "Last night Gabriel and Natasha saw its location while they were…"

Suora stopped short. The bishop had already told her of the amorous way in which the Book would be located.

"While we were meditating," finished Gabriel, smiling slightly.

The old bishop's eyes lit up as he began to understand.

"Ah, yes... Meditating," he said with a wink.

He looked at the others.

"Now who would have thought that old book would be showing up here of all places?" he asked. "Shall we go?"

"We need to find Bahadur first," said Gabriel. "The book's in a safe. We'll need explosives."

"Why, Bahadur is already in the dungeons, my son," said the old bishop. "And I would not be surprised if he had explosives with him."

"What do you mean?" asked Gabriel. "What would he be doing with explosives down there?"

"They are setting up defences," said Fra. "Earlier on we saw a large group of them going down, all of them armed to the teeth. They fear Nasrallah may try to retake the castle."

"But why would they be setting up defences in the dungeons?" asked Natasha.

"Tunnels, my child," said the bishop. "The Moors built them to flank enemies that were laying siege. Nasrallah used one of them to escape."

Gabriel nodded in understanding.

"And he could use them again to stage a surprise attack."

"Exactly, my boy," said the bishop. "But tell me. Why the packs?"

"Suora had a dream last night," said Gabriel. "We're just playing it safe. You'd best bring your gear as well."

* * * * * *

Admiral Sterling stared into the monitor in disbelief. The face of John F. Abbot, President of the United States was looking back at him, a stern expression knotting his brow. What the admiral was being ordered to do was unheard of.

"Mr. President, sir," said Sterling respectfully. "Am I to understand that I am to place this destroyer, along with its entire compliment of three hundred and twenty-three souls under the direct control of a civilian, sir?"

"That's correct, Admiral," said Abbot. "But keep in mind that this is no ordinary civilian. He's the Permanent Secretary of the Vanderhoff Group. I don't expect you to know who he is, but I'll have you know that his organization has aided our country since it was in diapers, and you'll take any of his orders as though they were coming directly from me. Is that understood, Admiral?"

"Understood, Mr. President, sir," he said. "And thank you for the explanation, sir. It was not necessary."

"Admiral," continued Abbot in a more friendly tone. "I want you to know that our country owes a great debt to the Vanderhoff Group. We've got a world war on our hands right now, and our chain of command is stretched too thin to deal with individual terrorist cells, no matter how dangerous they might be. Mr. Antov is privy to all U.S. intelligence. I'm much obliged for his assistance, as I'm sure you can understand."

"Yes sir, Mr. President, sir," said the admiral. "And I will do everything in my power to ensure that his every order is executed with the diligence and bravery that is characteristic of the United States Navy, sir."

"Thank you, Admiral," said the President. "Over and out."

"Over and out, sir."

The admiral swiveled in his command chair as the screen went black, swallowing another handful of Tums and pressing a blue button on his control panel.

"Attention all hands," he said, chewing. "Commence firing sequence Delta Fourteen-Thirty-Two on my mark."

Admiral Sterling paused for the final confirmation from his ballistics officer and then turned back to face his bank of monitors.

"Fire," he ordered sharply, shifting his eyes to an exterior view of the ship.

Like angry hornets exiting a burning hive, the fifteen Tomahawk missiles left the destroyer's gun ports, each one on its way to the same destination.

* * * * * *

Rounding the final bend of their descent, Gabriel and his small entourage were at last able to see the source of the orders they had been hearing. Scotty Roberts was directing a group of six men, and beside him were Bahadur and a fully recovered Amir. Their backs were facing them, and Gabriel was the first to arrive.

"You have no authority to be down here!" he barked in his best foreign accent.

Amir spun around with swinging dreadlocks, but Bahadur did not even flinch.

"Welcome to the dungeons, Dr. Parker," he said, without turning. "No evil tongue could ever deliver a voice so eloquent as yours."

"You're no fun," said Gabriel, putting his arms around both of them. "But I've still got a surprise for you, Captain. I brought you some visitors."

Bahadur turned to see the small group, his smile warming when he noticed that Suora was among them.

"A pleasant surprise indeed," he said nobly, his voice as deep as the dungeon. "And how do I have the honour of this great visit?"

Natasha took hold of Bahadur and Amir and pulled them back into the corridor with the old bishop at her side.

"We need your help," she whispered, and then she proceeded to explain what she and Gabriel had learned of in their trance.

Bahadur seemed astonished.

"I cannot help but recall how you mentioned your need to locate a lost codex in our meeting last night, my lady…"

"That's right," said Natasha.

"Had you said that this codex was the Book of Khalifah, I would have been able to speak of it."

"What do you mean?"

"I have heard tell of this book, Doctor," said Bahadur, glancing aside as the others joined them. "I was among those who unearthed an ancient scroll that spoke of its existence."

Natasha blinked back at the giant wide-eyed.

"A scroll?" asked the bishop, taking hold of Bahadur's forearm. "What scroll, my son?"

"It was found in Ceuta. We were expanding an underground hashish operation there. Nasrallah had built the site years before, in ancient tunnels that ran beneath the city. When production was not meeting his expectations, he ordered me to expand the site by digging new tunnels. It was then that we found the chamber."

"What kind of chamber?" asked Gabriel.

"It was like no other I had ever seen," said Bahadur, his brow furrowing as he remembered. "I was alerted to it by the cries of the workers. They were calling out a name. *Al Tariq! Al Tariq!*"

"The Moorish general," said Gabriel, rubbing the stubble on his jaw.

"It was a treasure house," continued Bahadur. "Built by Al Tariq. I could see the gold in the reflected light before I had even entered the room. There were many treasures there, and on a sole pedestal was a golden scroll, still open and undisturbed for centuries.

"I notified Nasrallah at once. When he arrived, he cried out in victory. *'The Cube and the Book are mine!'* he said. Nasrallah knew much about ancient things. He studied archaeology at the University of Cambridge."

"Did he really?" asked Natasha, surprised. "What a well-bred villain…"

"He is a dog, my lady," said Bahadur, a painful expression coming over his battered face. "Do not be fooled. There were four men digging there that day. They were good men, fathers of families. Nasrallah ordered them to build a door covering the entrance which he later locked. After that he invited us all to a dinner of celebration. We were taken in separate cars. I never saw the men again."

"What happened after that?" asked Gabriel.

"I arrived at Nasrallah's suite to find him with the scroll. He told me many things, just as they had been told to him by his grandfather."

"What did he say?" asked Natasha.

"He told me the legend of the *Cube of Knowledge*, and how it could transform the soul of a man and make him immortal. He then spoke of the Book of Khalifah, and how it had been created by sages from the four corners of the earth, so that the Cube's power could one day be unharnessed.

"He said that the scroll would lead us to both the Book and the Cube. I can still remember how he held it aloft. There was a madness in his eyes."

"What was on the scroll?" asked Gabriel.

"A map," replied Bahadur, frowning. "It showed the Strait of Gibraltar, and Cordoba as it would have been many centuries ago. On it was marked the resting place of the Cube, a burial chamber belonging to the Barghawata ambassador to Córdoba, *Abu Salih Zammur.*"

"His tomb was excavated in 1928," said Gabriel.

Bahadur nodded.

"Yes," he said. "And its contents were moved to the Tangiers Museum of Antiquities. Nasrallah told me that the Cube would have appeared to be an unremarkable relic to anyone not familiar with it, and that he believed it still resided in the museum. It was not long before we were planning the robbery."

"So that's how Nasrallah found the Cube," said Natasha, amazed. "His grandfather told him about it?"

"Ustadh Darrak was a good elder," said Bahadur. "The most learned in the medina. As a boy I would visit his home every day. He taught me of our Moorish forefathers and infected me with their incessant thirst for knowledge."

"Some people say he was an oracle," said Amir, nodding. "He was blind, but he walked around like he could see. Bahadur would have been a university professor today if old Darrak had had his way."

Bahadur's dark eyes were staring into the past.

"In the end the old man was not so wise," he said deeply. "He did not see the evil that lurked in his grandson's heart. Darrak was the reason why Nasrallah studied archaeology. His tales filled him with wonder. It was a great coincidence that we should have stumbled upon the scroll in those tunnels that night…"

"There are no coincidences, dear Bahadur," said the old bishop. "There is only universal order. Now, what of the Book of Khalifah? Did Nasrallah recover that as well?"

Bahadur shook his head.

"He did not. The map on the scroll showed the existence of a secret tunnel originating in the treasure room, but we could not find it. We spent weeks looking. In the end Nasrallah gave up.

"He seemed content to possess the Cube and all the treasures he had found in the chamber. When everything had been sold, the profits amounted to almost four million Euros. He used the money to purchase this castle."

"Not a bad haul," said Gabriel, shaking his head and looking over at Natasha. "But why did we see the Book of Khalifah in our trance then?"

He turned to Bahadur.

"Nasrallah must have found it. Can you take us to the chamber we told you about?"

"I can," said the giant. "It is next to the chamber where my family was being held."

He turned to look in that direction.

"I know now that Elakhdar did more than just save their lives," he added. "Nasrallah must have tried to get through him to retrieve the Book. If the pigdog does not have it now, it is thanks to Elakhdar. He killed two of his men and sent the rat fleeing into the tunnels."

"Where are they, my son?" asked Suora suddenly. "Where is your family?"

Bahadur smiled tenderly at the old nun.

"They are safe, sweet Sister. They left early this morning. I had two of my men drive them back to Tangiers."

"Let's go," said Gabriel suddenly. "I'm dying to find this book."

They followed Bahadur as he led them through the party of smugglers. As they passed, they spotted Scotty Roberts sending a group of his men off into a tunnel with sandbags and ammunition. Natasha saw him look suddenly over at her. He flashed a smile so charming that she felt herself blushing self-consciously.

* * * * * *

"This is the chamber," said Bahadur. "But I have never seen a strongbox here."

"That's because it's hidden under this masonry," said Gabriel, bending a knee.

By prying his hunting knife into a seam, he was able to lift a stone enough to get his fingers around it. In this way he cleared two other stones of similar size until an iron safe came into view.

"Now we've just got to blow the door off," he said, looking up at Bahadur. "Where do you keep your explosives?"

"I have a sufficient charge here on my belt," said the giant, tossing a fist-sized pouch down to Gabriel.

In a matter of seconds he had laid the charge, and all exited the chamber so that it might be detonated. Gabriel was the first to re-enter after the explosion.

"There's no book," he said through the clearing smoke. "But there's a scroll..."

All moved closer as Gabriel held up a gem encrusted cylinder. Even in the dim light it sparkled magnificently.

"It's beautiful," whispered Natasha, her eyes alight as she took hold of it. "It must be the one from the secret chamber."

No sooner had Natasha finished speaking, however, than they were all thrown to the ground. A barrage of gravel and sand was coming down around them as a series of earthshaking explosions ripped through the castle above.

CHAPTER 21

Central Jerusalem, Israel.

Doctor Bennington awoke to find himself in an enormous bed, in what looked to be the suite of a five-star hotel. Daylight was streaming in through the curtains.

"I dreamed the entire thing..." he muttered sleepily, rising and moving to the window. "I'm not even underground. It's a wonderful day outside..."

He arrived at the window and opened the curtains to find a beautiful view of southern France stretching off into the distance, the sounds of chirping birds and the gentle rustle of leaves filling the air.

"But what is this?" he muttered to himself. "This isn't real..."

Looking more closely, he was able to see that the view was in fact a holographic projection of exceedingly high resolution. He fell back onto the bed, sitting and watching as a group of sparrows swooped off his balcony and disappeared into the lush valley that lay beyond.

"Good morning, Doctor," came the voice of Christian Antov. "I see you are enjoying the view."

Bennington turned to see Christian's face on a monitor above the room's fireplace, and the events of the past days came flooding into his mind. He recalled with horror the terrible experiments he had been forced to witness in the secret research facility, and how Christian had commanded Cynthia to kill herself in the Holy of Holies.

Only then did he remember how he had lost consciousness shortly after that event, and how he had dreamed that Cynthia's corpse had been reanimated and possessed by a demon summoned from hell.

Thank God it was just a dream...

He looked with repulsion at the face that filled the monitor.

"You are a murderous monster," he whispered.

"I am what I am, good Doctor," replied Christian. "Now clean yourself up. You will be escorted to meet me for breakfast in precisely thirty minutes. I hope that leaves you with enough time."

* * * * * *

The breakfast room was as luxurious as Bennington's suite, and every bit as comfortable. He scanned the faces at the tables around him, observing what appeared to be a very normal collection of professionals, each chatting amiably amongst themselves, just as they might have done in any other restaurant setting.

They have no concept of what they are a part of...

Bennington scanned the surroundings, looking up to see a barrel-vaulted ceiling comprised entirely of curved glass panel monitors, each one giving a sectional view of a moving summer sky. The illusion was perfect. To his right, numerous French doors opened onto a terrace shaded in dense grapevines, a holographic view of Provence stretching off into the distance.

Were it not for all that had transpired, Bennington, like the many others who populated the dining room, would have certainly been filled with a sense of peace and relaxation. Even the air was fragrant with the scent of southern France.

"I hope you are enjoying our habitat," said Christian, approaching the table and seating himself opposite the doctor. "We have paid infinite attention to every detail here. As you can see, today we are in Provence. Next week we will be in Tuscany, and after that on an island in Greece."

Bennington said nothing. He could only think of the cold bloodedness that Christian had exhibited when he had commanded the girl to commit suicide.

"It had to be done," said Christian. "There was no alternative."

"You may be capable of fooling yourself, Christian," said Bennington in the most professional tone he could muster, "but you will never succeed in fooling me. There is always an alternative. You did not have to act on your impulses. You had the strength of mind to resist them."

"Come now, Doctor. You've seen all the movies, haven't you?"

"What are you talking about, Christian?"

"The virgin sacrifice, of course," said Christian, holding up a silencing hand as the waiter approached.

"Eggs Florentine, hot coffee, and extra Hollandaise. My guest will have the same but make his eggs Benedict."

"Very good, sir."

"Now then," continued Christian as the waiter moved off. "Where was I?"

"Why did you kill her?" demanded the doctor.

"So that the captains of my army might be assembled. I also wanted to see how well the virus worked outside the laboratory."

"What the hell are you talking about, Christian?" said Bennington, a little too loudly for Christian's liking.

Bennington leaned forward and whispered.

"You're confusing your delusions with reality."

"Am I, Doctor?" asked Christian. "Perhaps you are doing the same? Did you not also see what happened last night? Why do you deny it?"

Bennington was taken aback by the question. What had occurred after Cynthia had died had clearly happened in his dreams. It could not be real. Christian was simply reading his mind and trying to confuse him.

"But why the girl?" he asked painfully. "She was innocent. She had done you no harm."

At that moment Christian's phone rang.

"Why is the strike behind schedule?" he demanded.

There was a long pause as he listened.

"Are you telling me that you fired fifteen Tomahawk missiles and failed to destroy the target?"

Another pause.

"It is irrelevant that the castle has been demolished. The artifact is still intact!"

Christian's anger was merging with his frustration. His newly acquired powers were telling him that the Cube was in perfect condition. He could sense it, just as he could sense the approximate location of the Two.

"How I know this is not your concern!" he snapped into the phone. "I will inform you when the Cube has been destroyed!"

Christian listened intently, his brow knotting with anger.

"It is most likely below ground, you idiot!" he snapped. "Put Nasrallah on the phone."

There was a pause.

"You escaped the castle by means of a tunnel," said Christian. "Is this not true?"

He listened.

"If you need men, then get men," he said. "My agents will assist you. Search every tunnel. Block every exit. If they are still alive the only place they could possibly be is in the lower levels of the castle. Find them, kill them, and bring me the Cube and the scroll. Is that clear?"

He listened again.

"Go! I want a progress report every hour."

Christian pocketed his phone just as their food arrived.

"Enjoy your breakfast, Doctor," he said standing up. "Unfortunately, I cannot join you. I have pressing matters to attend to."

* * * * * *

Christian sat at a granite desk in an enormous room walled in the same cold stone. He slid a finger over a small, disc-shaped interface before him and watched as a holographic keyboard and monitor materialized. After keying in his instructions, he moved his fingers through the air to activate the necessary node points on the monitor.

"Initiate conference connection," he said, and a moment later the face of Admiral Chester B. Sterling appeared on the monitor.

"Mr. Antov," he said, giving a stiff salute. "An honour to meet you, sir. I've spoken directly with the President and have been ordered to put this ship, and its entire compliment, at your disposal. The missile strike has been executed and the target destroyed. Is there anything else I can help you with today, sir?"

"Yes, Admiral, there is," said Christian. "Am I correct to understand that you have helicopters on board?"

"Yes, sir, Mr. Antov, sir. We have two SH-60 Sea Hawk helicopters on board, sir."

"Very well, Admiral," said Christian. "I would like you to send both of them to the site we have just targeted. It's possible that some of the terrorists have eluded the attack and are escaping on foot. If this is the case, I want helicopters there to eliminate them."

The admiral frowned in consternation.

"Mr. Antov," he said respectfully. "The Tomahawks we fired went in below radar and are not officially traceable to the US navy. Helicopters would be picked up immediately by Moroccan radar. You do understand that deploying any military aircraft into Moroccan air space will be considered a deliberate act of war."

"I am aware of this, Admiral," said Christian dryly. "Please dispatch them as soon as possible, and have your technicians send me live feeds. I want to know what those Sea Hawks are doing. Can you do this for me, Admiral?"

"Yes, sir, Mr. Antov. My men will have your live feeds up and running in the time it takes for the Sea Hawks to arrive at the target."

"Very good, Admiral," said Christian. "I will be waiting."

CHAPTER 22

The Atlas Mountains, Morocco.

Scotty Roberts was the first to get back on his feet after the explosions. He burst into the chamber where the others were to find Bahadur rising from beneath a pile of rubble. Under the shelter of the brown-skinned giant lay the little nun.

"Are you hurt, Sister?" he said to her, his voice deep with concern.

"No," said Suora, a little shaken. "I am fine. Thank you, Bahadur. You saved my life."

She looked around.

"But how are the others?"

Under the dim glow of the emergency lights, their companions could be seen rising slowly in the dusty air. Gabriel had thrown himself over Natasha, and Amir had managed to cover Fra Bartolomeo. It had all happened very quickly, and they were still reeling from the attack.

"Where's Uncle Marcus!" coughed Natasha, spinning to look for him.

At that moment, a heap of rubble near the center of the room began to shift.

"That must be him!" said Scotty, rushing to the mound. "He's the only bloke still missing!"

The smuggler was soon digging through the rubble. The others joined immediately. It did not take long before the good bishop came into view. He sat huddled under an old wooden table, wrapped in his frocks.

"Good of you to dig me out," he said, coughing. "It was getting a trifle close in here."

"Uncle!" exclaimed Natasha. "Are you hurt?"

"I appear to be intact, young lady," he said. "I only hope that our treasure has fared equally well."

And just then the bishop opened his frocks to reveal the glimmering cylinder held safely in his lap.

"You saved it!" said Natasha. "I was sure it was lost."

"Not on your life, child," said the bishop, holding out the cylinder.

Natasha took it while Gabriel helped the old bishop to his feet.

"How'd you act so quickly?"

"Second nature, dear child!" he exclaimed, shaking the dust from his vestments. "As a boy I weathered the London blitzes of World War Two, don't forget! Much more than the bombs, I feared my mother's belt if I'd forgotten to take the china with me under the stairs!"

They all laughed, Scotty Roberts especially. He had never seen people taking to life threatening dangers so easily. He looked at the old nun, amazed. She had fallen into Fra's arms, and they were both laughing merrily.

"Have you all lost your minds?" he said at last, a sudden realization coming over him. "What are we doing laughing? We've got men in the tunnels! And what about all the blokes up top?"

With his words their laughter came instantly to an end. In the joy of their own survival, they had forgotten the severity of the situation.

"Gather the men!" said Bahadur to Amir, his basso voice booming. "See if the way up to the castle is still open! Roberts! Arrange to have the other four tunnels searched! I want to know which ones are still passable! We must move quickly! Nasrallah's men could already be here!"

Bahadur helped the others find their packs in the rubble. It was not long before they were all assembled in the outer chamber, ready for the next move. Amir was the first to arrive back. He was pale with shock.

"The way up's completely blocked..." he muttered. "There were four men in that passage..."

"What?" cried Gabriel. "We've got to dig them out!"

Amir was shaking his head in grief.

"It's impossible, boss. They're gone."

Gabriel kicked a piece of rubble in frustration and looked up at the ceiling.

"What could they have hit us with? I counted five explosions."

"Artillery strikes," said Bahadur, approaching. "There were several explosions in each strike. I was not aware that Nasrallah had such an arsenal."

"That was no artillery strike," said Scotty, appearing with only two of his men. "They were missiles."

"How can you be sure?" asked Gabriel.

"Because we found a way out," he said gravely.

Like Amir, he too was in a state of shock.

"There's nothing left up there, mate. The men in the tunnels have all been lost. We're the only survivors. Everyone else is dead."

"What are you saying?" exclaimed Natasha, waking to the extent of the tragedy. "How can that be? There were almost a hundred people up there!"

Bahadur turned to face Scotty and gripped his shoulders with both hands.

"What did you see, my friend?" he asked gently, his battered features etched with sadness.

"The castle's gone, Captain," said Scotty through tears of anger. "There's just a pile of burning rubble. Everything's been decimated. They're all dead. Bloody hell. Every last one of them."

"What weapons could have done this?" muttered Bahadur, swaying on his feet.

"We counted fifteen hits," said Scotty, stumbling backward and slumping to the ground. "I'm no expert, but by the accuracy of the strikes, and the damage, I'd say they were guided missiles, most likely American or British. They're the only ones with military forces in the area."

"All our friends are dead," muttered Amir, slumping to the ground with head in hands.

There had been almost thirty Gibraltarian men in the castle above, and twice that number of Moroccans.

"How can they all be dead?" said Gabriel. "There's got to be survivors."

"Anyone buried in the rubble won't survive long," said Scotty. "There's no way to get to them. Bloody hell! If you saw it, you'd understand. There's literally nothing left. God damn those bloody bastards!"

"How could the Americans be involved in this?" asked Gabriel. "Was Nasrallah a suspected terrorist?"

"Not to my knowledge," said Amir, bewildered. "But U.S. intelligence has been known to make mistakes before. We can't rule out the Brits either."

"At this moment it is of no concern who did this," said Bahadur suddenly, wiping the tears from his eyes. "Whoever it was who fired those missiles will be on their way here. We must leave this place at once, or we too will be dead. We have some ammunition and supplies, but we are few against such a force. What of the other tunnels?"

"All blocked," said Scotty, rising to his feet. "The only way out is by the front tunnel."

"That would be suicide," said Amir, unfastening the safety strap on his combat knife. "If they're not up there already, they'll be here any second. Even if we could get out in time, they'd just track us down and kill us."

"There might be another way," said Bahadur. "A secret tunnel that leads to the river. We must see if it is still functional."

Gabriel and Amir followed Bahadur out of the chamber. When they returned, they found the others sitting amongst the wreckage. Natasha had removed the scroll from its canister and was studying it intently.

"The tunnel to the river's still good," said Gabriel. "We've got to go now."

"Why, mate?" asked Scotty, dejectedly. "What's the use? We're already dead. The only safe place would be outside Morocco, and unless there's a chopper down there, I can't see what the point of running is. Nasrallah's got agents all over this country."

"I think you should all look at this," said Natasha, peering up from the scroll.

Gabriel went over with the others in tow. Spread out before them, and glimmering in precisely worked gold leaf and silver point, was an ornate map, fashioned in the style of ancient Islam.

"That is the scroll I told you of," said Bahadur deeply.

"Is that Tangiers?" ventured the old bishop, pointing to a coastal city on the Strait of Gibraltar.

"I'd say it was Ceuta," said Gabriel, pushing back his hair as he bent closer.

"And you would be correct, Dr. Parker," said Bahadur.

He pointed to a spot within the city.

"Marked here is the chamber where this scroll was found."

The old bishop produced his spectacles.

"Then this must be Gibraltar on the other side of the strait."

"And what's this?" asked Natasha, running her finger over a meandering golden line that began in the chamber that Bahadur had just pointed out. It stretched across the sea to Gibraltar.

"That, my dear girl," said the bishop, "must certainly be the legendary Tunnel of St. Michael."

"St. Michael's Pass?" said Gabriel. "How could that be? It's just a legend."

"What legend?" asked Natasha, her eyes alternating between the two of them. "What tunnel?"

"The Rock of Gibraltar's a honeycomb of tunnels and underground chambers," said Gabriel. "Some are ancient, others are as recent as the nineteen-forties. There's basically a small city in there."

"And St. Michael's Pass?" asked Natasha.

"There are natural caves under Gibraltar too. They're off limits to the public. If you descend deep enough, you come to an underground lake. I was there once on a military tunnel tour. When you traverse the lake you arrive at Lower St. Michael's Cave. It's basically a bottomless pit."

"It's marked here on the map," said Natasha, pointing to the place. "It's where the tunnel ends."

Gabriel shook his head in amazement.

"There's an old legend in Gibraltar," he said. "It claims the pit descends into a system of caves that traverses the strait, but it's never been confirmed. They've sent dozens of expeditions down over the centuries but the men in them always disappear."

The bishop tapped the spot on the map with an old finger.

"During one of Gibraltar's many sieges, a little boy was lowered down on a rope. He was given a drum and a bag of gold.

His instructions were to play the drum continuously so they would know he was still alive. The plan was to use the gold to bring back men and supplies from Africa, but just like all the others, he too disappeared."

"But how could he disappear if he was tied to a rope?" asked Natasha.

The bishop shrugged. Gabriel continued.

"Legend has it that when the drumming stopped, they pulled up the rope to find it severed."

Gabriel turned away from the map and began to pace.

"To all Gibraltarians, Lower St. Michael's Cave has always been an unsolved mystery. It's even rumored that the military once sent an unmanned probe down there but that they lost contact with it as well."

Natasha was amazed.

"Looking at this map," she said, "it would appear that those tunnels really do exist."

She pointed to what looked like a chamber near the halfway point, somewhere deep beneath the Mediterranean Sea.

"And what's this?" she asked.

"That is the Chamber of Khalifah," said Bahadur, frowning. "The place where the Book of Khalifah supposedly resides. But as I said before, we were unable to find an entrance to the tunnel that leads there."

Gabriel looked up from the map, his eyes locking with Natasha's.

"If the tunnel entrance exists, I can find it, but one thing's for sure though. It'll be heavily trapped."

The bishop cleared his throat and readjusted his black vestments.

"Traps would explain why so many people have gone missing over the centuries," he said.

Bahadur rose from his stooped position over the map.

"We will find and take St. Michael's Pass," he said. "Ceuta is thirty kilometres north of here. We will hide in the caves by the river until nightfall, and then follow it to the city under the cover of darkness. I will take you to the treasure chamber, Dr. Parker, and there you will find the tunnel entrance. The Pass will lead us to safety. We must leave at once."

He tossed Scotty a packet of explosives.

"Plant them in the short tunnel. Time them to detonate in fifteen minutes. I want that passage completely sealed so they cannot follow us. We leave now!"

CHAPTER 23

They were still descending when the explosives detonated. There would be no going back now. Bahadur had made sure of that. To eliminate any risk of pursuit, he had insisted on blowing the entrance to the tunnel they were in as well. The only way to go now was down, and they all hoped that the path would be open.

They proceeded in single file, each member of the party of ten clinging to the rough walls. The tunnel descended steeply, its perilous steps carrying them to the valley floor. Here a wide and fast-moving river stretched out before them, flanked by towering cliffs. Although swollen from heavy rains, there was just enough space to walk along its edge. The sun had yet to rise above the chasm and all was still in shadow.

"We must move north as quickly as possible," said Bahadur, breathing in the cool river air. "Nasrallah must not see us. If he does, there will be no hope of escape."

At that very moment the ground at their feet began to explode under a rain of bullets. Looking up they could see a cluster of men on the clifftops. They were shooting down at them.

"Get back against the wall!" bellowed Bahadur.

Everyone obeyed instantly, taking shelter beneath the outcroppings of rock. Two of the men that were with them, Miller and Stephenson, jumped out into the open to return fire. They were armed with assault rifles and the deafening rattle left Suora and Natasha bringing their hands to their ears.

"Get back in here, God damn it!" bellowed Scotty. "You're wasting ammunition!"

The two men did as they were told and the group remained pinned where they were, desperately thinking of a way out.

"How could Nasrallah have known we were down here?" asked Natasha. "And that we were even still alive..."

"The answer is obvious, my child," said the bishop. "He must be in communication with the Nautonnier."

"The who?" asked Gabriel as another barrage of bullets struck the rocks above them.

"The Nautonnier is the leader of a powerful organization, my son. I will tell you more of him later."

Amir shuffled over to Gabriel's side.

"Are you thinking what I'm thinking?" he asked, tying back his dreadlocks with a bandana.

"I've been thinking it the whole way down."

Natasha joined them.

"What are you two conspiring about?"

"Feel like getting to Ceuta really fast?" asked Gabriel.

Natasha nodded.

"As long as it doesn't involve getting shot."

Gabriel reached over and tapped Bahadur.

"I think there's a way out of here."

The giant frowned.

"There is very little time, Dr. Parker," he said. "Thirty minutes at most."

"That's more than enough to get to the raft."

Bahadur was confused.

"What raft?" asked Natasha.

Gabriel and Amir exchanged a glance.

"If it's still there," said Amir, producing a hot cinnamon toothpick from his pocket and slipping it into his mouth.

"What raft?" asked Natasha again. "What are you guys talking about?"

Another hailstorm of bullets commenced, this time sending blasts of sand and stone fragments down upon them. Gabriel took hold of Natasha and sheltered her with his body.

"When Amir and I came to steal the Cube, we used a river raft to escape," he said. "We took it down stream to where we had our truck parked, but we didn't have time to deflate it and take it with us."

"We hid it in the bushes instead," added Amir over his shoulder. "It might still be there."

"But Gabriel, my son," said the old bishop. "There are ten of us, and all of our equipment as well."

Gabriel nodded, shielding his face from yet another barrage of flying sand and grit. The bullets were coming down with increased ferocity now. Gabriel had to raise his voice to be heard over the maelstrom of bullets.

"When we tried to buy an inflatable raft, we couldn't find one anywhere!" he cried. "The only place around was an Australian white-water rafting company just upriver. They didn't have any small rafts, just those big round ones that hold eight people. We bought one anyway. I think it would hold us all if we squeezed in."

"And you think we could escape on it?" asked Natasha. "How could we possibly paddle that quickly?"

Gabriel shook his head and pushed back his hair. They did not understand.

"We're on the banks of a river that people from all over the world come to for white-water rafting," he said. "It flows fast; *really* fast. It goes through the mountains and empties into the sea right around Ceuta."

"Where is this raft?" asked Bahadur, frowning in disbelief.

"It's on this side of the river," said Amir. "Only about twenty minutes from here if it's still there."

"It might even be closer than that," said Gabriel. "It's hard to say."

"Then we must go at once," said Bahadur. "Already the firing has stopped. They will be moving away from us. South to the only place where they can descend into the gorge. They will come quickly."

He turned to the others.

"We go now!" he said. "Stay close to the rockface!"

They had only begun to move when the shots began again, but this time from a single sharpshooter that had been left behind. They jumped back under the cover of the rocks, but Gabriel was holding his shoulder. Natasha gasped when she saw blood soaking through his shirt.

"I'm all right," he said, wincing in pain. "It's just a graze. Let's go. We haven't got time."

They made their way downstream as quickly as possible, hugging the wall until they were confident that they were out of the sniper's range. The swollen river was already beginning to look dangerously turbulent.

"And will it be safe in this raft?" asked the old bishop, looking out over the swelling torrents.

"Safer than bullets, priest," said Scotty, squinting up at the cliffs.

Amir kept track of the time as they made their way along. They had already been walking for fifteen minutes with no sign of the raft. He frowned and chewed worriedly on his toothpick.

It had been dark that night, and their speed hard to measure. The distance that had only taken them minutes to cover in the raft was proving to be much greater than he had expected.

"They will soon be upon us," said Bahadur. "Are you certain that we have not already passed the site?"

"Not a chance," said Gabriel. "I'd recognize it in a second. It's in a little cul-de-sac. There was a lot of vegetation around it. I'm sure we're almost there."

Just then the blast of a rifle sounded behind them, and the rocks to the right of Gabriel's head exploded under the impact of a bullet.

"Stay close to the rockface!" bellowed Bahadur. "We must continue to move downstream at all costs!"

"We'll cover you!" said Scotty, slapping the backs of Miller and Stephenson. "Come on gents, let's do this!"

The three Gibraltarians tucked in as close to the rocks as possible, sending controlled bursts of bullets into the enemy. Bahadur and Amir joined them, their assault rifles singing. They could see at least fifty men running for cover, not three hundred yards upstream. They had come hard and fast.

"Keep moving!" cried Bahadur. "We must make it to that raft!"

They shot as they went, two of them stopping in turn to return fire while the others advanced. Alternating in this way, they managed to cover their flight with a continual spray of bullets.

The enemy was finding it very difficult to gain any ground on them. Already the only two marksmen who had attempted to emerge from their cover lay wounded on the sand. The twist of the river was working against them, allowing their prey to continue downstream while they remained pinned to the rocks and unable to advance.

In this way Gabriel led the party ahead, arriving at last at the cul-de-sac they had been looking for. He pulled the circular raft from the undergrowth and sighed with relief. It was in perfect condition. With the help of Natasha and Fra they moved it into the water and began loading it with equipment. Thanks to the rock formations, the shallow cul-de-sac offered decent cover from the incessant barrage of bullets.

"We're good to go!" bellowed Gabriel over the clatter.

Their guns rang out in unison as they jumped into the raft. Suora, Fra, the bishop and Natasha huddled in the middle, with Gabriel and Amir manning the paddles in front. In this way the four gunners were able to climb into the rear of the raft and cover their backs with a spray of bullets. It worked perfectly, forcing the enemy to take cover and return only sporadic fire.

"We are pulling out of range!" cried Bahadur. "Drop your guns and take up the paddles!"

Within seconds they had navigated the raft into the centre of the river where stronger currents accelerated them out of harm's way. Behind them in the distance they could see a large group of men, perhaps a hundred strong, emerging from their cover. They stood at the base of the towering cliff face, watching as their prey slipped away.

"We did it!" cried Natasha happily.

"So far so good," said Gabriel, "but we've saved the best for last."

In a matter of seconds, they were learning why the river was one of the most sought-after white-water rafting destinations in the world.

"Steer left!" bellowed Gabriel, the raft lurching over a massive boulder. "We need to get to the right of those rocks!"

Back at the rafting outfitters, Amir had casually studied a map of the river while Gabriel had arranged their purchase. He knew that the worst was yet to come. Before opening into a smooth flowing waterway, the river would first pass through a very tight gorge dubbed *The Eye of the Needle*. Here the ride would take on its most challenging aspects. It was an extremely dangerous run and not for the novice rafter.

"Have you ever done this before, boss?" hollered Amir to Gabriel over the roaring water.

"Only once when I was a kid!"

The raft was already dangerously low in the water and Amir swallowed hard, tightening his grip on his paddle and getting ready for the fight of his life.

"To the right!" yelled Gabriel, a sudden explosion of river water dousing them all from head to foot. "Hard! Now!"

The group responded instantly, each of them paddling with all their might. Up ahead Amir could see the Eye of the Needle approaching rapidly. It was still a ways off, but at the speed they were moving, he knew it would not be long before they were in the worst of the rapids. From that point of entry, they would travel over two kilometres before finally being ejected into the open river beyond. If they could get through the narrow gorge without capsizing, the rest of the way would be smooth sailing.

* * * * * *

Christian sat at his desk. The expansive holographic monitor before him held a dozen different windows, each containing a live video feed from helicopter cockpits, helmets cams, and satellite images. It was in several of these that he could see the river raft making its way towards the mountain gorge.

"Estimated time of arrival to target location, three minutes and counting," came the voice of one of the pilots.

Christian spotted the two Sea Hawks approaching the river on a satellite image.

"Fire on the target as soon as you see them," he ordered dryly.

"Roger that, Mr. Antov, sir," said a pilot. "Terrorist target will be destroyed at first visual."

Christian moved uneasily in his chair. He could see that the raft was rapidly approaching the narrowing of the gorge and knew that the helicopters would not be able to pursue them into it. He shifted his gaze between the various satellite feeds on his monitor and passed a hand through his hair anxiously.

* * * * * *

"Helicopters!" cried Fra, his keen hearing picking up the beating blades of the Sea Hawks before anyone else.

Gabriel turned to see the two military choppers descending to within an arm's length of the river's surface, not three hundred meters behind them. They were gaining quickly, their massive guns poised and ready to fire the moment they came into range.

Before them the Eye of the Needle was approaching rapidly as well. If they could make it there before the helicopters commenced their firing they would live a little while longer. Ultimately, however, Gabriel knew they had little hope. When their raft emerged on the other side of the gorge there would be no cover to be had. They would be sitting ducks.

At that instant the river behind them began to boil with a spray of high calibre rounds. They were just at the edge of the gorge now and the shadows of the towering cliffs were falling over them.

"Go! Go!" cried Gabriel, paddling frantically. "We're going to make it!"

They moved as one, paddling with every ounce of their strength. As of yet, no bullet had found them, and with every passing second they plunged deeper and deeper into the gorge. If they could make it a little further the helicopters would be forced to let off their chase and fly to the north side to await them there.

"We're in!" cried Amir just as two missiles slammed into the rockfaces directly to their left and right.

The fiery explosions were deafening, and the blasts sent large sections of cliff sliding into the river. A shower of boulders was raining down around them, and Gabriel could see dangerous rock fragments flying past on all sides. It seemed impossible that not a single projectile struck them.

He shook his head in disbelief and shifted his attention to where the river was leading them. Its surface was churning treacherously, and it seemed preposterous that any vessel could be expected to pass through such a furious mass of water without being utterly destroyed.

"Bloody hell!" screamed Scotty, paddling for his life. "Out of the frying pan and into the bleeding fire!"

The river was exploding beneath them, the raft lurching and bending as the angry countercurrents tried to suck them under. It was all Gabriel could do to pick a path through the chaos and hope for the best. With his lack of experience, it was more a guessing game than anything else.

"We must stop the raft somewhere in this gorge!" cried Bahadur amid powerful strokes. "They will be waiting for us on the other side!"

Gabriel scanned their surroundings and knew the order would be impossible to obey. The current had them in its grip. Merely staying above it without capsizing would be a feat in itself. Stopping was not even a possibility.

* * * * * *

"Take up positions on the other side of the gorge," said Christian calmly.

He had watched the raft disappearing into the dark chasm from the helicopter cameras, but he was not worried. Even if his prey managed to survive the rapids, there would be no escape for them on the other side. This time he had them. There was not a doubt in his mind.

"No," muttered Christian in disbelief.

He had just noticed ten objects on the long-range radar feed. They were approaching rapidly, and he knew by their speed that they could only be one thing: Moroccan fighter jets.

Christian cursed as he watched them converging on the helicopters. The two Sea Hawks would be no match against ten Mirage F1 fighters. Even still, there was a good chance that the Sea Hawks would be able to destroy their target before the fighter jets arrived.

In that moment he saw the helicopters beginning to move away.

"What's happening?" he screamed. "Where are you going?"

"Enemy fighter jets approaching, sir," came the voice of the admiral. "This is standard procedure."

"Return to your positions immediately!" bellowed Christian in fury. "Destroy the enemy target!"

Christian saw the admiral's face appear on his monitor.

"Mr. Antov!" he said. "The pilots will be lost! They must retreat to international airspace!"

"They will accomplish their mission!" snapped Christian.

"Then they will die," said the admiral.

Christian watched the helicopters return to their positions, and just then the voice of a Moroccan captain sounded over the radio feed.

"You are in Moroccan air space. Leave immediately or you will be shot down."

Christian peered at the opening of the cliffs on his monitor, his eyes darting back and forth between the helicopter view and the satellite image of the rapidly approaching fighter jets.

"Prepare for evasive action!" ordered the admiral.

"Belay that order!" commanded Christian. "You will hold your positions!"

* * * * * *

Gabriel looked ahead. A vertical sliver of light had only just appeared out of the shadows. Against all odds they had made it through, but he felt no elation. Along the entire run there had been no opportunity to dock the raft, let alone even slow it down. They now found themselves barreling to their doom at top speed. It would take a miracle to save them now.

As if in slow motion, Natasha spotted the two Sea Hawks hovering over the surface of the river. Their rotor blades were chopping the air, their missiles and guns on the verge of firing. She turned to face Gabriel. He had since stopped paddling and the others followed suit. The end had come, and they all made ready to be taken into the great unknown.

Natasha fell into Gabriel's arms as the missiles left the helicopters. Their raft had been ejected into open water now, and above them black clouds were amassing.

"It is a good day to die," said Bahadur with a grim smile.

"Maybe not!" cried Amir, suddenly noticing the trajectory the missiles were taking.

In seconds their raft was lurching in the turbulent air as the rockets flew past, missing them by a metre on each side and exploding onto the bluffs behind them.

A rain of gunfire had suddenly enveloped the helicopters, the deafening roar of jet engines clapping against the echoing cliffs.

The hovering Sea Hawks exploded in great fireballs a moment later, crashing to the surface of the lake amid chopping blades and burning hulls. They disappeared from sight almost instantly, and just then the fighter jets swept past in a chest-rattling pass, roaring upwards and away in tight formation.

By the swiftness of the attack, it appeared as though their small raft had gone completely unnoticed. Everyone let sound a cheer of relief and joy, unable to believe their eyes.

"Thanks be to Allah!" cried Bahadur.

"And long live the Moroccan air force!" exclaimed Amir.

Natasha hugged Gabriel as tightly as she could, unable to contain her joy. Beneath her she could feel the fast-flowing river pulsing under the raft's rubbery bottom. It would soon carry them northward to Ceuta, and to the mysterious tunnels of St. Michael's Pass.

* * * * * *

Christian sat at his desk, his face twisted with anger and frustration. On the satellite feed he could see the raft speeding its way towards the Mediterranean Sea. With both helicopters destroyed, he would be forced to pursue his prey on land before he could acquire more aircraft. All would have to be done according to military protocol. He cursed bitterly. He was the most powerful man on the planet, yet even he was a victim of bureaucracy.

CHAPTER 24

Los Picos de Europa, Northern Spain.

Isaac looked away from the computer monitor, his eyes burning as he struggled to make sense of everything he had just learned. He scanned the room, still amazed by its uniqueness. Comprised entirely of abandoned furniture, the decor resembled that of a nineteenth century boudoir, complete with hanging veils, glowing oil lamps, and a blazing silver candelabra. At his feet he could see Shackleton lying fast asleep on the tattered rug.

After having bathed and eaten, Isaac had settled happily into his new accommodations, dressed in the warm flannel pyjamas he had been given. It was the first bit of civilization he had seen in weeks, and the fact that their strange suite resided in a medieval dungeon made no difference whatsoever. The bath had been heavenly, and the hearty food rejuvenating. To his delight he had found a computer in the room, complete with an internet connection.

After informing himself of the dreadful events occurring around the world, Isaac had managed to gain access to the church orphanage database, his old password surprisingly still active.

"Incredible," he whispered, his eyes scanning the text.

There now remained no doubt that Gabriel and Natasha had been born on the same day and hour as his own son, and like his son, they too had both been in rare coma vigils at the time. Further investigation confirmed that one month after their births, Gabriel and Natasha had both awoken in a state of demonic possession. Accounts of their adoptive parents were mentioned as well. Professor Agardi Metrovich was named as Gabriel's adoptive father, and Father Franco as Natasha's legal guardian.

Isaac produced the old priest's diary. There was one more question he needed answered. He flipped through the book until he found an entry that spoke of the *Rex Angelus Monastery*.

Metrovich and Father Franco had planned to visit the place after the burial of his son, and it appeared to be a destination of great importance. Acting on an impulse, Isaac did an internet search on the name. The articles that came up left him perplexed.

In one of them, Rex Angelus was being referred to as a secret aristocratic bloodline, comprised of powerful leaders and nobility, both living and dead. The name appeared to be woven into the very fabric of European history.

Isaac had always been a loyal Roman Catholic, but if the information he had unearthed was true, it would forever change the way he viewed the church.

According to one of the articles, the Rex Angelus bloodline had descended directly from Jesus Christ. They were supposedly the keepers of what was being referred to as the *Original Teachings of the Kristos*; a body of knowledge that the Vatican had purportedly gone to great pains to wipe from existence.

Isaac bent closer to the monitor, his brow furrowed in confusion as he re-read the text.

The Rex Angelus families had allegedly kept the heretical teachings a secret, privately practicing the initiatory rights handed down to them from their ancestors, while maintaining an outward appearance of religious conformity.

Scrolling down, Isaac came upon an embedded video and clicked it despite his misgivings. In it a distinguished British historian was being interviewed, his elbow propped casually on a cluttered bookshelf as he spoke.

"Rex Angelus had become fully established in the European aristocracy by the early fourth century," he said. "By the Middle Ages they had not only assimilated themselves into the highest courts and parliaments, but infiltrated the innermost chambers of the Vatican. Their secret mission was a simple one: To overthrow the blasphemous Church and reveal to humanity the true initiatory teachings of Jesus Christ. This they would do through their newly formed Cathar religion."

Isaac had to force his jaw shut.

The blasphemous Church?

The video played on.

"The political sway of Rex Angelus reached a critical point at the beginning of the eleventh century, with the formation of over sixty-eight Cistercian houses, one of which was known as *The Poor Militia of Christ*, an organization later to be officially recognized by the Church as *The Knighthood of the Temple of Solomon*, or *The Templar Knights*, as they are more commonly known.

"It was this organization that provided the greatest impetus to the Rex Angelus bloodline, but one that would also, over the span of one hundred and eighty years, be responsible for the family's eventual fracturing.

"Notwithstanding, the Knights Templar would become the equivalent of history's first multi-national corporation, and their rise to power would be swift and radical."

Isaac gave a long sigh and shut down the computer. He needed sleep desperately and would finish watching the video the following morning. He rubbed his face and glanced down at the slumbering Shackleton.

"A bloodline of Christ..." he said to the sleeping dog. "A church of lies and deception.... How can any of this possibly be true?"

Swiveling in his chair, Isaac reached over and took hold of the topographical map he had only just printed. It showed the exact location of the Rex Angelus Monastery, the very same one that Father Franco and Professor Metrovich had been planning to visit. Considering its elevation, Isaac estimated it would take Shackleton and himself approximately twelve hours to reach it on foot. His mind went over the incredible story he had just read on the internet. It told of those who had built the monastery, and the incredible events that had led to its construction.

After obtaining enormous wealth, power, and an unhindered influence within the Vatican, the *Knights Templar* had become divided. On one side were those who still held to the strictures of the original teachings of Jesus. These knights worked diligently to support the ever-growing Cathar church.

On the other side, however, were the knights who had forsaken their Rex Angelus bloodline. They had aligned themselves with a secret society of corrupt power mongers who had been operating within the Vatican since its inception.

The new society they established would be called *The Illuminati*, named after Lucifer, who bore the Latin name *The Illuminated One*. In less than a year the *Illuminati* would take full control of the Vatican, crowning the first of a series of puppet popes and ordering a papal bull issuing the arrest of all nonconforming Templar Knights, and the immediate destruction of the Cathar church.

This would mark the beginnings of the Inquisition, and the subsequent massacre of hundreds of thousands of peace loving Christian Cathars in what would later be known as the Albigensian Crusades.

The monastery Isaac would soon be visiting had been built by a renegade group of these Templar Knights. They had eluded the papal bull centuries before and allegedly preserved the original teachings of Jesus Christ to this day.

Isaac climbed into the canopied bed and gave a great yawn.

"Tomorrow we shall see..." he murmured, and just then a deep slumber took him.

CHAPTER 25

Northern Morocco.

It had been over three hours since they had left the rapids behind, and as of yet they had seen no sign of Nasrallah's mercenaries. Bahadur and his men sat at the ready as they were carried downstream, their assault rifles propped on the hull of the raft, prepared to return any fire that might come at them.

Having weighed the options, they had decided that staying on the river would be the best course of action, even if it offered them little protection. An attack was inevitable, but at least in this way they would remain moving targets, as opposed to being surrounded and trapped.

Around them the chiseled gorge had now been replaced with a softer terrain, the swollen river coursing through a broad valley dotted with abandoned tier farms and the occasional empty village. Even as the waters had calmed, the weather had grown dark and ominous, and the small group found themselves under a tumultuous sky, its boiling clouds blotting out the sun. Amir had his radio on.

"Good evening," said the commentator. "You are listening to GNN's European radio broadcast. This hour: Violent storms sweeping across Spain and Italy, moving northward into France, Austria, and Switzerland. We have reports of massive devastation occurring in many points across the Iberian Peninsula, as well as severe flooding in Southern Italy. One hundred and fifty kilometre an hour winds have been reported in Paris, and violent electrical storms are blanketing most of Europe.

"What is happening to the environment? With us now is Dr. Walter Fischer of the European Meteorological Society. Dr Fischer, could you tell us exactly what's happening?"

"We cannot say we know exactly what is going on," he said in a Swedish accent. "These weather patterns are completely foreign to our climes. What is truly remarkable, however, is that these anomalies are occurring on every continent."

The commentator paused for effect.

"Are you saying that the latest earthquakes in California are a part of this same weather pattern?"

"Yes, I am," came the grave reply. "All these anomalies are most definitely linked."

The commentator spoke urgently.

"In California we've seen over a dozen very brief, very intense tectonic shifts along the San Andreas Fault. Some geologists feel that the plates will soon give way to a major earthquake. Could this be the Big One?"

"It could very well be," said the climatologist. "There have also been earthquakes registered over many parts of China and Russia. As we speak, violent storms are raging over South America, and massive volcanic activity is occurring in the Indian Ocean, as well as in Japan and Hawaii.

"Only one hour ago, I was speaking with a colleague at the Royal Society of London. He was telling me of the unprecedented activity being recorded along the entire mid-Atlantic ridge."

"So, what, in your opinion, is the cause of this, Doctor?"

"I believe that much of the weather we are experiencing is a direct result of climate change, but the severe variances that are occurring in the movement of tectonic plates is still a mystery."

"Will we see it getting any better soon?"

"We should be prepared to witness these patterns worsening before they eventually improve."

"What can families do to survive this crisis?"

The climatologist paused before answering.

"Stay indoors," he said slowly. "Get underground if you can, and never forget that storms always pass."

"Thank you, Doctor."

"You are very welcome."

"That was Dr. Walter Fischer of the European Meteorological Society. Coming up next in our broadcast: Citizens of the United States reel under the iron grip of its new police state."

Gabriel switched off the radio and looked up at the sky.

"We're getting closer and closer to that Dark Rift," he said, glancing over at Natasha. "This is precisely what the old gypsy woman said would happen."

Bahadur turned to speak, his voice deep with concern.

"What will occur if the earth enters into the Dark Rift before we find the labyrinth?"

Gabriel shrugged.

"The gypsy woman said something about perpetual darkness for all mankind. It didn't sound very promising."

Amir gave a grunt and spat out his masticated toothpick. The weather was getting worse. When the tempest struck, it would do so mercilessly. Already the wind was blowing in buffeting gusts, pushing their raft around as though it had been equipped with a sail.

"Bloody hell," cursed Scotty Roberts under a pummelling squall. "It feels like the bloody end of the world..."

Bahadur had to raise his voice to be heard.

"What is our distance from Ceuta, Dr. Parker?"

The sky had suddenly become as black as pitch. It was churning like a witch's cauldron. Gabriel pulled out his phone and checked their position.

"We're getting close," he said. "We're only twenty kilometres from the city centre."

"Take up the paddles!" cried Bahadur, rising suddenly to his knees. "We will bring the raft to shore here!"

"Why?" cried Natasha.

Bahadur grimaced.

"Nasrallah and his men have not yet attacked us," he said. "This can only mean they will be waiting for us outside Ceuta. We will visit a friend of mine here on the river. He will take us into the city by land."

They picked up their paddles and made their way to the banks of the river amid a deafening series of thunderclaps. With the widening of the gorge the current had become much more manageable, and it was not long before they were feeling the bottom of the raft scraping along the gravel at the river's edge.

It was at that very moment that the stormfront arrived, and the sky unleashed its fury. Grape-sized balls of hail were suddenly falling all around them, and the lightning strikes were blinding.

"Up there!" bellowed Bahadur over the rolling thunder.

He was pointing high and to the right, and Gabriel peered up to see what looked to be the abandoned ruins of a village, not a hundred meters away.

"Pick up the raft!" he hollered. "We can use it to shelter us!"

In this way the group made its way up the rocky terrain to the village, the inverted raft acting as a shield against the onslaught.

Like many other villages in the region, the hamlet lay abandoned after a decades-long drought. Bahadur squinted up at the ruins, remembering a time when it had been a happy, populated place. He was certain that one man still resided here however; an eccentric Sufi hermit whom he knew would assist them.

It was not long before Bahadur steered his company into the shelter of a small cave-like home carved directly into the mountain.

"Miller and Stephenson!" he ordered, pointing to a crude hearth in the corner of the chamber. "The temperature is dropping. Gather wood and light a fire. Amir and Scotty. Come with me. Bring your weapons!"

Natasha watched as they disappeared into the hailstorm, using their packs as shields. It was only early evening, but it was as dark as night. Along with the storm had come a strange, frigid wind.

"It's a good thing we found this village," she said, shivering. "I've never seen a storm like this before."

She smiled in thanks when Gabriel wrapped her in a blanket, a sudden clap of thunder making her jump.

"Neither have I," he said. "One thing's certain, though. If it hadn't been for this turn in the weather, I'm sure we would have seen more helicopters. We've been lucky."

"Luck has nothing to do with it, my children," came the old bishop's voice from behind. "We have been receiving special assistance."

Natasha turned to face him.

"I was thinking the same thing. They fired four missiles at us in the gorge and not even a splinter of rock touched us. What's happening? In the professor's journal it says that spirits can't interfere in the physical world, but it seems to me that's exactly what they're doing."

"They can interfere only according to divine law," said the old bishop, nodding. "With the coming of the hermaphrodite, many demonic entities have entered into our world. Universal law dictates that for every number of evil spirits that arrive on the earth sphere, a certain number of spirits from the world of God can come as well. Gutierrez claims that the ratio is approximately twenty to one."

"Twenty demons to one angel," said Gabriel, looking out into the storm. "That doesn't seem very fair."

"On the contrary, my dear boy," said the old bishop. "Angels are much more powerful than demons."

"And why's that?" asked Gabriel.

"Because one good act is far more powerful than many bad acts combined."

"Then why not bring in a whole bunch of angels and end this thing right now?"

"Because the battle between good and evil must be fought and won fairly," said the bishop. "In this way, Lucifer will be unable to make any excuses when he has lost. He will have no choice but to surrender to God's will. This is why it is so important that the playing field always be kept level. The universal laws ensure that this is always the case."

With that the bishop turned and went to join Suora and Fra. They had managed to find a few chairs and a table to sit at. In the light of the fire that Miller and Stephenson had just lit, Natasha could see the brother and the nun preparing some sandwiches. The bishop was soon pulling a bottle of wine from his pack, his eyes twinkling mischievously.

Natasha shook her head and smiled. Even under the direst of circumstances some things never changed.

"Come on," she said to Gabriel. "Now's a good time to try and locate that labyrinth."

They sat next to the fire and began their studies of both the professor's journal and the map they had found, but nowhere could they find any clues as to where the mysterious island might be.

"It's pretty clear that neither the Moors or Gutierrez wanted any written record of the island's location," said Gabriel, rolling up the map in frustration. "They couldn't risk it. I just can't figure out how both our dads knew where it was…"

"The father of the hermaphrodite must have told them," said Natasha.

Gabriel sat up, his eyes alight with hope.

"Well then all we've got to do is find him."

Natasha was shaking her head as she flipped through the old journal.

"Uncle Marcus already tried," she said. "His name is Isaac Rodchenko. He's gone missing. Even the police can't find him."

Gabriel slumped back against the wall in defeat. Natasha finished reading an entry she had found and looked up from the book.

"Gutierrez says that the Labyrinth of Sarras is constructed of cubes within cubes," she said. "The cubes are separated by seals, and passing through each seal takes you further into the labyrinth until you arrive at a central chamber.

"He says that each seal holds a riddle that needs to be solved before it can be passed through, but that ultimately, the only way to gain entry into the central chamber is by transcending duality."

Gabriel cocked an eyebrow.

"Is that all?" he asked sarcastically.

Natasha shot him a sidelong glance.

"He refers to this central chamber as *Ostium Sanctus.*"

"*The Sacred Gate,*" translated Gabriel. "Osiris and Isis were looking for a similar portal in the myth, weren't they?"

He paused for a moment to consider the implications.

"If the parallel is consistent," he said slowly, "and reality really does mirror the myth, then the central chamber of the labyrinth must be some kind of a gateway to—"

He stopped himself short. The idea was preposterous.

"A gateway to heaven," finished Natasha, her eyes wide with wonder.

"One that would apparently mirror the Portal of Ahreimanius," cautioned Gabriel. "Which is basically a gateway to hell."

Natasha shuddered at the thought.

"Gutierrez says that gaining access to the inner chamber will be the most difficult task imaginable. He says that no one has ever done it before."

Gabriel was going to say something but the roar of a loud engine stopped him. They looked over to see an old school bus pulling up.

"Get all your things together, mates!" ordered Scotty Roberts, rushing in.

To everyone's surprise he was carrying a portable anti-aircraft missile launcher, its stout barrel pointing to the ceiling. Outside the storm had grown into a raging tempest. It was nothing short of apocalyptic.

"Bahadur's friend is dead!" he cried over the thunderclaps. "We found two of Nasrallah's men downstream! We took their Stingers, but they got off a distress call before we could take them down! Nasrallah's men will be here any second, mates! We've really got to move!"

In a moment all was in chaos. Bahadur left the bus idling and came in to help the others gather the equipment. The incessant pounding of hail on the bus's metal roof sounded like battle drums, driving them all to quicken their pace.

"Their plan was to ambush us at the next village where the river is at its slowest!" boomed Bahadur.

He was carrying a huge load of packs and ammunition.

"They know we are here! They are on their way! Perhaps a hundred strong!"

"Bad timing..." said the bishop to Fra, taking a final bite from his sandwich before stuffing it into one of his vestment pockets. "We'll have to make this take-away, old friend."

In a matter of seconds they were boarding the bus, with Amir and Bahadur bringing in the last of the supplies. The door had not even closed before Gabriel gunned the old engine and sent the vehicle roaring out into the deluge.

"Hold on to your hats!" he cried over the pounding hail.

"Make for the south of the square!" bellowed Bahadur.

The smuggler captain looked enormous at the front of the bus, his battered head bleeding from where a chunk of ice had hit him.

"Miller! Stephenson!" he ordered. "Grab your guns and get to the back! Get ready to return fire! Amir! Roberts! Prepare the Stingers!"

Gabriel shot a glance over to see Bahadur use a fire extinguisher to punch out windows on either side of the bus. Amir and Scotty rushed up with the missile launchers they had taken from the enemy.

Gabriel cursed aloud. He was having a very difficult time seeing the road ahead. He squinted into the blur of lashing rain and hail, the windshield cracking more and more with every passing second.

"What the hell is that?" he cried, and only then was he able to make out the extent of their predicament.

The square they found themselves in had once served as a kind of village roundabout, and to Gabriel's horror, he could see that a huge procession of military trucks was converging on it, some from the left, and others from the right. Their escape route was closing before his eyes.

"Make for the exit!" bellowed Bahadur.

"I can't!" cried Gabriel. "They just blocked it off!"

"Make for the exit!" repeated Bahadur louder still, and just then Gabriel saw Scotty and Amir in each of the side-view mirrors. They were leaning outside, braving the hailstorm to point the Stingers directly ahead.

"Aim for the middle transport!" cried Bahadur. "Fire!"

Gabriel swallowed hard when he saw the missiles leave the launchers and converge on the truck that was blocking their way.

"This had better work!" he bellowed, shifting into a higher gear and slamming the accelerator to the floor.

The bus lurched forward, taking a path directly through the centre of the roundabout. A second later the missiles met their target.

"Get down!" he cried, grabbing the wheel with both hands and preparing for impact just as the Stingers detonated in unison.

The ensuing explosion had a far greater effect than they ever could have hoped for. In order to deny their prey any means of escape, the convoy had stopped bumper to bumper. As it was, many of the transports were carrying caches of ammunition, and in a matter of seconds the explosions were having a domino effect, ripping through the convoy in both directions.

With the momentum of a runaway train, the vintage bus crashed through the burning wreckage, sending what was left of the transport careening out of the way. Gabriel slammed his foot to the floor again, using the acceleration to bring the skidding tail of the bus back under control. The explosions were deafening.

"When you get to the main road, head north!" roared Bahadur, but Gabriel had already made the call.

Battered and broken, the old bus made its way through the icy deluge, its undercarriage lit by the flickering flames of the burning debris that still clung to it. Behind them, the chain reaction of detonating ammunitions continued, lighting up the stormy sky with flashes that rivaled the lightning itself.

CHAPTER 26

Central Jerusalem, Israel.

Christian stood in his new command centre, a glowing hologram of planet Earth hovering before him as tall as a man. Within the desecrated sanctity of the Kadosh Hakodashim, the globe could be seen. It was a high-resolution replica of the fragile planet, and its surface was rippling with activity. Ribbon-shaped sections of reconnaissance were wrapping themselves around the sphere in a constant state of update.

Covering its surface were hundreds of interactive icons, each one providing access to the thousands of real-time events occurring around the world. Demonstrations, terrorist bombings, troop movements, missile attacks, stormfronts, natural disasters, and staggering regional death tolls.

Amidst the clutter of electronic equipment, Christian worked the holographic interface like a conductor before an orchestra, rotating the globe effortlessly with one hand while circling areas on its surface with the other and directing them to monitors on the periphery.

Snaking over the golden floor were the countless cables that connected the equipment to the massive servers that had been assembled in the refrigerated chamber outside. From there, a dozen technicians monitored and maintained live feeds from NORAD, SIGINT, GCHQ, NSA, and the CIA, to name only a few.

Dr. Bennington left his armed escorts at the tunnel entrance and entered the holy chamber alone. The shock of what he saw there made him clutch the wall as he climbed the final step, his knees threatening to give way.

There could now be no doubt that the events of the previous night had not been a dream. The walls were still coated in the black vitriol that had desecrated chamber, and in the air still hung the fetid stench of rot and decay.

Before him, under the shadow of the two blackened Cherubim, Bennington could see Christian silhouetted against the giant hologram of the Earth, but it was not he that commanded his attention.

Chained to the defiled Arc of the Covenant was Cynthia's undead, demon-possessed corpse. She was hunched over, and in the act of devouring the gory contents of a bucket at her feet, her dead eyes radiating cold malevolence. Her movements were frenetic, and the guttural sounds that escaped her mouth echoed through the chamber as she fed.

Bennington shuddered when those fiendish eyes shot up to meet his own. Her distended jaw was snapping and tugging at a rubbery length of pig intestine held fast in her hand. The stench of the offal made him gag and cough.

"Thank you for joining me, Doctor," said Christian without turning. "I wanted you to be a part of this."

Bennington noticed something in Christian's voice immediately. It was very subtle and would have been undetectable to anyone other than an experienced psychiatrist. Even still, observing it was all the doctor needed to pull himself together. His patient needed help.

With a decisive effort Bennington shifted his attention away from the strange, paranormal events, and directed it at Christian. The relief he felt was substantial, even if a part of him knew that it was only temporary.

Bennington scanned the back of Christian's form. There was an unsteadiness in his body language, and something in his demeanor was amiss. In order to ascertain what it was, he would need to get him talking.

"What have you done to this sacred chamber, Christian?" he asked, gathering himself.

"I have transformed it into what it was destined to become," said Christian, turning momentarily to face him. "My throne room."

Bennington stepped over the cables to arrive at Christian's side.

"Why did you call me here?"

"I have called you here to witness the beginning of the end," said Christian. "Today, the Coalition will attack China in response to their recent occupation of Taiwan, and in so doing spark a tactical nuclear war that will eventually spread to the Middle East and Africa. From there it will graduate into a full-blown nuclear holocaust."

"Have you lost your mind?" said Bennington, forgetting his professionalism. "Christian, this is madness! You do not have to do this."

"Of course I do not have to do this," said Christian dryly. "But I *want* to do this. There are far too many souls incarnating in China and Africa. The populations in these places must be culled.

"Besides, the Asian and African Unions must begin to become more than fanciful ideas on these continents. They will soon become a necessity, established out of the ruin of the People's Republic of China.

"As the years pass, and the losses are compounded, all nations will at last concede and merge into a fully unified world government."

"This is madness," began Bennington, but Christian held up a hand to silence him.

A communication was coming in. Christian brought a finger to his earpiece.

"You what?" he said, beginning to grow angry.

Bennington strained to hear the tinny voice.

"They have escaped, Mr. Antov," it said. "They have killed seventeen of our men."

"Are you telling me that a group of archaeologists and senior citizens have defeated your entire battalion?"

"The weather here is severe, sir. We have lost them."

"Wait," ordered Christian.

Bennington watched as Christian closed his eyes in concentration.

"They are approaching Ceuta," he said. "Find them and kill them, or I will annihilate the entire coastal region and you along with it. Where is the scroll?"

"We are still digging, sir," came the shaky reply. "We are making good progress."

"I want those artifacts!" snapped Christian. "My patience is wearing thin."

"The Compostela Cube?" asked Bennington, seeing that Christian had severed the line.

"A thorn in my side, Doctor. But one that will soon be extracted and destroyed."

Turning suddenly, Christian made his way down the steps of the dais, past Cynthia's feeding corpse, and towards a bank of eleven monitors that were grouped on a nearby table. Bennington followed, observing Christian as he brought the monitors online.

Each one contained a video feed of a particular steering committee member. There was fear and anxiety in their faces, and it became clear to Bennington that they were no longer even tenuously in control.

"Well, my esteemed colleagues," said Christian, sitting down in a chair. "It would appear the time has come to officially start World War Three."

"The coalition governments have all been notified," said one of the old men in a grim tone.

"Our media infrastructure as well," said another.

"All military levels have ratified the action," said yet another. "Tactical missiles are ready and waiting to launch on your command, sir."

Dr. Bennington shuddered.

What could Christian have done to these men to break their wills so?

He thought of young Cynthia dying by Christian's hand.

How many of the committee's family members has he put to death to achieve this subservience?

Bennington watched Christian leave his chair and suddenly felt as though he were in a dream. An encompassing feeling of twisted *wrongness* was seeping into the ancient chamber now, permeating the air around him. He thought he could hear an echo of the demonic chorus that had assaulted him the previous night. It was faint, but nevertheless present. The supernatural quality of it sent an evil chill up his spine.

My God in heaven, can you not prevent this?

Banks of lights had been installed throughout the cube-shaped chamber. They sent a dimmed glow up onto the ceiling, with the blackened wings of the cherubim casting ominous shadows.

"Launch phase one!" cried Christian suddenly, and Bennington gasped in horror.

On the holographic globe, twelve missiles had emerged from the central Pacific Ocean. Christian magnified them with the wave of a hand, their tails glowing as they made their way to a dozen different targets.

Bennington swallowed hard. The projected planet seemed almost alive to him; as though it were trembling in anticipation of the blow it was about to receive.

"Witness the birth of a new era," said Christian.

A computer-generated voice of a woman spoke out.

"First impact in nineteen minutes and counting."

Bennington staggered backwards. He could see Christian standing before the glowing planet, a distinct climate of psychological uncertainty about him. The head of the most powerful organization in the world was doubting himself. Bennington was sure of it.

Looking to the globe, he could see the twelve ICBMs making their way ever closer to their targets. He brought his hands to his face as the grim realization set in. The world he had always known and loved would soon cease to exist.

"Dear God in heaven," he whispered, aghast. "Save the children."

CHAPTER 27

Ceuta, Spanish Morocco.

Natasha followed the others as they moved through a derelict tunnel beneath the ancient city of Ceuta. Around her was the clutter of what had once been a busy underground hashish factory, the overturned tables and dried out piles of marijuana stalks giving testament to the tunnel's former purpose. Having been tipped off by Vanderhoff operatives, the Spanish Civil Guard had raided the site a week ago, stripping Nasrallah of yet another operation, and driving him one step closer to complete Vanderhoff subservience.

Just ahead, Natasha could see that Bahadur had stopped before a metal door set in a wall of newly laid brick. The door looked to have been forced open during the raid.

"We are here," he said deeply, his bear-like hands on his hips. "This is the treasure room, the chamber where we found the scroll."

Bahadur entered first. He tripped a breaker that the smugglers had installed and the room was instantly flooded with light, revealing a golden interior.

"We searched extensively," he said as the party shuffled in behind him. "We could not find the secret entrance depicted on the map, nor any other entrance for that matter. There is only the hole we came in through."

Gabriel scanned the room. It was circular in shape, and relatively large for an underground chamber, measuring approximately thirty feet in diameter. Above him, some ten feet aloft, was a shallow domed ceiling of intricate geometric design, its abundant use of gold leaf and mosaic confirming the chamber's importance.

"This place is like a mini-Alhambra," he said, moving towards one of the many intricate niches adorning its walls. "Outstanding…"

Natasha and the others could not help but be amazed as well. Everything was shimmering magically under the bright lights.

"This must have been wonderful to see when it was full of treasure…" said Natasha, moving to the centre of the chamber and spinning slowly to take in the space.

What Bahadur had said was true. Apart from the haphazard hole the excavators had made when they had discovered the room, the chamber had no doors or exits.

"How could anyone have entered this place?" she said, looking over at Gabriel. "There's no entrance."

Gabriel pulled the bejeweled cylinder from his pack and spread the scroll out on the floor. Natasha knelt down next to him.

"What are you thinking?"

Gabriel pointed out a geometric pattern that was incorporated into the map's design.

"There are two entrances in this chamber," he said. "One of them is up there."

He used his thumb to point at the centre of the ceiling. Natasha looked up and saw the map's pattern duplicated in the carvings there.

"And the other entrance?"

Gabriel rose to his feet and moved to stand beneath the pattern. He bent down and ran his hands over a section of floor just as Bahadur was approaching. There was an expression of curiosity on the giant's face.

"We did not check the floor," he said deeply, raising a crooked eyebrow. "We were searching for doors."

"No doors in this kind of chamber," said Gabriel.

He brushed away some sandy gravel to reveal a large hexagonal stone depicting the map's pattern again. Natasha and Bahadur watched as he cleared away its edges with his fingers, and then peered up at the ceiling. He appeared to be counting.

"What are you doing?" asked Natasha.

He patted the hexagonal stone with the flat of his palm, thinking.

"This is the entrance to St. Michael's Pass," he said. "I'm sure of it."

He glanced over his shoulder at a section of the chamber's wall.

"The Moors were trading partners with Carthage," he said, rubbing the stubble on his jaw. "If this mechanism is what I think it is, they must have also traded engineering tips..."

Gabriel rose and walked over to the section of wall he had been looking at. Natasha and Bahadur followed close behind. It was covered in a three-dimensional honeycomb structure that mirrored the map's pattern perfectly. Gabriel frowned.

"What's wrong?" asked Natasha.

He pointed at a section of the design.

"Someone's been here already," he said, perplexed. "Look at that actuating stone."

"I see nothing," said Bahadur, bending closer.

"It's the only one not covered in dust," said Amir, coming up behind Bahadur. "Whoever it was knew exactly which stone to press."

Natasha chewed her lip.

"Maybe Nasrallah figured it out. Maybe he already has the Book of Khalifah..."

Bahadur frowned in confusion.

"There is no other man alive who knows of this chamber. Who else could it be?"

"There's only one way to find out," said Gabriel.

He looked over his shoulder and saw that the old nun was dawdling in the centre of the room.

"You might not want to stand there, Suora," he said.

"Oh dear me, child," she stammered, looking down to see the hexagonal stone that Gabriel had only just brushed off. "Do excuse me. Good heavens."

When Suora had moved aside, Gabriel gave the honeycomb structure one last look and then placed his palm on the stone that had been cleared of dust. All watched as it slipped effortlessly into the wall. Almost immediately a low rumbling could be felt reverberating beneath their feet.

"Is that normal?" asked Natasha, stepping back.

"As normal as ancient counterweights slipping along cast bronze tracks can be," said Gabriel.

"Gotta love Phoenician engineering," added Amir, biting down on a toothpick.

Amazingly, the section of stone where Suora had been standing dropped and slid aside, clearing the way for an elaborately carved spiralling wooden staircase to rise slowly from the floor.

At the same time, from a cleverly hidden section in the ceiling, there descended another staircase of the same design. Within seconds the two had met with a solid thump, forming a perfectly proportioned stairway that led up into the ceiling and down into the floor.

"Good work, Gabriel!" cried the old bishop, clapping his hands in delight. "Well done, man!"

Gabriel approached the staircase with hands on hips. He was looking up into the ceiling.

"Everybody wait here," he said. "And for God's sake, don't touch anything."

They all watched as Gabriel ascended in measured steps, the wandering beam of his flashlight remaining temporarily visible after he had vanished. Everyone waited expectantly.

"Where has he gone to now?" said Natasha, more to herself than anyone else.

"Have patience, child," said Fra.

He was standing beside her and could sense her concern.

"Gabriel has done things like this many times before."

As if in response to the brother's words, Gabriel emerged from the dark opening and began his descent in a carefree trot. Oddly enough, tucked under his arm were two floral bouquets, fresh and blooming.

"For the two loveliest ladies in the entire Moorish empire," he said with a bow, handing the flowers to Natasha and Suora.

"You're crazy!" said Natasha, smiling with delight.

"Wherever did you get these, my child?"

"It would appear the Caliph's primary residence has over the centuries become Ceuta's flower market," said Gabriel. "The passage led to a concealed door right behind the main steps."

Bahadur moved to the stairs and looked up, frowning with concern.

"We must seal this entrance immediately."

"You're absolutely right," said Gabriel, "We'd best get downstairs. With any luck we'll find a mechanism that'll do just that."

Gabriel went first, with Natasha close behind. Immediately the earthy smell of an underground chamber filled their olfactory, a cool and damp air engulfing them as they descended. By the echoing sounds of their footsteps, they knew they had entered a large chamber, but the walls could still not be seen. Only an inky blackness surrounded them, swallowing the beams of their flashlights.

"You'd all best come along," said Gabriel, glancing up at the others. "There's plenty of room down here. This chamber's massive."

They followed the spiralling steps down to what appeared to be a round platform, surrounded by a stone railing. Bahadur was last to descend, and he lit a flare when he had reached the bottom. In that instant their surroundings burst to life, revealing a scene that none of them had been expecting.

"Good God!" exclaimed the bishop. "This is outstanding!"

The other's gasped in surprise. Under the light of the flare, they could see that the secret staircase had descended onto a terrace of sorts. It was perched on the peak of a great rock formation, one that rose from the base of an enormous underground cavern.

Stretching out in all directions was a jagged sea of stalagmites and stalactites, clinging like teeth to the oddly shaped cave. In the light of the flare, glossy surfaces of rock glowed as though illuminated from within, with sporadic groupings of quartz crystals at the extremities of the chamber, shining like stars in a night sky.

"It's so beautiful," whispered Natasha in awe. "I've never seen anything like it."

However captivated by the sight, the party's attention soon turned to something far more pressing. The spiral staircase they had just descended was sinking into the ground, and above them, two slabs of stone were sliding into place over the opening they had come down through. A resounding boom echoed through the cavern as the heavy stones met.

"Well, Captain," said Gabriel to the giant. "Problem solved. The entrance to the treasure room is now shut."

"You were expecting this to happen?" asked Bahadur, his voice sounding even deeper than usual in the echoing gallery.

"Not exactly," said Gabriel, rubbing his chin, "but by the design of that mechanism, both exits will have closed, and that's what we wanted, right? Just don't ask me to open them again."

"Look at this, boss," said Amir suddenly.

He had moved to the side of the platform and found a section of intricately worked mosaic tiles.

"It's a map of the caves," said Natasha, coming up beside him.

Gabriel bent closer to read.

"You're absolutely right," he said, "but there's also a warning here. Under no circumstance is anyone to enter into the tunnels without royal escorts."

He read on and then turned to face the others.

"Well guys, it looks like we found it. Welcome to the legendary Pass of St. Michael."

"And which way is Gibraltar, my son?" asked the old bishop, barely able to contain his excitement.

Gabriel pointed at two ornate pedestals. They were waist high, and they marked where a flight of steps descended to the cavern floor.

"The pedestals are markers," he said, "All we need to do is follow them. They should take us directly there. The only thing we've got to worry about is bumping into Nasrallah."

Scotty Roberts tightened his hold on the assault rifle.

"And you're sure he came down, mate?"

Gabriel nodded slowly, pointing to the mosaic map that Amir had discovered. The dust that covered it had been recently wiped clean.

"And there was only one set of tracks on the stairs," he said to Scotty. "If they didn't belong to Nasrallah then who?"

Bahadur rubbed his colossal chin.

"It's not like Nasrallah to go anywhere alone," he said deeply.

He looked over at Miller and Stephenson.

"Follow up the rear and be on your guard. We go now."

CHAPTER 28

Central Jerusalem, Israel.

Christian awoke with a start. He was seated at a table in the desecrated Holy of Holies, his head still resting in his folded arms. He had been dreaming of his brother Isaac's death again. It was a repeating nightmare, brought on by what the Zurvanites had revealed to him only days before.

Through their eyes he had seen Isaac butcher the corpse of his son and open the Portal of Ahreimanius. Christian knew that no man could have survived the fires that ensued, and something in his heart cried out in pain. His brother had been the only person who had ever shown him kindness and love. He stifled his emotions at once and forced himself to sit up.

Christian glanced at the holographic earth suspended above him. It was glowing and rippling with life, as though it were a living organism. To his right a blinking bank of monitors offered views of a nuclear war that was rapidly engulfing the planet.

His eyes focused on one of the screens. A drone was flying a low surveillance route over a decimated city. There were countless dead littering the streets, their corpses like blackened logs in a burnt-out fire pit. Christian felt a spasm of grief despite himself. He denied it at once.

I don't give a shit. Let them all die.

His words did little to squelch the guilt that was welling up in him. For the first time since his childhood, Christian was experiencing traces of compassion, and its presence sent a deep wave of fear and uncertainty through him. He grew angry with himself.

I'll have none of this bullshit! Humanity is a scourge! They're rats needing to be exterminated!

He sprang to his feet, the room spinning as the blood rushed to his head. Compassion was weakness. It was his enemy, and he reacted to it as though his very life were at stake.

In a matter of seconds his dark self had surfaced in response, a reptilian shadow that claimed with unquestionable authority to be his true identity. It came on a wave of fear and hatred and exploded into fury.

Christian jerked his head around with murderous intent. The oscillating forms of the four Zurvanites had just materialized behind him, and his hatred of them merged with his wrath to produce a surge of unbridled dark power. Instantly he felt nothing for the dead that lay strewn in the streets. He cared not that tens of thousands lay trapped and dying in the rubble. They were a blight. They deserved to die. He pushed himself away from the table, drunk with rage.

"Kill them!" hissed the Zurvanites wickedly. *"Kill them all and you will be God!"*

Christian could see Cynthia's undead corpse as it squatted in the shadows. There was a cruel, demonic light in the cadaver's eyes, and it fueled his hatred and fury like gasoline to a flame. He was the one in charge, and now he would show everyone just how powerful he had become.

"Computer," he said with cold malice. "Prepare to execute the Lazarus Sequence."

Even within the Vanderhoff Group, the Lazarus Sequence was a covert and highly classified operation. Only the Nautonnier and Christian's father had been fully aware of its sinister, occult objectives.

By annihilating the populations in the mountainous regions surrounding the Portal of Ahreimanius, their new biological weapon would supply tens of thousands of reanimated corpses to an army of demons waiting to possess them.

Christian trembled with dark anticipation. Ever since he had seen how swiftly Cynthia's corpse had been taken, he had been filled with an irrepressible urge to set the Lazarus Sequence in motion.

"Viral components activated," said the computer in its seductive female voice. "Bringing drones online."

Christian waited. The sequence would utilize four unmanned drones stationed at a US airbase in Torrejon, Spain. Having given the orders to transport the virus from the Jerusalem complex the previous day, Christian knew that the drones would by now be fully armed. It was just a matter of deploying them.

"Drones will be fully functional in three minutes and counting," said the computer.

The bank of screens came to life next to Christian just then. Several of them were filled with the faces of steering committee members.

"Nautonnier!" cried one of them. "Please! You must not do this!"

Christian looked over his shoulder to see the mortified faces of his colleagues. He gave a dry chuckle. They only knew of the contagion, and the rampant undead that the virus would bring. They had no clue as to the throngs of demonic entities that would soon be taking possession of the newly made cadavers. He smiled coldly.

The dead shall walk.

"Your Eminence!" said another. "This is not part of our agenda. These drones must not be launched. Please reconsider!"

Christian muted their displays with the wave of a hand and continued to wait impatiently.

"All drones armed and ready to execute Viral Sequence Lazarus," said the computer. "Awaiting your order, Mr. Antov."

Christian could see that the entire muted Steering Committee was online now, speaking and gesticulating frantically. He dismissed them with a hateful scowl.

Weak and compassionate fools. They make me sick to my stomach.

Christian's mind was made up. He would not stop the killing until the prophecy had been fulfilled and two-thirds of the world's population was either dead or undead. He was the one in control now, and he would prove just how indifferent he was to the suffering of others.

"Computer," he said coldly. "Deploy the drones."

CHAPTER 29

Northern Morocco.

They had been descending for a little over an hour when Bahadur at last called for a halt. The path they followed had spiraled down from the platform where they had first entered into the caves, a series of markers guiding them through a landscape of fractured rock and tangled stalagmites. Although constantly on the lookout, they had as of yet been unable to find any tracks belonging to the mysterious person who had gone before them.

From where she stood, Natasha could see Bahadur squatting low with Gabriel at his side. The two were studying a marker and talking quietly amongst themselves.

"We're in good hands," said Amir, coming up beside her. "They're the two smartest people I know."

Natasha watched Bahadur lift a powerful arm to point at something. Gabriel looked and nodded in agreement.

"He isn't like the other smugglers," said Natasha. "Why didn't he become a university professor?"

Amir was looking at them as well.

"My cousin grew up in a family of pirates," he said, pushing aside his dreadlocks to look at her. "His father was a smuggler captain. Bahadur was expected to follow in his footsteps."

"He should have refused."

Amir smiled slightly.

"He did. He had already passed his university entrance exams when his father was arrested. Bahadur took a seven-year wrap for him."

Natasha turned to look at Amir in disbelief.

"Why would he do that?"

Amir slipped a cinnamon toothpick into his mouth and shrugged.

"He did it for the family. Things were at a point where everything would have been lost if his father got put away, but Bahadur was—"

"Bahadur was expendable," said Natasha, shaking her head. "What a waste of a good mind."

"He studied all the time he was in jail," said Amir. "Bahadur is obsessed with knowledge. He's like a caliph from the Golden Age. He believes knowledge can transform a person. That's why he got that tattoo on his neck while he was in jail. So that he would never forget his destiny."

Natasha shook her head again, but this time in amazement.

"A moth," she said softly. "The universal symbol of transformation…"

Amir looked back at his cousin.

"Bahadur is honoured to be on this quest, Doctor. The Cube stands for everything he holds sacred. It's funny, but we couldn't have found a better man to assist us. He's helping to finish something that our Moorish ancestors started a thousand years ago."

Natasha's eyes were wide with admiration now. Their battered and bruised captain was not only selfless and brave, he was also spiritually inspired. She was going to say something when Bahadur rose and turned to face the party.

"We will stay here for the night," he said in his deep basso. "It has been a long day, and we have made good progress."

Natasha looked around to see that he could not have chosen a better spot to make camp. There was even a trickling stream of sweet water here, and the floor of the cavern was smooth and warm to the touch.

It was not long before the party settled down to eat the sandwiches that Fra had prepared back at the village. They chatted excitedly while they dined, revisiting the many events that had transpired over the past few days, and trying to figure out what their best course of action would be once they reached Gibraltar.

Only Scotty Roberts remained silent and lost in thought. He was sitting next to Amir, quietly watching him pack his ancient chillum and stoke it to life.

Amir exhaled a billowing cloud of the fragrant smoke and pointed to Natasha's equipment case with the stem of the pipe. He had seen her carrying it since they had first met in Estepona.

"What have you got in there, Doc?" he asked, passing the chillum to Scotty.

"It's a BIRIS," she said, reaching for it. "A portable 3-D imagining scanner. We brought it to scan the Cube, but we haven't had a chance to do it yet."

"How does it work?"

"It uses lasers to image an object at varying depths."

Gabriel popped the last bite of his sandwich into his mouth.

"That thing runs on batteries, doesn't it?"

Natasha nodded.

"Let's scan the Cube right now then," he said, rising to his feet with a weary groan. "Maybe we can get an idea of what makes it tick."

Having finished eating, the others seemed less interested in the Cube and more interested in getting some sleep. Scotty in particular. He was not used to the potency of Amir's special blend and had soon returned the pipe to him with a bewildered expression on his face.

One by one they curled up in the blankets that Miller and Stephenson had salvaged from the village, leaving Gabriel, Natasha, and Amir to pursue their investigations alone.

It was not long before the three had set the Cube spinning on a platform in the BIRIS, watching as the computer began to render a three-dimensional scan of it. They were amazed by what they saw.

"That's really strange," said Natasha, frowning. "This artifact is comprised of thousands of layers. There seems to be no end to them..."

They watched as one image replaced the next, each comprised of chaotic patterns similar to that of snow on a television screen. To the bottom right of the computer's monitor, they could see the counter clicking forward as each new layer was detected. It was already nearing three thousand and showed no signs of stopping. Just then, an error window appeared in the centre of the monitor.

"What's the problem?" asked Amir over Natasha's shoulder.

"We're out of RAM," she said. "The file's too big, even though I've been scanning at low res."

Gabriel rubbed his chin. The monitor was showing that the BIRIS had penetrated less than a millimeter into the artifact.

"Would it be possible to dump all these files and just get a single, high-res scan of the first interior layer?"

"Sure," said Natasha, liking the idea. "But it'll take about an hour to do it."

"We've got nothing but time," said Gabriel, leaning back against the smooth cave wall and closing his eyes.

Natasha initiated the scan and then took up one of the blankets, curling up next to him. It was not long before they had both fallen asleep.

"Baby, wake up. I think it's done."

It was Gabriel who spoke, and Natasha opened her eyes to see Amir bent over the computer, encased in a cloud of smoke.

"It's covered in markings," he said, looking over at them through his dreadlocks.

Natasha rose to her feet, keeping the blanket wrapped around her. She was amazed by what she saw on the screen.

"They look like symbols..." she said, studying the rotating cube. "Thousands of them, and all lined up in perfect grids."

"They're too small to make out," said Gabriel, pushing back his messy hair. "Could we zoom in and isolate just one of the sides?"

Natasha manipulated the scan until the screen was filled with hundreds of triangular symbols.

"Look familiar?" asked Gabriel, peering over at Natasha.

"It's cuneiform," she said. "I saw something similar to this in your father's journal."

Gabriel brought out the diary, removing it from the watertight freezer bag he was using to store it in now. There, on the left side of two opposing pages, could be seen a square grid containing symbols similar to those on the screen. On the facing page was a grid comprised of standard numerals. Gabriel shook his head.

"Cuneiform numerals on the left, and their conversions on the right... I don't know where my father could have dug this up, but it matches the layout of our scan perfectly. I wouldn't be surprised if every layer of the Cube is structured the same way."

"But why Sumerian cuneiform?" asked Natasha.

Gabriel shrugged.

"Whatever the reason, these numbers are definitely based on the Sumerian sexagesimal system."

"Sexagesimal," repeated Amir. "What's that?"

"It's still around today," said Gabriel. "It's a numerical system based in sixty. We use it to measure time and degrees. Sixty seconds in a minute, sixty minutes in an hour, three hundred and sixty degrees in a circle.

"The ancient Sumerians and Babylonians used it to solve complex astronomical calculations. Sixty is an HCN, or a Highly Composite Number. It allows for calculations that would be impractical with the standard Arabic numerals we use today."

"But what do these numbers mean?" asked Natasha, her brown eyes wide with concern.

"They look to me to be matrices, my child," came the unexpected voice of the old nun.

"Suora," said Natasha, noting how drained she looked. "I thought you were asleep."

"I was, dear girl," she said weakly, "but nature calls the old more often than the young. I was only going off to have a pee when I saw you all gathered here."

"You're sure these are matrices, Suora?" asked Gabriel.

He passed her the journal, along with a flashlight so that she could have a better look.

"Most definitely, my child," she said, nodding. "They appear to be representing linear transformations. Do not forget. I taught mathematics for most of my life. I know linear algebra when I see it."

The old nun produced her glasses and squinted at the numbers.

"This is very complex," she said quietly, shaking her head. "It would appear to be a type of algorithm, but what it is expounding I could not even begin to say."

She rubbed her chin and took a closer look.

"It could very well be emulating a quantum mechanical model... It reminds me of Dirac and Heisenberg's work back in my university days…"

Gabriel and Natasha looked at each other amazed. They would never have suspected that Suora would have known such things, but doing the math, Gabriel realized that most of the quantum mechanics used today had been discovered around the time of Suora's birth. Her generation would have been the first to study these models.

"What else can you tell us about these matrices, Suora?" he asked.

"Not much without further study, my child," she said. "Only that they appear to be using different dimensional vector spaces at the same time... Solving this would be a challenge even for Albert Einstein. It would take a very powerful computer to make sense of these coefficients; much, much bigger than this little one you have."

Suora had no sooner said these words than Gabriel and Amir exchanged a glance, the same name popping into their heads simultaneously.

"Peralta," they said in unison.

"Who?" asked Natasha.

Gabriel scratched his head.

"He's a crazy Gibraltarian. A hacker and a smuggler. If he can't decipher these numbers, then nobody can."

"There's only one problem, boss," said Amir. "He's been AWOL for months now. Word was that he partnered up with Nasrallah last spring. Nobody's seen him since."

"Really?" said Gabriel, perplexed. "But Peralta hates Nasrallah. Why would he be doing business with him?"

Amir shrugged and pocketed his pipe.

"Nobody can figure it out. Not even Bahadur."

"I hope he's all right," said Gabriel.

"He's smart, boss," said Amir in his even tone. "I'm sure he's fine. I just wish there was a way we could contact him. I'll start asking around when we get back to Gib."

Gabriel nodded and passed a hand through his hair. He looked over at the old nun.

"Suora," he said, holding the journal out to her in its plastic bag. "You might as well hang on to this. If you get a chance tomorrow, it would be great if you could take a closer look at those numbers. The more we know about them the better."

"I most certainly will, my child," she said, taking the journal and shuffling off.

The three of them turned to see her disappearing into the shadows.

"Go to sleep, all of you," she said over her shoulder. "It has been a long day, and we can talk more about this in the morning. I am off to pee now. No peeking!"

CHAPTER 30

Gibraltar.

It was well past sundown by the time Major Roberts returned to the Governor's House. His day had been spent playing political ping pong with what seemed to be a divided and entirely dysfunctional European Union.

With the global climate in the state it was, it seemed there were no delegates available to help resolve the dispute that had erupted between Gibraltar and the Spanish Civil Guard. On the one side, he was being told to comply with their mandate, while on the other, that he should in no way do so.

With half of Europe now under martial law, it was becoming more and more obvious that regional authorities were disregarding statutes in order to accomplish objectives that would have normally been impossible.

"The Guardia Civil is accusing Gibraltar of harbouring terrorists," Roberts had told one of the officials at the European Commission in Brussels. "And the Spanish government is doing nothing to stop their aggressive behavior. There are no grounds for their claim. It's a fabrication created to validate what is nothing other than an aggressive act of war against Gibraltar.

"At this very moment our city is besieged by radical Spanish militia posing as EU anti-terrorist police. I would like it to go on record that Gibraltar will defend herself. She will not fall prey to Spain's new inquisition."

Passing through the main chambers, Roberts thought back on what he had said. Perhaps dubbing the incident as Spain's new inquisition had been a bit much, but he had been tired and frustrated with the EU's lack of coherence on the matter.

I'll phrase things differently in the letter.

He made his way through the convent, his footsteps echoing in the empty hallways. It was late now, and everyone had gone home, leaving him with an odd sense of foreboding. He was not looking forward to telling the governor the latest news.

He arrived at the old knight's door only to find it slightly ajar. Within he could hear the voice of a woman speaking in hushed tones. He knocked quietly.

"Come in," said the woman, and entering, Roberts recognized the pretty nurse at once.

"Hello, Clara," he said. "How's our governor feeling this evening?"

The nurse shot him a sad smile.

"Alas, Major," said the old man, summoning the little strength he had left. "The governor is feeling heartbroken if the truth must be told. I have asked young Clara if she would like to go out dancing with me this evening and she has regretfully declined."

Roberts smiled.

"She knows she could never keep up with you, sir."

The governor did his best to return the smile, and then seeing the major's face said:

"Ah, but I see you are troubled, my faithful Aide du Camp. Clara, be a lovely thing and do leave us alone for a moment. I fear the major has some important matters he wishes to discuss."

The young nurse made a quick alteration to the governor's blankets and then left the room, closing the door softly behind her.

"I could never have imagined I would have fallen in love again," said the governor between coughs, "but that pretty little thing has truly softened my brittle old heart."

"She's lovely, sir," said Roberts, smiling. "An angel, to be sure."

"Come and sit down, son," said the old man. "Tell me what has happened."

Roberts did as he was told, a deep concern furrowing his brow as he spoke.

"The United Coalition has responded to China's invasion of Taiwan, sir," he said solemnly, his right eye giving a few quick blinks. "There's been an exchange of tactical nuclear strikes in the region. Millions are dead."

The old governor gazed into Roberts' eyes without saying a word. He was digesting the news as best he could.

"We also had a small nuclear device go off in the Madrid airport," added Roberts solemnly. "It was similar to the one that went off in Atlanta last week."

"It has begun," said the governor at length. "It will not be long before the entire world is drawn into the conflagration."

Roberts held the governor's eyes.

"You warned me many times that this would happen, sir," he said. "And I always doubted you. I'll never doubt you again. What would you have me do, sir?"

"The time has come to prepare the people of Gibraltar for the worst," said the old duke. "As you know, the purpose for this war is to destroy the free world. The controlling elite want to build a global police state, run by a centralized world government. This has always been their plan."

The governor broke into a fit of coughing, and only after regaining his composure did he continue to speak.

"The destruction will happen on many levels," he said. "We are already experiencing one such level. Gibraltar is besieged by the enemies of freedom. Do not call them Spanish, for the Spaniards are a noble people. These are the pawns of those in higher positions. We must never overlook this fact and be fooled by what the media says. Should these forces enter onto the Rock, Gibraltar will never again be the same."

"They will not enter," said Roberts unfalteringly. "Gibraltar has never fallen to any siege, and thanks to your foresight we are well prepared, sir. Gibraltar will hold."

The governor smiled weakly. These were the words he wanted to hear from his Aide du Camp. He patted Roberts' hand and continued to speak.

"It is time that the people began growing accustomed to the possibility of having to retreat to the underground city," he said, even weaker now. "The nuclear war will soon spread to the Middle East and Africa. It will not be long before contaminated air makes its way here. Biological weapons will also be used.

Viruses will be propagated to cull populations. They will find their way here as well. It has all been planned."

"But, sir," whispered Roberts. "How can this be? How could something so monstrous be on our very doorstep?"

"Gibraltar's population will eventually have to go inside," strained the governor. "There is no other way. It will only be for a certain time, perhaps for a year, perhaps two."

"And what shall become of my wife?" said Roberts, more to himself than to the governor.

"There is still time to bring her over," whispered the old knight.

"But how, sir?" said Roberts, his heart sinking. "The border's closed and there's a blockade in the sea all around us. They'll shoot down any aircraft that attempts to leave our airport, sir. There's no way."

"Be patient," said the governor, patting his arm reassuringly. "A way will be made."

Roberts looked up at him. For some inexplicable reason he believed the old man.

"I'll contact the chief minister in the morning, sir," he said, composing himself again.

"Have them all underground as soon as possible," said the governor, slipping slowly into unconsciousness. "Give them time to make the necessary preparations, but don't let them dally. You know what needs to be done, Major. We have drilled this many times before."

* * * * * *

Major Roberts stood upon Princess Anne's Battery, overlooking the Bay of Gibraltar. The night was bright with the light of a full moon, and the heavy rains had left the sky clear and star-studded. Stretched out below him he could see the many ship lights of the blockade scattered across the water, and in that moment his thoughts went to his wife and the unborn child in her womb.

Roberts made the calculations in his head. Anita was not thirty-five kilometres away as the crow flies, but the distance could have been a hundred times that and it would have made no difference.

He turned himself in her direction, trying to feel her presence over the space between them. In that moment, he promised himself that he would get her back, despite the fact that he had no clue as to how he might do so. In the silence of the night, he could still hear the governor's encouraging words as if they had only just been spoken.

"A way will be made," Roberts said to the night. "A way will be made."

CHAPTER 31

Under the Mediterranean Sea.

They had been travelling for the better part of the morning, their path leading them deep into the entrails of the earth. By each of the directional markers they had found stockpiles of torches, and it was under their flickering light that they made their way through expansive caverns and along tight chasms.

The subterranean geography of the place had proven to be so diverse and breathtaking that the group spent much of their time in silent contemplation as they walked. It was in a particularly unique cavern that Bahadur called for a stop. They had come upon a new marker, and it would need to be consulted before they could proceed.

Bahadur bent over the stone to read its surface. The network of low pedestals had proven to be invaluable, guiding them faithfully past many deadly traps designed to prohibit southward passage, and through what would have otherwise been an unnavigable maze.

At present they found themselves in a steeply angled chasm, the massive rock shelf before them fragmenting into four possible directions. Gabriel squinted into the narrow spaces around them, feeling much like an insect in danger of being squashed should the planet so much as hiccup.

Turning to look in the direction they had come, it appeared to Gabriel as though a massive rock formation had been wrenched apart by tremendous forces, leaving between its two severed halves the meter-wide gap that the group had only just made its way along. Natasha was looking back as well.

"What do you think?" asked Gabriel, using the sleeve of his shirt to wipe the sweat from his brow.

The temperature had been growing progressively hotter as they descended.

"It's as though I could feel the weight of the entire Mediterranean Sea over my head."

Natasha touched the perspiring rock and then tasted the tips of her fingers.

"It's not salty."

"Not this far down," said Gabriel. "All the salt's been filtered out of it."

Natasha chewed her lip and looked around.

"Shouldn't we have found the Chamber of Khalifah by now?"

"I've been thinking the same thing," said Gabriel. "We've got to be really close. I'd wager we're at the halfway point to Gibraltar, and down at least a couple of kilometres, judging by this heat."

He glanced over at Suora and Fra, a look of concern coming over his features. They were both sitting on the chamber floor, their faces white from exhaustion. Out of the two, the old nun looked the worse. Her breathing was strained and irregular.

"I'm worried too," said Natasha, guessing Gabriel's thoughts.

"Uncle Marcus is doing great," he whispered, so as not to be heard. "He's like a giddy schoolboy, but Fra looks like hell, and Suora even worse. Maybe we should call it quits for the day."

At that moment Bahadur rose to his feet, his flaming torch held high. The rest of the party had dropped to the chamber floor, and the only one still standing was Scotty Roberts. He was perched on a rock, smoking a cigarillo, and silent as usual. Too many good men had been lost back at the castle, and the smuggler was still coming to grips with the tragedy.

"Dr. Parker," said Bahadur deeply, directing his gaze at Gabriel. "Perhaps you could assist me with this marker."

Gabriel and Natasha approached the brown giant. Following his lead, they squatted down beside the stone, the Islamic text merging with complex geometric patterns in the gold and alabaster.

"Of the four possible routes," said Bahadur, running a thick finger over the stone to tap a particular section, "there are only two that will serve us, and those barely so. I am gravely concerned for the elders. They will not endure this heat very much longer."

Gabriel nodded sombrely and bent to study the text. It did not take him long to decipher their limited options.

"This doesn't look good," he muttered, rubbing the back of his neck as he read.

"What is it, Gabriel," whispered Natasha. "What does it say?"

He replied in a hushed tone so as not to be overheard.

"By the looks of it, this igneous formation's the weakest point in the whole cave system. It's prone to seismic activity. The marker says that up ahead we're going to see the chasm we're in fall off into some kind of fissure, and that it's not uncommon for torrents of water to empty into it from the sea above. It warns of a great danger to travellers should this happen when they're in the vicinity."

Gabriel turned his gaze away from the stone marker and towards Natasha. Bahadur did the same.

"There are four ways to go," said Gabriel. "Two of them lead to galleries located east and west of here. They're basically dead ends unless you want to crawl on your belly for a kilometre in sweltering heat. The other two passages cross the fissure above us and below us."

He pointed at a heavy bronze door set into the cavernous wall behind Natasha.

"All four passages are behind that water lock."

Natasha glanced at the door and then looked back at Gabriel and Bahadur.

"So what's the problem?"

Bahadur frowned and spoke, his voice deep with apprehension.

"The marker warns that the lower passage is very treacherous. It is exceptionally hot and can often become flooded with seawater."

"No one is advised to take it," added Gabriel. "The one above us is the one they recommend. Apparently, there's a bridge that crosses the chasm there."

"So why not take that one?" asked Natasha.

"The Moors made the bridge retractable."

"And?"

"And it takes a guide to operate it. A guide who would, at that point, turn back to Morocco."

"I don't understand," said Natasha.

Gabriel frowned and pushed back his hair.

"Back when we first entered the caves," he said. "There was a caution that forbade anyone to proceed without royal escorts. All these markers along the way have basically been for their use. It would appear that at least two escorts accompanied each expedition. This marker's saying that one escort will stay behind in order to operate the bridge."

"Why would they do that?" asked Natasha angrily.

Gabriel shook his head.

"The Moors didn't want enemies using the pass to sneak into their palaces," he said. "My guess is that there's some kind of barrier in the lower passage as well."

"So what are we going to do?"

"We cannot take the lower route," whispered Bahadur, turning his massive head in the direction of the old nun. "It is utterly out of the question. Not just because the elders would never survive the heat, but also because the Chamber of Khalifah could easily reside on this side of the bridge."

Gabriel nodded.

"I was thinking the same thing. If the lower route's prone to flooding, the upper passage would be the place to build the secret chamber."

"Then what can we do?" asked Natasha. "One of us can't just stay behind…"

"We have no choice but to take the higher path," said Bahadur. "I will carry Suora. You and the others can help Fra and Bishop Marcus along. If anything, gaining altitude will offer them a break from this heat. If we cannot all pass the chasm, I will activate the bridge from this side and then proceed to the lower path. We will reunite at the first junction point on the other side."

Gabriel and Natasha nodded in agreement and rose to their feet. There were no other alternatives if they wanted to keep Suora and Fra alive and avoid the risk of accidentally skirting around the Chamber of Khalifah.

Gabriel checked the bronze door for traps and then worked the heavy iron wheel set into the wall next to it. Soon the door was rising noisily into the ceiling, a cool draft of air pouring in from the passage beyond.

"We go up!" announced Bahadur, turning to the others. "We will soon leave this heat behind."

When they had all passed through the door, Gabriel released the holding mechanism and the heavy barrier came down with a rattling crash. He turned to peer up the dark passage, holding up a flickering torch to dispel the gloom.

"All right," he said with a grimace. "Let's see where this goes."

CHAPTER 32

Los Picos de Europa, Northern Spain.

Isaac awoke to a violent pounding and opened his eyes in time to see the blue-haired girl burst into his room. Her boyfriend was clinging to her side, pale, frightened, and wounded. There was an open gash on his left shoulder.

"Something terrible has happened!" she blurted through her tears. "My Pedro has been hurt. Help us. Please!"

Isaac watched her lay the boy down on the floor and then turn to lock the door behind her. There was a frantic urgency to everything she was doing, one that Isaac could not understand.

"There is no need to panic," he said kindly, rising from his bed and beginning to dress. "I have some medical experience. The wound does not look life threatening. All will be well, young lady."

"You do not understand!" she cried, frantically sliding the room's armoire to block the door. "They've gotten inside!"

Isaac buttoned his shirt and watched as Shackleton approached the boy. The dog sniffed him suspiciously and then shot him an intense glare. Isaac frowned in confusion. They were obviously in danger, but from whom?

"My dear child," he said, putting on his shoes. "What are you saying? Who has gotten inside? What is happening?"

"The people of the village," stammered the girl. "All those poor people…"

The boy was only semi-conscious now, perched lifelessly against the wall. She turned from him to face Isaac, her expression grave.

"They walk around as though they were asleep, but they are not. They are dead. I am sure of it. They are dead yet they still walk!"

Isaac donned his ragged suit jacket and approached her.

"They're killing everyone!" she cried, clinging to him and bursting into tears. "Those they don't eat rise up again and join in the killing."

Isaac pulled away enough to see her face. As gently as he could he lifted her chin until he could look into her eyes.

"Start from the beginning, child," he said, his brow furrowed. "Tell me exactly what has happened."

The girl swallowed hard and brushed aside her frazzled blue hair.

"I was sleeping with Pedro in the room above here when we heard the screaming. Right after that my phone rang. It was my mother. She told me not to go outside. She said that early this morning a strange plane had flown by. She said that after it passed people started to fall dead in the streets; that it was spraying some kind of poison. Then I heard her screaming…"

The girl pressed her head into Isaac's chest and sobbed uncontrollably.

"They killed her! They killed my mama!"

Isaac's eyes scanned the room as the girl wept. He could hear movement outside the door. Something appeared to be scratching at its surface. Shackleton was sniffing the crack under the threshold. He growled suspiciously and then shot a glance back at Isaac, his amber eyes intense.

"What happened after that, my child?"

"When I told Pedro, he got up right away and left our room. I was so scared. I didn't want him to leave me alone. My mother had said not to go outside, but he didn't listen. Why didn't he listen?"

The girl pushed away from Isaac and bent to tend to her boyfriend again. He had fully lost consciousness now. Before Isaac could do anything, he saw the boy's body go into seizure and then fall suddenly still.

"No!" cried the girl. "No Pedro! Don't die! I love you!"

Shackleton turned and began to bark at the boy. Isaac did not understand what was happening. He searched for a pulse but found nothing. Although deep, the wound in the boy's shoulder had severed no arteries.

How could he have died so quickly?

Isaac moved away. If the boy had been infected with some kind of virus, it would be best if they kept their distance.

"I am so sorry, my child," he said, taking the girl by the arm. "He is gone. Come over to the bed. You must rest now."

In that instant, several things happened at once. No sooner had the girl risen to her feet than the armoire began to shake violently under a barrage of forceful blows. The door behind it had already come off its hinges, and the tips of bloodied fingers came into view, probing the crack that separated the armoire from the wall.

"It's too late," whispered the girl, her eyes wide with fear. "They've found us."

Isaac looked down in time to see the dead boy's eyes jerk open, his hand darting out to take hold of the girl's leg.

Merciful Father in heaven!

Isaac could not understand. In the space of a moment the boy's body had somehow reanimated, and in his mind there came a vivid recollection of the corpse of his son.

"No," he gasped, shaking his head from side to side. "This cannot be..."

The boy was jerking spasmodically now, his mouth snapping at the girl like a rabid dog. Isaac watched as Shackleton came suddenly to the rescue, taking the dead boy by the throat, and dragging him away from her.

The girl, who had only just loosed herself from the clutching hand, now struggled to free herself from Isaac's embrace, desperately wanting to stop Shackleton's attack. Isaac held her fast, looking over to see that the armoire was already sliding away from the wall.

The probing fingers had now been replaced by grey and bloodied arms. There were at least four victims prying their way into the room and it was utterly obvious that just like the boy, they too had transformed.

"Let me go! Can't you see he's killing him?" screamed the girl, but just then Shackleton finished his grisly work, tearing the head from the jerking torso.

The girl was in hysterics now, fixated on the corpse of her boyfriend and screaming incessantly.

"Is there another way out of this chamber?" cried Isaac, turning her away from the source of her panic. "Listen to me!"

The effect was almost instantaneous.

"The service stairs to the laundry room," she whispered, wide eyed.

"Show me where it is!" said Isaac, releasing her and taking up his belongings.

They made their way to a sliding door in the corner of the chamber. Opening it they found a narrow flight of stone steps winding upward. Shackleton bounded up first, followed by the girl, and then by Isaac, who managed to slide the door shut behind him just as the armoire came crashing to the floor.

Moments later they had gained access to a laundry room with a single door and window. They were on the ground floor now, and outside, laundry could be seen hanging from a clothesline.

"We've got to get out of here!" cried the girl.

She rushed to the door and took hold of the knob.

"Wait!" cried Isaac, but he knew it was too late.

The girl turned to face him just as the door splintered behind her. A dozen groping arms took hold of her instantly, dragging her back into a mob of at least twenty undead. A loud bark sounded, and Isaac spun to see Shackleton looking back at him from the other side of the window, his amber eyes insistent.

"Dear Father in heaven," he sobbed, climbing over the sill. "Save their souls..."

CHAPTER 33

Central Jerusalem, Israel.

Christian looked blankly at the video images. The sweeping devastation caused by the viral weapon was like nothing he could have imagined. This was not death, but rather a desecration of life, and something in him was appalled that he could have instigated such a monstrous act of destruction. He found himself repeatedly confirming the reality of the events to himself, as though he were somehow unable to accept them.

These are live feeds. This is actually happening.

Through the enhanced satellite imagery, Christian could see the macabre spectacle unfolding before his eyes. A plethora of high-resolution videos were offering him every grim detail. Four drones had flown along precise aerial routes, spreading the virus in a fine spray of specially engineered bio-gel. By taking advantage of wind currents in the mountainous landscape, they had managed to spread the virus along the entire northern coastline, and about twenty kilometres inland.

Christian's eyes scanned the affected region on the hologram. The virus itself would not affect everyone, only those caught outdoors, and only during a short window of time. In open air the genetically engineered pathogen could only survive an hour at most, but once absorbed into a host it would sustain itself indefinitely.

After terminating all brain functions, the virus would proceed to alter the host's DNA, and in this way attain the unsettling reanimation that gave the virus its horrific characteristics. Endowed only with the primordial instinct to feed, the infected corpses would then spread the virus via the bite wounds they inflicted. Christian knew this would soon become a plague of biblical proportions. He recalled what he had learned from the Zurvanites.

The demons will soon take possession of these corpses...

Writhing masses of humanity stretched out before Christian in real time. Some were in the process of being taken by the virus. Others had already reanimated and were feeding. He could see hordes of cadavers filling the streets like walking zombies, but it was the undead children who affected him the most.

Christian passed his hands over his face, pushing his fingers into his eyes as he rubbed them. He was struggling to regain his apathy but there were too many children among the infected. Their faces were horrific.

I don't give a shit. I don't give a shit!

He turned away from the hologram to spot the thick-necked admiral Chester B. Sterling appearing on one of his communications banks. In the shadows behind the monitor, he could see Cynthia's ragged grey corpse devouring a glistening mound of pig offal. His eyes lingered on her for a long moment.

I don't give a fucking shit.

"We've searched the entire strait, Mr. Antov, sir," said the admiral. "There's no sign of them."

Christian's eyes returned to the monitor and scanned the admiral's ruddy face, his mind starting as it remembered the temporarily forgotten Cube. This was his priority. What had he been thinking? The artifact had to be either recovered or destroyed. He turned away from the monitor to clear his mind, just as his father's insistent hiss exploded in his brain like a bursting tumour.

"All power is based in fear! Fear must be maintained at all costs!"

Christian cringed visibly as the ghost of his father wormed into him yet again, violating his personal boundaries and filling him with an uncontainable urgency to destroy the Cube. He began to tremble uncontrollably, and looking down at his hand, saw that his body was shifting and jerking in and out of solidity. For fleeting moments his skin was reptilian.

"Mr. Antov, sir," said the admiral. "Is everything all right, sir?"

"Everything is fine," said Christian, keeping his back to the monitor. "Did you complete the underwater search?"

"Affirmative. If they were under there, our sonar would have picked them up. They've vanished, sir."

Christian closed his eyes in concentration. His ability to determine the exact position of the Two was lessening as the spiritual separation between them disappeared. He ground his teeth in frustration. Everything was falling apart. He jerked around to face the monitor.

"Look again!" he barked, his eyes cold and reptilian. "Report back to me in sixty minutes!"

"Aye-aye, sir," said the admiral, his monitor going black.

It was at that moment that a video communication from Nasrallah arrived. He was in Ceuta, and his countenance resembled that of a greasy rat. Behind him could be seen the upper torsos of two Vanderhoff operatives, their burly arms crossed over their chests.

"What news do you have for me?" asked Christian in disgust.

"We located the safe where the treasure was kept, Master. The scroll is missing."

"Missing?" asked Christian, a deep rage beginning to boil in him. "You are an incompetent fool! I have no more need of you!"

"Please, Master," pleaded Nasrallah, knowing that his death would come swiftly. "Perhaps I can still be of use. Parker will go to Ceuta. I have many connections there. I can aid you in your hunt. He will not escape that city."

"He has left Ceuta!" bellowed Christian in frustration, "They have all disappeared somewhere in the Strait of Gibraltar!"

"They are in a boat, sir?"

"No they are not in a boat!" cried Christian. "They are not in a plane, or in a submarine! They have disappeared you useless fool! And with them the Compostela Cube. I have no further need of you. Now you will die."

"Wait, please!" cried Nasrallah, cringing in pain as one of his captors clamped a hand onto his shoulder. "I believe I know where they are."

"You lie!"

"On the scroll was a map," stammered Nasrallah hurriedly. "A map of the strait! It showed a passage beneath the waters; a passage that began in Ceuta and that led to Gibraltar!"

Christian bent close to the monitor, his face filling the screen and sending waves of fear through Nasrallah. Christian Antov did not appear human anymore. Perhaps he was losing his mind, but for fleeting instances it seemed to Nasrallah that he was looking at a reptile; a lizard-man…

"What did you see on that map?" asked Christian slowly, his fury on the verge of explosion.

"I do not know exactly," lied Nasrallah. "I did not have an opportunity to study it in detail."

"What kind of map was it?"

"I do not know, Master," pleaded Nasrallah. "Please have pity on me. I only know that I saw a passageway. I can be in Ceuta in a few hours, Master. I can find the entrance of the tunnel for you."

Christian could sense that Nasrallah knew more than he was saying. The roach of a man was planning something, but it mattered not. He would be accompanied by an entire task force. He had nowhere to run.

"You *will* find the entrance to that passage," said Christian menacingly.

"Yes, Master," said Nasrallah, nodding emphatically. "Immediately, Master. Thank you, Master!"

CHAPTER 34

Ceuta, Spanish Morocco.

Nasrallah made his way through the familiar underground tunnels, the sight of his ravaged hashish operation intensifying his hatred of Christian Antov. Over the past few days, he had learned from his taunting captors that Christian had been the one responsible for his ruin, having given the orders to inform Interpol of his numerous drug operations.

Nasrallah smiled wickedly as he passed the ransacked debris. He would have his revenge shortly. Having led his captors to a place where he knew it would be easy to disappear, he had slipped away unnoticed, and left them searching for him in the upper tunnels. Accompanying him now were the six hired men he had secretly arranged to meet; filthy cutthroats who would have gladly turned him over to his captors for a reward, were it not for the promise of riches that Nasrallah had made them.

"The treasure chamber is just ahead," he said. "There we will find the entrance to the tunnels I spoke of."

The plan was simple. Ambush the unsuspecting group in the tunnels and take the Cube and the scroll. With any luck they would have already recovered the Book of Khalifah, and they would take that too. Christian Antov had made it very clear how much he valued these artifacts. Now he would pay dearly for them.

Nasrallah opened the door to the treasure chamber to find the lights still on.

They have been here recently. It is just as I suspected...

Like a rat following a scent, he made his way to the wall where the actuating device was located. He could see that one of the stones was free of dust. The swarthy cutthroats gathered around him.

"Where did you hide the treasures that filled this room?" said one of them, his lips drawn back in a snarl.

"Those treasures are gone!" snapped Nasrallah, but he calmed down immediately. "Nevertheless, still greater ones await us."

He laid a filthy hand on the stone and gave it a push. It sunk inwards effortlessly, and within moments, a deep rumbling could be felt at their feet.

* * * * * *

"So what you are telling me is that the existence of an underground passage is theoretically possible."

It was Christian who spoke. He was seated in the Holy of Holies, his face showing signs of a fatigue that was taking everything in his power to hold at bay.

"Yes sir, Mr. Antov, that is correct," said the admiral over the monitor. "We've consulted with our geologists, and they have confirmed that there is a divergent tectonic plate boundary located directly beneath the strait. It is at the point where the African and European plates meet, sir."

"And what does that mean?"

"Well, sir," said the admiral, looking down at a report on his desk. "It would appear that about six million years ago there was a tectonic shift in these plates and the Strait of Gibraltar closed up tight, effectively locking out the Atlantic Ocean.

"Over a period of about seven hundred thousand years, the Mediterranean Sea repeatedly evaporated and flooded, sir, the result of which created extensive sedimentary formations to a depth of several kilometres, sir.

"About five million years ago there was another tectonic shift and the strait opened up again, this time permanently filling the Mediterranean with seawater from the Atlantic. Our geologists believe it's very likely that there are pockets within the sedimentary rock that could have produced underground caves. They would be highly unstable, but they could nevertheless exist, sir."

"What do you mean by highly unstable?"

"Well, sir, there's always been a history of seismic activity in the area, but most of it's minor. Even still, with all that pressure from the sea above, it wouldn't take much for those caves to flood. Many of them have probably done so already, sir."

Christian sat back in his chair, an idea forming in his mind.

"Admiral," he said. "I remember hearing about newly developed weapons capable of penetrating bunkers. Do you know of these?"

"Yes, sir," said the admiral. "They are nuclear devices designed to target underground installations."

"Could these missiles be used to target the sea floor?"

"I can't see why not, sir," said the admiral, raising an eyebrow. "I'm sure they would need to be modified slightly, but I know for a fact that they can be launched from submarine installations. It would simply mean reprogramming their guidance systems."

"Very well, Admiral," said Christian. "I want you to consult your geologists again. This time I want to know where the weakest point in that fault line is. We will detonate one of these weapons there and see if we cannot create an earthquake to collapse the underground caves."

"Very good, sir," said the admiral. "I will update you the moment I have this information."

"Thank you, Admiral," said Christian wearily. "Our target must be destroyed at all costs."

* * * * * *

Having descended the spiralling staircase, Nasrallah bent over the mosaic panel at the cave's entrance. The six dark characters gathered in close behind.

"The way will be marked clearly for us as we proceed," he said, passing his fingers over the stone as he read it. "It will not be long before we find them. There will soon be riches for us all."

Having said this, there sounded a deep rumbling, and they turned to see the staircase vanish into the floor. A deep and inky void encapsulated them, and Nasrallah shuddered unintentionally.

The thump of the stair's closing mechanism had sounded to him like the sealing of a tomb.

CHAPTER 35

Gibraltar.

Major Richard Roberts watched as the ranks of chattering civilians filed into the tunnels, each with their allotted piece of luggage in hand. The recent detonation of a nuclear device in a Madrid airport, coupled with reports of biological weapons being used in Northern Spain, had proved to be sufficient motivation for the majority of Gibraltar's population to wish to take shelter.

"Private Henderson here, sir," came the crackling voice over Roberts' radio. "The governor wishes to see you, Major."

"Very well, Private," replied Roberts. "Tell him I'm on my way."

From his perch atop an old fortification, the major made his way down a narrow flight of stone steps, emerging into a crowded area by the tunnel mouth. Much to his satisfaction, he had earlier that morning seen the governor installed into his private apartments within the complex. Knowing the old duke would now be in close proximity to Gibraltar's best military doctors gave him one less thing to worry about.

With a light step he slipped past the entry checkpoint and hopped onto an electric golf cart waiting for him inside.

"Take me to the governor's lodgings, Private."

"Yes sir, Major Roberts," said the soldier at the wheel, jerking the cart into motion.

Even under the grim circumstances, there was a palpable excitement in the air as they drove into the underground city. The hustle and bustle of the entering populace made the gallery appear more like a busy hotel lobby than a bomb shelter. The people of Gibraltar were a close-knit society, and under the crisis they were becoming even more so.

Groups of them milled about peacefully and chatted amongst themselves, their preparations appearing more like a holiday excursion than an emergency retreat. Roberts looked around in satisfaction. His cart was moving along the central tunnel now, passing lines of pedestrians as they made their way towards their new lodgings.

The majority of the spaces they would be inhabiting had been excavated by Canadian miners during the Second World War. What had before been damp and musty chambers in the rock, had recently been transformed into warm and comfortable abodes, with thousands of cubic meters of freshly scrubbed air being pumped through the complex every minute.

"Good work, men," said Roberts as his cart slowed to pass through a check point. "We're making excellent progress."

The soldiers saluted proudly as the Aid-du-Camp's cart sped off again. The operation was running smoothly, and all were pleased, on both civilian and military sides. In just a few more hours the sanctuary would be fully locked down, its main doors secured, and the bio-support systems activated. When this had been accomplished, the underground city would be able to provide food and shelter for its occupants almost indefinitely.

The governor's apartments were located directly below the Central Command Centre. Wanting a status report, Roberts decided to take a quick detour up to the facility before visiting the old governor.

Leaving the golf cart behind, he entered a broad cargo lift and soon found himself immersed in the command centre's lively environment. It was an expansive, semi-circular chamber, excavated high within the northern face of the Rock, and fully renovated. Dozens of personnel bustled around here, surrounded by batteries of surveillance monitors, communications arrays, and defence system terminals. In control of power generation, life support, and sanitation, this room constituted the central brain of the underground city.

"Corporal," said Roberts, stopping a supervisor as she passed. "How are we making out with the hydrogen generators?"

"Steady as she goes, Major, sir," came her enthusiastic response. "They should be online in twenty minutes."

"Any hiccups I should know about?"

"Smooth sailing, sir."

"Excellent," said Roberts, his right eye twitching. "Keep up the good work, Corporal."

Roberts circled the facility and returned to the main lift when he was satisfied that all was well. Within seconds he was back in the golf cart and passing through the maze of tunnels and chambers that comprised the military residences. Complete with a hospital, a restaurant, a pub, and even a cinema, the military sector boasted all the amenities of the civilian complex.

After whisking past a group of doctors and nurses, Roberts' cart arrived at a set of dark oaken doors, flanked on either side by the Gibraltar coat of arms, and those of the Gibraltar regiment.

"Thank you, Private," said Roberts to the driver. "Please wait here. I shan't be long."

Roberts made his way through the heavy doors, entering into an oak-paneled chamber. He was greeted by the governor's secretary.

"Good morning, Major," she said with a smile. "Welcome to the New Governor's House."

"Thank you, Silvia," said Roberts with a smile. "It certainly looks familiar."

Silvia returned the smile, knowing that Roberts had been referring to the fact that all the furnishings had simply been moved here from the original Governor's House. The effect was quite agreeable, lending a familiarity to the apartments that would have been otherwise impossible to obtain.

"He's particularly weak this morning, sir," she added quietly as Roberts passed. "The doctors have only just left."

Roberts knocked softly and entered slowly. Were it not for the lower ceilings, it would have been impossible to tell that the governor's abode had changed, so similar was it in size and layout. In the dimmed lights, Roberts could make out the old duke in his bed. He seemed to be sleeping.

"Are you awake, sir?" he asked quietly.

"Indeed I am, my son," said the old man, opening his eyes.

"You called for me, sir?"

"Sit down, Major," he said, waiting until Roberts had seated himself next to the bed before continuing. "What is the condition of our defences?"

"Fully operational, sir," said Roberts, bending closer. "We've left a contingent of men arming the exterior posts, but everything is prepared so as to continue our defence from within, should the need arise, sir."

"And the civilians?"

"Almost all have been relocated, sir," said Roberts proudly. "Those remaining outside are either foreigners who have decided to remain in Gibraltar, or citizens either not willing to enter the sanctuary, or wishing to wait until the danger is more imminent."

"And the siege?"

"Still fully in effect, sir. There's been an increase in patrol ships and a slight decrease in troops at the frontier. It would appear they're planning to lock us in until we run out of supplies, sir."

"Good," said the governor weakly. "This tells us that they are unaware of our resources. Geothermal hydrogen generators and hydroponic gardens are the last thing they think we have."

"That's correct, sir," said Roberts, nodding. "They think we're still burning coal over here."

CHAPTER 36

Somewhere under the Mediterranean Sea.

Gabriel reached out just in time to stop Fra from falling. The old brother had insisted on making his own way, but it was becoming more and more obvious that he was in no condition to do so. Both he and Suora had been severely affected by the heat of the lower passages, and though the air was slightly cooler now, the strain of their earlier endeavors was weighing heavily on them.

"Thank you, my son," said the old brother, his face pale and drawn. "It would appear that this old body of mine is giving me some trouble."

"You're doing great, Fra," said Gabriel. "I'm feeling half dead myself. The heat down there was crazy."

Gabriel looked up from his place at the rear of the procession to see Suora riding weakly on Bahadur's back. Their captain was leading them up a narrow tunnel, his flaming torch casting flickering shadows as they passed.

Behind Bahadur, were Miller and Stephenson, followed by Scotty Roberts and Amir. Directly in front of him, Gabriel could see Natasha sticking close to the old bishop.

In this way they continued their slow ascent until the tunnel leveled off and then dipped into a small, open area. Just above them, a fracture in the rock was giving vent to a steady gust of cool air being channeled down from above. In an instant everyone had thrown themselves onto the cavern floor, lying flat on their backs with smiles of relief lighting up their faces.

After some time, Natasha sat up to find that Suora and Fra were talking quietly among themselves, seated with their backs against the cavernous wall. The fresh air was helping them tremendously, but their faces still seemed dangerously pale to

Natasha, and this concerned her greatly. She tilted her head in their direction to hear what they were saying.

"We have lived a wonderful life together, my love," said Fra, smiling peacefully. "We have been blessed."

"*E vero, il mio tesoro,*" said Suora, resting her head on Fra's shoulder.

Natasha's eyes welled with tears, and seeing this, Gabriel put a hand on her shoulder.

"What's wrong?"

"Suora and Fra are talking as though they're going to die down here," she whispered.

Gabriel frowned.

"They're just being silly," he said. "They're going to be fine."

* * * * * *

Nasrallah and his men were making fast progress now, navigating the passageways at a brisk trot. Unlike the group they pursued, his men were young and unencumbered, driven by a lust for riches that served well to fuel their pace. The sooner they could kill their prey, the sooner they would receive payment.

Knowing their greed, Nasrallah pushed them harder still. He was anxious to get his hands on the artifact, and in so doing win back the life that had been taken from him.

"They have three elders with them," he said as they ran. "They will not have gone far."

Already Nasrallah had covered the distance it had taken the others an entire day to complete. At this pace they would be on them within the hour.

* * * * * *

Not fifteen minutes had passed before Bahadur ordered the party to rise again, stating that with the cooler air, the way would now be much easier for them all. What he did not relate to them was that his smuggler's intuition was warning him of an impending danger, urging him to press onward despite the fatigued state of his company.

"We will all rest in Gibraltar," he said in his deep basso, hoisting Suora gently onto his back. "Let us press on. We are very close now."

They had not been walking long before Bahadur's fears were confirmed.

"Stop!" came a hoarse whisper, and turning, Bahadur saw that all eyes were fixed on Fra.

Both of the brother's hands were held up in an urgent plea for silence. He turned his old head to face the tunnel behind them and listened intently for a moment longer.

"There is someone there, my friends," he whispered. "They have opened that metal door that we passed through."

All listened but could hear nothing. Knowing well of the brother's uncommonly keen sense of hearing, Bishop Marcus was the first to take heed of the warning. He turned to Bahadur, a look of consternation on his old face.

"But how can that be?" asked Bahadur, frowning. "The door is too far away to be heard."

Gabriel put a hand on Fra's shoulder.

"You're absolutely sure?"

Fra nodded confidently.

"These old ears have never lied."

Scotty was already moving off with Miller and Stephenson at his side.

"We're going to check it out, mates," he said, patting his assault rifle. "I've got a little something I want to give to that rat."

Bahadur was perplexed. He looked over at Gabriel.

"Dr. Parker. Is it possible that we could have passed Nasrallah somewhere along the way, if it is indeed him?"

Gabriel looked back at him, thinking.

"He must have taken a wrong turn down one of the passages, and then found his way back."

Bahadur nodded and turned to Scotty.

"Go with great care, my friend," he said. "A cornered rat can be very dangerous. We will continue forward."

Scotty gave them a wink.

"We won't be long, mates."

It was only a short while later that the group finally came upon what they had been longing to find. Hewn directly into the granite was a low archway leading into a widened area of tunnel, the complexity of its architecture showing its obvious importance.

"The Chamber of Khalifah!" exclaimed Natasha. "We found it!"

She was going to rush in but Gabriel took hold of her shoulders and held her back.

"Careful," he said. "Let's do this slowly."

He took a cautious step forward and aimed his flashlight into the space. Within was a natural formation, measuring a dozen feet in diameter. The granite was particularly fractured here, with deep crevices and fissures all around. A soft rumbling sound was emanating from the walls.

"There's a gallery behind this portico," he said, looking back over his shoulder. "The chamber's got to be close by."

"What's that sound?" asked Natasha.

"Seawater," said Gabriel, looking around suspiciously. "It's coming down from above. We must be at some kind of fault line."

With practiced stealth, Gabriel made his way forward. He was scanning every surface for traps but paid particular attention to a horizontal crevice high and to the left. He hoisted himself carefully upwards so that he could aim his flashlight into the space, and then turned to survey the gallery. He was amazed by what he saw.

Much of the stone had been very carefully worked here, and the floor was perfectly level. Across from him was an elaborate stone wall covered in ornately designed fist-sized symbols, each set into a grid that stretched from floor to ceiling. Positioned at its centre was what looked to be two peepholes, complete with an indentation to accommodate a viewer's face. It resembled the backside of a mask. He hopped down and waved the others forward.

"It's all right," he said. "Come in and take a look at this."

As they entered, he brought their attention to the mysterious wall of stone carvings. Its textured surface danced under the flickering light of their torches. Gabriel began to examine the friezes in more detail.

"It looks like the Chamber of Khalifah could be directly behind this wall," he said, "but for God's sake, don't touch any of these stones. They might have been designed to trigger some kind of mechanism. I've never seen anything like this before."

CHAPTER 37

Central Jerusalem, Israel.

Christian could see the admiral's face in the monitor before him, but his voice was almost inaudible over the icy whispering that filled his mind. The desecrated Kadosh Hakodashim loomed around him, and Cynthia's possessed corpse was particularly agitated.

The demonic voices were feverishly insisting that the Cube be destroyed at once. They infected Christian's psyche with a frenzied urge to act immediately; to obliterate anyone or anything that stood in his way.

"Mr. Antov. Is everything all right, sir?"

Christian heard the admiral's voice at last and clung to it desperately.

"Yes, yes," he managed to say. "I'm fine. Continue."

"Our geologists inform us that there's an igneous formation one kilometre south of Gibraltar that appears to be the weakest point along the tectonic rift, sir. There's only one problem."

Christian battled to regain control of himself. He made a concerted effort and at last managed to lower the volume of the voices in his head.

"I don't like problems, Admiral," he said with a final shudder. "What is the issue?"

"Well, sir," said Sterling, "on the positive side, our geologists all agree that if a nuclear device were to be detonated on this fault line, the chances are almost one hundred percent that any underground cave systems would begin to collapse immediately. The only problem is that the explosion would also create widespread damage in other areas."

Christian nodded. Dr. Bennington had just appeared at the entrance of the chamber.

"Yes," said Christian. "Please continue."

"First of all, sir, an undersea explosion of this size, at this depth, would create significant disturbances in the water, sir. A good example would be the WIGWAM test that was carried out in the South Pacific in 1955.

"A nuclear device was detonated at a depth of two thousand feet, sir. It created three high-velocity shockwaves before surfacing as a nine-hundred-foot spray dome. In the strait we would be detonating at three thousand feet, sir. We could most likely count on generating four to five shockwaves."

"And?"

"Well, sir, they stir up the water something awful. The WIGWAM test created massive waves, sir. Something similar to a tsunami. We're dealing with some enormous forces here. The device you want to explode is about ten times the size of the device used at the WIGWAM test, and it would be detonated at an even greater depth.

"The waves generated from a blast such as this would basically take out all the coastal regions in the vicinity, and severely damage coastlines as far away as Malta and Greece."

"Is there anything else?"

"Well, sir," continued the admiral, swallowing hard, "there's also the question of the radiation that would be released. The spray dome would be well over twelve hundred feet high. It would scatter millions of tons of radioactive water into the atmosphere, sir. It would be an ecological disaster."

"Is that all?"

"Well sir, no it isn't," said the admiral. "What I've just described to you is the damage we are guaranteed to obtain. There is another effect this detonation could possibly have that would make this other stuff look like a walk in the park, sir."

Christian bent closer to the monitor; his eyebrow raised ever so slightly.

"And that is…?"

"Ground zero would basically be right on the active fault line between the African and European plates, sir. The Strait of Gibraltar registers low-level earthquakes almost monthly. Our geologists warn of the possibility of a massive earthquake being unleashed if this detonation were to occur; an earthquake that could rival the one that measured 8.8 back in 1755. Back then, the number of casualties amounted to one hundred thousand, sir, but our geologists estimate that a similar quake would take out ten to fifteen times that amount of people in the present day."

"Good work, Admiral," said Christian with a nod. "Notify all military installations in the affected areas to be on high alert should the worst-case scenario come to pass. I want that missile fired within the next thirty minutes."

"But Mr. Antov, sir," said the admiral, a shocked look of dismay overriding his normally hardened features. "There are coalition boats in the Strait of Gibraltar that would need several hours to move out of range, sir. Perhaps by tomorrow…"

"You have my orders, Admiral," said Christian coldly. "Proceed immediately."

"Yes, sir, Mr. Antov, sir," stammered the admiral. "Immediately, sir."

Christian ended the call. His face had become pale and damp with sweat, as though he had just awoken from a nightmare. He rose to his feet, swaying dizzily before the glowing holographic planet. He reached up and turned it, pinpointing the area of the Mediterranean that would soon be decimated.

Let them all die. I don't give a shit.

He could see Dr. Bennington approaching out of the corner of his eye. The atmosphere was warping around Christian now, a tremendous pressure mounting in his head. He battled to silence the voices as they began their litany once again but failed hopelessly. Everything was in turmoil. He feared for his sanity.

"Destroy the Cube! Destroy it now!"

"Christian," came the doctor's sober voice. "You asked to see me."

Christian turned to face him but said nothing. Bennington could see that he was crying out for help. Christian's defences were collapsing. For better or worse, the time had come for Bennington to intervene.

"Dear, Christian," he said. "Can you not see what you are doing?"

He put a calming hand on his patient's shoulder.

"Let's talk for a moment. It's important you understand something, my friend."

The four Zurvanites appeared to Christian just then, jerking and shifting, and filling his mind with even more madness. They were insisting that the doctor's life be terminated at once. Christian reeled under their attack. He pushed Bennington away viciously.

"Kill the doctor!" they hissed. *"Kill him now!"*

Bennington fell and struck his head. He looked up from the floor to see Christian's eyes filled with murder. He could feel a trickle of blood running down his face. He dabbed it with a handkerchief and struggled to lift himself into a chair.

"More killing will not make the pain go away, Christian," he said dizzily. "You are trapped in a vicious circle. You must extract yourself from it."

Christian was hunched over in rage.

"What are you talking about!" he bellowed, the veins on his neck bulging.

An encompassing confusion had taken him. He was reacting like a cornered animal.

"What the fuck are you talking about?!"

The dark reptilian beast in Christian had surfaced once again, and this time it wanted nothing more than to strangle the doctor where he sat. Christian battled with himself. The doctor was all he had. He was his only friend. Even still, Christian found himself moving slowly towards the old man, the urge to exterminate him too great to resist.

"I am talking about *numbness*, Christian," said Bennington, his eyes widening at the impending danger. "I am talking about your only defence against the pain."

Christian stopped in his tracks and dropped into a chair, kneading the armrests with clenched hands. He was looking straight ahead, his eyes glazed from the tempest of his inner conflict. He wanted blood, but Bennington's words had struck a chord in him. Numbness was what he most yearned for. It was the one thing he desperately needed to regain.

Even still, the murderous urges continued to engulf him nonetheless. They were impossible to resist. He shot his head around to see Cynthia's corpse jerking in the shadows behind him. His rage was on the verge of exploding. It needed to be vented.

"Give me another injection!" he snapped, then he pulled open his desk drawer and produced a large calibre handgun, complete with silencer.

Bennington rummaged through his bag hastily, watching as Christian staggered over to where Cynthia crouched. The first bullet struck her in the chest with a dull thud, but she continued with her feeding as though nothing had happened.

Christian ground his teeth. His face was spattered with her coagulated blood, but he had garnered no satisfaction. The next shot severed Cynthia's hand at the wrist, and the third left her jaw hanging by a tendril of flesh, but still there was no reaction in her; no cries of pain; no suffering.

Instead of being quenched, Christian's rage was only growing. He stepped forward, his eyes gaping. With shaking hands, he unscrewed the silencer and proceeded to empty the remaining fifteen rounds point blank into her skull.

Deafening reports filled the chamber, and though Christian's face and body were soon painted with blood and gore, his rage was still undiminished. He dropped the heavy gun to the floor and turned to face the stunned doctor, drawing up his bloodied sleeve with a trembling hand.

"Give it to me now or I swear I will murder you!"

Bennington tore his eyes from the pulpy mass that had once been Cynthia's head. There was no time to waste. He got up and administered the sedative at once. Christian slumped into a chair; the lids of his eyes heavy. Seeing this, Bennington took a deep breath and returned to his seat.

"I want you to try very hard to understand what I am going to tell you, Christian," he said, sitting forward. "As a boy, your only defence against all of the cruelty you suffered was to become numb to it. Is that not correct?"

Christian nodded.

"It's true," he said quietly. "I never let myself give a shit."

"Precisely," said Bennington. "And you found that the best way to be apathetic to your own pain was to be apathetic to the pain of others. If you could witness somebody else suffering, and be unaffected by it, that meant you could also be unaffected by your own pain. Is that not also correct?"

Christian looked up at the doctor. He had never thought of it that way, but it was true. To this day, seeing someone suffer pain or humiliation was always a pleasurable experience for him. It proved to him that he truly did not care. It validated his sense of numbness. It made him feel strong and secure.

"And for this reason," continued Bennington, "as a child you were sometimes driven to be cruel to others, perhaps to animals, just so that you might demonstrate your numbness."

Christian nodded.

"As a boy I used to catch field mice and dissect them alive. I never knew why I was doing it. It was just something I did..."

Bennington smiled gently with understanding. It was important that Christian did not feel judged. Cruelty to animals was a typical compulsion in abused children.

"The trouble with this kind of validation is that it always creates the same problems, Christian," he said. "It makes us feel guilty, and the pain from this guilt gets added to the original pain, so that we have to become even more numb to deal with it."

"What are you talking about?" asked Christian, sitting up in his chair.

He had hoped the doctor would assist him in regaining his numbness, but he suspected that Bennington was moving in a very different direction.

"I feel no guilt whatsoever," he lied. "You're wrong."

"You know that's not true, Christian," said Bennington firmly. "You are caught in a vicious circle. Each time you lash out at the world, you do so to prove to yourself that you are numb to the suffering of others, and thus to your own suffering, but it is not working anymore. You only find that your pain increases. So you lash out again, thinking that more of the same remedy is all that is needed."

"Shut up!" said Christian, rising to his feet. "Shut your mouth!"

"The solution you used as a child will no longer work for you, Christian," said Bennington, rising to his feet as well. "You are in an emotional crisis, my friend. Your numbness has broken down, as it was always destined to do. Such defences cannot last indefinitely. They are based in denial."

"That's not true," said Christian, beginning to tremble.

His reptilian self was returning more forcefully than ever now. He could resist it no longer. Bennington's words were a direct assault on his last remaining subterfuge; they were awakening in him a primordial urge to defend himself.

Christian approached the doctor with clenched fists. He would not accept what he was being told. Without numbness he was lost. He needed to regain it immediately. What did he care if this pathetic old man lived or died? He would throttle him now with his own hands and prove to himself how numb he really was.

Bennington backed away from Christian in fear. His patient's face was blood-spattered and dripping with gore. There was murderous intent in his eyes.

"The only solution available to you is to confront the guilt you're feeling, Christian," he said unsteadily. "You must accept what you have done and allow yourself to grieve over it. More killing will not alleviate your suffering. It will only make the pain worse."

Christian said nothing in response. He had not even heard the doctor's words. His eyes had become like those of a snake, and Bennington knew in that moment that he had failed. He could see Christian shapeshifting before his eyes, his body jerking and oscillating violently from side to side as his reptilian self battled for dominance.

"You must not identify with the entity that controls you at this moment, my friend," he said, feeling Christian's trembling fingers wrapping around his neck. "It is just a fragment of your personality, a culmination of all the pain and fear that you have repressed throughout your life. It is a shadow, Christian. It does not really exist."

Bennington was struggling to breathe but he made no effort to free himself from Christian's stranglehold. When he felt the strength leaving his legs, he let himself fall back into his chair, his eyes bulging from the mounting pressure.

"You are not wicked, Christian," he strained to say as consciousness left him. "In your heart you are good."

* * * * * *

Christian looked down at the cold corpse of the doctor, his eyes glazed over with glorious numbness. He could see the repugnant Zurvanites oscillating around him, but he paid them no heed. A gaping void had opened in Christian's heart, and he cared not.

Before him lay the lifeless body of his only friend, and he felt no pain. A part of Christian knew that he himself had died in this murderous act, and that it was through his own self-destruction that he had come to obtain the numbness he had so longed for.

There remained only the reptile in him now. Christian Antov was dead. He recalled Oppenheimer's famous quote from the *Bhagavad Gita*, uttered shortly after the world's first atomic bomb had been detonated.

"Now, I am become death," whispered Christian, as all went black. "The destroyer of worlds."

CHAPTER 38

Under the Mediterranean Sea.

Natasha examined the little clay bottle that Gabriel had given to her. Its neck was sealed in wax.

"What is it?" she asked.

"It's lamp oil," said Gabriel, still studying the slot in the wall where he had found it.

"But I see no lamp," said the old bishop, surveying the area. "Are you certain, my son?"

Gabriel nodded and pointed the beam of his flashlight at two oval niches to the left and right of the peepholes.

"The lamps are on the other side of the wall."

A reflection came from within the niches as Gabriel's beam of light passed over them. Natasha moved to get a closer look.

Within each niche could be seen the wick of a lamp, and a small reservoir for oil. It was what lay behind the wicks that caught her attention however; hundreds of crystal lenses comprising what appeared to be optical instruments. They reminded Natasha of the astrolabe they had found in the Chamber of the Sphere.

"Have you seen this?" she asked, turning to face Gabriel.

He was shining his flashlight into one of the peepholes and looking intently through the other. He pulled away and turned to her.

"Take a look in there."

Natasha peered inside. Shining back out of the darkness were dozens of tiny reflections, delineating a sizable chamber within. She looked back at Gabriel.

"They're mirrors," he said. "Just like the ones that were inlaid in the dome back in the Chamber of the Sphere. It's the same optical technology. These lamps are projectors."

Gabriel was stepping back to examine the wall in its entirety when the faint rattle of gunfire could be heard.

"They must have found Nasrallah," said Amir, pricking his ears.

Bahadur frowned and moved to the chamber's entrance, readying his assault rifle.

"Be on your guards," he said over his shoulder.

Gabriel nodded and returned his attention to the wall.

"This is definitely a trap," he said with hands on hips.

He looked up to study the ceiling and then returned his gaze to the wall.

"I really don't think the Book of Khalifah's in there."

Amir held back his dreadlocks and peered through the peephole.

"What if it's not a trap, boss?" he asked. "What if we need to light those lamps to see where the book is?"

Gabriel shook his head and pointed to his feet.

"This floor isn't carved into the rock," he said. "It's a slab, and my guess is that it's hinged somewhere."

He turned to study the facing wall and was about to say something when a loud explosion sounded. Seconds later Scotty burst into the gallery with Miller at his side. The two smugglers were shaken and clearly out of breath.

"We're in trouble, mates," said Scotty, his face grave.

Bahadur put a hand on his shoulder.

"Where's Stephenson?"

Scotty grimaced and shook his head.

"He's dead. Nasrallah's back there with six ugly blokes and they're armed to the bloody teeth. We're totally out gunned. We've got to get the hell out of here fast! We set off a grenade, but it won't hold them back long. They'll be on us in a minute."

"But there was only one set of tracks on the stairs when we entered the caves," said the old bishop. "I do not understand."

"There's no time to understand," said Gabriel. "But I'm thinking this could work to our advantage."

He hurried over to Suora and Fra and brought their attention to the horizontal crevice he had examined earlier on.

"Do you think you guys could make it up there if we helped you?"

"Most certainly, my child," said Suora.

"We still have some life left in us yet, young man," added Fra.

Gabriel gave a half-smile and nodded, moving to where the crevice was.

"There's plenty of room up there for all of us," he said to the others. "I say we let Nasrallah figure the hologram thing out for us. He can show us what not to do."

Bahadur took charge immediately, ordering Miller and Scotty to go up first so that they might help the others as he hoisted them up. In a short while they had all hidden themselves away in the crevice. Gabriel and Natasha were the last to ascend, and they took up lookout positions, lying side by side on their bellies and peering down into the chamber below.

A minute had not passed before the patter of trotting feet could be heard. Moments later Nasrallah burst into the gallery, his six cutthroats filing in behind him with rifles poised and torches ablaze.

"Wait!" barked Nasrallah. "Guard both exits and touch nothing!"

Gabriel and Natasha watched as Nasrallah examined the wall, his experience in archaeology leading him to the discovery of the niches and lamps almost immediately. He took hold of the little clay bottle that Gabriel had replaced in its slot and pried open the lid. The rogues gathered around.

"What is that?" grunted one of them.

Nasrallah dipped his finger into the bottle and tasted its contents.

"Lamp oil," he said, spitting on the floor. "Just as I thought."

He directed his attention to the peepholes, producing a flashlight and shining it into one of them while looking through the other.

"What do you see?" asked one of the mercenaries. "Is there treasure?"

Nasrallah said nothing, but instead moved the beam of his flashlight to the niches and examined each one of them in turn.

"What do you see?" repeated the cutthroat impatiently.

Nasrallah turned.

"Nothing yet, but we will light these lamps and find out."

Taking great care, Nasrallah poured oil into both of the lamp reservoirs and proceeded to light each of their wicks. He stepped back and addressed the man nearest him.

"The honour shall be yours," he said. "See with your own eyes what lies beyond this barrier."

With a mixture of distrust and excitement the swarthy character made his way to the wall. No sooner had he brought his face to the peepholes than he gasped in surprise.

"Great Allah!" he cried. "What heavenly place is this?"

"What do you see?" demanded Nasrallah, and noting that there was no danger, he attempted to squeeze his way in. "Stand aside!"

"There is much treasure here!" said the rogue, remaining where he was. "How it shimmers and glows!"

Gabriel exchanged a glance with Natasha. This was precisely what he had wanted to happen, and he looked on with great curiosity to see how things would unfold. Nasrallah had by now pushed the man aside and was staring covetously into the chamber.

"I have never seen its like…" he whispered in awe.

He turned to the others; their sodden faces consumed with greed.

"The Book of Khalifah lies within," he said. "It sits upon a podium surrounded by a mountain of treasure. We must gain entry to this chamber at once."

"And why have the others not done so?" asked one of the mercenaries. "They were just here. The smoke from their torches still lingers in the air."

Gabriel and Natasha pulled back into the shadows as the band of thugs began to scan the room.

"We have them on the run, idiot!" snapped Nasrallah. "We arrived before they had a chance. We will take this treasure, and then we will hunt them down and take the Cube as well!"

Gabriel and Natasha exchanged another glance, and then resumed their surveillance. Nasrallah was running his hands over the wall now, studying each of its many carvings.

"There is an assortment of images here," he said at last. "But only one is of any relevance to the Book of Khalifah."

He pointed to a carving that depicted an apple with its peel arranged around it in a coil.

"This is the image that resides on the Cube of Knowledge, and as the Cube and the Book are linked, it can be the only image that is of any importance here."

With arrogant confidence Nasrallah pushed the carving, jerking back his hand as the surrounding stones sank unexpectedly into the wall along with it. The movement was accompanied by the loud rumbling of coursing water and a split second later the floor fell suddenly away.

In the blink of an eye Nasrallah's men were tumbling into a chamber below, their surprised cries cut short as they were impaled upon the many spikes that lined its bottom. Only Nasrallah and two others were able to escape death, grabbing hold of the walls and clinging to the edge of the precipice.

"Where have you led us!" sneered one of them. "You will die for this!"

A curved dagger flashed into view and went straight for Nasrallah's throat. The latter reacted instinctively, pushing himself off the man next to him to avoid the blade, and sending him careening into the pit. A second later he had scampered up the angled floor and disappeared into the tunnel. His attacker did the same and vanished as well.

Gabriel and Natasha watched as the floor returned to its original position, sealing itself with a resounding boom. It was followed shortly after by a light clinking sound as another bottle of lamp oil was dispensed into the slot.

"Ingenious," said Gabriel, rubbing the stubble on his jaw. "The trap just reset itself..."

He looked over at Natasha in relief.

"If we hadn't seen that holographic tech in the Chamber of the Sphere, I probably would have fallen for it too..."

When the rumbling sound of rushing water stopped, Gabriel turned to face the others at the back of the cave.

"We're good to go," he said. "Nasrallah figured out the booby trap for us."

"Are they all dead?" asked Bahadur from his crouched position.

Gabriel shook his head.

"Just five of them. Nasrallah got away and one of his thugs went after him. He chased him back in the direction they came."

Gabriel hopped from the sill and helped Natasha down.

"I think that rat will be more concerned with saving his own hide than killing any of us right now," he continued. "We should be safe for the time being at least."

"Seawater-powered, you say..." pondered the old bishop when they had exited the hiding place. "Remarkable. But where is the Book of Khalifah?"

"Right behind this wall," said Gabriel, bringing their attention to an inconspicuous part of the gallery.

Partially hidden behind an outcropping of rock, six square-shaped stones had been inlaid into the cavernous wall. They were arranged in the form of a cross, and each was crudely carved with runes.

"Why, they look identical to the carvings on the Cube," said the bishop in surprise.

"I noticed them just before Scotty and Miller got back," said Gabriel, examining them closely. "They're very similar to the runes on the Cube, but if I'm not mistaken, only one of them will be identical."

He produced the glowing artifact and handed it to Natasha.

"Why don't you do the honours."

While Natasha compared the carvings with those on the Cube, Gabriel studied the rock wall itself. Unlike its counterpart on the opposite side of the chamber, this one had been made to resemble a natural formation.

"I found it," said Natasha. "You were right. Only one of the carvings is identical."

Gabriel returned to her side.

"Give it a little push."

Natasha bit her lip and looked at the others, following their eyes to the floor beneath them.

"Don't worry," said Gabriel. "It won't move an inch. I promise."

Natasha took a deep breath and pushed on the stone. Moments later, a section of the rock face before them pivoted silently away, revealing a humble circular chamber, with a single book podium at its centre. In that instant they all saw their worst fears confirmed.

"It's missing!" gasped Natasha. "The Book of Khalifah's gone!"

CHAPTER 39

Los Picos de Europa, Northern Spain.

Isaac Rodchenko looked up from the map. The light was fading rapidly and at some point Shackleton had gone off, leaving him alone atop a rocky perch. A cold mass of dead air was settling down around him, and the mild shivering he had been experiencing up to then was growing more intense.

They had been travelling all that day, and even though Isaac should have been thinking of setting up camp, a voice in him was insisting that he not stop. The monastery could not be far now, and something around him did not feel right. It was only after a few minutes of observation that he was able to pinpoint what was wrong.

An unnatural silence had fallen over the land. Not a single bird or insect could be heard anywhere. Overhead, the daunting sky hung heavy and immobile, an impenetrable blanket of somber cloud. Isaac scanned his surroundings in the dying light. A dense fog was forming in the hollows.

"Where is that dog?" he muttered to himself, frowning with worry.

At that moment he saw Shackleton trotting up the path towards him, a sense of uneasiness expressed in his movements.

"What's the matter, boy?"

Shackleton did not stop to greet him; instead, he moved briskly past, climbing to the place where the path continued upward. Only then did he turn to look at Isaac, a deep urgency filling his amber eyes.

He is trying to tell me something, but what?

Turning on an impulse, Isaac peered down the path that Shackleton had just come from. There was a group of shadowy figures approaching, numbering a dozen or so. It was difficult to see them through the failing light and fog, but they appeared to be stumbling up the mountain towards them, their movements slow and clumsy.

"Dear God in heaven," gasped Isaac, straining his eyes. "How can this be?"

They had not encountered any of the undead since they had made their escape from the village, and Isaac had begun to believe that the anomaly had been localized to that particular place.

Looking down at the approaching horde, he could see that this was not the case. He turned back to Shackleton and found that the dog had once again vanished, only this time the disappearance caused him great concern.

"Shackleton!" he called out in a sharp whisper. "This is no time to be disappearing!"

Isaac hurriedly collected his things and moved to follow, turning one last time to look down, but seeing nothing in the fog. It was creeping upwards in waves now, each crest followed by another, and advancing quickly.

Moving around a rocky bend, Isaac found Shackleton again. The dog was up ahead of him, a grey silhouette against a darkening sky. He moved off the moment their eyes met, and in that instant, it became clear to Isaac that Shackleton had been telling him to make haste. Now he knew why.

Isaac scrambled his way up the twisting path and Shackleton only returned to his side when he was convinced that Isaac was moving as quickly as he could. Even still, there was a continued urgency in the dog's demeanor; a ridged body language that communicated the grave danger they were in.

Isaac hurried along, and below them they heard the muted and strangled cries of a small animal rising from the fog, only to go suddenly silent. Shackleton's eyes opened wide at the sound, and Isaac swallowed hard as he stumbled forward. The undead behind them were drawing closer with every passing second. They desperately needed to find somewhere to hide.

Rounded stones were lining the path now, and the irregular gravel was soon giving way to the occasional step or section of cobblestone. The cold fog was rising ever quicker, curling over Isaac's feet and in some areas wading up to his knees. He moved forward with haste. An inky shadow of fear had engulfed him, carrying with it flashes of his ordeal at the Portal of Ahreimanius.

Isaac looked around with haunted eyes. Ancient stone structures were materializing out of the mist now, their forms dark and dripping with moisture. They had come into a solemn village and were moving along a cobbled lane flanked by low buildings. Not a soul could be seen anywhere, not a single light in any window. Isaac made the connection at once. This was the village from which the mob had come.

He could see Shackleton just ahead, turning nervously and continuing to communicate haste. It was only then that Isaac spotted a throng of figures emerging from the fog behind them. They were twisted and stumbling and numbered fifty at least. To make matters worse, vague shadows of yet more undead lurked in the mists to their left and right. Isaac peered into the gloom and realised they were surrounded.

It was only then that a potent demonic force came upon him, paralyzing him with a coursing fear that drove the breath from his lungs. A full recollection of the time he had spent possessed pushed itself into Isaac's mind just then, filling his eyes with flashing images of the gore and carnage he had endured as he was made to butcher the corpse of his son.

Isaac's breath was coming in short pants now. The mob was approaching swiftly, and he dared not budge, fearing that the slightest movement would send him plummeting into insanity. He could only watch dumbly as the space that separated him from the shadowy horde diminished.

Shackleton darted to his side and nudged him hard with his muzzle, and just then Isaac broke from the spell. He watched the brown dog dart off and followed him at an awkward gait, the closest thing to running his panic-seized body would allow him to do. His flight ended at an old monastery, its ancient wooden doors crouching under a mist-enshrouded portal of gothic masonry.

Isaac's throat was too constricted with fear to shout, so he pounded on the heavy wood instead. Try as he might, the reports he made were weak and muted, and the thick fog swallowed them instantly. It was only when Shackleton let sound three barks that he dared hope again. They were loud and sharp, and they cut through the fog.

Isaac turned and pushed his back hard into the doors, trying in vain to force them open. A full moon had just appeared from behind the cover of an overhead cloud, its cold light shining down like a graveyard lamp.

Dear God in heaven...

The walking cadavers were almost upon them. It was only then that a small hatch slid open in the door behind him. He jerked around to see a shadowy face appear on the other side.

"Melchizedek?" it said in a loud whisper. "Is that you?"

Shackleton barked in confirmation, but Isaac was sure it was too late. Looking over his shoulder he could see that the shadowy figures had arrived, their arms outstretched, their jaws snapping hungrily. A second later he felt them tugging at his pack. He struggled frantically against their clawing hands. Their bodies were grey and festering, their eyes bereft of life.

"For the love of God!" he cried in desperation. "Let us in!"

Isaac squirmed out of his backpack, using it to push away the undead who had already taken hold of it. In that instant he heard the scraping friction of an iron deadbolt, followed by the clank of an ancient latch.

Within seconds a pair of strong arms had pulled him into a dark, medieval courtyard, and slammed the door behind him. Almost instantly the inhuman sound of clawing and scratching filled the air. Isaac turned instinctively, peering through the door's open hatch to see the throngs of undead gesticulating outside. He threw his body against the door and turned to face his rescuer.

"I am Isaac Rodchenko," he panted, his eyes wide with fear. "I owe you my life."

"You owe me nothing, my son." said the man, ruffling the fur atop Shackleton's head.

He had a large build and was bearded and dressed as a monk, with an ample belly and a bald, chiseled head. His height, combined with his strong jaw, gave him a powerful appearance, but it was tempered by a pair of gentle, patient eyes.

"If you owe your life to anyone," said the monk in a thick Spanish accent, "you owe it to Melchizedek. Were it not for his bark, I would never have heard your call. This evil fog swallows all sounds."

"But how is it that you know this dog?" asked Isaac, still breathing heavily. "Who are you?"

"I am Brother Bernardo," he said. "You are now in the care of *The Order of St. James the Just*. Melchizedek is an old friend of ours. He comes and goes, but he is always welcome."

"He saved my life," said Isaac, patting Shackleton's rump.

The fat monk looked up at him urgently.

"Have you been touched by the dead?"

"I have not," said Isaac. "I was speaking of this dog's miraculous appearance not three days ago. After my plane crashed, I came to be in a lake. He appeared out of nowhere and saved me from drowning."

The monk raised his eyebrows in wonder.

"It would appear you have been through much, my friend," he said. "Were there many others on the plane with you?"

"Only three," said Isaac, still catching his breath. "All of them perished. One of those killed was Father Franco Rossi. I found his journal amongst the wreckage. He was planning to come here."

"Father Franco?" asked the monk urgently, taking Isaac suddenly by the shoulders. "You say he is dead?"

Isaac nodded solemnly. By the expression of loss in the monk's eyes, he could see immediately that the two had been good friends.

"Are you Rex Angelus?" asked Isaac.

"Yes," said the monk sadly. "I am. But there are few outside the walls of this monastery who would know that, apart from Father Franco and Professor Metrovich, that is. Was the professor on the plane as well?"

Isaac nodded solemnly.

"I do not know why I am here, Brother," he said. "I was guided by powers greater than my own. Like you I am a man of faith, and I say to you that something of unparalleled importance is occurring; something that is for the most part a mystery to me. It would seem to revolve around an artifact known as the Compostela Cube."

At the mention of the Cube, the monk's knotted brow seemed to relax, an air of perfect understanding engulfing him as he looked at Isaac. He reached past him and slammed home a second deadbolt in the gate.

"There is much to talk about, my good Isaac," he said. "But first you must come with me."

The monk laid a gentle hand on Isaac's shoulder, glancing back at the heavy door. Outside, the undead had retreated into the night fog, but he knew they would return.

"You and Melchizedek will need food and rest," he said. "You have both been through a great ordeal."

CHAPTER 40

Under the Mediterranean Sea.

Bahadur led the group in a single file, their treacherous path hugging a narrow ledge that clung to the side of a deeply fractured fissure. With all hopes of finding the Book of Khalifah gone, the giant had no choice but to push the company forward.

His priority was to get them out of St Michael's Pass and deliver Fra and Suora to the Gibraltar hospital as soon as possible. The tunnel expedition had proven to be too much for the octogenarian couple, and it was clear that they were both suffering from severe exhaustion.

"Unbelievable," muttered Gabriel, holding out his flaming torch. "Who would have thought that all this could be hidden beneath the Mediterranean?"

To their left, the fractured wall of rock had fallen suddenly away, exposing a black void. The stone here was dark and slippery with dampness. Gabriel cast a small stone into the divide, counting to five before hearing it strike something far below. For all intents and purposes, the chasm was bottomless, just as the marker said it would be.

"We made it!" cried Amir suddenly. "The pass is just up ahead!"

Within moments, all realized he was not mistaken. After arriving at an open ledge, they discovered their path had come to an abrupt end. A dark shadow on the opposite side of the chasm showed where the tunnel continued on.

In the centre of this open area, they found a marker, but unlike the others before it, this one was flush with the cavern floor. In it were set two shoe-sized depressions, each of them oval in shape and adorned with the familiar Islamic text.

"This is the actuating device for the drawbridge," said Gabriel, moving his torch closer to the marker so that he could read its carvings. "As long as one of these ovals are depressed, the bridge will remain open."

"Let's just push one down with a rock," suggested Natasha. "That way we can all cross."

Gabriel shook his head and frowned.

"There's a catch," he said. "After one has been depressed, the other will need to be depressed while the first returns to its original position. To keep the bridge open, the ovals need to be stepped on in alternating cycles, kind of like an exercise machine. Rocks wouldn't do it."

Natasha looked over to see Bahadur standing fearlessly on the edge of the precipice.

"I was hoping we might have been able to jump across," he said, gauging the distance. "But this would be an impossible leap. Even if we had a rope, there would be nowhere to secure it."

Natasha looked around and saw that it was true. The walls in the chamber were utterly smooth. The Moors had gone to great lengths to ensure that the chasm could not be crossed by any means other than the bridge.

"Let's give this a try," said Gabriel, taking Natasha's hand. "Would you like to do the honours?"

Natasha nodded and stepped into one of the two ovals.

No sooner had she done so than it dropped several inches.

"Now switch," said Gabriel.

She stepped into the other oval and found that it lowered just as the former returned to its original position. With each alternation, it became easier to depress the steps, and a slow rumbling could soon be felt at their feet. Below them, a hidden flywheel began to pick up speed.

After alternating her steps a few more times, the sound of rushing water sounded beneath them, and in the space of a minute, a narrow wooden catwalk emerged from a concealed opening in the cliff's edge. It shot suddenly across the chasm and found home in a slot on the other side, forming a bridge.

The catwalk remained extended while Natasha continued to shift her weight from oval to oval, but it retracted immediately when she discontinued her work.

"Well," said Gabriel, "so much for stepping on these stones and then trying to make a run for it. This mechanism uses water pressure to pull the bridge back the moment the pumping stops."

Natasha frowned.

"We wouldn't make it to the middle of the gorge before it disappeared under our feet."

Scotty went to stand beside Bahadur at the edge of the chasm.

"I'll take the lower route with you, comrade," he said solemnly, putting his arm around the brown giant.

Bahadur smiled and gave a nod of deep appreciation. They walked back to where the others were.

"Let us begin to cross," said Bahadur, his voice deep with resolve.

Seeing that the old nun and brother were still resting on the chamber floor he added:

"We will begin by moving the equipment. Suora and Fra may continue to rest until we are ready to proceed."

The five-hundred and sixty-one-foot Ohio Class submarine made its way through the dark waters of the Strait of Gibraltar, its enormous belly gliding mere meters above the sandy sea floor. Its crew had only just completed the last scans of the fault line, and they were steering the black goliath out into the Atlantic Ocean to take up their launching position. In the submarine's metal bowels, a ground-penetrating nuclear missile lay armed and ready for launch, specially modified, and a tactical twenty-five kilotons in size.

"The submarine will be in attack position in T-minus three minutes and counting," said the sultry voice of Christian's computer.

Christian glanced up at the hovering holographic planet. Across from him, and under the shadow of the enormous, blackened cherubim, Dr. Bennington's lifeless corpse had been propped up in its chair. Christian stared at it blankly, his face empty of emotion.

"As you can see, Doctor," he said, raising an eyebrow, "I feel no guilt or pain. I feel nothing whatsoever."

The chamber was quiet around him, the dark voices silent with anticipation. Christian felt sated. Killing the doctor was the best thing he could have done. He was in control of himself again. Nothing would stop him now.

"The missile is fully operational," said the computer. "Standing by for launch sequence."

Christian glanced up at the glowing holographic planet, his eyes panning over the banks of monitors that flanked it on all sides. Each one was showing its own live video feed, combining to form a flickering wall of war, carnage, and devastation. He shot a glance over at Bennington's slumped corpse, and for a moment he thought he could see it smiling.

"Fire," he said, a pang of self-doubt running suddenly through him. "Fire, God damn it. Fire, fire, fire!"

CHAPTER 42

Under the Mediterranean Sea.

Even after a long respite, Suora and Fra had still not managed to regain their strength. They were reclining on a blanket that had been laid out for them, watching the others as they gathered around a stone marker on the opposite side of the chasm.

"Have strength, my love," said Suora weakly to Fra. "There is only one kilometre left. We must try with all our might."

She was wrapped in her blanket with only her face visible, looking over at Miller who had remained behind to work the bridge mechanism.

The old brother was nodding wearily, knowing full well he would be incapable of such a feat. He had managed to sit up but he was still deathly pale, and try as he might, he could not stop shivering.

"One kilometre straight up, *mi tesoro*," he said hopelessly. "May God help-"

A booming blast shook the chamber, cutting off his words. It had sounded like a muffled thunderclap, and a moment later the entire gallery began to shake violently. From high above, large sections of stone began to fall in tumbling masses, disappearing into the void of the chasm.

Suora saw Miller jump to his feet, and in that moment turned to find Fra looking directly at her. For a timeless moment they gazed into each other's eyes.

"Could it already be time, my love?" asked Suora, a deep peace engulfing her.

"I believe it is, my darling," replied the old brother, smiling sadly.

No sooner had the ground begun to grow still again than another blast sounded, followed by yet another. This time it seemed that the explosive force was beginning to resonate within the stone itself. The chamber seemed to be lurching from side to side almost rhythmically.

At that moment the old brother rose slowly to his feet, pulling Suora up with him. He turned to face Miller, a newfound strength filling his body.

"Go and get Bahadur!" he ordered. "I will man the bridge!"

Within seconds he had stepped into the ovals and begun pumping them, the ancient mechanism shooting the long wooden catwalk out across the chasm.

Amid a rain of falling rocks they watched Miller arrive safely on the other side, just as the others appeared from within the tunnel mouth. Suora could see Natasha's face among them, and the expression of horror it bore when Fra stepped off the mechanism. The bridge retracted instantly.

"Suora!" cried Gabriel over the tumult. "Fra!"

There was panic in his eyes.

"Activate the bridge!" he screamed. "We're coming to get you!"

Natasha saw Suora move into Fra's embrace, and in that moment knew what was happening.

"No," she said quietly, her eyes filling with tears. "No, it can't happen here. Not like this..."

The ground shook again as the final shock wave detonated in the sea above them. The chamber was beginning to shudder in a peculiar way now, and across the chasm they could see Suora and Fra standing arm in arm, dwarfed against the backdrop of the massive rock formations.

"You will activate the bridge mechanism immediately!" bellowed Bahadur, moving dangerously close to the edge of the precipice. "That is an order!"

Those around him were not sure what boomed more deeply, the shuddering earth or the desperation in his voice.

"Leave this place now!" cried Fra with his last remaining strength. "Make haste!"

A tremor ripped through the chasm and were it not for the strong arm of Scotty Roberts, Bahadur would have fallen to his death. With a mighty heave, the smuggler drew the giant back from harm's way, bringing his battered brown face within inches of his own.

"Are you our leader?!" bellowed Roberts over the crashing tumult, and at that very moment, tumbling masses of seawater began to fall from above, partially obscuring their view of the brother and nun.

Like Gabriel and Natasha, Bahadur too was in a state of panic, wanting nothing but to leap the impossible distance and come to the aid of his dear friends. His heart went out to Suora and Fra in desperation. This had not been the plan. He and Scotty were to have taken the lower passage. It was they who should have been on the other side.

Bahadur looked down to see that he was still being clutched by the smuggler. He stared blankly into his eyes.

"Are you our leader?!" bellowed Roberts again, his face straining from the effort.

"Yes..." said Bahadur, at last regaining control of himself. "Yes, I am!"

"Then lead us out of this Godforsaken hole, God-damn-it!"

In that moment all hell broke loose. A force so powerful jarred the ground that it made the recent blasts seem tame by comparison. Mighty as they were, the other explosions had been manmade. What they were experiencing now was Mother Nature's tectonic response to their insolence, and it was by no means subtle.

"Come on!" bellowed Gabriel over the crashing of falling rocks and water. "We can't save them! We've got to go now!"

He had his hands wrapped around Natasha's shoulders, trying to get her to turn and run.

"Suora," whispered Natasha, suddenly seeing the frail little nun through a gap in the wall of falling water.

She stood next to Fra, but whereas he was waving his arms frantically, yelling out orders for them to flee, she was calmly smiling, and for an instant Natasha's eyes locked with hers and time seemed to stop. The chamber grew oddly silent.

"Run, my child," came her familiar voice. "Escape this place and complete the task you were born to do. Bring peace to the hearts of those who will make the crossing. Darkness surrounds us now, and you must be brave. We will meet again soon, my child. Run now. Run as fast as you can!"

In that instant a great churning mass of water descended on the nun and brother, washing them away in a fraction of a second. Natasha felt herself being turned around forcefully. The crashing tumult was deafening. Directly before her she could see Gabriel's face. He was drenched in seawater, but his eyes were calm with resolve.

"Natasha," he said in earnest. "They're gone. It's time to go."

* * * * * *

Najiallah Nasrallah threw down his bloodied knife and gripped a stone outcropping with all his might. His surroundings were shaking with indescribable violence, and already the rising seawater was beginning to cover the corpse at his feet.

He had been forced to run a considerable distance before arriving at a place where he could ambush the man who pursued him. The chase had led him into a formation of fractured rock, in the middle of a meter-wide gap that separated two towering sections of granite.

Nasrallah looked around in horror. He could clearly see that the rock faces were drawing closer together as they shook. If they continued to do so, it would only be a matter of time before he was crushed. He frantically looked around. There was nowhere to run.

"Dear, Allah!" he gasped, jerking his head from side to side. "Have mercy on me, I beg you!"

As if in response to his plea, a particularly violent tremor shook him to the core just then, and the rock walls jerked suddenly together with a grinding crunch. Nasrallah was swiftly pinned, and panic took hold of him.

"No!" he screeched. "Please!"

Very slowly, the rock face continued to close in upon him, and as his ribs shuttered and popped under the pressure, Nasrallah cursed Christian with every fibre of his being. The stabbing pain in his chest was unbearable, and things were about to get much worse. Without warning his flashlight slipped from his grip and sank into the frigid seawater, plunging him into an inky black hell.

For a long while Nasrallah struggled there like a pinned sewer rat, trying to keep his head above the turbulent water. In the end, however, his frenetic refusal to die ended in vain, despite his best efforts.

After what seemed to him like an eternity, the stone walls finally moved in to obliterate him, just as the seawater rose to cover his face. In this way Najiallah Nasrallah perished in the bowels of the earth, to be missed by no living thing that walked upon its surface.

CHAPTER 43

Under the Mediterranean Sea.

"We must move quickly!" bellowed Bahadur, shoving the others into the tunnel one by one. "The water will reach us the moment the lower galleries have been filled!"

Still in shock, Gabriel and Natasha found themselves first in line, leading the others through a narrow tunnel at a brisk run. It climbed steeply before them, a natural formation that looked to have once been an underground river. From behind them came a powerful current of air that was growing in intensity.

"Why's it so windy?" asked Natasha as she ran.

Mighty gusts were blasting past them now, pushing them forward with incredible strength.

"The seawater's forcing the air out of the lower galleries!" cried Gabriel over the tumult. "This must be the only way for it to get out!"

Luckily for the party, the compressed air was having a tremendous impact on the speed of their ascent. The wind was helping to push them up what would have otherwise been a very challenging incline. Because of its consistent flow, it became easier and easier for the party to measure its effect on them, and they were soon proceeding upwards in great leaps and bounds, the smooth tunnel walls speeding past them in a blur.

"We're going too fast!" cried Natasha over the buffeting air, her ears plugged from the rapid change in altitude.

"We'll be fine!" bellowed Gabriel from his place in front of her.

He was scanning the dark tunnel ahead of them.

"Just stay on your feet!" he cried. "And keep your flashlight trained straight ahead!"

Behind them the rest of the party was doing the same, each one focusing their jerking beams into the dark depths that rushed towards them.

Bringing up the rear of their procession came Bahadur, clutching the old bishop to his side. The buffeting wind was catching the enormity of his body and carrying him as though he were a tenth of his weight.

They had been ascending in this way for almost five minutes when Bishop Marcus at last began to feel a cold mist at his back. Shining his flashlight behind him, he could see hints of spray beginning to appear in the distance. There could be no doubt. The tumultuous seawater would soon reach them. If they did not find an exit soon, they would all be drowned.

It was only then that the tunnel opened suddenly into a wider chamber, and the flow of air lessened instantly. There was a stone marker in the centre of the space, and they gathered around it in the buffeting wind.

"We cannot stay here!" cried Bahadur.

He was bending over the stone now, reading it as best he could.

"The water is almost upon us!"

Gabriel joined him. It was imperative that they make the right decision. There were several openings to choose from, and a wrong turn would cost them their lives.

"It says that Gibraltar's directly above us!" cried Gabriel, looking back to see a wall of sea foam exploding from the tunnel mouth.

"Follow me!" bellowed Bahadur. "Now! Now!"

Within a matter of seconds, the giant had ushered the party through one of the portals and into a chamber. To their great relief the room had been equipped with a massive bronze door.

In an instant Scotty, Miller, and Bahadur were bent on closing it, but the ancient hinges were seized and not budging. Gabriel squeezed in to lend a hand. Outside, churning masses of white spume were quickly filling the chamber. The raging seawater would be upon them in a matter of seconds.

"Push!" bellowed Bahadur as the veins popped from his corded neck. "HEAVE!"

With a resounding crack the hinges at last gave way, and the massive door slammed into place with a boom, just as a deluge of seawater exploded into the chamber outside. With a final consolidated effort, a heavy iron crossbar was lowered into place. Outside, the angry seawater pummelled the bronze door violently.

Bahadur slumped to the ground, his back leaning against the door as a pool of shallow water formed beneath him. Natasha's anguished sobs filled the darkness. She had curled herself up in Gabriel's lap, crying uncontrollably as the reality of what had just happened set in.

Amir found a basket of torches nearby and lit one. In its flickering light the shocked faces of all those present could be seen with utter clarity. Two of their dearest companions had sacrificed their lives so that they all might live. The bishop stood swaying on his feet, the blow proving to be more forceful than all the explosions they had experienced.

"They were our dear friends," he said, his grief and fatigue overcoming him.

He fell to his knees.

"They were our family."

A long time passed before Bahadur ended his reprieve and stood up at last. He lit another torch and held it aloft.

"Take heart, comrades," he said bravely. "Our dear friends are with Allah. My faith tells me that they are well, and that we need not be sad for them. We must continue on."

And then looking down at Gabriel he said:

"Dr. Parker. I believe that only you can find a way out of this chamber."

Gabriel and Natasha glanced up at the giant, their faces still torn with grief. It was only then that they noticed they were in an exact replica of the antechamber they had found on the opposite side of the strait.

Gabriel kissed the top of Natasha's head and came to his feet, making his way over to an elaborately carved wall. It was identical to the one they had encountered in the original space. He cleared away a mass of cobwebs and dust to reveal the surface of the actuating mechanism.

"We're in a twin chamber," he said, looking back at the others. "If I'm not mistaken, the same stone that got us in will get us out."

CHAPTER 44

Los Picos de Europa, Northern Spain.

Their footfalls echoed hollowly off the dark stone masonry. The heavy monk was leading Isaac along the isles of a large gothic church and past a long row of life-sized statues. The effigies depicted angel warriors in full armour, and at their feet lay a long battery of flickering prayer candles. The shifting light cast shadows over their angelic wings, imbuing them with life.

Isaac moved forward in silence, his eyes scanning the strange house of worship. It was clearly of Christian denomination, but whereas most church altars had as their central element a crucifix, this one had instead a large tree of the purest white marble. Every leaf and stem was masterfully carved from what appeared to be a single piece of stone.

"The Tree of Life," said the monk, seeing where Isaac's eyes lingered. "To the early Christians it symbolized far more than a wooden crucifix ever could."

Isaac turned to find that the monk was looking directly at him.

"The cross was an instrument of death, dear Isaac," he continued, "while Jesus was, after all, concerned with life above all else. It is only the dark Vatican that is concerned with death, and it is for this reason that the crucifix has always been used as its primary symbol."

Isaac did not know how to respond. This was not the first hint of heresy he had heard in the few hours he had been in the monastery. Before their meal, Brother Bernardo had led him and a small group of monks in prayer, reciting the Our Father with slight variations to the version promulgated by the Church.

"And lead us in our temptations," he had said, *"So that we may deliver ourselves from evil."*

Isaac thought back on what he had read on the internet, and how this group of monks believed themselves to be the decedents of Jesus Christ. What could he expect to find here but heresy? Even still, doubt had somehow been instilled in his mind. It was not doubt in the existence of God, but rather in the Church itself. History was rife with far too many examples of the Vatican's corruptness, and of its murderous and hypocritical acts.

Leaving the church, Isaac followed Brother Bernardo into a long corridor, with Shackleton leading the way. He was amazed at how well the animal knew the monastery, and once again found himself wondering why the dog had saved his life. He considered the many strange synchronicities that revolved around the mysterious Cube, and now more than ever wanted to find answers.

"Brother Bernardo," he said on an impulse. "Could I ask you a question?"

"Certainly," said the monk, slowing to walk beside him.

"Does the name, *The Portal of Ahreimanius*, mean anything to you?"

The heavy monk stopped in his tracks and turned to grasp Isaac by the shoulders.

"Where did you hear that name spoken?" he asked, his brow furrowing. "Did Father Franco mention it to you?"

"Why, no," said Isaac, encompassed by guilt and shame. "I was made to go there by what I can only describe as a supernatural force..."

The monk continued to frown as he bent closer.

"By a demonic force?" he asked in a whisper.

Isaac bowed his head and shuddered at the memory of it all.

"Yes," he said quietly. "They made me do abominable things..."

"I see," said Brother Bernardo, and it seemed to Isaac that the monk somehow understood. "Were you made to do things to the corpse of your son?"

Isaac was taken aback.

"I was," he said. "How is it that you know?"

The monk looked deeply into Isaac's eyes.

"I was a fool not to heed my intuition. Follow me, please."

They changed direction and walked for some time before descending into a circular crypt. It had a low ceiling and was encircled by twelve arched openings, each emptying into dark, unlit corridors beyond. At the centre of the crypt was a single stone sarcophagus, unadorned and of simple construction.

"This is a very sacred chamber," whispered the monk, falling to his knees as he spoke. "Do not be fooled by its humble appearance. Please wait here. I shall not be long."

Isaac watched the heavy monk rise and disappear into one of the arched openings, then he turned to face the crypt. A powerful paranormal energy seemed to be radiating from the place, but unlike what he had experienced on the island, its vibration was utterly benign.

What is this?

The crypt was cold and damp, and its odour was that of antiquity, combined with the pungent bite of stale earth. Isaac glanced over to see Shackleton sniffing at the base of one of the stone arches, but when he looked away, he found that was standing at the foot of the sarcophagus now, though he could not recall having walked there.

At that very moment he was overwhelmed by a feeling of such warmth and safety; of such blissful peace, that he bent on an impulse and kissed the stone tomb.

"Dear Lord in heaven," he whispered, falling to his knees. "What joy is this that fills me?"

Isaac's heart was overflowing with a sensation of the purest love imaginable, and he could not understand why. It seemed to him that he was no longer alone in this world, and that the many tragedies that had befallen him in the past had all occurred so that he might be led to this very spot.

A sense of identity and purpose was welling up in him now, but more encompassing still was the feeling of unhindered redemption that permeated his soul. In that very moment, he knew that he had been absolved of all his actions at the Portal. He could only feel atonement now, perfect and complete atonement.

Isaac looked up with teary eyes to see that Brother Bernardo was standing next to him.

"Rise, dear Isaac," he said kindly. "You have passed the test. The *Logos* is strong in you."

Coming to his feet, Isaac saw the forms of what appeared to be twelve fully armed knights standing in each of the twelve niches that encircled the crypt.

"What is happening?" he whispered.

"Behold the sacred tomb of Jesus Christ," proclaimed the monk. "Few are those who have been given to drink of his Logos, as you have just done."

Isaac looked down at the sarcophagus in utter disbelief. Engraved into its top was the image of a sword with a single Greek word below its pummel.

Χριστός.

Isaac staggered backwards in shock. In his heart of hearts, he knew what the word meant.

The Anointed One. The Christ.

"Dear God," he gasped. "This cannot be…"

Throughout his entire life, Isaac Rodchenko had been taught that Jesus Christ had risen from the dead; that his body had vanished from his tomb only to come back in spirit after the third day. A sarcophagus claiming to contain the remains of Jesus Christ was heresy on every count.

A great conflict ignited in Isaac. A part of him could not accept what his heart was telling him, but at the same time, he could not deny the sublime reality of the events that had only just transpired. He was still overflowing with the love that had engulfed him upon kissing the sarcophagus, a love whose existence could in no way be denied.

After a brief moment the battle had ended. Religious dogma might be captivating, but experiential wisdom was irrefutable.

"Never in my life had I considered…" he whispered, running his hands over the tomb and falling to his knees again.

"Rise, dear brother," said the monk, smiling. "You are truly the *Consilio*. Long have we awaited your arrival, dear friend."

Isaac looked up at the monk, his brow furrowed with confusion as he rose slowly to his feet.

"Who did you say I was?"

"You are Rex Angelus, my brother," smiled the monk. "You have come to mend that which was split, and to assist the Two in their noble endeavor."

Isaac was going to speak, but Brother Bernardo held up his hands in a gesture of patience.

"The elders are gathering as we speak," he said. "The Final Council of the Apocatastasis has been assembled. All your questions will soon be answered."

CHAPTER 45

Gibraltar.

I just can't figure this out," said Gabriel, clearly stumped.

Having exited the twin chamber, he had led the group along a short tunnel only to find that it ended abruptly at a stone wall. After examining it he had found the hairline cracks of a concealed door but could find no way to open it. He had been searching for an activating mechanism for the past ten minutes.

"It just doesn't make any sense," he muttered, pushing back his wet hair.

He looked over his shoulder to see that the others had all seated themselves along the tunnel wall, taking the opportunity to rest while he plied his trade. Only Bahadur remained on his feet, pushing random bricks in the hopes of finding the actuating device.

"Perhaps we should return to the twin chamber, Dr. Parker," he said, coming to his side. "Is it possible that there might be another exit there?"

Gabriel turned to look at the giant, an idea suddenly occurring to him.

"I'll be right back," he said, vanishing into the shadows of the tunnel.

Not a minute passed before Bahadur heard a deep boom and saw the hidden door swing silently inward. A broad chamber lay on the other side. Gabriel returned a moment later.

"The mechanism was at the entrance of the tunnel," he said with a shrug. "Sorry about that."

He held out a hand and pulled Natasha to her feet.

"How are you making out?" he asked gently.

Natasha smiled sadly.

"It's so strange, Gabriel," she said. "It's as if I can feel Suora inside me. I feel even closer to her now than I did when she was alive."

The bishop interjected.

"That is because you truly are closer to her, my child," he said. "When our body dies, we do not go somewhere *out there*, but rather *in here*. We return to the great *One*, and that can only be found within."

He pointed to his solar plexus and gave a cheerful wink.

"We must not be sad even for a moment," he said. "Suora and Fra are very much alive. Do not be fooled by appearances!"

He gave a broad smile and turned to follow the others out of the tunnel.

"Death does not exist!" he added over his shoulder, and a moment later he was gone, leaving the two of them alone.

Gabriel took Natasha into his arms.

"Do you know what?" he said. "I think that crazy old man's right."

Natasha squeezed him tightly, her sorrow transforming.

"Come on," she said, her eyes bright and shining now. "We've still got to save the world."

Gabriel and Natasha found the others gathered in an open chamber. The walls here were bound by sturdy interconnecting arches made of ancient clay bricks. It was clear that they had found the foundations of Gibraltar's Moorish castle, and that their journey had at last come to an end.

No sooner had they passed into an adjacent chamber however, than an alarm sounded with piercing intensity. A blindingly bright light was suddenly illuminating the area around them.

"YOU ARE IN A RESTRICTED ZONE," boomed a computerized voice. "DO NOT MOVE OR YOU WILL BE SHOT."

Everyone looked up to see a crudely fashioned robotic bank of guns whir into position above them, its three gigantic barrels pointing directly into their midst.

The warning repeated itself again, and Bahadur turned to face the others, not knowing what to do. There was, after all, no enemy to be seen, only a makeshift bank of high-calibre guns seemingly aware of their every move.

Resigning themselves to their fates, Bahadur and the others lowered their guns and waited. It was not long before the alarm subsided and was replaced by an oddly familiar sound.

"Who are you, and what are you doing in here?" barked a hoarse and scratchy voice.

Gabriel and Amir turned to look at each other immediately, their eyes wide with surprise. There was only one person whose voice that could belong to.

"Peralta?" they asked in unison, amazed beyond belief. "Is that you?"

"All right," came the reply after a brief pause. "So you recognize my voice. Big deal."

Amir looked around the room for a camera.

"Peralta!" he said, pulling back his dreadlocks to expose his face. "It's me! Amir Mustafa. What the hell are you doing down here? And why the hell are you pointing those guns at us?"

All watched as the bank of weapons altered its position to face Amir, the lens of a camera that was hose-clamped to its frame buzzing as it zoomed in.

"Amir!" came the raspy voice again. "It really *is* you, man! What in God's name are you doing in here, and so close to the surface at that? Do you have any idea how much radiation there is up there?"

In an instant the robotic cluster of guns retracted, and the floodlights dimmed to a more comfortable level.

"Just stay where you are," came Peralta's raspy voice. "I'll come and get you myself."

It took about fifteen minutes before the stout and messy Peralta appeared wearing a white lab coat and green surgeon's pants. His glasses were exceptionally thick, and he possessed bushy white eyebrows that protruded out over their rims. Peralta had an uncommonly large head, with tangled white hair that proved beyond a doubt that he was his own barber.

Gabriel spoke into Natasha's ear.

"He's the crazy hacker we were telling you about in the caves," he whispered. "He'll know all about the matrices."

Natasha shook her head in amazement. She had just noticed that Peralta was walking amidst an entourage of miniature drones, each one whirring and buzzing around him.

He said nothing as he approached, but instead raised both his arms to exchange warm embraces with Amir, Bahadur, Miller, and Scotty Roberts alike. The latter hesitated a moment before returning the hug.

"I should shoot out your knees for what you did to my suppliers," said Scotty, pushing Peralta away but keeping hold of his shoulders. "But I'm too happy to see your sloppy face, mate!"

Peralta smiled back. In his eyes there was great affection for the smuggler, coupled with sincere regret.

"I had no choice, old friend," said the uncombed hacker. "I'll explain later. I'm really sorry."

Peralta turned to Gabriel, bowing his head respectfully.

"Dr. Parker," he rasped, shaking Gabriel's hand. "Always a pleasure."

When Peralta's eyes fell on Natasha his demeanor changed. His tight face seemed to relax, and his eyes opened a little wider.

"My name's Peralta," he said, shaking her hand. "But yours must certainly be Venus."

"I'm Natasha," she said, laughing.

She was instantly taken by the eccentric engineer and puzzled by the feeling of undefended familiarity that seemed to exude from him. If anyone could be said to be comfortable in his own skin, it was Peralta.

A tiny drone buzzed past them just then and Peralta produced an instrument from his pocket. There was a look of consternation in his eyes as he studied its display. He muttered something under his breath and stroked the side of the instrument as though it were a little mouse.

He looked up at the others.

"It's just as I thought," he rasped. "There are dangerous levels of radiation here. We've got to leave right away!"

"What do you mean?" asked Gabriel. "Why would there be radiation down here?"

Peralta cocked a quizzical eyebrow.

"Didn't any of you happen to hear a few little explosions around twenty minutes ago?"

He spread his arms and managed to herd the group down the passage he had emerged from.

"Do you mean the earthquake?" asked Natasha, stumbling forward as he pushed.

"No," said Peralta, perplexed by her ignorance. "I mean that silly little nuclear detonation that *caused* the earthquake!"

At these words, Bahadur, who was at the head of the procession, came to a complete stop. All bumped into him as he turned to face Peralta, his brow furrowed with severity. Bahadur knew well of his old friend's intellectual playfulness and was in no mood for it now.

"What are you talking about?" he said in his booming basso. "Be clear about it, man. We have been deep under the sea, navigating a tunnel that began in Ceuta. We heard many blasts. What is this talk of a nuclear device?"

It was only then that Peralta understood why he had found them where he had, and his eyes grew wide with amazement.

"You found it too!" he exclaimed; his voice particularly hoarse. "St. Michael's Pass! How the hell—"

"Of what detonation do you speak?" repeated Bahadur, and the firmness with which he asked the question seemed to take Peralta off guard.

"A nuclear device," stammered the engineer. "It must have gone off right above you. Not even an hour ago, I intercepted a coalition radio transmission warning that a terrorist attack was imminent in the strait. It ordered all personnel to prepare for a nuclear strike and the possibility of a resulting tsunami."

Everyone was speechless, and the horror in their eyes was more than enough to communicate their concern for all those who lived above. Peralta picked up on it immediately.

"Gibraltar's population is safe at least," he rasped solemnly. "There were still some people above, but they all got inside in time. The day before yesterday the governor called for an immediate evacuation into the galleries. It's a good thing he did too, or almost everybody on the Rock would be dying from radiation sickness right now."

They were partly relieved, but their concern hardly vanished. Hundreds of thousands of people along the coast would be dead or dying. Peralta tried to get them moving again.

"We've really got to go," he insisted, looking at the still stunned Bahadur. "We've already been exposed longer than we should."

Like Amir, the brown giant was thinking of his family, and praying that Tangiers had remained upwind from the blast.

"Where exactly are we?" he asked.

"Directly under the Moorish Castle's inner courtyard," rasped Peralta. "There's a hidden passage that leads up to the main entrance from here, but that's the last place you'd want to go right now. We need to head down, not up. Now come on. Please!"

With a grunt, Bahadur produced a flashlight and led them down the dark passage at a quick pace. He had to bend over so as to not strike his head on the low ceiling. Peralta took the opportunity to explain how he had come to be here.

"I always suspected there were natural caves on the Rock's eastern face," he began. "But I had no idea the military would have had so much interest in them."

Amir dodged one of Peralta's miniature drones and slipped a cinnamon toothpick into his mouth.

"What military interest?" he asked. "And how the hell did you get down here anyway?"

Peralta switched on his flashlight and trained its beam onto the roof of the tunnel.

"The Moorish Castle up there used to be Gibraltar's prison before it became a tourist attraction."

"So?" asked Amir.

"So, a long time ago, one of the inmates dug an escape tunnel…"

Amir frowned.

"Are you talking about Gavin's Hole? That's a smuggler's myth."

Peralta shook his head.

"It's not. I used it to get down here. I couldn't exactly take the hidden passage."

"Why not?"

"Because it opens onto the castle's main entrance. They nearly caught me when I used it to get out of here the first time. I couldn't take that chance again."

Amir looked back at the engineer in confusion.

"What are you guys talking about?" asked Gabriel.

Amir was shaking his head in disbelief.

"Gavin Binks was a convict back in the nineteen-forties," he said. "The story goes he spent years digging a shaft under his bed. One day he broke through into an old Moorish tunnel and supposedly used it to escape."

Peralta was nodding emphatically.

"It's all true," he said. "He tunnelled down here and then used the hidden passage to get out. I know because I found the old prison warden in the retirement home. He told me where Gavin's old cell was. As it turned out, it was in a part of the castle that's off limits to the public. I broke in and did some tunnelling after business hours. The rest was easy. I inherited this whole place."

As if to confirm Peralta's story, they arrived at an ancient brick wall that he claimed to have broken through. They had to bend low to traverse the short passage, but on the opposite side was a broad tunnel reinforced with concrete.

"And here we are," he rasped, sending the beam of his flashlight into the shadows. "This was all built by Canadian miners in World War Two."

He pointed the beam of light into the darkness.

"Down there's where the tunnel collapsed back in nineteen-fifty-three. The military never fixed it. I guess they figured the lost equipment was all outdated anyway."

Amir looked around through his dreadlocks. There was a three-wheeled service vehicle parked there. It had a flatbed trailer connected to it and resembled something from the nineteen-forties.

"Is that the equipment you're talking about?"

Peralta chuckled knowingly and approached the little truck.

"Hop in," he said, starting up the puttering engine. "It'll be faster than walking."

There was only space for one passenger in the little driver's cab and Peralta offered it to Marcus.

"God bless you, dear boy," said the old bishop, making himself comfortable. "It feels like I haven't sat in a proper seat for months!"

The other's piled into the trailer and they were soon bumping along the dark, humid tunnel.

"Where's he taking us?" asked Natasha, peering into the darkness behind them.

Gabriel produced a flashlight and checked his compass.

"We're heading east," he said. "Judging by our angle of decent, I'd say we were probably around sea level by now."

Ten minutes had not passed when they arrived at a single iron door at the tunnel's end. It had a large wheel at its centre and resembled something that might have belonged in a ship. Gabriel came up next to Peralta.

"Exactly what kind of military equipment were you talking about back there?" he asked.

Peralta gripped the rusty wheel at the centre of the door and gave it a turn.

"The kind that's been making me a fortune ever since I took possession of it."

After a short struggle with the mechanism, the door swung open to reveal an elevator-sized compartment within. Its walls were comprised of riveted iron, with another hatch directly in front of them.

"It's an old airlock," said Peralta, inviting them in and cranking the door closed behind them. "The military put it in to nullify the effects of the tide on the water level inside."

The old bishop was going to ask a question, but his words caught in his throat. Peralta had just opened the forward hatch to reveal a completely unexpected sight.

There, in an expansive subterranean cave, could be seen an old submarine. It was berthed in a dark, glassy pool, and was surrounded by a battery of pulsating electronic equipment.

Everyone blinked in amazement, their eyes scanning the tiny fifty-foot sub. It was dramatically lit; its dark hull rippling with reflections from the lapping waters beneath it. In its cavernous setting, it would have appeared to be part of an elaborate movie set, were it not for the smell of stale diesel fuel in the air.

"Bloody hell!" exclaimed Scotty, his eyes wide with surprise. "What the hell have you got going on in here, mate? You sneaky son of a bitch!"

Peralta was beaming with pride.

"It's a 1944 Royal Navy X-Class midget submarine," he rasped. "There are only two others like it in the entire world, and the one you're looking at is currently being used in one of the most lucrative smuggling operations in the entire history of the Rock."

The group shuffled their way into the secret military submarine port, with the entourage of miniature drones buzzing in ahead of them. The sight was impressive to say the least.

Set against a backdrop of old military crates and hanging cargo nets, were dense banks of electronic equipment, and dozens of monitors shimmering with rolling streams of data. A plethora of equipment filled the chamber, ranging from machining tools to laboratory devices. The gear occupied almost every square foot of available space, but the central attraction was most definitely the submarine.

"You're smuggling in that?" asked Amir, pointing to the vessel with a toothpick.

Peralta sat down at a workstation that looked like something Batman might have used.

"How else do you think I've been paying for all these toys?"

He began to type into one of the numerous keyboards before him.

"Cassano!" he bellowed unexpectedly, and instantly from out of the clutter there appeared a small man with a trimmed goatee, gold earrings, and a colourful scarf wrapped around his neck.

The latter looked at the group of visitors with wide eyes and removed the pair of oversized headphones that had prevented him from hearing them as they came in.

"Don't just stand there gawking," said Peralta, his voice particularly rough. "Go and make sure all the drones have docked into their stations!"

The scrawny pirate disappeared with a nod, leaving the others even more confused than before.

"That was Cassano!" exclaimed Amir. "Everybody thought he was dead; vanished on that run to Tangiers."

"He's been working for me down here," said Peralta, his attention focused on the monitors. "We've been moving tobacco, booze, hashish, marijuana, and pretty much anything else that's needed out there on the Med. The cargo gets brought down from the upper galleries through that."

Peralta used his thumb to point out a secondary airlock that led to an old service elevator.

"It really didn't take much to make it operational again," he said. "When seen from above, the shaft looked like it was caved in, but if those lazy military engineers had taken the trouble to go down and investigate, they would have found the damage to be quite minimal. The lift itself was in perfect nick. We use it all the time."

"But wouldn't they see you coming and going?" asked Amir. "The tunnels might be off limits to the public, but there are still military personnel walking around up there."

"Only occasionally," said Peralta, "and we've got hidden cameras that tell us when it's safe to go up. We're in a very isolated wing."

"This is brilliant, man," whispered Scotty in awe, his eyes scanning the miniature sub. "There's no way they can catch you."

"Not at sea," rasped Peralta.

He had just finished bringing up some images of the nuclear detonation.

"Any approaching customs boats or helicopters show up on the sub's radar, giving us plenty of time to dive. It's the perfect smuggling machine."

"And how exactly did you find out about this place?" asked Gabriel. "How did you know it was even down here?"

"I found out last year when Nasrallah had me locked up in his castle doing his dirty work," rasped Peralta. "I used his computers to hack into the S.A.S. mainframe one day and got a big surprise when I looked at their file on Gibraltar. The hard part was finding a way to get down here. After the tunnel collapse it was completely inaccessible."

"Until Gavin's Hole solved your problem," said Amir, shaking his head in amazement.

Peralta smiled impishly.

"But couldn't divers have gotten to it from the outside?" asked Gabriel.

"Nope," said Peralta. "They couldn't get through the bay doors. They'd been constructed to withstand direct hits from enemy torpedoes and could only be opened from the inside."

"Hang on a second, mate," said Scotty. "Back up. Tell me more about Nasrallah's dirty work."

Peralta scratched the back of his head as he recalled the events.

"When Nasrallah found out that Cassano and I had bought a shipment of hashish from his competitors, he nabbed us and forced me to plant RFID chips in every kilo of it. He made me put together a tracking network, and then return the hash, saying that I'd been found out, and that I couldn't distribute it.

"I gave Nasrallah's competitors five grand for their trouble, and then used the tracking data to find their warehouses and get them busted."

"That was a slimy thing to do, mate," said Scotty, leaning forward. "I lost fifty grand because of you."

Peralta looked down at his feet.

"I know," he said. "And I'll pay it all back to you. I just didn't have a choice at the time. Nasrallah was going to kill Cassano if I didn't do exactly what he said. It wasn't until a month later that I found out about this submarine port."

"So what did you do?" asked Amir.

"Cassano and I planned an escape. When we got back, I figured out a way to get down here and went looking for the old prison warden. You know the rest. We've been hiding down here ever since."

Peralta directed their attention to the monitors.

"Check this out. I just hacked into the dry dock security cameras, and this is what came up."

All looked over in time to see the massive detonation that had occurred not forty minutes before. A dome of seawater was rising over a thousand feet into the air.

"Good God," stammered the old bishop. "How could we ever have survived such a blast?"

All watched in amazement as Peralta replayed the video.

"Fortunately for everyone living on the coast, the detonation only triggered a minor earthquake," he rasped. "Anything larger would have wiped out coastal cities from here to Greece."

"That blast was aimed at us," said Gabriel to the others. "Whoever sent those military choppers was also responsible for this attack. I'm sure of it."

"But those helicopters were American," said Scotty.

Natasha turned to Gabriel.

"Are you saying that the American military would risk killing millions of people just to destroy the Cube? How could that be possible?"

Gabriel looked hard into Natasha's eyes.

"I don't know what I'm saying," he said. "A part of me still can't believe that any of this is happening."

"One thing is certain," said Bahadur, his voice sounding even deeper than usual. "Our enemy can track the artifact. They will know that it has not been destroyed. They will come for us."

Peralta turned away from his monitors, a look of confusion transforming his features.

"Are all of you insane?" he asked. "This was a terrorist attack, just like the nukes that have been going off all over the world. Americans could never have done it. Besides, what artifact could you possibly have in your possession that would make them detonate a nuclear bomb to destroy?"

"This artifact," said Gabriel, producing the Cube from his duffel bag and passing it to Peralta. "We'd planned on looking you up as a consultant, but it would appear that you found us first, and for some crazy reason, that doesn't even surprise me. Very strange things have been happening lately. Inexplicable things..."

Peralta looked at Gabriel, straining to comprehend what he was being told. The scraps of information he had received thus far were disjointed, and difficult to understand. He took hold of the Cube and tried to piece together what he had learned.

"What could possibly be so special about this?"

Peralta gasped as the Cube burst to life, a strange blue light erupting from its core. He stared into it, struggling to understand.

"Believe it or not," said Gabriel, "the artifact you're holding is probably about two hundred and fifty million years old, and not only does it light up like a Christmas tree, it somehow interfaces with both Natasha's brain and mine. For the last thousand years it's been disguised as an unassuming medieval quadriform."

Peralta looked up over the rims of his glasses.

"With pictures of peeled apples on each of its sides?"

Gabriel and Natasha exchanged a quick glance before looking back at Peralta.

"Yes," they said in unison. "How did you know that?"

Peralta returned his gaze to the Cube.

"Because I've seen this artifact before," he said, frowning with confusion. "Nasrallah made me run some tests on it one night when I was his prisoner. It was emitting scrambled alpha-wave sequences. Human brain waves. Very, very strange. I didn't tell him a thing about them, but I think they made me dream things... It's difficult to explain..."

"What kind of things, mate?" asked Scotty, leaning closer.

Peralta looked up at the smuggler pirate, a distant look in his eyes.

"The morning after I'd examined it, I woke up knowing a way out of the castle," he said faintly. "There was a secret tunnel in the lower levels... Cassano and I used it to escape."

On hearing this, Bahadur took a step closer.

"That is very strange indeed, my old friend," he said in his deep basso. "Only Nasrallah and I knew of the existence of those tunnels."

"Look," said Gabriel, putting a hand on Peralta's shoulder. "We've got a big problem. If we don't get that Cube to the north coast of Spain before the winter solstice, this whole world is going to go to hell. As it stands, it might go there regardless. We needed to retrieve an Islamic codex that was supposed to be hidden in St. Michael's Pass, but we failed. It was the only thing that could tell us what we needed to do with the Cube."

Peralta tore his eyes from the artifact and looked up at Gabriel, his jaw hanging open with surprise. He was about to say something, but Amir spoke first.

"How the hell are we supposed to get the Cube up north?" he asked. "We can't exactly leave Gibraltar right now. The radiation would kill us."

Everyone looked at Amir in shocked realization. He was absolutely right. The levels of radiation outside would be lethal. Gabriel's eyes met Natasha's, a look of defeat coming over him.

"We'd have to wait at least two or three weeks," he said. "By that time, it'd be too late."

Peralta held up a hand.

"Hang on a second," he rasped, rising from his chair. "You said that you were looking for an Islamic codex in St Michael's Pass?"

Gabriel glanced over at Natasha and then looked down at his feet.

"That's right."

Peralta frowned and placed the Cube on the desk decisively. He walked to a nearby filing cabinet and opened a drawer, producing a medium sized package.

"Take it," he said, handing it to Natasha. "Consider it a donation to the cause."

Natasha took hold of the package, a quizzical expression on her face. She laid it down on a table and removed its wrapping, exposing a jewel encrusted book that was beautiful beyond description.

"The Book of Khalifah!" she gasped. "I can't believe it!"

Everyone looked at Peralta to find him oddly silent. His eyes were fixed on the golden book.

"Where did you find that?" demanded Bahadur, coming to Peralta's side.

The messy scientist looked up at him and shrugged.

"I found it in St. Michael's Pass," he said. "It was in a secret chamber not far from here."

Gabriel could not believe his ears.

"How did you find the chamber?" he asked. "And how the hell did you get into St. Michael's Pass to begin with?"

Gabriel looked over at the others, the answer to his own question coming to him at that very moment.

"He's the one who left the tracks on the stairs," he said, looking back at Peralta again. "They never belonged to Nasrallah. They were yours the whole time. What the hell happened?"

Peralta sat down in his chair and removed his glasses.

"When Nasrallah gave me the Cube to examine, he also gave me a scroll to look at."

He wiped the lenses with his lab coat and put them back on.

"I guess he figured he was going to kill me anyway, so it didn't matter if I knew about the secret treasure room. He desperately wanted to find the Book of Khalifah. I guess he hoped I might see something in the scroll that he'd missed."

Bishop Marcus could sense the scrappy engineer's distress as he recalled the events. He laid a comforting hand on his shoulder.

"All is well, my son," he said. "Go on."

Peralta looked up at the old bishop and smiled gratefully.

"I took a picture of the map with my phone when he wasn't looking. When Cassano and I escaped, we headed to Ceuta. We'd bought tickets for the ferry that morning, but I changed my mind at the last minute. I couldn't resist. I told Cassano I'd meet up with him in Gib and went to look for the treasure room."

"You sneaky little devil," said Gabriel. "And you figured out the way in."

Peralta shrugged.

"It wasn't so hard," he said. "All the clues were right there on the map."

Amir stared at the slipshod scientist in disbelief.

"And how did you manage to get into the Chamber of Khalifah?"

Peralta nodded as he remembered.

"That was trickier," he rasped. "The big wall of symbols reminded me of a trap I'd come across in a game of D&D once. Something about it just didn't feel right. I wasn't about to start lighting any lamps. When I found the runes on the opposite wall, I thought they'd be a much better bet."

"And how did you know which of the stones to push?" asked Natasha, still amazed. "There were six to choose from, and the others would certainly have triggered the trap."

Peralta shrugged.

"I pushed the one that had the highest electromagnetic reading."

"What?" demanded Amir. "How the hell would you know that?"

Peralta produced his smartphone. It was housed in a bulky case that had obviously been fashioned by him.

"I used this," he said, lifting up the device.

A slim rectangular sensor emerged suddenly from its side, buzzing momentarily. The screen of the smartphone showed a complex looking meter application.

"It's an electromagnetic field sensor," said Peralta. "It occurred to me that the mechanism behind the secret door's actuating stone might give off a different reading than the stones that would trigger the trap. There might be more bronze in there, or even a different kind of metal altogether. As it so happened, I did get a different reading in one of the stones, so I took a chance and gave it a push."

Gabriel was astonished by the device.

"May I?" he asked.

He had barely taken hold of the contraption when a sharp blue flame burst suddenly from its side. Peralta snatched it back.

"Sorry," he said, tapping the screen to extinguish it. "I should have told you about the blowtorch app."

Scotty laughed aloud.

"What else does that bloody thing do, mate?"

Peralta seemed suddenly self-conscious.

"Lots of things," he said bashfully, putting the gadget back into his pocket. "The case I built for it uses the phone's processor to drive all of its physical applications."

"All right," said Amir, beginning to pace. "So you used your special phone to get the Book of Khalifah. How'd you get across that chasm by yourself?"

"I couldn't," rasped Peralta. "I had to double back and take the lower passage. It really wasn't that difficult to get through. There were a couple of traps, but they were designed to kill people coming in, not going out."

Natasha had been leafing through the Book of Khalifah as Peralta spoke, and only now looked up from its gold encrusted pages.

"This book is not only the most beautiful thing I've ever seen," she said, looking over at Peralta, "It's also filled with important information about the Cube and our mission. I can't believe we have it. How can we ever repay you?"

Peralta picked up the Cube from where he had left it on the desk and held it up for all to see.

"Tell me everything you know about this artifact, and we'll call it even."

Cassano took the rest of the party on a tour of the submarine after they had dined, leaving Gabriel and Natasha to relate the complex history of the Cube to Peralta. This in itself was no small task. Beginning with the story of their coinciding births, Gabriel and Natasha went on to tell him everything they knew.

Oddly enough, and taking into account the extent of their adventures thus far, Peralta was much less shocked and disbelieving than one might have suspected him to be.

Having briefly experienced the Cube's strange qualities himself, he could instantly appreciate the significance of the issues at hand. He took a particular interest in the events that had transpired in the Chamber of the Sphere, and the solar system's impending crossing of the galactic plane.

"I'm well aware of this hypothesis," he rasped, "but I had no idea that the actual crossing was so imminent. The last I heard; astronomers were saying it would happen in three thousand years. Not two days… It's quite scary really…"

He paused for a moment as though considering something.

"You know, Einstein would have had a field day with the Dark Rift," he said, shaking his head. "It's very likely that its gravitational field will cause severe temporal distortions in our solar system."

Gabriel and Natasha looked at Peralta, trying to imagine what this could possibly mean. Peralta had, in the meantime, picked up the Cube again. He was studying it closely.

"Speaking of Einstein," said Gabriel. "When we scanned the Cube, we found that it was comprised of thousands of layers, each one containing data encrypted in what appears to be Sumerian sexagesimal cuneiform.

"Suora had a chance to look at some of the scans we made in the tunnel last night. She said they were *matrices representing linear transformations in a state of quantum invariance.* Whatever that's supposed to mean."

Peralta nodded knowingly, his bushy eyebrows gathering together as he examined the artifact.

"I see," he said. "Did she say anything about them being arranged using different dimensional vector spaces simultaneously?"

"I think she did," said Natasha, looking over at Gabriel, amazed. "How did you know?"

Peralta turned his head to face them both, an excited smile spreading across his rumpled features.

"Let's just say I'm a fan of Heisenberg too," he rasped, rising to his feet with the Cube in hand. "Have you still got those scans?"

Natasha nodded and rushed off, returning with the 3-D scanner and her laptop computer. She placed them together on the table.

"Isn't that a cute little BIRIS," said Peralta, smiling.

"You know what it is?" queried Natasha, arching an eyebrow.

"Of course I know what it is," said Peralta, petting the machine's dome-shaped processor unit as though it were the head of a little animal. "I've got one myself as a matter of fact. Picked mine up in Switzerland..."

He pointed to her laptop computer.

"Why don't you boot up your little friend and follow me."

Peralta walked them over to an area that lay hidden behind a wall of empty WWII munitions crates. In amongst a tangle of wiring harnesses and other clutter, were various pieces of equipment, including an x-ray machine, a scanning electron microscope from the late nineteen-fifties, and a BIRIS that was considerably larger than Natasha's portable model.

He placed the Cube on a turntable within the apparatus and powered it up.

"What the hell have you got going on down here?" asked Gabriel, examining the vintage microscope.

"I've collected most of this equipment over a lifetime," said Peralta. "But I've also acquired some new pieces of late. I moved my entire laboratory down here shortly after I found the place."

"And what do you do with it all?" asked Natasha, peeking behind an adjacent wall only to find another grouping of machines.

"I explore, I resolve, and I build," said Peralta.

He was bent over and began typing into a keyboard as he spoke, absently reaching for a half-eaten sausage roll on the desk and popping it into his mouth.

"Let's take a look at those scans of yours while the BIRIS boots up."

Natasha opened her laptop and brought up the scans they had made of the Cube the night before.

"These are just of the first layer," she said, pointing to the screen. "I didn't have enough RAM to render anymore of them."

Peralta looked impressed.

"Great scans," he said, bringing the screen up to his face to get a closer look.

Gabriel peered over Peralta's shoulder.

"We used to have a sample page of conversions from the cuneiform into standard numerals," he said, "but it was lost in St. Michael's Pass."

"Not a problem," said Peralta, proceeding to upload Natasha's files onto a memory stick. "I've got AI software that'll scan and translate all of this."

Natasha turned to Gabriel while Peralta busied himself. Her face was troubled.

"Suora had your father's journal?"

Gabriel nodded in consternation.

"I gave it to her last night."

"What are we going to do without it?"

"I have no idea..."

It was just then that the bishop appeared from behind a pile of crates, having returned from the submarine tour ahead of the others.

"You underestimate Suora greatly, my dear children."

Gabriel and Natasha turned to find him with the professor's journal in hand.

"She gave it to me for safe keeping early this morning."

Natasha took the book.

"She knew she was going to die?" she asked solemnly, passing her hand over the battered cover.

The bishop smiled gently.

"She must have suspected something," he said. "But she was not fearful."

When they returned their attention to Peralta, they found he had already uploaded the scans and fed them into the AI. A scrolling array of glowing green data was tumbling down a monitor before him.

"This is certainly an algorithm," he said, nodding as he studied the speeding script.

Natasha frowned.

"What exactly *is* an algorithm, Mr. Peralta?"

The messy engineer turned to look at her for a moment.

"It's a series of instructions," he rasped. "In this case it's for completing a very complex task."

"And what task is that?" asked Gabriel.

Peralta squinted at the monitor.

"To activate some kind of transponder that appears to be housed within the Cube," he said. "All of this falls into the realm of *Algorithmic Information Theory*. The complexity of these strings is absolutely massive, and what's more, it looks like it requires some kind of universal decryption language to make it work."

Peralta stopped his typing and looked over his shoulder at them.

"If this artifact truly is capable of synching with your brains, there's a good chance that the decryption language is based on a combination of both of your alpha wave patterns."

"By that do you mean our thoughts?" asked Gabriel.

Peralta nodded absently as he scanned the rolling data.

"But that's not all..." he said. "There appear to be some other factors involved here as well..."

He resumed his typing for a moment and then sat back in his chair as the AI did its work.

"You mentioned a labyrinth," he said, his eyes glued to a different monitor now.

"Yes," said Natasha. "The Labyrinth of Sarras. We need to find it before the planet enters the galactic plane."

Peralta turned to face her.

"And what happens if we don't find it?"

Gabriel cleared his throat.

"Perpetual darkness…" he proffered. "That and the complete extinction of the human race."

Peralta shifted his eyes to Gabriel and held his gaze for a long moment before speaking.

"I see," he said at last, nodding. "That does in fact put a bit of a rush on things…"

Natasha led Gabriel to the table where the Book of Khalifah lay. With the bishop having wandered off in search of a snack, and Peralta engrossed in his work, she thought it might be a good time to study the codex. She passed Gabriel his father's tattered diary and bent over the Islamic tome to get a closer look.

"I saw something in here about the *Ostium Sanctus...*"

"Latin for *The Sacred Gate*," said Gabriel. "The Chamber that lies at the centre of the labyrinth."

Natasha took hold of the book reverently. With the practiced hands of an artifact restorer, she made her way through the fragile pages until she had found what she was looking for. There, inscribed in what looked to be silverpoint, was an Arabic poem referring to a cube-shaped labyrinth.

"Here it is," she said, translating it as she read. "Listen to what it says."

In the belly of the mountain are two gateways,
Made by the ancients before the coming of man.
One is descending.
The other is ascending.
Like the cart that follows the wheel,
So are these two gateways married and joined.
Interdependent yet separate.
United yet divided.
So that in descending one may ascend.
And in ascending, one may know what it is to be free."

"Descending so as to ascend," said Gabriel, leafing through his father's journal. "That's a dualistic transcendency concept. A paradoxical contradiction."

He stopped at a double-page spread and tapped the diary. On it was a detailed diagram of the Labyrinth, depicted as a series of cubes within cubes. He held it out for Natasha to see.

"The only way to get out of the labyrinth is to go deeper into it," he said.

Natasha shook her head in confusion and turned her attention back to the ancient tome.

"Listen to this entry. It refers to *The Two*. And again there's that double meaning of the primordial-king-queen in its usage… Only this time it's in Arabic…"

Natasha read the excerpt aloud.

"For the mountain's belly is also a prison, and that prison is called the Firmament. Its walls are of earth and sky and flesh and bone, and the curtain of matter is drawn shut. The prison's six sides are equal. Its nature is impenetrable. But The Two are like the water that finds its way through to the other side. It seeps into the darkest of places where no man will enter, and breaches the six veils."

"I'm seeing a lot of sixes in this stuff," said Gabriel, and at that moment they looked at each other, the same idea occurring to them both.

"Each level of the Labyrinth corresponds to one of the six sides of the Cube," said Natasha, moving quickly through the ancient book until she found the page.

"Here it is. The translations of the proto writings that are carved into the Cube."

"Made by the Council of Six," said Gabriel, looking down at the book in amazement. "There's that number again."

At the top of the page, a page written solely in Arabic, were the Latin words *Illac Domus*.

"*The Path Home*," he whispered, translating. "The way for the fallen angels to return to their place of origin."

He rubbed the back of his neck.

"A pathway to heaven…"

Gabriel's eyes locked with Natasha's. Once again, the same idea had just occurred to them both. Mapping this mysterious path was the Cube's primary purpose.

Natasha pointed to the line of text directly below the title. It was inscribed above a two-dimensional representation of a labyrinth, with the crude image of a man standing at its entrance. At its centre was an All-Seeing Eye.

To transcend the Cube is to see it in all things.

Gabriel opened his father's journal to the first page.

"That's the first thing he writes… What does it mean?"

Natasha shook her head and continued to read through the texts.

"Each side of the Cube appears to demarcate a spiritual milestone that's reached on the path of Illac Domus," she said. "They're calling them the *Six Divine Actions*, and each is directly linked to one of the six major world religions. It says here that a *Seal* will only open when we've fully understood the wisdom behind its corresponding Divine Action."

She held up the book, pointing out a collection of verses.

"These riddles hold the clues," she said. "But an intellectual understanding of the knowledge they relate won't be enough. We need to understand them experientially.

"It's like the difference between imagining that a flame can burn you, and actually being burned by it. The first way is knowledge by deduction—"

"And the second is knowledge by *experience*," said Gabriel, finishing her sentence. "…also known as *Gnosis*."

He skimmed over the verses. Above each one was a heading. He read each of them aloud.

"*Prajñā, Pu, Jihad al-akbar, Atma-Jnana, Logos,* and *Binah-Chokhmah.* Which is which?"

"Prajñā is Buddhist," said Natasha, drawing from her schooling in theology. "Pu is Taoist, Jihad al-akbar is Islamic, Atma-Jnana is Hindu, Logos is Christian, and Binah-Chokhmah is Judaic."

"And what do *these* mean?" asked Gabriel, pointing to a series of symbols that were drawn on either side of the headings.

"They represent the seven steps of alchemy and the seven Hindu chakras," said Natasha. "This is fascinating, Gabriel. The

Cube draws on all the wisdom that humanity possesses, regardless of its place of origin."

"Six spiritual stages," said Gabriel, trying to understand. "Each one containing a key that can be used to get through each of the six seals, so as to arrive at the labyrinth's central chamber."

Natasha nodded slowly, her mind working.

"These Divine Actions are nothing less than the six fragments that the *Original Gnosis* was split up into," she said in awe. "Your father was right, Gabriel. At the root of each world religion lies a fragment of the *Original Knowledge*. The purpose of the Labyrinth is to unify all of those fragments."

"But what about the Seventh Seal?" asked Gabriel. "What about the key to the Ostium Sanctus? It says nothing about it anywhere."

"Perhaps that seal is always open," said Natasha, looking at the eye in the centre of the drawing. "There's no mention anywhere of it being locked."

Gabriel paused to think.

"And does anything in there talk about what actually happens if someone passes through that Seventh Seal?"

Natasha chewed her lip.

"According to this, one would gain entry to the higher spheres without having to actually die. Gutierrez refers to it as a kind of de-materialization."

"Like a transporter in Star Trek."

Natasha rolled her eyes and shook her head at Gabriel's nerdiness.

"He describes the Seventh Seal as the *Alpha and the Omega*. It could be a reference to the Book of Revelations."

"The apocalyptic prophecy that talks about a second coming of Christ?" asked Gabriel.

"Yes," said Natasha. "But Gutierrez interprets the second coming symbolically, referring to it as a higher *Christ Consciousness* that will be adopted by the collective consciousness, as opposed to Jesus actually coming down from the clouds."

Gabriel snapped his father's journal closed and crossed his arms.

"So there's our mission in a nutshell," he said. "All we've got to do is get to the north coast of Spain in the middle of a raging third world war, uncover the entrance to a long lost, proto-Celtic labyrinth, find our way through it by transcending duality, and then go to heaven without dying. And all this before a cataclysmic, extinction level event occurs just two days from now. Sounds simple enough. I don't think we should have any problems at all."

Natasha was looking for something to hit Gabriel with when she heard Peralta's scratchy exclamation.

"It's at the centre of everything!"

They turned to see the scruffy engineer pacing.

"What?" asked Natasha.

"The Labyrinth…"

Gabriel frowned.

"How so?"

Peralta was holding the glowing artifact out before him and shaking his head in amazement.

"The first layer of this Cube is a living testament to Gödel's Incompleteness Theorem," he began. "Your combined alpha waves won't be enough to satisfy it."

He continued with his pacing.

"My guess is there will be a master transponder located at the Labyrinth; one that'll provide the axiomatic systems needed to make the artifact fully functional."

Natasha and Gabriel exchanged a puzzled glance.

"There's only one problem," continued Peralta. "Even if we find this labyrinth, there'll still be something else needed."

"What?" asked Gabriel, moving closer with Natasha at his side. "What's missing?"

"It's a fourth factor," said Peralta, scratching his head. "I'm not completely clear on it yet."

He returned to his computer and scanned the rolling data.

"Is there somebody else involved in this? Somebody who can access the artifact with his thoughts as well?"

Gabriel and Natasha looked at each other.

"Not that we're aware of," said Gabriel. "What are you getting at?"

"It's difficult to say at this point…"

He shook his head in an effort to clear his thoughts.

"Either way, if we're going to try and figure out how this Cube works, it's going to take a huge amount of computational power to extract all this data."

"Is that a problem?" asked Natasha.

"A big one," said Peralta. "The only way I can think of pulling it off in such a short period of time would be to utilize a *Boink*."

Natasha glanced over at Gabriel in confusion.

"A *Berkeley Open Infrastructure for Network Computing*," said Peralta. "It's a middleware system for grid computing. It was originally developed for SETI."

"The Search for Extra-Terrestrial Intelligence?" said Gabriel. "They've got over two million PCs hooked up to that thing worldwide. How the hell are we supposed to put together a network like that in two days?"

"Well," said Peralta, looking down at his fingernails. "I'm sure they wouldn't miss a few Teraflops of processing power. I mean there's so much of it out there…"

"Are you suggesting we hack into SETI?"

Peralta looked intently at Gabriel.

"We've got to find that labyrinth right away," he said. "It's the key to everything."

Gabriel looked back at him hard. The nerdy engineer had touched on a problem that had been plaguing him since they had arrived back in Gibraltar.

"The Labyrinth is somewhere in the mountains of Northern Spain," he said. "How the hell are we supposed to even get there? We can't exactly leave Gib right now. The radiation out there would kill us. We'd have to wait at least two weeks, and by that time it'll be too late."

Peralta pointed to the submarine.

"There's a lot of lead in that hull, Dr. Parker."

"You think that old sub would make it all the way to the north of Spain?"

"I'm absolutely certain it would," said Peralta. "But there's one little problem. We don't have enough fuel to do it, and there's no way of acquiring any."

"I know a bloke who can get you the diesel, mate!"

All turned to see Scotty Roberts approaching.

Having completed their inspection of the submarine, he and Amir were making their merry way towards them enshrouded in hash smoke.

"And exactly who might this diesel-dealing gentleman be?" asked Peralta, propping his hands on his hips skeptically.

"My brother Richard, mate," said Scotty offhand. "He's practically the bloody governor, and he's in charge of the entire Gibraltar Regiment. If anybody's got access to fuel, it's him."

The smuggler snatched the chillum away from Amir and took a deep haul from it.

"I'll get him to give you all the bleeding diesel you need, mate," he said, releasing a billowing cloud of smoke. "Whether he bloody wants to or not."

CHAPTER 48

Central Jerusalem, Israel.

Christian entered his private chambers, overcome with frustration and rage. Even though he had obliterated most of the Mediterranean coastline, the Cube appeared to still be intact. To make matters worse, he had utterly lost his ability to pinpoint its location.

Oddly enough, the frenzied demonic whispering that had threatened his sanity up to that point was having no effect on him anymore. The reason for this was simple. There was nothing vulnerable left in him. Christian's reptilian self was fully in control now. Its demonic, multi-dimensional form had fully merged with his own. With the murder of his only friend, Christian had truly become the son of Lucifer.

He made his way to his desk. More disconcerting than his sudden inability to locate the Cube were the things he had learned from the Zurvanites in their last appearance. His brother had not died after all, but rather survived, and was on the verge of engaging in a plan that would assist the Two in their mission to unlock the gnosis contained in the Cube. The thought of his brother's betrayal made Christian's blood boil.

I will destroy him. I will drink his blood.

Now that he had embraced his dark, reptilian self, he knew it would always govern his actions, and he felt a certain comfort in this. At present, it was telling him that there was one more task for him to complete; one last element of an age-old agenda, which when enacted, would ensure the transference of all earthly power into his hands. He clenched his fists with resolve.

Let the will of Lucifer be done.

The Vatican church that Christian's forefathers had created as the seat of Lucifer's throne would now be destroyed, along with the entire city of Rome. The results of this *terrorist* attack would have global reverberations, affecting more than a billion Catholics worldwide. It would pave the way for a new world religion, one that would have at its root the cleverly hidden tenants of the left-hand path.

"Computer," said Christian dryly. "Activate *Terminus Sanctus.*"

A holographic representation of Vatican City materialized suddenly over his desk. Located deep in a crypt beneath St. Peter's Basilica could be seen a massive nuclear device awaiting detonation. Christian smiled darkly. The Vatican, as it so happened, had been doomed since its inception.

In 1139, during an audience with Pope Innocent II, the Irish Archbishop St. Malachy had experienced a 'holy mystical vision' and shortly after named the one hundred and twelve Popes who would reign from that day until the Day of Judgment.

His predictions had of course been fabricated by the Church, but they would over the centuries prove to be forebodingly accurate, adding to the Vatican's multi-armed campaign to achieve subservience through fear.

To the very last Pope, Malachy had given the name, *Peter the Roman*, and it was a Pope by this very name who currently resided in office.

Christian studied the hologram. According to Malachy's prophecy, the utter destruction of both the Vatican and *The City of Seven Hills*, which was Rome, would come to pass under the reign of the last Pope. It was an ominous foreshadowing of an event that had, in reality, been planned since the Vatican was first created in the fourth century.

"*Terminus Sanctus* is armed and ready to deploy," came the computer's sensual voice. "Awaiting further instructions."

Christian could not help but marvel at the size of the explosive. Built during the Soviet era, it was a one hundred megaton version of the fifty megaton *Tsar Bomba*, the most powerful explosive ever to be detonated in the history of humanity.

That an artifact such as this had been sitting in the bowels of the Vatican since the early nineteen-sixties was incomprehensible; that it was on the verge of being detonated, unthinkable.

A sensation of baleful ecstasy encompassed Christian. This would be the event that would mark the world's transition into darkness and misery.

"Computer," he said with perfect equanimity. "Let us fulfill the holy prophecy that St. Malachy so graciously gave to us. Detonate *Terminus Sanctus* at sunrise, local Rome time."

BOOK THREE
THE SACRED CHAMBER

CHAPTER 1

Los Picos de Europa, Northern Spain.

Isaac passed through a broad set of doors to find himself in a great circular hall of dark and somber stone. Its domed ceiling was soaring and supported by a ring of twelve gothic arches. Enormous stained-glass windows encircled the space, flashing brightly under the light of an electrical storm outside.

At the hall's centre was a heavy round table, and around it were placed twenty-five elaborately carved chairs. All but one were occupied.

Isaac took a deep breath and readied himself. The air smelt of incense and antiquity. Brother Bernardo's whisper sounded hoarse in his ear.

"The Final Council of the Apocatastasis," he said, and just then a succession of flashes sent the stained glass aglow.

Isaac smoothed down his hair and arranged his dark suit as best he could. It was tattered and travel worn and in need of a good cleaning. Studying the faces of those at the table, he counted twelve elders, six male and six female. They were dressed in crimson robes, with the exception of an ancient couple whose gowns were deep blue.

Flanking this couple, and the elders who sat to their left and right, were the twelve armed knights he had seen earlier in the crypt. They were unhelmed now, and he took note of their youthful appearance. The chair that was reserved for him lay directly in their midst.

"You must go and sit down," whispered the hefty monk. "I will be waiting outside."

As Isaac approached, all but the couple in blue rose to their feet. Their smiles of welcome did nothing to mask the deep concern in their eyes.

"Welcome, dear friend," said the seated elder. "I am Alulim, named for the first Sumerian King who came to possess the gnosis of the ancients. This is my wife, Ursula. You are in the house of the Order of St. James the Just, and this special council has been called so that the future glory of the Apocatastasis may be duly preserved."

Isaac bowed low, unsure of what to do. He was still trying to assimilate everything that had happened since he had arrived at the strange monastery. He felt as though he had been transported back in time.

Alulim and Ursula were clearly the leaders here, not only because of their blue robes, but because of the regal way in which they held themselves. Alulim was tall and clean shaven and sat erect despite his advanced years. Ursula possessed an elegance and beauty that defied her age. Her silver hair was long and still thick, her green eyes almond shaped and sparkling with kindness and wisdom.

Isaac could not help but feel like a pauper before monarchs.

"I thank you for the honour of being in attendance here, your Excellencies," he said as formally as he could. "Any help that I can offer is humbly yours."

"Isaac Rodchenko!" cried Alulim officially, rising to his feet. "Do you reject Lucifer and all his works?"

Isaac looked at Alulim with a questioning frown.

"With every fiber of my being, your Worship."

Alulim smiled softly and sat down.

"Be seated then, dear friend. I am convinced of your sincerity. The Final Council of the Apocatastasis can now begin."

Even as everyone sat, one knight remained standing. He appeared to be older than the other knights, perhaps forty. His hair was thick and matted, and his jaw was square and strong. Whereas the other knights wore red over their shirts of mail, his tunic was the same deep blue as Alulim's, and it was clear to Isaac that this man was their captain.

"Our families and friends are dead," he said solemnly, his eyes moving over all those present. "Their bodies are just outside, roaming the streets like rabid dogs. Our once happy village has been destroyed by this plague, and it is clear that the prophecies we have kept in trust for so many centuries have come to pass in ways more horrific than any of us could have imagined."

The knight leaned over the table, planting both of his fists on its dark wood.

"I should like to ask who our guest is," he said bluntly, looking over at Isaac. "And what role he has to play in these events. My men and I are anxious to act!"

Alulim nodded slowly, inviting the knight to sit down with the wave of his hand.

"The souls of our brethren are happily in the beyond, Sir David," he said reassuringly. "We can never allow ourselves to forget this, or despair will surely take us. As far as Mr. Rodchenko is concerned, he is the *Betrayer.*"

No sooner had Alulim uttered these words than all the knights leapt to their feet, their hands moving to their swords. According to the Ascender's Prophecy, the Betrayer was the harbinger of doom; the one who would open the Portal of Ahreimanius and release the demons from the lower spheres. If the truth was being spoken, seated at their table was the very hand of Ahreimanius.

"Please sit down, good knights," said Alulim, turning his gaze to a confused Isaac. "Just as good can come from an act of evil, and evil from an act of goodness, so too is Mr. Rodchenko both the Betrayer and the *Consilio* at once."

The knights took their seats. As opposed to the Betrayer, the Concilio would be a great hero, assisting the Two in their noble mission. That both friend and foe could exist within the same man seemed the greatest contradiction to them, but like many spiritual concepts, the paradoxical was often the crux. It would be as Alulim said.

The council soon fell into discussion, addressing the subject that was the primary reason for the order's existence. Every member present was a humble servant of The Two, and each had sworn to aid them in their mission to release the gnosis that was housed in the Compostela Cube.

Their order constituted the side of the Rex Angelus bloodline that had remained faithful to Jesus Christ. What Isaac did not know, and soon learned, was that he himself was a member of their bloodline, his family belonging to the side that had formed an allegiance with the Luciferic captains at the core of the Vatican; the ones who had called themselves *The Illuminati*.

"You are of unimaginable importance to the great plan of Illac Domus," said Alulim. "Through you, Isaac, shall come the long-awaited reconciliation of the two houses in our bloodline, and the fulfillment of the prophecies."

"I'm afraid I do not understand," said Isaac, more confused than ever.

Alulim smiled kindly.

"In order for you to fully understand your role in all of this, you must hear our story from the very beginning, and the beginning was indeed a very long time ago."

Alulim sat silently for a moment, gathering his thoughts before he spoke.

"If you sincerely consider how ancient this planet is," he said at length, "and how tiny a sliver of time has been occupied by our civilization, it will not appear illogical to you that humanity was not the first civilization to inhabit this world. There were others before us, and their societies were as large and diverse as our own, but these people were not human."

Isaac furrowed his brow in confusion.

What is this man saying?

That a secret society of people should inhabit a village lost in the Cantabrian Mountains was difficult enough to accept. That they had raised their children to be knights, trained in outdated forms of battle, and sworn to protect a pair of saviours spoken of only in obscure prophecy, was even more outlandish.

But to be inferring that another race of beings inhabited the planet before humans did; this was insanity. Even still, Isaac listened politely. Outside, the strange lightning was increasing in frequency and intensity.

"Long ago," began Alulim, "there existed a race of reptilian creatures who possessed the same souls that we possess today, albeit in far less developed states. In essence, we were these creatures, and our primitive souls resided within them as we first incarnated upon this earth."

"If I may ask," interjected Isaac humbly. "How could it be that there are no traces of this civilization?"

Alulim nodded, as if expecting Isaac's skepticism.

"Two hundred and fifty million years will erase many traces, my friend. In the Permian period, life on earth was flourishing, but the planet was an utterly different place. There was but one supercontinent, which geologists have since named *Pangaea*, and it was comprised mostly of desert and savannah. It was within the oceans where the vast majority of life existed, and it was there where the reptilians lived and thrived."

Isaac listened intently as an exceptionally strange story was related to him. Speaking at intervals, the different elders explained that when the first shattered soul fragments of the fallen angels had begun to incarnate on the newly formed earth-sphere, they could do so only in the form of raw minerals and other innate substances.

Slowly, they said, over billions of years of spiritual evolution, these same soul fragments began to unify themselves to the extent that they could now incarnate as plants, and then as brachiopods, arthropods, vertebrates, and so on.

The elders claimed that it was not until much later that the first fully sentient, self-aware beings came to exist on the earth, and that this occurred approximately two hundred and fifty million years before the birth of Jesus Christ.

"Primitive and utterly evil," continued one of the elders, "a race of reptilian beings developed deep on the ocean floor, where the environment was similar in both density and darkness to that of the lower spheres; the spheres from whence they had come.

"Although not human, they were nonetheless manifestations of the countless fallen spirits that longed to return to the world of God. As such they would incarnate again and again, life after life, in the slow process of spiritual purification."

The elder went on to explain that this race of reptiles would continue to evolve over the millennia that followed. Their societies were brutal and merciless, eventually developing sophisticated social structures, and a technology more advanced than our own.

Through the tens of thousands of years of their existence, they came to build vast cities in the deepest regions of the ocean floor, and like humanity, they too warred amongst themselves. Eventually, they developed weapons of enormous power, and the day came when they used these weapons against each other and destroyed themselves as a result.

"Because of the tremendous depths of their cities," said Ursula, "and the tectonic activity that has all but reshaped the ocean floors since their passing, remnants of their civilizations have yet to be discovered. Their skeletons, which were formed mostly of cartilage in order to withstand the tremendous pressures, have left no distinguishable remains either. Bearing in mind these points, you might now understand why no evidence has ever been found to prove their existence."

Isaac listened in amazement.

"Among the many sub-aquatic nations," continued Alulim, "there existed a small and peaceful realm of more evolved reptilians. Their kingdom was ruled by a benevolent King and Queen.

"Through their court oracle, this King and Queen learned that their race would soon perish in a great war and cataclysm, and that every soul but theirs would be taken by Lucifer and imprisoned in the lower spheres."

Isaac listened intently, his amazement transforming into stunned disbelief as he was told of the approaching Dark Rift, and the destruction that would soon befall the earth. It was an event that had happened before, a very long time ago.

"Although they were powerless to avert the cataclysm," said Ursula, "the King and Queen suspected there might be a way to set things right. Their oracle had informed them that it would take hundreds of millions of years of spiritual evolution for the reptilian souls to fully escape their prison in Hades."

"When they finally did accomplish this feat, however," added Alulim, "their souls would be ready to incarnate as a race of human beings that would populate the earth in the distant future. If the King and Queen could save this future race of humans, they would in essence be saving themselves."

"And what was the King and Queen's plan?" asked Isaac.

Alulim exchanged a glance with Ursula and then spoke.

"Using their most advanced technology, they would incorporate all their knowledge and wisdom into a cube-shaped artifact, and build a complex, multi-dimensional labyrinth through which this knowledge might be revealed.

"One galactic year later, when the crossing was once again imminent, the King and Queen would incarnate as two human beings and unlock the gnosis that they had preserved."

"In this way," added Ursula, "they would use the temporal anomalies of the galactic plane to protect humanity from Ahreimanius during the crossing, and give to humanity the knowledge it needed to ascend into the next higher level of spiritual evolution. This would of course bring each of us one step closer to the Apocatastasis."

Isaac struggled to understand.

"But what is this Apocatastasis?" he asked. "I have never heard this word before."

The first to reply was Ursula.

"The Apocatastasis signifies the eventual return of all the fallen angels to their original home in the House of God," she said. "It is our evolutionary fate, and the meaning behind our cyclical life incarnations here on earth.

"The Apocatastasis is the reason why we suffer and die. It is the reason why we learn. The Tree of Life grows towards it, and the wheels of the universe turn solely to arrive there. We are all on a great pilgrimage back to the paradise we left long ago, regardless of whether we know it or not. The Apocatastasis marks our triumphant return."

Alulim leaned forward in his chair.

"The Apocatastasis is Lucifer's bane," he said. "His power is measured solely by the number of souls he holds under his sway. Every soul that ascends into the higher realms weakens Lucifer tremendously and makes it easier for other souls to escape him as well."

Isaac looked up at the towering panels of stained glass, lit as they were by the electrical storm outside. They were in fact a visual representation of what the elders had just described; a complex and brilliantly composed work of art dedicated to what these people claimed to be the meaning of humanity's existence here on earth.

In these panels could be seen many tree-shaped timelines, showing humankind in its various levels of physical and spiritual evolution. Isaac looked at the tunics that the knights wore, understanding now why each was adorned with the image of a tree. They were depictions of the Tree of Life, growing from what appeared to be a single seed. In the hall's central panel, to the right and left of this seed, could be seen images of a King and Queen.

"The Two," said Isaac, at last understanding. "The reptilian King and Queen are the Two."

"Indeed, they are," said Alulim. "And it is our purpose to help them in any way we can."

"But why should they require our help?" asked Isaac. "If they built the Cube and the Labyrinth, they should know exactly what to do."

"There are two reasons," said Ursula. "The first being that the moment any soul is incarnated into the world of matter, all memory of life in the spirit world is lost. Just as we cannot remember our past lives, neither can the Two remember theirs. For this reason, the King and Queen left clues for themselves to follow, and with the help of the divine world, they created institutions such as ours to aid them in their task."

Isaac considered what the elder was telling him. Earlier that day, Brother Bernardo had explained to him that when a soul incarnated, it arrived on the earth anesthetized, the majority of its knowledge being made inaccessible to it. This occurred so that the purification of its lower aspects could take place. The retention of past-life knowledge would make this process impossible.

"And the second reason?" he asked.

Ursula folded her hands and focused her gaze on Isaac.

"After some time, Ahreimanius became aware of the King and Queen's intentions to disseminate the true gnosis to humanity, and he devised a plan to thwart them. He founded a sinister society whose mission it was to not only destroy the Cube, but to infiltrate the Vatican and corrupt the truth behind the meaning of mankind's existence."

Alulim leaned forward in his chair.

"This would be done so that humanity might be in spiritual darkness as we entered into the Dark Rift," he said. "In this way we would be made powerless to escape the trap that he had laid for us there."

"The Two require our help to undermine this sinister plot," added Ursula. "And this is where you play a key role, dear Isaac."

Isaac frowned in confusion.

"But how could I possibly help in this matter?"

"Your father was the leader of the wicked society of which we speak," said Alulim. "It was he who manipulated you so that a hermaphrodite child might be born of your seed. According to the Ascender's Prophecy, your son would be a vile desecration of the Divine Androgyne, conceived through the incestuous union of the Rex Angelus Illuminati bloodline. Only in this way could the Portal of Ahreimanius be opened, and Lucifer's plan be put into action."

Isaac recoiled in shock.

"Incestuous union?" he exclaimed, rising to his feet. "Are you suggesting that my wife was also my sister? Are you mad, sir?!"

As gently as possible, Isaac was told of how Father Adrianus Vanderwerken (or the Nautonnier, as he was also known) had conspired with his father to not only bring about the incestuous birth of the hermaphrodite, but also to groom his younger brother Christian as the new Nautonnier.

Isaac learned that the demons he had released from the Portal of Ahreimanius were none other than the Fourteen Emissaries of Lucifer, and that they would soon captain an immense host of demons due to pass through the Portal at any moment. Their ranks would constitute an army of darkness that, unless stopped, would overrun the entire earth.

Upon hearing these things, Isaac collapsed back into his chair.

"I truly am the Betrayer," he said solemnly. "I am a blight to humanity."

"Not so!" exclaimed Alulim, rising to his feet. "Your actions were extremely necessary! You have drawn out the hidden evil so that it can now be seen in the light."

Ursula came to her feet as well.

"An invisible enemy can never be defeated, dear Isaac," she said gently. "Your purpose as the Betrayer has been fulfilled so that you might now be redeemed as the Consilio."

Isaac brought his hands to his face in frustration.

"I do not understand!" he cried. "How can I be cursed and blessed at once?"

Alulim placed both his hands on the table and spoke with commanding authority.

"Only through you can the *Two* enter into the Labyrinth and release the gnosis held within the Cube!"

"But where are they?" asked Isaac weakly.

Sir David rose to his feet as well.

"They are most likely on their way to the Labyrinth," he said, bending over the table. "It is time to act!"

Isaac looked over at the captain.

"But have any of you ever even met them?" he asked.

The knight shook his head gravely.

"We have not," he said, sitting down. "We know only their names and titles. They are Gabriel, Hero of God, and Natalia, Day of our Saviour's Rebirth."

Isaac locked eyes with the knight.

"Gabriel and Natasha," he said. "I know these names."

He looked back to Alulim.

"Father Franco wrote of them in his diary. They are orphans, children born of unwanted teenage pregnancies."

Alulim nodded knowingly and sat down again. Ursula followed suit.

"*The Two* symbolize a union between the bloodline of Jesus, and the common bloodlines of humanity," she said. "They are not pure Rex Angelus, and for this reason they were given up for adoption."

"The Rex Angelus line does not intermingle with other bloodlines," added Alulim. "They were given up in accordance with our laws."

"But did their families not know of the Ascender's Prophecy?" asked Isaac. "Why would they have given up children who could have potentially been *The Two*?"

"Because the prophecy could not have been fulfilled if they had not done so," said Alulim.

"All this is of no concern!" exclaimed Sir David. "The Portal of Ahreimanius widens with every passing moment! If not stopped, Ahreimanius will use it to draw every human soul into the lower spheres, just as he did with the souls of the reptilians at the time of the last crossing! He endeavors to prevent the Apocatastasis from ever occurring!"

Isaac grew silent as the magnitude of the danger set in. Over the period of the past few minutes the ground beneath their feet had begun to rumble. Outside the undead had begun to respond with horrific, strangled cries. Everyone sat quietly, listening in fear to the unearthly tumult. Alulim was the first to speak, and he did so unfalteringly.

"Know that the dead will not cease their unholy litany until our planet has entered into the Dark Rift," he said. "Nor will the ground stop its quaking until the final tribulation has come to pass. We are arrived at the apocalypse, my brethren. Be stout, and be strong in faith, for God and all his angels are with each and every one of us."

No sooner had Alulim said these words than a ghastly scream was heard, followed by a resounding bark from Shackleton, who had been lying under the table. In an instant every member of the council leapt to their feet. The scream had come from within the monastery itself. A fraction of a second later Brother Bernardo burst into the hall, a bloodied sword in his hand and a frenzied panic in his eyes.

On the floor behind him was the decapitated corpse of the undead child he had just found squatting in the shadows outside the council door. A choking gust of air rushed into the hall, replacing the pleasant scent of incense with the stench of rotting flesh.

"They have breached the walls!" he cried, jerking his head around as yet another horrific scream sounded behind him. "They are everywhere! Hundreds of them!"

At that moment many things happened at once. With a deep and resounding boom, an explosion sounded from within the earth itself, and the ground beneath their feet began to shift so violently that all but the dexterous knights were thrown to the floor. The entire hall was rocking upon itself now, and the mortar between the massive stone blocks was cracking and crumbling before their eyes.

In that instant, each of the towering stained-glass windows exploded into the hall without warning, and hordes of living dead poured in through them like maggots from a bursting corpse. Those in front were being cut to pieces by the heavy shards of falling glass, but even still they continued to advance.

"To the shelter!" cried Alulim. "Brother Bernardo! Instruct all those within to retreat to the shelter!"

The fat monk turned and disappeared through the doors, his sword flashing. The shrieks arising from the undead were deafening, and they sent paralyzing waves of fear through the elders. The latter had gathered together in a tight group now, sheltering behind a line of battling knights.

Like butchers in a slaughterhouse, the swordsmen felled the slow-moving hordes as they poured into the rotunda. With their heads dislodged, the bloodless corpses fell lifelessly to the ground, and it was not long before their gruesome cadavers formed a great mound in front of the knights. It served to slow the advance of the undead that poured in, but the grisly terrain made it even more difficult to fight those that did.

"Go!" ordered Sir David, pointing to four of his men. "Lead the elders to the shelter and secure the entrance!"

He singled out another three knights.

"Keep this horde back until you are called! The rest of you follow me!"

Isaac felt himself being forcibly directed towards the doors and saw four of the knights follow Sir David into the sanctuary, their swords raised and their crimson surcoats flowing. Looking to his left, he saw that Alulim was next to him now. The old man stood tall for his age and not a trace of fear could be seen in his eyes.

"Quickly now!" he said to the other elders. "We must reach the shelter at once!"

CHAPTER 2

Gibraltar.

The underground cavern was holding together remarkably well, given the intensity of the tremors they were experiencing. In its bay, the X-class midget submarine lay safe and undamaged, the seawater rippling around its dark hull.

Gabriel was inspecting the cavernous ceiling for cracks. Unlike the caves they had traversed in St. Michael's Pass, this one was free of stalactites and seemed very solid. Any areas that might have been questionable had long ago been reinforced with concrete.

He thought of Natasha and the others, and hoped they would be faring equally well in the upper galleries. They had taken the service elevator and gone in search of Scotty's Roberts' brother, Major Richard Roberts, in the hopes that he might be able to supply them with the diesel they needed.

Gabriel walked over to where Peralta was sitting. The disheveled engineer was engaged in a flurry of typing, writing computer code with the relish of a concert pianist. He looked up for a second as Gabriel approached.

"The sheer quantity of layers that this artifact is comprised of boggles the mind," he said, shaking his messy white head in amazement. "I've already extracted over ten million of them, and I haven't even penetrated a centimeter into the thing."

The BIRIS had not stopped its scanning since it had begun over five hours earlier, and the data it was amassing was of such an enormous scale that Peralta had been forced to hack into several external data banks to store it. At the sound of an electronic bell, the messy scientist stopped his typing and turned to face one of the dozens of monitors that were positioned around him.

"The results of the tomography are just coming up now."

He squinted at the data.

"Of course," he said in a captivated whisper. "This explains everything. The strange density of the artifact. Its ability to interact with your brain. And its ability to have maintained such an immense quantity of data in such a pristine state for so long..."

He looked around as though searching for something. There was a kind of madness in his eyes.

"It's been regenerating itself the whole time..."

"What do you mean?" asked Gabriel, leaning closer.

Peralta turned to face him with unrestrained urgency. He spoke in a low rasp.

"This artifact is no conventional piece of hardware, Dr. Parker. It's an advanced artificial intelligence. It's made up of densely packed synthetic cells... Living circuits of synthetic DNA. Instead of electricity it uses the equivalent of neurotransmitters to move data around. This is incredible. It's perfect biomimicry."

"Are you saying that the Cube's a synthetic brain?"

"Absolutely," said Peralta. "A super brain. By the looks of how many millions of instructions it's processing every second, it's close to eight billion times more powerful than a human brain."

Peralta paused.

"Wait a minute," he muttered. "What the hell..."

He tapped away at a keyboard, bending closer to one of the monitors as his brow tightened.

"I've never seen anything like this before..."

He scratched his head excitedly and adjusted his glasses.

"It's utterly inconceivable..."

Gabriel turned to face him only to have the lapels of his jacket taken. Peralta pulled him to within an inch of his face, a tiny crumb of hamburger bun still clinging to his white mustache from lunch.

"This artifact exists in many times *at the same time!*" he whispered frantically. "It's not only conscious, it's *inter-dimensional!*"

He released Gabriel and seated himself in his chair, calming down at once.

Gabriel approached him cautiously.

"If it's alive," he asked, "what does it feed on?"

Peralta seemed lost in thought.

"It feeds on the same thing that gives it its inter-dimensional properties..." he said to himself, and then looking up at Gabriel he added:

"It feeds on gravity."

Gabriel frowned as he struggled to remember what he had read in a science magazine not so long ago.

"Membrane theory..." he said. "There are four different forms of free energy that we know of. Two are nuclear; strong and weak. Then there is magnetism, and the weakest force of all is gravity. Membrane Theory postulates that gravity is weaker than the other three because it's being spread out over an almost infinite number of adjacent dimensions..."

Gabriel scratched his head before continuing.

"What you're suggesting is that the Cube resides in numerous dimensions simultaneously, and that it's somehow using the force of gravity to fuel itself."

"That is *exactly* what I am suggesting, Dr. Parker!" exclaimed Peralta. "And the really inconceivable thing is that all those infinite dimensions are being processed from the same location inside the Cube; a kind of ethereal mind..."

"What do you mean?" asked Gabriel, confused. "Who's mind?"

Peralta stopped to think.

"Your mind," he said. "My mind. Everyone's mind."

"But how's that possible?"

"Because all consciousness is *One*," whispered Peralta reverently. "And what's more, if this artifact has the power of close to eight billion brains, it's only because it's linked to every brain on the planet. It's like a huge Boink! It's directly hooked up to the collective consciousness!"

Gabriel was silent for a moment before he spoke.

"The gypsy woman in Toledo said that the Cube would communicate to the world through the collective consciousness."

Peralta's eyes opened wide with urgency.

"That's why it's imperative we get to that labyrinth," he exclaimed, "and activate the transponder in this thing! This artifact employs a technology that operates on two metaphysical platforms. The collective consciousness, and the universal field of intelligence."

"What's that?" asked Gabriel.

"I'll tell you in a second," said Peralta, "but first consider this: What if the Cube has been evolving with humanity? What if that was the reason why it's using an ancient Sumerian sexagesimal system to run its internal functions? Why else would it be running website architectures?"

"Hang on a second," said Gabriel, holding up a hand. "Did you just say *website?*"

Peralta nodded rapidly and then removed his glasses to rub his eyes.

"You're not going to believe this," he said, "but ciphered into the outer layers of the Cube is a code that's a dead ringer for XHTML. I couldn't begin to tell you what it's about, but it's definitely a website."

Gabriel was speechless. The idea sounded absurd. Peralta was nodding in silent agreement.

"The only explanation is that the Cube has been evolving with humanity," he said. "That would explain why it's chosen to apply itself through the use of a conventional, twenty-first century website. It must have learned this from us; from humanity. Don't forget. For all intents and purposes this artifact is *conscious.* "

"Tell me about that universal field of intelligence you mentioned," said Gabriel, shaking his head in an attempt to clear it.

Peralta clutched the table as yet another tremor shook the ground.

"Do you know what happens when a man is starving to death?"

"He gets grumpy?" offered Gabriel.

"He also has a very hard time thinking. Ask him what five times five is and he won't be able to tell you. His brain stops working properly."

"And?"

Peralta rose to his feet and moved to one of the neighbouring monitors. He bent over and tapped something into a keyboard before continuing.

"Regardless of how weak he is, that starving man will still know how to tie his shoelaces, even if he doesn't have the strength to actually do it. In short, he will have full unhindered access to all his memories and all his knowledge, right up to the point of brain failure and death."

"So what?"

"So what?" repeated Peralta, frustrated. "Can't you see? If his brain is out of fuel, how can it possibly be accessing and processing all that information? He's dying of starvation, remember? There's no glucose to power the brain's functions anymore, yet somehow, he still manages to know everything. The answer is that our minds are not located in our brains, but rather somewhere else. That's why a guy who's dying from hunger can still access all of his knowledge and memories."

"So our minds reside in the universal field of intelligence."

"Yes," said Peralta, pacing. "It's like cloud computing. Our brains are tuned into it. Synaptic activity is nothing more than a three-dimensional projection of what's happening in that field. And this is the really cool part. Because of the fixed nature of the space-time block, the UFI contains thoughts that haven't even been thought of yet. Ideas from the future. Human growth and learning is all based on our evolving ability to access the UFI. The better we do it, the wiser and more intelligent we become."

"And the Cube's plugged into the UFI," said Gabriel.

Peralta nodded.

"That's why it's been able to evolve with us."

"Let me ask you a question," said Gabriel. "If a certain individual was to uncover knowledge from this field of intelligence, would that knowledge then be propagated to the rest of the world through the collective consciousness?"

Peralta sat down next to Gabriel and let out a long breath.

"Absolutely," he rasped, running both of his hands through his disastrous hair. "The two platforms work together seamlessly. That's why things tend to get invented in different parts of the world at the same time. We're all connected."

Peralta leaned forward.

"Something else occurs that's very fascinating. The greater the number people who acquire a specific piece of knowledge from the field, the easier it gets for others to adopt that same knowledge."

"I've heard of this phenomenon," said Gabriel. "You can see it happening everywhere. Take using electronics for example. The interfaces haven't changed all that much since gadgets started to appear, but whereas only the brainiest types could use them at first, now all kinds of people are using them, even seniors who are supposed to have trouble learning new things."

"That's because a tipping point was reached," said Peralta. "It happens with everything that's learned on a societal level. The mechanism became evident when our species first started using tools, and it's followed us right through to using electronic gadgetry. There comes a point when enough people have adopted something, that it becomes almost second nature for everyone to adopt it."

Gabriel sat up as the realization finally gelled.

"That's what's supposed to happen with the Cube," he said. "Natasha and I are supposed to somehow release the knowledge that's stored in it. That knowledge will then get injected into the collective consciousness. When enough people have worked to assimilate it, larger segments of the population will follow, until a tipping point is reached. After that, everyone will adopt the new knowledge and the world will jump to the next level of societal evolution."

The sound of an opening airlock filled the cavern, and Gabriel and Peralta turned in time to see their friends emerge from the service elevator. First out was Natasha, followed by a hand-cuffed officer with a black hood covering his head. Behind them were Scotty Roberts and the giant Bahadur. Only Miller was missing, having opted to remain in the tunnels above.

"I hope you don't mind a military presence in your laboratory, Peralta my mate," said Scotty, snatching the hood off their captive.

Peralta and Gabriel looked on in surprise. Their prisoner was none other than Major Richard Roberts. The latter was in the process of taking inventory of his new surroundings, an expression of shocked amazement transforming his features. The ground rumbled as if to punctuate his displeasure.

"Scotty," he said calmly to his brother. "I've agreed to your silly games, now get these blasted handcuffs off."

CHAPTER 3

Los Picos de Europa, Northern Spain.

Christian's private jet was making its way eastward over the Cantabrian Mountains when the sun broke the horizon. Its hue was that of blood-soaked crimson, and in the dawning light, the night's strange electrical storms could still be seen flashing through the thick clouds below the plane. High above, like an extended aurora borealis, the entire outer atmosphere was ablaze with ruby and emerald light. A massive, magnetospheric storm was engulfing the planet and it was a sight like no other.

With the galactic plane drawing ever nearer, the intensity of the Dark Rift's gravitational field was playing havoc with the plasma being emitted by the sun. Its solar wind had intensified a hundred-fold, and as such was bombarding the earth's magnetic field with an unprecedented concentration of charged particles.

The result was the appearance of a sky on fire, and this, coupled with the altered hue of the sun itself, made it very clear that there were immense changes taking place, not only on the earth, but in the entire solar system.

Christian wiped his mouth nervously, his face damp with cold sweat. Shortly after takeoff he had been visited by the Zurvanites again. Through the sharp ears of an undead child, the Four had overheard Alulim speaking at the Council of the Apocatastasis and had learned of Isaac's important role in their enemy's plan to activate the Cube.

The destruction of the artifact would no longer be necessary if Isaac Rodchenko were to be eliminated. Without him, the Cube would be unable to disseminate its gnosis and humanity would fall.

To drive the point home, Ahreimanius had shown himself to Christian, manifesting briefly in the horrific form of the hermaphrodite, only to vanish a moment later. His short-lived appearance had been enough to fill Christian with a frenzied urgency to kill his brother. It pressed in on him, causing him to experience uncontrollable jerks and spasms throughout his body.

"Kill him! Kill him! Kill him!"

Christian slapped his face repeatedly, struggling to regain control. Everything was going according to plan. There was no need to panic. The ancient city of Rome would soon be wiped from the face of the earth, and in less than a minute, all of its three-and-a-half million inhabitants would be incinerated instantly. He forced himself to breathe.

"Forty-five seconds to detonation," said the seductive voice of his computer, as if to confirm his thoughts.

Christian produced a pair of protective goggles. As instructed, the pilot was veering the plane northward so as to facilitate a better viewing of the spectacle that would soon be taking place in the eastern sky.

The Vatican was about to offer herself up so that a new "holy institution" could be built from her ashes; an institution that would surpass the church's most monumental achievements and eventually govern the hearts and souls of every man, woman, and child on the planet.

Christian's work was nearing completion. All that remained was that he locate his brother and kill him.

A cold smile of self-satisfaction appeared on Christian's face. The Zurvanites had made it very clear to him that Isaac would be travelling to the Portal of Ahreimanius, and bearing this in mind, Christian had made careful preparations to reach the small island before his brother did. In the back of the plane sat four special forces officers, each being awaited by select units of coalition troops on standby in Santander.

Because of the tempestuous weather, helicopter access to the mountain lake would be impossible. The distance of forty kilometres would need to be covered on all-terrain vehicles, following a footpath belonging to the Camino de Santiago. This trail would take them along an ancient Celtic route, directly to where the Portal lay. It was here where Christian would find his brother and slay him.

"Ten, nine, eight…"

Christian put on his goggles as the AI began its countdown. Even at this distance the light emitted from the blast would damage human retinas through atmospheric focusing.

"Three, two, one, detonation."

Christian's jaw fell open as the blast lit up the horizon, making the rising sun seem pale in comparison. The explosion was over a moment later and Christian was amazed that something so catastrophic could come to pass in such a short period of time.

He removed his goggles, looking down at his computer to study the live feeds coming from cameras along the Italian coast. The mushroom cloud over Rome was gargantuan and still rising, measuring over eighty kilometres in height and fifty in width.

"Taller than Mount Everest," he muttered to himself. "And hotter than the surface of the sun…"

The plane banked sharply to resume its westerly heading, and Christian was suddenly gripped by a crippling pain. It shot through his head and into his eyes. Squinting up from his computer he saw that the four Zurvanites were standing an arm's length away, their grainy forms jerking and twisting in and out of being.

He gripped his head and writhed in agony. Their frenetic chanting was driving the sanity from his mind.

"Kill him! Kill him! Kill him! Kill him!"

CHAPTER 4

Gibraltar.

Major Roberts continued to stare at the monitor even after it had gone black, his right eye twitching and blinking repeatedly. He was still struggling to assimilate everything he had learned.

Earlier on, Cassano had created a video on Peralta's orders, one that explained every aspect of the artifact, and even included a brief interview with Gabriel and Natasha. It was to be sent out to all those friends of Peralta whose assistance was desperately needed, and had proved to be the final piece of information needed to leave the major utterly convinced.

He looked up as his brother struck a match.

"Well?" asked Scotty from his perch on a nearby desk. "See what I mean, bro?"

He exhaled a cloud of smoke.

"It's not just Gib that's in a bind," he added. "It's the whole bleeding world."

Major Roberts was still speechless. He shifted his gaze to Peralta and locked eyes with the rumpled scientist. Yet again the ground shook violently beneath them.

"You can see how urgently we need to get Gabriel and Natasha to the Labyrinth, Major."

Roberts nodded slowly, his expression still blank with shock. He looked over at the old submarine in its berth, as if to confirm that this was all really happening.

"Perpetual darkness," he said dazedly. "That and the complete annihilation of the entire human race..."

Natasha approached and handed him the Cube. He looked up at her and accepted it with hesitation, noting its odd density the moment he had taken hold of it. He peered into its glowing, iridescent depths.

"Incredible…" he mumbled.

In that instant Roberts made up his mind. He looked over at his brother and gave him a single nod. Scotty hopped down from his perch with a grin and gave his brother a heavy pat on the back.

"I knew we could count on you, bro," he said, and then looking to Peralta added:

"You've got your diesel, Captain, but on one condition."

Everyone including Roberts looked at Scotty, curious as to what the stipulation might be. Scotty spit out a shred of tobacco.

"The condition is we pick up Anita and bring her back first," he said. "She's holed up in a cellar, and she's as pregnant as a bloody rabbit."

All looked at the major. His face was chiseled with concern. He gazed back at his brother. There was a deep gratitude in his eyes.

"Thanks, Scotty," he said. "But I'm afraid it's impossible. There's too much radiation out there. Even a few minutes of exposure would be lethal."

"Where is she?" asked Peralta, rising to his feet with sudden concern. "Why didn't you say anything about this?"

The major shook his head, struggling with his emotions.

"What was the point?"

Everyone braced themselves as another tremor shook the cave.

"He's right about the radiation," said Gabriel. "But even still, there's got to be a way to get her out of there."

Peralta took off his glasses, wiped them, and then began to pace.

"The radiation in the first minutes of a detonation will exceed all the accumulated radiation a person could be exposed to in the first week. The first week of exposure exceeds all the radiation that a person could ever be exposed to in a lifetime at the site…"

He looked over at Roberts.

"How pregnant is she?"

The major ran a hand through his short-cropped hair.

"She's due in ten days," he said, frowning. "Maybe less."

"Well then we've got time," said Peralta. "We'll collect her on the way back. By that time the radiation will have dissipated sufficiently."

Everyone looked at the scrappy engineer.

"Look," he said. "We've got to be realistic here. If we fail, we're all dead anyway. If we succeed, we'll have plenty of time to make it back."

Gabriel put a hand on the major's shoulder.

"She could come out just as we arrived and get into the sub before the radiation could harm her."

"It'll be an easy pickup, man!" added Scotty reassuringly. "There's a bloody pier right in front of your place for Christ's sake. Just get her to put on lots of layers. She can strip them off before she gets into the sub."

Roberts' face was alight with hope.

"My God," he said. "Could this really be possible?"

Natasha put her arms around Gabriel.

"It's more than possible," she said. "It's probable. Everything's going to be fine, you'll see."

The major rose to his feet and handed Natasha the Cube.

"You're absolutely right," he said, looking over at his brother. "There's plenty of time, and you guys are going to get the job done!"

He produced his radio.

"Captain Brown. Is the fuel ready?"

"Affirmative, Major," came the response. "It's on the skids and ready to move."

Roberts looked at the others, an excited smile on his face.

"Get it here right away, Captain. There's not a moment to lose. My brother will give you the details."

CHAPTER 5

Los Picos de Europa, Northern Spain.

Isaac squinted up at the bleeding sun, watching it for a moment before it disappeared back into the cauldronous clouds. He was high in the mountains, looking down over the trembling lands. The planet seemed to him like a feverish mother, its curving surface appearing to expand and contract ever so slightly, as though it were struggling to breathe.

"We will rest in the upper gallery!" bellowed Sir David from a raised outcropping of rock.

He was not five meters away, but the wind made his voice barely audible. Isaac turned to look where he was pointing and spotted some fortified walls in amongst the rocky terrain.

He could feel his legs almost giving out with relief. For over three hours now they had climbed, stealthily leaving the monastery behind, along with the teaming hordes of undead who had besieged it. Isaac found comfort in knowing that Alulim and the others were safe inside their shelter.

"You have done well, Consilio," said an approaching knight.

He put a hand on Isaac's shoulder.

"This is a favourite outpost for us. It is equipped with many comforts and will take our minds off our suffering, even if for just a little while."

Isaac tried his best to smile.

"Have you lost many loved ones to the plague?"

The young knight frowned.

"I lost a brother, my lord," he said, "but I am fine. I take courage from our captain. Seeing how he endures brings strength to us all."

Isaac laid a hand on the young knight's arm as they resumed their trek upward.

"Has Sir David lost someone too?"

The youth's eyes were still on his captain. He had stopped atop a steep crag and was pulling up his men as they approached.

"He was our village doctor before all this happened," said the knight, his eyes alight with admiration. "He lost a wife and two daughters to the horde. She was pregnant with a third."

Isaac wanted to say something to show his sympathy, but just then they arrived at the crag. He gave Sir David a nod of thanks and reached up to take hold of his arm.

* * * * * *

The cave proved to be as warm and accommodating as the young knight had promised, resembling more of a clubhouse than a military outpost. It was not long before a fire had been lit in a large stone hearth there, and the strange cataclysmic day was shut out and temporarily forgotten. Only the constant rumbling of the earth gave any reminder of its continued presence.

"Thank you," said Isaac, accepting the piping hot bowl of stew that Brother Bernardo was handing him.

The heavy monk invited him to sit on a sofa by the fire and then fell into a neighbouring armchair. Shackleton, having already eaten, was asleep at their feet.

"We must be well into the rift by now," said Isaac, swallowing a mouthful of food.

"We are merely approaching it," said Sir David.

He was squatting beside the fire.

"Things will get much, much worse."

"Nevertheless, we have nothing to fear," said the monk. "The angels of God are here with us. They will help us succeed in finding and assisting the Two."

"Ours is an ancient plan," added Sir David. "One that the spirit of the Christ himself created."

"In that he came to redeem us," said Isaac, but his words struck an odd chord.

It was as though the monk and the knight knew something he did not.

"Contrary to what the Vatican would have you believe," said Brother Bernardo, "Jesus Christ did not come to redeem, but rather to reveal. He taught an ancient gnosis, the same gnosis that resides in the Cube. It is based on the correlation between personal freedom and personal responsibility."

"I don't understand," said Isaac.

"It means that we are the only ones who can redeem ourselves," said Sir David. "Nobody else can do it for us, no matter how wealthy or powerful their organization happens to be."

The monk took up an iron and poked the fire.

"The Vatican has one central tenant," he said. "It states that Jesus Christ was murdered in order to appease a vengeful, yet somehow compassionate god. They claim that this god willingly allowed the death sacrifice of his only son so that the price for humanity's sins might be paid."

Sir David frowned bitterly.

"This is a reprehensible lie," he said. "The true meaning behind the crucifixion of Jesus' body was to symbolize the crucifixion of the personal ego, with its vanity, neurosis, and selfish will. His life, death, and the resurrection of his spirit, demonstrated the stages of development that each of us must go through in order to regain the kingdom of heaven."

Brother Bernardo nodded knowingly.

"The Vatican's literalist version of the crucifixion metaphor not only misses this point entirely, it also serves to induce a heavy guilt in Christians, along with a feeling of morbid indebtedness to Jesus, and a deep existential fear of God."

Sir David leaned forward in his chair.

"And in order to repay this debt, and assuage the guilt and fear it induces, we are urged to give our wealth and obedience to the Church."

Isaac was taken aback by the knight's words.

"But it was only through Christ's death and resurrection that our salvation was made possible," he said weakly. "Jesus paid the price so that our transgressions might be forgiven..."

"Every one of our sins was forgiven long before Jesus ever incarnated, dear Isaac," said the monk. "Long before they were even committed. Forget your biblical Yahweh for a moment and try to think of God as the ineffable entity he truly is. There is nothing we could possibly do that could offend him, for behind our worst actions lie causes that he fully understands. God wants to help us, not condemn us. He wants us to come home."

Isaac remained silent.

"In the time of Jesus," said Sir David, "the entire Roman Empire was mostly at peace, but this was not the case in Jerusalem. It was a hot bed of insurrection. Early Christianity, with its message of personal empowerment, posed a direct threat to Roman rule. They needed to control this new religion, and the manner in which to do this was given to them by a Pharisee named Saul of Tarsus."

"But Saul of Tarsus was St. Paul," said Isaac. "He was the father of the church. St. Paul could never have been a Pharisee."

"Saul of Tarsus was not only a Pharisee," added Sir David, "he was a cousin of King Herod himself, and as such, a member of the ruling family of Jerusalem. As a young man he had been a member of the temple guard, authorized by the high priests to persecute Christians. He occupied this position even when Jesus was arrested and killed."

Isaac looked at Sir David, unable to respond. St. Paul had freely admitted to persecuting Christians before he had been converted to Christianity.

"Through St. Paul, the Romans would, over time, remove the self-empowering aspects of Jesus' original teachings, and replace them with a dogma that was specially designed to repress and control," continued the knight. "They would equate Jesus with God, making any realistic emulation of him impossible. They would revoke personal responsibility and replace it with blind faith in the church's doctrine. They would take the reincarnation taught by Jesus and replace it with eternal hellfire. Any salvation to be had would come solely through the sanctity of the church, and a sinner's humble adherence to its laws."

"You must forgive us if we appear passionate about this subject," said Brother Bernardo, "but you must try to understand how difficult it has been for our society over the centuries, knowing what we have known about the Vatican, but being sworn to secrecy."

Isaac could not believe what he was hearing.

"But what of all the wonderful things that have been done by the Church?" he asked. "What of all the love that has been spread, and the countless people who have been helped? Surely the Vatican cannot be so evil."

"The blessed things you describe have come from the hearts of individual Christians throughout history," said the monk, "and the incorruptible truth of what Jesus Christ stood for. These blessings did not come from the captains of the Vatican. You must not confuse the government of a nation with its people. A government can be corrupt and vile, while its people remain good and true. It is the Vatican that is evil, not the people who do good work in its name."

Isaac stared into the flames of the fire, reflecting on the early church and its actions to secure power. He knew that in 325 CE the pagan Roman Emperor Constantine had summoned the First Council of Nicaea, where he had made official the doctrine of his new Roman Catholic Church.

With a mighty government to back him, he had proclaimed that any who did not follow the church's new creed would be proclaimed a heretic, and an enemy of Rome. From that council, Constantine had established the papal seat of supreme governance, creating an institution that claimed to be the sole representative of God on this earth. To go against this church was to go against God himself. The power that resulted from the formation of this organization was unimaginable.

Isaac also recalled Theophilus of Alexandria, and the destruction of knowledge and culture that he had reaped throughout the fourth century. He thought of the dark ages that had followed, where the rights of the individual to read and write had been revoked, and given only to those in the clergy, who would in turn perpetuate the repressive dogma, instilling even more fear, more guilt, and more unworthiness into the hearts of men.

He thought of the Crusades, and the slaughter of Muslims, Jews, and Orthodox Christians in the Holy Land, as well as the systematic eradication of the peace-loving Cathars in Europe.

Right into the modern day he saw the damage and destruction that this institution called the church was responsible for. Was this a church of Jesus Christ? How could it possibly be? Jesus Christ stood for freedom and love.

Since its inception, the Catholic Church had perpetuated repression, intolerance, and hatred through its policies, along with guilt, fear, superstition, and unbridled violence in its countless wars. The Vatican was a clear and indisputable distortion of what Jesus Christ had stood for; a complete inversion. It always had been. It was a blasphemous deception, a great and terrible lie.

"If Jesus Christ was not God," asked Isaac suddenly, "then who was he?"

The ground shuddered violently beneath them.

"Just as we are all incarnations of the angels who fell," said Brother Bernardo, "Jesus was an incarnation of the angel of the Christ; the most exalted spirit in all of God's world.

"For thousands of years the Kristos was spoken of in myth. He is the personification of God in the body of a man. He was Horus to the Egyptians, Dionysus to the Greeks, Mithras to the pagans, and known by a hundred different names across the globe. He was, and is, the highest of all the angels and archangels, but he is not God. He is the Christ, and when he incarnated, he was simply Jesus. A man like any other; and not…"

"But how could he be like any other man if his spirit was that of the highest angel?" asked Isaac. "He would have been perfect."

"Yes," said Brother Bernardo, "but he did not know it. You forget the universal law. When incarnated into matter, a being's knowledge of the spirit world is lost, and this applied to the incarnation of the Kristos as well.

"It was for this reason that Jesus struggled like all the rest of us. Much more so, in fact, because Ahreimanius knew who he was, and was bent on defeating him. He desired nothing more than to make Jesus renounce God and join the forces of darkness."

Sir David spoke out.

"Unlike the many sages who have been teachers of the ancient gnosis throughout history, Jesus was the first to successfully apply the teachings in his own life, and gain liberation from the wheel of death and rebirth. Jesus made it to the higher spheres, but the important thing to remember is that he did this as a man, and not as some omnipotent godman, as the Vatican would have you believe. If he could do it, then everyone can do it. It is humanly possible."

Brother Bernardo poked the fire again.

"Jesus introduced a new modality into the collective mind of humanity," he said. "A Christ Consciousness, if you will. This modality or mindset has been spoken of since the time of the ancients. It embraces the fact that God can always be found directly within us, immediately accessible to anyone who cares to make the effort to establish contact.

"Without this contact, one cannot follow the path of gnosis and advance to the higher spheres. It is a paradox. One has to do it by oneself, but one cannot do it without the help of the Divine."

Sir David rose to his feet.

"The Kristos merges with our true self and the two become one," he said. "It is through this merger that liberation from death can be achieved, and the higher realms be entered into. Before Jesus came, this was not possible for us. For this reason, we owe him much gratitude, but it is nothing to feel guilty about. It is only something to be delighted about."

And then placing a hand on the monk's shoulder he said:

"Come, Brother. The Consilio must sleep now."

Brother Bernardo rose to his feet with a groan.

"Rest well, dear Isaac," he said, turning to leave. "You will need all your strength in the coming hours."

CHAPTER 6

Under the Mediterranean Sea.

The midget submarine slipped silently into the dark waters of its secret berth, turning to pass through a short tunnel before entering into the radioactive waters on Gibraltar's eastern face. Echoing through its hull could be heard a strange cacophony of sounds rising from the sea floor. The reverberations lent a surreal quality to the interior of the sub, and reminded its occupants of the tremendous geological stresses that the earth's crust was currently experiencing.

After having removed its weapons systems and installed a new, more efficient engine, Peralta had managed to significantly increase the sub's usable space, improving both its smuggling capacity and its performance. As it was, its contingent of six were finding the quarters ample enough, with only the giant Bahadur having a difficult time moving around.

"Radiation levels are well within limits," said Gabriel, reading a newly added gauge among the high-tech gadgets retrofitted by Peralta. "I've got to say, that was a great idea you had to line the hull with lead."

"A lucky decision," rasped Peralta over his shoulder.

He was busily tapping away at one of several keyboards.

"When I removed the old engines and all the weapons systems, I had to replace the ballast with something that was heavy and took up as little space as possible. Lead sheeting was the best solution. I hid it behind the paneling. I had no idea I'd ever be using it to shield us from beta and gamma radiation."

Gabriel looked around, shaking his head in amazement. Whereas the sub's exterior had been left entirely in its original state, its interior had undergone a complete transformation. Gone were the sweaty steel walls and riveted seams typical to subs of that era. In their place had been installed rich mahogany paneling and buttery leather upholstery, similar to that which could be found in a luxury yacht.

Although nowhere near as extensive as Peralta's laboratory in the underground port, the bridge of the X-Class sub was equipped with many high-resolution monitors, and technologies like those found in the most modern submarines. From his helm, Peralta not only had fly by wire navigation and state of the art communications, but also remote access to his mainframe computers on land, and the many others he had hacked into.

It was for this reason that he had insisted on leaving as soon as Major Roberts had arranged to have their fuel delivered. There was basically no computing that could be done on land that could not also be done at sea.

Gabriel felt a sudden wave of grief come over him and turned in time to see Natasha bring her hands to her face and burst into tears. She was seated before a monitor that showed the face of Bishop Marcus on a live feed from the submarine port. Cassano was standing behind him.

"I am so sorry, my dear child," the old bishop was saying, his face pale with sorrow. "It has only come to our attention at this very moment."

"What is it?" said Gabriel, moving to the monitor with Amir and Scotty bumping in behind.

Natasha stood up and threw her arms around Gabriel, burying her face in his chest.

"Everyone in Rome is dead!" she cried. "All my friends! All their families!"

Gabriel looked to the monitor in shock.

"What happened?"

"Rome has been decimated," came the bishop's frail voice. "There was a massive nuclear strike on Vatican City. There is nothing left. Close to three million people have been incinerated. Many more are wounded and dying in the outskirts."

* * * * * *

The sub's only cabin was located at the very rear of the ship, directly above the engines. Like the rest of the sub, it too had been completely refurbished, its cozy rosewood paneling and amply cushioned interior turning it into a sanctuary of sorts. It was here on a comfortable bed that Gabriel lay with Natasha, her body curled up against his as great sobs of grief escaped her.

Although she had lived in Florence, Rome had been where she had grown up, and the city was not only filled with all the special places of her youth, but also with her closest friends. The event had been devastating, and lying beside her, Gabriel was at a loss as to how to comfort her.

"Why Gabriel?" she sobbed. "Everything I had is gone. They took away Suora and Fra, and now all of my friends. All the people I called my family…"

Gabriel kissed the top of her head and held her close. He could find no explanation for the injustice of the catastrophe and was on the verge of expounding on the meaninglessness of life when a thought occurred to him.

He remembered something he had read in his father's journal; something that seemed to offer an explanation. He ran a hand through his hair.

"It's all about truth," he said, more to himself than to Natasha, but his words caught her interest, and she looked up at him.

"What do you mean?"

"Well," began Gabriel, and the words seemed to come to him as he spoke. "If you keep in mind the truth behind the suffering, it all makes sense."

"But what truth could make sense of millions of people being incinerated, or worse still, being left to die slowly in agony?"

Gabriel tried to be as gentle as possible.

"You know I'm not big on religion, Natasha, but what if the crazy things we've been reading about in the journal are actually true? According to the ancient wisdoms, suffering brings spiritual growth, which eventually leads people to the truth."

"And what's the truth?"

"The truth is that death doesn't exist," he said, surprised to hear himself saying the words. "The physical body dies, but people keep on existing. Come on, Natasha. You know this. You're a theologian."

"But why?" she sobbed. "Why the children?"

"There could be a million reasons. People have been suffering, dying, and being reincarnated for aeons now. It's the way we evolve."

Natasha sniffled through her tears. She understood what Gabriel was saying, but something in her resisted it, nonetheless. The mindset he was describing seemed so cold and so unfeeling, even though she was certain it was based in truth.

She could not be sad for the people who had died, for they, in truth, did not really die. As well, she could not be sad for those who were suffering, because in its ultimate sense, their suffering was a blessing; a way for them to evolve spiritually so that one day suffering and physical death would no longer be necessary.

The only thing she could possibly be sad for was herself, and this amounted to nothing but self-pity, a blight that she had resolved to rid herself of years ago.

"Look," said Gabriel slowly. "I'll be damned if I'm going to acquire all this knowledge about how the universe really works, and then not apply it. If the demons that possessed us were real, then angels and alternate dimensions must be real too. It's getting pretty obvious that an afterlife exists. We need to be able to stand on that truth like it's the solid ground it is, and to do that, we've got to believe in it."

Natasha smiled affectionately. Who was this Gabriel? Surely, he was an angel as well. In the most difficult times, she had never once seen fear in his eyes, only compassion, understanding, and an unwavering resolve to do the right thing. Now she had seen something new in him. A willingness to change his beliefs.

"Knowing the truth really does set you free, doesn't it?"

Gabriel found himself surprised by Natasha's words. He had heard the saying countless times before, but he had never understood its meaning until just now. When one knew the truth about life, death, and suffering, fear lost all its power. He was going to say something when Natasha reached up and put a finger over his lips.

"Make love to me, Gabriel. Make love to me right now."

* * * * * *

The X-class Midget submarine made its way northward along the coast of Portugal, its dark hull slipping silently through cold and lightless waters. In a tiny aft cabin of the boat, Gabriel and Natasha lay entwined in their lovemaking. And whereas most lovers would have been confined to the limited space of the small berth, they had left the world of earthly matter, and through Mithuna, entered into an astral plane that knew no boundaries.

To Gabriel and Natasha, it seemed that they were swimming beneath the surface of a clear and tropical ocean, with soft sunlight filtering down upon them. Here there was no pain or sorrow, only limitless beauty, and an indescribable sense of euphoria.

They could see a shimmering being of translucent light approaching through the waters, and they knew in a moment that it was the same being they had encountered during their first ascension into Mithuna.

"Greetings, my dear friends," it said in the most harmonious voice imaginable. "From the House of God, I bring you many divine blessings."

* * * * * *

Six hours had passed by the time Gabriel and Natasha emerged from the sub's cabin. With over five hundred nautical miles lying between their current location and the north coast of Spain, their journey would still take another eighteen hours to complete, leaving them only six hours to find the Labyrinth of Sarras before the galactic plane was entered into. Even still they were not worried. Their guide had not only revealed to them the exact location of the Labyrinth, but an unexpected route that would carry them there swiftly.

Gabriel and Natasha entered the bridge to find Scotty looking through the periscope. Peralta was busy tapping away at a keyboard, a tiny dragonfly robot perched on his shoulder.

"Hello, Captain Peralta," said Natasha. "When are you going to show us the Cube's website?"

Everyone on the bridge turned to find her and Gabriel standing by the hatch. Amir was about to say something, but Natasha spoke first.

"Don't worry about me," she said, seeing the compassion in their faces. "I'm fine now."

Peralta smiled and nodded, scrubbing at his face and hair in an attempt to revitalize himself.

"Well, now's as good a time as any to show you," he rasped, punching some instructions into the navigation system.

He looked back at Scotty.

"Bring down that periscope. It's time to dive."

All eyes turned to a monitor positioned at the front of the bridge, its large display lighting up to show a forward-facing view. Choppy seawater began to cover the screen as the vessel angled downward into a dive, its twin floodlights probing the murky depths.

"Autohelm is now engaged," announced Peralta, bringing the Cube's website up on a monitor next to him. "Why don't you guys pull up a chair?"

Gabriel and Natasha did as they were asked, with Amir and Scotty filing in behind. Only Bahadur was not present. He was stretched out on the deck at the back of the sub and sound asleep.

"What we've got here is a website with no content," said Peralta in his raspy voice. "Even still, you'll be able to see how it's set up, and what it's capable of doing."

On the lower corner of the screen were two cube icons rotating slowly. Peralta dragged his mouse over one of them and caused it to expand. Each of its six sides moved away from its centre, providing links to six separate areas within the site.

"One cube deals with the practical aspects of life. The other one deals with something spiritual. Let's look at the first one. It serves as a portal to a social networking site. Its purpose is to create governmental directives."

"Like mandates?" asked Gabriel.

Peralta nodded.

"Each of the six sides pertains to a specific category. Government, health and welfare, education, business and trade, environment, and foreign relations. Each of the categories contains local and international forums. It looks like the objective here is to democratically create petitions that can be presented to government officials."

"What is this thing?" asked Gabriel, confused.

"It would appear to be a new form of world governance," said Peralta. "It's a massive content management system that has the ability to process and organize billions of votes in real time, and on any given issue. It uses our existing governments to enact the directives."

"But our governments are a mess," said Natasha.

"Not really," said Peralta. "If you think about it, they coordinate vast arrays of super complex tasks. It's taken centuries for them to evolve. Our governments keep the world running like a well-oiled machine. Problems only exist because of the leaders we put at the controls of that machine. Having democratically generated mandates to tell them what to do would fix things pretty quickly, I would think..."

Gabriel had long been a critic of the current state of democracy in the world, and a fan of the direct democracy that was being implemented in Switzerland. He found the idea fascinating.

"What's stopping politicians from just ignoring the mandates?"

Peralta shrugged.

"I suppose if an official can't execute the directives he's been given by a community, he'll lose their votes. The bigger the communities get, the more he'll have to do what they tell him to do, or he'll be out of a job."

Gabriel looked around the sub. The strange noises consistently emanating from the ocean floor seemed to be intensifying. They were sending strong vibrations through the hull of the boat and felt similar to air turbulence in a plane.

Peralta noticed them as well. He swivelled in his chair to check the sub's navigation system. The minor earthquakes had been continuing unabated for the last twelve hours now, and he was concerned they might be affecting the delicate instrumentation. He spoke over his shoulder as he typed.

"I think this website's capable of ushering in a new age of democracy," he said. "The Cube's a powerful AI. It knows what it's doing. It would probably make all the mundane decisions that nobody wanted to vote on."

"And what about the spiritual cube?" asked Natasha.

Peralta nodded and moved the cursor, expanding the second cube into six different links: Buddhism, Taoism and Confucianism, Hinduism, Islamism, Christianity, and Judaism.

"I can't even guess at what this is about," he rasped.

"It's about the six divine actions…" whispered Natasha, looking at Gabriel as she made the connection. "A spiritual path made up of the wisdoms housed within each of the world's religions…"

"What wisdoms?" asked Amir. "What are you guys talking about?"

Gabriel looked at him for a moment without speaking. The global implications of such a social networking platform were beginning to dawn on him.

"Originally there was only one religion," he said. "If you could even call it a religion. It contained a body of knowledge that eventually became fragmented, with each fragment becoming its own religion.

"If the parts were reassembled again, the original knowledge would be revealed. It could potentially change the way humanity thinks and acts. It looks like this website is where the reunification is supposed to take place."

"Why is that gauge flashing?" came a deep and unexpected voice.

All turned to see Bahadur. He was hunched over and pointing to a blinking gauge on the instrument panel, his shoulders rubbing the ceiling.

"Is that normal?"

"Buoy grid warning!" exclaimed Peralta, jumping from his seat. "Shit! This does not look good! This does not look good at all!"

The scrappy engineer bolted to a different section of the instrument cluster, caressing one of the gauges and muttering words of encouragement as he turned some knobs.

"What is it?" asked Gabriel, coming to his side.

"There's been a massive tectonic shift in the mid-Atlantic ridge!" exclaimed the scrappy engineer, his eyes wide with horror.

"It's created an immense shockwave! It's coming directly towards us! We've got to dive as deep as we can! Everybody tie yourselves down! This might get very ugly!"

CHAPTER 7

Santander, Northern Spain.

The plane was rapidly losing altitude as it made its way into Santander. The massive geomagnetic storm was playing havoc with its instrumentation, and while the ride had been relatively smooth in the upper atmosphere, things had changed dramatically as they descended into the churning clouds. The fuselage was shuddering violently, and they had lost all their navigational aids.

"I *will* kill you, brother…" whispered Christian ardently, his face damp with sweat.

The combined influence of the Zurvanites and Ahreimanius was affecting him in ways he could never have imagined. His sanity was slipping away, just as his body was transforming.

Christian looked down at his hands to see them oscillating between ghostliness and solidity. He was becoming reptilian.

He made a concerted effort to regain control of himself and unbuckled his seatbelt, stepping out into the aisle as the plane lurched underfoot. With great difficulty he made his way to the plane's cockpit, bursting in to find both pilots in a state of emergency. A series of alarms were sounding, and the instrumentation was smoking dangerously. Neither of them had even noticed his appearance.

"We've lost control of the rear aileron!" exclaimed the pilot at the yoke. "I'm sending more power to the left engine!"

Christian spotted an unconscious stewardess on the floor and woke suddenly to the gravity of the situation. Her head was gushing blood.

"What's happening?" he demanded.

Only the co-pilot looked back at him.

"Mr. Antov, sir!" he cried, struggling to find something in a manual. "You must return to your seat immediately!"

Christian's eyes opened wide when he saw what lay below them. Stretching out in all directions was a vast body of floodwater, littered with the ruins of the coastal city of Santander. The plane was hurtling towards it at an alarming rate.

"What the hell happened down there?" he cried.

"A tsunami, Mr. Antov!" blurted the pilot.

He was struggling to control the small jet.

"It's wiped out the entire Atlantic coast, sir. The airport's gone! There's nowhere to land!"

The noise in the cabin was rising, and the toxic smoke from the burnt wiring was making Christian's head spin. To make matters worse, the Zurvanites had appeared again.

"Kill your brother! Kill him! Kill him!"

Christian tried frantically to ignore them.

"Go inland!" he cried, shuddering uncontrollably. "Put us down in a field for Christ's sake!"

"I can't keep her up, sir!" exclaimed the pilot, battling with the yoke. "The electrical storm's crippled us. We're going down! There's nothing we can do! Get back to your seat and buckle in, sir! Put on your life jacket! If you stay where you are you'll be killed!"

Christian scanned the ruined city as it sped past below. They were descending far too rapidly, and he knew they would be in the water in a matter of seconds. He turned back into the passenger compartment only to find his four military commanders making their way towards him.

"Get into your seats and tie yourselves in!" he cried. "We're going down!"

They obeyed immediately, and Christian had only managed to secure his own belt when the plane made contact with the water.

In the span of seconds, the luxurious interior had transformed into a living hell, the fuselage screaming as the plane skipped over the treacherous flood water.

Christian shot a glance outside to see that the pilots were bringing them down over what had once been a major avenue. A second later he was thrown forward violently, the door to the cockpit exploding open and sending a deluge of seawater and wreckage into the cabin, along with the bodies of the two dead pilots. The plane began to list.

"Move it! Move it!" came the resounding order from one of the officers.

Christian felt himself being forcibly removed from his seat as the four soldiers burst into action. The plane had come to a standstill now, but the front of it was slipping quickly into the water.

In an instant Christian was being pulled up to the back of the plane and shoved through the service doors into the rear cargo area. After that, things happened very quickly. In a blur of activity, the captains gathered up their gear and ammunition, using their assault rifles to blast away an aluminum hatch as the plane began to sink.

"Get out of the way!" bellowed one of them, and Christian was yanked aside as an officer pushed through with a raft that was already beginning to inflate.

Christian watched as it was thrown from the opening, landing in the water just outside the sinking plane.

"Go! Go!" screamed another, throwing Christian through the opening and into the raft.

In a matter of seconds their escape had been executed, and Christian found himself lying safely in the raft surrounded by three heavily armed soldiers. He watched the twisted fuselage slip under the water and vanish without a trace.

"Wilkinson!" bellowed the captain next to him, his head craning over the side of the raft. "Wilkinson!"

A long minute passed, and then to everyone's surprise the lost officer broke the surface, his resolute face drawing a deep breath of air as he took hold of the raft. Seconds later he was aboard, collapsing back onto the inflated rubber to catch his breath.

"This doesn't look good," said one of the captains, examining the gaping wound on the man's shoulder. "What happened? You were fine on the plane."

"Something was down there," said Wilkinson, his strong jaw trembling. "It grabbed me and took a chunk out of me. I don't know what the hell it was, but there was more than one. If it didn't sound so crazy, I'd say there were people down there."

Christian frowned and scanned the waters. The red light filtering down from above revealed little, but the irregular flashes of lightning told a different story. In the murky depths, Christian could discern movement. And whereas no corpse could be seen anywhere above the water, the same could not be said for what lay below.

"What the hell…" muttered one of the captains, looking overboard.

The undead were clear to see now. They resembled black wraiths in the oily water, slow moving and ghostly.

"What are you doing?" blurted the captain, but Christian had already snatched away his rifle.

Without a word of explanation, he leveled the weapon at Wilkinson and pulled the trigger, releasing it only when the man's head had been reduced to a pulpy mass. The officers recoiled instinctively, a grim spray of brain, blood and bone fragments dripping from their faces.

"You crazy son of a bitch!" screamed one of the soldiers, reaching for his gun.

Christian was faster. He trained the sites of his rifle on him and waited for them to calm down.

"Throw his body overboard!" he ordered, blinking away a shooting pain in his head.

The demons were worming into his brain.

"Kill your brother! Kill him! Kill him!"

Working together, two of the captains took hold of the headless corpse and threw it overboard. The water boiled with a frenzy of motion where it had gone down.

"What the hell's going on?" asked one of them, turning to look at Christian.

"This area's been exposed to an experimental virus," he managed to say.

The screaming whispers in his head were growing louder with every passing second.

"Kill your brother! Kill him! Kill him!"

Christian struggled to speak.

"Your colleague was bitten by one of the infected… He would have killed us all."

The three officers fell silent, trying to understand what Christian was telling them.

"Are you saying there are people down there?"

"Yes!" snapped Christian, a madness in his eyes. "And they are all dead!"

"But we just saw them moving," exclaimed another. "Why haven't they drowned?"

"The dead don't breathe!" barked Christian, snapping his head around. "Don't let them touch you!"

"Ahreimanius! Lucifer! Lucifer!"

Christian battled with his aggressors and managed to regain a semblance of control.

"The water is full of them…" he said, willing himself to grow calmer. "The surrounding hills too. Reanimation can only be prevented by destroying the brain."

He pointed his gun at the captains.

"Two of you pick up those oars and get us to dry land," he said. "You! Shoot at anything that moves. They'll attack when we reach the shallow water."

Christian's prediction proved accurate. No sooner had they reached the shore than the dead began to rise from the floodwater, stumbling slowly and inching ever closer. There were suddenly hundreds of them, and the eerie red light of the aurora filtered down over their ranks.

No sooner had they exited the raft than one of the officers became infected with fear.

"Get away from me you mother fuckers!" he bellowed, and a deafening rattle exploded from his gun.

He was firing directly into the mob, but only the corpses that had received numerous rounds to the head went down. The others were driven back by the force of the bullets, but soon began inching their way forward the moment the firing had stopped.

"For Christ's sake, they don't even bleed!" cried the officer in despair.

Christian turned in his direction, a demonic chorus screeching through his mind.

"Their blood has coagulated," he muttered, wincing under the pain of the icy whispers. "It cannot flow."

Christian let himself be herded to a new position on higher ground. From there the hordes could be seen rising from the waters in their multitudes, illuminated by flickering barrages of lightning. There were tens of thousands of them, all coming towards Christian in twisted, black reverence.

"And the sea gave up the dead which were in it," Christian heard himself say.

He was quoting from the Book of Revelations.

"And death and hell delivered up the dead which were in them…"

"What the fuck are you talking about?" screamed one of the officers.

He jerked around with his rifle only to see they were surrounded.

"Squadron one, squadron one!" barked another into his radio. "Do you read me! This is captain Ronald T. Curtis. We are down. I repeat. We are down! Do you read me!"

"Your troops are all dead," said Christian, a wicked smile of realization suddenly transforming his features.

He threw aside the assault rifle he was holding.

"Everyone here is dead, Captain, including yourself."

And as the ground lurched and shuddered beneath their feet, and as the floodwaters seethed and trembled with the approaching hordes, the soldiers' guns exploded into fire, their bullets vanishing into the throngs like droplets of rain into a jungle, their grenades dismembering corpses that continued forward regardless.

"Die, you bloody sons of bitches!" cried one of them, rushing into the horde in a suicidal rampage of gunfire.

The others watched in dumb horror as he was swallowed up and consumed. Only Christian was without fear. He could see grainy, demonic shadows rising from the floodwaters everywhere now. They were flowing into the undead like black hornets into nests.

Christian watched the corpses transform the moment the demons had taken possession of them, their rotting faces taking on reptilian features, and their movements becoming fiendish and jerky.

No longer were these the thoughtless shells of the undead. They were his subjects now, and he was their lord and master.

From every corner they were coming to worship at his feet. This was his army, and they would serve him now and in the future.

Christian saw that the four Zurvanites had appeared around him again, and as always, their frantic desperation was poisoning him to the core. Everything was hinging on his success; an aeon of plotting and conspiring all culminating in a single event. Failure to kill his brother would result in irreversible loss. The Apocatastasis would become unstoppable. Isaac had to die. Failure was not an option.

"Kill your brother! Kill him! Kill him!"

Christian jerked his head around to face the Four. An ocean of dark power was suddenly swelling within him, and his hatred for his brother surged to an unimaginable intensity.

"Feel the Dark Lord within you!" hissed the Zurvanites in unison. *"Your time is at hand. By the fist Ahreimanius will you conquer this world and rule it in darkness!"*

And then, in one instant, the glorious numbness that had always been Christian's fortitude was returned to him. He could feel the strength of Ahreimanius surging in his body, and the panicked screams of the two remaining officers only served to accentuate the majesty of the moment.

With the cartridges of their guns empty, they had gathered closer and closer to Christian, only to be ripped away and devoured by the teeming hordes.

"GET THEE DOWN!" boomed Christian suddenly from his mount, and in that instant every corpse as far away as the distant hills lowered itself before him, writhing and twisting on the ravaged earth like beaten dogs.

High above a single eagle flew, scanning the wasted domain. Under the cataclysmic sky it could see a vast army assembling over the lands, rank upon rank of twisted undead, milling and seething, and armed with a plague that if left unchecked, would devour the entire planet.

CHAPTER 8

Los Picos de Europa, Northern Spain.

Isaac awoke to the clank of armour and the thud of many boots. The knights were preparing to depart. There was an unmistakable haste in their movements and Isaac knew that something must have happened whilst he slept. He rose to his feet, his head still heavy with sleep. He could see Brother Bernardo approaching.

"What's happening?" he asked, rubbing his face awake.

"The demons have taken possession of the dead," said the monk in a low voice. "They are reptilian now, just as the Ascender's Prophecy foretold. They use their hands and feet to propel themselves and they are fiendishly fast. A rogue group of them attacked the knights on watch. They were destroyed, but not without cost. We lost two of our men."

He threw Isaac his pack.

"The scouts have spotted a horde behind us. They are approaching fast."

Sir David burst into the cave just then, his sword drawn and bloodied.

"We move now!" he barked, vanishing a second later.

In the space of a minute Isaac found himself rushing along a narrow mountain pass, with Shackleton at last appearing at his side. The state of the planet's surface had worsened considerably over the time they had been in the cave. Its atmosphere was now heavy with the toxic expulsions of recently formed volcanoes, and in the blood red sky could be seen great blankets of gaseous green fires.

The relentless barrage of charged solar particles was breaking down atmospheric water molecules into oxygen and hydrogen, only to be ignited by the sheets of lightning. The result was the birth of a cataclysmic world that no longer even resembled Earth, but rather a strange and foreign planet in some cursed region of space.

"The horde is upon us!" cried a knight suddenly.

He had been on the rear guard but had run up to warn his captain.

"Three hundred strong! Perhaps more!"

Sir David wasted no time, ordering the party to gain higher ground immediately. To their good fortune, the path at this point ran along an almost sheer precipice. The rocky terrain above the trail would at least slow the attackers.

"God help us," he said, taking a last look over his shoulder before following the others up.

He had witnessed firsthand the metamorphosis that had taken place in the undead. They could travel over the rocky terrain with freakish speed now, and he knew there would be little they could do to defend themselves against such a mob, regardless of their strategic position above the path.

"Form a ring around our charge!" he cried, and his knights scrambled to obey, their shields interlocking to form a formidable barrier bristling with the blades of their swords.

In the blink of an eye, Isaac, the monk, and Shackleton found themselves completely enclosed. It was not long before they felt a strange rumbling in the ground. It rode atop the regular churning of the earth's crust.

Moments later the horde came into view, a macabre mass of shadowy grey corpses leaping like rabid animals along the narrow path below them. Through the gaps and spaces between the knights, Isaac could see them passing. There was a cold malevolence in their lizard-like eyes, but they were all looking eastward, never once glancing up.

Isaac felt a hand on his shoulder. It forced him down behind the boulders. The defensive ring of knights was breaking apart, and he turned to see Sir David's face only inches from his own.

"Stay down!" he whispered, his eyes alight with hope. "They have not seen us!"

Isaac swallowed hard, fighting back the urge to bolt. Brother Bernardo had not been exaggerating. The undead were truly reptilian now, and it seemed to him that a horrific nightmare was playing out before him.

Many of them were plunging from the cliff's edge as they stampeded past, only to rise from wherever they fell to continue their maddened flight into the east. In this way the mighty horde came and went in the space of just a few minutes.

"Where are they going?" asked Isaac, struggling to compose himself.

He had come down to join the knights on the path and was having to step around the fetid gore that covered the earth. Amid the sludge of clotted blood, bile and excrement could be seen grey swaths of skin, severed digits, and grisly sections of tooth and gum.

"They go to the Portal," said Sir David, grimacing. "Just as the Ascender's Prophecy foretells. There will be no stopping them until the demons have been exorcized and forced to descend again."

Isaac let his head fall, knowing that it was he who was responsible for this. In that instant, however, he felt a comforting hand on his shoulder, and looking over saw that Brother Bernardo had come to join them.

"For a large wound to be healed," said the monk softly, "it sometimes requires that a smaller wound be inflicted first. Do not regret your actions, dear Isaac. In opening the portal, you also made it possible for *The Two* to descend into it. Therein lies our only hope."

Isaac turned to face the monk. In the eastern sky behind him a funnel of churning clouds had amassed. It loomed black over their destination, a sinister finger pointing to the very same island where he had committed his atrocities.

Isaac felt his eyes burning with tears as he gazed out over the tortured lands. It was a panorama of oblivion, writhing under the force of an ever-worsening cataclysm. Despite the brother's kind words, he could not shake the feeling that he was responsible for all this, and it weighed on him heavily.

"I had a dream whilst I slept..." he said quietly, his gaze lingering in the east.

Brother Bernardo drew close, his eyes solemn but compassionate.

"What did you dream, dear Isaac?"

"I dreamed of a shadowy emperor," he said. "Attended to by the Fourteen Emissaries of Lucifer. They were at the head of an army that covered the earth like a blanket of cinder."

Isaac looked down to find Shackleton loyally by his side. He fell to one knee and ruffled the fur atop his head.

"The emperor was my brother," he continued, squinting up at the monk through the stinging rain. "He's coming to kill me."

CHAPTER 9

Somewhere under the Atlantic Ocean.

"This is unbelievable!" exclaimed Amir.

His eyes were wide with surprise as he gazed into the monitor. Peralta looked up from his work at the control panel, wondering what all the fuss was about.

After having been hit by the underwater shockwave, the small sub had tumbled to depths that had threatened its structural integrity. It was only by a miracle that they were still alive. As it was, many systems on the boat had been damaged as a result, and repairing them was proving to be no small task.

"What is it?" asked Peralta, looking up from his calculations.

He had only just managed to get the internet systems online again, but there was still a long list of configurations that needed to be made. Amir looked over at him, his face beaming with excitement.

"You're gonna love this."

Peralta rose groaning from his seat. A stretch would do him good. He hobbled over to Amir's station and peered into the monitor. The video Cassano had made was online and streaming. Gabriel and Natasha were presenting the three-dimensional scans and describing the Cube's ability to interface with their brains.

"All right," said Peralta, yawning. "He did a great job on the video. What's the big deal?"

"You haven't looked closely enough," said Amir, chewing on one of his cinnamon toothpicks. "Look at the number of views it's had."

He watched Peralta's eyes shift.

"What the hell…"

In a split-second Peralta's sleepy expression had transformed into utter surprise. He craned his neck forward to be absolutely certain he was reading it correctly.

"That's right," said Amir proudly. "Over twenty million hits and counting!"

"But how?" stammered Peralta.

"It's gone viral, my friend," said Amir, sitting back and crossing his arms. "We've already got over six hundred thousand people hooked up to our Boink worldwide. As soon as you get your systems working, I think you're going to be seeing some crazy amounts of fully extracted algorithms in your data banks."

Peralta stood in silent amazement, his arms dangling at his sides as his mind struggled to understand.

"But what could have been in the video that made the world embrace it like this?"

"Hope," came Natasha's voice from behind.

Peralta turned to see her smiling happily.

"Just when the planet's lost all hope, the Compostela Cube comes along."

Amir nodded in agreement, his dreadlocks swaying.

"A communications artifact created by an advanced civilization that lived on earth two hundred and fifty million years ago," he said merrily. "That's pretty big news, especially if it's holding a secret that's going to solve all our problems, man.

"I'm sure people are thinking if this isn't a hoax, it's the biggest discovery ever made. And the fact that there's a mysterious website you can interact with just makes it even more exciting."

"But there's no content on the website," said Peralta, scrubbing at his messy head in an effort to get the blood flowing.

"Maybe that's where the hope comes in," said Natasha, turning to see Gabriel entering the bridge.

To their relief his thumbs were both held up in a gesture of success. Behind him came Bahadur, bending low to squeeze in through the small hatch. The two of them were drenched from head to foot, having been outside repairing the communications antenna while the sub continued its race northward.

Given the turbulent state of the ocean, making the repairs had not been an easy task. Peralta wasted no time in darting to his workstation to reactivate the central telemetry. In an instant the old bishop's face had appeared on the main monitor as the connection was made, his eyes alight with relief and happiness.

"Thanks be to God," prayed the bishop, and then turning his head he exclaimed:

"Cassano! You must come at once, my son! We have re-established contact! They appear to be safe and sound!"

"Uncle Marcus!" exclaimed Natasha, delighted to see the old man's face. "We're all fine! We were hit by a tsunami."

"I know, child, I know!" came his reply, beaming with joy.

"Good God," exclaimed Cassano, his face appearing behind the bishop's. "I've just had a look at your transponder. How did you cover so much distance?"

"The tsunami must have sucked us northward," said Peralta, "We lost our positioning system when the initial shockwave hit. Where exactly are we?"

"You're at the top of Spain, Captain," said Cassano. "You'll be able to take up an easterly heading within the hour. I'll send you the data so you can recalibrate."

"Much has happened since you lost contact," said the bishop as Cassano disappeared to do his work. "Your video has circled the globe."

Peralta was nodding in amazement.

"I still can't believe it..."

"Well, that is not all," said the bishop. "It would appear that leaders from the six world religions have also joined our cause."

"What do you mean, Uncle?" asked Natasha.

The old bishop shrugged.

"An official World Religion Consortium has been formed. It is momentous, my child. Planet Earth has risen to its feet and is rallying behind the Cube!"

"But that's crazy," said Gabriel, waking from his initial shock. "There's no real proof out there that the Cube even exists. How could all this come from a single video?"

"The video represents something that the world hungers for," said the bishop. "It represents democracy and solidarity. The Cube has six equal sides, my son. One for every religion. Its very existence sings of unity.

"Just as people are drawn together by crisis, so has the entire world been drawn together by this cataclysm. You do not fully understand. You have been out of touch with the world for the past ten hours. Everything has changed. As far as proof of the existence of the Cube is concerned, there is a substantial amount readily available."

"What proof?" asked Gabriel.

"Why, the social networking platform," said the old bishop matter-of-factly. "Already there are millions of citizens interacting on it. Word is spreading like wildfire. There are democratic forums already planning cease fires in numerous countries worldwide."

Peralta darted back to his workstation and brought up the Cube's website.

"Twenty-two thousand forums in attendance..." he said over his shoulder, still having difficulty believing what he was seeing.

"Response has been overwhelming!" exclaimed the bishop. "And it is only natural given the circumstances. Everyone is locked in their homes as a result of the tempestuous weather and curfews. They are glued to the internet. People want to resolve this crisis, and the website is giving them a way to do it."

Peralta returned his attention to the monitor, an expression of concern coming over his features.

"It'll all be for nothing if we can't locate that labyrinth and activate the Cube..."

"For nothing?" said Amir, "I hardly think so. The new directives they're formulating could end this stupid war."

"Sure, but it won't make a difference," said Peralta.

"What do you mean?"

Peralta took a deep breath and centred himself.

"When we cross the galactic plane, the gravitational field is going to do a lot more than move some tectonic plates around. It's going to affect our *brains*. Our sense of perception will be shifted and distorted. Time will literally be warped. It'll be as though everyone in the world's been given a massive dose of LSD for God's sake! It's going to be disastrous..."

Amir held Peralta's gaze without saying a word. He himself had experimented with psychotropic substances in university and knew what it was to have one's mind enter into such altered states. If Peralta was right, it would be the final blow to end society.

Gabriel had assisted Amir in the experiments, and his attention was fixed on Peralta as well.

"Of course," he said slowly. "That's how the whole thing works. That's why the Cube is the way it is."

"What do you mean?" asked Natasha. "What do psychotropic drugs have to do with the Cube?"

Gabriel turned to face her.

"The effects of any mind-altering drug are directly related to the participant's state of mind," he said slowly. "In other words, after consuming a psychotropic substance, the ensuing experience will be positive or negative, euphoric or hellish, depending on what one's mental attitude was before the drug was ingested."

"It's the difference between a good trip, and a bad trip," said Amir with a shrug.

"Exactly," rasped Peralta. "And the present state of the global consciousness pretty much guarantees a bad trip. The world population is currently experiencing an unprecedented level of fear and anxiety, as well as bitterness, hopelessness, and doubt. A crossing of the galactic plane under these conditions would have a devastating effect on the minds of every person on this planet. We'd be plunged into despair and come out of the crossing in a state of general insanity."

Gabriel interjected immediately.

"But just as with all psychotropic hallucinogens," he said, holding up a hand, "the mind-altering effects could also be a profoundly positive and deeply spiritual experience."

Gabriel paused for a moment before continuing.

"Speaking for myself, my limited experiments with peyote and hallucinogenic mushrooms were enlightening, but my mental state was healthy and peaceful going into them. I can see what you're saying, Captain, but perhaps this is where the Cube can make a difference."

"Which is exactly my point!" rasped Peralta. "The Cube is plugged into the collective consciousness, and it has been for the past quarter of a billion years. If we can get to the Labyrinth on time, and you two can activate the Cube's systems, it's very likely that something beneficial will occur."

"Like what?" asked Amir.

"I have no idea!" said Peralta, frustrated. "All I can tell you is what I know from the numbers we've decrypted. Some kind of data pattern will be injected into the universal field of intelligence at the time of the crossing."

"Peace," said Natasha softly.

She had suddenly recalled Suora's last words.

Bring peace to the hearts of all those who will make the crossing.

She looked at the two rotating cube icons on the monitor.

"It's going to be a profound feeling of peace and serenity that'll get injected into the collective consciousness," she said quietly. "Like the warm fuzzy feeling you get on Christmas Eve. Do you know the one I mean?"

Everyone turned to face Natasha. Her words had struck a chord. From the outset, they had all known that the Cube's purpose was to usher the world into a new and better age, but it was not until this very moment that they fully understood how the artifact was going to accomplish this feat.

The Cube would first endow humanity with the peace of mind needed to survive the crossing, and it would then imbue humanity with the wisdom it needed to socially evolve after the crossing had been made.

Now, more than ever, an urgency to complete the mission surged within each of them. Locked in this Cube lay a gift so wonderful, so benevolent, that they could not even begin to imagine the benefits it would bestow upon humanity. They simply had to find the Labyrinth of Sarras, and as quickly as possible. Time was running out.

Peralta was the first to break from the silence that had come in the wake of Natasha's realization.

"Cassano," he said. "I just looked at the data you sent me."

While the others had been lost in thought, the scruffy engineer had returned to his workstation and got down to the more practical matters at hand.

"Our position is good," he rasped, "but we're still approximately six hours from Santander. Less than eight hours remain before we cross the galactic plane. How are we supposed to locate this labyrinth in two hours, especially if we don't know where it is?"

Gabriel rose to his feet. Because of the tsunami crisis, he had not yet had a chance to share what he and Natasha had learned of in their trance.

"Where exactly are we?" he asked, moving to Peralta's side.

"Approaching the northern tip of Spain. We've just got to head west along the coast, and we'll be on our way to Santander."

Gabriel looked back at Natasha.

"We forgot to mention something," he said. "We don't need to go to Santander anymore."

"What do you mean?" asked Peralta. "If not Santander, then where?"

"Do you know a village called Finisterre?" asked Natasha, stepping closer.

Peralta checked his navigation system.

"Finisterre is on the west coast, directly east of our present location," he said, frowning. "I could have us there in twenty minutes. But if the Labyrinth is south of Santander, it would be way faster for us to travel there by sea rather than over land."

Peralta saw Gabriel and Natasha exchange a knowing glance, a smile appearing on both of their faces. He stood up, his fists propped on his plump hips.

"Perhaps you might like to share your little secret with us now?" he said, clearly annoyed. "What's it going to be? Over sea, or over land?"

"Neither," said Gabriel with a wink. "Take us into Finisterre and we'll show you how to get us to the Labyrinth on time."

CHAPTER 10

Los Picos de Europa, Northern Spain.

Christian moved forward like someone passing through a dense and viscous liquid, his concentration bent solely on putting one foot in front of the other. Blanketing the lands around him was a host of undead so large that its numbers were uncountable, and still more came with every passing minute.

Christian was encased in them as he stumbled forward, held aloft by fetid reptilian arms, with each frenzied corpse herding him to the place where all would be decided. His body was jerking and trembling uncontrollably now, his advance resembling less the procession of a powerful emperor, and more the parade of a captured lunatic.

For over eight hours he had travelled in this way. Overhead the sky bled and boiled, lit by fires of molten gas, and expanding sheets of verdigris lightning. With the Dark Rift now only hours from being crossed, the planet was shuddering fitfully, its crust expanding and contracting with the force of falling mountains; enraging the sea and the air, and all that was ever once calm.

Christian squinted up into the acid rain, his eyes burning and his lungs on fire. For hours now he had been accompanied by the silent ghost of Dr. Bennington, conjured by his unconscious mind in an attempt to regain the confidence he had exhibited while under the doctor's care.

"As you can see, my good Doctor," muttered Christian, stumbling over a rock made slippery with gore. "Everything is moving according to plan. Soon all of humanity shall bend to my will."

But whereas the doctor had always been kind and patient with him in life, his specter had been made cruel and wicked by the tremendous guilt that Christian harboured.

"Your will means nothing!" hissed Bennington, his eyes glowing red. *"You are a piece of refuse, adequate only to be used as a vessel for the sexual gratification of your superiors."*

Bennington's words cut Christian to the bone, reopening the wounds that lay at the root of his torment. His body fell into uncontrollable spasms and seizures, and soon after, everything went black.

* * * * * *

Christian awoke to find himself lying on the rocky ground, surrounded by a frenzied mob of demonically possessed corpses. The stench of them was outlandish, and as he rose unsteadily to his feet, he realized that his numbness had once again been revoked. It had been replaced by a seething, baleful force that wormed through his mind like a nest of maggots.

He could hear his father's hissing voice in his head, and whereas before it had been a great torment to him, it was now almost comforting, reminding him of a time when he had been impervious to pain.

All power is based in fear. Fear in the masses must be maintained at all costs.

Christian pushed his fingers into his eyes, straining to regain his mind and set straight something that was driving him into madness.

In times such as these, when his reptilian self prevailed, he experienced strange sounds and visions. They were brief glimpses of scenes, where he found himself in other parts of the mountains, but always among the undead.

The visions were becoming clearer to him now, and in that moment, he understood that he was seeing through the eyes of the undead themselves. The demonic corpses were a part of him now, and along with this new understanding came a sudden realization. He now possessed tens of thousands of eyes through which to look for his brother. It would only be a matter of time before he found him.

Christian made his way to the edge of a high precipice, the undead hordes clearing a path before him. From here the earth could be seen writhing in agony, the expulsions of newly formed volcanoes belching poison into the toxic air. The ground was shaking and lurching constantly now, and Christian had to make an effort to stay on his feet.

Far below him lay a small mountain lake, its surface black like carbon. Even the burning sky, with its fiery clouds and rippling sheets of lightning could do nothing to illuminate it. Only a tiny island was visible there, its burnt trunks rising from it like charred fingers from a shallow grave.

Christian passed his hands over his face in an attempt to revitalize himself. He had at last arrived at the Portal of Ahreimanius. Here, with the help of his army, he would find his brother and kill him.

CHAPTER 11

Isaac looked down at the lake from his elevated perch. His arrival had coincided perfectly with Christian's, but he and his knights were on the western side, directly opposite his brother, and considerably closer to the island.

Christian's army of corpses could be seen on the eastern shore, a gargantuan host of seething cinder-grey shadows amassed on the hilly terrain. Shackleton was at Isaac's side, and the fat monk behind him. In their worst nightmares they had never foreseen such a large force opposing them. Their numbers were literally in the millions.

"What do we do now?" asked Isaac, turning to see that the knights had grouped to form a protective barrier behind him.

"We wait," said Brother Bernardo. "We wait and we hope."

"But we have no boat. How will we reach the island?"

Sir David approached just then.

"Our way into the City of Sarras will be shown to us when the Two arrive, just as it is written in the Ascender's Prophecy."

Isaac was perplexed.

"What city? There is only a tiny island here."

"We will wait, and we will see," said the captain. "In the meantime, we shall rest. My men are tired, as must you be, dear Isaac. Sit and eat. We are safe here for the time being."

CHAPTER 12

Finisterre, Northern Spain.

All eyes scanned the images being shown on the bridge's main monitor. Having arrived at Finisterre, Peralta had followed Gabriel's directions and turned the sub into the sheltered port. Using what he proudly referred to as his Synthetic Aperture Sonar, Peralta had located some unique rock formations about thirty meters below sea level.

"Could that be it?" asked Natasha, pointing to the monitor. "The dark section there, next to that big rock."

Peralta used the joystick to nudge the sub a few degrees starboard until its lights fell on the feature that Natasha had pointed out.

"That's definitely a cave," he rasped. "By the looks of it, I'd say it was big enough to steer this boat into as well."

A tremor shook the submarine and he turned to exchange a worried glance with Gabriel.

"Are you sure about this, Dr. Parker?"

Peralta rubbed his temples when he saw Gabriel nod. He was still having difficulty believing what he had been told. He made some adjustments to the navigation system.

"A two-hundred-and-fifty-million-year-old tunnel," he said, shaking his head. "Built by an ancient race of hyper-intelligent reptilians. All so they could get to an underground city they built in the middle of the mountains…"

He swiveled in his chair and adjusted some knobs.

"A tunnel that has not only survived countless geological events, but one that also travels horizontally for approximately three hundred kilometres."

He finished his preparations and looked over at Natasha.

"Forgive me if I'm a little skeptical."

All eyes were glued to the monitor as Peralta eased the submarine into the cave. It did not take long before it became obvious that they had found what they were looking for. The sonar showed a long and spacious tunnel heading due east, its trajectory perfectly level. A moment later Peralta was increasing the sub's speed.

"Well then," he said, shaking his head again, but this time in amazement. "This tunnel is definitely not a natural formation. Those reptilians knew what they were doing. It's perfectly straight."

Gabriel's eyes met with Natasha's. The tunnel seemed familiar to them, and not just because they had seen it while in Mithuna. There was something remotely familiar about this place, as though they had been here many times before.

"Captain Peralta," said Natasha on an impulse. "Do you think you could turn off the headlights for a moment?"

The messy engineer raised an eyebrow at her odd request, and then flipped a few toggle switches on the instrument panel. The exterior monitor went black.

"Well I'll be damned…" whispered Peralta.

The tunnel had begun to glow with iridescent blue light. He bent to tap on a keyboard and adjust a few knobs.

"We're definitely going to need to find out what's causing this…"

Scotty and Amir entered the bridge as Peralta went about his work. They had been in the engine room with Bahadur.

"What the bloody hell…?" said Scotty, his attention fixed on the sub's main monitor. "Don't tell me that's the tunnel you were talking about. That's a video game you're playing, right, mate?"

Peralta's face wore a mask of astonishment.

"Judging by these scans, it would appear that the walls are lined with the same material that the Cube's made of. They're synthetically alive… And flexible…"

"That'll do it," said Gabriel. "Couple that with the fact that the Precambrian rock formations here are over two billion years old, and we can see how this tunnel's stood the test of time."

Amir was shaking his head in disbelief.

"You'd think that would surprise me, but it doesn't."

He paused to scratch behind an ear, thinking.

"What I don't get is why they would have to build the Labyrinth so far inland... Why not just build it on the coast and save themselves all the trouble of having to dig such a long tunnel?"

"The Labyrinth had to be built where the portal was located," explained Gabriel. "From what I gather, the portal's some kind of wormhole located in outer space. It's in a very specific location that our planet actually moves through as our solar system orbits the centre of the galaxy."

Peralta turned to look at Gabriel.

"A wormhole?"

"I think so," said Gabriel, frowning. "It's located directly on the galactic plane. I guess it just so happened that these mountains are the place on the planet where it all lines up."

Peralta held up his hand, wanting to be absolutely sure he understood what Gabriel had said.

"Bear with me, please," he rasped. "The Labyrinth is built precisely on the point of land that will align itself with a wormhole, just as we pass through the galactic plane."

"That's right," said Gabriel. "That specific place happens to be located deep underground, directly beneath that island we keep talking about. That's where they built the City of Sarras."

"Of course..." said Peralta. "That explains everything. The natural place for a wormhole to form would be in an ultrahigh gravitational field, just like the one in the galactic plane..."

A shadow of fear passed over his face.

"What the hell are we heading for?" he whispered, peering into the depths of iridescent blue tunnel as it sped past. "Going through the galactic plane is going to be crazy enough, but to do it right beside a wormhole? Have you any idea what we're in for? Wormholes are very enigmatic things, Dr. Parker. They're suspected of connecting utterly different dimensions outside of space and time. We could be lost forever!"

"I guess that's why they call it a labyrinth," said Gabriel, cocking an eyebrow. "This location seems to be some kind of a gateway. One that runs in two very different directions."

"One gate goes to heaven," said Natasha slowly, "but the other one goes to hell."

Peralta swallowed hard, recalling what the bishop had spoken of earlier that day. There had been very disconcerting reports coming from the Cantabrian Mountains. The area had been quarantined by the military, but news of the atrocities that had befallen the people living there was still leaking out.

Unbelievable as it sounded, the dead were said to be walking, their corpses infected with a strange experimental virus that was highly communicable. If this were not bad enough, Natasha had earlier informed him that Professor Metrovich had written of these evils in his journal, stating that the victims would soon be possessed by demons from hell, and that the only way to destroy them would be through decapitation.

Peralta removed his glasses and rubbed his weary eyes.

What are we driving into?

CHAPTER 13

Six hours had passed when they finally reached the end of the tunnel, leaving only two hours before the earth began its descent into the gravitational field of the galactic plane. Despite the heightened seismic activity in the earth's crust, the small sub had smoothly navigated the tunnel, reaching an enormous underwater cavern beneath the island. It was perfectly spherical in shape.

"This is unbelievable," whispered Peralta in awe, looking at a three-dimensional sonar-generated image of the space.

On the sub's main monitor was the section that lay directly before them, its entire surface aglow in the same blue light as the tunnel.

"What's that over there?" asked Natasha, gesturing to the corner of the monitor. "It looks like a flight of steps."

Peralta manoeuvred the sub to face where she had pointed.

"That's exactly what it is," said Gabriel, taking hold of the control panel as yet another tremor shook the boat. "It's just like it was in our trance."

The image became clear as the sub approached. Before them was a wide platform, with a broad flight of steps glowing in phosphorescent blue. It led up to a raised portico.

"Why would aquatic reptilians need to build steps?" asked Amir. "Couldn't they have just swam up there?"

Natasha scanned the image.

"Nothing was underwater when we visited this place in our trance. We were walking around."

She looked at Gabriel.

"There was a slot at the top of the steps where we inserted the Cube. Do you remember?"

"I do," he said. "The doors opened right after that."

"So what are we supposed to do now?" asked Amir. "How are we supposed to get to those doors if everything's underwater?"

"This sub is equipped with an access hatch," rasped Peralta. "It's down below. The trouble is there's only one diving suit."

"That's all we'll need," said Gabriel. "How much time have we got?"

"Just a little under two hours."

The submarine lurched violently as another tremor shook the tunnel.

"Then we'll have to hurry," said Gabriel. "We're running out of time."

* * * * * *

Gabriel made his way through the frigid water, turning to see the little submarine floating in the centre of a colossal chamber shimmering with blue light. What had been an impressive glow through the sub's external camera was in fact an awe-inspiring iridescent splendor. He had been diving since he was a boy, and seen incredible things, but this literally took his breath away.

Turning to face forward, Gabriel could see an enormous wall comprised of gigantic stone pilasters. It measured at least thirty meters in both height and width and had a broad flight of steps leading to a massive portico at its top.

"This is unbelievable..." he stammered, swimming forward.

Peralta's raspy voice sounded in his helmet.

"How close are you to the entrance?"

"I'm here. I can see the slot."

Gabriel approached an enormous pair of doors that looked to be ten meters in height. They were adorned with an intricately carved image of the Tree of Life. Next to the doors was a small, square-shaped indentation. He produced the Cube.

"I'm inserting it now," he said. "Here goes nothing."

Natasha looked intently at Gabriel's grainy silhouette, dwarfed as it was against the massive entrance. She gasped in alarm. The submarine had begun to shake violently.

"Something's happening!" came Gabriel's crackling voice. "There's a loud rumbling coming through the water. It started as soon as I put the Cube in the slot. It sounds mechanical. Something big's going down. Can you feel that?"

"Affirmative!" said Peralta, taking hold of the control panel to stabilize himself. "Now get back to the sub!"

"But the door hasn't opened!" cried Gabriel amid the rising tumult. "I'll try something else!"

"Gabriel!" barked Natasha, her hands making fists. "Get back to this submarine right now!"

Gabriel turned to face her.

"All right, all right," he said, putting away the Cube. "I'm on my way. Jeez, you'd think it was the end of the world or something."

CHAPTER 14

Shackleton rose swiftly, protectively moving to Isaac's side moments before the strange rumbling began. An instant later everyone could feel it too. Unlike the irregular shuddering of the earth's crust, this was a steady, mechanical vibration, accompanied by a deep, chest shaking hum.

"What is this?" asked Isaac, standing up.

He saw the knights jump to attention around him.

"Something is happening to the lake!" hollered Brother Bernardo over a clap of thunder. "Look at the island! The water level is dropping!"

The monk was not mistaken. In the few minutes that had passed since the mechanical rumbling had begun, the lake's waterline had already dropped considerably.

It was not long before they saw that the island was in fact the tip of an enormous pyramid-shaped structure that had been hidden beneath the waters. It was covered in dark green algae, and intricately adorned with a latticework of strange and complex architectural details.

"The ancient city of Sarras!" cried Sir David, amidst a barrage of thunderclaps. "Make ready to descend!"

Isaac looked back to see the knights assembling themselves. Far below, massive vortexes had appeared on the lake's surface, and as the water level continued to drop, a way down opened up before them. Sir David wasted no time leading them into the valley. They were soon making their way along a treacherous path, slippery with mud and algae.

"Where are we going?" cried Isaac over the roaring thunder and tumult.

"An opening will soon be revealed!" bellowed Sir David. "We must get to the city before the hordes, and then seal the entrance behind us!"

With the lake almost entirely drained now, Isaac could see the colossal structure in its entirety as they descended. He estimated it to be at least three hundred meters in height, twice the size of the Great Pyramid of Giza. He was amazed that such an awesome thing could have remained hidden for so long.

Its builders must have diverted rivers to fill this valley.

The pyramid was now towering ominously above them, its ancient surface lit by pulsating sheets of verdigris lightning. Underfoot, the earth was lurching violently. It took the ground suddenly from beneath Isaac and were it not for the stout knight who caught him, he would have fallen to his death.

No sooner had they reached the valley floor than they were made aware of a new and pressing danger. Something, it seemed, had alerted the undead to their presence. What had once been a dense body of milling corpses had now formed into a single, coherent mass; one that was rushing towards them in a maddened frenzy.

"Make haste!" bellowed Sir David over the din. "The entrance to the city is there!"

Isaac followed the captain's pointing finger to see a tiny opening at the base of the structure. A narrow flight of stone steps wound precariously up to it. It would have been indistinguishable amid the countless niches and alcoves, were it not for the strange blue light that emanated from it.

"Move!" bellowed Sir David, turning to look again at the advancing hordes. "We must secure that entrance!"

Having reached the floor of the valley, only a level stretch of land now separated them from the base of the pyramid, and the stairway leading to its entrance. It was not a hundred meters away but with the lake now drained, a thick and slippery silt coated the ground, making their progress slow and treacherous. Looking back, Isaac could see that the charging undead were unaffected by the sludge. They were gaining on them rapidly.

The company arrived panting at the stairway just as the first wave of undead arrived, their twisted corpses frantic and filled with indescribable hatred. The shields of the knights strained under their onslaught, and Isaac gasped as strong arms hauled him up the steps. Two knights had remained below while the rest of them sprinted upwards to establish a defensive position above.

Fortunately for them, the thick algae covering the pyramid was thwarting the attempts of the undead to scale the structure, making the steps the only means of ascent. Their narrowness, in turn, was limiting the frontal attack to no more than two or three undead at a time, and in this way, fighting side by side, the two knights who remained below were able to hold back the advance. Even still, it would only be a matter of time before the horde overwhelmed them.

"Hurry!" bellowed Sir David. "Move! Move!"

They were almost at the entrance now.

"Good God…" muttered Isaac, aghast.

Having reached the top, he had turned to look out onto the lakebed below. That such an immense army could have amassed there so quickly seemed impossible. A sea of teaming undead was now covering the entire valley floor; hundreds of thousands strong, each one ravenous and frenzied, and lit by the burning sky. Their ranks swayed with the lurching earth like black weeds in a festering sea.

Isaac glanced down the steps in time to see the knights of the front guard falling. Seconds later a densely packed host of savage undead were leaping and bounding up the steps towards the next line of defence. There, another two knights held them back with flashing swords and straining shields.

This was no longer the slaying of slow-moving zombies. Being possessed by demons, their assailants were now as quick as cobras, and more frenzied than rabid beasts. It would only be a matter of time before this next bastion fell as well. Already two more knights had filed in behind them, waiting for their turn to die in the service of the Two.

"We must not linger here!" said Sir David to Isaac, bellowing so as to be heard over the unearthly cries. "I will escort you into the city whilst our brothers hold back the dead!"

But even as Sir David spoke these words, there came crashing down from above a group of seven undead who had managed to scale the slippery walls. It was all the knights could do to cut them down as they moved past Isaac. Even still, four managed to escape into the city entrance, their dark forms hurtling down a long, glowing tunnel that plunged into the depths of the pyramid.

Glancing down, Isaac could see that Shackleton was in a dilemma, shifting his attention between him and the fleeing undead. In a second the dog had made up his mind, sounding a resounding bark and darting off into the tunnel after his prey.

"Shackleton!" cried Isaac, feeling a sharp pain in his neck just as the words left his mouth.

He brought a hand to the spot and when he pulled it away, it was covered in blood.

"No!" gasped Brother Bernardo, tearing open Isaac's collar to examine his neck. "This cannot be!"

Isaac said nothing. His eyes were wide with surprise as the scene replayed itself. A filthy hand had slashed at him when the corpses had passed, its blackened nails carving a deep gouge in his neck. Almost instantly he began to feel engulfed by a cold fog as the virus made its way into his system.

Isaac slumped to the ground and let out a shuddering breath. The clangor of the attacking hordes was merging with the laboured beats of his heart. He was beginning to lose consciousness.

CHAPTER 15

Natasha turned and looked down to see Peralta standing atop the submarine. She was climbing the ancient steps with Gabriel at her side, the very same steps he had been swimming above a few minutes earlier. Behind them was Amir, with Bahadur and Scotty Roberts following up the rear, their assault rifles poised.

Shortly after his return to the sub, Gabriel and the others had watched in amazement as the chamber emptied itself of over half its water, becoming a massive subterranean port in the space of ten minutes. With the platform now serving as a dock for the sub to berth at, it was becoming increasingly obvious that the edifice had been built for humans.

As it was, the small party now found themselves before two massive doors leading into the mysterious city, their surface still wet from waters that had covered them for the past quarter of a billion years.

"Let's try this again," said Gabriel, producing the glowing Cube and inserting it once again into the slot.

Shortly after, a loud boom reverberated through the chamber and the massive doors swung silently inward. Gabriel spun to face the sub. He could see it floating far below, dwarfed under the chamber's enormous, towering dome. The ground was shaking incessantly now. The planet was just one hour away from entering the Dark Rift.

"How's the signal?" he said into his radio, peering down at Peralta's tiny form.

"It couldn't be better," came the response. "Good luck!"

After collecting a sample of the glowing bio-synthetic substance that coated the chamber's walls, Peralta had found that it was an excellent transmitter of radio waves. By reconfiguring their communications devices, he had not only managed to sync their radios through it, but also re-establish a perfect connection with the satellite feed that kept them linked to their base in Gibraltar.

"The reptilians must have used this blue goo to communicate with their underwater cities," he had explained. "It's faster than fibreoptics and its constantly emitting the axiomatic codes I need to decrypt the Cube's data streams. We shouldn't have any problems with communication as long as things continue to glow blue, no matter how deep you go."

Gabriel took a breath and stepped through the ancient threshold, his trained eye scanning his surroundings as he proceeded. The others followed close behind. In the iridescent blue light, the strange organic quality of the architecture was easy to see.

Carved from the living rock, their surroundings took on the nature of having been constructed by insects, the rounded edges and curving walls expressing proportions characteristic to all naturally occurring structures.

"This place is a testament to the Fibonacci sequence," said Gabriel, looking around in awe. "The proportions are perfect."

The chambers they passed through were exceedingly beautiful, but it was not long before they had left them behind. They were traversing a long glowing passageway now. It ascended at an even incline and brought them to a junction where another passage led off into the centre of the structure.

"There's a good chance this could be the entrance to the Labyrinth," said Gabriel, pointing down the passageway. "From the configuration of these tunnels, I'd say we were in the descending passage of a pyramid, and if that's the case, the central chamber should be right down there."

He dug into his pack and produced the Cube, exchanging a glance with Natasha to set it aglow.

"I think we should be keeping an eye on this from now on," he said. "Peralta mentioned there'd be some kind of transponder near the entrance that would communicate with it."

Gabriel stopped short. A mass of fetid air had suddenly engulfed them. It was thick with the putrid reek of rotting flesh.

"What the hell is that stench?" asked Scotty, grasping the wall to balance himself during a particularly aggressive tremor.

Gabriel frowned.

"It's coming from an exit up there."

"Something is not right," said Bahadur, peering up the tunnel.

It was at that very moment that they saw four dark shapes hurtling towards them.

"What the hell are those things?" cried Gabriel.

Bahadur wasted no time finding out. In a matter of seconds, he had leveled his assault rifle and opened fire.

"Scotty!" he bellowed, and in a second the smuggler's gun was sounding as well.

The effects of their salvo seemed to have only a moderate effect on the advancing beasts, serving to slow their advance but not stop them. Bahadur suddenly remembered what the old bishop had said earlier that day.

"Aim for their heads!" he bellowed.

The frenetic corpses were almost upon them now, and with them came an indescribable sensation of evil. Natasha felt herself shuddering with fear. It was the same paranormal force she had encountered in the storeroom that day, only much more potent.

It was as though the beasts had tentacles that were reaching into her. She fought them back with all her strength. Something demonic was attempting to take her. She jerked herself around to face Gabriel, only to see that he was engaged in a similar battle.

"What the hell is this?" he grunted; his fists clenched as he fought off the invisible enemy. "Get the hell out of me, you sons of bitches!"

The assault ended as suddenly as it had begun, coinciding with the empty clicking of the assault rifle cartridges. Four corpses lay on the tunnel floor, their heads reduced to lumps of grey flesh.

Bahadur and Scotty turned to look at the others. The last of the undead was not two meters from where they stood. They were lucky to be alive.

"Got any more ammo, mate?" asked Scotty, looking over to Bahadur.

The fearless smuggler was clearly shaken.

"I do not," he said, his voice deep with concern.

Natasha was still trembling.

"What just happened, Gabriel?" she asked. "There were demons in those people. They tried to come into me…"

Gabriel took her into his arms.

"It's all right," he said, gathering himself. "They can't get into you if you fight them."

He lifted her chin and looked into her eyes.

"Don't ever let yourself be scared of them, Natasha," he said, remembering something he had read in his father's journal. "Demons are pathetic cowards. Fear's their only weapon, and the minute you call them on it, they scatter and run."

Natasha nodded with resolve. Behind Gabriel she could see Bahadur examining the crumpled bodies, a large combat knife in his hand. It was at that moment that one of the corpses began to shake violently. It launched itself at his back before she could cry out in warning.

It would have reached him were it not for a blurry form that appeared out of the glowing tunnel. It leapt through the air to impede the attack, taking the corpse by the neck and ripping off what was left of its head. Bahadur turned instinctively, ready to do battle with the new assailant.

"Don't hurt him!" cried Natasha. "We know that dog!"

Bahadur shot his head around, surprised to see the brown dog bound past him and into her arms.

"Shackleton!" exclaimed Natasha. "I can't believe you just did that!"

Bahadur frowned in confusion, walking cautiously up to the fallen corpses, and bending to sever what remained of their heads. As grisly as the task proved to be, he wanted no more surprises.

He returned to the group with a scowl on his face. Never before had he been required to do anything even remotely similar, and it was comforting for him to see Natasha smiling happily. Shackleton was attempting to nuzzle his head into her lap as she repeatedly pushed him away.

"No, Shackleton!" she said, laughing. "You're covered in zombie gore. Get away from me!"

Scotty was squatting on the floor next to his pack. He looked over at the corpses and then up at Bahadur.

"That was a little too close for comfort, mate," he said, snapping a cartridge into his gun and tossing the weapon up to the giant.

Bahadur snatched it out of the air and looked down at the smuggler, a puzzled expression on his face.

"I fixed a jammed cartridge that was in my pack. It's half empty so use it sparingly."

Amir put up a hand in a plea for silence. Footsteps were approaching from the passage above them. Bahadur spun instantly, levelling the gun. He had spotted several figures approaching.

"Who goes there?" he bellowed. "Stop or you will be shot!"

The figures came to a standstill at once, swaying as the earth shifted under foot. There were four of them in total. One of them was wounded and being held erect by two figures.

Oddly enough, they appeared to be dressed in medieval armour. Bahadur could see shields slung over their backs and drawn swords in their hands. The fourth figure wore the robes of a monk, and it was he who called out to them.

"Do not fire!" he cried. "We are friends of the Two!"

CHAPTER 16

Christian made his way along a route that cut through the last of the throngs. Almost an hour had passed since he first saw the great pyramid begin to emerge from the water. He had been high on a cliff then, and the way down had been fraught with danger. In some places he had been forced to call upon his servants for assistance, letting himself be lifted and carried by their festering hands.

Now he had arrived at last, and amid the panicked demonic whispering in his head he could see that only two knights remained to defend his brother's position. They were perched high atop a narrow flight of steps, their swords flashing as they held back the unrelenting hosts. Christian made his way towards them, the frantic hissing in his mind blotting out all other sounds.

He had seen his traitorous brother only moments before through the eyes of the undead, and watched in frustration as a group of his minions disobeyed his orders to kill him. Instead, they had charged down a long, glowing tunnel, overwhelmed by their frenzied attraction to the Two, and their insatiable desire to possess them.

Before the four renegade minions had fallen however, Christian had caught a glimpse of the Cube in Gabriel's hands. The Two were on the verge of finding the entrance to the Labyrinth. They had to be stopped immediately, but the last remaining knights still stood in his way.

"Kill your brother!" hissed the demons in his head. *"Kill him now!"*

At that moment one of the knights fell, leaving only one to defend the entrance.

"I am coming, dear brother," said Christian, his body shifting in and out of its reptilian state. "I am coming to destroy you."

CHAPTER 17

"He is the Consilio!" exclaimed the sturdy monk, gesturing to the unconscious Isaac. "Without him you cannot gain entry into the Great Labyrinth!"

Gabriel and Natasha looked at each other.

"Peralta," said Gabriel into his radio. "Did you just hear that?"

"I did," came the engineer's raspy reply. "He's got to be the missing alpha-wave sequence! You've got to get him to the entrance right away!"

"Boss!" said Amir suddenly, brandishing the timer.

Gabriel's eyes opened wide at the sight of it. Less than fifteen minutes remained.

My God... We're running out of time...

In a matter of seconds all were sprinting up the tunnel. Sir David and the remaining knight were carrying Isaac, with the bulky monk following close behind. He was last to arrive at a towering chamber located directly in the centre of the pyramid. Like everything else, its walls were organically shaped and glowing blue, its soaring ceiling held aloft by arching columns fashioned to resemble trees.

On a swelling mound in the centre of the chamber sat a dais. Three sculpted thrones were set upon it, each carved from stone and made to look as though they were comprised of tangled boughs.

At the foot of the thrones were two stone sarcophagi of simple design. A waist-high obelisk rose between them, emerging from a circular slab of black stone that measured a metre in diameter.

Brother Bernardo approached, pointing to the thrones as he struggled to keep his balance. The ground was shifting violently now, and a deep groaning sound came from it, ever-increasing in volume.

"The King must sit to the right of the Consilio!" he cried. "The Queen to his left!"

"We're not the King and Queen!" cried Gabriel over the tumult. "We're the Two!"

"They are one in the same, my liege!" hollered the monk. "Your souls are those of the ancient King and Queen, the builders of the Great Labyrinth!"

The tremors in the earth were becoming deafening now, and the sound of cracking stone and volcanic explosions filled the air.

"Only the two of you can help humanity survive this crossing! Only the two of you can open the way of Illac Domus, so that all may follow you into the higher spheres!"

Gabriel glanced over at Natasha.

"Ready?"

Natasha gave a decisive nod and Gabriel shot a glance at the knights. They acted immediately, carrying Isaac up the steps to the dais and placing him on the central throne. Brother Bernardo approached, bending next to him.

"Isaac," he said softly. "Wake up, dear friend. You must focus all your thoughts on the Cube."

Isaac opened his eyes and smiled weakly.

"I am ready," he whispered.

He was shuddering violently now, and his face was ghastly pale.

Gabriel looked at Natasha and then sat down in his throne.

"Let's do this."

Natasha followed suit, holding the Cube aloft as she did so. Nothing was happening. All eyes fell on Brother Bernardo. He was still kneeling beside Isaac. He looked up to face them, his brow knotted with grief and fear.

"The virus has taken him!" he cried. "The Consilio is dead!"

Gabriel rushed over and put two fingers on Isaac's neck, looking for a pulse.

"Amir!" he called back. "How much time have we got?"

"Eleven minutes, boss!"

"He's just unconscious!" cried Gabriel, his eyes alight with hope. "We've got to wake him up!"

Gabriel's eyes scanned Isaac's face in desperation. Natasha brought her hands to her head.

"What's happening?"

The room around her was warping and distorting in a manner that she could not understand. Peralta's raspy voice sounded suddenly over their radios. It was barely audible over the tumult.

"I'm totally feeling the gravitational effects on my brain!"

"Is that what this is?" cried Natasha.

"It's going to get way worse!" said Peralta. "It's not your sanity! It's just the Rift!"

Gabriel was battling with the effects as well. A desperation was taking him. He simply had to revive Isaac. There was no other option.

Acting on an impulse, he pulled him from the throne and laid him down on the shifting ground. The noise in the chamber was deafening.

"Breathe!" he cried, pumping his chest rhythmically.

When no response came, he increased his efforts and shot a glance over at Amir. The fate of the world was at stake, and they were almost out of time.

"Breathe, you stupid son of a bitch!"

"Gabriel!" screamed Natasha. "Gabriel!"

Gabriel stopped what he was doing and looked up at her, his eyes vacant. He could see her, but she seemed so distorted, so out of context. It was only then that he began to recall his experiences ingesting peyote cactus.

He had been assisting Amir with a university project on the Yaqui Indians of North-Western Mexico. They had experimented with the plants and herbs used in their shamanistic rituals. The symptoms he was experiencing now were almost identical, and the knowledge of the fact made everything change. He looked up at Natasha, a strange lucidity encompassing him.

"I'm sorry," he said, his anxiety slipping away. "I lost it there for a second..."

He rose unsteadily to his feet and took her hands into his. The ground was shaking violently.

"We're in big trouble, baby," he said. "The clock's running out."

The bishop's voice sounded suddenly over their radios. Peralta had patched him through from Gibraltar.

"All hope is not lost, my children!" he cried, and his voice showed signs that he too was experiencing the same mental distortions. "Remember that only truth and love will serve you now!"

"Gabriel," said Natasha, glancing down at Isaac. "The Cube can bring him back."

Gabriel looked deeply into her eyes.

"Of course it can," he said, nodding slowly. "We've still got nine minutes. We've still got a chance."

Natasha held out the Cube only to see it warping and shifting before her.

"We'll heal him just like we healed Amir."

The explosive rattle of Bahadur's assault rifle called everyone to attention. A mob of undead had just arrived at the chamber's entrance.

In a matter of seconds one had already fallen, its head turned to pulp by the last of Bahadur's bullets. Three more crumpled to the ground as Sir David and the other knight lopped off their heads. Even still the situation was deteriorating rapidly.

Unlike the narrow stairway they had earlier defended, the wide opening into the tunnel allowed for dozens of undead to attack simultaneously. The knights could do nothing to prevent them from entering into their midst.

"Dear God!" gasped Brother Bernardo.

A crippling force of the purest evil had entered into the hall now. Combined with the mind-altering effects of the Dark Rift, the demonic presence was paralyzing.

Strangled and discordant screeches were filling the space, and Brother Bernardo moved his hands to his ears instinctively, his eyes gaping in terror when he saw the younger knight fall. The chamber was teaming with undead now. It was only a matter of seconds before they arrived at the dais. After that, death would come quickly.

Only Gabriel and Natasha were unaffected by the attack. The chamber was shifting and lurching around them, but their minds were focused on something else; something not of this earth.

The demons had come to accost them with their age-old weapons of doubt and fear. They had filled the chamber with a coursing evil designed to distract them from their purpose, but Gabriel and Natasha were fully aware of their tactics. They negated the illusory darkness with ease, and in that instant the Cube exploded with blinding light. It was so intense that everyone in the chamber was forced to shield their eyes, and the undead recoiled from it in excruciating pain.

Outside the earth fell into its final cataclysmic seizures; its crust cracking, its mountains tumbling, and its oceans exploding. All around the planet those who were not perishing in horrific natural disasters were one by one falling into a void of dark insanity.

A paralyzing fear and confusion was taking root in the very soul of humanity, and like a spreading virus, it infested every living person, driving any hope of salvation from their twisting and contorting minds.

CHAPTER 18

Christian made his way down the glowing passage, consumed by his desire to end this insurrection, and secure his reign as emperor once and for all. A frantic mob of undead was flowing past him, rushing to replace those who had been felled by the knights.

Before their heads had been hewn from their bodies, Christian had seen his brother through their eyes. He had been unconscious at the time, with a gaping wound on his neck.

Christian scanned the twisted reptilian faces that surrounded him. He would have no shortage of help to destroy his enemies, but if his brother was still alive when he got to him, he would slaughter him with his own hands.

The ground lurched underfoot as he moved forward. He could sense the mind-warping effects of the Dark Rift but compared to the ordeals he had suffered at the hands of the Zurvanites, the mental distortions were inconsequential. Instead, he channeled his murderous rage to remain focused, ensuring he never lost sight of his objective.

"Kill your brother!" hissed the Zurvanites. *"Kill him! Kill him!"*

It took Christian longer than expected to arrive at the central chamber, and frustration was consuming him as he approached it at last. Near the halfway point the undead had begun to fall to the ground, shrieking in agony for some unknown reason. He had been forced to clamber over their ranks to complete the route.

Now, with the mind-contorting effects of the rift subsided, his purpose rang as clear as his wrath. He would kill his brother. He would bathe in his blood.

Christian scrambled over the last of the cowering undead to stagger out onto the hall's expansive threshold. What he saw before him made the Zurvanites in his mind explode with fury.

The Two were already sitting on their thrones, and his brother was occupying a smaller throne between them, his eyes open and impossibly alert. The sight of him well again transformed Christian's rage into turmoil and confusion. The wound on his brother's neck had completely vanished.

To make matters worse, in Natasha's upraised hand he could see the Compostela Cube, but its light was now white and blindingly intense. It was this that his army of undead were cowering from. By the intensity of their torment, he knew that the demons infesting them could not bear the Cube's emissions. Their wailing was ear-splitting.

Christian looked down at the beasts that trembled at his feet and pointed to the dais.

"Kill them!" he bellowed, but his voice was inaudible over their shrieks.

He looked up in time to see the Cube's energy suddenly double in intensity. It became so bright that he was forced to shield his eyes. Through his fingers he could see the lids of the two sarcophagi slowly opening, and at that moment a radiant sphere of blazing light exploded from within the stone arches above. What followed left Christian swaying dizzily on his feet, his jaw slack with disbelief.

A glowing procession of what could only be described as angelic warriors was swooping down towards him. They were comprised of translucent light and possessed of mighty wings and fiery swords. They were a thousand strong at least, and in the blink of an eye their multitudes were rushing past him like a coursing river, disappearing into the glowing tunnel that led to the lands outside.

Their effect on the demons was instantaneous. Not just in the great hall, but across the surrounding mountains and valleys as well. These angels constituted the most potent army ever assembled, and they attacked the undead everywhere they stood, their blazing white broadswords slicing through dozens of them at a time, leaving the corpses untouched but vanquishing the dark entities that resided within them.

Everywhere demons were exploding from their hosts like swarms of black hornets from their nests. An even louder wailing ensued just then, and these cries only subsided when all the unholy entities had plunged into the ground to disappear forever.

"Behold the glory of the higher spheres!" cried an elated Brother Bernardo, rising to his feet. "The angels of heaven have come to our rescue! The Cube of Compostela has been restored!"

It was at that moment that Christian locked eyes with Isaac. His brother was sitting on the central throne, his face alight with love and compassion directed solely at him.

"My little brother," said Isaac softly, and impossibly, Christian could hear his words. "My dear sweet brother. What have they done to you?"

Christian ground his teeth until they cracked, his features twisting into a mask of hatred and violence. It was because of Isaac that all this had come to pass. Every torment and degradation he had been made to endure throughout his life, had now been for nothing. His brother's love felt like a dagger in his back.

It was only then that the dark self in Christian reacted, and its wrath was unimaginably potent. It brought with it that final burst of vigour that comes to every entity on the threshold of death, and it served to detonate a conflagration of such hatred in Christian, that his sense of identity was stripped away. All that remained was pure destruction, and the desire to bring to oblivion anyone or anything he could drag down with him.

In the Cube's white light, the recently exorcized undead could now be seen stirring from their stunned positions. They were everywhere in the chamber, but they were moving slowly now, as they had done before they had become possessed.

Thankful of the reprieve, an exhausted Sir David had lowered his sword to catch his breath. Bahadur and Amir had done the same with their weapons. Christian saw this and blinked in disbelief as he scanned his surroundings.

Nothing lay between him and his brother except Natasha and the upraised Cube. Everyone in the chamber was staring at the artifact in amazement, and no one but his brother had seen him enter the hall.

Christian could feel his heart pounding in his chest. Out of nowhere a newfound hope had been given to him. It was still not too late. He would tear the life from Natasha and his brother and stop the Apocatastasis from ever happening. The Cube might have been reawakened, but victory was still within reach.

It was in the wake of this realization that an unexpected change began to take place in Christian. Black acid vitriol was pounding through his veins now. His slitted pupils had begun to dilate, and his scalp was tightening as the skin on the back of his neck began to thicken. He could feel the intoxicating power of Ahreimanius swelling in him like a cancer, and the metamorphosis it brought was almost orgasmic. The bones in his body creaked and snapped as they altered in size and shape, his joints popping as his muscles became imbued with outlandish strength.

Isaac's eyes were still locked with Christian's as the transformation took place, and his rapturous expression soon gave way to one of horror. What he saw across the chamber was no longer a man, but rather a venomous reptile, jerking in and out of existence like a phantom or wraith.

Gripped by shock, Isaac could only manage to point a finger and sound a muted cry as he saw the beast leap towards him. Natasha noticed his gesture and shot a glance over in time to see the creature advancing, her eyes going wide with fear.

With unimaginable strength and agility Christian was rapidly closing the gap between them. His hands and feet had grown talons, and he was clawing over the awakening dead like a lizard over loose rubble.

Sir David spotted him coming as well but could do nothing. Christian was moving too quickly, and his bloodied sword came up a fraction of a second too late. As it was, the knight had been the only line of defence between Natasha and Christian. The others could only look on in stunned disbelief. It would only be a matter of seconds before the beast reached her. Soon everything would be lost.

Christian's dark self watched as the space between him and his first victim closed. He could already feel his clawed fingers tearing her eyes from her face. He could already taste her blood. He would extinguish her pathetic life, and then he would take his brother's as well. He would eat their flesh. He would drink their blood. He would crush the Cube underfoot and cast the angels of God to hell.

For Natasha, everything had slowed into a lucid frame by frame succession. She watched dumbly as Gabriel leapt over Isaac but knew he would never get to her in time. His cry hung heavy in the air around her, and there was a desperation in it that confirmed what she already knew.

The beast that barrelled towards her carried with it too much speed and momentum. When it reached her it would be unstoppable. There was nobody close enough to save her. Natasha swallowed hard. The hour of her death had come.

How can this be? How could we fail now?

It was only when Christian was on the verge of bounding up the final steps to the dais and taking into his hands that which he had sought to destroy for so long, that he felt something snag his foot. His momentum allowed him to jerk free of it, but when his other leg became entangled, he felt himself being pulled to a stop.

In fury he looked down to see a slow-moving corpse grasping his ankle. Pain shot up his other leg a moment later, and he jerked around to see the bloodied teeth of an adolescent boy sinking into his thigh.

Christian bellowed in rage. All his will was bent on conjuring the wrath of his dark self again, but this time it did not respond. Ahreimanius had abandoned him, leaving him weaker and more vulnerable than ever before. It was only then that Christian lost his balance.

All watched as he toppled backwards into the hungry mob. Natasha's fate had seemed sealed, and now her assailant lay at their feet, prey to the beasts he had once commanded. Christian's reptilian state was collapsing rapidly as well, and in the space of a few seconds he had reverted to his pale self again.

A pressure of unspeakable magnitude was weighing down on him now, and he brought both his hands to his head in an effort to stave it off. Not only were the Zurvanites and the Fourteen Emissaries accosting him, but the Dark Lord Ahreimanius as well.

"You will pay dearly for this failure!"

Christian writhed in agony. His ears were bleeding from the mounting pressure, and his leg was exploding with pain as it was masticated and consumed. He looked around in horror. More and more of the undead were converging on him now, their distended jaws snapping hungrily, and their arms outstretched and grasping.

In one desperate attempt he kicked frantically at the corpse that was feeding on him. It recoiled from his repeated blows and chewed ravenously on the piece of flesh it had managed to tear free. A moment later Christian was back on his feet, limping towards the mouth of the tunnel. He was bleeding badly, and desperately fighting off the groping hands that sought to pull him down.

"I am your master!" he bellowed in desperation. "You will do as I bid! GET THEE DOWN!"

Christian was surrounded on all sides now. He scanned the hideous faces. These were no longer his reptilian servants. They had reverted back into mindless human cadavers again, and they were following the single, primordial instruction that had been programmed into the virus that infected them: A genetically imbued compulsion to feed.

He screamed in fury when a hungry mouth found his kidney. Everyone in the chamber was looking at him now, and his broken pride pained him more than all his wounds combined. He could see Natasha safe in Gabriel's arms, and his hatred of them felt as though it would consume him. He could see the gossamer angels, and his brother looking at him from the central throne above. He could feel their pity. He could sense their love. His humiliation burned like a white-hot furnace.

Christian screamed in rage and just then felt another jolt of pain. He jerked his head around to see the twisted visage of an old woman clamping her teeth into his shoulder.

More undead were latching onto him with every passing second now. One of them had succeeded in tearing the fingers from his hand, but Christian's attention was bent on something even more horrifying. In amongst the throngs, he could see the ghost of Dr. Bennington, its eyes glowing red.

"This was your doing, Christian," it hissed. *"You have no one to blame but yourself…"*

Christian felt his knees buckling under him. The doctor's eyes had suddenly burst into flames. His voice was like a surgical probe, stabbing into his brain without mercy.

"Now you will know the torment of the dungeons of Hades…"

Christian recoiled and crumpled to the ground. The grim irony of the situation was penetrating into him like a fast-moving poison. His organization had developed this virus. He himself had loosed it upon the world. The weapon designed to imprison humanity would instead imprison him. The horde closed in. He could see nothing but distended jaws and bloodied teeth now.

"In the name of Lucifer!" he screeched. "I order you to release me!"

But the teeming undead pressed down upon him nonetheless, feeding upon the flesh of what would have otherwise been their lord and master in another, darker world.

CHAPTER 19

Isaac looked at Gabriel and Natasha in turn, his eyes wide with wonder. The fourteen angel-warriors who had remained in the hall were gathering around them now, their gossamer forms indescribably beautiful and comprised solely of translucent light. Their presence had also purified the air, restoring the great hall to its former glory.

"Dear Father in heaven," whispered Isaac fervently. "How wonderful…"

The noble angels were radiating so great a peace that even the lurching earth had been temporarily stilled. Only a tranquil serenity remained. It was felt by everyone in the chamber, including Sir David and Bahadur, who were still engaged in the slaying of the slow-moving dead.

They had already decapitated the group of corpses that had taken Christian's life, and left their cadavers piled over his remains in a kind of macabre burial mound.

"It is the Two who have called this peace upon us," announced Brother Bernardo, looking at Gabriel and Natasha in turn. "In saving the life of the Consilio, they have not only opened their way into the Labyrinth but completed the primary part of their mission."

Natasha was the first to register his words.

"To bring peace to the hearts of those who will make the crossing…" she said, remembering what Suora had told her. "Only through an act of love could it have been accomplished…"

She looked down at the Cube in her lap, recalling the power that she and Gabriel had conjured in order that Isaac might be healed. By leveraging the gravitational energy of the galactic plane, the Cube had propagated their harmonious alpha-wave pattern to the entire collective consciousness, in effect, reaching and penetrating every sentient mind on the planet.

The results had been dramatic to say the least, awakening a peaceful, psychotropic bliss in the world's population. Across the planet, all traces of anxiety had given way to a state of pure rapture. In every region, every man, woman, and child had seen their terror transform instantly to serenity; every plant, animal, fish, and insect becoming peaceful and silent as the planet itself grew calm.

This reprieve had stretched on for a timeless moment, and when the earth finally did begin its quaking again, the peace and serenity of its inhabitants remained intact. Amir approached the dais with a profound calmness in his eyes. He was holding the timer out for everyone to see.

"Our alignment with the wormhole's getting close."

"Five minutes," said Natasha, her eyes focusing on the clock.

Brother Bernardo was first to awaken to the reality of the situation. The grinding sounds of shifting tectonic plates were once again filling the hall, and they were growing louder with every passing second. He had to holler in order to be heard.

"The Two must descend!" he cried. "They must find the entrance to the Labyrinth!"

"I thought *this* was the entrance!" cried Gabriel.

"The Labyrinth lies in the lowest sphere of Hades!" bellowed the monk.

Gabriel and Natasha exchanged a concerned glance and then looked back at Brother Bernardo.

"You will become separated!" he continued. "Only to be reunited at its entrance! You must open the Seals of Gnosis and enter into the Ostium Sanctus! All this must be done before the portal moves out of the Dark Rift!"

"And how long will that be?" cried Gabriel.

Brother Bernardo furrowed his brow.

"I do not know!"

"Well I do!" came the voice of Peralta from their radios. "If the vertical velocity of the solar system remains constant, it'll take precisely seventy-two hours to pass through the galactic plane! But that's of little use for the two of you! Time has no meaning where you're going!"

The chamber shook so violently that it seemed on the verge of collapse. The angels began to rise and exit the hall. The tumult was deafening.

"Hey!" cried Scotty, looking up as their translucent forms vanished into the ceiling. "Where are they going? Even they don't want to be in here!"

Brother Bernardo was also watching them depart.

"The Emissaries of the Kristos are ascending! Sarras will soon be destroyed! Every living person on Earth will be made to lose consciousness! Only when the first seal has been opened will the Cube reawaken the world!"

Amir was the first to do the math.

"Are you saying we're going to be unconscious for three days?"

Gabriel locked eyes with Natasha.

"Peralta!" he bellowed. "You guys have to leave right now!"

"I'm programming the navigation system to take us home!" hollered Peralta from the sub's helm.

He was tapping away at his keyboard furiously.

"Whoever's coming had better hurry up! Even that blue goo can't hold up the weight of a collapsing mountain, and that wormhole is right on top of us!"

Gabriel looked for Bahadur and found him standing with Scotty and Sir David. They were near the entrance of the chamber. All of the undead had either wandered off or been hewn down.

"Bahadur!" he bellowed. "Get everyone back to the sub!"

Bahadur turned to face him, with Scotty Roberts following suit. Amir was the first to voice what each of them was thinking.

"But what about you guys?" he asked. "How the hell are you going to get out of here?"

"We will be leaving this sphere," said Brother Bernardo, looking over at Isaac.

The latter was ruffling the fur atop Shackleton's head.

"You mean you're all going to die!" screamed Amir. "Boss! We're in a pyramid for Christ's sake. This is a tomb! There's no labyrinth in sight! Just two coffins with your names on them!"

"Amir's right!" said Peralta over the radio. "There's no labyrinth here! It's a dead end! You've got to come with us! The world will make the transition in peace now! Your job's done! There'll be another way to release the gnosis!"

"No, Mr. Peralta!" cried Natasha, looking with resolve at Gabriel. "You're wrong! There *is* a labyrinth, and we know the way into it!"

Gabriel nodded in agreement.

"We've got to do this!" he cried. "We're just going to be going somewhere else, that's all! We'll be fine!"

A deafening crash sounded suddenly from above, only to be followed by massive shards of falling stone. Amir looked down at the clock. Only a few minutes remained until the rift was entered into. When this happened, the poles of the planet would shift, and the real destruction would begin. Even with the sub's autopilot engaged, there was no guarantee they would survive the trip home.

"All right, boss!" hollered Amir reluctantly, pushing back his dreadlocks. "You've managed to slip out of every mess you've ever been in! I can't see why this one should be any different!"

Gabriel gave Amir a confident wink and then looked over to Bahadur.

"You've got three minutes!" he bellowed.

In a split-second Bahadur had burst into action, gathering the company together and herding them into the shifting tunnel outside. Only Brother Bernardo refused to leave.

"My place is with the Consilio, and with the Two!"

Isaac put his arm around the fat monk and smiled.

"We go to inner sanctum!" he cried, and then giving Shackleton a slap in the rump he bellowed:

"Go home, you silly dog!"

Shackleton darted to Natasha's side.

"You heard what Isaac said!" she hollered, pushing him away. "Go with Amir!"

Gabriel watched as a reluctant Shackleton joined the others.

"Now all of you get the hell out of here!" he cried over the tumult. "Now!"

In a matter of seconds all had evacuated the chamber, leaving the four of them standing in the midst of the towering hall. The tree-like columns were swaying above them as though they were being blown by some invisible wind.

"The Cube must be placed upon the gate!" cried the monk, pointing to the top of the waist-high obelisk that was positioned between the two sarcophagi.

Gabriel and Natasha hurriedly approached, inserting the Cube into a square-shaped slot at its top. The column sank quickly into the slab of black stone at its base, leaving only the top surface of the glowing Cube visible at its centre.

"This gate will mark the entrance to the Labyrinth in the lower spheres," cried the monk, pointing to the black slab. "The Consilio must now stand upon it!"

Brother Bernardo bowed to Gabriel and Natasha and gestured towards their sarcophagi, inviting them to enter.

"*To transcend the Cube is to see it in all things!*" he cried.

Gabriel took Natasha's hands in his. The chamber was literally collapsing around them.

"Ready?" he asked, trying to be heard over the clamour.

Natasha smiled bravely and nodded, giving him a quick kiss on the lips.

"Scared?"

"Very!" cried Natasha. "But nobody ever gets off the rollercoaster when it's about to go over the top!"

* * * * * *

Natasha was lying on her back in the sarcophagus. The clamour in the hall was deafening. To her right she could see Isaac standing fearlessly on the stone slab, the top surface of the Cube still glowing white at its centre. Brother Bernardo was standing at his side.

Natasha swallowed hard. The lid to her coffin was closing slowly on its hinges above her. She kept her eyes fixed on Isaac. He was standing erect in his tattered suit, his arms hanging loosely at his sides as he swayed with the lurching chamber. Around them, more and more debris was falling, and Natasha thought it remarkable that no one had been struck.

"Only by finding himself shall the King lose himself!" bellowed Brother Bernardo over the din. "And only by losing herself shall the Queen find herself! This is the way of the universe! For Truth is Love! And Love is Truth! And they are both the same!"

Natasha screamed in horror. A massive section of stone had come down on both him and Isaac as his words ended, obliterating them instantly. A split second later the lid to her sarcophagus began to seal itself shut. It closed with a stony thump and Natasha's cry was swallowed by the darkness.

All became still and icily cold, and Natasha began to shiver uncontrollably. Something was very wrong. A complex, stereoscopic pulsing sound was filling her ears now, and from within the tight confines of that lightless sarcophagus, the same demonic force that had accosted her and Gabriel not fifteen minutes before, was once again attempting to gain entry into her. Like a poisonous fog it twisted and pitched around her, and it was all she could do to keep it at bay.

A moment later she was falling, as though from a great height, and with her descent there came upon her a terrible and pressing weight. It was as though a great ocean of liquid density had enveloped her. It threatened to crush her, and it filled her head and body with excruciating pain.

In that moment Gabriel and Natasha were swallowed body and soul; sucked into the lightless void of the lower spheres as the planet slipped at last into the time-warping gravitational field of the galaxy's equatorial plane.

CHAPTER 20

When Natasha regained consciousness, she was enveloped in a pale fog. She was no longer in her sarcophagus but rather walking alone at night. A frigid gust broke the mist into tattered patches around her. Through bare and tangled boughs, she could see a waxing moon above. It cast a cold pallor on everything.

"My God..." she whispered, shivering with cold. "Where am I? Where's Gabriel?"

Around her lay groupings of crooked and ancient tombstones. She was standing in a neglected graveyard, its terrain disappearing into the gloom. She scanned the shadows, her eyes probing the crumbling graves.

The hissing whispers that had plagued her throughout her descent still echoed in her head. If what Brother Bernardo had said was true, she was now in the lowest sphere of hell. A cold shiver ran up her neck and along her scalp. There were shadowy, robed figures walking among the tombs. She could sense their evil.

They can't get into you if you fight them.

It was Gabriel's voice in her mind and Natasha found strength in it as she picked through the gravestones. Just then an iron gate emerged from the fog, with a gravedigger's cottage appearing behind it a moment later. It was a blackened dwelling, surrounded by thick briar, all dry and brittle and twisting. A path of greasy flagstones carved its way through to its door. Next to it was a tiny window glowing orange and warm.

Natasha looked up to see that the moon was no longer visible, and in the growing darkness the cozy window became impossible to ignore. It was not long before she found herself beside it, her hand reaching out to sound the knocker. The door began to open.

"My child," said the old woman before her.

"Suora?" whispered Natasha. "Is it really you?"

The old nun turned to open the way for Natasha to enter. The cottage had a low ceiling and a crude wooden floor, with two of its walls comprised entirely of packed earth. It was furnished with nothing but a single chair.

"Sit down, my child."

Natasha did as she was instructed. Outside a storm was approaching, and in a sudden flash of lightning she saw Suora's face change and distort unexpectedly. Her features were reptilian.

Natasha's eyes went wide with fear. Seven lightless figures were suddenly emerging from the earthen walls, their twisted bodies repugnant, and comprised of densely packed cinder. The whispering in her head was growing louder. These were the demons who had possessed her as an infant. She was sure of it. Seven of the Fourteen Emissaries of Lucifer. Of all the demonic entities in existence, they were the most powerful.

Natasha tried to move but found her body paralyzed with fear. The demons were gathering around her now, and each was pressing itself into her. She battled to keep them out, only to find that she was lying in a sumptuous bed now, in a dark and frigid room. Bending over her were Father Franco and Bishop Marcus. They were chanting in an ancient tongue, but their faces were twisted and evil, and their eyes glowed red.

Natasha jerked her head around to see an open window beside her. Its diaphanous curtains were billowing in the night wind. Outside, amidst twisted boughs and tombstones, a pyramid-shaped mausoleum was coming into view. It seemed to Natasha that blue light was emitting from the cracks around its door.

"The Labyrinth..." she thought frantically, her wide eyes darting from demon to demon as they pressed into her. "I'm forgetting why I'm here..."

Natasha knew she had to escape at once, but her fear was still too great. Try as she might she could not make her body move. It was like being in a nightmare.

The emissaries were sending their tentacles into her now, attempting to gain entry to her soul. It was taking everything she had to keep them out.

"You belong to Ahreimanius," hissed the demon who had taken the shape of Father Franco. *"Who do you think you are, coming into our*

realm as you have done? What did you expect would happen? You are Lucifer's now."

It was only then that Brother Bernardo's final words came to her mind.

Only by losing herself shall the Queen find herself.

Natasha closed her eyes and focused her thoughts. The solution to her dilemma lay in those words. She was sure of it.

Losing and finding...

With a flash of insight, the answer came to her.

Negative and Positive. Feminine and Masculine.

Ancient wisdom postulated that the human psyche was comprised of two halves: Two divine modes of being. The divine female was inward moving. Receptive, passive, negative. The divine masculine was outward moving. Creative, assertive, positive.

Her salvation lay in her ability to contact that part of her which was masculine. It was there where she would find the strength she needed to oust the demons. This was what Brother Bernardo had meant by the Queen finding herself.

Natasha struggled to think clearly. To lose herself was to do something inherently feminine. The riddle was suggesting that only by doing something feminine, could she gain access to the masculine part of her.

I need to let go... I need to let go now!

With all the will she could muster, Natasha did precisely what her instincts screamed she should never do. She let go of all her defences and became vulnerable to the demonic tentacles. She opened the doors of her soul to them.

No sooner had she done this than there appeared behind her a great void, and taking a leap of faith, Natasha let herself fall back into it, finding to her great relief that she did not fall at all, but rather floated safely above it, completely unharmed.

A great strength was pouring into Natasha now. It was masculine, assertive, and extremely proactive. When she opened her eyes, she could see that the demons had already withdrawn.

CHAPTER 21

Gabriel made his way through dark labyrinthine tunnels, their tangled paths plunging him deeper and deeper into the bowels of the earth. He was already being forced to walk in a stooped position, and the ceiling was becoming progressively lower as he advanced.

It seemed to him that he had been lost for hours, although it was difficult to be sure. Just as Peralta had predicted, time seemed to be distorted here, and his malfunctioning wristwatch only served to confirm this. To make matters worse, the batteries in his flashlight were beginning to show signs of expiring. His situation did not look good.

Gabriel stopped to make another addition to a rough map he had been drafting. By pacing off the distances and keeping note of all the turns and divergences, he hoped to at least not have to revisit the places he had already been.

He wiped the sweat from his brow. The winding passages had stripped him of all his confidence. He felt hopelessly lost and on the verge of panic. The earthen walls were closing in.

I'll never get out of here...

Gabriel scanned his surroundings. The beam of his flashlight had just fallen on yet another demon lurking in the shadows. He had counted seven of them so far, and although he tried his best to ignore them, he knew they would not be going away. They were poisoning his thoughts. It was only a matter of time before they began their attempts to possess him.

Gabriel pushed a hand through his messy hair and struggled to clear his mind. Natasha was surely in need of him, and he was of no use to her lost in this maze. He remembered how Brother Bernardo had warned them that they would become separated, only to meet again at the entrance to the Labyrinth. What if she were there already? What if she were in danger?

Gabriel plodded onward as quickly as he could, counting each pace and adding the data to his map. The ceiling height had been dropping consistently for the last while, and it was not long before he found himself navigating the passages on his hands and knees. A short while later he found himself gripped by a frantic desperation. Ashy black forms were emerging from the earth all around him now, whispering in cold, nefarious voices.

"We are the Emissaries of Lucifer."

Gabriel could feel himself starting to panic. He knew that these were the same demons that had possessed him as an infant, and this only made matters worse.

He battled forward in vain. He could see that not only was the way before him constricting, but the way behind him as well. It was only then that his flashlight failed, and an inky blackness enveloped him. The demons began their assault. He fought them with all his strength.

Get away from me you sons of bitches!

The air was becoming thick and difficult to breath now, as though he were running out of oxygen. Gabriel rolled onto his back and reached into his pocket, producing a half-used book of matches. He gasped aloud as he struck one to life. The earth had entirely closed in around him. He was in a grave, buried alive with seven twisting demons. He could feel them clawing at him. Their filthy nails were cutting into his skin.

Gabriel tried desperately to pull himself together. Something in him was insisting that this was not really happening. It was a dream. It had to be.

Only by finding himself shall the King lose himself.

They were Brother Bernardo's words, and Gabriel understood them at once. Finding himself meant making contact with his inner core. He pushed aside his fear and centred himself, feeling the tormenting demons recede almost instantly. Even still, he suspected that the full resolution of his dilemma lay in the second half of the riddle.

Why would the King need to lose himself?

Gabriel lit another match and forced his body to relax.

This isn't just about the King and the Queen. It's about the masculine and the feminine...

He looked down at the match. Its flame was brighter. There was more oxygen in the air.

Losing yourself. What could that mean?

A sudden thought came to his mind, and he spoke it aloud.

"Losing yourself is just another way of describing the act of letting go, of letting yourself be vulnerable."

Gabriel's voice was muffled by the proximity of the earth, but the sound of it was also sobering. It helped him to concentrate.

"Letting go is a psychological prototype of femininity," he said. "Discipline is a prototype of masculinity. Both of them exist within the human psyche."

The concept had been introduced to Gabriel in the Cube diary. His father had transcribed an ancient text into the journal. In his side notes he had written about masculine and feminine powers. True mastery over oneself, he had explained, could never be obtained unless the two forces were in perfect balance.

With sudden clarity, Gabriel recalled every word of the ancient text.

When the initiates fear their sexuality, the men let go when they should be exercising discipline, and the women exercise discipline when they should be letting go. Only by finding himself shall the King lose himself. And only by losing herself shall the Queen find herself. This is the way of the universe.

Gabriel struggled with the words. He could still not fully understand. If he were the King, why would he want to let go of himself in this of all places? Surely remaining in disciplined control here would be the best thing to do. Now more than ever, he had to be in contact with his masculine core; his inner King.

Gabriel noticed that the spaces around him were slowly increasing in size, as though the earth itself were pulling away. He lit another match and looked down at his feet. The tunnel was opening there as well.

It was not long before he could sit up, and just then he remembered the spare batteries in his pack. In his panic, he had completely forgotten about them.

Gabriel rose to his feet. The passages of the catacombs could now be seen branching off in all directions. He had followed the monk's advice and found himself. Because of this he had pulled himself out of danger, but now what? He was back where he had started.

Why would the King want to lose himself?

He produced his map and was about to resume his work when a complete understanding came flooding into him.

Up to this point, he had been relying on his masculine faculties to find a way out of the maze. He had kept a disciplined record of all his movements, but this was the last thing he should have done. The monk's words made this explicitly clear.

"What an idiot I've been!" he said, stuffing the map into his pocket. "My God, I hope it's not too late."

A second later Gabriel was speeding through the tunnels, listening into himself for directions at every branch he came to. Natasha had led them out of the catacombs in Rome by following her intuition, and intuition could only be accessed by letting go of the need to be in control. It was a feminine thing, and it was precisely what Gabriel would need to do if he ever wanted to find Natasha again.

He needed to contact his feminine core, but in order to do this, he first needed to be in complete control of himself, and this could only happen by contacting his masculine core first.

Only by finding himself, shall the King lose himself.

Gabriel sped through the tangled passages at full speed, putting all his faith in his gut. He could distinctly feel directions being called out to him as he ran.

Right, straight, right, left, straight.

The passages were becoming broader now, and in a few moments he came to single wooden door. He threw open the latch only to find himself in what looked to be a pyramid-shaped burial chamber. Everything was glowing in the familiar iridescent blue.

He sprinted across the room, passing a central tomb to arrive at a broad door in the opposite wall. He opened it to find Natasha standing directly before him. She looked radiantly beautiful.

"Natasha," he said, catching her as she fell into his arms. "How long have you been waiting here?"

She was beaming with joy.

"About ten seconds," she said, covering his face with kisses. "What took you so long?"

CHAPTER 22

Somewhere under the ocean.

Bahadur was the first to stir. He opened his eyes to find they were all well, and safely strapped into their makeshift harnesses. It had been a precaution that Peralta had insisted on, and Bahadur saw what a good idea it had been. Evidence of their tempestuous voyage could be found everywhere, yet apart from the general disarray, the bridge seemed undamaged.

"Bloody hell, mate…" came Scotty's groan.

Bahadur turned to see the smuggler untie himself and rise to his feet. He was rubbing a bump on the side of his head.

"That autopilot ought to have its license revoked."

"At least we're still alive," said a waking Peralta, his voice particularly hoarse. "And that's more than I expected. I wonder how Gabriel and Natasha are faring…"

"Are we receiving any communications from them?" asked Bahadur. "If we are awake, it must mean that the first seal has been opened."

"All our systems are down," said Peralta. "We have no way of knowing if they're trying to contact us."

"I feel like I spent the night drinking bad tequila," groaned Amir, rubbing his temples.

They heard a bark and then Shackleton burst onto the bridge with tail wagging. Sir David followed behind. They had been in the rear cabin during the voyage. Peralta rose from his seat and made his way to the back of the sub.

"Where are you going?" asked Amir.

"To find out why we're only running on emergency power," he said. "I'll be right back."

Not ten minutes passed before Peralta returned. He was muttering to himself, his hand scrubbing absently at his messy white hair.

"What's wrong?" asked Amir, slipping a cinnamon toothpick into his mouth. "Are we out of fuel?"

Peralta looked at him intently.

"The little diesel we have left is all gummed up. I'm polishing it right now, but it's going to take some time."

He returned to his control panel and began bringing the systems back online.

"It's really strange," he rasped. "I'd swear that fuel was ten years old. It's a good thing the emergency generator runs on butane, or we'd be in the dark right now."

Moments later, the bridge was aglow with the light of electronic gadgetry again. Peralta scrutinized one of the monitors before him, shaking his head.

"Amazing," he said. "There isn't a single satellite in the sky, or at least none that are functioning. It's a good thing I programmed the navigation system to use our topographical scans to get us out to sea. If I'd used the compass or GPS we would have probably run aground. As it is I have no idea where we are. It looks like the earth's poles really did shift."

Bahadur looked down at him.

"What exactly does that mean?"

Peralta took hold of the ballast controls.

"It means the earth's equator is in a completely different place than it used to be. If we're going to find out where we are, it's going to have to be the old-fashioned way."

Everyone watched the main monitor as Peralta brought the sub to the surface, their eyes opening with surprise at what they saw. There before them, shining in the sunlight, was the Rock of Gibraltar in all its glory.

"You did it, Captain!" said Scotty, slapping him hard on the back. "You brought us home, mate!"

Peralta shook his head in disbelief. Although he had programmed the navigation system to bring them back, with the tectonic shifting of the ocean floor, the chances of it succeeding had been a hundred to one at best.

"It looks beautiful out there," said Amir. "I thought I'd never see the sun again."

"We must not forget the radiation," warned Bahadur morosely. "The planet is poisoned and will remain so for many decades to come."

The giant smuggler turned to Peralta, only to find that the messy engineer was shaking his head, his white eyebrows gathered in confusion. Behind his thick glasses his eyes were darting between several gauges on the control panel, his fingers tapping away at two different keyboards simultaneously.

"I've triple checked these readings," he muttered. "There's no doubting they're correct..."

He sat back in his chair, scratching his head in confusion.

"What?" said Amir, coming to Peralta's side. "What are you looking at?"

In a moment Amir had himself spotted the strange anomaly on the control panel.

"What is wrong?" asked Bahadur, stepping closer,

Peralta swiveled in his chair.

"There would appear to be no significant levels of radiation outside," he said, shrugging with amazement. "Only trace amounts."

"How can this be possible?" asked Bahadur.

Peralta produced a pad of paper and began making hurried calculations.

"I'd need more time to really figure this out," he said, scribbling, "but the dissipation of radiation would appear to be directly related to the gravitational forces in the galactic plane."

He scribbled a bit more.

"It looks like a form of accelerated quantum tunnelling, just like in the Schrödinger equation... Beta particles, antineutrino's, gamma rays, they're all barely traceable. It's as though the detonation happened more than two hundred years ago."

"Are you suggesting that it's safe to go outside?" asked Amir, dumbfounded.

"Not only safe," said Peralta, moving back to the sub's controls. "Highly advisable. I didn't want to say anything before but we're running dangerously low on oxygen. If it weren't for the fact that we've been comatose for the last three days, we would have all suffocated in here."

"Well then let's get the hell out!" said Amir, smiling suddenly. "I don't know about you guys but I'm dying for some fresh air and sunshine."

He swung open the main hatch and everyone looked up to see a clear blue sky. A warm gust of air flooded the bridge.

"Something is not right," said Sir David as Amir climbed out. "It is still December. The air is much too warm."

Amir called down.

"You guys should really get up here," he said. "You're not going to believe this."

Peralta was last to emerge, poking his messy head out of the hatch in time to see a strange tropical seabird flying past. The others looked down at him, their faces alight with happiness. Surrounding the submarine were waters typical of the South Pacific, the air carrying a fragrant scent foreign to that of the Mediterranean Sea. Behind them the Rock of Gibraltar was covered in lush vegetation.

"My God," whispered Peralta in awe. "Look at all this plant growth. The galactic plane must have spit us out a couple of centuries into the future... I suspected we would be experiencing some distortions in time, but nothing like this..."

He scratched the back of his head.

"What I can't understand is why we haven't aged when everything else has. We should all be skeletons by now."

"It is as the Ascender's Prophecy foretold," said Sir David, a serene smile on his face. "The world has been born anew."

Scotty struck a match to light his cigarillo.

"We'd best fetch Anita then, mates," he said, exhaling a cloud of smoke. "The world ain't the only thing being born. She's probably ready to pop by now."

CHAPTER 23

Deep in Hades.

"There was a tomb in the centre of the mausoleum. It consisted of two sarcophagi. Natasha moved towards them.

"The gateway to the Labyrinth has to be around here," she said. "Brother Bernardo said we'd be reunited at its entrance."

Gabriel followed, noting the circular slab of black stone lying between the stone caskets. It was the same one that Isaac had stood on before they had descended, and at its centre, resting in the slot where they had placed it, was the Compostela Cube, glowing in iridescent blue again.

Gabriel looked over at Natasha to find that her attention was still focused on the sarcophagi.

"They're so beautiful..." she said, dazedly.

The stone caskets were identical to the ones they themselves had lain in, and there was something about them that demanded all their attention. Gabriel shook his head in trepidation.

"Those things are really creeping me out," he said. "Let's get out of here."

No sooner had he said this than their stone lids began to open. They both gasped in horror. Within the coffins were decomposing replicas of their own bodies, with sinister black vapours curling around them.

"What the hell is that?" stammered Gabriel.

He bent to get a closer look, but the toxic gasses had already engulfed the corpses. The mists cleared a moment later to reveal the mummified remains of two reptilian humanoids lying where the corpses had been. Each was arrayed in rich clothing and adorned with strange and beautiful jewelry.

Resting upon the body of the male reptilian was an elaborate shield, its surface adorned with the image of an elegant tree growing from a single seed. At his side was a beautiful lance, its shining blade engraved with the image of intertwining boughs. Gabriel was captivated.

"The Reptilian King and Queen..." he whispered in awe, "According to Brother Bernardo, we're looking at the remains of our own bodies from a previous life..."

He glanced over at Natasha and then back to the sarcophagi.

"Do you realize that these tombs are two hundred and fifty million years old?"

Natasha, who had initially turned away in horror, was now peering into the stone casket as well.

"I don't understand..." she said, her eyes wide with fear. "Why did we just see our own dead bodies in there?"

Gabriel looked at her but said nothing. There was a distinctly sinister presence in the chamber now. He tried to ignore it. He wanted nothing to distract him from the splendor of the archaeological find. The mummified bodies were irresistible to him. He bent closer to examine the spearhead. It was glowing in a ghostly hue of blue.

"Gabriel!" gasped Natasha, grabbing his arm.

He looked up to see that four robed figures had appeared immediately around them. Their forms were grainy and oscillating, and they exuded an air of icy wickedness. They were jerking violently from side to side, their robes grey and shadowy. Unlike the other demons, these figures had bodies similar to men, and they were soon reaching up to pull back their dark hoods.

Their voices were like venom.

"Insolent fools. You will bow to Lucifer at once!"

Gabriel and Natasha gasped when they saw their faces. Similar to the mummified remains, they too were reptilian, but still living, and looking older than anything could possibly be. A moment later Gabriel and Natasha were under attack, but this was like nothing they had ever experienced before. The assault was entirely psychic.

For Gabriel it came as an irrepressible urge to climb into the king's tomb, and he knew that Natasha was being manipulated in the same way. He could see her inching towards the queen's sarcophagus, her face growing more and more pale as the psychic assault continued. He made a concerted effort to speak. It took everything he had.

"Natasha..." he grunted through clenched teeth. "Stay away... from that coffin..."

But even as he said these words, he could see that he himself was climbing into his own sarcophagus. With all the strength he could muster he forced himself to look over at Natasha again. She was already settling herself down onto the mummified body, its brittle bones crackling beneath her.

Gabriel was mortified. Natasha's face was as white as parchment, and around her a black vapor was rising. The oscillating forms of the Zurvanites were so close they were almost touching him now. Gabriel heard himself trying to speak. It was like somebody else was saying the words.

"Let go... of her..."

He knew he had to act now or never. With desperate resolve he summoned all his strength and broke from the spell. In one swift motion he took up the king's lance and plunged it into the nearest Zurvanite. No sooner had he done so than all four ceased to flicker in and out of existence. They had suddenly become solid in form.

"What have you done?" hissed the Zurvanite who had been pierced, its reptilian eyes wide with surprise as it looked down at the spear in its chest. *"This is impossible... We are immortal..."*

The Four fell to the ground as one, and their tortured screeches were deafening. Gabriel watched in amazement as a flurry of insect-like particles exploded from their midst. Their ancient reptilian bodies were disintegrating before his eyes.

He looked at the spear in his hands, noticing only then that its head was glowing in the same blue as the Cube. He rushed to Natasha's side and lifted her out of the coffin.

"It's all right, baby. It's over."

She smiled weakly and Gabriel kissed her gently.

"Are you in pain?"

Natasha shook her head.

"I just feel tired..." she whispered, her eyes closing. "I need to sleep..."

Gabriel laid her down beside the circular slab in the floor. As they neared it, the Cube rose up from its slot and hovered an inch above it, as though it were being supported by a magnetic field.

"We'll use the Cube to make you better," he said.

No sooner had Gabriel taken hold of the artifact than the stone slab beneath it dissolved with a hiss, revealing a spiralling flight of stairs leading down into a chamber of glowing blue.

Gabriel wasted no time. He picked up Natasha and in a matter of seconds was laying her down on the floor of a cube-shaped room below, folding his jacket and placing it under her head. He looked up in time to see both the entrance and the flight of stairs melt into the glowing walls. The chamber had no exits now.

Gabriel took Natasha's hand in his. It was icy cold.

"Hey," he said, patting it gently. "You need to wake up."

He looked down at the Cube. It was beginning to grow dim.

"Ok," he said to her. "I want you to focus your thoughts on me. We're going to light up this Cube and use it to make you better again. Got it?"

Gabriel closed his eyes and concentrated, but no matter how hard he tried, he could not get the Cube to glow any brighter. On the contrary, in the ten minutes he had been trying it had grown even dimmer. Knowing that the Cube needed both of them in order to glow made it easy to see what was happening. He was losing Natasha.

Gabriel shot a worried glance over his shoulder. A circular pool had appeared in the centre of the room and water from it was already beginning to fill the chamber. When he turned back to Natasha, he saw that the liquid was already lapping around her head. There would be nowhere to escape if it continued to rise.

It was not long before Gabriel was treading water and trying to keep Natasha afloat on her back. He had searched desperately for a way out of the chamber but found nothing. He could only watch in horror as the last of the space filled. He took one last breath from the disappearing gap of air at the chamber's ceiling and let himself sink to the floor with Natasha in his arms.

My God, can it be that they really have won?

He looked down at her, his heart surging with grief and love, and the panic of approaching death. How could this have happened? They had come so far and at such great odds…

A deep serenity was coming over Gabriel now. They would at least die here together. He embraced the fact bravely. But just as Gabriel felt his lungs begin to spasm, he saw something that he could not understand. Natasha's chest was rising and falling rhythmically. She was breathing.

This is impossible…

Gabriel summoned all his courage and emptied his lungs, feeling his body inhale by reflex. He felt a burning pain as his lungs filled with water, only to be followed by the immediate relief of oxygen rushing through his system.

Within seconds he had grown accustomed to the strange feeling, and he recalled, as though from a long-forgotten dream, a distant memory of having breathed water before.

We were once reptilian….

Gabriel's eyes fell on the opening where the water had originated and swam towards it with Natasha in tow. He saw that it was in fact the mouth of a cave, one that led straight into the depths below them. Like the chamber, it too was covered in the glowing blue goo.

Gabriel descended into it with Natasha in his arms and soon found himself in an enormous underwater expanse. He looked down at Natasha and saw that she was opening her eyes.

"Gabriel," she said through unmoving lips.

She was smiling warmly now, but her voice seemed to be coming to him telepathically.

"What happened?" she asked. "I was in a dark prison, and then the water came to free me… Was I dreaming?"

Gabriel was smiling from ear to ear. He hugged her tightly.

"You gave me quite a scare, kid," he said without speaking. "From now on, no more sleeping on the job, OK?"

A formless being of translucent light approached them just then.

"Greetings, my dear friends," it said in the most harmonious voice imaginable. "From the House of God, I bring you many divine blessings. Follow me and I will take you to the Oracle. He will be the one to guide you through the seals."

CHAPTER 24

Gibraltar.

Peralta eased the submarine into its secret military port, steering the boat towards its berth on the south side of the cave. Amir opened the main hatch as soon as its hull broke the surface. He jumped onto the dock and secured the sub to its moorings, noticing just then that everything in the cave was covered in a thin layer of dust.

It's been two hundred years since we've been here...

He attached the gangway to the submarine and stood by while Bahadur and Sir David carried Anita out.

"Easy does it," said Peralta coming up behind them. "She might still be asleep, but she's also on the verge of giving birth. The last thing we want is to induce labour."

It was not long before everyone had settled into the familiar surroundings of the secret cave, with Peralta administering immediately to the old bishop and Cassano. They had found them lying unconscious on sofas in the common room, and just as he had done with Anita, Peralta administered intravenous drips, though he was unsure they would help. Anita's blood pressure had continued to drop regardless of the hydration she had received. Something more was at play here, something metaphysical.

Sir David squatted next to her, noticing the concern on Peralta's face.

"Before the apocalypse, I was the village doctor," he said. "No medical treatment will save our friends, Mr. Peralta. It is clear that the Two have not yet opened the first seal. Humanity will remain unconscious until they do."

"What I can't figure out is why *we* woke up," said Peralta. "It must have had something to do with our proximity to the wormhole when we made the crossing..."

Amir poked his head into the room. There was a lit chillum pipe in his hand. Peralta frowned.

"I see you found my stash in the cryogenic freezer."

Amir flashed an impish smile and exhaled a billowing cloud of smoke.

"You'd both had better come out here and take a look at this."

With their patients now cared for, Peralta and Sir David followed Amir into the main area, only to find Scotty and Bahadur waiting there with Shackleton at their side. Peralta sat down at his workstation and examined the monitor that Amir was pointing to.

"A trailer's appeared on the Cube's website," said Amir, exhaling another cloud of smoke.

He bent over and tapped a key to start the video. Bahadur came up next to him.

"It is called *Apocatastasis*," said the brown giant, frowning down at Peralta. "It appears to be based on a creation myth called *The Fall of the Angels.*"

Peralta glanced up at him and then looked back in time to see a line of blood-red text fade up on the monitor.

TO TRANSCEND THE CUBE
IS TO SEE IT IN ALL THINGS.

Moments later the trailer began, its dramatic computer-generated cinematography setting the stage. It told the story of how the earth had been formed as a means for the fallen angels to return to heaven, and how their lost souls had congregated here to evolve both physically and spiritually. The migration back to heaven would take hundreds of millions of years to complete.

The video played on. The reptilian race was at war and destroying itself with advanced weapons, all while the solar system plunged into the galactic plane. The ensuing cataclysm was absolute, and the destruction of the earth complete. Everything grew silent and faded to black.

An ancient rain forest appeared. Two hundred and fifty million years had passed now, and out of the primordial mists came the first human beings. They were the highest incarnations of the fallen angels yet; crude and primitive, but capable of greatness. A female human appeared superimposed over the scene. She stood floating in the centre of the screen, rotating slowly. Everything dissolved to white.

"That's where it ends," said Amir, looking over at Peralta. "Any idea why it's there?"

The scrappy engineer rolled his chair up to a keyboard and started to type.

"Go and get yourselves something to eat," he said, engrossed by the discovery. "I'm going to need some time to figure this out."

* * * * * *

Three hours passed before Peralta summoned them back. Several times they had gone to check on him, but they had always found him either bent in concentration or lying back in his chair with his eyes closed and his headphones on. This time he was fully present.

"All right," he rasped, gathering his thoughts. "I know this is going to sound crazy, but it appears that the Cube has created a video game."

"A video game?" asked Scotty, puzzled.

"The Cube's an advanced AI," said Amir. "Anything's possible, but why a game?"

Peralta rose to his feet and began rummaging through cluttered drawers while the others looked at him in bewilderment. He did not stop until he had produced four sets of earbuds and given them each a pair.

"This isn't your conventional video game," he said, inviting them all to sit down. "You don't play it by looking at a monitor. The technology uses binaural frequencies to stimulate the brain. Each ear gets its own set of frequencies, and the interference pattern in your head makes your brain think it's asleep and dreaming. The simulation's very convincing."

"How do you interact with it?" asked Amir.

"Just as you would interact if you were really dreaming," said Peralta, picking up a wireless tablet and plugging his headphones into it. "The Cube knows what you're thinking, and it knows what you want to do."

"How can it know that?" asked Amir.

"Because it's connected to every brain in the collective consciousness, remember? It knows what *everyone* is thinking."

"But why a game, mate?" said Scotty.

"I'll tell you inside."

Peralta tapped the screen of his tablet. After a few moments spent listening to a series of complex, stereoscopic pulses, they all fell asleep, only to awaken in a dark and densely populated city. The illusion was as real as waking life.

"Where are we?" asked Amir in awe.

The air was heavily polluted, and a bleak drizzle was falling. Amir looked over and found Peralta standing beside him.

"This is what is referred to as *Outer World*," he said, looking up at the jagged skyscrapers. "It's where the game begins."

"And who are all these people?" asked Scotty, looking at the dense throngs that filled the streets.

"Simulants," said Peralta. "If you told them they lived in a computer-generated world they'd say you were crazy. It's like the Matrix in here."

"Why are there so many people?" asked Bahadur.

"So they can be interacted with," said Peralta. "An avatar advances in levels through his or her interaction with people and events."

"I do not understand," said Sir David.

"The objective of the game is to find the *Seven Seals of Gnosis* and pass through each of them. It's all about going deeper and deeper into the game, but it's not as easy as it sounds."

"And why's that?" asked Amir.

Peralta paused to collect his thoughts.

"Seals are personal," he said, recalling everything he had learned. "They're unique to each avatar. They could be hidden anywhere on the planet, or even on other planets. To find them, you ask questions and get involved. You keep an eye out for clues that the Cube sends you. You follow your gut, and you watch your back. There are evil forces that are constantly working to stop you from finding the seals."

Everyone looked at Peralta, trying to understand.

"Moving through the game is like moving through life," he said with a shrug. "It's all about learning and evolving. The gnosis for the first seal isn't unlocked yet, but if it were, a player could study that gnosis, think about it, and then apply it to everything his avatar did in the game.

"Once you've amassed enough experience points and fully assimilated that seal's gnosis, you can pass through it and move into the next inner level. The Cube's constantly scoring you on your avatar's reactions to the tests and trials it sends."

"Tests and trials?" asked the smuggler.

"They're designed to bring out your weak points so that you can eventually learn the skills you need to get through your seal. Finding each seal and passing through it is the objective. I can't begin to describe how brilliant this game is. Apocatastasis is the most awesome MMORPG imaginable."

"What's a MMORPG?" asked Scotty, cocking an eyebrow.

Amir was shaking his head in disbelief.

"It's an acronym that computer geeks use. It stands for *Massively Multiplayer Online Role-Playing Game.*"

Peralta manipulated his tablet, and they appeared in a circular room of grey, polished stone. At its centre was the shell of an avatar in the process of being formed. It was hovering weightlessly over a stone dais and connected to dozens of liquid-filled tubes that emerged from the ceiling above.

"Bloody hell," muttered Scotty, scrutinizing the body.

Its skin was still only partially formed.

"Every player gets to build his or her own avatar," said Peralta. "It's really cool."

"When can we start playing?" asked Amir.

Peralta shrugged and tapped the tablet to terminate the simulation. They awoke simultaneously a moment later, as though from a deep sleep. Peralta yawned.

"I think we'll be able to create our avatars once Gabriel and Natasha open the first seal and wake up humanity."

He looked over at the bishop and Anita as they slept.

"I just wish they'd hurry up…"

CHAPTER 25

Deep in Hades.

Gabriel and Natasha broke the surface of the water to find themselves close to a tiny beach. Behind them a half moon was hanging over a mist enshrouded lake. They swam forward and made their way onto the sand, doubling over in fits of coughing as the water left their lungs. Their angelic guide had just disappeared.

"That was a very strange experience," said Natasha, gulping in the air.

Gabriel was looking around and shaking his head in disbelief.

"This has got to be some kind of a lucid dream..."

It was only when he had fully come to his feet that he noticed a hermit's cabin not a stone's throw away. He turned to see that Natasha had spotted it as well.

"Shall we go?"

Natasha took Gabriel's hand and pulled him forward.

They arrived to find a crude image painted on the cabin's door. It consisted of a seven-pointed star, with the bearded face of a man crudely drawn at its centre. Behind the star was an inverted triangle, its outer points holding a sun and moon, with the image of a cube at its bottom-most point. Natasha recognized the icon immediately.

"This is an alchemy mandala," she said, looking over at Gabriel. "It was used by ancient alchemists to illustrate the seven operations of the Philosopher's stone; a method for turning lead into gold."

"And what's with the cube at the bottom?"

"It represents the physical body, or matter," said Natasha, pointing out various parts of the drawing. "The Sun represents the soul; the moon represents the spirit. If you notice, there's a second upside-down triangle drawn over the bearded face in the middle. That's a symbol of cosmic consciousness, or the Christ consciousness."

Gabriel scanned the cabin's facade.

"Let's see if there's anyone inside."

He had no sooner knocked on the door than it opened instantly.

"I have been expecting you, my Lords," came a voice from within.

They entered to find a black-robed priest standing in what could only be described as an alchemist's den. It was a cluttered, smoky chamber crammed with overflowing bookshelves, half walls of scrolls, and rough-hewn worktables laden with bubbling beakers and primitive laboratory equipment.

The man appeared to be in his sixties, with a full beard and raven black hair. On his breast hung the same Tree of Life symbol that they had seen engraved on the reptilian king's shield, as well as on the massive doors that had led into the City of Sarras. He gave a low bow.

"Dear King and Queen," he said reverently.

Gabriel shot a puzzled glance at Natasha.

"We're looking for the oracle," she said. "Can you help us?"

The man bowed low again.

"You have grown into a beautiful woman, my Queen."

"Thank you," said Natasha with a smile. "Have we met?"

"But of course," he said. "The two of you helped me find the tomb of James the Just, and with it, the Compostela Cube."

Natasha tore her eyes from the priest and glanced over at Gabriel.

"You're Gutierrez de la Cruz?" she asked, looking back at the man.

"That is I," he said. "Come in. You are both cold and wet. I will light a fire so that you might dry yourselves."

Gabriel and Natasha were just finishing the soup they had been given when Gutierrez emerged from an adjoining room. He came and sat down near them, moving aside a pile of scrolls.

"Thank you," said Natasha, laying down the empty bowl. "Will you be taking us to see the oracle now?"

"I am the oracle," said Gutierrez, turning to gaze into the crackling fire, his eyes distant. "Long ago I stood at your side and assisted you with your great plan."

He paused for a moment and then added, "Life is a labyrinth and truth is its only exit."

Gabriel exchanged another confused glance with Natasha.

"You said you were expecting us."

Gutierrez's eyes returned to the flames.

"I foresaw this meeting."

Gabriel looked around at the cluttered laboratory.

"What year is it?"

"It is the year of our Lord, eight hundred and ninety-eight," said the priest. "It was thirty-three years ago to this day that you both visited me in a dream. It was also the day I landed on this island."

He turned to look at Gabriel and Natasha over his shoulder.

"You are much more than you think you are, my King and Queen. It will be my task to help each of you regain the knowledge that you once possessed."

Gabriel rose and moved to the window. Over the last few minutes, a thick fog had engulfed the cottage.

"Is this the island of Sarras?"

The alchemist rose to his feet with groan.

"It is, my liege."

"Above the reptilian city," ventured Natasha. "By the Portal of Ahreimanius."

Gutierrez gave a nod.

"You must never forget that your physical bodies are not present here, my Queen," he said, "but rather your ethereal bodies. You are experiencing an altered state of consciousness; a simulation created by an ancient technology. It is similar to a dream, but unlike a dream, there is little difference between it and waking life. Harm can befall you here. You remain mortal."

Natasha looked at Gabriel and then back to the priest.

"Are you saying that our real bodies are still inside those coffins?"

Gutierrez remained silent.

"But what will happen to them?" she asked. "The chamber we were in was collapsing all around us. We'll be buried alive."

"If you do not find the Ostium Sanctus," said Gutierrez, looking back into the flames, "your fate will be much worse than that."

He snapped from his reverie and made his way briskly to the door. The night fog spilled over the threshold as he opened it.

"We have spoken enough, my lords," he said. "You must begin your final quest. I will take you to the first Seal."

Gabriel and Natasha followed Gutierrez through foggy woods until they arrived at a circle of standing stones. The place was unsettlingly familiar to them both, and a dim recollection of having once been here surfaced in each of their minds.

At the centre of the clearing, where the large monolith had been, could now be seen a jagged pit, with a flight of crudely hewn steps descending into it. A viscous fog spilled down over them, sinking into the depths.

"I cannot instruct you as to how to navigate this labyrinth," said Gutierrez. "My role is solely to help you remember what you have forgotten."

Gabriel peered into the gloom and reached into his pack for his flashlight. Gutierrez put a hand on his shoulder.

"Let the Cube light your way, my King."

Gabriel gave a nod of understanding and brought out the glowing artifact instead. He looked over at Natasha to find her smiling back at him.

"Stay close," he said, stepping into the pit.

It seemed that more than an hour had passed before the narrow tunnel they had been traversing arrived at a chamber at last. It was circular in shape, and barely three meters in diameter. Seven blazing furnaces lit the space, and their rounded openings were spaced evenly around the room. At the centre of the floor was a flat, golden disc about the size of a manhole cover. Cast into its surface was the image of a four-petaled lotus flower.

"That's the symbol of the *Muladhara*," said Natasha, wincing at the heat from the surrounding furnaces. "It's the Hindu *root chakra.*"

Gabriel wiped the sweat from his brow.

"That means we're here. This is the first seal. What do you know about the Muladhara chakra?"

"It sits at the base of the spine," said Natasha. "We both have a scar there."

Gabriel nodded and squatted next to the seal.

"What else?"

"It's associated with calcination," she said. "The first of the Seven Stages of Alchemy."

Natasha passed her hands lightly over her face and sat down next to Gabriel. She tried to forget the heat and think clearly.

"What exactly is calcination?" asked Gabriel.

"It is the fire of introspection," announced Gutierrez from the entrance of the chamber.

"Why fire?" asked Gabriel.

Gutierrez raised an eyebrow.

"Pride is always the biggest hindrance to spiritual evolution," he said. "It must be recognized and eliminated so that the ego might be ousted from its customary seat of power. The humbling of the ego is an uncomfortable process. It feels to the initiate like a kind of burning."

Natasha pulled the Book of Khalifah from its watertight bag in Gabriel's pack. It was heavy from the abundance of gold leaf on its pages. She laid it down on the stone floor.

"This seal is paired with Prajñā," she said, opening the gem encrusted book. "Prajñā is the first Divine Action."

Gabriel nodded.

"The Buddhist contribution to the Cube."

"It's the first stage of *The Noble Eightfold Path*," said Natasha as she scanned the page. "It says here that Prajñā means Wisdom, or Discernment. It's about seeing things the way they truly are, as opposed to the way you think they are, or the way you'd like them to be.

"Once you've learned how to apply Prajñā to yourself, it becomes possible to apply it to life, and to other people, but it always begins with the self. Know yourself, and you will know the world."

Natasha turned the page and read aloud a riddle that was written there.

The eyes of the mind are many.
The truth is always illusive.
An infant's vision is nearsighted.
Its conclusions must always be questioned.

In the Royal Palace,
Bejeweled curtains are never hung where there are no windows.
Therefore, the Two say:
Better an ugly hole in the wall
And self-loathing.

To seek perfection is noble.
To embrace imperfection is majestic.

Natasha looked up from the book, her face lit by the fiery furnaces.

"What do you think?"

Gabriel frowned.

"I think self-truth is a monster nobody wants to look at."

He studied the seal and noticed a square indentation at its centre.

"It seems about the right size, doesn't it..."

Natasha watched as he inserted the Cube into the indented slot. In that instant the artifact began to glow in a deep crimson, and both she and Gabriel clasped their heads in pain.

"Ouch!" exclaimed Natasha. "Did you feel that?"

Gabriel nodded. No sooner had the Cube changed its colour than they had experienced a brief, stabbing pain in their temples.

"The discomfort arises as your temporal lobes are synchronized to the Cube," said Gutierrez. "When you fully understand the wisdom the riddle is relating, your brains will generate the correct alpha wave sequence and the seal will be opened to you. Do not dally, the heat in this chamber will soon become lethal."

Natasha wiped the perspiration from her face, noticing only then that the entrance to the chamber had completely vanished. The only way out was through the seal. She began to feel claustrophobic.

"The first two lines are easy," she said. "There are so many different ways to look at something, that it's always hard to know what the truth is."

Gabriel nodded in agreement.

"The next two lines struck a chord in me," he said, thinking. "Babies are all born nearsighted. Taken as a metaphor, it could mean that as children, our understanding of things is limited."

"And?" asked Natasha.

Gabriel shrugged.

"A few years back it occurred to me that many of the opinions I had about myself had been formulated when I was a kid, using childish logic. They weren't true at all, but I'd had them so long I never thought of questioning them."

"I understand," said Natasha. "And if this Divine Action is about seeing yourself as you really are, what better place to start than with your childhood images?"

Gabriel nodded.

"The trouble is they're really hard to find. They operate like subroutines in your mind."

Natasha chewed her lip and then drew the connection.

"If traumatic circumstances in a person's childhood made them form the opinion they were inadequate, then they're always going to believe they're inadequate, until they realize that it was just a childish conclusion they made, and that they're really not inadequate at all. Until the person does this, they'll always be trying to act in ways to counter their perceived inadequacy."

Gabriel nodded.

"And those counter measures will literally make them inadequate. When you try to fix a problem that doesn't exist, you're bound to create a real problem."

Natasha's eyes opened wide as the realization struck her.

"The result is that you become what you're struggling not to be," she said. "It's a vicious circle. The more a person tries to act in ways that counter an imaginary problem, the bigger the problem gets, and the more he or she has to try to act in ways to counter it.

"It goes round and round. The only way to break the cycle is to fully understand that the original problem was based on a childhood image, and that the image was false. The truth is there's no problem."

Gabriel nodded.

"So, the first part of the riddle is all about questioning the things you've always believed to be true about yourself."

Natasha read the second stanza aloud. It was getting unbearably hot.

In the Royal Palace,
Bejeweled curtains are never hung where there are no windows.
Therefore, the Two say:
Better an ugly hole in the wall
And self-loathing.

"This is all about seeing yourself for what you truly are," she said, looking up from the book. "And not trying to cover up the ugly things with pretenses or shifting the blame away from yourself."

"All self-deception has got to be eradicated," said Gabriel, amazed by his deep understanding. "The truth about yourself has to be relentlessly searched for at all costs, even if it makes you hate yourself when you find it. *Better an ugly hole in the wall, and self-loathing.*"

"Calcination is the most unpleasant of all the alchemical stages," said Natasha. "It's a direct attack on personal pride, and it truly does feel like burning."

"As you can now see, my Lords," said Gutierrez, bowing. "You are already in possession of the gnosis. You acquired it when you were King and Queen, long ago. All that is required is that you remember it."

Natasha looked up at the priest. He was right. She knew these things, even if she could not recall where she had learned them.

"And the last two lines?" asked Gabriel.

"That's easy," said Natasha. "The key to true self-honesty is your willingness to embrace your imperfection. As long as your ego is fixated on being perfect, you'll never be able to walk the path of Illac Domus. Your pride won't let you."

Gabriel nodded as a full recollection of the first stage of the gnosis flooded into him.

"Prajñā's all about striving to be perfectly imperfect..."

"Look!" exclaimed Natasha. "It's dissolving!"

Gabriel snatched the Cube from its slot just as the seal disappeared beneath it. It left a dark hole in the ground with a ladder descending into it.

"Come on," said Gabriel, rising to his feet and shouldering his pack. "Let's get out of this oven."

CHAPTER 27

Gibraltar.

Major Richard Roberts awoke on a sofa just outside the governor's chambers. His head was aching, and his mouth was parched. He sat up and looked around, waiting for the fog in his mind to dissipate. It took a while before he could remember what had happened.

His eyes fell on the coffee table before him, and he spotted a copy of the emergency bulletin he had circulated after Bishop Marcus had given him the news about the galactic plane.

The Governor of Gibraltar has issued an
EMERGENCY NOTICE
Please be advised of the possibility of dizziness and temporary loss of consciousness occurring as the result of a rare cosmological event to take place at precisely 11:11am on Dec. 21st. You are advised to find a comfortable place to sit or lie and remain there until the event has completed its natural course.

What had occurred just prior to this event, however, had been completely unexpected. Roberts could still feel evidence of the profound euphoria that had overcome him just before the crossing had taken place, and apart from his tremendous thirst and aching head, a happy excitement still seemed to be surging in his heart; one that was completely at odds with the gravity of the situation.

This is ridiculous. Why do I feel so merry?

Roberts sat up and looked around to make some very peculiar observations. He reached over and picked up the bulletin, only to find that the paper it had been printed on was yellow and brittle, as though it were very old.

What was more, everything in the room, including himself, was covered in a fine layer of dust. Studying his surroundings, the major noticed that all the plants in the room were missing. Only the soil in their pots remained. He rubbed his face in an attempt to fully awaken.

I saw those plants being brought in from the Convent only the day before yesterday. What the hell is going on?

Just then the governor's nurse entered the room. She was carrying a tray with a pitcher of water and some glasses. She seemed dazed, but like the major, she was at peace. In her eyes was a glimmer of the same excitement that Roberts was feeling.

"Hello, Clara," he heard himself saying. "Is everything all right?"

She stopped and gave him a smile, her pretty eyes sparkling.

"I think so," she said. "But I must say, sir, everything seems rather odd today. I think that cosmological event left me a little out of sorts. I woke up so thirsty... I thought I'd check on the governor and see how he was doing. Would you like a glass of water, sir?"

Roberts took the proffered glass and drained it in a single draught.

"Thank you, Clara," he said. "I was parched as well."

She walked to the door of the governor's chambers, but stopped and turned to face him before entering, her hand still on the knob.

"Why is everything covered in dust, sir?"

The major held her gaze, his brow furrowing ever so slightly.

"I'm not really sure," he said, and then he looked down at himself. "Tell me, Clara. Do you find that your clothes feel," he searched for the right word but drew a blank, "...funny?"

"Why, yes, sir," she said, nodding in earnest. "I do. They seem almost brittle. It's quite strange."

She gave a shrug and then followed it immediately with a cheerful smile, disappearing into the governor's bedroom.

Roberts rose to his feet, his head finally clearing. He produced his mobile phone but found it was not working, only to check his two-way radio and discover the same.

"Faulty batteries...?" he muttered to himself. "Very strange..."

He shot a glance at the phone behind the receptionist's desk and walked over to pick up the receiver.

"This is Major Roberts," he said after dialing. "Get me Captain Brown, please."

There was a pause.

"Captain," he said, his right eye twitching. "Can you give me a status report?"

"Yes, sir," replied the officer happily. "And it's good to hear from you, sir. Happy Christmas!"

"Thank you, Captain," said Roberts, cocking an eyebrow. "But Christmas isn't until the day after tomorrow."

"I'm afraid that's not the case, sir. It would appear that we've been asleep for quite some time. It's Christmas morning, sir. We only just checked our clocks with Geneva."

For a moment Roberts was speechless.

Three days. That's why I feel so groggy.

As odd as it seemed, it truly did feel like Christmas morning, and his heart was happy, though he could not understand why. There had been a nuclear strike in the Strait. Tens of thousands were dead. The world was at war, and Anita and his unborn child were still trapped in a cellar with supplies running low. He had absolutely no cause to be happy, yet he was, and this confused him more than anything else.

"There's something else, sir," continued Brown over the phone. "It's difficult to explain."

"Well spit it out, Captain," said Roberts, emerging from his thoughts.

Brown cleared his throat.

"For starters, sir, almost everything is offline," he said. "The only thing that's still working is our geo-thermal generator, and even that's shown signs of exceptionally heavy wear, sir. It's on the final redundancy system, and the electrode clusters are on the verge of failure. The technicians are amazed that they can still be producing hydrogen and oxygen in the state they're in. If they go, we're as good as dead, sir."

"I'm well aware of that..." said Roberts. "What do they think the cause is?"

"Entropy, Major," said Brown. "It would seem that all our systems have experienced substantial amounts of decay over the last three days."

Roberts thought about the batteries in his phone and the yellowed quality of the bulletin paper.

"What's the life span of an electrode cluster under continuous use, Captain?"

"Just a minute, sir," said Brown. "I'll find out."

There was a brief pause.

"Fifteen to twenty years, sir, maybe longer. There's no reason why we should have gone through all ten clusters."

The nurse emerged from the governor's suite.

"Major," she said quietly, her eyes filled with tears. "The governor wants to see you."

Roberts gave her a concerned nod.

"Captain," he said. "What the hell's going on?"

"We're not entirely sure, sir."

Roberts turned to look at the nurse, doing the math in his head. If the clusters were any indication, two hundred years could have passed in the space of three days.

"I'm going in to see the governor now," he said, moving to hang up the phone. "I'll be in the control centre as soon as I'm done. Get a team on the redundancy electrode clusters right away. We can't afford to run out of power."

Roberts entered the governor's chamber to find the room dimly lit. The nurse approached and clung to his arm. Her face was wet with tears, and she was smiling sadly.

"What's wrong, Clara?" whispered Roberts, trying to comfort her.

The nurse shook her head. She was unable to speak, and Roberts knew why. The old Duke was dying. He made his way to the bedside and laid a hand on the governor's shoulder.

"I'm here, sir," he said gently. "You wanted to see me."

The governor opened his eyes and smiled tenderly.

"My faithful Aide de Camp," he said weakly. "Give me a status report. What is the condition of the Rock?"

"It took us three days to pass through the galactic plane, sir," said Roberts. "We've suffered some damage. It would appear that the increased gravity has not only affected our instrumentation and mechanical systems. It appears to have also altered the way time has passed, sir, as odd as that might sound. Our technicians are looking into it as we speak. Many of the systems are showing signs of severe entropy. It's as though a couple of centuries have passed in the period of three days."

The old knight nodded slowly and then smiled.

"That would make me very old indeed, now wouldn't it, Major," he said with a weak smile. "I needn't feel bad about moving on."

The governor pointed feebly to his night table and Roberts saw an envelope there. He picked it up. It was yellow and brittle, just like the bulletin.

"Open it," whispered the governor, smiling softly.

Roberts obeyed. Within was a document announcing his official appointment as the new governor of the now independent Gibraltar. Along with this was the duke's last will and testament.

"Everything I have shall be passed on to you, Richard," he said weakly. "You are the son I never had."

"But, sir," said Roberts. "There's no need for any of this. You'll soon be well."

The old governor smiled affectionately.

"Tell me about Anita," he managed to say.

Roberts could see that the life was beginning to leave the old duke.

"She's still locked up in the cellar, sir," he said, looking down.

"All will soon be well, young man," came the weak reply. "Do not fret..."

The governor released a long breath and then closed his eyes. Roberts bent closer, his gaze glassy and sad.

"Watch over Gibraltar..." whispered the dying knight. "Keep her safe..."

With these words the governor passed away, his face a mask of serenity. Roberts lowered himself to his knees next to the bed. He had loved the old man like a father.

Goodbye old friend...

Five minutes had not passed when Roberts heard the door opening slowly behind him. He glanced over his shoulder with tear-filled eyes, amazed to see his brother Scotty enter the room.

"I always liked that old bloke," said the latter, nodding sadly. "Even though the bastard would have locked me up without a second thought."

Roberts' heart was pounding in his chest upon seeing his brother, but he would not allow himself to rejoice just yet; not until he was certain. His words came out in a choked whisper.

"Did you bring her back?"

Scotty's smile was warm.

"Just like I promised, big brother. She's waiting to see you."

CHAPTER 28

In the Labyrinth of Sarras.

Gabriel and Natasha pushed their way through tangled and encroaching passages. They had been doing this for more than an hour now and Gutierrez was nowhere to be seen. They needed to find the seal that would take them into the next inner level of the Labyrinth, but there had been no trace of it anywhere.

"We've got to be getting close," said Gabriel, holding out the Cube to light their way.

The tunnels they traversed burrowed their way into the densely packed earth, moving within what Gabriel and Natasha knew was a cube-shaped structure. Forks in the warren appeared constantly, and their intuition always told them which path to take. It was as though they knew the way.

"I think it's here," said Natasha, wiping her brow with the back of her hand.

A low breach had appeared suddenly to their left. It opened into a somber, cavernous hall. There was a black pool at its centre, echoing the chamber's oval shape. There was something out of context in the space as well.

"Are those what I think they are?" asked Gabriel, cocking an eyebrow.

"I don't get it..." said Natasha.

Oddly enough, the dark pool was encircled by dressing mirrors, each as tall as a man and numbering fourteen in total. As they approached them, they could see a flight of concentric steps leading down into the pool's opaque, black water.

Natasha opened Gabriel's pack and removed the Book of Khalifah while he scanned the chamber for Gutierrez. The alchemist was nowhere to be seen.

"Which seal are we looking for?"

"Taoism and Confucianism," said Natasha, sitting down cross-legged and opening the book on her lap. "The Divine Action for this seal is called *P'u*."

Gabriel frowned.

"What does that mean?"

Natasha looked up at him from the book.

"Roughly translated it means, *The Uncarved Block*."

Gabriel held her gaze.

"It's a symbol for an unbiased state of awareness," she explained. "In the state of P'u, nothing is good or bad, there's only what is, without judgment. The metaphor of an uncarved block describes an object or an event in its original state, before the mind has been able to shape it into something with its judgments and labels."

Gabriel nodded.

"And how does the second stage of alchemy fit into this?"

"That would be Dissolution," she said. "It refers to the dissolving of the constructs that make us want to judge and classify things. It opens the initiate's mind so that he can adopt new vistas and re-evaluate his opinions."

Gabriel understood at once.

"So basically, the ugly character traits that were found and calcified in the last stage, are now dissolved into a new substance that's neither good nor bad."

Natasha nodded and looked down at the pool.

"There's something symbolic about those mirrors, Gabriel."

Gabriel moved away from Natasha and approached one of them. They were supported by armatures that allowed them to be angled upwards or downwards, but unlike regular mirrors, these had warped surfaces that offered severely distorted reflections. The pool itself was no less mysterious. Its water was as black as a void and seemed to be warning them that its surface should in no way be disturbed.

Gabriel walked back to where Natasha was sitting and squatted down behind her, looking at the book over her shoulder.

"Could we go so far as to say that P'u is the absolute positive state of anything that can be? Good or bad, beautiful or ugly; it's positive simply because it exists?"

Natasha looked up from the book and paused to think.

"I think that would be correct," she said.

Gabriel nodded and sat down next to her.

"What does the riddle say?"

Natasha read it aloud.

When searching for something that is lost,
One first finds the places where it is not.
In a bowl of bitter salt crystals lies a diamond in the rough.
Each piece is tasted until the treasure is found.
Therefore, not finding leads to finding,
And bitterness becomes sweet.
The Two find the One by finding the places where it is not.
They look to the left and to the right,
And loath not the seven sins that lie there.
Although veiled in darkness, the sins are a blessing,
For they point to the Kingdom that was lost.

Gabriel considered the mirrors grouped on either side of the pool.

"The Two," he said, pointing to each side. "Male and female. Left and right."

Natasha pondered on the observation.

"What are the seven deadly sins?" asked Gabriel. "Can you remember them?"

Natasha smiled.

"That's easy. There's pride, covetousness, lust, anger, gluttony, envy, and sloth."

"Can sins have male and female aspects?"

"A sin committed inwardly would be its feminine expression, and one committed outwardly would be its masculine."

Gabriel rubbed the stubble on his face.

"What if the mirrors represented the seven deadly sins?"

"That would explain their distorted reflections," said Natasha. "If you think about it, a sin is nothing but distorted behavior; a misconception that's acted upon."

Gabriel got up and began to pace.

"The riddle says that the Two find the One in the places where it is not. In other words, they find the truth by finding the misconceptions first; by being aware of them."

"That's what we learned to do in the last seal," said Natasha. Gabriel shook his head.

"None of this tells us where the next seal is."

"If these mirrors represent the seven sins, then the next seal should be in the pool."

"How's that?"

Natasha turned to face Gabriel.

"Because the mirrors would be *veiled in darkness* if we angled them down towards the pool."

"Why would they be veiled in darkness?"

"Because they'd reflect the black water."

Gabriel nodded slowly. He was beginning to see where Natasha was going with this line of thinking.

"If we pivoted them to face the pool, that would mean they'd be pointing to the *Kingdom that was lost*, which is just another name for the higher spheres…"

Natasha smiled.

"And because the seal is a door to the higher spheres, it has to be in the pool."

Gabriel pointed a finger at her.

"You think you're pretty smart, don't you…"

Natasha beamed.

"I'll do the ones on the left. You do the ones on the right."

Moving to their respective sides, Gabriel and Natasha angled the mirrors downward so they would point to the pool. They did so in unison, one at a time, until only one set remained unchanged.

"All right," said Gabriel. "Let's do it on the count of three. One, two, three—"

Natasha gasped aloud. No sooner had the mirrors been aligned, than the black water became suddenly clear. She could see the second seal at the bottom of the pool, glimmering in solid gold. Moments later the water began to drain away, leaving the manhole-sized portal readily accessible.

Gabriel wasted no time, carefully making his way down the concentric steps towards it. Natasha followed close behind.

"This is the symbol for the *Swadhisthana* chakra," she said, kneeling beside the seal. "It's the second chakra, located in the genital area."

"Marked by the scars below our bellybuttons," said Gabriel.
Natasha nodded.

"It's the centre of unconscious emotions and sexual desires."

Gabriel studied the golden disc. The image of a six-petaled lotus flower covered its surface in bas-relief, with a square indentation for the Cube at its centre.

"Are you ready?" he said, holding the Cube over its slot. "This is probably going to hurt again."

Natasha nodded and Gabriel lowered the Cube into place. They immediately felt a spasm of pain in their heads. With the connection now made, the Cube began to change in colour, this time turning from crimson into a rich orange.

Natasha moved to sit on the steps, carefully placing the Book of Khalifah down beside her.

"I can understand how the seven sins represent the destructive aspects that were unearthed in the first seal, but how could any of them possibly be good, as the Divine Action of P'u would suggest?"

"Because, my Queen," said Gutierrez, appearing suddenly above them at the top of the steps, "when we use denial and self-deception to hide our *destructiveness*, we bury much of our *constructiveness* along with it. Because of this fact, the bad things actually become good things when they are exposed and removed. The process of purification releases vast amounts of creative power."

"*Bitterness becomes sweet,*" said Gabriel, looking up at the alchemist. "Tasting each bitter salt crystal is like finding each misconception. It brings you one step closer to finding the hidden diamond of creative power. If you don't expose the bad, you'll never find the good. In that way the bad becomes good. *Not finding leads to finding.*"

"Provided the initiate does not identify with the evil that he unearths in himself," said Gutierrez, holding up a finger. "There is always that danger."

Natasha nodded in agreement.

"The initiate needs to realize that the dark things are only a small part of him. They're not the whole of him. He can never let himself forget that he's an evolving person, prone to mistakes and misconceptions."

"That's easy to say," said Gabriel, "but harder to do when real, justified guilt is involved."

"It is simply a matter of applying the Divine Action of P'u," said Gutierrez. "In their ultimate sense, good and evil are both good. If a person does or says something that causes harm to another, to that same degree, he does the other person a great service."

Gabriel cocked an eyebrow.

"How can that be?" he asked. "That sounds completely illogical."

"It's not illogical at all," said Natasha, turning away from Gutierrez to look at Gabriel. "But first you have to understand this concept: A person can do the same bad thing to two different people, perhaps say something offensive, and one person will be harmed, while the other will just let it slide. In other words, it's not the person's action that hurts us, but our reaction to it that causes the harm."

Gabriel considered what Natasha was saying. It was an odd concept, but he could see some truth in it. He nodded slowly.

"I think I understand," he said. "If we're ever hurt, it's only because there's something in us that makes us susceptible to being hurt. It's always due to some kind of misconception that we house.

"By hurting us, the perpetrator is actually aggravating our misconception, and giving us a chance to become aware of it. You can't get rid of something if you're not aware that it exists."

"Yes," said Natasha, "but the gift is lost when we try to blame the person who inflicted the harm on us, instead of taking full responsibility for our reaction to their act. It works the same in the opposite direction too. Any harm that we might have inflicted on others in the past was also a gift to them, no matter how horribly we acted."

"We can never know what the other soul needs in order to evolve," said Gutierrez, "but there is comfort in knowing that the universal laws will never allow anything to befall anyone that is not in strict accordance with universal justice."

"But what about innocent victims?" asked Gabriel. "What about the child who's been murdered? How could that possibly be a gift to the child, or its parents for that matter?"

"As long as you continue believing in death, my King," said Gutierrez, "you will never acquire this wisdom. The child's soul is very old and is in need of experience regardless of its bodily age. Its particular incarnation might appear to have been cut short by human standards, but this is not so on a larger scale.

"We do not know the workings of the universal intelligence, but if such a seemingly unjust things occurs, it is certain that both the souls of the child, and its parents, were in need of the experience in order to advance and evolve.

"There is a positive evolutionary reason behind all human suffering. That is why suffering must be respected, and never pitied; why it must be embraced and never rejected."

Natasha was nodding in agreement.

"Nothing can ever happen to us that we don't need to happen to us," she said. "There are no victims."

"Suffering occurs because of misconception," said Gutierrez. "It occurs because of untruth. A mind must be fully in truth if it is to create a heavenly world in which to abide."

"Heaven's a state of mind..." said Gabriel pensively, recalling what Bishop Marcus had once said.

Gutierrez smiled and nodded.

"For this reason alone, suffering is a blessing, my Liege," he said. "It creates pain in the areas where we are not seeing things clearly. Were it not for the pain of suffering, we would never be motivated to address the problems within us, and as such, we would never be able to create the mindset needed to return home.

"The prideful ego does not want to accept this. It becomes outraged and insulted when things do not go its way. As a result, it makes every effort to skirt the truth, and project the blame outside of itself."

Natasha rose to her feet.

"The fact is we all have a choice," she said. "We can take responsibility for everything bad that happens to us and know that it's what our soul needs to evolve, or we can decide to be powerless victims. The choice is ours, and I choose power over helplessness."

"Agreed," said Gabriel. "And because of the inherently positive nature of suffering, we can forgive ourselves for the harm we might have done to other people in the past, as well as to ourselves. It was all part of our individual and collective evolution."

"Yes, my King," said Gutierrez. "But that is not to say that we should go out and purposely try to harm other people, in order that we might help them. We would only end up hurting ourselves if we were to do this. What one does always comes back to oneself."

Gabriel rose to his feet.

"True, and that's why the next time somebody wrongs me, I'll know that I had it coming, and I'll try to figure out which of my past thoughts or actions brought it on, instead of just blaming the perpetrator, or life in general."

"Good is positive," said Natasha. "But evil is also positive in the long run. Both opposites make up the Uncarved Block."

Gutierrez pointed to the golden seal. It was quickly vanishing.

"The Divine Action of P'u has now been unlocked to the world."

CHAPTER 29

Gibraltar.

Major Richard Roberts arrived at the submarine port just minutes after his son had been born. He was in the company of Scotty Roberts, and the two medics they had brought along. Anita had gone into labour shortly after Scotty had gone off to fetch his brother, leaving Peralta no alternative but to assist Sir David in birthing the child where they were.

To the great delight of all, the delivery had gone off without a hitch.

"Well, that was definitely interesting," said Peralta, leaving the room with Sir David at his side. "Can't say I'll ever forget that…"

"Blessed be that little boy," said the old bishop, peering into the room. "He is most probably the first to be born into the new age of the Christ Consciousness, and just like the baby Jesus, he too was born in a secret cave on Christmas!"

Peralta shook his head in resignation.

"It won't be a secret cave for long," he rasped. "The military will be taking possession of it soon enough, and I'll be going to jail for good."

The others all looked at the rumpled scientist, realizing for the first time what the discloser of the submarine port meant. Peralta had broken many laws in occupying the military bay. He would surely pay for his crimes. It was as they contemplated these facts that the medics emerged bearing Anita on a stretcher. She asked them to stop so that she could have a word with Peralta.

"Thank you, Captain," she said in earnest, taking Peralta's hand. "You saved my life, and the life of my baby."

Peralta smiled genuinely.

"The pleasure was all mine."

Major Roberts emerged from the room carrying a bundle of Anita's things.

"I owe you a great debt, Captain."

"I'm no captain, sir," said Peralta, looking down at his feet. "I'm just an old smuggler on his way to jail."

Roberts put a firm hand on his shoulder.

"I'd sooner lose an entire platoon than lose you, Captain," he said. "I'm going to arrange a full pardon for your past activities. I'm the new governor now, and from this day forward you'll be an honoured officer in the Gibraltar Regiment. That submarine and this entire bay will be officially under your command."

Peralta blinked in surprise, scratching his messy head.

"You'll have a full salary," continued Roberts, liking the idea. "And a pension when you retire. You'll also have a seat of honour in the officer's mess. You're a hero, Captain Peralta, as are all your friends. You'll be received as nothing less!"

Peralta looked at him, speechless.

"There would be one caveat however," added Roberts, bending in closer and lowering his voice. "If you continue to find it necessary to engage in your old trade, do make sure to keep it all underwater, so to speak."

Peralta removed his glasses to wipe the tears from his eyes.

"Those days are over, sir," he stammered. "I would much rather attend to my research and serve Gibraltar in any way I can."

The major took hold of Peralta's hand and shook it enthusiastically.

"Well said, man!"

Everyone applauded when Anita and the baby were carried into the freight elevator. They could never have wished for a happier outcome to their impossible expedition. Being the attending physician, Sir David went with her to complete the required paperwork. Behind were left Peralta, the old bishop, Amir, Bahadur, Scotty, Cassano and a very jovial Shackleton.

"Well then!" said the old bishop. "I do believe we have done it. Humanity is out of the rift and the planet is saved!"

"So far so good," rasped Peralta. "Now it's just up to Gabriel and Natasha to complete their mission."

"They're well on their way," said Amir from the computer banks. "The game's active."

Peralta and the others rushed over to the workstation.

"The website's a flurry of activity," added Amir. "The gnosis from the first two seals has already been released."

Peralta told the bishop and Cassano about the game, and everything else they had learned whilst the two of them had been unconscious.

"And have we had any word from them?" asked the bishop of Gabriel and Natasha.

He was still trying to come to terms with the fact that two hundred years had elapsed in the period of three days.

"Unfortunately, not," said Peralta, pulling up a chair and beginning to tap away at a keyboard. "But something occurred to me while we were delivering the baby. There's a possibility that I could use the game's binaural interface to establish a connection with them."

"How do you plan on doing that?" asked Amir.

Peralta looked up at them.

"I haven't said anything up until now, but I found data paths in the descrambled algorithms that we extracted from the Cube. They're carrying alpha-wave signatures identical to the game's dream simulation interface."

"What the hell's that supposed to mean, mate?" asked Scotty. "Speak in English, God damn it."

Peralta rose to his feet and walked to a different section of the workstation, throwing himself into a chair and beginning to hammer away at a keyboard.

"The reptilians who built the Cube used the binaural interface to enter into its internal architecture. I'm going to do the same thing. I've managed to decrypt their entry codes using the fractal equation that operated the transponder back at the Labyrinth entrance. I have no idea where I'll end up but it's worth a try."

Cassano pushed his way up from the back of the group.

"Are you sure that's a good idea?" he asked. "You're going to be hacking into the most sophisticated piece of technology ever created."

Peralta looked hard at Cassano before responding. The scrawny pirate was right to feel reticent about the plan. The odds of getting lost inside the multi-dimensional artifact were very high. Peralta would be relying on the Cube's intelligence to guide him.

"I just can't shake the feeling that Gabriel and Natasha need our help," he rasped. "It's imperative we establish a connection with them as soon as possible. Going into the Cube is the only way I can think of to do it."

He turned away from Cassano and looked up at the others.

"I've got to put my trust in the Cube."

* * * * * *

Peralta opened his eyes and yawned. He gazed languidly around at his new surroundings as the grogginess left him. He was sitting in a room that he recognized at once, and his heart skipped a beat when his eyes fell on that which lay before him.

There on a worktable was the Compostela Cube, as it had been before Natasha had removed its ornate framework and illuminations.

"My God," he gasped. "Why did it bring me back here?"

He had appeared in Nasrallah's laboratory. The very place where he had been held prisoner. What was more, he could see himself fast asleep on a cot, not four paces away.

I'll be nice and quiet. Waking me up probably wouldn't be a good idea.

Peralta took inventory of the equipment that surrounded him. There was a portable x-ray machine, an old oscilloscope, and a computer monitor filled with x-ray images of the Cube.

"I've definitely come backwards in time," he whispered, amazed. "Back to the night when Nasrallah gave me the artifact to examine…"

Peralta rose to his feet and stood there silently looking around.

"Cassano will be in the dungeons below," he muttered inaudibly. "Nasrallah will be upstairs in his quarters. He didn't come to take the Cube back until midnight. I remember because that old grandfather clock was sounding when he came in and woke me up."

Peralta turned to find the clock and gasped when he saw the time.

Eleven fifty-five!

He looked down and just then noticed a bright orange light shining from the cracks in the Cube's coverings.

"It's active," he muttered, bending over to examine it more closely. "But it's not glowing blue. It must be emitting a different frequency..."

Peralta reached over and switched on the oscilloscope, connecting the Cube to it as quickly as he could.

"Four hundred and seventeen hertz," he said, his brow furrowed. "I know this frequency. Where have I seen it?"

He scratched his messy head and struggled to remember. Something else puzzled him as well. Why had the Cube decided to bring him to Nasrallah's castle to show him this new frequency? Why not some other place in time? Why not back to when he was working with Gabriel in his own laboratory?

It was at that moment he heard the deadbolt outside the chamber being thrown back. Nasrallah was on the verge of entering. The grandfather clock began to chime, and Peralta could see himself stirring on the cot.

My God. I've got to get out of here.

In one swift motion Peralta produced his tablet and terminated the simulation, opening his eyes to find the massive head of Bahadur looking down at him. He was smiling with relief.

"You have been unconscious for almost six hours," he said in his deep basso. "We were beginning to worry, my friend."

CHAPTER 30

In the Labyrinth of Sarras.

Natasha did not like their new surroundings at all. After having spent over two hours navigating the damp worming passages of the Labyrinth, they had crawled into a tiny crevice that had nothing in it but an old well. To make matters worse, the ring of stonework that encased the pit was crusted in bat dung, and the air stank of sewage and rot.

Gabriel dragged himself over to the edge and looked down. An iron ladder had been set into the masonry, disappearing into the murky depths.

"What's that sound?" asked Natasha, crawling up beside him.

The darkness was inky and oppressive here, and there was a dry rattling filtering up from below. It was barely perceptible in the dead air, but Gabriel frowned, nonetheless. An eerie chill was running up his neck and over his scalp. He pushed back his hair.

"I'll go first."

It was not until they had descended a dozen metres that they were able to see the source of the rattling sound. The well had led them into a large, torch lit chamber. They were entering it through the ceiling and the ladder they were on descended all the way to the floor below; a floor that was seething with a carpet of insects.

"Cockroaches," grunted Gabriel, half gagging. "Why did it have to be cockroaches?"

Natasha looked down at him with panic in her eyes. For a long moment they both remained where they were, clinging to the iron ladder but unable to continue downward. It was Gabriel who first broke from the spell.

"We've got to get over there somehow," he said, pointing.

Natasha turned to look. Gutierrez had appeared on a raised area in the corner of the chamber, not twenty paces away. The floor at his feet was curiously free of insects and behind him was the room's only exit: An arched opening leading into a dark corridor. The only way there would be through the cockroaches.

"I'm going to jump down," said Gabriel. "Then you're going to climb on my shoulders. Got it?"

Natasha was shaking her head, her big eyes wide with fear.

"I can't do it, Gabriel."

"Of course you can do it," he said, stepping off the rungs.

He groaned in disgust. The milling nest came up to his knees.

"Get on!" he cried.

He was on the verge of panic. The insects were already in his trousers.

"Now!"

Natasha screamed as she lowered herself onto his shoulders. Gabriel did not waste any time after that. With a grunt of pure repulsion, he moved out into the seething nest, fighting to keep the panic at bay. He forced himself to be deliberate with every step he took. Tripping and falling was not an option.

The repugnant cockroaches were soon crawling all over his body, and to make matters worse, there were also millipedes in the swarm. He used his hands to keep them off his face, but their burning bites were making him feel dizzy and nauseous.

"Hang on!" he cried through clenched teeth.

Natasha could feel the millipedes burrowing through her hair and over her scalp. Dozens of cockroaches were scurrying over her too, no matter how furiously she brushed them away. It was all she could do to remain coherent.

At long last they arrived at the raised area where Gutierrez had stood. He was nowhere to be seen now. They scrambled up a flight of stone steps and proceeded to strip themselves naked, shaking the insects from their clothing and hair.

"That was horrible," said Natasha, wiggling back into her jeans.

Gabriel frowned and buckled his belt.

"Let's not dwell on it," he said, turning to face the tunnel.

Natasha aimed her flashlight into the passage, seeing its light fall onto a thick wall of fog within. There was something unsettling about its density. It was oily and viscous.

"So, what's the next seal?" asked Gabriel, trying to get his mind off the insects.

Natasha cleared her thoughts.

"It belongs to the Islamic side of the Cube," she said. "It centres on the *Jihad bil qalb*, the most difficult of all the greater Jihads of Islam. It's a battle with the devil himself."

"Lovely," said Gabriel, peering into the foggy passageway and then back into the den of cockroaches. "Can't wait for that. Someone in here's hell bent on freaking us out..."

He extended his arm to Natasha.

"Shall we?"

Natasha took it and smiled.

"I thought you'd never ask."

They entered into the fog without hesitation, leaving behind the chamber of insects only to find the passageway infested with hundreds of angry bats. In seconds they were forced to let go of each other to defend themselves. It was only when the onslaught had passed that Natasha reached out for Gabriel and found that he was no longer at her side.

"Gabriel?" she called. "Gabriel!"

She heard him cry out as if from very far away.

"Natasha! Where are you?"

"I'm over here!" she cried, but even as the words left her lips, she knew that Gabriel would never hear them.

The fog was as dense as soup now. It swallowed her voice entirely.

"My God," she whispered, half choking. "What is this?"

She could feel the air growing very warm around her. A second later the fog vanished to reveal an enormous subterranean cavern. She was standing on a stone platform no wider than she was tall. It sat atop a massive fragment of rock that rose from the depths like a jagged finger, surrounded on all sides by a fiery chasm of lava and ash.

"What's going on?" she gasped, and just then a terrible clamor arose from all sides.

It was as if masses of people were crying out in agony. Natasha spun around, looking over the edge to see that there were thousands of figures writhing below. They clung to rocks, or cowered in crevices, their bodies burnt and mutilated by the splashing lava and sulfurous explosions.

If this were not enough, she looked up to see something that amazed her even more. There, on the opposite side of the burning chasm, was an enormous dragon fast asleep on a mountain of golden treasure.

"The fire and brimstone make it clear where I am," she whispered quietly, gawking at the beast. "But why a dragon?"

Natasha spun around on the platform. There was clearly no way off. With a sigh of resignation, she sat down on the hot stone and took a tiny sip of the little water that remained in her canteen.

"*Accidenti,*" she said in Italian gloomily. "Where are you, Gabriel?"

* * * * * *

Gabriel moved forward through the dark fog, fumbling with his radio.

"Natasha," he said. "Can you hear me? Peralta. Are you there? Can anybody hear me?"

He pocketed the device in frustration, only then noticing the fragrant scent in the air. It smelt of hardwood fires on a crisp winter's night, and he breathed it in deeply, his eyes attempting to penetrate a brighter section of fog that was located directly above him.

In moments it thinned into tattered wisps and a full moon materialized in the sky. Snow laden tree boughs formed a canopy above him, and he could see that he was in an olive orchard on a clear wintry night. The ground was covered in a fresh blanket of snow, and jagged moonlit mountains towered in the background.

"Who goes there?" came a haggard voice, and Gabriel spun around to see a robed man approaching.

No sooner had he spotted the *Tree of Life* pendant hanging from his neck than he knew it was Gutierrez. Gabriel watched intently. Gutierrez was carrying a large wooden staff and was using it to help himself plod through the ankle-deep snow.

"It's me," said Gabriel. "Natasha and I just got separated."

The alchemist came up to him and threw back his cowl. It was only then that Gabriel noticed how old Gutierrez had become.

His black beard was now long and white, as was his hair and eyebrows.

Gabriel was amazed. The minutes that had passed for him had been decades for Gutierrez. It was only after a long moment that the old man recognized him.

"Hero of God!" he proclaimed suddenly. "Long has it been since I gazed upon your noble face, my King!"

He lowered himself reverently to a knee and would have been unable to get up again had Gabriel not helped him.

"Do you remember when we last met?" asked Gabriel.

Gutierrez smiled and nodded.

"We parted ways in the Labyrinth," he said, his brow furrowing as he remembered. "We had arrived at the dragon's lair."

The dragon's lair?

Gabriel cocked an eyebrow but decided not to comment. Instead, he looked around, noticing only then the snow-covered village that lay behind them. It was medieval in style, and warm firelight was coming from the windows of its inn.

"You wouldn't know where Natasha was, by any chance," he asked, watching a pair of drunken men staggering out onto the cobbled streets.

Gutierrez moved to Gabriel's side.

"She is in the den of the dragon *Ialdabaôth,*" he said, frowning. "To rescue her you must learn the ways of the *Mujahid.*"

Gabriel nodded slowly.

"The Holy Warrior."

"Yes," said Gutierrez, motioning towards the inn. "Come with me, my Liege. We must begin your training at once."

CHAPTER 31

Gibraltar.

Peralta opened his eyes and looked around. He was in the secret submarine port, sitting at his workstation by the dark, lapping waters.

"Bahadur," he rasped, rising to his feet and stretching. "Where are you hiding?"

Peralta could distinctly remember having seen the brown giant when he had awoken but realized that he must have drifted off again without knowing it.

"Shackleton!" he called out. "Are you here?"

He scanned the submarine port. There was not a soul in sight.

"They must have gone up top," he muttered with a shrug. "I might as well get started on the communications array."

He opened a nearby drawer and produced the glowing sample of *blue goo* that he had taken from the Labyrinth entrance. It was the size of his fist, and still covered in the tangled circuitry he had connected it to.

Thinking back on his recent adventure, Peralta recalled why the Cube's new frequency had seemed so familiar to him. It belonged to the *Solfeggio Scale*; a set of seven mysterious notes originating from ancient India and adopted in medieval times by Gregorian monks in their chants.

Apart from the scale's professed powers of spiritual enlightenment, the sequence of notes had been found to contain inexplicable properties. Amazingly enough, biochemists were using the scale's third frequency to repair human DNA.

"If these notes can fix damaged cells then there's a good chance they can at least stimulate the goo."

Peralta bent over an adjacent computer and launched a program that would generate the special sine wave needed for his experiment.

"Four hundred and seventeen hertz is the second frequency in the scale," he muttered, entering in the data. "Let's see what happens..."

He plugged in his headphones and placed them carefully over the reptilian-made substance, turning the volume to its maximum setting. No sooner had he initiated the sine wave than the blue-glowing sample began to glow in a rich hue of orange.

"Yes!" cried Peralta, rubbing his hands together. "It's matched the Cube's new frequency! This ought to work now!"

"Gabriel!" he said into his radio. "Natasha! Can either of you hear me?"

The response came almost instantly.

"You son of a gun!" cried Gabriel. "You couldn't have had better timing!"

Gabriel checked his voice, noticing only then that he was drawing attention to himself. He was sitting in the inn's common room, and although masked for the most part by the drunken din of merriment, those at a neighbouring table had heard Peralta's tinny voice coming from his radio and were looking over at him suspiciously.

Gabriel lowered the volume and brought the radio closer to his ear.

"How's everybody doing?" he asked. "Give me an update."

"Everybody's fine!" came Peralta's reply. "The world was unconscious for a total of ninety-one hours. Everyone woke up when you and Natasha opened the first seal. Anita had her baby about ten minutes after that. Oh yeah, I almost forgot. We popped out of the rift two hundred years in the future."

"What?" exclaimed Gabriel, and then lowering his voice he added:

"How the hell did that happen?"

"Severe time dilation," said Peralta. "But it's a good thing. All the radiation's gone now. A game appeared on the website. I think it's an extension of the Labyrinth, complete with seals that have to be traversed. It works on a binaural dream simulation interface. How's Natasha?"

"She's great," said Gabriel, turning his back on his inquisitive neighbours. "But we got separated about an hour ago. We've been encountering some pretty surreal stuff. Right now I'm sitting in a ninth century pub while Natasha is being held prisoner by a dragon."

"Are you being serious?"

"Very," said Gabriel.

Peralta scrubbed at his head.

"Well, I wouldn't take things too literally if I were you. I'm pretty sure the Labyrinth is like the game. It's a dream simulation that interfaces with the Cube. I wouldn't be surprised if you could actually shape events if you tried. My guess is that your physical bodies are still in the sarcophagi."

"They are," said Gabriel. "And they're being buried alive as we speak."

"The sarcophagi would have been specifically designed for that purpose," said Peralta. "I'm sure your bodies will be safe in them."

"I hope you're right," said Gabriel. "Now how can I get a hold of Natasha?"

"You'll have to wait until she turns her radio on," said Peralta. "The Cube's emitting a different frequency now. The blue goo I used to link our radios is now orange goo. I'll be keeping an eye on our connection from this end."

"It'll be changing colours every time we pass through a new seal," said Gabriel, seeing only then that three ruffians were approaching his table.

"I've got to go," he said. "I've got company. Stay in touch."

"Will do," rasped Peralta. "And good luck!"

Peralta severed the connection but left his radio on standby. Seeing that his work was done, he decided to visit the upper galleries and search for his friends.

It was not until the elevator door opened that Peralta noticed things were not as they should be.

"This looks like something straight out of Star Trek," he muttered.

The tunnel walls were glowing with light, and the floor appeared to be made of glass.

"Coolmaster!" said a voice, and Peralta turned to see a young man approaching. "Welcome! The oracles be blessed! I must have missed their announcement of your coming!"

Peralta looked at the boy in confusion.

"The oracles?" he rasped, cocking an eyebrow. "And who are the oracles?"

The boy nodded as though Peralta had said something very profound.

"It is true, Coolmaster," he said respectfully. "They are only people. The same as you and I. We are all divine."

Peralta was going to respond, but a group of children engulfed him before he could do so. They could barely contain their excitement. Peralta made the connections. The young man who had spoken to him was obviously their teacher. He could hear some of the children whispering behind his back.

"Look at his old skin!" said a little girl.

"…And his white hair!" said another.

In moments the children had taken hold of Peralta's hands and were guiding him down the passage, crying out in happy voices.

"A Coolmaster has come! A Coolmaster has come!"

Peralta let himself be herded along until a large door opened before them. On the other side was Gibraltar's main street, crowded with people. A regular stream of flying cars was passing by overhead, but other than that, the place seemed unchanged. The air was fresh and clean.

"My God!" gasped Peralta, looking down at the children who surrounded him. "What year is this?"

They all laughed at his question, their eyes alight with joy.

"Yes, we know!" they cried. "Tonight is New Year's Eve! That's why you've come, isn't it, Coolmaster?"

Peralta decided to play along.

"Of course," he rasped. "And what year will it be tomorrow?"

"One thousand of the New Era!" they cried in unison.

Peralta looked around at his surroundings, amazed that he was seeing his hometown ten centuries in the future. The original structures of Gibraltar had been perfectly preserved. He breathed in the fresh sea air, reveling in its cleanliness.

"I like what you've done with the place," he said, nodding in approval. "Is there still a governor in Gibraltar?"

The children laughed at his question as though it were silly.

"Can you take me to him?" he asked.

"We would be delighted, Coolmaster," said the young teacher approaching.

CHAPTER 32

In the Labyrinth of Sarras.

Gabriel turned to see that Gutierrez was making his way towards him through the inn's crowded common room. He took a sip from his mug and leaned back in his chair. Three ruffians approached him as the old priest arrived.

"This is the knight of whom I spoke," said Gutierrez, gesturing towards Gabriel. "He requires sparring partners, but it must be with naked steel. You will all be paid, but the man who brings him down will receive this prize."

He held up a small leather pouch and emptied its contents onto the palm of his hand. Twenty pieces of gold. The eyes of the men lit up at the sight. Gabriel rose to his feet.

"Now hang on a second," he said, looking at Gutierrez with shocked anger. "I'll be having no quarrel with anyone in this place."

Gabriel sized up the burly men, taking special note of the heavy swords that hung from their belts.

"Least of all with these good gentlemen," he added, flashing the most charming smile he could muster.

The men frowned and turned their attention back to the gold coins.

"If you kill him, you shall have double," said Gutierrez.

Gabriel tore his eyes from the ruffians and turned to face the priest.

"Are you crazy?" he whispered. "What are you saying?"

Gutierrez ignored him entirely.

"Do you accept my offer, gentlemen?"

The three ruffians grunted in unison and moved off to wait outside. Gabriel was going to speak but Gutierrez held up a hand.

"Come with me, my Liege," he said. "I have arranged so that you might be dressed and armed."

* * * * * *

Gabriel walked through the common room with Gutierrez at his side, surprised by how unencumbered he felt in his chainmail armour. He put a hand on the broadsword that hung from his belt, his fingers running over three slots in its pummel. It seemed odd that they should be there. A circle, a square, and a triangle.

"You do realize I have no idea how to use this," he said, looking hard at Gutierrez while motioning to the sword.

"Is that so," said alchemist. "Are you sure of that, my King?"

They left the inn and made their way into a snow covered square in the centre of the night enshrouded hamlet. Gabriel could see the three men Gutierrez had hired, accompanied by a drunken mob of spectators, all lit by the flickering light of torches that had been set around the courtyard.

No sooner had they laid eyes on Gabriel than the crowd began to place bets, and in no time a clamor of excitement had infected everyone. More and more people were emerging from the inn as word of the spectacle spread. Gutierrez paid them no heed.

"If you are to slay the dragon and open the third seal," he said, shuffling forward through the snow, "you must learn the ways of the *Mujahid*. The time has come to reawaken your Inner Warrior, my King."

Gabriel looked over at Gutierrez.

"And how exactly am I supposed to do that?"

"You must establish a connection with him."

Gabriel watched the brutes begin to spar with one another.

"And exactly who is this inner warrior I'm supposed to connect with?"

"He is the greatest of all warriors," said Gutierrez. "He is the Kristos."

Gabriel turned to face Gutierrez.

"Jesus Christ?" he asked, his hands on his hips. "Are you crazy? I think I'll need to connect with someone a little more assertive than a hundred-pound weakling in sandals."

Gabriel noted the force with which the sparring blows were being dealt and looked back at the old alchemist.

"I think someone like Conan the Barbarian would be much more suitable, given the circumstances."

Gutierrez frowned.

"I will have you know that Jesus was not the emasculated man that the Vatican invented, my Liege," he said soberly. "He was neither poor, weak, celibate, nor timid. He achieved the highest possible state of body and mind that a man can achieve, and he did this by connecting fully with the inner Christ Consciousness."

"He connected with himself?"

"Indeed, he did," said Gutierrez. "And so can we all. The Christ Consciousness resides at the core of every human being. It has been called many names over the ages, but it has always been one with our higher-self, and one with the Creator himself. Jesus was simply the first man to establish a full and unobstructed connection to it."

"And that made him a warrior?"

"Many and powerful were the demons who fought to prevent this connection from taking place," said Gutierrez. "They attacked him viciously and incessantly, in both physical and psychic ways. He defeated them all. Jesus Christ was, and is, the greatest warrior in existence, my Liege. He was the first Mujahid. He is the Kristos."

Gabriel looked at Gutierrez, trying to understand.

"And you say he wasn't celibate?"

Gutierrez shook his head.

"Contrary to what the blasphemous Vatican might have you believe, my King, sexual union is not a bestial sin. It is a great and wonderful blessing that draws us ever towards unity consciousness."

Gabriel considered what he was being told.

"Your Jesus seems a lot more real than the one I've always heard about," he said. "He actually sounds human. How do I make contact with him?"

"To connect with the Inner-Christ, you must allow yourself to feel his love for you."

Gabriel groaned.

"Couldn't we just leave out that whole *Jesus loves you* part?"

Gutierrez gave him a puzzled look.

"It is the only way to shed the hidden contempt that you have for yourself, my Liege. There is not a human being alive who does not house this self-contempt, whether he or she is conscious of it or not. Unless you allow yourself to feel the Christ's unconditional love for you, you will never feel worthy of merging with so great a force as he."

Gabriel considered what the old alchemist was saying. It aligned perfectly with the gnosis of the last two seals. He turned and saw that his opponents were now waiting to engage. The crowd was growing impatient.

"You cannot defeat Ialdabaôth if you are not Mujahid," said Gutierrez. "And you cannot be Mujahid if you cannot experience *Tawhid*, or true Oneness with God. Jesus Christ was the first to accomplish this state, and having done so, he opened the way for others to follow."

Gabriel nodded with understanding.

"He injected his ability to connect with the Inner-Kristos into the collective consciousness," he said. "That's what Natasha and I are supposed to be doing with the gnosis as we open the seals."

"In the three days that passed between his death and symbolic resurrection," said Gutierrez, "Jesus Christ gathered his archangels and led a war against the hosts of Lucifer in Hades. He was victorious, and he opened the Seventh Seal of Ostium Sanctus; the gateway to the higher spheres. Your task is to help the world make their way through that seal."

Gabriel looked at Gutierrez, understanding at last why the seventh seal required no divine action to open. Jesus Christ had unlocked it two thousand years earlier. Gutierrez sensed Gabriel's new understanding and smiled.

"Do not forget who you truly are, my Liege," he said. "In your ancient incarnation you already established a full connection with the greatest warrior of all time. Make a silent prayer to the Inner-Kristos and ask him with humility to help you remember how to do battle. The rest will come naturally."

Gabriel nodded and moved forward, reminding himself of what Peralta had only just confirmed. The truth was that he was in a dream simulation, a virtual reality. Everything here was symbolic. He would be able to control events if he could establish the correct mindset. At the same time, he recalled what Gutierrez had told him when they had first met. He could still die in this dream.

"All right," he said. "Here goes nothing."

Gabriel met his opponents in the centre of the square, drawing his sword and thrusting it into the ground. He bent on a knee before it.

"Jesus," he prayed. "I'm seriously and humbly asking for your help. I've had my doubts that you exist, but if you really are who Gutierrez says you are, you'll understand. Please help me remember my connection to the Inner-Kristos. I need to make this sword work."

Gabriel rose to his feet, but before he could think he had already acted on a strong gut feeling, spinning around to deflect an overhead blow that would have cut him in two.

The battled that ensued was nothing short of miraculous, with Gabriel showing a proficiency that was unmatched by anything the spectators had ever seen. Not only did he defeat his opponents, but he did so without inflicting any mortal wounds. They were soon lying in the snow, either groaning in pain, or completely unconscious.

"Well done, my Liege," said Gutierrez, shuffling past Gabriel as he stood there panting. "Come along now. We have a dragon to slay."

* * * * * *

It seemed to Natasha that she would surely die in this heat. Across from her the dragon still slept on its mound of treasure, oblivious to the incessant wailing of the damned. The beast had broken from its slumber only once, opening one of its emerald eyes to lazily spy on her just before turning over and falling asleep again.

It was only then that Natasha remembered her radio, and she reached into her pack to retrieve it, switching it on.

How could I have been such a dummy?

"Gabriel, are you there? Can you hear me?"

"Natasha!" came Gabriel's crackling voice. "Yes, I'm here. I've been waiting for you to turn your damn radio on!"

"I completely forgot about it," she said apologetically. "Oh, thank God."

"Are you all right?"

"Yes, but it's really hard to breathe down here," she said. "I'm trapped on a rock shelf, surrounded by a fiery chasm. It's filled with screaming people, Gabriel. Can you hear them? It's straight out of Dante's Inferno. There's something else here too. Something that doesn't really belong..."

"What?" asked Gabriel with concern. "What is it?"

"There's a dragon," she said. "It's sleeping on a big pile of gold."

"I know."

"You do?"

"Gutierrez told me all about it."

"Well then get me out of here!" she cried. "What's taking you so long?"

CHAPTER 33

Gabriel looked over his shoulder, taking in the expansive moonlit view. He and Gutierrez were high in altitude now, on horseback and picking their way along a narrow, frigid trail. It stretched out before them, making its way to the top of a jagged, snow-covered mountain. The little hamlet could still be seen far below. It was shrouded in blue, with gossamer threads of moonlit smoke emerging from its chimneys.

Gabriel drew his pelt around him and looked ahead at Gutierrez. He too was wrapped in furs, and for all his years was managing his horse like the best of equestrians.

Gabriel inhaled the mountain air. The cold was intense and there was not a breath of wind. Above him the stars glowed, twinkling through waves of heat that appeared to be rising from the mountain itself.

"We have arrived at the entrance," said Gutierrez over his shoulder. "We now can dismount."

They led their horses into a sheltered area, finding the ground littered with crumbled masonry. Warm, sulfurous gusts were rushing from the mouth of a cave.

"Looks like the villagers tried to shut him in," said Gabriel, surveying the decimated fortifications.

"Ialdabaôth cannot be locked away and forgotten," said Gutierrez. "He will always break free, no matter how fervently one denies him."

It was not long before they were making their way through round, fire scorched lava tubes. Even after having stripped themselves of all their furs, they were still sweating profusely, and for the first time Gabriel was feeling the weight of his chainmail and sword.

He stopped before a fork in the passage as Gutierrez came up beside him.

"To the left lies the easiest way to the lair, but it is sure folly to travel that route. We will take the right-hand path, which is the more difficult of the two. It will take you where you want to go, but it will bring hardships."

"Why doesn't that surprise me?" muttered Gabriel, watching as the old priest shuffled off ahead.

They continued onward until they arrived at a deep chasm that split their path. It was only a meter across, but it spanned the entire width of the tunnel. Further ahead they could see a cavernous chamber with three monsters standing motionlessly at its centre. Their disfigured forms were draped in shadow, and each was armed with a massive, two-handed battle axe held point down before it.

On the ground behind the beasts was a circular opening, glowing with the light of unseen lava below. It was enclosed by bars of black iron, and from it came the tortured wailing of the damned. Next to the pit lay a thick length of coiled rope. One of its ends was fastened to a sturdy iron ring anchored into the ground.

"Below lies the lair of Ialdabaôth, my Liege," said Gutierrez. "It is there where you will find both your queen, and the seal."

"And what are *those* things?"

Gutierrez scowled at the shadowy monsters, his mouth contorting with disgust.

"They are the Wormlords, my Liege," he said, turning to face Gabriel. "Insidious demon-kings. They command the many legions of devils and wraiths that prey upon humanity."

"I don't understand."

Gutierrez returned his gaze to the shadowy beasts.

"In the same way that there are angels around us at all times, so too are there demons, my Liege. Those who are close to self-realization can have many demons assigned to them at any given moment. Those who are further from self-realization, and do not pose an immediate threat to Lucifer, will have fewer demons assigned to them."

"And what do these demons do?"

"They attempt to burrow into the human soul substance," said the old alchemist. "Apart from weakening us by feeding on our life force, it is the demon's task to separate us from God, from our fellow man, and from ourselves. They do this by influencing us with mental attitudes that sever our connection to the divine world."

"Why do they look like they're made of earth?"

"Demons are comprised of very dense matter," said Gutierrez. "Much denser than the matter that we are comprised of. It is for this reason that we cannot normally see them. They have a very low energy frequency."

Gutierrez bent closer.

"Demons do everything in their power to distance us from the higher, ethereal states of being. They trick us into believing that the physical world is the only thing that is real. Their presence fills us with confusion, and false rationality, so that it seems that truth does not exist; that it is only a relative concept. This weakens us by undermining our ability to have faith in what we intuitively believe to be true."

Gabriel's eyes opened wide. The old alchemist was slowly dissolving.

"How do I dispel these demons?" he asked urgently.

"By hunting them relentlessly," said Gutierrez. "And by using the positive aggression of the Warrior Christ to vanquish them once they have been found."

"I didn't know there was such a thing as positive aggression," said Gabriel. "I thought aggression was a bad thing."

Gutierrez smiled.

"That is because aggression is most commonly released through destructive means. We fail to see that aggression can also be used for constructive purposes.

"The Mujahid uses it to vanquish the Wormlords, and the many demons that they command. In this way his attitudes remain in alignment with the truth. The demons flee from him. They cannot abide his aggression. It burns them."

"What happens after you dispel a demon? Is it gone for good?"

"Yes," said Gutierrez. "But another might come to take its place if it has the courage. You see, when a demon has been dispelled, it suffers great humiliation in the eyes of its peers. This pain causes it to cry out for God's mercy despite itself, and an upward movement is initiated in the demon's soul.

"For this reason, the Christed Mujahid always strikes without mercy. He knows that by vanquishing a demon, he helps it to evolve, and so furthers the Apocatastasis."

With those words Gutierrez disappeared. Gabriel turned to look across the pit at the demonlords and then brought out his radio.

"Natasha, can you hear me?"

"Yes," came her parched reply, "but please hurry, Gabriel. I don't know how much longer I can stand this heat."

"I'm right above you, baby," he said. "Just look up. Can you see a round opening anywhere?"

She scanned the cavernous ceiling.

"Yes," she said, rising to her feet. "There's one about ten meters above me."

"That's where I'll be coming from," said Gabriel. "There's only one problem. I've got to fight my way past three monsters to get to you. What do we know about this seal?"

Natasha looked over at the sleeping dragon.

"Its alchemical stage is Separation," she said. "Calcination brought out all of our destructive aspects through the fire of introspection. Dissolution dissolved all those faults into a homogenous mass. Separation is the step where the faults are analyzed so as to learn their causes. Truth gets separated from misconception. Read the riddle. I marked the page in the book."

Gabriel sat down on the edge of the chasm, his feet dangling over the side. He opened his pack and brought out the Book of Khalifah, removing it from its watertight bag.

"All right," he said. "My Arabic's nowhere near as good as yours but I'll give this my best shot."

He translated the text as he read it.

At the root of all evil lies the triad of death.

Self-will endeavors to confuse and twist the truth.
Pride limits vision to all but what is apparent.
Fear labours incessantly to separate and divide.

The warrior crosses the threshold and passes into the realm of shadows.
He engages his enemies and so obtains the three keys of purification.

When mother and father are seen in truth,
Religious tradition can be questioned.
Enmity then becomes tolerance,
And tolerance becomes Unity.
After the false god has been slain,
What before seemed impossible, becomes feasible.

Only when the triad is revealed and conquered,
Can there be unity between all nations and creeds.

Gabriel put down the book and picked up his radio.

"What do you think?"

"I remember reading something about self-will, pride, and fear in your father's journal," said Natasha. "You need to find that entry, Gabriel. It was somewhere near the middle of the book."

Gabriel produced the diary and located the page.

"My father's saying that nobody's entirely free of self-will, pride, and fear," he said, scanning the text. "While one might be more prevalent than the other two, all three are always present at the same time. He says they're the sole cause of all our suffering, both individually and collectively."

Gabriel read the rest of the entry aloud.

Self-will is not to be confused with free will. Self-will comes from the desires of the little ego. It strives to get what it wants at any cost, regardless of the harm it does along the way. Self-will resides mostly in the unconscious mind, and conflicts with the good intentions of the conscious mind.

Pride means that our little ego is more important than the other person's; that we desire advantages for ourselves, and that we have vanity. If we feel the humiliation of another person less than our own humiliation, then we have pride. Only by detaching ourselves from our vanity, can we have the same reactions for ourselves as we do for others.

Fear that our pride will be hurt, and fear that the desires of our self-will will not be obtained, makes us cling to self-will out of pride, and to pride out of self-will. This is what the ancients referred to as the triad of death; a vicious circle linking the three destructive attributes. The triad can only be broken by observing its mechanisms in the depths of our own unconscious mind.

Gabriel closed the book.

"The three Wormlords have got to be the enemies in the riddle," he said. "They represent the triad."

"If that's the case," said Natasha, "then they also embody confusion, materialism, and separation. The demon of confusion makes truth appear to be untrue, and untruth appear to be true."

Gabriel nodded.

"Confusion is also linked to self-will in the riddle," he said. "Mixing up truth and lies is always great for rationalizing destructive acts and manipulating people."

Gabriel scratched his head.

"What about the second element of the triad?"

Natasha wiped the perspiration from her face and tried to ignore the incessant wailing around her. She was feeling a deep wisdom rising up from within her. She was remembering.

"The second element is materialism," she said. "It denies the existence of anything other than the surface appearance of things. It negates the invisible world of spirit, and as a result, the true meaning and purpose of life. Materialism is linked to pride because it takes humility to accept that there are spiritual laws that must be obeyed."

"And the third?" asked Gabriel.

"Fear," she said, concentrating inwardly. "It's the central instrument of the left-hand path. It divides and conquers wherever it's present. Fear keeps us isolated from everything, and from everyone, including ourselves."

"Done," said Gabriel. "There's a chasm directly in front of me. That's got to be the threshold to the realm of shadows that the riddle speaks of."

"The unconscious mind…" said Natasha.

Gabriel nodded. He too was remembering.

"The unconscious mind is where our real enemies exist," he said. "I can see them standing on the other side of the chasm.

They'll hold the three keys of purification that the riddle speaks of."

"But what about the false god in the riddle?" asked Natasha.

"It's Ialdabaôth," said Gabriel, packing away the books and rising to his feet. "He's the dragon."

"Of course," said Natasha. "Ialdabaôth was humanity's first monotheistic god. He's false because he's obsolete. I still don't understand Ialdabaôth's connection to the triad though."

"Give it some thought while I take these Wormlords down," said Gabriel, drawing his sword and stepping across the chasm.

"Be careful!"

"Don't worry about me," he said, swinging his sword with expert proficiently. "I seem to have developed some very useful skills of late."

Gabriel made his way into the chamber, watching as the three Wormlords gathered in front of the opening in the ground. He could see that its bars were held fast by three golden padlocks. He said a quiet prayer to Jesus Christ, requesting his assistance again, and then moved forward, grunting with disgust.

In the light that came from the opening, he could at last make out the repugnant forms of his adversaries. Although similar to the other demons he had encountered, these were crawling with pale maggots. They stank of decay and putrescence.

"I believe that you gentlemen are in possession of keys to that pit," he said, fighting back an urge to vomit. "Why don't you make this easy for all of us and just give them to me?"

Gabriel received an answer to his question in the form of a powerful attack from the middle beast. At the last second, he dodged aside as its massive axe hissed by. Another attack came from the next fiend immediately afterwards, followed by a stabbing thrust from the third.

In a matter of seconds Gabriel was engaged with all three demons, emptying his mind of all thoughts so as to follow every signal that came to him through his newfound intuition. The result was a fluid dance of sorts, each movement placing his sword in the perfect position to parry the incoming blows.

With a decisive thrust Gabriel sunk his sword deep into one of the beasts. The Wormlord imploded with a sickening crunch as the blade found home, and it did not take long before Gabriel had felled the others in similar fashion. In the end they laid in dead heaps on the ground, the seething worms and maggots already beginning to break apart their corpses.

Gabriel moved to study the padlocks, finding that they each contained a differently shaped slot, identical to those in the pummel of his sword. One was square, one circular, and the other triangular. Embedded into the soles of each of the monster's feet, Gabriel found three shining gemstones bearing the exact same shapes. He used them to open the padlocks and then stuffed them into his pocket, pulling out his radio.

"Natasha," he said, poking his head down through the opening. "Look up."

Natasha's expression transformed with relief.

"I can't tell you how good it is to see your face, Gabriel."

She squinted through the rising waves of heat and brought the radio closer to her mouth.

"Are you wearing armour?"

"Chain mail," replied Gabriel proudly.

He picked up the rope and threw it down.

"I'll be right there."

No sooner had Gabriel set foot onto the stone platform than Natasha threw herself into his arms. He handed her his canteen and watched as she drank. In an effort to lessen the heat, Natasha had ripped the hem from her blouse, and used it to tie up her hair. It fell in thick ringlets around her face.

Gabriel's eyes found the dragon. Natasha had not been exaggerating. From head to tail it must have measured a hundred feet. He shifted his gaze to the throngs of writhing bodies that filled the cavern. They were steeped in lava and ash and wailing in agony.

"I can see why people have always listened to angry priests…" he said, shaking his head.

Gabriel produced the gemstones and fit them into the pummel of his sword. They began to glow as soon as they were embedded in their slots. He looked over at Natasha and held out his hand.

"Are you coming?"

"Where?"

Gabriel feigned surprise. No sooner had she taken his hand than he pulled her over the precipice with him. In that instant they were swallowed by an eruption of smoke and ash, only to find themselves standing face to face with the dragon when the air cleared. Natasha snapped her jaw shut.

"How did you know that would happen?"

The dragon reared up and spread its wings. It was enormous.

"I didn't," said Gabriel, craning his neck to look up at the beast. "I just followed my gut."

Natasha was eyeing the dragon as well.

"Does your gut know a way to stop this thing from burning us to a crisp?"

Gabriel gave her a wink and held up his sword. Its blade was shimmering with the light of its three glowing gemstones.

"It sure does…"

The dragon was by now in a furious rage, and the fire that spewed from its mouth was blanketing the cavernous ceiling in a wash of rippling flames. Around them the damned were screaming in terror, but Gabriel was unaffected. He simply scrambled up the mound of golden treasure until he was directly below the beast, and then thrust his sword up into its belly.

The dragon roared and collapsed backwards, shaking the ground as it fell. The wailing of the damned ended shortly after. Gabriel turned to look down at Natasha.

"That was impressive," she said, arching an eyebrow. "A bit anticlimactic but impressive…"

Gabriel gave a knightly bow, his face a mask of relief. On his way back down the treasure shifted under his boots, exposing the third golden seal in the ground before them.

"This is the symbol for the *Manipura* chakra," said Natasha, bending over the seal. "It's a ten-petaled lotus flower; the energy centre for willpower and achievement. It's located where we have the scars on our upper abdomens."

Gabriel squatted down next to her, producing the Cube from his pack. It was still glowing bright orange.

"Willpower fits this seal perfectly," he said, inserting the artifact into its slot. "This gnosis is all about positive aggression, and not taking any bullshit."

Natasha brought her hands to her head as the new alpha-wave link was established.

"I'll never get used to that," she said. "It really hurts!"

Both watched as the Cube transformed in colour, this time becoming bright yellow. Gabriel pulled it out of its slot and packed it away. He brought out the Book of Khalifah again and handed it to her, laying himself back onto the mound of golden treasure.

"All right then," he said, stretching himself. "All we have to do now is figure out the rest of the riddle."

Natasha leafed through the ancient pages.

"Tell me about the glowing stones in the handle of your sword."

Gabriel held the pummel out to better study it.

"I took one from each of the Wormlords," he said lazily. "They opened three padlocks in a gate that barred the hole I came down through."

Natasha chewed her lip as she considered.

"So symbolically speaking, your victory over self-will, pride, and fear not only allowed you to gain entry to the place where the dragon of the false god exists in your unconscious mind, but it also gave you the means to kill it."

"It would appear so," said Gabriel, impressed by Natasha's insight.

"Ialdabaôth," she muttered, continuing to study the book. "This was the name the gnostic priests had for Yahweh. He fizzled out two thousand years ago, but subconsciously we all still try to appease him, hoping he won't destroy our lives."

"What do you mean?" asked Gabriel, propping himself up on an elbow.

Natasha looked over at him.

"Most of us have a completely distorted view of what God is," she said. "That's why so many people reject God's existence.

"Take Yahweh for example. He was a primitive god for a primitive people. When he came onto the scene three thousand years ago, humanity was much less evolved than it is now. We needed fear to make us obey the law, and a terrible father figure to enforce it. Yahweh was perfect. He was monotheistic, which was a great step forward from polytheism, but he was not at all the way God really is."

"And how is God, really?" asked Gabriel.

Before Natasha could answer, Gutierrez appeared from behind the dead dragon.

"God is the substance that makes up all things, physical and metaphysical," he said, studying the remains of the dragon. "He comprises the laws of nature and of being. He is truth and love. He is beyond good and evil. In short, the true ineffable God is infinitely more than a vengeful old man who lives up in the sky."

"So God's impersonal then," said Gabriel. "Kind of like a powerful super-computer."

"Certainly," said Natasha, giving Gutierrez a warm smile, and noting how much older he was. "But he's also *everything*, so that makes him personal too. He's out there, and in here, all at the same time."

"People often think of God as being on one side, and the devil on the other," added Gutierrez. "This is not the case at all. Even Lucifer must abide by God's laws, for no matter how far away he goes from God, Lucifer is always surrounded by God, made up of God, whether he likes it or not."

"We all are," said Natasha. "It's kind of like living in God soup. We're all soaked in it; permeated by it. Anything that can possibly be, is made of God. Even our thoughts and emotions are made of God."

"Humanity's concept of the Creator evolves as humanity evolves," said Gutierrez. "Religious conflict occurs when we do not allow our concepts to change; when we rigidly defend the views handed down to us by our forebears. This always comes about as a result of pride, self-will, and fear."

"So when Jesus came to the Jews with a new concept of a loving, all forgiving God," said Gabriel, "they didn't accept him because of their pride, self-will, and fear?"

Natasha considered.

"I think that people would have accepted Jesus if their corrupt religious leaders had helped them accept him," she said. "The Jews were ready and eager to take the next spiritual step."

"Contrary to the Vatican's inflammatory dogma," said Gutierrez, "it was not the Jews who killed Jesus at all."

Natasha nodded in agreement.

"It was the Romans," she said. "Herod was a Roman, and the Sadducees were his political puppets. Jesus was an upstart that threatened the Roman system, so they killed him. The Sadducees were not the only ones who held on to the outdated Yahweh, though. The Roman fathers of the Christian church found him very useful too."

"Yahweh instills fear in the people," said Gutierrez, "and fear is power. This is why such a contradiction exists between the God of the Old Testament, and the God described in the New Testament and in the Koran. The fathers of the church could hardly deny the true version of God that Jesus and Muhammad brought, but they kept the old version to help them manipulate and control."

"Of course," said Gabriel. "The new version of God, or Allah, was merciful and all forgiving; a much more evolved concept of God than the one that followed the ancient Jews around, killing people and tearing down cities."

"Yahweh, or Ialdabaôth, is the god of the ego," said Gutierrez. "And like the ego, he behaves like a selfish little child who thinks itself omnipotent. The child demands complete obedience, loyalty and servitude, and if it does not get these things, it becomes angry, jealous, and punishing.

"But as humanity evolves, Yahweh's threats become empty. Eternal hell is seen for the lie it is; a deception devised by the same religious authorities that have led humanity astray for so many centuries."

"They altered the gospels," said Natasha. "They turned Jesus into a meek and passive figure that preached poverty and submission. It's all nonsense, Gabriel. The real Jesus was not like that at all. His teachings were about achieving abundance and self-empowerment."

"You're absolutely right," said Gabriel, recalling his recent experiences in battle. "What Christians need to do is separate the truth from the lies. Jews and Muslims need to do the same, just as all the people from every religion in the world.

"As it stands, most of humanity is throwing the baby out with the bathwater. We're either rebelling and dumping religion entirely, truths and falsities alike, or we're submitting and making ourselves swallow everything that our religious leaders tell us to believe."

Gutierrez held up a finger.

"We fear that if one thing in the doctrine is untrue, then it must all be untrue. Our pride does not want to admit that our ancestors could have been mistaken about some things. Our self-will works to resist change in any way it can. It always does this by denying the truth of the matter. Namely, that religions are both right and wrong at the same time."

"This is what the riddle means when it talks about questioning religious tradition," said Natasha, "and seeing our parents, or forebears for what they really were: Human beings prone to error and misconception."

"We've all been lied to by our leaders in one way or another," said Gabriel. "It's a matter of separating the truth from those lies."

"And separation is the third alchemical stage," said Natasha.

Gabriel sat up, thinking of the final three lines in the riddle.

"With this new frame of mind, something that always seemed impossible suddenly becomes feasible…"

"The fusing of the six world religions," gasped Natasha with sudden realization. "One of the primary purposes of the Cube. When the six fragments of truth contained in each of the six religions are brought back together again, the original gnosis will be re-established. What was broken will be made whole again…"

All watched as the golden seal dissolved, revealing yet another passage leading down into the Labyrinth.

"Well, that solves that," said Gabriel, rising to his feet and pulling up Natasha. "Slowly but surely, we're getting through this maze. Let's see what this next seal has to offer."

CHAPTER 34

Gibraltar.

Peralta looked out of the window, watching the rocky terrain pass below. He and the governor were in the back seat of a self-driving flying car, the luxurious interior oddly simple, and reminiscent of the styles popular in the nineteen-forties. He peered out the forward-facing window to see their destination come into view. It was a small observatory, built on the Rock's topmost peak.

"Don't you find it even a little incredible that I've come from the past?" he asked, turning to face the governor.

"Not in the least," replied the latter. "We were expecting you."

Peralta had met the governor the moment he arrived at the Convent. The bureaucrat was exceedingly young for his position, appearing to be in his thirties, but he showed the confidence and wisdom of a man twice his age.

Peralta had told him who he was, and where he had come from, and had been very surprised at how readily the governor had accepted his farfetched story. The fact that he had travelled through time had not fazed the bureaucrat in the least.

"I'm afraid the world is once again in a bit of a crisis, Mr. Peralta," said the governor as the car began to decelerate.

"What kind of crisis?"

"Your friend will tell you everything."

"My friend?" asked Peralta, watching as the car navigated its way into the observatory's loading bay. "Who?"

The governor pointed outside.

"The oldest Coolmaster on Earth."

Peralta turned to look just as the car came to a stop. Standing beside them was a well-preserved senior citizen in a nicely tailored suit. He had perfectly groomed, snow-white dreadlocks.

"Amir?" exclaimed Peralta through the glass. "What the hell are you doing here?"

* * * * * *

Peralta moved to the centre of the planetarium, taking in the nebulous expanse that had been projected onto the domed surface above. It was a three-dimensional representation, and as his line of vision followed Amir's pointing finger, he could see what looked to be a planet.

"That's Niburu X," said Amir.

His voice was that of an old man's, but his demeanor was identical to what it had always been.

"The earth's under imminent attack, my friend. The hosts of Satan are on that planet."

"What?" exclaimed Peralta, turning to look at Amir. "That's ridiculous. Niburu X is an internet myth. It doesn't exist."

"I'm afraid it does…"

Peralta had to force his jaw shut. Niburu X was the central theme of one of the most ludicrous conspiracy theories he had ever encountered. It stated that there existed a planet whose orbit crossed with the Earth's once every ten thousand years. Discovered and named by the ancient astronomers of Sumer, Niburu X was said to be home to an evil race of beings that would usurp the earth at the next planetary conjunction.

"The Nephilim of Niburu X," said Peralta, shaking his head incredulously. "The ancient race of giants that were said to have once ruled earth…"

The governor came to their side.

"Astronomers all over the world have been monitoring its approach for the past twenty-four hours," he said. "The planet came out of nowhere and is approaching very quickly. We will cross paths with it in precisely twelve hours and forty-three minutes. We really don't know what to expect. Its velocity is tremendous."

Peralta turned to look at the man.

"And is the world armed and ready?"

The governor trained his eyes on Peralta.

"The Earth has not possessed military forces for over six hundred years," he said. "There has been no need even for police."

"No military," said Peralta aghast, and then turning to Amir he asked:

"How do you know that Satan is even on that planet? Doesn't that sound a little superstitious and paranoid?"

"It's in the Book of Revelations," said Amir, his white eyebrows gathering. "There would be one thousand years of peace after the second coming of Christ. After that, Satan would return for his final battle."

"The second coming of Christ?"

"Of course," said Amir matter-of-factly. "It occurred when Gabriel and Natasha activated the Cube. That's what that feeling of euphoria was when we made the crossing. It was the mass induction of the Christ Consciousness into the Collective Consciousness."

"I see," said Peralta, adjusting his glasses, "It wasn't a literal second coming... And the thousand years of peace are up tonight at midnight..."

"They are indeed," said the governor.

"But I would have thought the opening of the seals would have negated that part of the prophecy," said Peralta.

"And you would have been correct, my friend," said the governor, "if all the seals had in fact been opened."

"I don't understand."

Amir put an old hand on Peralta's shoulder.

"Gabriel and Natasha never succeeded in opening the sixth and final seal," he said. "Humanity's been waiting a thousand years for them to finish their mission."

"But what are you saying?" exclaimed Peralta. "That would mean that Gabriel and Natasha are still trapped in the Labyrinth!"

"Most certainly," said Amir, "but as I'm sure you know, time has no meaning in the Dark Rift. To them, thousands of years could pass in a few hours."

Peralta nodded slowly. He knew well of the time-warping characteristics of the galactic plane. When considered from this perspective, Amir's words did not seem so farfetched.

"What the hell is going on here, Amir?" asked Peralta, fully awakening to the situation. "How did you know I'd be popping up in the future? And what the hell are you still doing alive?"

* * * * * *

It was only when they had seated themselves in the observatory's small pub that Amir and the governor agreed to answer Peralta's questions. A young waitress arrived with their pints.

"God bless you, girl," said Amir. "Talking's a parched business without a nice bit of stout to sooth the throat."

Peralta took a sip and wiped the froth from his mustache. He looked at Amir and the governor in turn.

"It's good to see that the Irish are still getting the planet into trouble."

He put down his glass.

"Now if you'll please be so kind," he rasped, directing his attention at Amir. "You don't look a day over eighty. How did you manage to live for a thousand years? And what the hell is a Coolmaster? Why did the children think I was one?"

"Because of your white hair," said Amir, putting his glass down pensively. "If you haven't noticed, people here don't age past thirty-three."

Peralta looked over at the governor and found that it was true. He had not seen a single elderly person since he had arrived in the future.

"Thirty-three's the maximum age of genetic development in humans," said the governor, sipping his beer. "We stop ageing once we've reached it."

Peralta was going to say something, but Amir spoke first.

"It was no advancement in science that made people stop aging," he said. "It happened as a result of slow and steady spiritual evolution. You see, the more a person embraces the gnosis, the longer he lives and the happier he becomes."

"Then why do you look so old?" asked Peralta.

"Because I was born before the crossing," he said. "Most of us have died. The ones that still live are what you might call holy men and holy women. We're called Coolmasters."

"And why are you called Coolmasters?" asked Peralta.

Amir took a long, slow draught from his stout.

"It was observed that the more one advanced on the spiritual path of Illac Domus, the cooler one became."

"How so?" asked Peralta.

"People on the path become very laid back," said Amir with a shrug. "They're self-confident, relaxed, non-judgmental, easy-going, loving, considerate, or in other words, cool.

"If you really think about it, cool people have always been around. They rarely say brainless things. They rarely do things that aren't cool, like forcing their will on other people, or committing destructive acts. They never need to impress anyone. They don't have hang ups about sex or letting loose and having a good time. But they're also extremely responsible, dependable, and fearless. They live life in a rich, full, and spontaneous way. That's what it means to be cool."

Peralta considered what his friend was saying.

"I never thought about it that way before," he said, thinking. "Cool people are spiritually evolved people, even if they don't consider themselves to be spiritual at all…"

"They rarely consider themselves to be anything," said Amir. "They just *are,* and that's what makes them cool. Of course there have also been the poser types; those who try to act cool by being detached and aloof, but it's all just an act, and they're often more insecure than anyone else."

Peralta watched in muted shock as Amir produced his chillum pipe along with an old-fashioned box of matches. It was the same pipe he had always seen him with; an ancient, carrot-shaped artifact covered in Sanskrit texts.

"And what kind of a holy man drinks beer and smokes hash, for God's sake?" said Peralta, watching in disbelief as Amir stoked the pipe to life.

"A true holy man," he said, exhaling a great cloud of very pleasant-smelling smoke. "One who's not pretending to be anything he's not."

He smiled happily and leaned back in his chair.

"Genetically modified marijuana kief," he said, admiring the pipe. "It's quite good for you. The smoke vapor is comprised of antioxidants, coupled with a variety of vitamins and minerals. It actually scrubs your body of toxins as you smoke it."

He took a long sip of stout and looked at Peralta over the rim of his pint glass.

"It's got a crazy buzz too," he said, tilting his dreads to the side and taking another haul from the chillum. "Way more mind-expanding than the old stuff."

He proffered the pipe to Peralta, but the latter just looked at it and shook his head in disbelief.

"You're no holy man," he rasped. "You're a bloody fraud! A one-thousand-year-old fraud!"

Amir only winked happily.

"A very strange thing happened after the crossing."

"What?" rasped Peralta irately.

"All stress, everywhere, just vanished. Within a few weeks the whole planet had become so calm you wouldn't have even recognized the place. It was incredible. It happened to everyone, in every country. Hatred and fear just dissolved."

Peralta seemed genuinely surprised.

"How's that?"

Amir shrugged.

"Hatred and fear belonged to the world before the cataclysm," he said, leaning back. "After the crossing, there was nothing it could latch onto anymore. Everything lost its severity. Anxiety disappeared."

"I've been feeling that way since I arrived..." said Peralta, realizing it only then. "I feel like I haven't got a problem in the world."

"And you don't."

"But how can you even begin to say that?" exclaimed Peralta. "Satan is about to attack the planet with a race of evil giants from the planet Niburu X! This is serious shit, man!"

Amir smiled affectionately.

"I missed you, old friend," he said, waving the waitress over. "You've got to try and understand the universal laws. Nothing can happen in the outer world that isn't a reflection of the inner world. This applies to individuals, and to humanity as a whole.

"Consider the shadow government that tried to take over the world at the time of the crossing. It was just a reflection of the shadowy self that resided in every individual, vying for control. Once that lower self was exposed and vanquished, shadow governments couldn't exist anymore."

Peralta struggled to understand.

"So World War Three was just a reflection of an internal war?"

Amir nodded.

"Absolutely. That's why it was called Armageddon; the final battle between the higher-self and the lower-self; between good and evil. It was being waged in every heart a long time before it manifested in the outer world."

Peralta understood at last.

"So then climate change was just a reflection of the changes happening in the collective consciousness. The outer world has always been a product of our inner state of mind. It's a quantum projection... Collectively and individually..."

Amir gave a nod and just then the waitress arrived.

"We'll have another round, my little Venus," he said flirtatiously.

To Peralta's surprise, the girl smiled and gave Amir a sultry look. When she left, he leaned closer and spoke in a low voice.

"A Coolmaster's longevity is partly due to his heightened sex drive."

"At your age?" said Peralta in shock. "You should be ashamed!"

Amir shot him a mischievous wink.

"The young ones always come looking for me."

Peralta turned to the governor for support but found the bureaucrat nodding knowingly.

"It's very true," he said. "Quite incredible, really."

"All right," rasped Peralta, waving his hands. "I've heard enough. Tell me what else has happened to this crazy planet."

Amir sat back in his chair.

"Things altered rapidly after the cataclysm," he said, nodding as he remembered. "People began to question everything they thought they knew. There came about massive changes in politics, education, and religion. The truth about our place in the universe, coupled with the knowledge of the true meaning of life, altered the way we looked at ourselves. It also altered the way we looked at each other, and at life in general. You see we'd moved into the next higher sphere without even knowing it. Society was transformed."

Peralta leaned forward in his chair.

"In what ways?"

"No more money for one thing," said Amir, looking over at the governor.

"No more war," added the bureaucrat. "Transparent direct democracies everywhere. No more hunger."

"How could there be no money?"

Amir shrugged again.

"Seven centuries ago, the publicly owned and operated Cube Corporation bought out the last of the private corporations, and took over the United Nations, forming a single world government that was democratically run by the citizens of the planet. Profits were spread evenly throughout the entire population."

"A tipping point was also reached in the collective consciousness at that time," added the governor.

Amir nodded in agreement.

"Everyone was playing a lot of Apocatastasis," he said. "They really began to understand the gnosis as a result of that game. It became easier and easier for them to apply what they learned in the game to their lives."

"But what about the global financial system?" asked Peralta.

"All the money anybody needed came from their Cube Corp dividends," said the governor. "As such, people started giving products and services away."

Amir took another haul from his chillum.

"Currency became less and less necessary," he said. "Until it was finally phased out entirely."

"So who does all the work around here?" asked Peralta. "If there's no need to earn money, then there's no need for anyone to work."

"People go to work because they want to give," said Amir, glancing over at the young waitress. "They do what they feel most inclined to do, and for this reason, people generally love their jobs. The jobs that nobody wants to do are done by humanoid robots."

"One of the biggest lessons humanity has learned is that a person's happiness is directly related to giving," explained the governor. "If you give to your maximum potential, you can't help but be happy."

"It's all about giving, old friend," said Amir. "And receiving is just another form of giving."

Peralta struggled to understand.

"How's that?"

Amir shrugged.

"You give someone a gift when you accept what they want to give you. It works the same with the universe. God wants us to have everything we desire, so you give him a gift when you let yourself receive universal abundance."

"Weren't there any problems at all?"

"Growing pains," said Amir. "Over the years, the population continued to increase, albeit at a much slower rate than before. As third world nations were transformed, their birth rates naturally fell. Even still, when we reached nine billion, we began to dedicate our collective attention to developing space travel and terraforming technology.

"Interplanetary colonization became an obsession for many people, and science made an exponential leap shortly after that. The knowledge given to us by the reptilians, combined with the spiritually inspired minds of our scientists, gave birth to an entirely new technology."

"Could you be more specific?" asked Peralta, his professional interest peaking. "What kind of technology?"

"The long-awaited unification of physics and metaphysics," said Amir. "Through it we learned how to isolate gravitons and dark matter. Our scientists used them for everything from free energy to inter-galactic space travel. They opened up new worlds that could rapidly be terra-formed and populated. Human colonies can now be found all over this galaxy. The earth is no longer overcrowded."

"I can't believe it," said Peralta. "Gravitons. Dark matter. Incredible. What's next then? Where is humanity headed?"

"Inward," said Amir. "There's nowhere to go but *in*. There never was."

"But what about Niburu X?" said Peralta, feeling a sudden wave of sleepiness begin to take hold of him.

"Niburu X is a test," said Amir. "Like everything else in the outer world, this invasion is simply a reflection of our inner state of mind. It comes as a result of the upward spiral movement of spiritual evolution."

"Resistances have to be revisited before they can completely be dissolved," explained the governor. "Niburu X will be humanity's last encounter with the echo of fear it once had. This will be like a final exam."

"I didn't know we were in school."

"That's precisely where we are," said the governor.

"Ever since the crossing," explained Amir, "we've learned that every event and occurrence in life has a lesson behind it. Everything is symbolic, no matter how meaningless it appears to be. If you stub your toe, or drop something, try to remember what you were thinking of when it happened, and you'll see the symbolic connection."

"Sure," said Peralta, yawning, "but you could look at anything that way, and come up with a million symbolic interpretations."

"Most certainly," said Amir, "and isn't it amazing that out of all the interpretations you could have possibly chosen, you chose the one you did?"

"I see your point…"

The governor leaned forward in his chair.

"You'll find that if you empty your mind, the first interpretation that pops up will always be the true one. If you follow your intuition, life will always reveal a lesson in every event you're experiencing."

"It's the only way to advance on the path of Illac Domus," said Amir. "This kind of observing has to be done constantly. It's a lot of fun. It turns life into the mystery-solving game it was always meant to be."

Peralta rubbed his face in an effort to wake himself up. The Cube's dream interface was on the verge of taking him. Amir produced a little canister from his pocket and emptied a blue pill onto the table.

"What's this for?" asked Peralta, picking it up.

"It'll help you find answers once you get back into the Cube's central interface," he said. "Take it."

Peralta looked at Amir and then swallowed the pill, washing it down with a gulp of stout.

"I still feel sleepy as hell," he said.

Amir smiled.

"As you should, old friend. I want you to relay a message to Gabriel and Natasha for me."

"What shall I tell them?" asked Peralta, yawning.

The governor bent forward and looked at Amir.

"He really doesn't know, does he..."

Amir shook his head.

"He hasn't a clue."

"Know what?" asked Peralta, struggling to keep his eyes open.

Amir put a hand on his forearm.

"You'll learn all you need to know when you're in the central interface," he said. "But there's also something you've got to figure out for yourself. Think of the *Tree of Life*. Think of the structure of the Cube and compare it to the structure of the universe. Think of the dream interface and compare it to waking life. When you find the answers, you'll understand."

"But what am I supposed to tell Gabriel and Natasha?" asked Peralta, barely managing to remain awake.

"You've got to make them see the truth, and you can only do that if you know the truth yourself. It's not the same if we tell you, but I can give you some clues. There are four dimensions in this universe. There is length, width, height, and depth.

"Think! Where is depth? How is it connected to the other three dimensions, and to the gravitational singularity? Use that messy head of yours. Find the answers and apply them. If you can't make Gabriel and Natasha understand the truth, they'll never make it through the last seal, and the Nephilim of Niburu X will destroy Earth. We're all depending on you, old friend."

Peralta wanted to ask another question, but the pull of sleep was too strong. He struggled to open an eye, but instead fell headlong into slumber.

CHAPTER 35

In the Labyrinth of Sarras.

After what seemed like hours spent traversing the winding passages of the Labyrinth, Gabriel and Natasha came at last to a cavernous chamber, its jagged low ceiling lit by dozens of oil lamps.

The golden seal could be seen in plain view here, adorning the ground below what appeared to be a prehistoric cave painting. It depicted a crude target or sorts; a large round dot surrounded by a circular ring.

Gabriel wasted no time. He bent over the seal and inserted the Cube into its slot. After the customary jolt of pain, he and Natasha watched as its colour changed from yellow into a rich hue of emerald green. Natasha explained that this was the colour of the fourth *Anahata* chakra, the energy centre located in the centre of the chest, just above the heart.

"A dot within a circle," she said, looking up at the crude painting on the wall. "This is the alchemical symbol for gold, but it's also a circumpunct, an ancient symbol for the higher-self."

Gabriel examined the painting.

"There's a second outer circle here," he said, running his hand over its surface. "It's very faint."

Gabriel opened his duffel bag and produced the Book of Khalifah, handing it to Natasha. She read the fourth riddle aloud.

The Two look inward to the divine core,
But first come to the walls that enclose it.
One is of deception.
The other of misconception.

There is a fragment here that never sleeps.
To transcend it one must be relentless.
If the child is to mature,
The teacher must be patient.
Only then can the apprentice become the master.

"I'm completely lost," said Gabriel. "What's the alchemical stage for this seal anyway?"

"Conjunction," said Natasha, putting the book down on a nearby boulder and moving closer to the painting. "The bringing together of two parts to make a single element."

Gabriel rubbed the stubble on his face as he considered.

"And what's this seal's divine action?"

Natasha was examining the painting's surface.

"*Atma-Jnana*," she said. "It's the Hindu contribution to the gnosis. It means self-realization, which is the experience of the true self, and its oneness with *Brahman* or God."

Gabriel nodded.

"So the riddle and the cave painting are both referring to the same thing: The higher-self."

"Yes, but it's not just a cave painting," said Natasha, turning to face him. "It's a mandala; a meditative symbol. The central dot represents our divine core. The outer circles represent our lower-self."

"So the outer circles are the walls that the riddle talks about," said Gabriel. "The ones that prevent us from reaching our divine core. One circle symbolizes deception, and the other circle symbolizes misconception. Which is which?"

"The outer circle is definitely deception," said Natasha, pausing for only a moment before continuing. "It represents our mask-self."

"The person we pretend to be," said Gabriel, thinking.

Natasha went back to where she had laid the Book of Khalifah and began to search through its pages.

"This is starting to make sense, Gabriel," she said, finding the passage. "Listen to these lines. I remembered having seen them in the cleric's letter to the Umayyad Caliph of Cordoba."

She translated from the Arabic as she read.

"Know, oh prince, that the divine core is hidden like an emerald in a cake of muddy clay. Only when the mind's eye unites with this core can the mud be washed away, and the inner child exposed and re-educated. In this way the lower shall be raised to the higher, and the two conjoined at last."

Natasha looked up from the book.

"The lower-self is the inner ring in the mandala," she said. "It's being likened to an ignorant child full of misconceptions. The child can be re-educated only if the teacher is patient, and that's where the love from the heart chakra is taken into account. It's not a question of destroying the lower-self, it's a matter of helping it to grow up. After that, the inner child sees things clearly, and it merges with the divine core, or the higher-self."

Gabriel went to investigate a shadowy area of the chamber and soon found a rough bench carved into the rock.

"I think I might have just found that *mind's eye* you were reading about," he said, directing the beam of his flashlight to a crude image on the ground.

Natasha came up next to him. At the foot of the bench was the painted image of an eye.

"This bench symbolizes the objective point of view," she said, sitting down upon it.

She patted the space beside her and smiled. Gabriel sat down too. From their new position they could see that the oil lamps in the room had in fact been strategically positioned. Their light was reacting with a reflective material in the paint and giving the mandala a magical glow.

"Mandalas are meant to be meditated upon," said Natasha. "Try to concentrate on the symbol and think about the knowledge it's relating to you."

Gabriel did as he was told, emptying his mind of all other thoughts. Natasha continued.

"The alchemists believed that the human personality was comprised of three basic components," she said. "The mask-self, the lower-self, and the higher-self. Once the mask-self is dissolved, the lower-self can begin to be integrated into the higher-self."

"Conjunction," said Gabriel. "The fourth stage of alchemy."

"Yes," said Natasha, "and when it's accomplished, one becomes the *Jivanmukta*."

"What's that?" asked Gabriel, looking over at her.

"It's Sanskrit for a person who has experienced the state of Atma-Jnana and attained *Moksha*."

"Which is...?"

"Liberation from the cycle of death and re-birth," said Natasha, turning to look back at Gabriel. "Ascension to the higher spheres. Moksha is the reason why we incarnate on Earth."

Gabriel returned his gaze to the glowing mandala.

"Tell me more about this mask-self," he said. "Why is the ring that represents it in the mandala so hard to see?"

"Because the mask-self doesn't really exist," said Natasha. "It's a fabrication."

"A psychological image?" asked Gabriel.

"Yes. A master image. It comes into being during childhood. It's designed to bring us happiness, but it brings the exact opposite."

"How so?"

"It's basic psychology," said Natasha. "When a child misbehaves, the parents usually take away their love as punishment. This is the most traumatic thing a child can experience. On the other hand, when the child is good, the parents reward him with even more love. The basic image the child formulates is that he must be good and saintly and avoid being bad at all costs."

"So the child tries to be good," said Gabriel with a shrug. "What's the damage in that?"

"He ends up creating a mask-self," said Natasha. "One that's always good. The trouble is, the child knows he's nowhere near as good as his mask-self is. It's just an act, and he can sense there's something really dishonest about it. Because of that guilt, the whole construct eventually gets buried in his unconscious mind, but the feeling of being a fraud never entirely disappears."

"I get it," said Gabriel. "And as we grow up, we start to identify with our mask-self, instead of with our true, imperfect self."

"Yes," said Natasha. "And as we can never live up to the mask-self's ridiculously high standards, we begin to hate ourselves, or feel we're failures. Either way, we put more and more energy into maintaining our mask-self, thinking that if we pretend hard enough, we'll eventually become that person.

"Of course we can't do this because that person's been a lie from the start, but the more we try, the more separated we become from our real self. We can't bear to look at our lower-self attributes, because admitting we have them would mean we're not who we think we are."

"And that's when things start getting messy," said Gabriel. "If we can't see our faults, we can never grow out of them. That's what the first and second seals were all about."

Natasha nodded, her eyes trained on the mandala.

"The mask-self can be found in almost everyone," she said. "At least to some degree. It's hard to uncover it because in one respect, it seems like the right thing to do. After all, how could it be wrong to be decent and loving, and never get angry or envious; to always try to be perfect?"

"You're right," said Gabriel, nodding. "But in the meantime, the unconscious fear of getting found out as a fraud rots you from the inside, even if you can't put a finger on it."

"That's why the mask-self has to be uncovered and dissolved before anything else can happen," said Natasha. "It's not hard to do once you've seen it in action and understand the damage it causes on so many different levels."

Gabriel crossed his arms.

"The initiate has to learn how to become perfectly imperfect…"

As he said these words, the outer ring of the mandala began to slowly disappear, leaving only one ring around the central circle.

"Well, there you go," said Gabriel. "We just dissolved the mask-self. All we have to do now is make that outer ring merge with the inner circle and we'll be through this seal. What about the *fragment that never sleeps*. What's that all about?"

Natasha concentrated on the riddle's fifth line but drew a blank. It was only then that Gutierrez appeared suddenly behind them.

"The lower-self and the inner-child comprise what is often referred to as the ego," he said. "They are one and the same thing."

"Hey!" said Gabriel, turning in his seat. "Where do you keep wandering off to?"

Gutierrez shrugged and then gave a courteous bow.

"You were both doing so well that I did not want to disturb," he said. "But here I must interject and remind you both that the human ego must be considered as a part of this mandala. The ego's transcendence is directly related to Atma-Jnana."

Natasha looked at Gabriel and then back to the priest.

"Of course it is," she said. "Please continue."

"The ego is comprised of two parts, my Queen," said the old alchemist. "The higher ego, and the lower ego. The higher ego is the mind's eye that the riddle speaks of. It can look at the entire personality objectively and can ask the divine core to take over, so that the ego might begin to transcend itself. The lower ego wants no part of this and works incessantly to prevent any of this from happening."

"So the lower ego is the *Fragment that never sleeps,*" said Gabriel.

"It is," said Gutierrez. "The lower ego is but a small fragment of a person's entire consciousness. It is the initiate's task to re-educate this aspect of himself so he might expand his field of operations. His awareness. His capacity to create.

"The trouble is that to the limited ego, expansion of this kind is synonymous with annihilation. The lower ego says, 'If my higher-self takes over, then I will cease to exist.' This, of course, is not at all the case.

"The ego is a divine aspect of the whole personality. It has its place in life. All that is required is that it allow the divine core to take control. Its resistance to do so must be overcome, again and again, until this is accomplished."

"And the initiate has to be relentless in order to make this happen," said Natasha, thinking of the riddle.

"Yes," said Gutierrez. "The lower ego uses pride, self-will, and fear to trick us into believing that the ego is all we are. Its attitude is always, *I versus you*. This is pride. The ego's defiance and rigidity comprise its self-will. It is always stubborn and spiteful. It says, "I will stay as I am." Finally, the ego uses fear to make free expansion seem like a mortal threat. Life is always growing and changing, but the ego wants no part of this."

Gabriel understood at last.

"And almost everyone alive is living in this fragmented ego state," he said. "Cut off from our divine core and everything that we truly are and can become."

Natasha smiled. She knew that they had solved the riddle.

"But the more we identify with our higher ego and use it to ask our divine core for assistance, the more we obtain the wisdom we need to teach our lower ego the truth about things; so that it can step down, and let the higher-self take over."

"*Only then can the apprentice become the master,*" said Gabriel, quoting the riddle.

In that instant the cave painting transformed into a single circle, exploding with light as the seal beneath it dissolved.

"Done," said Gabriel, rising to his feet and holding out his hand for Natasha. "Come on. Just two more to go and we can get the hell out of this place."

CHAPTER 36

Gibraltar.

Peralta opened his eyes to once again find the massive head of Bahadur looking down at him. The reflected light of the submarine port's waters was animating his bear-like features, accentuating the depth of his frown.

"You have been unconscious for almost six hours, my friend," he said in his deep basso. "We were beginning to worry."

Peralta rose groggily from his chair and rubbed his face.

Didn't he say that already?

He leaned on the worktable beside him, his eyes finding Shackleton. He was sitting erectly on his haunches, staring intently at him, as though waiting for an explanation.

"What was it that you experienced?" asked Bahadur.

Peralta stared back at the giant.

"I need caffeine," he rasped. "I need a lot of caffeine…"

By the time Peralta had finished his third cup of coffee, Scotty, Amir, Cassano, and Bishop Marcus had also joined them.

"Very well, my son," said the old bishop. "You have now most certainly had enough time to wake up."

"Spit it out, man," said Amir, putting a heavy hand on Peralta's shoulder. "Let's hear it. What happened?"

Peralta looked at them all in turn. He scrubbed at his messy head again, furrowing his brow in an effort to gather his thoughts.

"The Cube took me into the past, and into the future."

Amir cocked an eyebrow.

"In the game, you mean to say," he said. "In Apocatastasis, the dream simulation."

Peralta did not respond. He looked at Amir, still seeing him as an old man. He struggled to find a place to begin his story.

"Do you remember the symbol that Sir David and his knights had on their shields and tunics?"

"The Tree of Life," said Bahadur. "It was also carved into the doors that led into the City of Sarras."

Bishop Marcus pulled up a chair and sat down.

"The Tree of Life is an ancient analogy, my son," he said, adjusting his travelworn vestments. "Why do you bring it up now?"

Peralta held his gaze.

"Because it isn't just an analogy," he said. "It's also a map."

They heard a match flare and glanced over to see Scotty Roberts lighting up one his cigarillos. He pushed aside some clutter on a nearby workbench and sat himself down.

"A map of what, mate?" he asked offhand.

"A map of spacetime," said Peralta. "A map of the multiverse..."

Everyone looked at the unkempt engineer, waiting for an explanation.

"Einstein's theory of relativity states that past, present, and future, all exist simultaneously," he rasped. "They coincide in a block of what he called spacetime."

"What the hell are you blabbering on about now?" said Scotty, spitting out a shred of tobacco.

Peralta adjusted his glasses.

"I'm talking about the illusion behind our perception of time," he said carefully. "Think of a movie reel. It's made up of thousands of still images. When the images are projected one after the other, we get the illusion that they're moving, but they're not moving at all. They're just a collection of still images."

Amir was as lost as Scotty.

"So?"

"So, our perception of time is no different," said Peralta. "Think of every moment in time as being frozen, just like a single frame in a movie reel. All those frozen moments are contained inside the spacetime block, just like all those individual frames are contained in the movie reel."

Amir frowned as he considered the concept.

"So every moment in time, from the distant past, to the present, to the distant future, is a stationary moment frozen in the spacetime block?"

"Precisely!" cried Peralta. "Time isn't what moves. *We're* what moves. Our consciousness moves through the spacetime block. That's what gives us the illusion that time is passing. Time doesn't really exist. Einstein called it a stubbornly persistent illusion."

"And how does the Tree of Life fit into this, my son?" asked the bishop.

Peralta thought for a moment, and then opened a nearby drawer. He produced a deck of cards and tossed it into the air.

"I could do that a million times," he said as the cards fluttered to the ground, "and each time, the cards would fall in a slightly different pattern. As far as spacetime is concerned, all those millions of patterns happened simultaneously just now, even though we only experience one of them. The same thing happens with absolutely every event that could possibly take place. All variations occur simultaneously."

"I'm afraid I do not understand..." said the old bishop. "If all those other possibilities exist, then where are they?"

"They exist in physical universes that are adjacent to our own. The whole structure is called the multiverse. If you could map them, they would take the form of a tree."

"But with so many different universes being created at every moment, the cosmos would be impossibly huge," said Amir. "Each variation would create an infinite number of other variations that would stem from it, and each of those variations would do the same."

Peralta nodded.

"Absolutely," he said. "The size and complexity of the Tree of Life is so vast that it's beyond human comprehension."

"And you're saying we live in this tree," said Scotty.

"Yes," said Peralta. "We make our way through it much like a character makes his way through a video game. Any event we could possibly encounter, already exists within the program, or in our case, within the Tree of Life.

"Anything is possible because everything that's possible already exists in spacetime. Achieving your goals in life is just a matter of correctly navigating your way through the tree. It's all about cause and effect; making the right decisions and doing the right actions so as to move along the right branches."

"And how does the Cube play into all of this?" asked Amir, a cinnamon toothpick in his mouth as he spoke.

Peralta paused to gather his thoughts.

"The Cube appears to be directly synced to this tree," he said, frowning. "I still don't know exactly to what extent, but what I do know is that the reptilian king and queen used the Cube to travel back to the birth of spacetime; to the root of the tree."

"Why?" asked Amir.

"To build the Labyrinth," said Peralta.

"But why the beginning of time, my son?" asked the old bishop.

Peralta gave him a nod of gratitude. It was a good question.

"The purpose of the Labyrinth is to disseminate the gnosis," he said. "That gnosis has to filter up through the Tree of Life. If they'd built the Labyrinth any time after the birth of the universe, there'd be branches of spacetime that the knowledge could never reach.

"Any fallen angels inhabiting those branches wouldn't be able to access the gnosis and would be lost forever. In order for the Apocatastasis to occur, every fallen angel has to return to the higher spheres; even Lucifer, but he'll be the last to ascend, because he was the first to fall."

"Incredible," said the old bishop.

"It gets even crazier," said Peralta. "Building the Labyrinth was a suicide mission. It would need to be built in the lowest level of Hades, and the king and queen knew there'd be no way to get out after they'd finished. They'd be forced to go through another two hundred and fifty-million-year cycle of evolution, even though they'd already reached enlightenment, and could have ascended to the higher spheres if they'd chosen to."

"This was an inconceivable sacrifice they made..." said Bahadur.

"I'd say," said Peralta.

"But why didn't they ascend and then incarnate as humans to build the Labyrinth?" asked Amir. "Why did they have to do it as reptilians?"

"Because of two factors," said Peralta. "Energy requirements and the wormhole. To build the Labyrinth would require an inordinate supply of energy. The universe is powered by gravity. It's the strongest of all the forces, even though it appears to be the weakest because of its dispersion through the infinite dimensions of the multiverse.

"The only place to access the kind of gravitational force needed to build the Labyrinth was in the galactic plane. They needed one pass through it to harvest the energy required to build the Labyrinth, and another pass through it to activate the Cube."

Amir nodded.

"The galactic plane is a flattened-out black hole. It has an incredibly strong gravitational field…"

"Yes," said Peralta, rising to his feet and beginning to pace. "That's why we were thrown forward in time when we came out of it, and that's why Gabriel and Natasha are racing towards the future the longer they remain in it."

Peralta seemed deeply troubled.

"What is the matter, my son?" asked Bishop Marcus.

"There's something about the Cube that I can't seem to make any sense of, and it's driving me crazy."

"Tell us," said the bishop, leaning forward. "It will ease your mind."

Peralta turned to face the old man.

"All the reptilian technology is based in biomimicry," he said, pointing to a bank of monitors that were blinking with streaming reptilian data. "They copied the way nature works. The Cube is a perfect replica of the multiverse. It's so precise, that I don't know where it ends, and where our present universe begins. It's as though the two were quantumly entangled."

"Back to your bloody blabbering again," said Scotty, lighting a second cigarillo. "Speak in English, mate!"

Peralta resumed his pacing and proceeded to relate all the events that had befallen him while in the Cube's dream interface. He told them of how he had visited the governor of Gibraltar and found Amir one thousand years in the future. He related all the strange things he had seen, telling them of the planet Niburu X, and what he had learned after taking the blue pill that Amir had given him.

"But none of that was real," said Amir. "I wasn't real. It was all just a simulation, can't you see? It was a dream."

Peralta stopped and turned to face him.

"Was it?" he asked. "And what exactly is a dream, my friend? The exact same number of neurons fire in your brain when you're dreaming as they do when you're awake. To our brains, there's no difference whatsoever between being awake and dreaming."

Peralta turned to look at the submarine. It sat in the centre of the cave, the black water lapping around its dark hull.

"In the future," he said at length, "Amir and the governor knew something I didn't know. They said they couldn't tell me what it was; that I had to figure it out for myself…"

Bahadur came to his side.

"To transcend the Cube is to see it in all things," he quoted. "Perhaps the answer to your mystery is contained in those words."

Peralta turned and looked up at the giant, his face transforming as a thought occurred to him.

"But that would mean that all this time…"

"What are you thinking?" asked Amir, rising to his feet.

Peralta rubbed his face.

"How could I have been so stupid?" he said, understanding at last. "It's not a matter of the Cube and our universe being tangled up. It's a matter of the Cube and our universe being one and the same thing!"

He returned to the computers and tapped away at a keyboard, watching as a new series of exponents ran across the screen. He shook his head incredulously as the mathematical proof was offered up to him, and then turned to face the others.

"I've just initiated a computer simulation to confirm the data, so I won't know all the facts for at least another few hours, but this much I can tell you. We, my friends, have been squeezed into a three-dimensional, cube-shaped multiverse for the past 14.6 billion years. Ever since we fell!"

"What do you mean?" asked Amir.

"I mean this whole world; the one we think is so real, is in actual fact a simulation! It's no different to the Cube's dream interface. It came into existence when Lucifer opened up the Einstein-Rosen Bridge that we call the Portal of Ahreimanius.

Lucifer made some promises, and we followed him into it, despite all the warnings that we'd been given. As it stands, the only way out of this prison we're in, is to dream our way out!"

"But surely this is just a theory," said Bahadur.

Peralta shook his head.

"Math doesn't lie. The fractal equation that the reptilians used in their axiomatic decryption code is a constant in the fabric of spacetime. It's the bloody mathematical recipe of creation! We're living in a dream simulation. We always have been!"

"What the hell is a fractal equation?" asked Scotty.

Amir answered the question for Peralta.

"It's a mathematical pattern," he said, still contemplating the magnitude of what Peralta had just said. "It's the same on all scales, no matter how big or small it gets."

Scotty exhaled a mass of cigar smoke and Amir pointed to it.

"Clouds are a great example," he said. "If you zoom into them, the shapes you see are identical to the shapes you were just looking at. If you zoom out, the shapes you see are the same too, even if they're in a nebula that measures millions of light years in diameter.

"Fractals go on forever in both directions. They're like algorithms that nature's built on. They govern everything from the way a blood vessel grows to the way a galaxy forms."

"The micro is in essence the macro," said Peralta. "And vice versa. For this reason, everything can be seen within everything else. *To transcend the Cube is to see it in all things.* The reptilians mimicked this characteristic of the universe to create the Cube, and in the same way, the Cube has mimicked the characteristics of life to create the game."

"How so?" asked Amir.

"The game's a metaphor of life," rasped Peralta. "It performs the same function as a myth."

"And how the hell does it do that?" asked Scotty.

Peralta turned back to the monitors and spoke as he studied the data that was coming up.

"Myths have always had to relate sublime universal concepts in terms that primitive people could understand," he said, scanning a line of code. "That's why they always sound so primitive. A shaman would delve into the unknown depths of his psyche, uncover profound universal truths, and then try to relate what he'd found by coming up with stories that his villagers could understand."

"And?" asked Scotty.

Peralta turned away from the monitors to look at him.

"And that's exactly what the reptilians have done," he rasped, taking off his glasses to wipe them. "Only they had it a lot easier than the shaman did. The reptilians knew that people would be a lot less dumb in the future.

"Instead of the meaning of life having to be likened to a hero cutting his way out of the belly of a whale, the reptilians are telling us that the meaning of life is like a hero making his way through a video game, so that he can *escape* from the video game!"

Amir shook his head incredulously. Peralta was making perfect sense. He removed the toothpick from his mouth and used it as a kind of talking stick.

"In the Cube's game," he said. "You incarnate as an avatar and collect experience points by getting past barriers and going through good times and bad times. You assimilate knowledge and move up in levels until you eventually ascend as a god. It's just like life. The only difference is that the Cube's world isn't real. It's a myth. It's true, and not true, all at the same time."

"Every myth is true!" exclaimed Peralta, moving away from the monitors to where he had placed his electrode-covered sample of reptilian goo. "Even the most primitive ones. They all point at the same existential facts. I tell you, our universe is like the Matrix, but unlike the movie, it's our souls that are plugged into it, not our bodies."

"But what's outside of the Cube?" asked Amir. "That's the real question."

Peralta had a look of awe about him as he replied.

"Countless inhabitable dimensions that we are totally incapable of experiencing in our current state of awareness…"

"What dimensions?" said Scotty, unimpressed.

Peralta glanced over at him, still lost in amazement.

"Take for example our three dimensions," he said. "There's length, width, and height. They're easy for us to understand, right? Well, when Amir was an old man in the future, he told me that there was also a fourth dimension to our world. He called it *depth.*"

"But depth is just another way to describe length," said Bahadur. "The depth of the ocean can be measured."

"Old man Amir wasn't referring to that kind of depth," said Peralta. "Think of depth in terms of feelings and emotions. It's hard to grasp, but you can easily sense it if you try. Depth can be felt within you. It goes into a place that can't be measured with a ruler. That place is an inner world. It's every bit as real as the outer world we live in, but it's sitting in a different dimension."

"So what's your point?" asked Scotty.

"My point is that if it's hard for us to grasp a dimension like depth, imagine how impossible it would be for us to imagine other dimensions that are completely foreign to us?"

"Yet they're every bit as real as our four dimensions…" said Cassano, assisting Peralta with the wiring.

"Exactly," said Peralta. "We're like fish trapped in an aquarium. The first step out of the tank is to know that we're *in* the tank. The real world is much bigger than our limited little universe. If we could get out of this Cube, we'd be able to experience it."

"What on earth are you up to now?" asked Scotty, watching as Peralta placed a set of headphones over the orange glowing goo.

"When I was in the future, Amir told me that it was imperative that we make contact with Gabriel and Natasha. He said the fate of humanity depended on it. Gabriel and Natasha need to know the truth. Without it, they'll never be able to open the sixth seal."

"What truth, mate?" asked Scotty.

Peralta turned away from his work and looked back at the smuggler, his expression dumbfounded.

"Have you been asleep this entire time?" he asked, amazed. "We're in the bloody Cube, man! Humanity is, and has always been, trapped inside a holographic simulation! Knowing that kind of changes our perception of things a little, don't you think?"

Scotty Roberts only shrugged and produced yet another cigarillo.

"Keep your bleeding shirt on, mate," he said, striking a match. "If life's just a video game, then there's no point getting stressed about it now is there? Bloody hell…"

CHAPTER 37

In the Labyrinth of Sarras.

Natasha looked over at Gabriel. They were still squeezing their way through the worming passages, burrowing deeper and deeper into the Labyrinth. For quite some time now a sound similar to that of the ocean had been getting progressively louder.

"Can you smell that?" she asked.

Gabriel inhaled and nodded.

"It smells like the sea."

In that moment a briny gust engulfed them both, and Natasha grabbed Gabriel's hand, tugging him forward.

"This is the first fresh air I've breathed in what feels like months. Come on!"

It was not long before the constricting tunnel opened onto an expansive ocean, its untamed waters crashing on giant rocks below. A full and waxing moon lit the scene, and they could see that they were at the outermost point of a promontory, at the base of a towering cliff. Below them, a sturdy breakwater made its way out into the pounding surf.

"My God," said Natasha, her hair blowing in the wind. "This is so beautiful…"

Gabriel scanned the moonlit cliff face that they had emerged from. It looked to be over six hundred feet high and was comprised of glossy wet granite. At its top was an old Roman watchtower, crumbling and overgrown.

Gabriel turned back to find that Natasha had made her way down the rocky crags to the water. She was sitting down on a narrow shelf overlooking the pier, her legs dangling over the side and swinging contentedly.

"Come down!" she cried over the crashing waves. "It is wonderful here!"

Gabriel sauntered down the craggy steps, awestruck by the unbridled power of the ocean. The waves looked to be over fifty feet high and were crashing with such force that they shook the bedrock.

"This has got to be Finisterre!" he hollered over the pounding surf.

He sat down next to Natasha and put an arm around her, pulling her close.

"*La Costa de la Muerte*," he said into her ear. "The druids called this Land's End."

"What do you think that is?" asked Natasha, pointing to the end of the jetty.

Gabriel frowned and rose to his feet to get a better look.

"I have no idea..." he cried, squinting into the wind. "It looks like a crate..."

He offered Natasha his hand.

"Shall we investigate, pretty girl?"

Natasha let Gabriel pull her up and then fell into his arms, giving him a passionate kiss that ended with a beaming smile. She was glad to be with him, and out of those horrible tunnels. She took Gabriel's hand and led him down to the jetty.

At the end of the pier the two of them came upon an antique, iron-shod trunk. It was battered by the elements and slick with ocean spray.

"It's an old sea chest!" hollered Gabriel over the howling wind.

He opened its latch and within found a Viking's blowing horn, ornately carved with Nordic runes. Gabriel produced his flashlight to better study the thing.

"This is weird!" he cried, pointing to a string of text engraved around the horn's open end. "There's a Latin inscription."

"*Manifestabo Desideriis Renuntians Eos.*" cried Natasha, reading the text. "Manifest your desires by renouncing them."

"In other words," shouted Gabriel, handing Natasha the horn and rising to his feet. "Make your dreams come true by giving them up. I thought we were supposed to hold on to our dreams!"

He turned to look out over the raging surf, only to find that Gutierrez was standing beside him. Strangely enough, the roaring of the ocean and the howling of the wind lessened just then. It was as though the old alchemist had cast a spell.

"Well?" asked Gabriel, welcoming the reprieve. "Got anything to offer up on this one?"

Gutierrez scanned the ocean, the silent wind billowing through his robes.

"Desire is like sculptor's clay, my Liege," he said. "One must learn how to work it, or one will always make a botch of things."

Natasha came up on the other side of the alchemist, amazed by the sudden silence. It lent a surreal quality to the turbulent scene that surrounded them.

"Eastern philosophy claims that true happiness can only be attained when all desire is eliminated," she said. "They believe that desire is a hindrance."

"This is only partly true, my Queen," said Gutierrez, with a bow. "It is untrue in the sense that it is impossible to be motivated to create anything if desire is absent, even if what you want to create is desirelessness. Desire in itself is neither right nor wrong. Its creativeness or destructiveness is a direct result of its expression. It is a vital force, even if it has been feared and repressed throughout the ages."

"If desire's so important," asked Gabriel, "why would we want to renounce it?"

Natasha answered before Gutierrez could.

"Because if you can't give a desire up," she said, "it was never a desire in the first place. It was a demand; a product of self-will, not love."

Gutierrez nodded.

"Whatever your demands create will never fulfill you," he said. "Only the life force can manifest what you truly long for, but the life force can never be threatened or coerced. It must be induced with a patient and harmonious soul movement."

"And what exactly is a soul movement?" asked Gabriel.

"A soul movement is comprised of the feelings and attitudes that are connected to any desire you might have," said Gutierrez. "The movement can be healthy or unhealthy."

"I don't understand," said Natasha.

Gutierrez turned to her.

"If you observe how a particular desire makes you feel as you contemplate it, my Queen," he said, "you will easily discern the nature of the soul movement behind it. A disharmonious soul movement will feel tight and urgent, while a harmonious one will feel soft and flowing. For a desire to be truly fulfilled, no urgency can be attached to it. You must be so content and fulfilled in your present situation that the desire need not even be realised."

"But that would mean that it wasn't even a desire anymore..." said Gabriel, suddenly realizing that this was what renouncing a desire meant.

Gutierrez took the horn from Natasha and handed it to him.

"You must be able to say of your desire, *My life is already full, and as such, I can live without it. I can go through the pain of not having it.* In this state of mind, you allow the life force to make that desire become manifest.

"Tell me, my King, what is it that you most desire at this moment?"

Gabriel looked at Natasha.

"To get past these last two seals and get the hell out of this labyrinth."

"Very well," said the alchemist. "Relate this desire to your innermost being and then sound the horn. But be sure to keep everything that I have said in mind as you do so."

Gabriel reached over and took Natasha's hand, pulling her towards him.

"Any last suggestions?"

Natasha smiled.

"I think you're the kind of man who usually gets what he wants. Just do what you normally do. I'm sure it'll work."

Gabriel looked over at Gutierrez and held up the horn.

"What I normally do is not let myself give a shit."

The old alchemist gave a single nod.

"That is what is more reverently known as *Holy Indifference*, my Liege."

Gabriel shrugged and then blew into the horn with all his might. In an instant a loud note sounded, and no sooner had it done so than the pounding surf became suddenly calm.

Gabriel lowered the horn, amazed. The raging ocean had turned into a sea of glass.

"Look," said Natasha. "There's a boat on the horizon."

It was not long before the craft arrived, and they saw that it was a medieval bark, with a high prow and stern, and a single mast holding aloft a tattered, square sail. It had no pilot, and inlaid into its otherwise empty deck was a shining, golden disc.

"That's got to be the fifth seal," said Gabriel as the boat pulled up to the peer.

Gutierrez drew their attention to a sign that was affixed to its hull.

BE WARNED, ANY WHO WOULDST SET FOOT IN ME, THAT THOU BE STRONG OF FAITH AND PURE OF SOUL, FOR I AM NAUGHT BUT LOVE AND TRUTH, AND I WILL CAST DOWN ANY WHO SPEAK THE POISONED WORD AGAINST ME.

Gabriel looked over at Gutierrez.

"Well that's definitely something to keep in mind before going aboard."

Natasha hopped onto the boat without a second thought.

"Wait!" cried Gabriel. "What are you doing?"

"Do you really think we would have made it this far if we weren't strong of faith and pure of soul?"

She knelt down beside the seal.

"Really, Gabriel. I'm surprised at you."

Gabriel looked back at Gutierrez only to find that the old alchemist had vanished.

"I was just playing it safe..." he said, hopping aboard.

"This is the *Vishuddha* chakra," said Natasha, studying the symbol on the seal. "It's located in the throat region, but it governs hearing."

Gabriel's fingers found the scar on his neck.

"Hearing..." he pondered, pacing the deck. "Wasn't the Divine Action for this seal, *Logos*, or *The Word?*"

Natasha looked up and nodded.

"It's the Christian contribution," she said. "Logos is at the root of all creation. *In the beginning was the Word, and the Word was with God, and the Word was God.*"

"The first lines in the Gospel of St. John…" said Gabriel, looking around. "Tell me, is there anything familiar to you about this boat?"

Natasha scanned the bark.

"Not really," she said. "Should there be?"

"Of course there should be," said Gabriel. "It's straight out of *The Quest For The Holy Grail*. Don't you remember the chapter about the boat that King Solomon built to serve the last of his bloodline?"

Natasha made the connection at once.

"It had a similar warning attached to its hull," she said. "It took Galahad and the Maiden to the heavenly City of Sarras, where they healed the Fisher King."

Gabriel smiled and nodded.

"That boat was the method of transport between the earth and the higher realms," he said. "If that boat is *this* boat, then we're standing on our ticket out of this labyrinth."

"Sarras was Holy Jerusalem," whispered Natasha in awe. "The City of God in heaven. If the legend is being mirrored, the king would have to be healed before we could get there. How are we supposed to do that?"

Gabriel produced the glowing Cube and turned it in his hands. Its rich emerald light was breathtakingly beautiful.

"The infirmed Fisher King wasn't just a guy," he said, looking into the Cube. "You yourself said it. He was a metaphor for the corrupt Catholic Church, and all the world's corrupted religions for that matter. We heal him by unlocking the gnosis and plugging that knowledge into the collective consciousness with the Cube."

He held up the shimmering artifact.

"You're absolutely right, Gabriel," said Natasha, amazed.

"Once that's done," he continued, "all the screwed up religious beliefs in the world will begin to get set straight, and just like in the legend, the land will be restored. Remember what my father said? The Cube is the Holy Grail, Natasha. It always was."

Natasha was shaking her head in astonishment.

"It also makes sense if you draw a comparison between us and the characters in the Grail legend. Brother Bernardo said that we're both Rex Angelus; direct descendants of Jesus Christ. In the story, it was hinted that Galahad and the Maiden were as well.

"Think about it. We've arrived at Finisterre, or at the End of the World, and now we're on the legendary boat that Solomon built for us. It's clear that we're going to be taken to Sarras, which is basically where this whole thing began. Sarras is heaven, or the higher spheres. It's our true home; the home we all left long ago."

Gabriel squatted down beside the disc and looked deeply into Natasha's eyes.

"What's the alchemical stage connected to this seal?"

"Fermentation," said Natasha, suddenly realizing how close they were to completing their mission.

"Fermentation in what sense?"

"In the sense of allowing all the knowledge we've unlocked so far to merge and ferment."

"So that it can be applied to a single purpose," said Gabriel. "So that it can be applied to Logos; to speaking the Word of Creation."

Natasha removed the Book of Khalifah from his pack.

"I'm getting the feeling that we're about to unlock something really big..."

She read the fifth translation aloud.

In the soil of the Earth there exists a power that brings forth life,
Yet it cannot be seen.
In the depths of the ocean there exists a power that sustains the world,
Yet it cannot be seen.
In wind, and in fire, there exists a power that governs all existence,
Yet it cannot be seen.

Therefore, that which is invisible is the true power,
And that which can be seen is the result of it.
Earth, water, wind, and fire are servants of the Master.
The Two speak the Word and are obeyed.

Mighty is he who knows the invisible.
The power of powers will be his to command.
Cursed is he who is blind to the invisible.
His struggle will only cease when the poison has been revealed.

Wealth cannot come from poverty.
Abundance cannot be born from lack.
Therefore, the Master finds the great richness within.
He sees what he desires and possesses it in faith.
He tempers his will and waits patiently for the arrival.
In this way he brings heaven to the earth.

"All right," said Gabriel, holding the Cube over the seal. "Are you ready?"

Natasha watched as he inserted it into its slot. No sooner had he done so than they felt the familiar jolt of pain in their heads and saw the Cube change from green to a deep purple.

"That is so beautiful..." whispered Natasha.

Gabriel was equally enthralled. The colour seemed to be of the same frequency as black light. He looked out over the becalmed ocean, noticing only then that the bark was taking them out to sea.

"You know, there's no way this boat could have brought the seal to us if the waves hadn't died down."

"A symbolic event," said Natasha, watching the jetty grow smaller and smaller as they slipped away. "The turbulent ocean was like a turbulent mind. It became still because your soul movement was healthy and harmonious when you made your wish."

"And what about the sign on the hull?" pondered Gabriel. "It says that the boat will cast down anyone who speaks the poisoned word."

Natasha scanned the bark.

"This boat must represent the life force," she said. "It'll take you to what you want, but only if you're pure of soul and strong of faith. If you're not, and you're speaking a poisoned word, it'll give you what you need, which might mean going down, before you can go up again."

Gabriel pushed back his hair and ran the riddle over in his mind.

"If Logos is the *Power of Powers*, then Logos must be invisible to us, like the things in our unconscious mind..."

Natasha nodded slowly.

"And if we harbour negative unconscious thoughts, we're going to create negative events. Remember what Uncle Marcus was talking about at the picnic. The physical universe is made up of malleable stuff. We literally shape it with our thoughts. That's what the riddle's saying when it states that the four elements are the servants of the master. They serve us by becoming what we tell them to become."

"And that's why making the Word visible is the key," said Gabriel, amazed by his sudden comprehension. "The Word is nothing but an unconscious thought that tells the life force what to create. The life force doesn't differentiate between good or bad. It just makes what you tell it to make. To take control of the creative process, the initiate has to find the screwed-up words that he's unconsciously speaking and then exchange them for healthy words."

"That's the divine action of Logos," said Natasha.

"You know," said Gabriel, thinking. "There's probably not a single person out there, including myself, who's wanted something so bad and gone through all the effort of working towards it, only to watch it all fall apart when it was just about to happen."

"There can only be two reasons for a failure like that," said Natasha. "A poisoned unconscious word, or an urgent, disharmonious soul movement behind the desire. In most cases it'll be a combination of the two."

Gabriel frowned.

"I guess the big question is, what does a poisoned word sound like, and how do you change it up for a healthy word?"

"I don't think that Logos is just about the words that are being spoken unconsciously," said Natasha. "It's also got to be about the general intentions and motives behind those words. Maybe there are fears or hidden agendas there, or negative things that we're only half aware of.

"Do you want the thing you desire for the sake of having it, or do you want it so that you can appear to be better than other people, or have power over them? That kind of thing…"

"The Triad of Death," said Gabriel, rising to his feet and beginning to pace again. "If what you want is in any way connected to self-will, pride, or fear, then your inner word will always be poisoned. This is precisely why the alchemical stage for this seal is fermentation. Everything the initiate has learned up to now has to be combined if he's ever going to find the unconscious poison that screws up his life."

Natasha nodded in agreement.

"In other words, we teach ourselves how to create good things in our lives by fully understanding how we've unconsciously created the bad things in our lives."

Gabriel smiled. Natasha had summed it up nicely.

"And that means not putting the blame on anything outside of ourselves when things don't go the way we want them to go," he said. "It means accepting that it was us who sabotaged our success, and no one else. There are no victims of chance here. There's only complete self-responsibility."

Natasha looked at Gabriel but said nothing. A deep understanding was pouring into them both. Logos truly was the secret of secrets. With this knowledge people could create anything they desired.

"I think that deep inside most of us feel we don't deserve the desires that continue to elude us," said Natasha. "We're scared of what might happen if we were to get them. The child in us thinks that maybe we'll be punished somehow, or we'll not be able to live up to the expectations and responsibilities connected to the desires. Maybe we feel guilty…"

"There could be a million reasons," said Gabriel, "but the bottom line is if you're not getting something you want in life, it can only mean that somewhere inside you're speaking a poisoned word against that thing."

He moved to the boat's railing and looked down at the water as it rushed past. He could feel the gnosis flooding into him. He was remembering. He looked over his shoulder at Natasha.

"The easiest way to prove you're speaking a poisoned word is to visualize actually having the thing you want, but can't seem to get, and listening into yourself as you do it. If you're ruthlessly honest with yourself, chances are you'll find a voice in you that says no to your desire, or maybe you won't even be able to make yourself visualize the desire in the first place. You'll put off doing it, or your thoughts will drift when you try. Either way it'll be pretty clear there's a blockage in you."

Natasha came to his side.

"In the same way," she said, "if you think about the wishes you've had in the past that have come true, you'll find there's no blockage in you with regard to those particular issues. There's only a deep inner yes that says you can have them; that you deserve them."

Gabriel bent to pick up the Book of Khalifah and read the last lines of the riddle aloud.

Wealth cannot come from poverty.
Abundance cannot be born from lack.
Therefore, the Master finds the great richness within.
He sees what he desires, and already possesses it in faith.
He tempers his will and waits patiently for the arrival.
In this way he brings heaven to the earth.

"The last three lines remind me of Mark 11:24," said Natasha. *"What things so ever ye desire, when ye pray, believe that ye receive them, and ye shall have them."*

"What about the first three lines?" asked Gabriel. "And how does, *The master finds the great richness within* fit into any of this?"

Natasha sat down with her back against the railing and chewed her lip. She was stumped by the question. The fact that wealth and abundance could not be born from poverty and lack was obvious. The rich always tended to become richer, while the poor seemed to always grow poorer. But this inner richness that the riddle spoke of... What was it?

It was only after Gabriel had sat himself down next to Natasha, and they had both pondered the riddle for some time, that Gutierrez appeared before them.

"My dear King and Queen," he said with a formal bow. "What can a rich man do that a poor man cannot?"

Gabriel looked at Natasha before responding.

"He can spread his wealth."

Gutierrez nodded.

"And what if the rich man was to give away all of his wealth? Would he still be rich?"

"What are you getting at?" asked Natasha.

Gabriel answered before the old alchemist could.

"He's saying that a rich man can have nothing and still be rich, because inside he knows that his true nature is abundance. He can give away his entire fortune and never feel poor because he knows he already possesses everything. He can acquire another worldly fortune whenever he wants."

Natasha understood at once.

"There's no urgency in his desire to get rich again; no poisoned unconscious word that stops him. He always reacquires his fortune because being rich is his natural inner state, regardless of his current life situation."

"I guess that's what being truly rich means," said Gabriel. "It's got nothing to do with what you've got in your bank account, and everything to do with what you know you've already got right now."

Natasha's eyes lit up.

"So finding our inner richness means realizing our higher-self is just like the rich man. It's only our poisoned words that make us think otherwise."

"The fact of the matter is that no one is ever poor, my Queen," said Gutierrez, smiling kindly. "Even the most wretched of us is a very wealthy person. They just fail to realize this fact."

"At worst we're just broke," said Gabriel. "But there's a huge difference between being broke and being poor. One's a temporary state that we'll eventually evolve out of. The other is a lie."

"There goes the seal!" cried Natasha. "Gabriel, we're through!"

CHAPTER 38

A long minute passed before Gabriel or Natasha were able to voice their astonishment. After the seal had vanished, they had passed through the opening and descended a short ladder into the bark's lower cabin, only to find the most sumptuous room imaginable.

"This is incredible..." muttered Gabriel, stooping under the low ceiling.

Natasha remained silent. Her eyes were wide with wonder. Before them, under the golden light of many shimmering oil lamps, was a spacious canopied bed, laid out in deep crimson damask. It sat within a structure that was comprised entirely of polished tree boughs, their tangled branches strangely beautiful, and serving to hold aloft a veil of intricately embroidered silk.

At their feet were plush rugs, their rich hues merging with the dark wood that made up the cabin's walls and ceilings.

"This is the bed that Chrétien de Troyes wrote about in the Grail Quest," said Natasha, still in awe. "The one that King Solomon's wife built using boughs from the Tree of Life."

"You're absolutely right," said Gabriel, making his way to the bedside. "I never could figure out why the only thing that Chrétien de Troyes put on the boat was a bed. It seemed like such an odd thing to do."

He drew aside the diaphanous veil, seeing only then the silken sheets and sumptuous pillows that bordered the mattress on all sides.

"It's like a little world in there," said Natasha, peering over his shoulder. "It smells so fresh..."

Gabriel ran his hands over the strange boughs and then moved away to inspect the rest of the cabin. He looked back to see that Natasha had already climbed onto the mattress. She was luxuriating on it, a happy smile on her face.

"You're not going to find anything out there, you know," she said, her eyebrow arched suggestively.

Gabriel looked at her with a puzzled expression and then continued with his inspection of the room, walking around the bed to look for anything that might be relevant to the seal.

Not fifteen seconds had passed before he began to find it extremely difficult to ignore Natasha. As she had said, the cabin was empty, and he found himself increasingly engulfed by a very strong desire to lie with her. He turned in her direction.

"See what I mean?" she said from behind the veil. "This cabin's all about the bed. Come and see for yourself."

Gabriel watched as Natasha stretched her slender, ballerina's body out over the pillows, writhing with pleasure. He swallowed hard.

"I'll be right there."

No sooner had Gabriel spoken however, than Peralta's raspy voice sounded over his radio, the harsh static shattering the mood entirely.

"Are you guys receiving this?" rasped the engineer. "Can you hear me?"

Gabriel looked down at the device on his belt and hesitated.

"Gabriel Parker," said Natasha soberly.

He looked up to see that she was now on her knees, her hands clasping the polished boughs as she strained to look through the embroidered veil. Gabriel groaned and then pressed the speaker button.

"This had better be good."

"I've got them!" cried Peralta to the others before continuing. "Wow, you guys are really moving! At the sixth seal already! I had to reconfigure this goo three times before establishing this link! We've pretty well gone through the whole Solfeggio scale!"

Gabriel climbed into the bed not knowing what the quaky engineer was talking about. He drew the veil behind him as he entered.

"Hello? Hello!" rasped Peralta's voice. "Are you receiving?"

"Affirmative, Captain," said Gabriel, watching Natasha's fingers as they unhooked his armour. "How's everything on your end?"

"All is well, my son!" exclaimed the old bishop unexpectedly. "Did we catch you at a bad time?"

"Uncle Marcus!" cried Natasha, her words cut short by a loud bark on the other end of the line. "Shackleton! I'm right here!"

"I hate to cut this short," said Peralta, "but we can't waste any time with pleasantries. The goo's losing power fast, and this connection's already beginning to decay. I learned some important stuff when I hacked into the Cube's dream interface. I need to tell you about it."

"You hacked into the Cube?" asked Gabriel, cocking an eyebrow. "What did you dig up?"

"For starters, both of you are the same person."

"Say again?" asked Gabriel, exchanging a confused glance with Natasha.

"You guys were a single angel before the universe happened," said Peralta. "You *fell* on purpose, and you were split into two halves as a result."

"Why would we fall on purpose?" asked Gabriel.

"It was the only way you could help the other fallen angels get back to the higher spheres," said Peralta. "But there's no time to explain. What's important is that you understand that you're not two people. You're one."

Gabriel looked at Natasha and nodded.

"What else?"

"Waking life and the Cube's dream interface are essentially the same thing," continued Peralta. "One's just a reflection of the other. Simply put, humanity's been living in a holographic dream simulation since the beginning of time. We're all trapped in a three-dimensional Cube. The higher spheres are the innumerable dimensions that lie outside of the Cube. In short, life as we know it is a kind of super-high-tech video game."

"Like the Matrix?" asked Natasha.

"Yes," rasped Peralta. "But it's not our bodies that are plugged into the machine, it's our souls. The Cube is part of that machine. It's directly linked to a massive CPU that runs every aspect of the simulation. The CPU is alive and conscious, and extremely intelligent. You might call it God, or at least an aspect of God… There's only one catch, and I just figured it out about three minutes ago when the results of a simulation I've been running came in. The CPU only has one user slot!"

"Are you saying that only one person can interact with the dream interface at any given time?" asked Gabriel.

"I'm saying that there is only one person *in* the dream interface. Period."

"What are you talking about?" asked Gabriel. "That can't be right. There are close to eight billion people on this planet. They've all got to be in the interface too."

"I don't know how all this works," said Peralta. "Everything about the Cube and this universe is a paradox. The only thing that's important right now is that we get you out of that Labyrinth, out of this Cube, and into the higher spheres. The fact that there's only one user slot completely changes the game."

"How so?"

"If there's only one person plugged into the simulation, then only one person can be unplugged from it. It can't work any other way. You guys are going to have to be that person if you want to get back to the higher spheres. But you can't be that person until you become the *SAME* person."

"The alchemical marriage," said Natasha, looking over at Gabriel. "The unification of male and female aspects. Its metaphorical expression would be a man and a woman fusing into a single entity. Remember what the old gypsy woman said? We need to transcend duality and become like the divine androgyne…"

Gabriel nodded.

"Like Isis and Osiris in the pre-Egyptian myth. We need to become like Atum."

"Atum!" exclaimed Peralta, remembering. "Yes, that's right!"

Gabriel scratched his head.

"Natasha and I weren't the only angel that split into two halves after the Fall," he said. "Every angel got split. Nobody can get back into the higher spheres until they've merged with their other half and become a single entity again."

"And how the hell are we supposed to find our other half, mate?" came Scotty's voice. "I know for damn certain that it ain't the bloody witch I've got waiting for me at home."

"The universe takes care of the details," said Natasha, struggling not to laugh. "The two halves are brought together when they are both ready, and not a moment before. It can happen in this lifetime or in a future incarnation."

"But what about the single user slot thing?" came Amir's voice, the static growing increasingly louder. "If you guys end up being the person in the higher spheres who's wired up to the Cube, or the multiverse, or whatever it is, and this is your simulation, then who the hell is everyone else?"

"We must all be computer generated simulants," said Peralta, disappointedly. "It's the only possible explanation. None of us exist outside the Cube."

"You're very mistaken, Mr. Peralta," said Natasha. "The ancient wisdoms state that we are all One."

"Like in the Beatle's song," came Amir's crackling voice. "*I am he, as you are he, and you are me, and we are all together.*"

"Exactly," said Natasha. "If there's only one user slot in the Cube, it's because there's only one person who can be plugged into it, and we're all that person."

It was only then that the connection at last began to fail.

"Guys!" cried Gabriel, picking up the radio. "Can you hear us?"

He looked at Natasha. It sounded like Peralta was speaking.

"The goo... losing... temporal coherence... need to say goodbye..."

Natasha spoke into the radio urgently.

"We love you all so much!" she said. "Thank you for all of your help! Thank you!"

The bishop's voice could be heard coming through the interference.

"God speed, my children. We shall meet on the other side!"

The connection terminated. Gabriel put down the radio and shrugged.

"Well, I guess that's that."

He looked up and saw that Natasha was crying.

"Now why on Earth are you doing that?"

"We'll not be seeing them again for a long time, Gabriel. They can't come where we're going. They're not ready yet..."

Gabriel touched her cheek and bent closer to her.

"You don't know that," he said gently. "And chances are you're wrong. I'll bet we see them all again, and very soon. Time doesn't exist in the higher spheres, remember?"

Natasha smiled and kissed Gabriel. He could taste the salt from her tears.

"You always have the right answers..."

"Always," said Gabriel, smiling.

He turned to hang his sword on the headboard only to notice a symbol carved into its surface. It was of a single eye at the centre of a square, with the image of a boat just above it.

"Now what could that mean?" he asked.

Natasha wiped away her tears and smiled radiantly. She pulled open the veil and looked under the bed, turning to face Gabriel with shining eyes.

"Give me the Cube."

Gabriel shot her a puzzled glance and produced the artifact from his pack. Natasha snatched it out of his hands.

"Ready for a little pain?" she asked.

Gabriel leaned over the side of the mattress to watch Natasha crawl under the bed and lie next to the sixth seal. It sat directly beneath the mattress. He watched her insert the Cube into its golden slot and felt the familiar pang of pain as the new alpha-wave link was established.

Both watched as the Cube changed back to its original hue of iridescent blue. Seconds later, Natasha was back atop the bed, leafing through the Book of Khalifah.

"How'd you figure out where the seal was?" asked Gabriel, still amazed.

"It was easy," she said. "The eye on the headboard is the same eye that we've seen depicted at the centre of every labyrinth symbol we've come across. It's the *All-Seeing Eye*. It represents enlightenment, or the Seventh Seal.

"The square in the carving represents the Cube, and the boat on top of it is where we are. We're literally right outside the Sacred Chamber, Gabriel. There was only one place where the seal could be. Directly beneath us."

Gabriel shook his head in amazement.

"Nice job," he said. "I couldn't have done it better myself."

"Here it is," said Natasha suddenly, placing the Book of Khalifah between them so that he could see it as well. She read the sixth riddle aloud.

The gateway to heaven is the mother of All.
It resides at the centre of the universe.
In this place the many souls are but one,
And the ten thousand places the same.
To transcend the Cube is to see it in all things.

Gabriel rubbed the stubble on his face.

"What's the alchemical stage for this seal?"

"Distillation," said Natasha. "What was fermented in the last stage is now distilled into an entirely new substance with no impurities in it."

"And the seventh stage?"

"Coagulation," said Natasha, looking deeply into Gabriel's eyes. "It's the final stage of the transmutation of the soul. If you think of the lead into gold analogy, the liquid gold that was distilled in the sixth stage is allowed to cool and gather itself into a solid metal."

"And what about the sixth chakra?" asked Gabriel, "The one that's related to this seal?"

"It is called *Ajna*, and it signifies the end of duality. Its seed syllable is the mantra, *OM*. You must have heard of this word before."

"I have," said Gabriel. "It's supposedly the name of God, and when properly uttered, it duplicates the natural frequency that the universe resonates at."

Natasha looked at Gabriel in surprise.

"I can't believe that you knew that!"

"I'm not as crude as I look," said Gabriel, frowning in mock offense. "I took a yoga class once."

"Well then you must know that the Ajna chakra is where the third eye is located."

Gabriel reached over and passed his thumb over the faint scar on Natasha's forehead, his eyes scanning her pretty face.

"What exactly does the third eye do, anyway?" he said softly.

"It's what we look through to see non-physical things," said Natasha, gazing deeply into his eyes. "It's the *mind's eye* from the fourth seal; the *mystical eye; the inner eye.* They say that to see through it is to be in harmony with the mind of the Kristos, or the Christ Consciousness."

"And how does all this tie in with the sixth divine action?"

"It ties in seamlessly," said Natasha, shaking her head in astonishment. "To see through the third eye is to temporarily transcend duality and experience things in their true, unified state.

"Transcending duality is what the sixth divine action is all about. It's called *Binah-Chokhmah*; the Judaic contribution to the gnosis. The Ajna chakra is directly attributed to it. The whole spiritual concept is referred to as *Unity Consciousness.*"

"Binah-Chokhmah," repeated Gabriel. "What does it mean?"

"In the Jewish Kabbalah, the Tree of Life is made up of ten *Sephirot*, or enumerations, through which the Infinite reveals itself to mankind. Binah and Chokhmah are the two topmost sephirot. Only the sephirot *Keter* is above them."

"And what's Keter?"

"The ineffable mind of God," said Natasha. "Something we can't possibly experience with our normal consciousness. The seventh chakra, the crown chakra, is directly related to it. It's called *Sahasrara;* the thousand-petaled lotus."

"Then Keter must be the state of mind that allows you to inhabit those multiple extra-dimensions that Peralta was talking about," said Gabriel. "The ones that exist outside of our three-dimensional world; outside of the Cube…"

"The higher spheres," said Natasha, her eyes alight.

"And how do we attain this mental state of Keter?"

"Binah and Chokhmah have to become one," said Natasha. "Binah represents Understanding, which is the supreme feminine trait. Chokhmah signifies Wisdom, which is the supreme masculine trait. The sixth divine action fuses the two and opens the way to the seventh seal."

"The end of our journey…" said Gabriel. "The Labyrinth's exit."

Natasha nodded and pointed to the carving on the headboard.

"The *Ostium Sanctus* is located directly below us," she said. "But the only way to it is through Mithuna. We need to become *one*."

Gabriel understood at once.

"That's why Chrétien de Troyes put a bed on the boat," he said. "It's for Mithuna. He even made it from the boughs of the Tree of Life. It was a direct reference to Jewish mysticism."

Natasha reached over and resumed her task of unbuckling Gabriel's armour.

"It certainly seems that way," she said, smiling excitedly. "But there's only one way to find out…"

CHAPTER 39

Gabriel and Natasha's entangled bodies were moving in a slow, tantric dance. Their skin was bathed in the ship's warm lamplight, glistening with the sweat of hours of lovemaking. It was not long after they had been joined in Mithuna that they had begun to experience the mysterious, transcendental effects brought on by the ancient sexual positions.

All was fueled by the enigmatic Kundalini energy the professor had written of. It was a mystical force that rose and circulated through them with the power of a small sun. In this ancient ritual, two distinct individuals could occupy a single mind and body, bathed, as it were, in the golden light of the purest love imaginable.

Natasha was immersed in joy and bliss, her big eyes heavy with ecstasy. The cyclical pattern of their lovemaking was carrying her and Gabriel along a truly magical trajectory. What had begun as a slow, almost sleepy cadence, was gradually increasing in pace and intensity. Their physical surroundings were transforming as well, and soon their interwoven bodies had left the bedchamber entirely. They were hurtling through what could only be described as a rushing tunnel of plasma light.

A potent current of orgasmic pleasure was coursing up through Natasha's body now. It felt like cool, slippery water, and from her heart and breasts it passed into Gabriel's chest, transforming there into a molten flow of desire that descended through his torso to gush from his penis.

In Natasha's vagina, his fire was quenched, only to rise up through her body again, cool and shimmering, to begin the rapturous Kundalini cycle yet again. This was the fabled *Circle of Light* that Gutierrez had written of, and its radiant energy was carrying the two lovers into uncharted regions of body, mind, and spirit.

At ever-increasing intensity, they soared forward and inward simultaneously. The tunnel of plasma light was rushing past them at impossible speeds now, until even it could withstand the flight no longer. They had arrived at a critical velocity, where their passion could no longer be retained and controlled.

In a sudden bursting flash of sublime existentiality, the Circle of Light detonated like a sun in supernova. It stole the breath from their lungs and left them spinning slowly and weightlessly in a formless void of light and love.

The result of this culmination was pure ecstasy, and as the effects of the transcendent orgasm began to slowly ebb away, Gabriel and Natasha fell into a deep state of peace and relaxation. They were fully out-of-body now, and their consciousness floated unhindered in a vast and infinite cosmic landscape.

Gabriel... It's so beautiful...

As before, they had once again astral travelled to a distant star constellation; one that was easily recognizable to Gabriel by the shape of the giant nebula that lay before them. It resembled a proud eagle, light years across, and it was breathtakingly beautiful in its enormity.

Natasha could hear Gabriel's thoughts as if they were her own.

We're in the Serpens Constellation. The wormhole's taken us to the Eagle Nebula.

Natasha recognized it at once from the famous photo taken by the Hubble Space Telescope.

The Pillars of Creation...

It was only then that the effects of their trance began to wear off, and they quickly found themselves in the bark's bed chamber once again, lying in each other's arms.

Natasha wiped the perspiration from Gabriel's forehead, giving him a deep and passionate kiss.

"That was incredible," she cooed. "I think I'll keep you around."

She pushed herself off Gabriel and bent over the side of the mattress to look under the bed.

"Well?" asked Gabriel, propping himself up on an elbow.

Natasha returned to his side.

"The seal's still there..." she said with a pout. "Shouldn't it have opened by now?"

"We're missing something," said Gabriel. "We've got to figure out the riddle. I don't think we're going to be able to just shag our way through this seal."

Natasha nodded; her face still flushed from their lovemaking. She opened the Book of Khalifah.

"This shouldn't be so hard," she said. "It's only five lines long."

She read it aloud again.

The gateway to heaven is the Mother of All,
It resides at the centre of the universe.
In this place the many people are but one,
And the ten thousand places the same.
To transcend the Cube is to see it in all things.

Gabriel sat up.

"The *gateway to heaven* has got to be the seventh seal, Natasha. I think it's being called the *Mother of All* because it's the user slot Peralta was talking about."

"I don't understand."

"If a user slot existed, it would be the *mother* of the entire simulation."

"Why?" asked Natasha.

Gabriel collected his thoughts.

"If life's a simulation being created by the Cube, then anything on this side of the user slot is part of that simulation, and anything on the other side of the user slot is the real, multi-dimensional world where the user, or the *player*, lives. The higher spheres."

Natasha made the connection.

"That's why the final line of the riddle says that in order to transcend the Cube, it has to be seen in all things. If the Cube can be seen in everything, it's only because everything here is being generated by the Cube."

"Exactly," said Gabriel. "Our bodies are like characters in a video game. They're part of the game's software, and so is anything you can see, hear, smell, touch, taste, and even think. Everyone and everything is part of the Cube's software."

Natasha shook her head in amazement.

"Anything we can experience is made of *Cube stuff…*"

They were both silent for a while, thinking.

"That would put the Seventh Seal at the centre of our cosmos…" said Natasha at length.

Gabriel was confused.

"How's that?"

"If the Seventh Seal is what's projecting our three-dimensional universe," she said, "then it would have to be at the centre of that projection, right?"

"That could be the reason why we've been astral travelling while in Mithuna…" said Gabriel. "We've been trying to find the centre of the universe."

He passed a hand over the stubble on his face.

"The first time we ended up in the Crab Nebula in the Taurus Constellation," he said, thinking. "And we just came back from the Eagle Nebula in the Serpens Constellation. The two are over fourteen thousand light years apart. We've certainly been looking for something."

They fell into silence once again, thinking. Gabriel was first to speak.

"I still can't get my head around everybody being the same person," he said. "Even if we are all part of the same software program. How can everyone be the same person if we're different people? It just doesn't make sense…"

"Maybe we just think we're different people," said Natasha. "I've always found it amazing that we all feel the same emotions. They're like energy currents that each of us moves in and out of. If I feel sadness, it's not some unique emotion that only I can experience. It's the exact same emotion of sadness that people have been feeling for hundreds of thousands of years. It's like that with all our emotions. So really, how different can we be?"

Gabriel's expression suddenly changed. Natasha's words had struck a chord. He closed the Book of Khalifah with a thump.

"Let's suppose that I was the single player in the simulation's only user slot," he said. "According to what we've learned, I'd be creating the world I live in, right?"

"Always," said Natasha. "Thoughts create things and events."

"All right," said Gabriel, holding up his hands in a gesture of patience. "Now what if the world's population was made up of elements from my own unconscious mind?"

"What are you saying?" asked Natasha, confused.

Gabriel groaned in frustration.

"What if the person in the Cube's only user slot was a schizophrenic with eight billion alternate personalities?"

Natasha's eyes lit up with understanding.

"That would make everyone on this planet elements of a single, very confused, mind!"

Gabriel shrugged.

"What do you think?"

"I think you're on to something," said Natasha. "The only way a schizophrenic can truly be healed is when the impermeable barriers that separate his personalities are made permeable again."

"So the only way humanity can be healed," said Gabriel, "is for everyone to realize that we're all unique aspects of the same mind, and as such, we're all essentially the same person."

Natasha shook her head in amazement.

"The billions of people on this planet are nothing more than individual fragments of a consciousness that fell and exploded into this three-dimensional, dualistic multiverse."

"Everyone alive is the single user," said Gabriel. "It's kind of like how the entirety of a hologram is contained in each of its parts..."

"How's that?" asked Natasha.

"It's got to do with the way holography records light wave interference patterns," he said. "In our case, the entirety of the original mind would be contained in each of its fragments."

Natasha smiled.

"A mystic would say that an entire ocean is contained in every drop of seawater."

"All, truly, is One..." said Gabriel in stupefaction. "All the angels that fell... We all came from the same consciousness..."

He paused for a moment.

"But who's consciousness was it?" he asked. "Who's plugged into the user slot?"

Gabriel looked up at Natasha, his eyes wide with wonder.

"It's God, Natasha," he whispered. "There's only one consciousness, and that consciousness is God. It got fragmented after the fall, but it never stopped being God. We're all God. Everything is God."

Natasha bent over the edge of the bed again but saw that the seal was still intact.

"There must be something else, Gabriel," she said. "Something we're missing…"

"I know what it is, baby," he said, taking her hands into his. "Let me take you there."

* * * * * *

The nebula that stretched out before them was beautiful beyond description. Its form took the shape of a great golden eye with an iris of translucent blue.

"The Helix Nebula. It's also been called the Eye of God."

It was Gabriel's thought that came to Natasha's mind. The effects of their orgasm had still not fully dissipated in her, and she felt drunk with the beauty she was experiencing.

"We made it, Gabriel. We're here."

Gabriel's response came almost immediately.

"The nebula's not the centre of the universe, Natasha… This is."

Natasha felt a tingling sensation in her solar plexus.

"Look around," came Gabriel's thought. *"What do you see in every direction?"*

Natasha did as she was asked, her eyes wide with rapture.

"I see infinity…"

"Exactly, and that puts you directly at the centre of the universe."

"I don't understand."

"It's called triangulation. It's simple math. If you're surrounded by infinity in every direction, you can't be anywhere else but at the centre of the universe."

Natasha gazed into the Nebula.

"So then the Eye of God is at the centre of the universe."

"Yes and no," came Gabriel's thought. *"We were surrounded by infinity back in the Serpens Constellation too. That place was the centre of the universe as well, even though it's six and a half thousand light years from where we are right now."*

"I don't get it," said Natasha. *"How can the centre of the universe be in two places that are so far away from each other?"*

"It can't be," said Gabriel. *"The centre of the universe is always in the same place. It's right here."*

Natasha felt the tingling in her solar plexus again, and this time she understood why.

"So, no matter who you are, or where you go," she said, *"no matter how many thousands of light years you may travel, you're always going to be surrounded by infinity in every direction. That puts you at the centre of the universe wherever you happen to be..."*

Gabriel looked deeply into the nebula, the enormity of the cosmic landscape filling him with unbounded awe.

"Each and every one of us is the source of the projection, Natasha."

She was silent for a moment before responding.

"That can only mean one thing, Gabriel. The Seventh Seal is directly within us..."

In the blink of an eye they found themselves back in the bedchamber again, but this time everything, including their own entwined bodies, seemed to be in a state of dematerialization.

Below them, through the dissolving bed, they could see the golden seal and the Cube. Moments later everything was melting into nothingness, leaving a black and lightless void looming beneath them.

Natasha began to feel a deep fear overcoming her.

"Gabriel... I can't go in there..."

At that very moment the voice of Gutierrez came to them both.

"Do not be frightened, my King and Queen," he said. "Have faith in faith. Trust in trust. Fear is an illusion, a ghost without substance. It is easily dispelled. Love is the only true reality!"

And just then a radiant light seemed to ignite deep within Gabriel and Natasha, and it filled them with courage. Their ascension into Mithuna had fused them, body, mind, and spirit, and now, as one, they took the great plunge, letting themselves be taken by the black void that had engulfed the chamber.

In the blink of an eye a golden light returned to encapsulate them again, only this time with unparalleled splendour. They began to feel themselves dissolving into its radiance, but there was no more fear or dread, only joy. Tremendous joy.

Back in their sarcophagi, Gabriel and Natasha's physical bodies were breaking down into their base components of energy and information. It felt to them like a buzzing, orgasmic tingling, and it was profoundly comforting; like being lowered into a cradle, or a warm and cozy womb. The frequency was comprised of the purest essence of love imaginable, and it pulled them into a deep and blissful sleep.

"Praise be to God in the highest!" came Gutierrez' radiant call. "We are victorious!"

* * * * * *

Gabriel opened his eyes to see that he was lying in a clearing in the woods, surrounded by a circle of standing stones. Natasha was fast asleep in his arms, and he knew that he himself would not be able to stay awake much longer. The pull of sleep was far too potent.

He could vaguely recall having visited this place a long, long time ago, in a previous incarnation. He and Natasha had been children during the time of the druids then. They had unwittingly been drawn into the Portal of Ahreimanius, so as to fulfill certain requirements of their mission.

But whereas then the stones had been the source of a tremendous evil, they were now indescribably beautiful, and exuded a feeling of such tranquil peace that Gabriel was instantly filled with bliss.

It's so wonderful, but I don't understand…

It seemed that everything around him was veiled in a tingling, fragrant mist. It was only when sleep began to take him that he saw two diaphanous figures approaching. Their bodies were emitting light, and as they drew nearer, he recognized them at once.

"Suora? Fra?" he managed to utter. "What are you guys doing here?"

"Dear, Gabriel," said Suora, smiling tenderly. "Sleep, my child. You have been through a great ordeal. We have only come to take you home."

Gabriel felt a great happiness and tried to smile, but the urge to sleep was far too encompassing. A moment later he had slipped back into a deep and blissful slumber.

CHAPTER **40**

Gibraltar.

The old bishop helped himself to another slab of prime rib roast, drowning both it and his Yorkshire pudding in thick, rich gravy. He was in the Royal Convent's officer's mess, seated at the bottom of a table laden with food and drink, and surrounded on all sides by his dearest friends. Each was dressed in his finest and flanked by his own personal waiter.

Directly across from Bishop Marcus, at the head of the festive table, lay the empty ceremonial armchair traditionally reserved for the Prince of Wales. In his jovial state, Scotty Roberts was in the process of dropping a generous slab of roast beef onto the prince's golden plate. Everyone was laughing merrily.

"It's time for an official toast!" said Major Roberts, standing up and raising his glass of wine. "I call upon our worthy bishop to do the honours!"

"And I second that motion, mate!" cried Scotty, rising alongside his brother.

All came to their feet, their faces bright and proud. The old bishop, preparing himself to rise, saw the heroic company of men standing at attention before him and his heart was joyful beyond description.

To his right was Captain Peralta, and beside him Amir, and the noble giant Bahadur. To his left was Sir David, wearing the elegant cloak that bore the seal of his order, along with Cassano, Scotty and the handsome major, in full uniform.

"My dearest friends!" said Marcus, coming to his feet.

His old eyes shone proudly.

"We have at last come to the end of our great adventure! The world has been saved, and humanity has happily entered into a new age of enlightenment. Let this toast be to Gabriel and

Natasha, for without them, our victory would not have been possible!"

"To Gabriel and Natasha!" cried all in unison, and just then they turned their heads to see what the astonished bishop was pointing at.

In the time they had been toasting, Shackleton, who had been residing under the table, had climbed into the Prince of Wales's armchair, and sat himself stiffly upon his haunches, as though he too were partaking in the toast.

He was looking proudly back at the congregation, a puzzled expression on his handsome canine face. There could be no doubt that the dog was questioning their sudden interest in him.

"To Sir Shackleton!" cried Amir, raising his glass.

The resounding reply came from all those present.

"To Sir Shackleton!"

"And long live the new Prince of Wales!" bellowed Scotty drunkenly.

And as all returned merrily to their meals, so too did Shackleton begin his, bending over his plate of solid gold to gobble down all the meat that Scotty Roberts could heap upon it.

CHAPTER 41

When Gabriel at last awoke he found himself lying alone in what looked to be a hospital room. A soft, golden light was filtering in through the open window, and the bright chirping of birds outside told him it must be morning.

He had no sooner sat up in bed than Natasha entered, more beautiful than ever. She was wearing a glowing white summer dress, and her dark chestnut hair fell in thick ringlets over her bare shoulders. Love and happiness were shining from her eyes.

"Well, look who's up!" she said, stopping in her tracks and putting her hands on her hips. "It's about time!"

Suora and Fra entered the room just behind her. Gabriel could see that they were much younger now, just as they had been when he was a boy. He rubbed his eyes and then broke into a broad smile.

"You two," he said groggily, rising to his feet and embracing them both. "I thought I dreamed the whole thing…"

He put an arm around Natasha and drew her close, kissing the side of her head.

"And you!" he added affectionately. "Fancy not waking me up sooner."

Natasha only shrugged and motioned to Fra.

"I must confess that it was under my strict orders that she did not," he said. "Now is a time for rest. You must both be fully restored before you can proceed."

Gabriel went back to his bed and sat down. He was still feeling drained.

"Proceed?" he asked, looking around. "What is this place? I thought the spirit world was multi-dimensional and unlike anything I could imagine. This place looks pretty damn normal to me."

"We're on a hospital island," said Natasha, sitting down beside him. "It's a place where people come to rest before they proceed."

Gabriel looked at her incredulously.

"You're telling me that there are hospitals in the spirit world?"

Suora chuckled knowingly.

"Most definitely, my child," she said. "Everything on the Earth-sphere is an imitation of what has always existed in the spirit world. Here we have hospitals, schools, theatres, golf courses... Absolutely everything that can be found on Earth, and much, much more."

"And everybody who dies comes to this hospital island first?" asked Gabriel, amazed by what he was hearing.

"Not everyone, my son," said Fra. "Only those who have suffered traumatic deaths or endured rigorous ordeals leading up to their transition. From this island are portals that lead into all the various spheres of the spirit world.

"An entity's level of spiritual purification will dictate through which portals he or she may pass. Most will go to spheres where they can be reunited with loved ones and begin the process of planning their next incarnation on the Earth-sphere."

"We plan our lives on Earth ahead of time?"

"Most definitely, my son!" said Fra. "There are special advisors who assist people in this task. It is a lengthy process. Recent incarnations are evaluated and compared with previous ones. It is similar to watching a movie of your life. You can see where you succeeded in satisfying the life plan goals you set out to accomplish, and where you still need improvement."

"What kind of goals?"

"Goals of spiritual purification," said Natasha. "If you still have problems with self-will, for example, your advisor will help you to create a life plan that will focus on bringing out those faults so you can become aware of them and fix them."

Suora elaborated.

"Any impurities that are preventing you from entering into the next higher sphere will be focused on, my child. One does have to be patient though. You do not want to bite off more than you can chew in a single incarnation. People with very trying lives are usually people who have been very aggressive in their life plan."

Gabriel was amazed by what he was hearing.

"And how do these advisors make life plans happen?" he asked. "Is everyone's life pre-destined?"

"Not at all, my son," said Fra. "Life incarnations are predetermined by who an entity incarnates with, and in what historical period they take place. The actual events of a life incarnation are never planned, but factors are chosen that will direct universal laws to make a specific life plan manifest itself."

"Parents and other authority figures will be specially chosen for the person to be incarnated," said Suora. "Their faults and virtues will help him or her to evolve, just as he or she will help them to evolve as well. The geographic and political conditions that he or she lives in are also chosen for the same reason. Everything works seamlessly, my child. The Earth-sphere is a vast training ground."

Gabriel was shaking his head in amazement.

"A virtual school projected inside a cosmic, three-dimensional Cube…"

Suora put a reassuring hand on Gabriel's shoulder.

"You and Natasha are no longer required to incarnate on Earth anymore. You are sufficiently purified to move to the next higher spheres. The resistance of matter, and all the hardships it brings, are no longer necessary for your purification."

"And how many more spheres are there before we reach the top?"

"We are not moving to the top, Gabriel," said Fra, smiling kindly. "We are moving to the *Centre;* to the *One.* This place is called *The House of God.* It cannot be measured or quantified. It is indivisible. We will arrive when we arrive."

"Try not to dwell on any of this now, my child," said Suora. "You will understand soon enough. For now, you must rest. Think of this island as a kind of holiday resort. Anything you could possibly want can be had here. All you need to do is visualize it and it will immediately materialize before you."

Gabriel rose and walked to the window, astounded by what he was hearing.

"Now ain't that something," he said, gazing out onto the lush, tropical grounds. "We've been teleported to Fantasy Island for God's sake..."

He turned to face the others.

"Will we be having dinner with Mr. Roarke and Tattoo this evening?"

Natasha clapped her hands and laughed aloud.

"Yes!" she exclaimed. "We can definitely make that happen!"

* * * * * *

Gabriel sat at the wheel of his sportscar, its tuned exhaust note rising and falling rapidly as he revved the engine. They had been on the island for over a month now, and while it had been a wonderful stay, they were both anxious to move on.

He looked over at Natasha. She was sitting in the passenger seat, her face lit by a sun that was setting over a beautiful tropical ocean. The sky was ablaze with orange and crimson light.

"It kind of looks like a star gate," said Gabriel, studying the portal that lay directly ahead of them. "You know...? Like the ones from the TV show *Stargate*...?"

Natasha rolled her eyes.

"You're such a nerd."

Gabriel shot her a sidelong glance and returned his attention to the portal. It sat at the end of a hundred-meter-long stretch of road; a circular disc of what looked to be rippling water. It stood vertically within a golden hoop measuring about ten meters in diameter. Gabriel had caused a stunt ramp to materialize directly before it, and it was at this that the car was pointing.

"We don't have to drive through it you know," said Natasha, looking over at Gabriel. "Every other enlightened person has just walked..."

Gabriel shook his head disapprovingly.

"We're about to enter into a cosmic realm of unlimited possibilities," he said, his heart thumping. "Its dimensions are so vast and so exciting that Suora and Fra couldn't stay on this island for more than a few hours before feeling stifled and claustrophobic. You seriously want to just walk into something like that?"

Natasha shrugged and then smiled excitedly.

"Certainly not!" she said suddenly.

Gabriel revved the engine again.

"Nervous?"

Natasha turned to face him; her eyes alight.

"A little…"

Gabriel gave her a reassuring wink.

"No need to be nervous, my darling," he said, reaching over and giving her knee a squeeze. "I've covered every angle."

He put the car into gear and slipped one of Amir's hot cinnamon toothpicks into his mouth.

Natasha was surprised.

"You told me that you hated those things."

Gabriel only shrugged.

"People change. Now let's go see what all this multi-dimensional hype is about."

With these last words Gabriel released the clutch, launching the car forward, and accelerating to a frightening velocity. In seconds they were at the ramp and then airborne, the car vanishing through the portal without causing so much as a ripple in its surface.

It was only then that the two spectators who had been secretly watching stepped out from their hiding place behind the bushes.

"I thought they'd never leave, boss," said the shorter of the two.

"Neither did I, Tattoo," said Mr. Roarke, rolling his eyes. "Neither did I."

EPILOGUE

He who had first come to Earth in an ancient incarnation long, long ago, opened his eyes and took in his new surroundings. In his arms lay a sleeping woman of riveting beauty, her tussled blond hair falling over her naked body, accentuating her flawless, golden skin. He took in a breath of her and smiled, his sleepy eyes shining with love as he continued his survey.

They lay in a sun spattered clearing, in the midst of a springtime wood. Around them was a circle of standing stones, their ancient forms seeming to crackle with magical energy. He kissed the woman tenderly.

"Wake up, my love. Wake up."

Her soft eyes opened, and she smiled drowsily. Only then did he see a lone figure approaching. It was bathed in light.

"Brother?" he said, at last recognizing his face. "Is that really you?"

"It is," said the man, smiling. "It's good to see you here, Lucifer. I've come to take you home."

The visitor smiled, struggling to understand why his dead brother had just called him Lucifer. He went over the recent events in his mind. He and his lover had traversed the Great Labyrinth of Sarras and had assimilated each of the six stages of gnosis. They had transcended duality, passed through the Seventh Seal, and then arrived here.

"Why do you call me Lucifer?" he asked sleepily, struggling to remain awake.

"Because that's who you are," said his brother with a casual shrug. "You're the *Bringer of Light*, and your crazy stunt only confirms it. The Kingdom of God is fulfilled because of you. This might sound strange, but you are a hero here; truly the *Morning Star*."

"I don't understand," he said, gazing down to see that his lover was fast asleep again. "If I truly am Lucifer, how could I possibly be a hero? Lucifer caused the Fall. One third of heaven has suffered in agony for aeons because of him."

"All that's water under the bridge," said his brother, smiling affectionately. "All's well that ends well."

It was at that moment that memories of the man's many past life incarnations flooded back into him. He realized that the person who stood before him was none other than his older brother Jesus, and that he himself truly was Lucifer; the first angel to fall, and the last angel to ascend.

With his arrival the apocatastasis had at last come to its fruition. Every fallen angel had now returned home, and Hades had been vanquished forever. The Kingdom of God had been restored at last.

"But a hero?" asked Lucifer, laying his head back.

The urge to sleep was overpowering. Jesus bent down next to him and put a hand on his shoulder.

"*The end of all our exploring will be to arrive where we started, and know the place for the first time,*" he said, quoting T.S. Eliot. "You unwittingly gave us a priceless gift, brother. You showed us all what home really is."

Lucifer looked sleepily into his brother's eyes, and in that moment knew that all the horrible acts he had committed were completely forgiven. A great happiness spread over him, coupled with the peace that only true redemption can bring.

"*And the Spirit and the bride say, Come,*" said Lucifer, quoting the last lines of the Holy Bible.

Sleep was taking him rapidly now, and it was all he could do to keep his eyes open. Jesus smiled tenderly, continuing the quote.

"*And let him that heareth say, Come. And let him that is athirst come.*"

Lucifer's eyes filled with tears. He knew that he was home now, and that he would never leave this place again.

"*And whosoever will,*" he quoted, as sleep finally took him. "*Let him take the water of life freely.*"

THE END